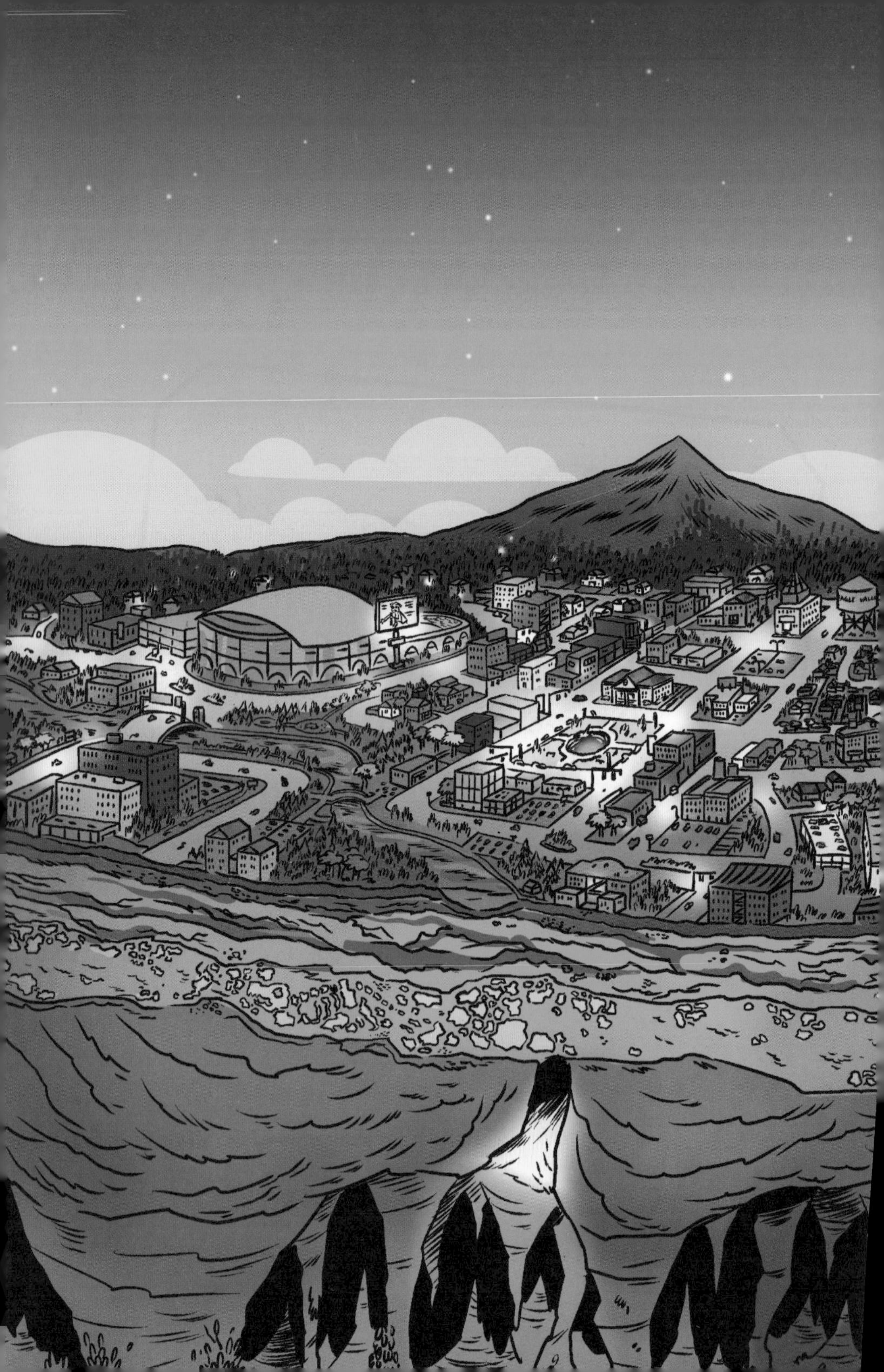

TALES OF A SEVENTH-GRADE LIZARD BOY

JONATHAN HILL
color by Nyssa Oru

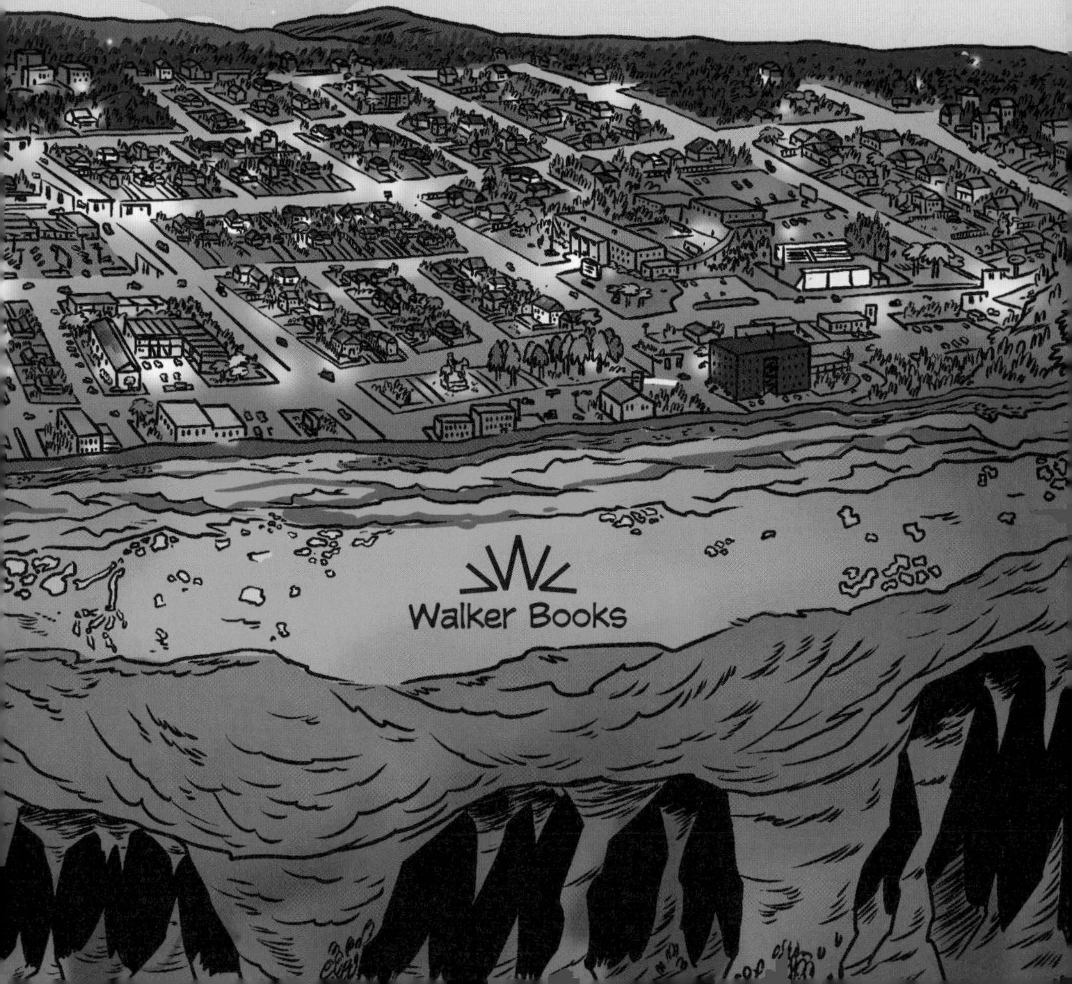

Walker Books

Copyright © 2022 by Jonathan Hill
Color by Nyssa Oru

Excerpt from *Sigh, Gone* copyright © 2020 by Phuc Tran. Reprinted by permission of Flatiron Books, a division of Macmillan Publishing Group, LLC. All Rights Reserved.

First edition 2022

Library of Congress Catalog Card Number 2021953238
ISBN 978-1-5362-1646-2 (hardcover)
ISBN 978-1-5362-1650-9 (paperback)

22 23 24 25 26 27 APS 10 9 8 7 6 5 4 3 2 1

Printed in Humen, Dongguan, China

This book was typeset in CCComicrazy.
The illustrations were created digitally.

Walker Books US
a division of
Candlewick Press
99 Dover Street
Somerville, Massachusetts 02144

www.walkerbooksus.com

For Uncle Phuc,
who always encouraged us to be ourselves

CHAPTER 1

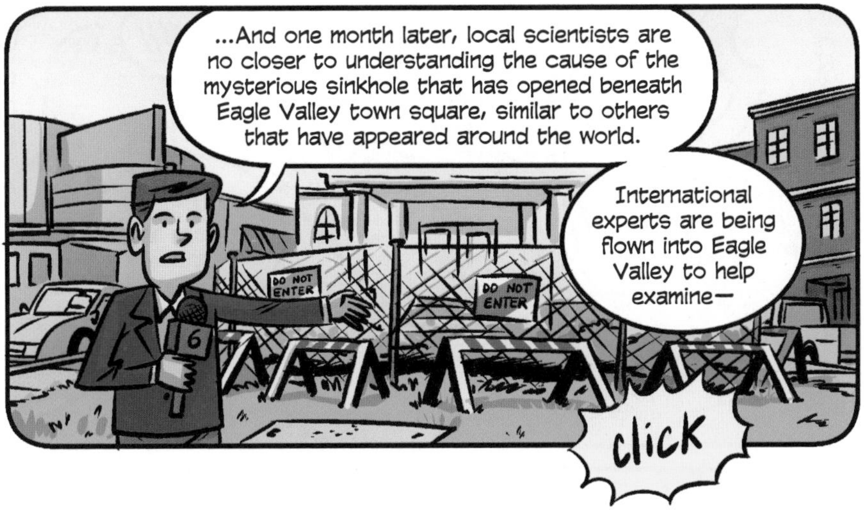
...And one month later, local scientists are no closer to understanding the cause of the mysterious sinkhole that has opened beneath Eagle Valley town square, similar to others that have appeared around the world.
International experts are being flown into Eagle Valley to help examine—
DO NOT ENTER
DO NOT ENTER
6
CLICK

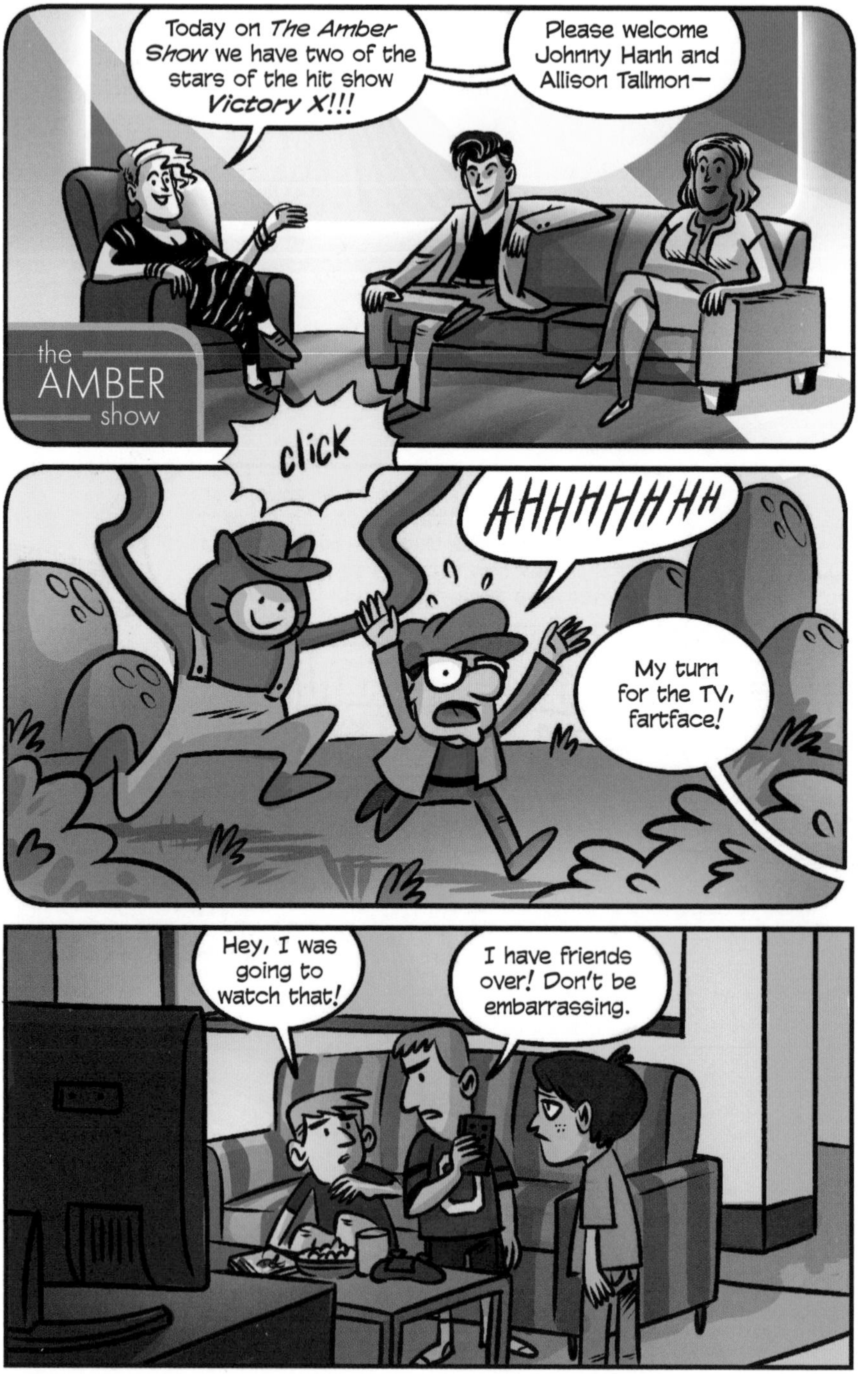

Today on *The Amber Show* we have two of the stars of the hit show *Victory X*!!!
Please welcome Johnny Hanh and Allison Tallmon—
the AMBER show
click
AHHHHHHH
My turn for the TV, fartface!
Hey, I was going to watch that!
I have friends over! Don't be embarrassing.

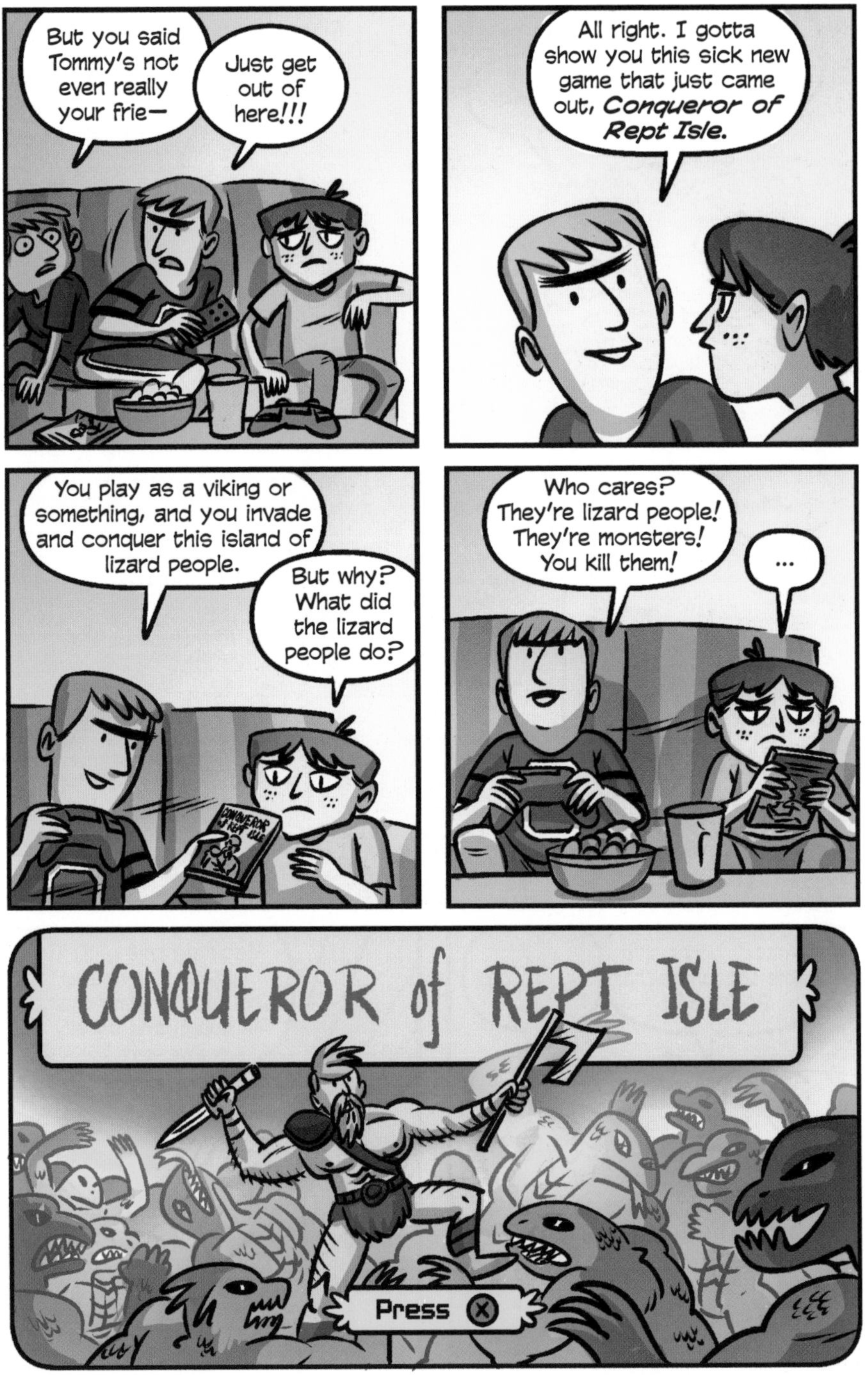
But you said Tommy's not even really your frie—
Just get out of here!!!
All right. I gotta show you this sick new game that just came out, *Conqueror of Rept Isle.*
You play as a viking or something, and you invade and conquer this island of lizard people.
But why? What did the lizard people do?
CONQUEROR OF REPT ISLE
Who cares? They're lizard people! They're monsters! You kill them!
...
CONQUEROR of REPT ISLE
Press ⊗

OK. You can play first. Go ahead and name the character.

OK...

Name

_____

A B C D E

I J K L M

Um...

click

click

click

click

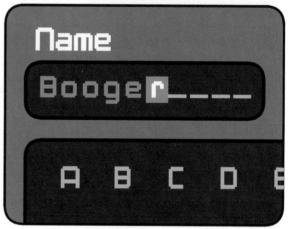

Name

Booger_____

A B C D E

What?! You can't name the character BOOGER!

Um... Why not?

Because this is THE HERO. They need to have a name that is tough and totally awesome!

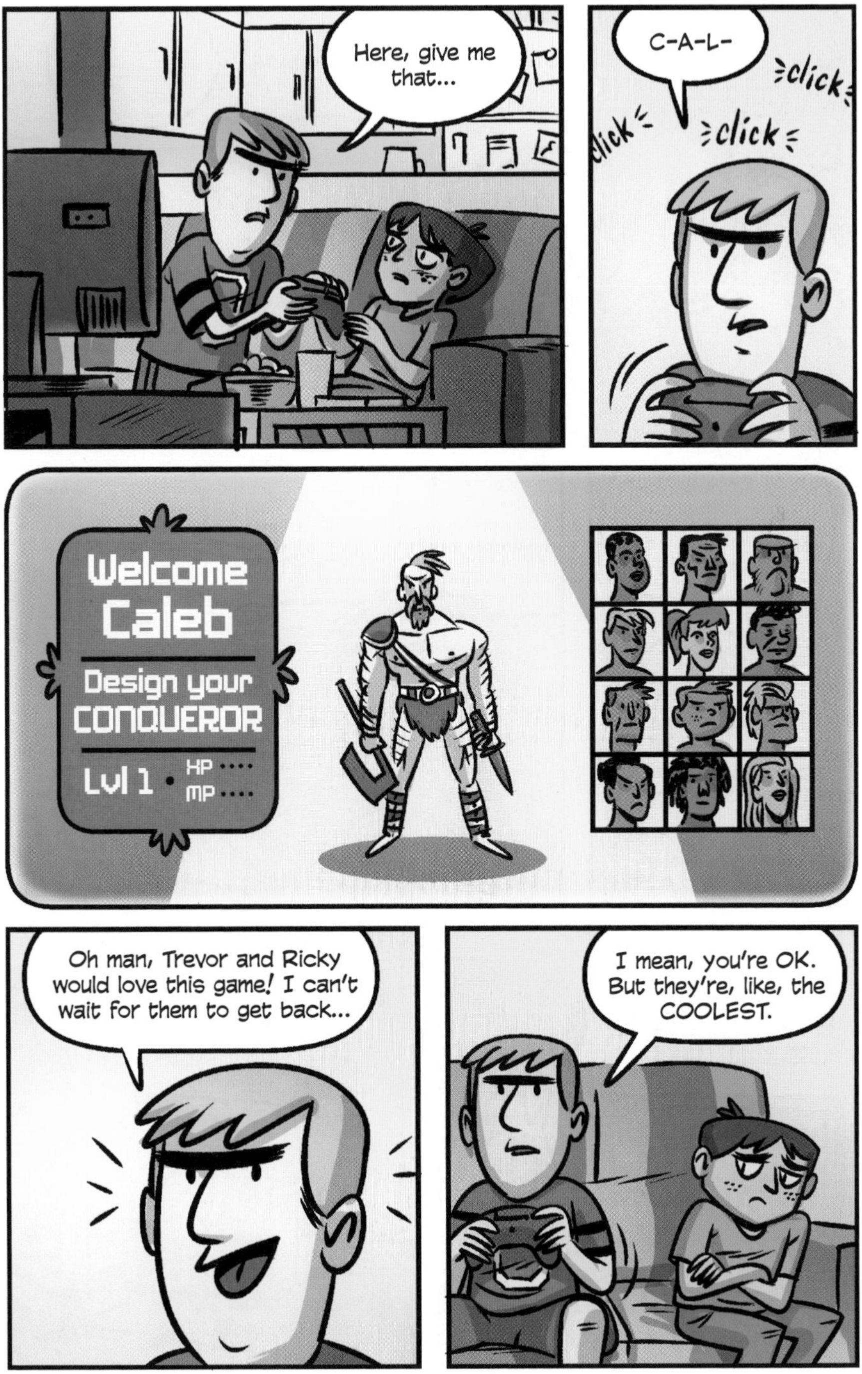
Here, give me that...
C-A-L-
click
click
click
Welcome Caleb
Design your CONQUEROR
Lvl 1 • HP .... MP ....
Oh man, Trevor and Ricky would love this game! I can't wait for them to get back...
I mean, you're OK. But they're, like, the COOLEST.

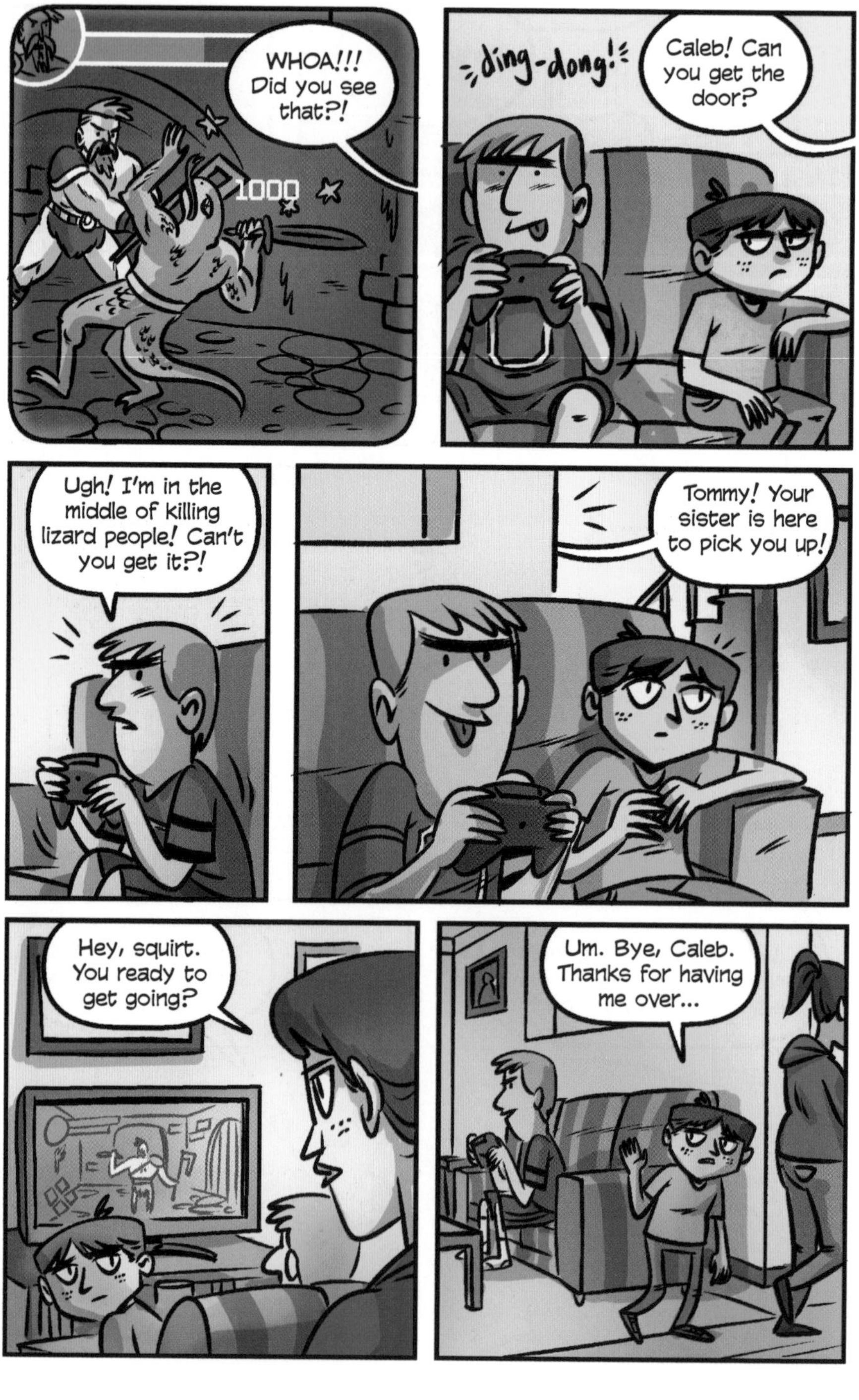
1000
WHOA!!! Did you see that?!
ding-dong!
Caleb! Can you get the door?
Ugh! I'm in the middle of killing lizard people! Can't you get it?!
Tommy! Your sister is here to pick you up!
Hey, squirt. You ready to get going?
Um. Bye, Caleb. Thanks for having me over...

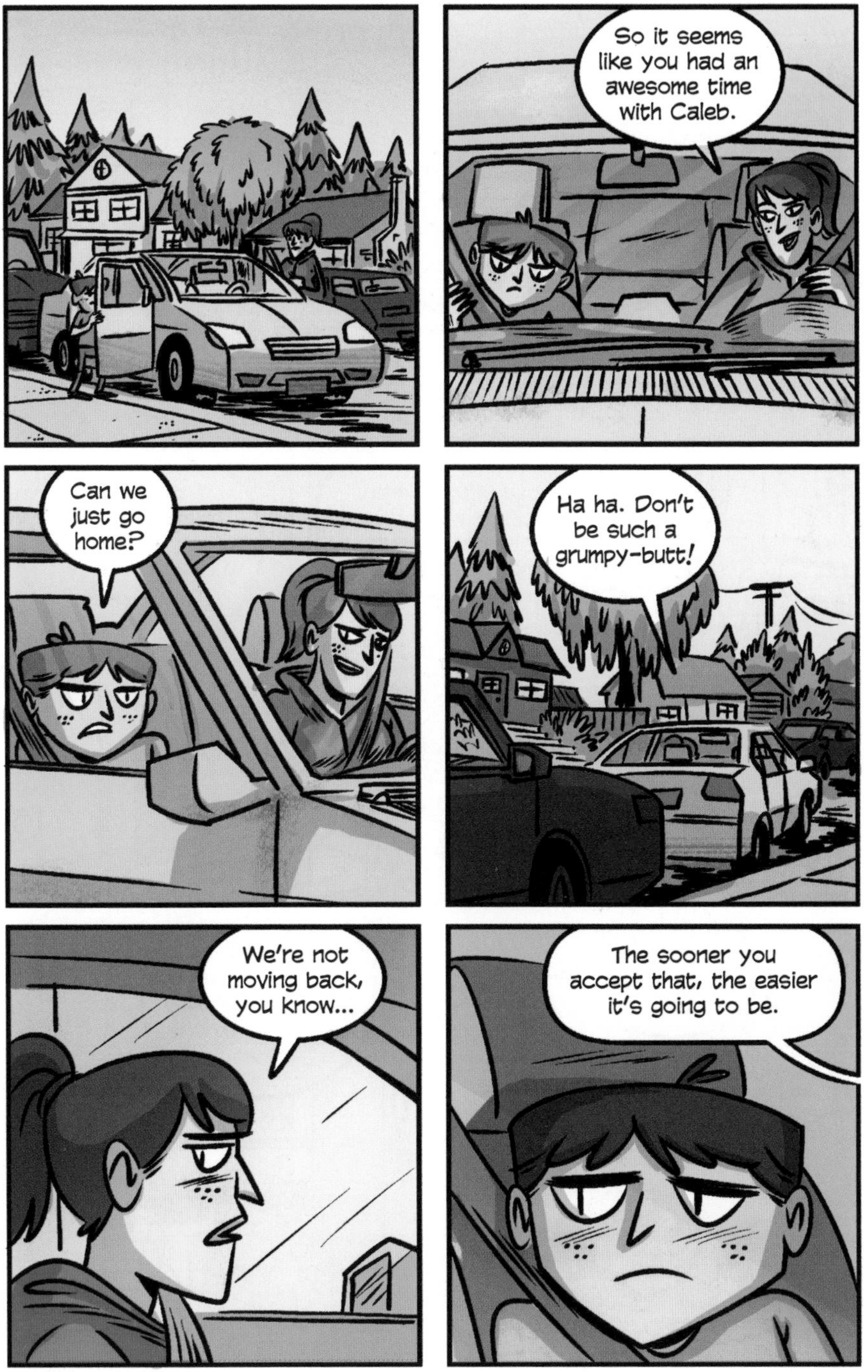
So it seems like you had an awesome time with Caleb.
Can we just go home?
Ha ha. Don't be such a grumpy-butt!
We're not moving back, you know...
The sooner you accept that, the easier it's going to be.

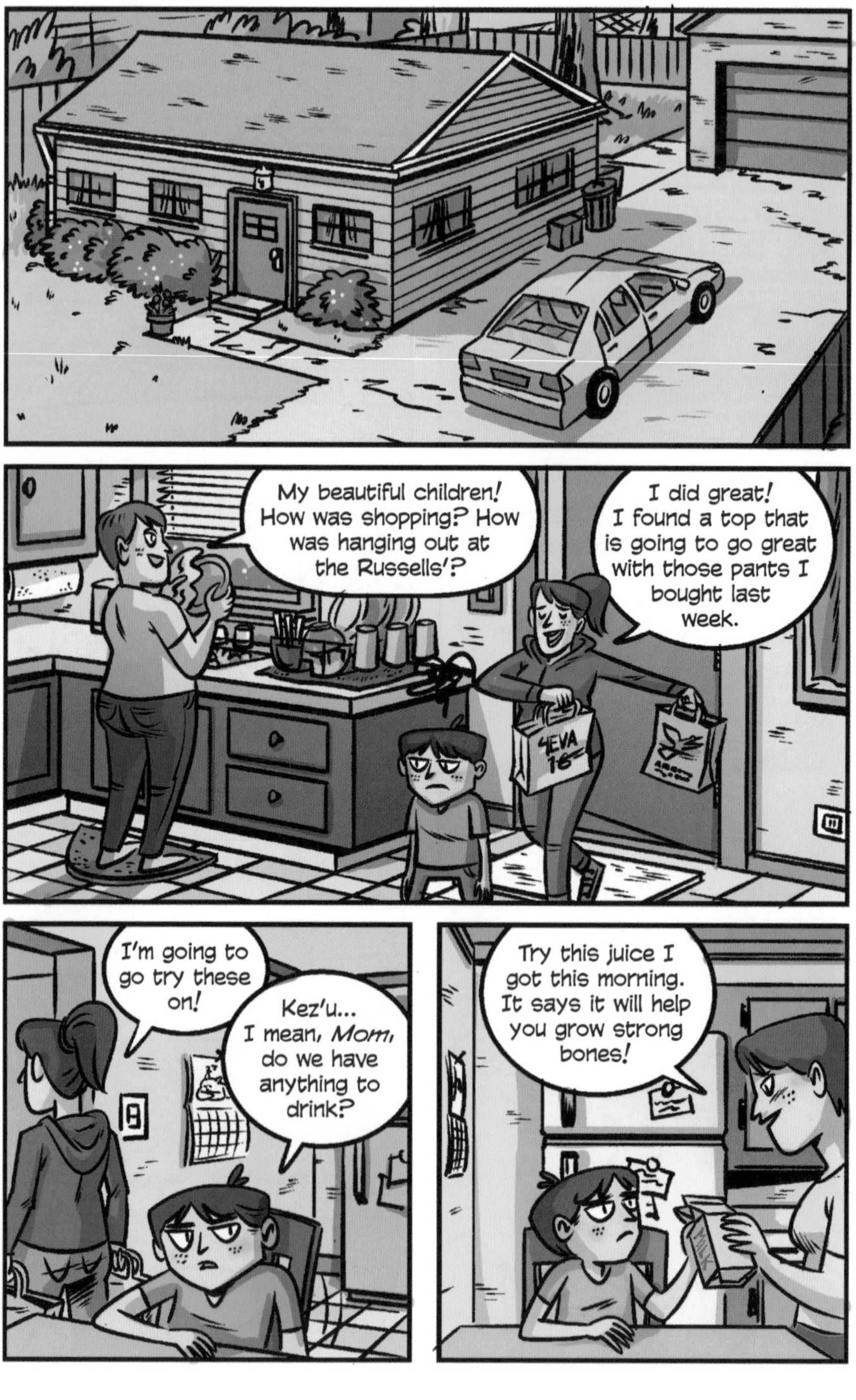
My beautiful children! How was shopping? How was hanging out at the Russells'?
I did great! I found a top that is going to go great with those pants I bought last week.
I'm going to go try these on!
Kez'u... I mean, *Mom*, do we have anything to drink?
Try this juice I got this morning. It says it will help you grow strong bones!

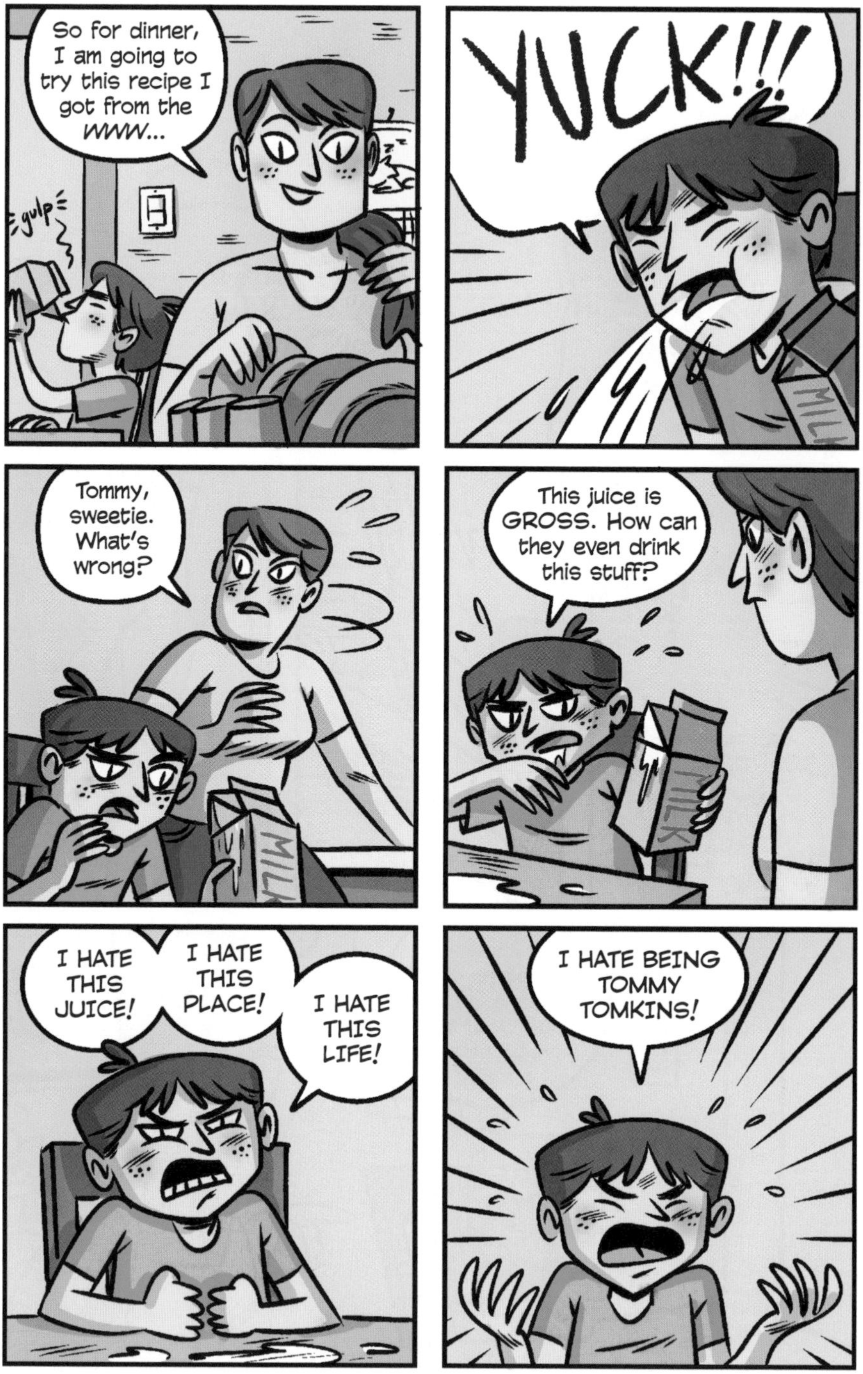
So for dinner, I am going to try this recipe I got from the WWW...
gulp
YUCK!!!
MILK
Tommy, sweetie. What's wrong?
MILK
This juice is GROSS. How can they even drink this stuff?
MILK
I HATE THIS JUICE!
I HATE THIS PLACE!
I HATE THIS LIFE!
I HATE BEING TOMMY TOMKINS!

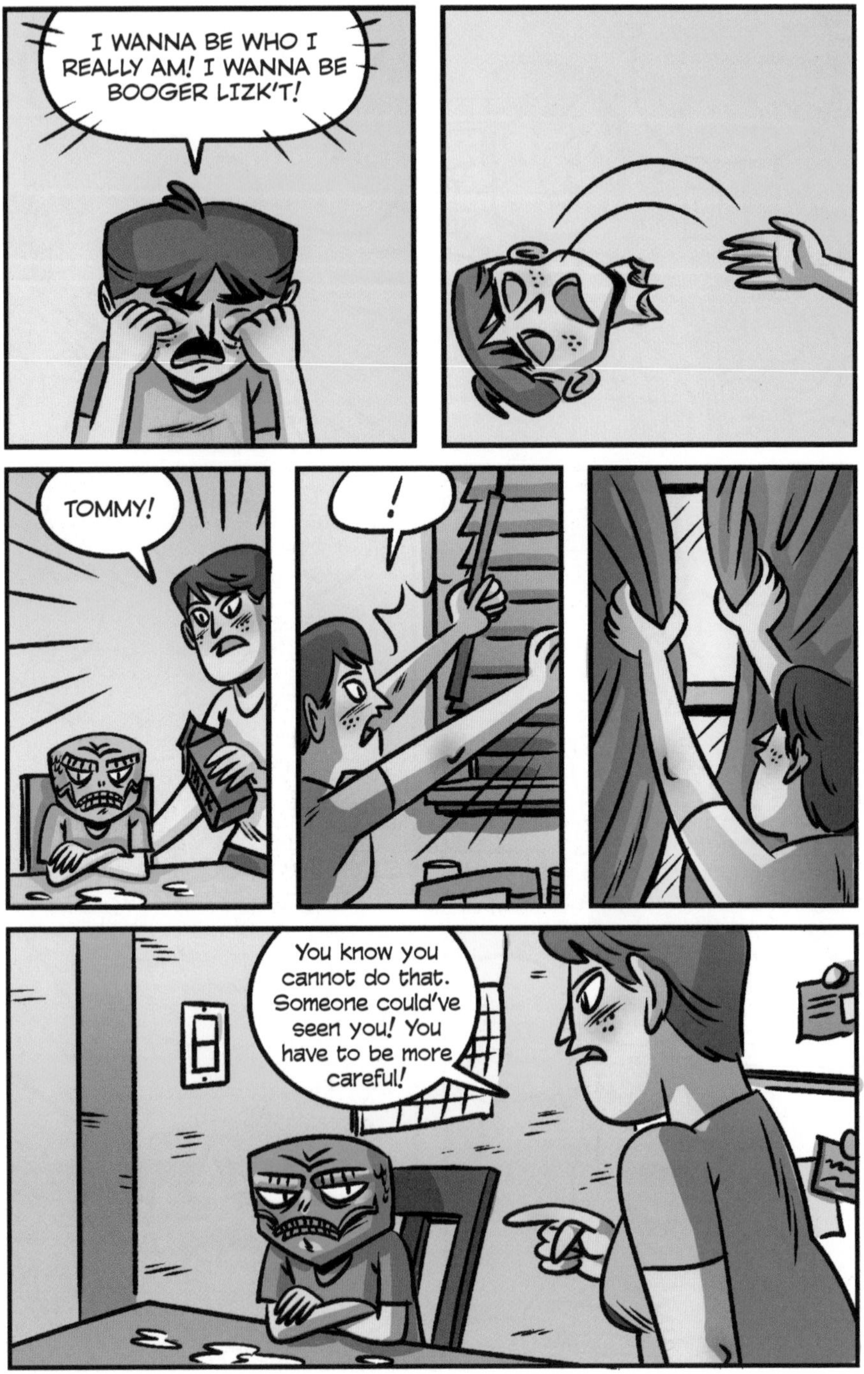
I WANNA BE WHO I REALLY AM! I WANNA BE BOOGER LIZK'T!
TOMMY!
!
You know you cannot do that. Someone could've seen you! You have to be more careful!

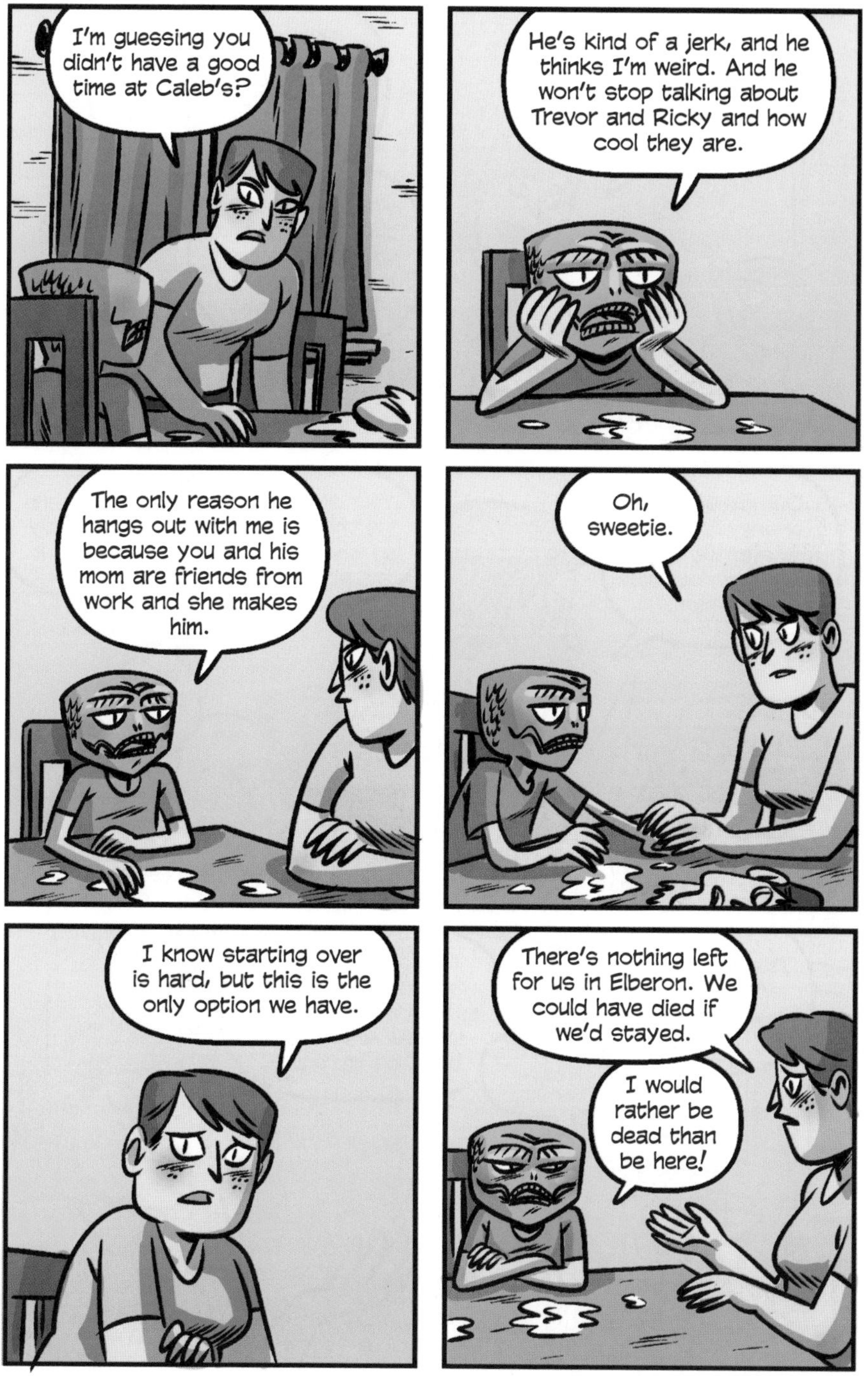
I'm guessing you didn't have a good time at Caleb's?
He's kind of a jerk, and he thinks I'm weird. And he won't stop talking about Trevor and Ricky and how cool they are.
The only reason he hangs out with me is because you and his mom are friends from work and she makes him.
Oh, sweetie.
I know starting over is hard, but this is the only option we have.
There's nothing left for us in Elberon. We could have died if we'd stayed.
I would rather be dead than be here!

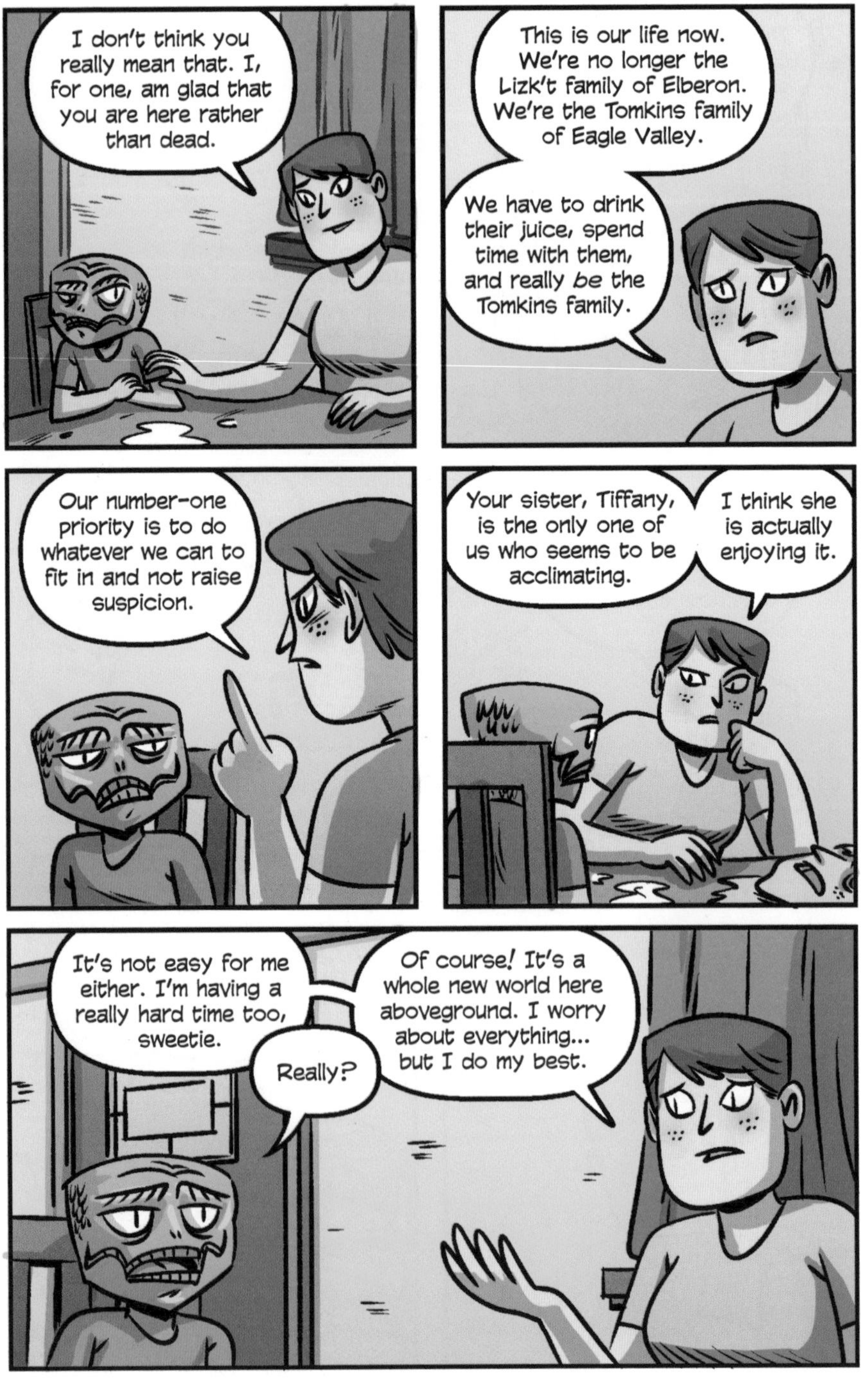
I don't think you really mean that. I, for one, am glad that you are here rather than dead.
This is our life now. We're no longer the Lizk't family of Elberon. We're the Tomkins family of Eagle Valley.
We have to drink their juice, spend time with them, and really *be* the Tomkins family.
Our number-one priority is to do whatever we can to fit in and not raise suspicion.
Your sister, Tiffany, is the only one of us who seems to be acclimating.
I think she is actually enjoying it.
It's not easy for me either. I'm having a really hard time too, sweetie.
Really?
Of course! It's a whole new world here aboveground. I worry about everything... but I do my best.

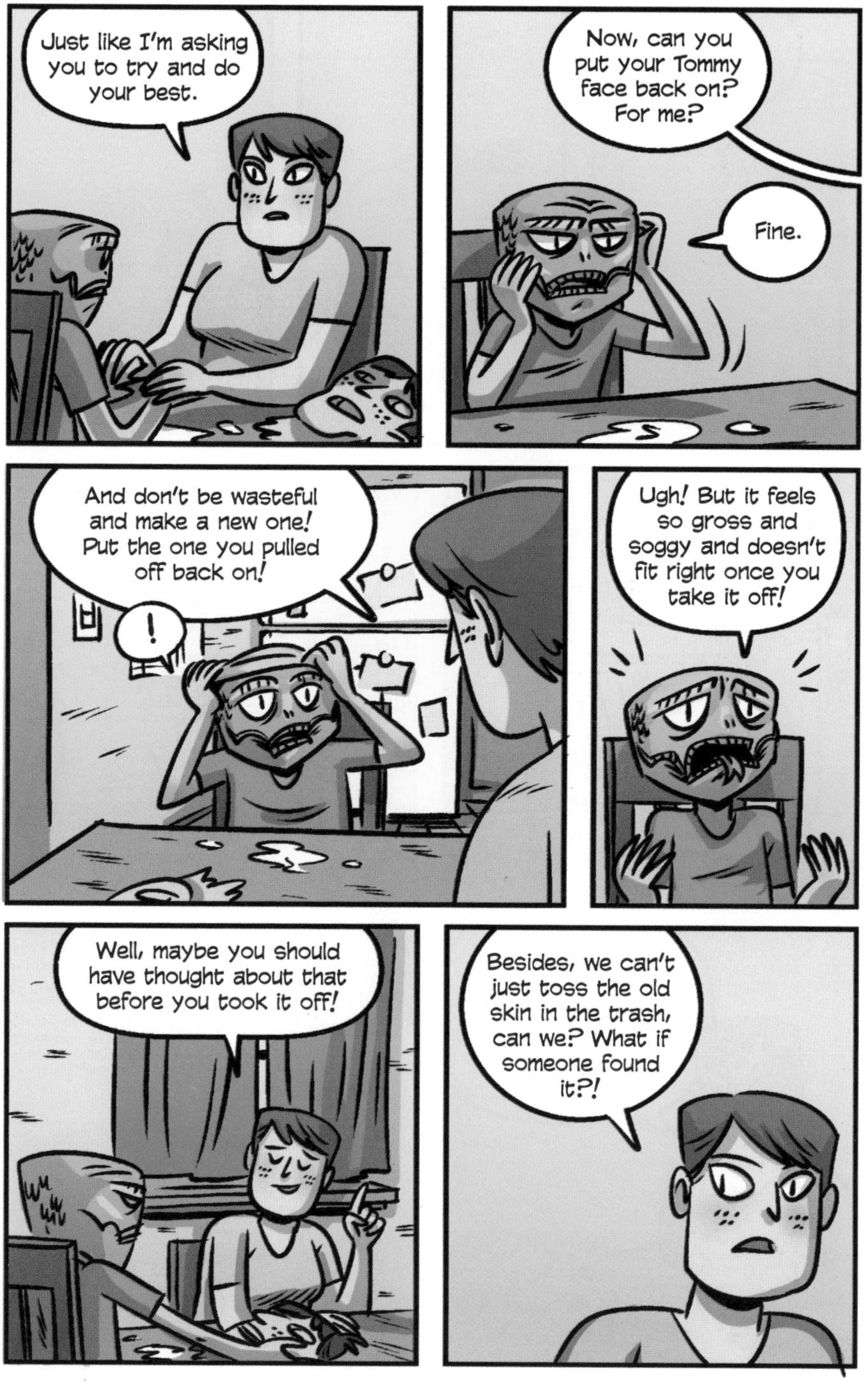
Just like I'm asking you to try and do your best.
Now, can you put your Tommy face back on? For me?
Fine.
And don't be wasteful and make a new one! Put the one you pulled off back on!
!
Ugh! But it feels so gross and soggy and doesn't fit right once you take it off!
Well, maybe you should have thought about that before you took it off!
Besides, we can't just toss the old skin in the trash, can we? What if someone found it?!

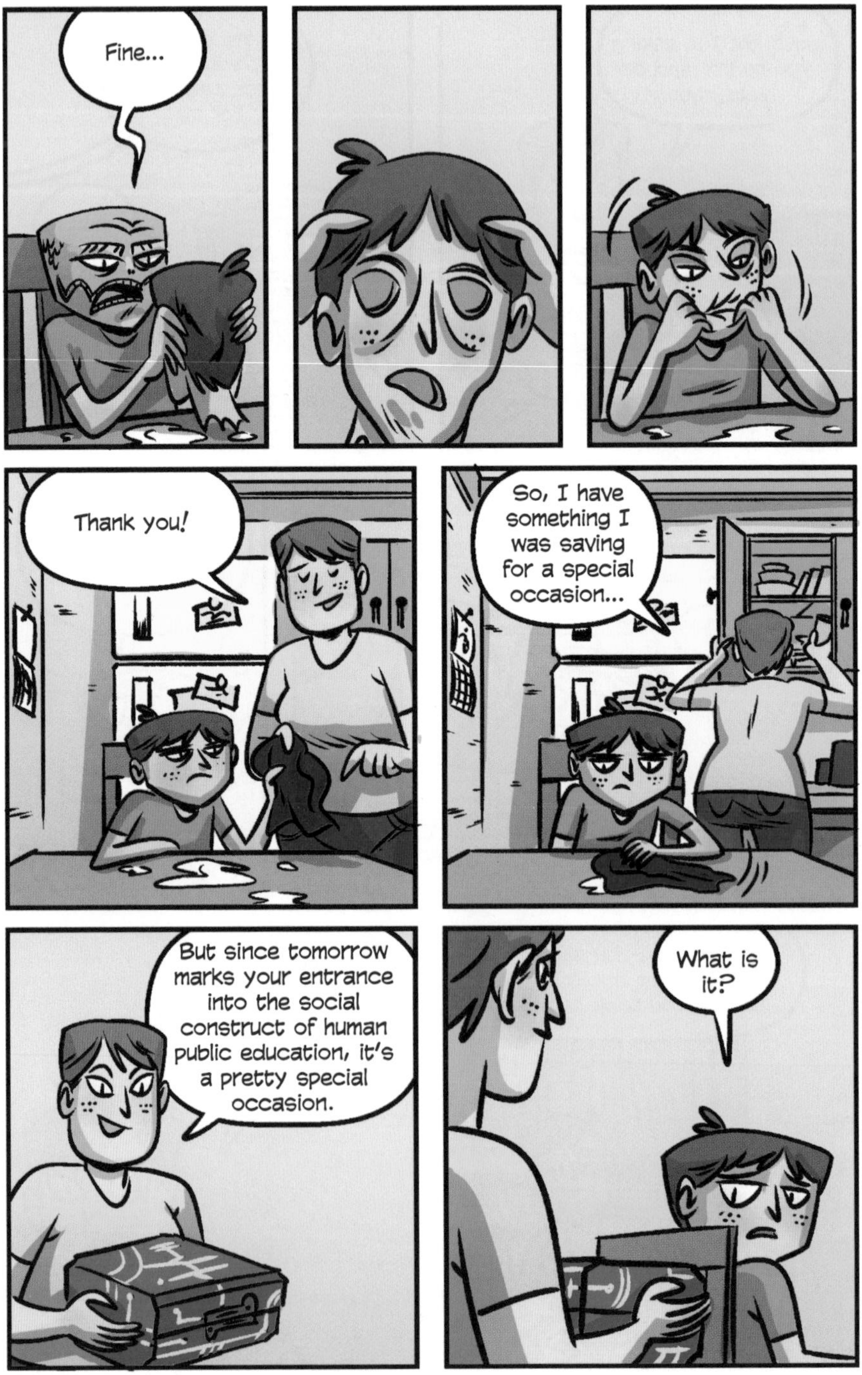

Fine...
Thank you!
So, I have something I was saving for a special occasion...
But since tomorrow marks your entrance into the social construct of human public education, it's a pretty special occasion.
What is it?

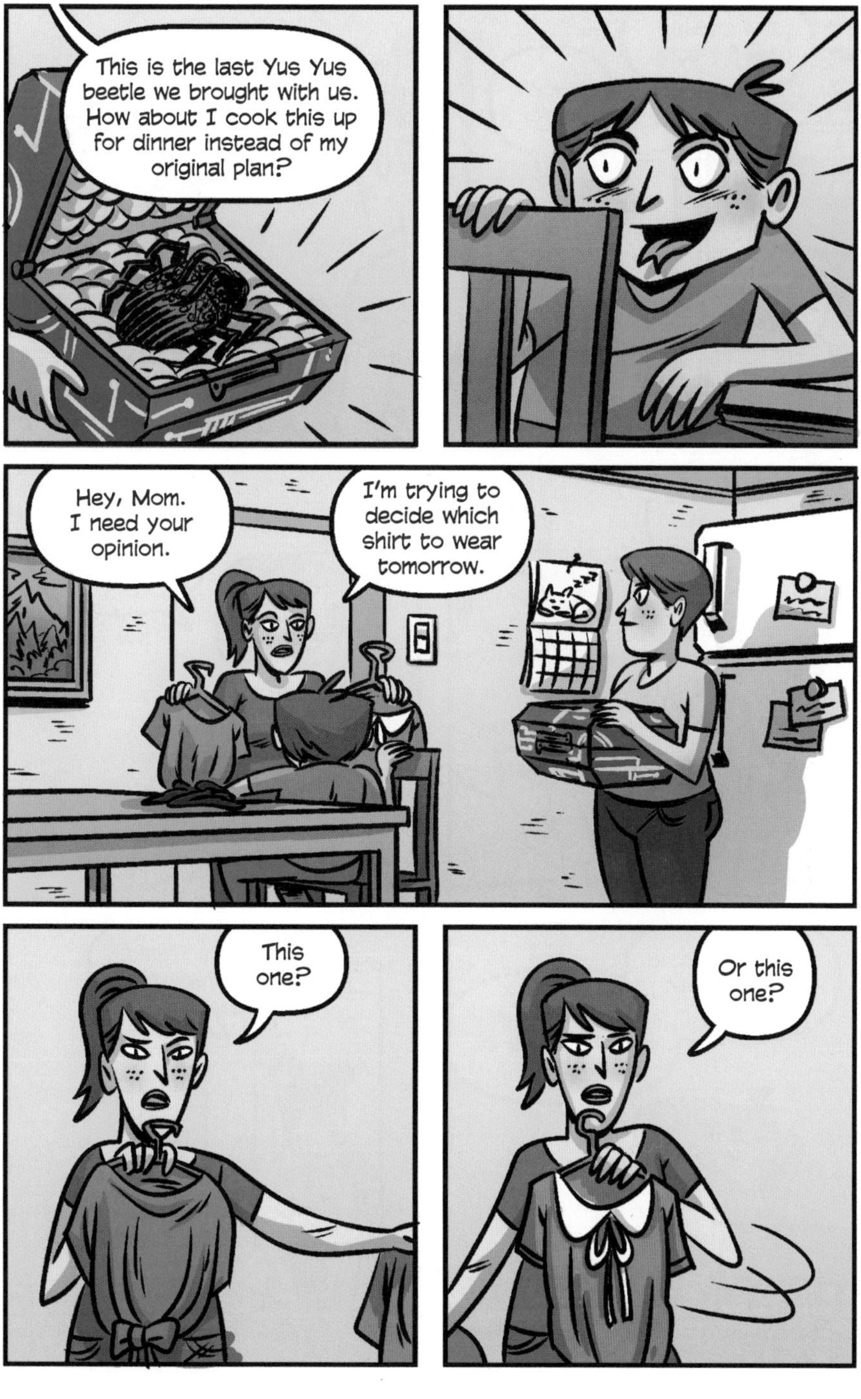

This is the last Yus Yus beetle we brought with us. How about I cook this up for dinner instead of my original plan?
Hey, Mom. I need your opinion.
I'm trying to decide which shirt to wear tomorrow.
This one?
Or this one?

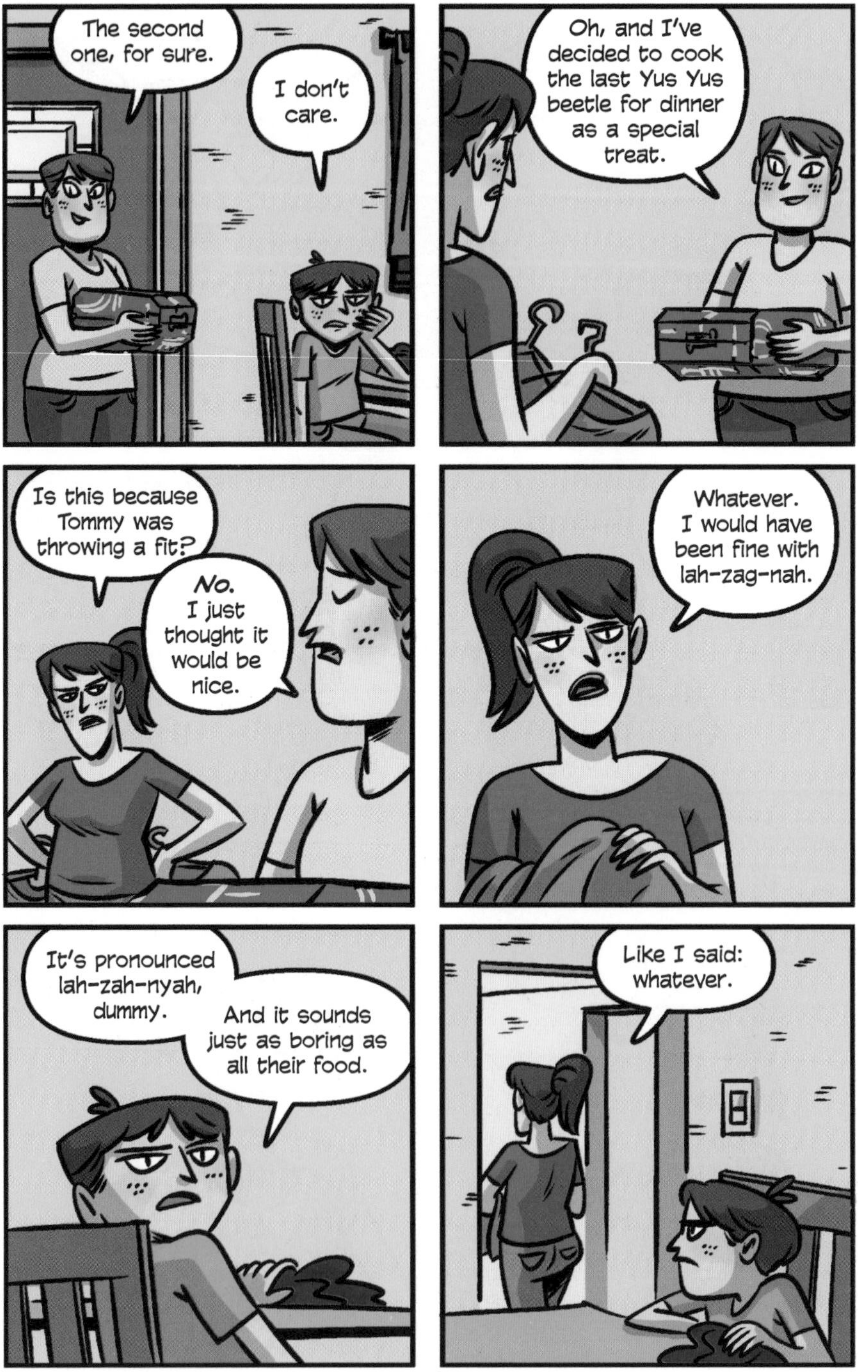
The second one, for sure.
I don't care.
Oh, and I've decided to cook the last Yus Yus beetle for dinner as a special treat.
Is this because Tommy was throwing a fit?
No. I just thought it would be nice.
Whatever. I would have been fine with lah-zag-nah.
It's pronounced lah-zah-nyah, dummy.
And it sounds just as boring as all their food.
Like I said: whatever.

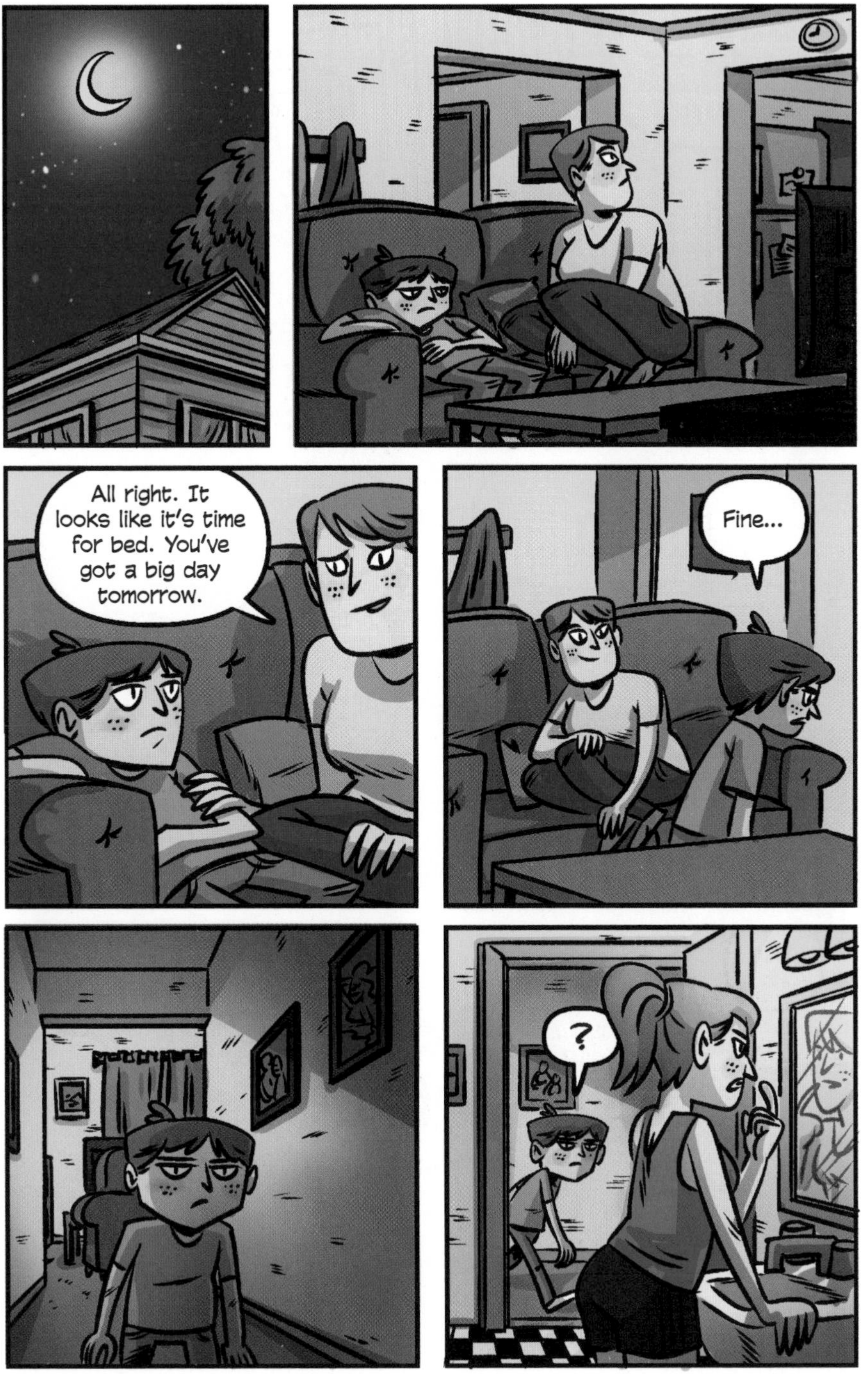
All right. It looks like it's time for bed. You've got a big day tomorrow.
Fine...
?

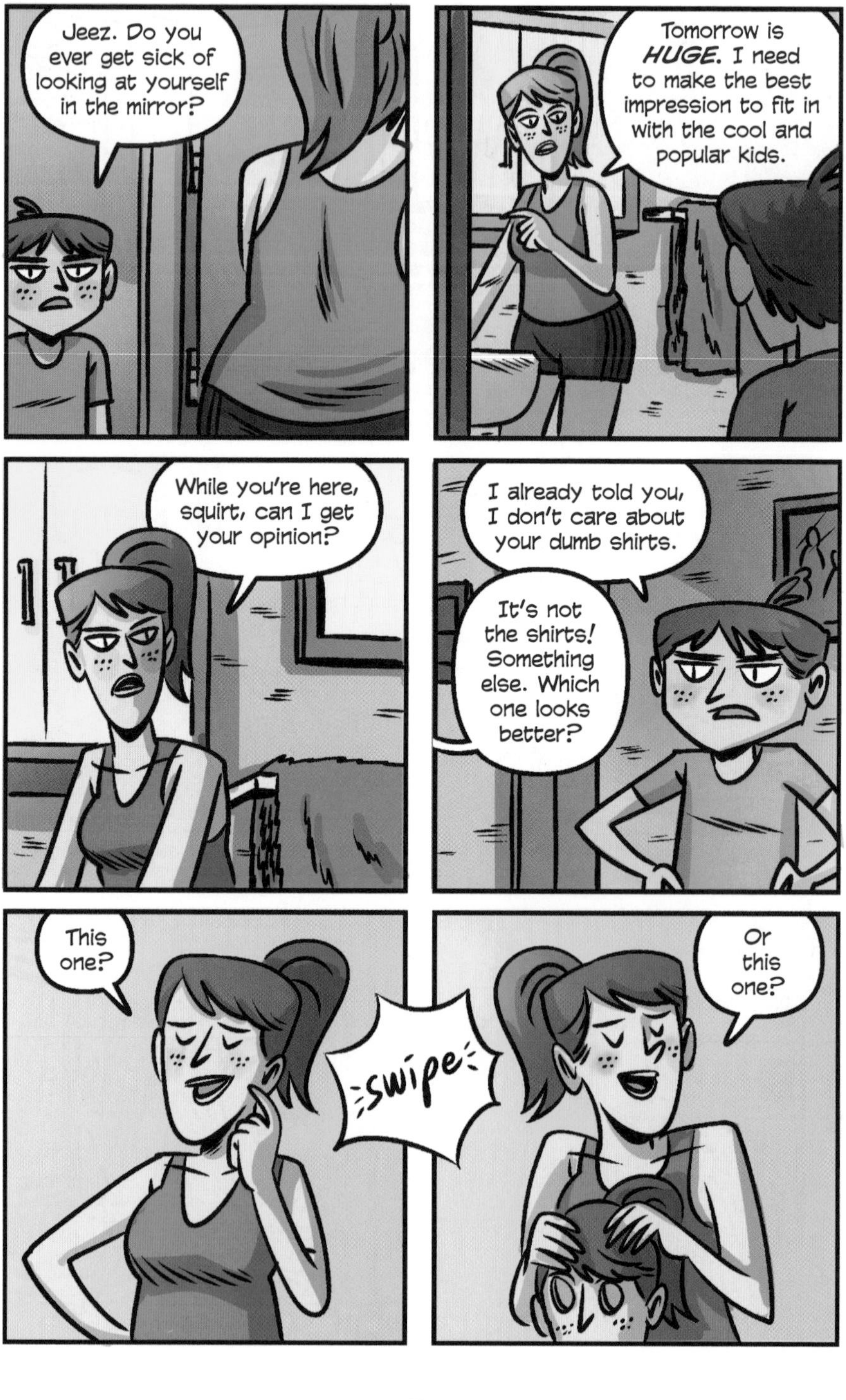

Jeez. Do you ever get sick of looking at yourself in the mirror?
Tomorrow is *HUGE*. I need to make the best impression to fit in with the cool and popular kids.
While you're here, squirt, can I get your opinion?
I already told you, I don't care about your dumb shirts.
It's not the shirts! Something else. Which one looks better?
This one?
SWIPE
Or this one?

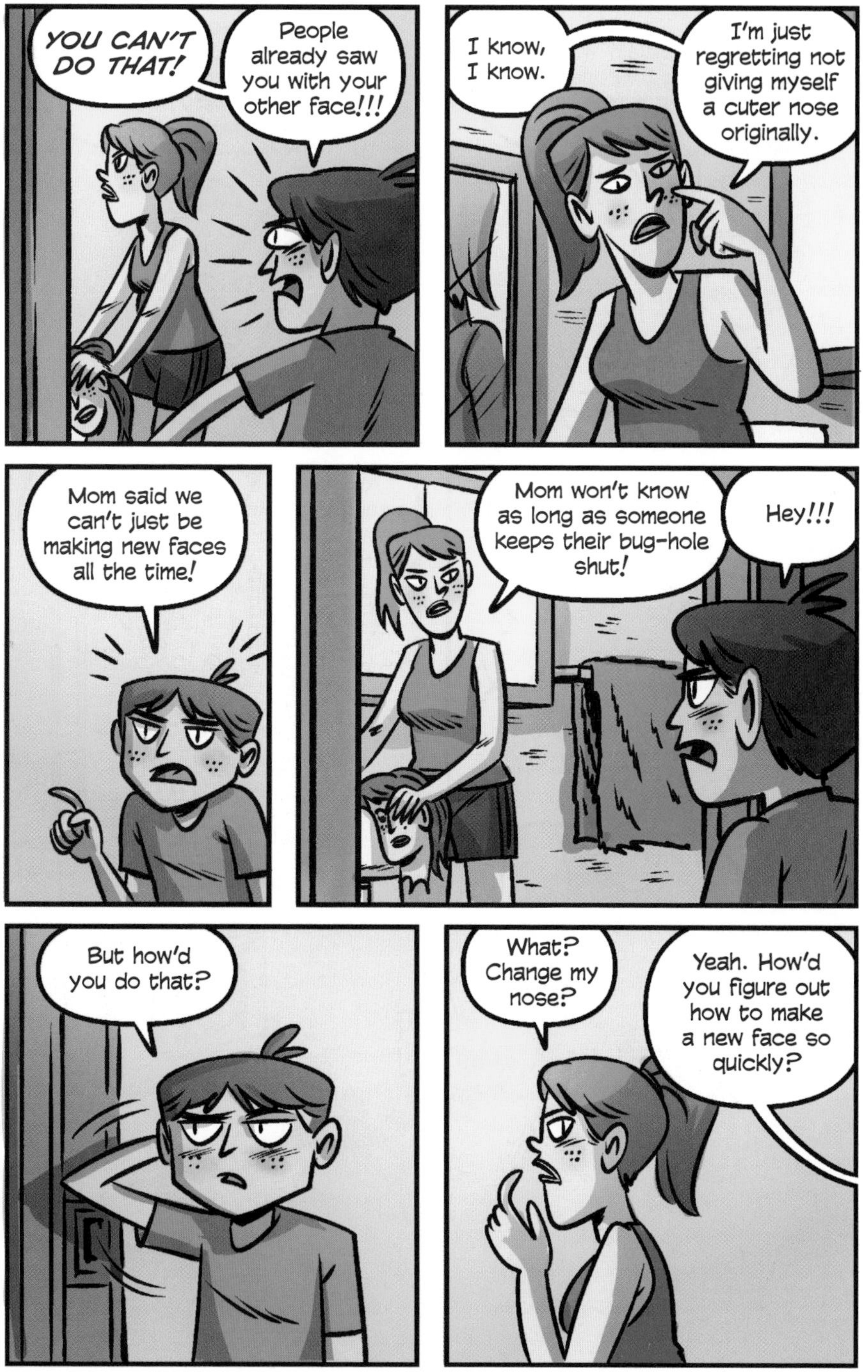
YOU CAN'T DO THAT!
People already saw you with your other face!!!
I know, I know.
I'm just regretting not giving myself a cuter nose originally.
Mom said we can't just be making new faces all the time!
Mom won't know as long as someone keeps their bug-hole shut!
Hey!!!
But how'd you do that?
What? Change my nose?
Yeah. How'd you figure out how to make a new face so quickly?

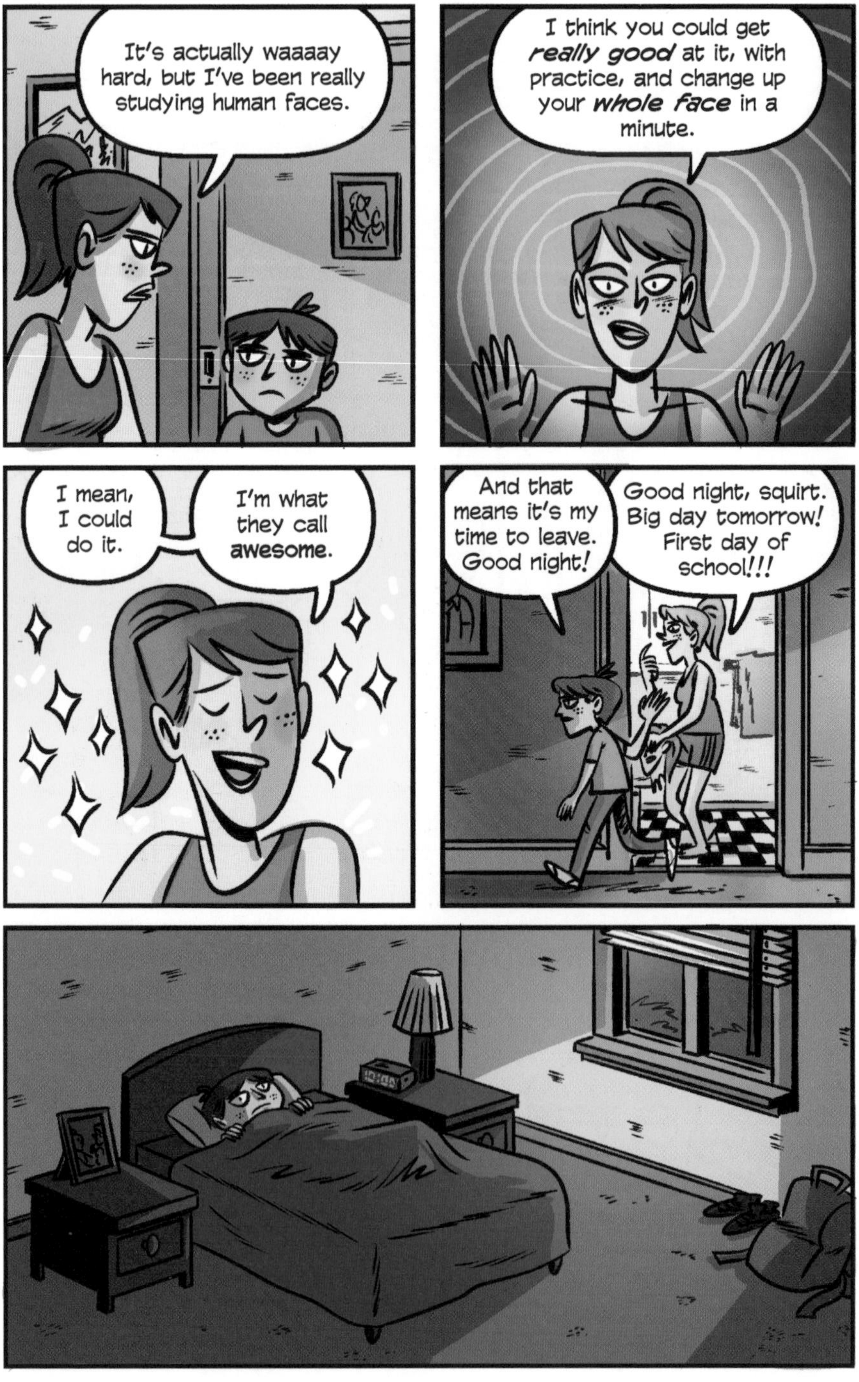

It's actually waaaay hard, but I've been really studying human faces.
I think you could get *really good* at it, with practice, and change up your *whole face* in a minute.
I mean, I could do it.
I'm what they call **awesome.**
And that means it's my time to leave. Good night!
Good night, squirt. Big day tomorrow! First day of school!!!

CHAPTER 2

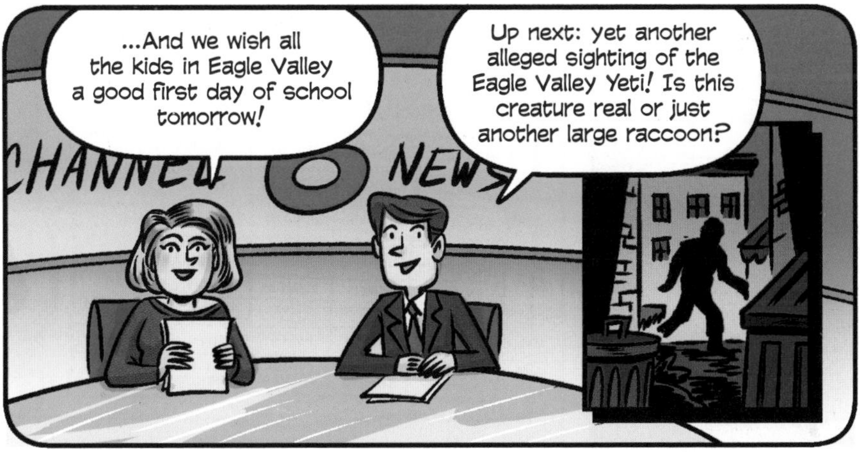
...And we wish all the kids in Eagle Valley a good first day of school tomorrow!
Up next: yet another alleged sighting of the Eagle Valley Yeti! Is this creature real or just another large raccoon?
CHANNEL 8 NEWS

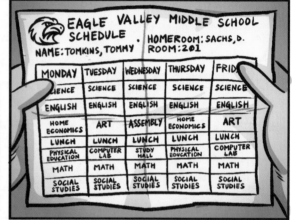

MONDAY	TUESDAY	WEDNESDAY	THURSDAY	FRID
SCIENCE	SCIENCE	SCIENCE	SCIENCE	SCIENCE
ENGLISH	ENGLISH	ENGLISH	ENGLISH	ENGLISH
HOME ECONOMICS	ART	ASSEMBLY	HOME ECONOMICS	ART
LUNCH	LUNCH	LUNCH	LUNCH	LUNCH
PHYSICAL EDUCATION	COMPUTER LAB	STUDY HALL	PHYSICAL EDUCATION	COMPUTER LAB
MATH	MATH	MATH	MATH	MATH
SOCIAL STUDIES	SOCIAL STUDIES	SOCIAL STUDIES	SOCIAL STUDIES	SOCIAL STUDIES

EAGLE VALLEY MIDDLE SCHOOL SCHEDULE

NAME: TOMKINS, TOMMY

HOMEROOM: SACHS, D. ROOM: 201

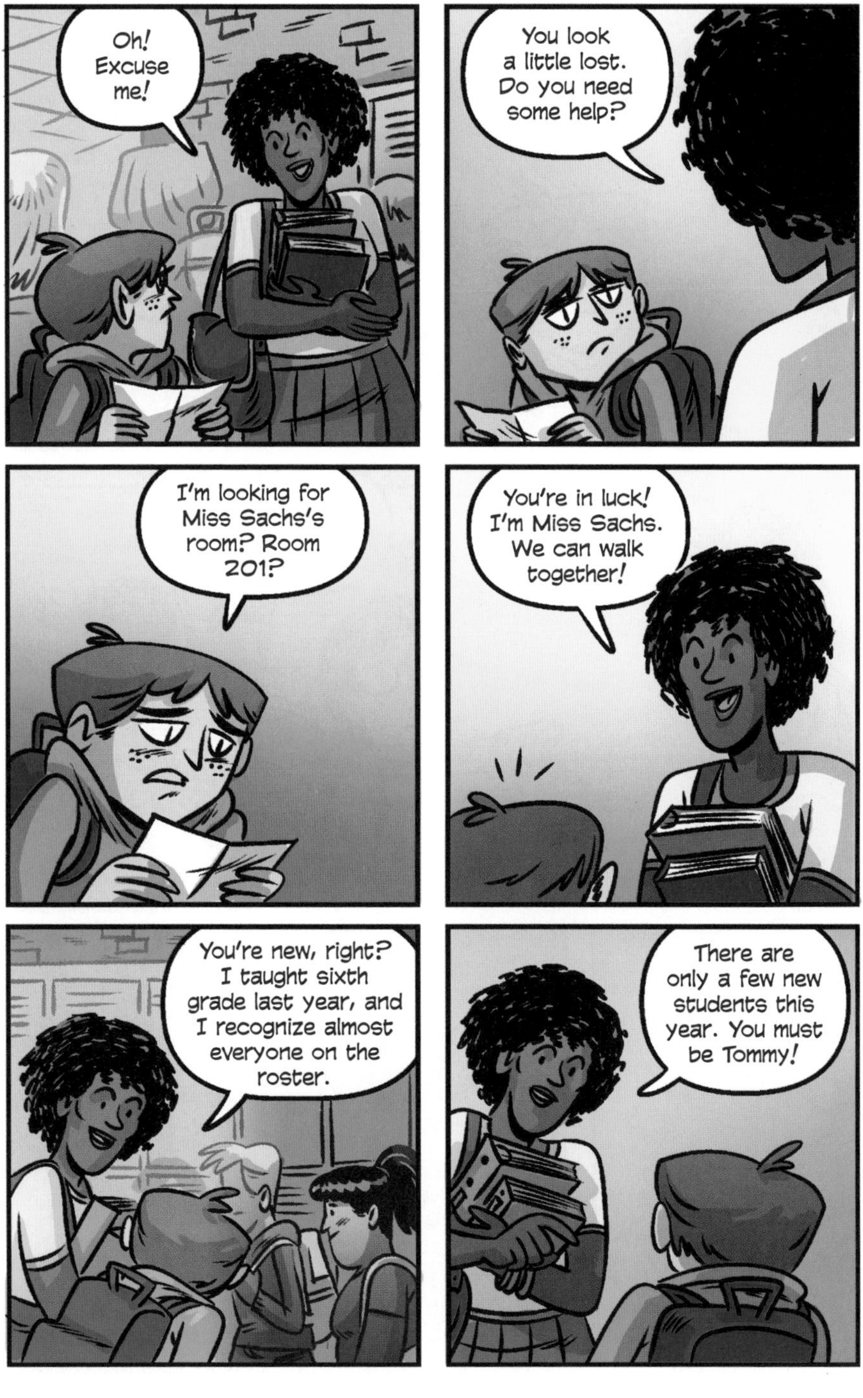
Oh! Excuse me!
You look a little lost. Do you need some help?
I'm looking for Miss Sachs's room? Room 201?
You're in luck! I'm Miss Sachs. We can walk together!
You're new, right? I taught sixth grade last year, and I recognize almost everyone on the roster.
There are only a few new students this year. You must be Tommy!

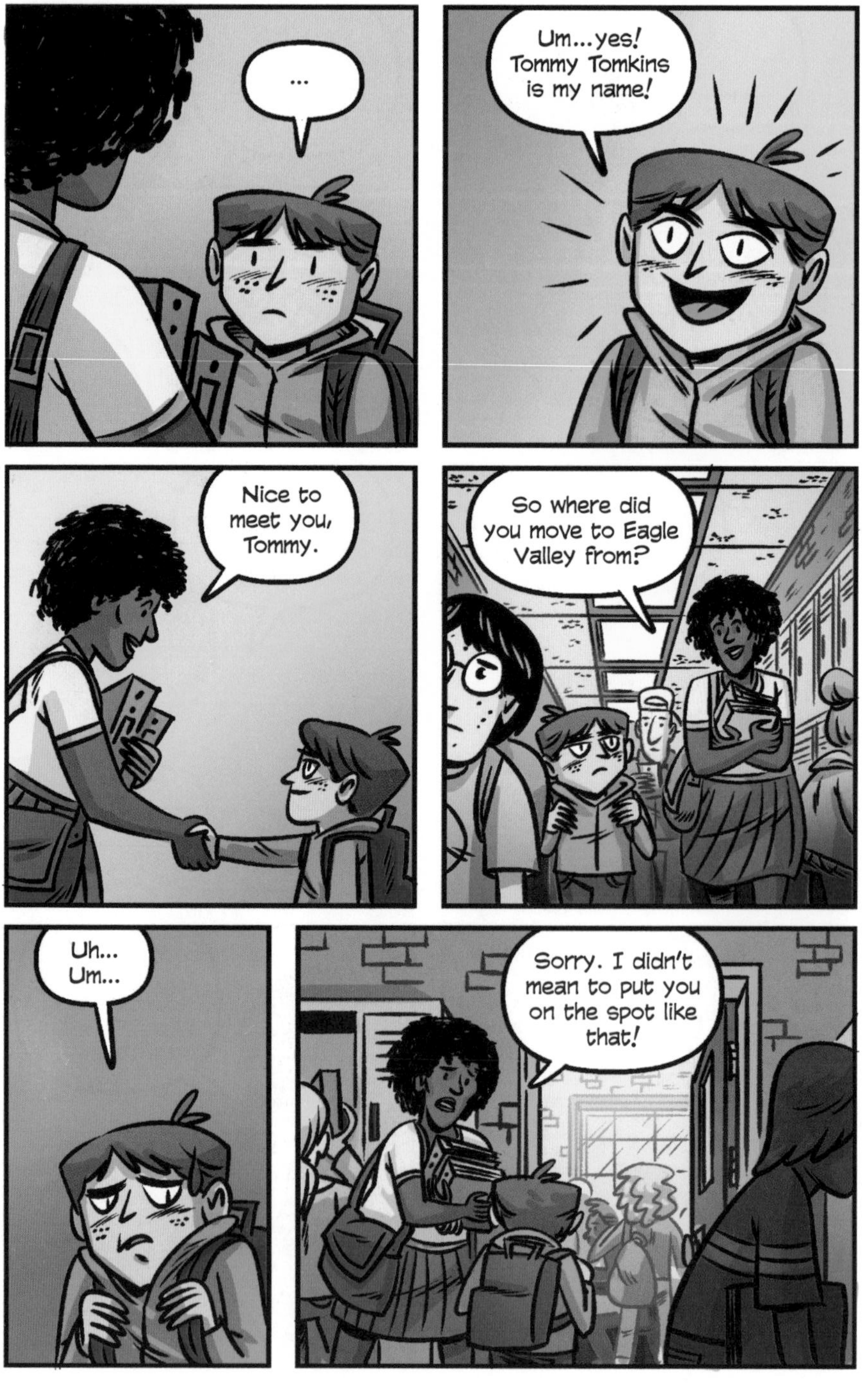
...
Um...yes! Tommy Tomkins is my name!
Nice to meet you, Tommy.
So where did you move to Eagle Valley from?
Uh... Um...
Sorry. I didn't mean to put you on the spot like that!

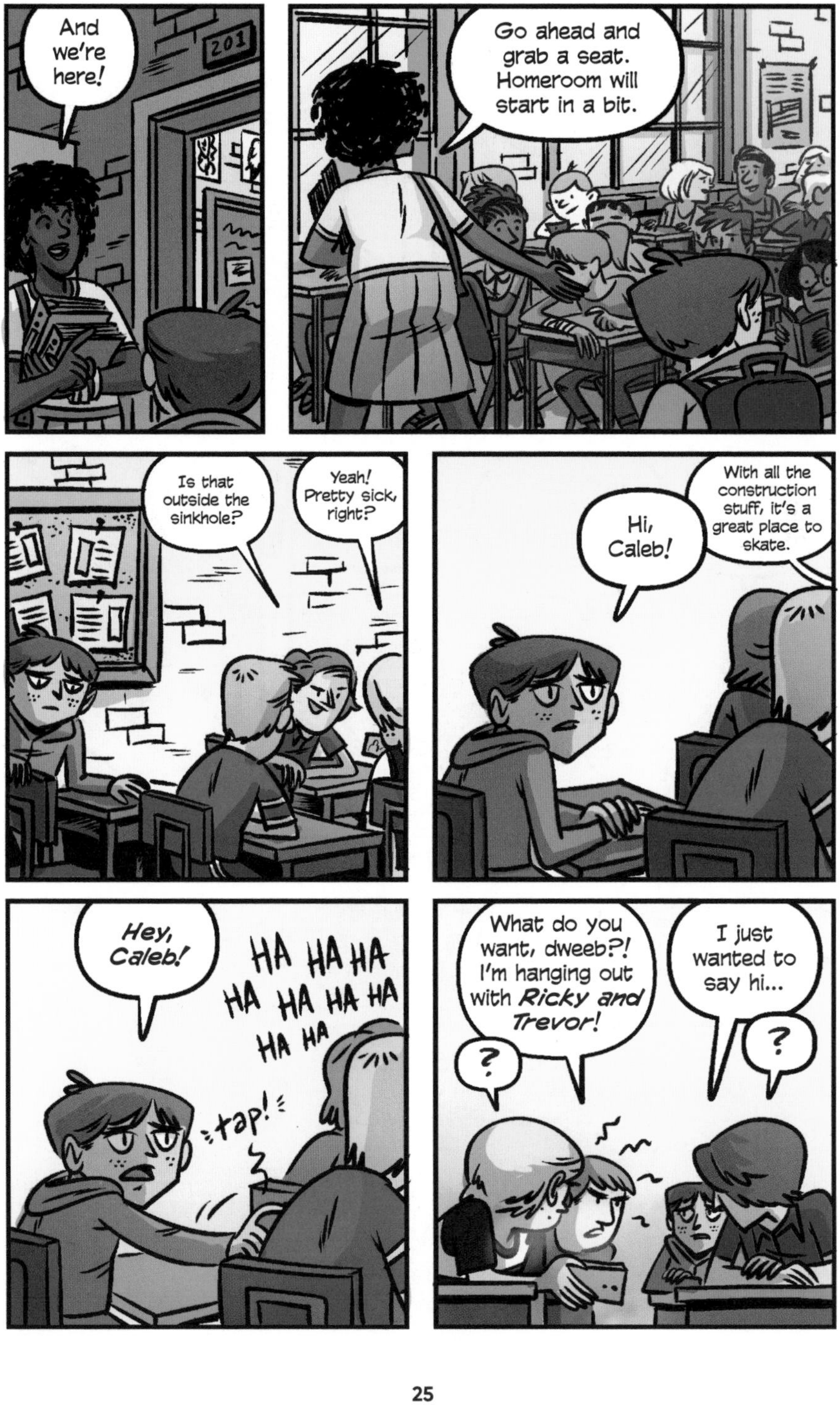
And we're here!
Go ahead and grab a seat. Homeroom will start in a bit.
Is that outside the sinkhole?
Yeah! Pretty sick, right?
Hi, Caleb!
With all the construction stuff, it's a great place to skate.
Hey, Caleb!
HA HA HA HA HA HA HA HA HA
tap!
?
What do you want, dweeb?! I'm hanging out with Ricky and Trevor!
I just wanted to say hi...
?

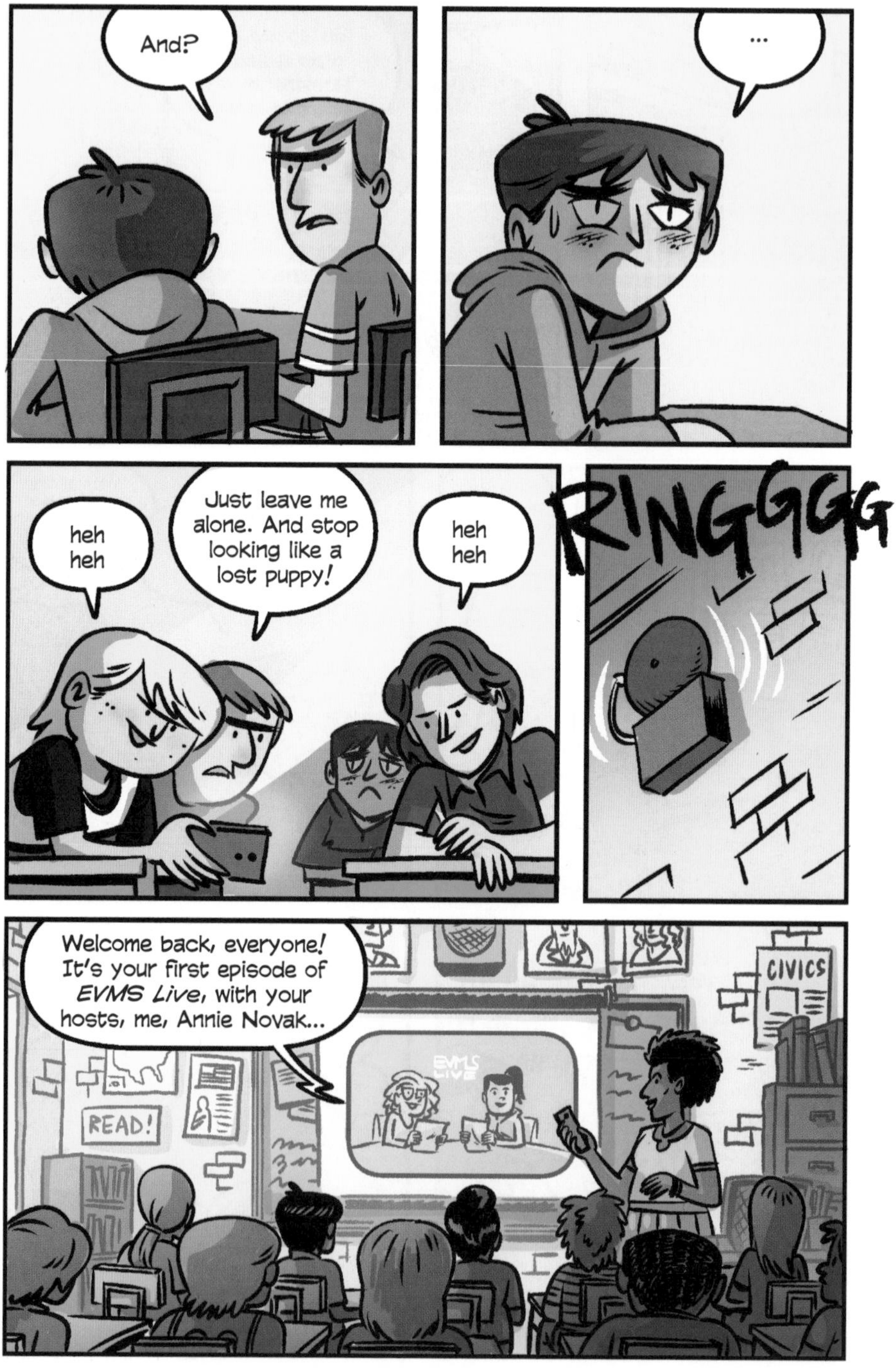
And?
...
heh heh
Just leave me alone. And stop looking like a lost puppy!
heh heh
RINGGGG
Welcome back, everyone! It's your first episode of EVMS Live, with your hosts, me, Annie Novak...
EVMS LIVE
READ!
CIVICS

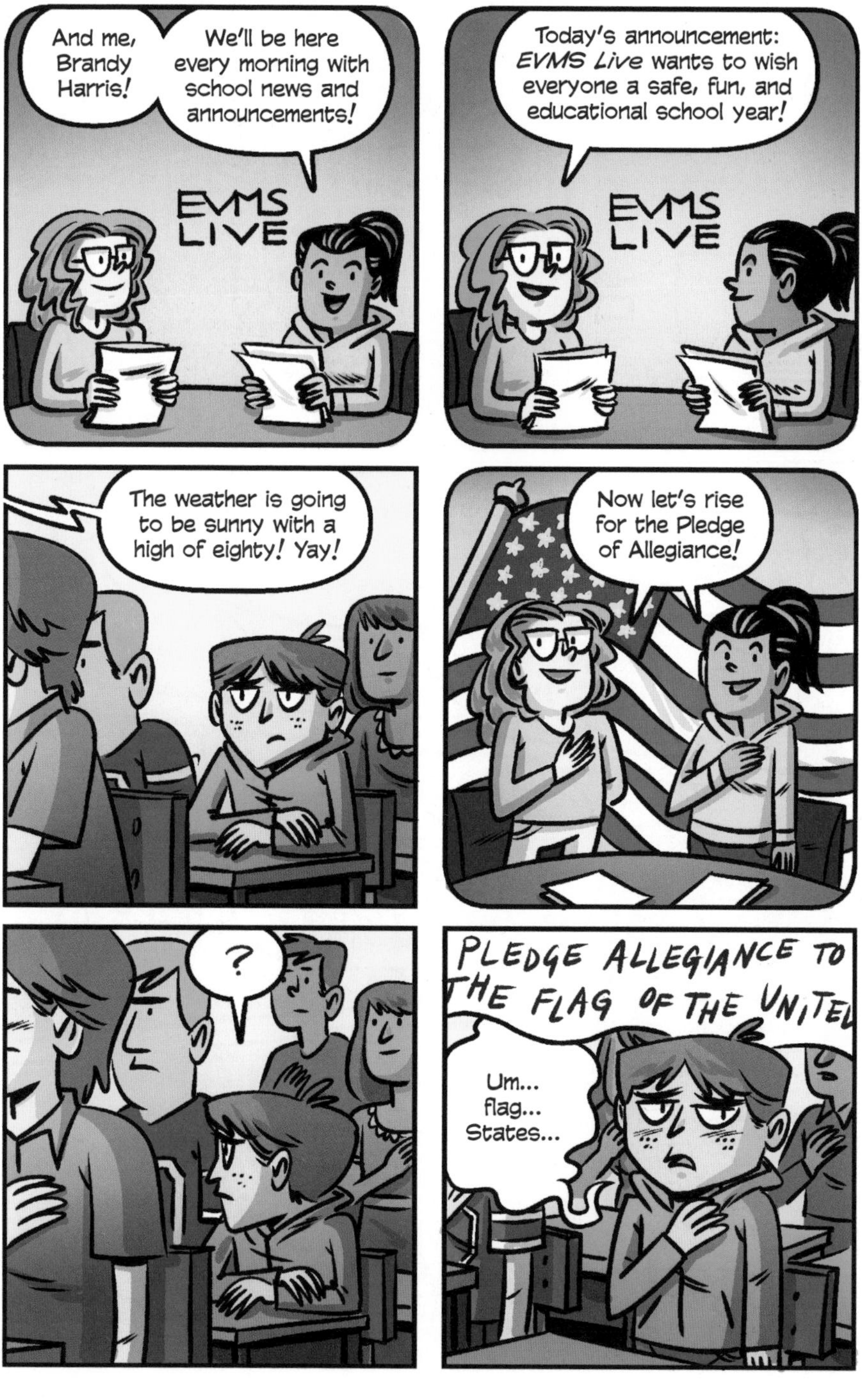
And me, Brandy Harris!
We'll be here every morning with school news and announcements!
EVMS LIVE
Today's announcement: *EVMS Live* wants to wish everyone a safe, fun, and educational school year!
EVMS LIVE
The weather is going to be sunny with a high of eighty! Yay!
Now let's rise for the Pledge of Allegiance!
?
PLEDGE ALLEGIANCE TO THE FLAG OF THE UNITE
Um... flag... States...

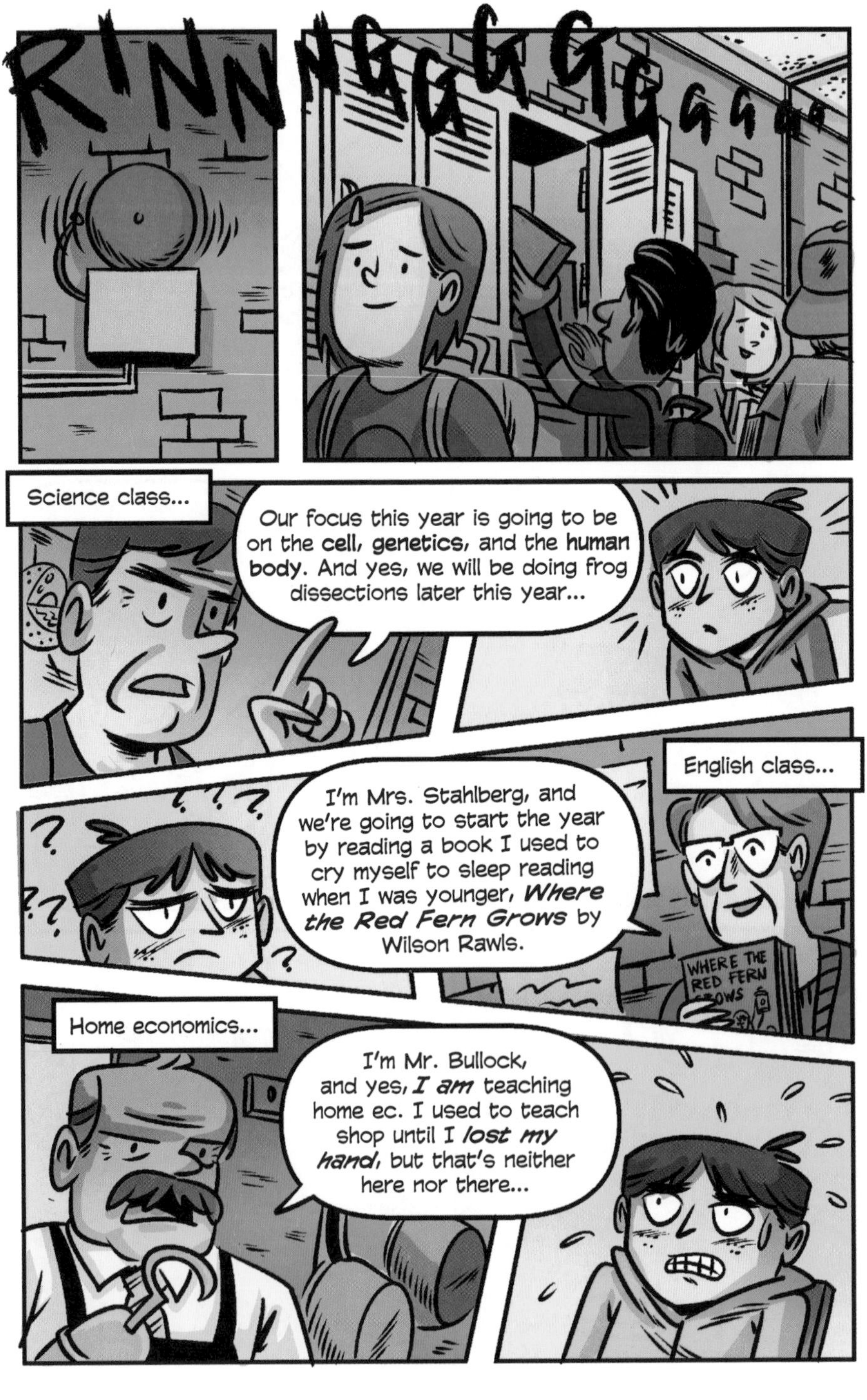
RINNGGGGGggggg
Science class...
Our focus this year is going to be on the **cell**, **genetics**, and the **human body**. And yes, we will be doing frog dissections later this year...
English class...
I'm Mrs. Stahlberg, and we're going to start the year by reading a book I used to cry myself to sleep reading when I was younger, ***Where the Red Fern Grows*** by Wilson Rawls.
WHERE THE RED FERN GROWS
Home economics...
I'm Mr. Bullock, and yes, ***I am*** teaching home ec. I used to teach shop until I ***lost my hand***, but that's neither here nor there...

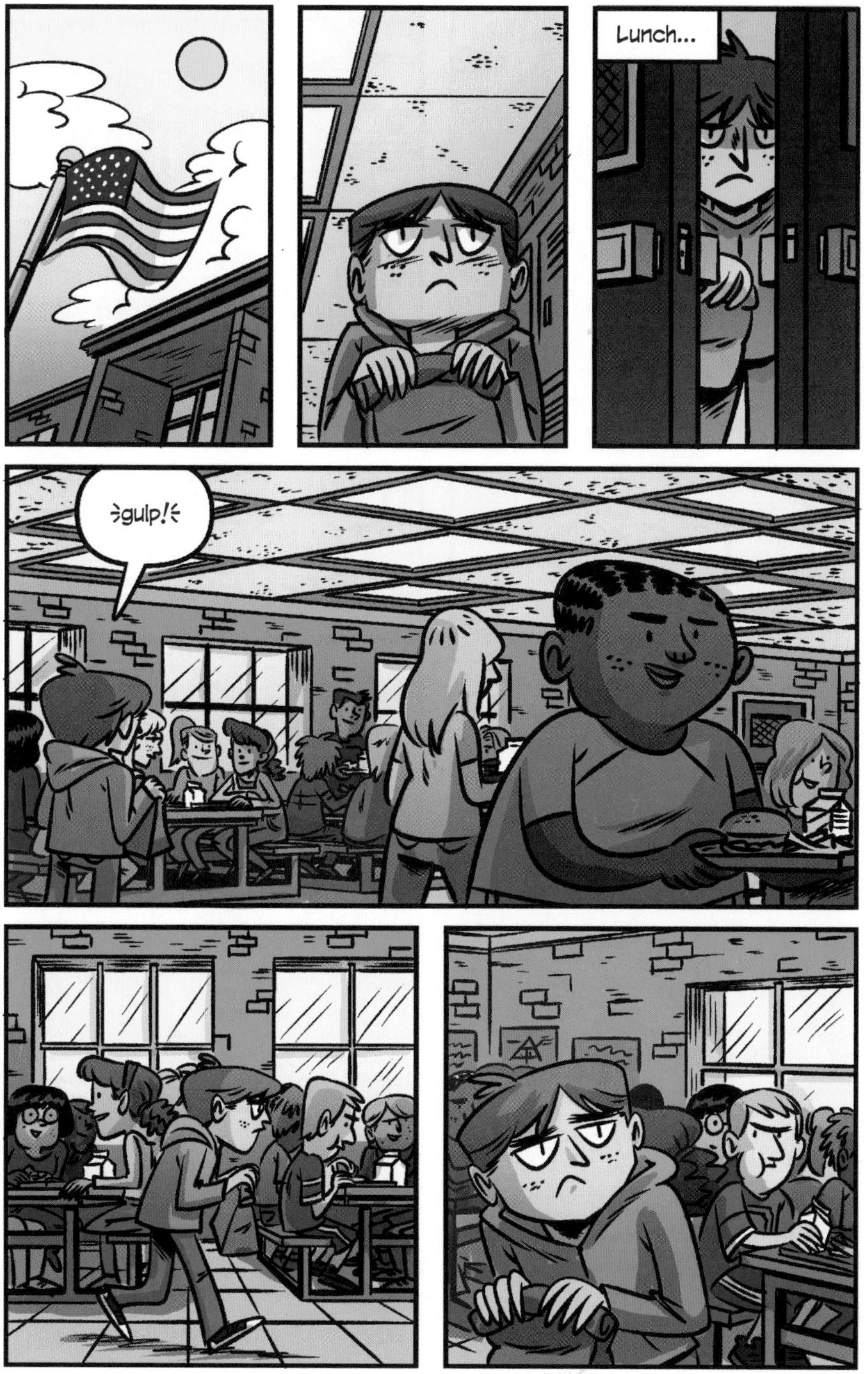
Lunch...
gulp!

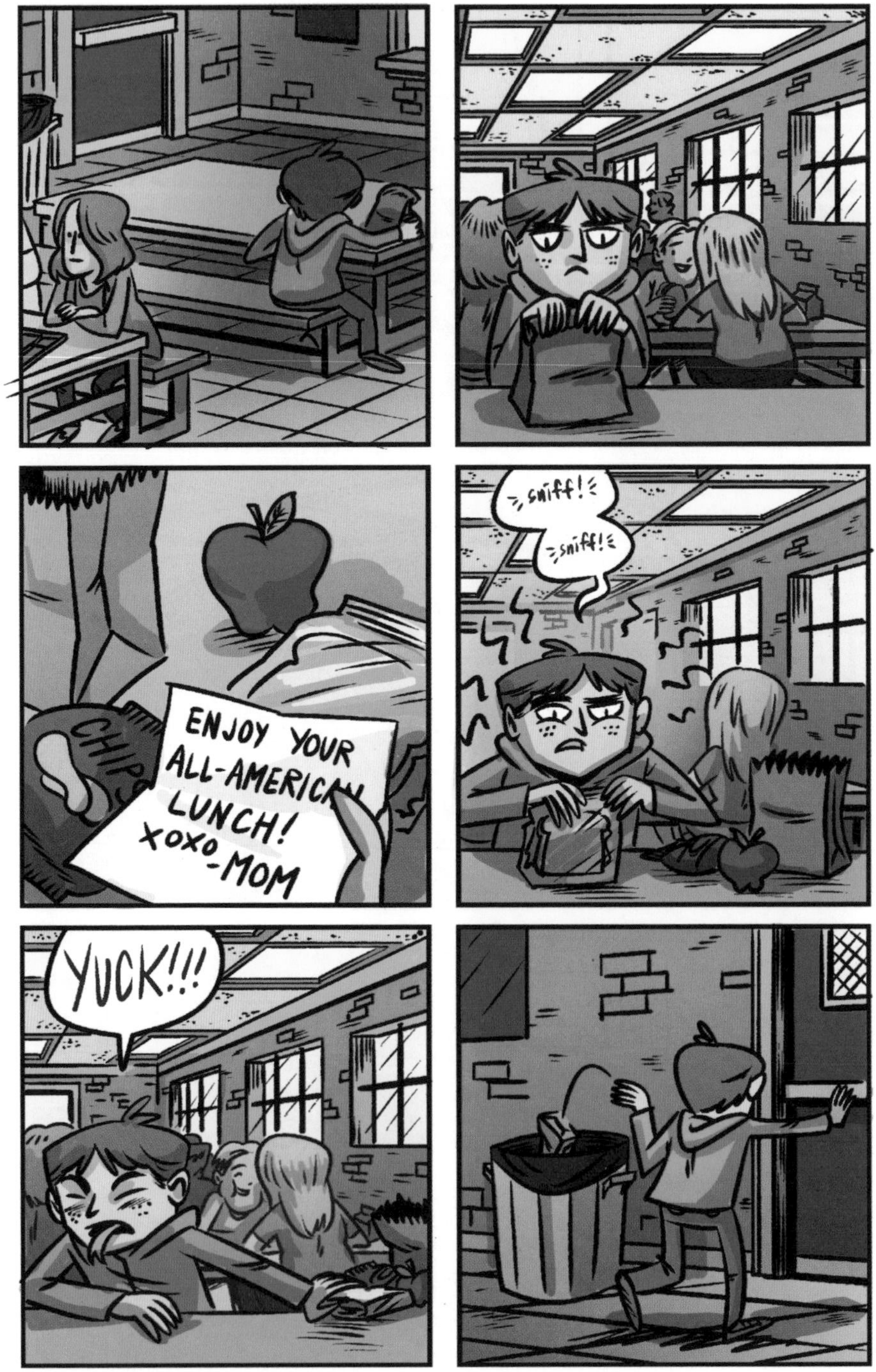
ENJOY YOUR ALL-AMERICAN LUNCH! XOXO-MOM
CHIP
sniff!
sniff!
YUCK!!!

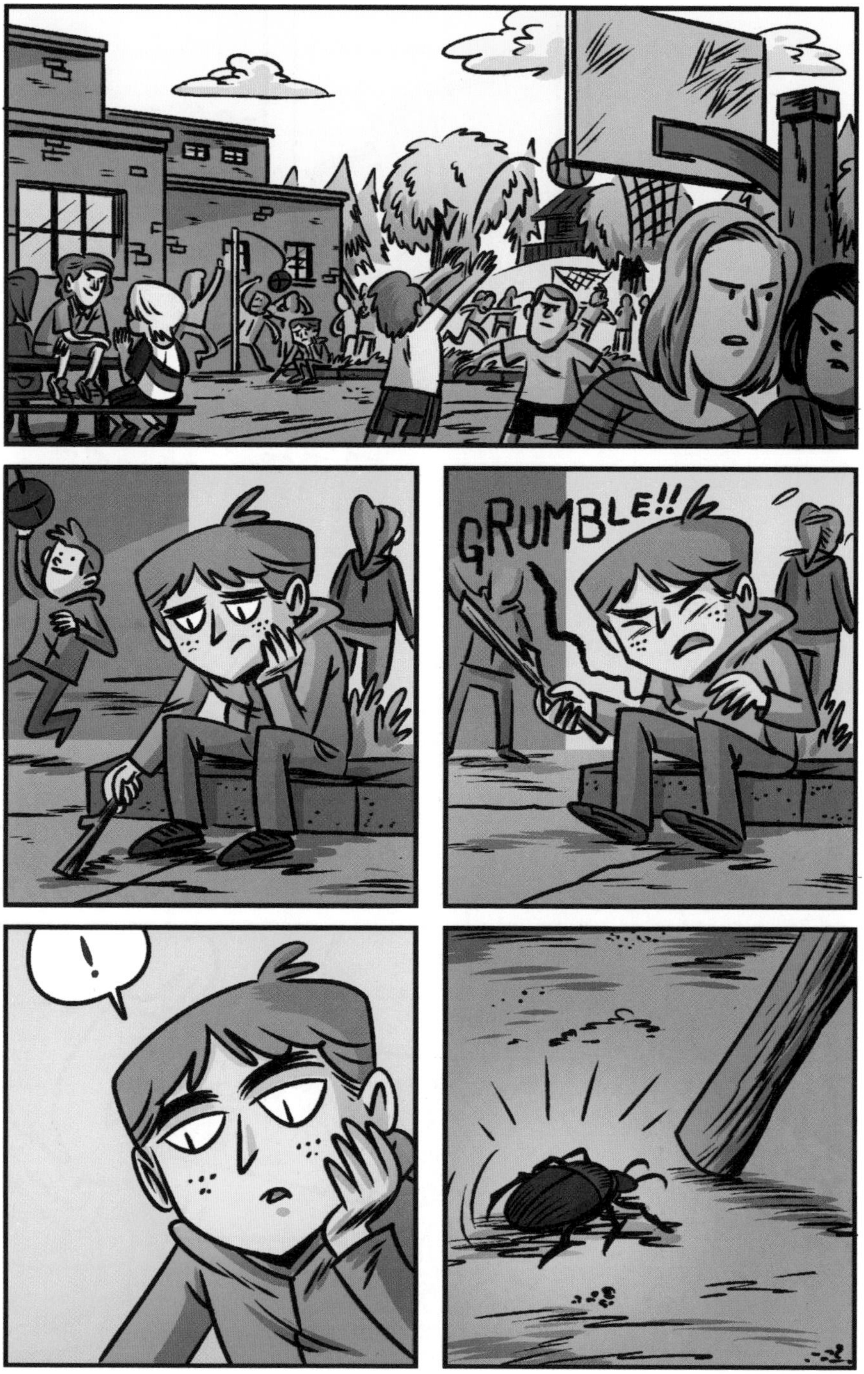
GRUMBLE!!
!

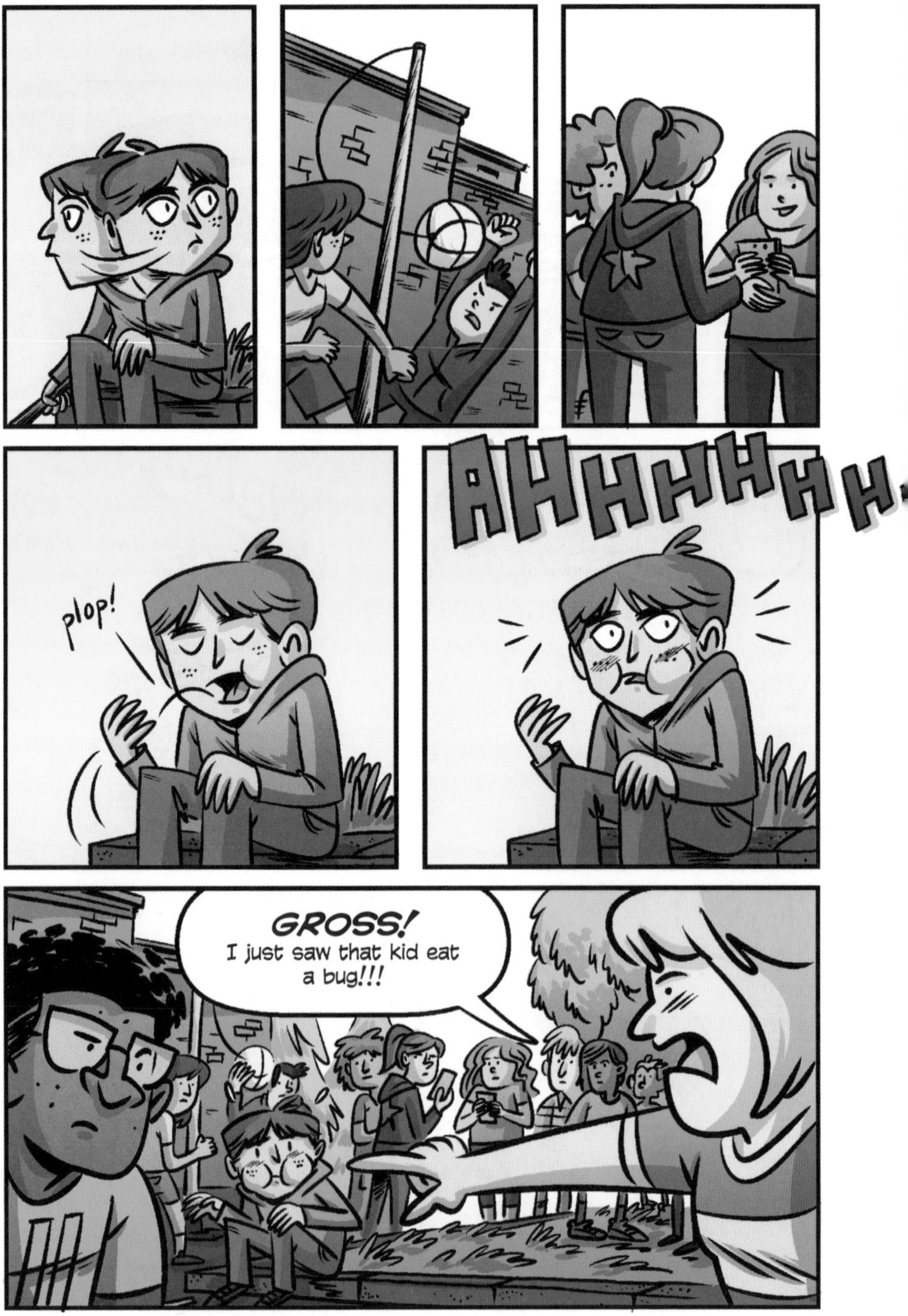
plop!
AHHHHHH
GROSS!
I just saw that kid eat a bug!!!

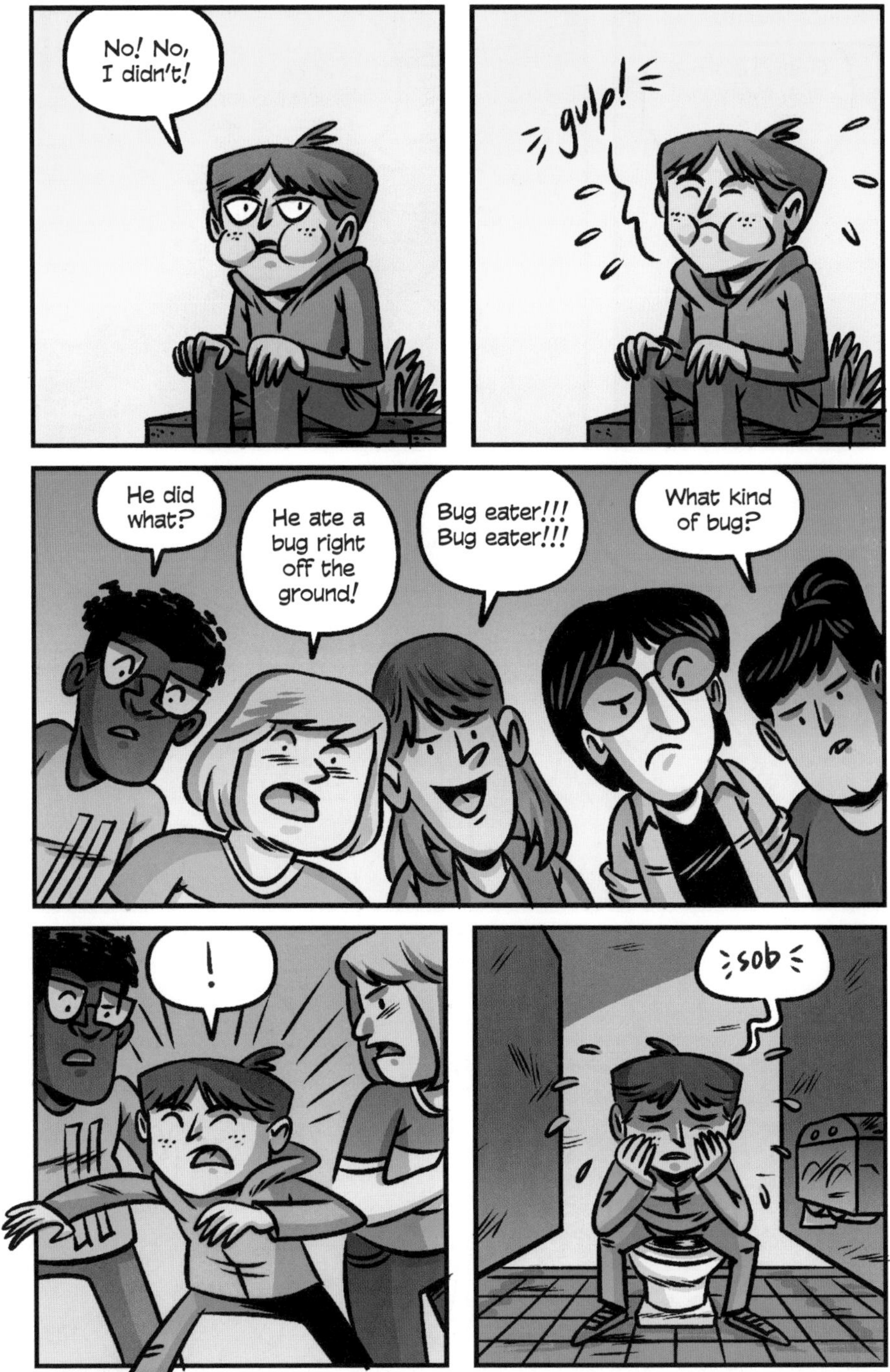
No! No,
I didn't!
gulp!
He did
what?
He ate a
bug right
off the
ground!
Bug eater!!!
Bug eater!!!
What kind
of bug?
!
sob

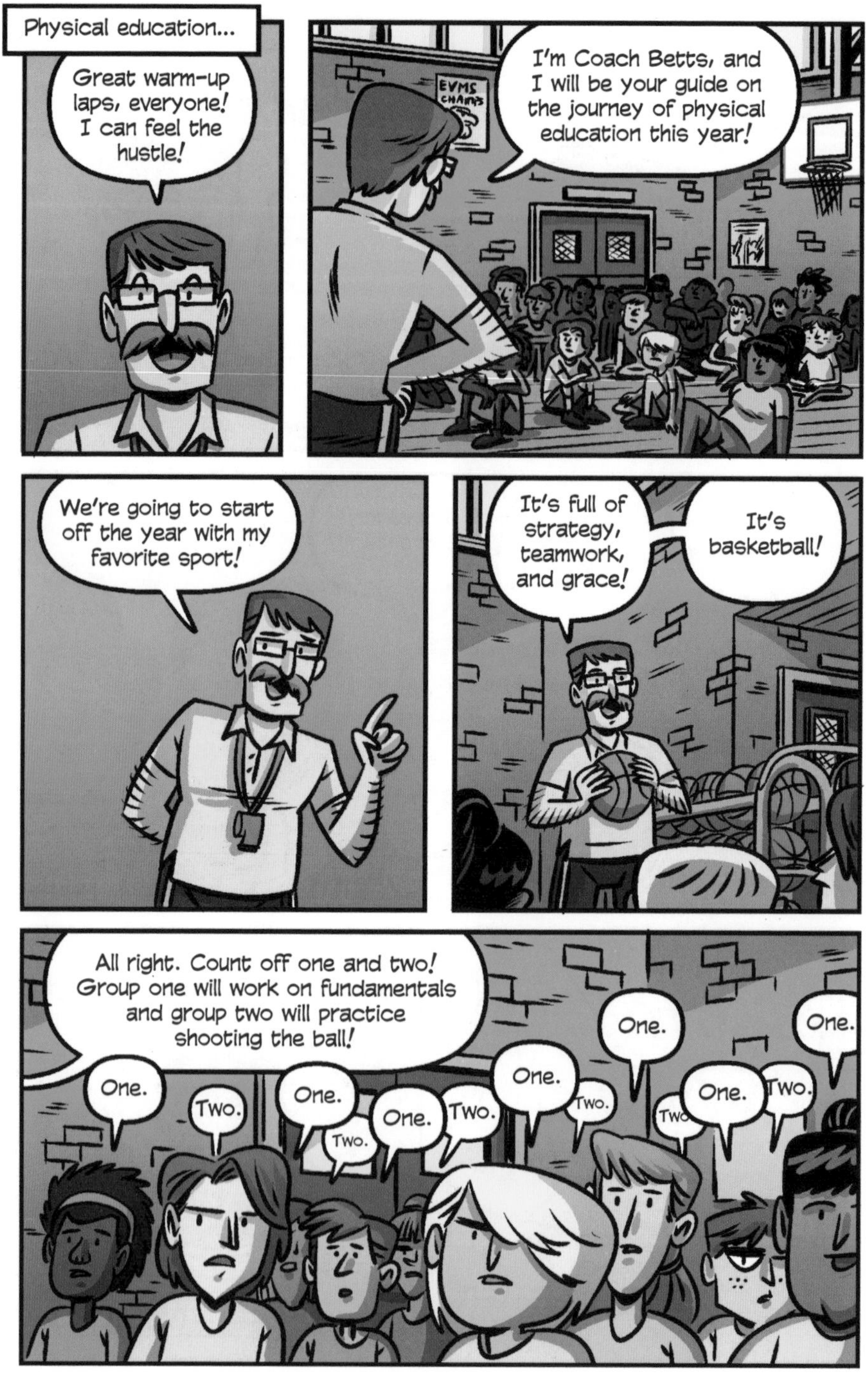
Physical education...
Great warm-up laps, everyone! I can feel the hustle!
I'm Coach Betts, and I will be your guide on the journey of physical education this year!
EVMS CHAMPS
We're going to start off the year with my favorite sport!
It's full of strategy, teamwork, and grace!
It's basketball!
All right. Count off one and two! Group one will work on fundamentals and group two will practice shooting the ball!
One.
Two.
One.
Two.
One.
Two.
One.
Two.
One.
One.
Two.
One.

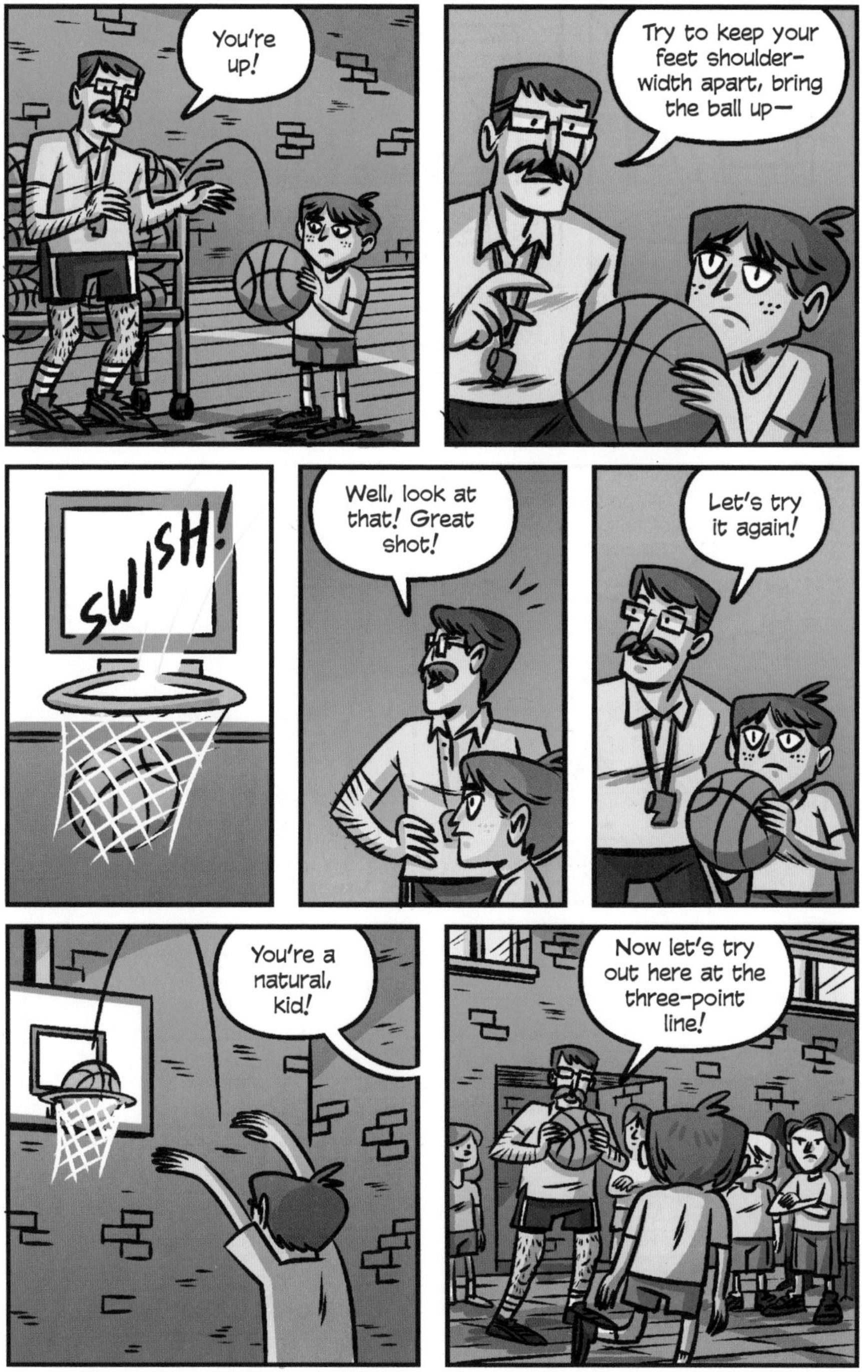
You're up!
Try to keep your feet shoulder-width apart, bring the ball up—
SWISH!
Well, look at that! Great shot!
Let's try it again!
You're a natural, kid!
Now let's try out here at the three-point line!

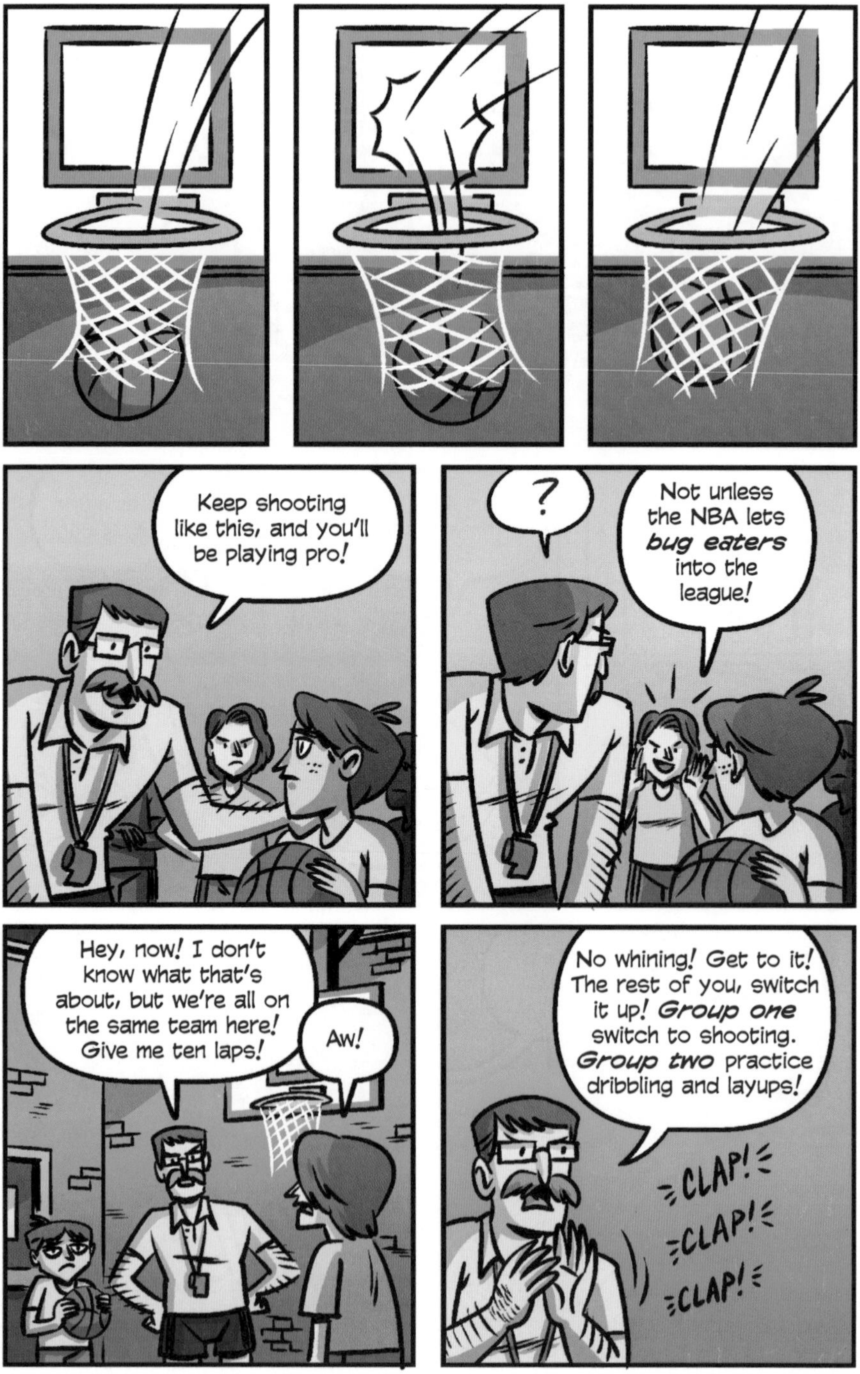
Keep shooting like this, and you'll be playing pro!
?
Not unless the NBA lets ***bug eaters*** into the league!
Hey, now! I don't know what that's about, but we're all on the same team here! Give me ten laps!
Aw!
No whining! Get to it! The rest of you, switch it up! ***Group one*** switch to shooting. ***Group two*** practice dribbling and layups!
CLAP!
CLAP!
CLAP!

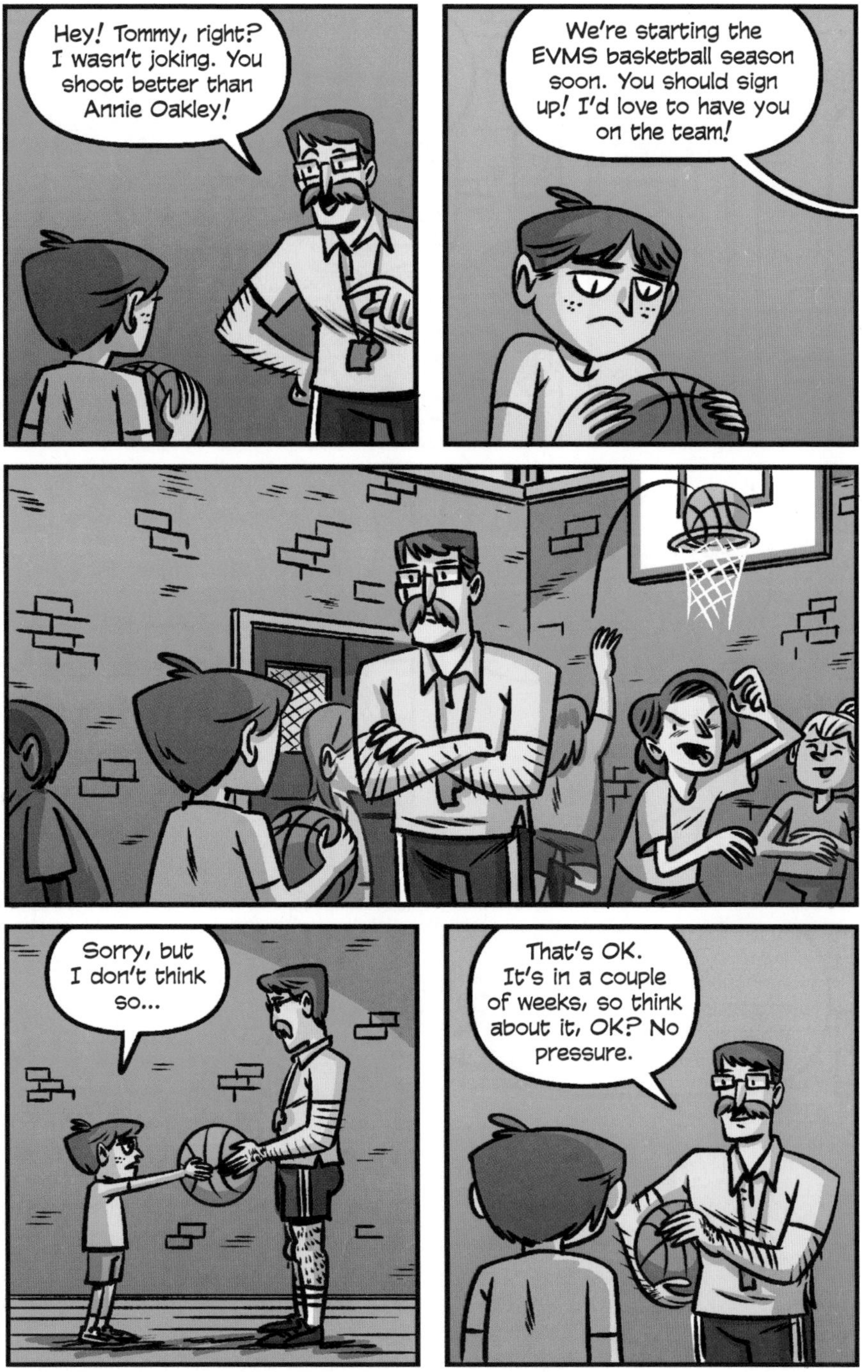
Hey! Tommy, right? I wasn't joking. You shoot better than Annie Oakley!
We're starting the EVMS basketball season soon. You should sign up! I'd love to have you on the team!
Sorry, but I don't think so...
That's OK. It's in a couple of weeks, so think about it, OK? No pressure.

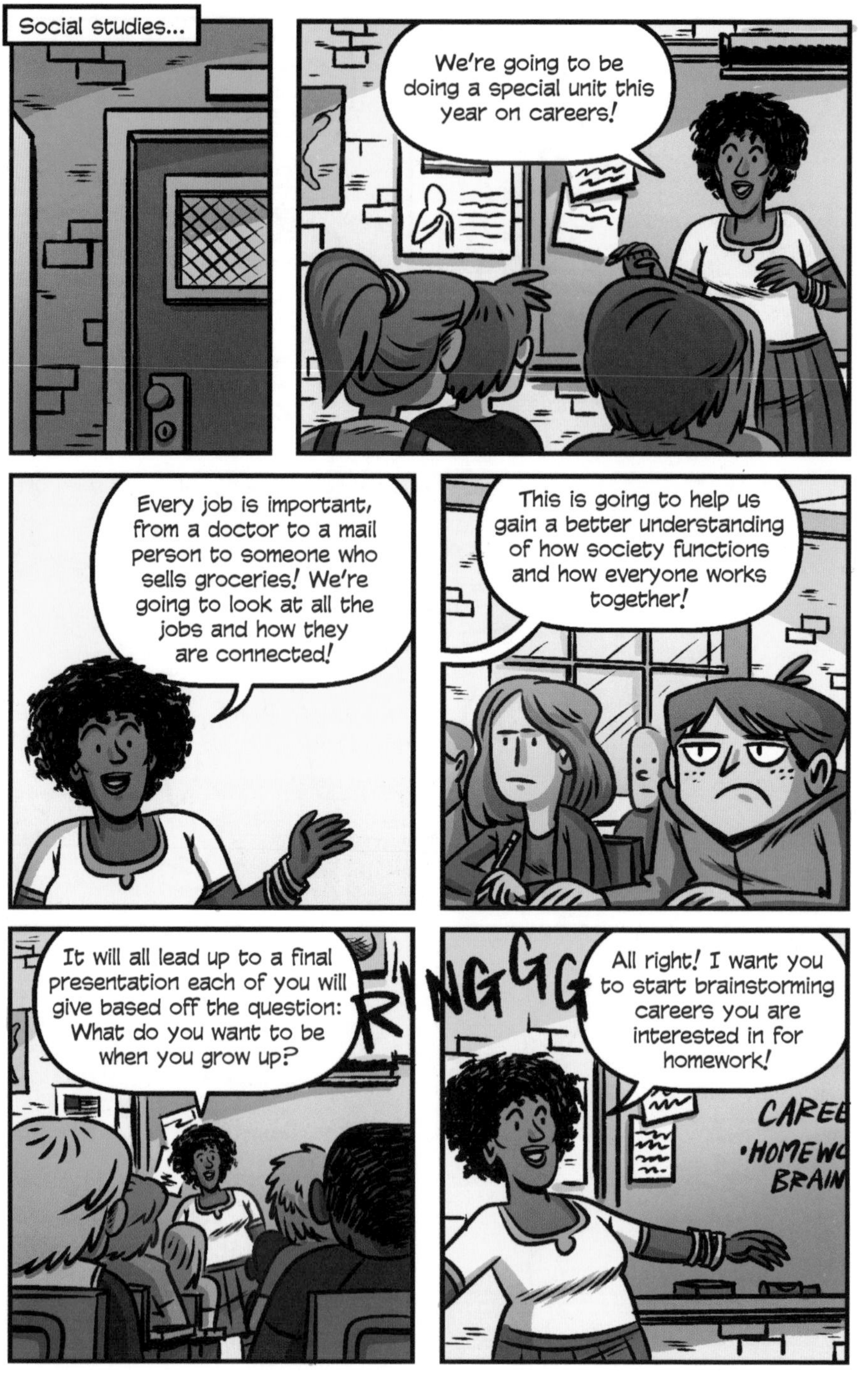
Social studies...
We're going to be doing a special unit this year on careers!
Every job is important, from a doctor to a mail person to someone who sells groceries! We're going to look at all the jobs and how they are connected!
This is going to help us gain a better understanding of how society functions and how everyone works together!
It will all lead up to a final presentation each of you will give based off the question: What do you want to be when you grow up?
RINGGG
All right! I want you to start brainstorming careers you are interested in for homework!

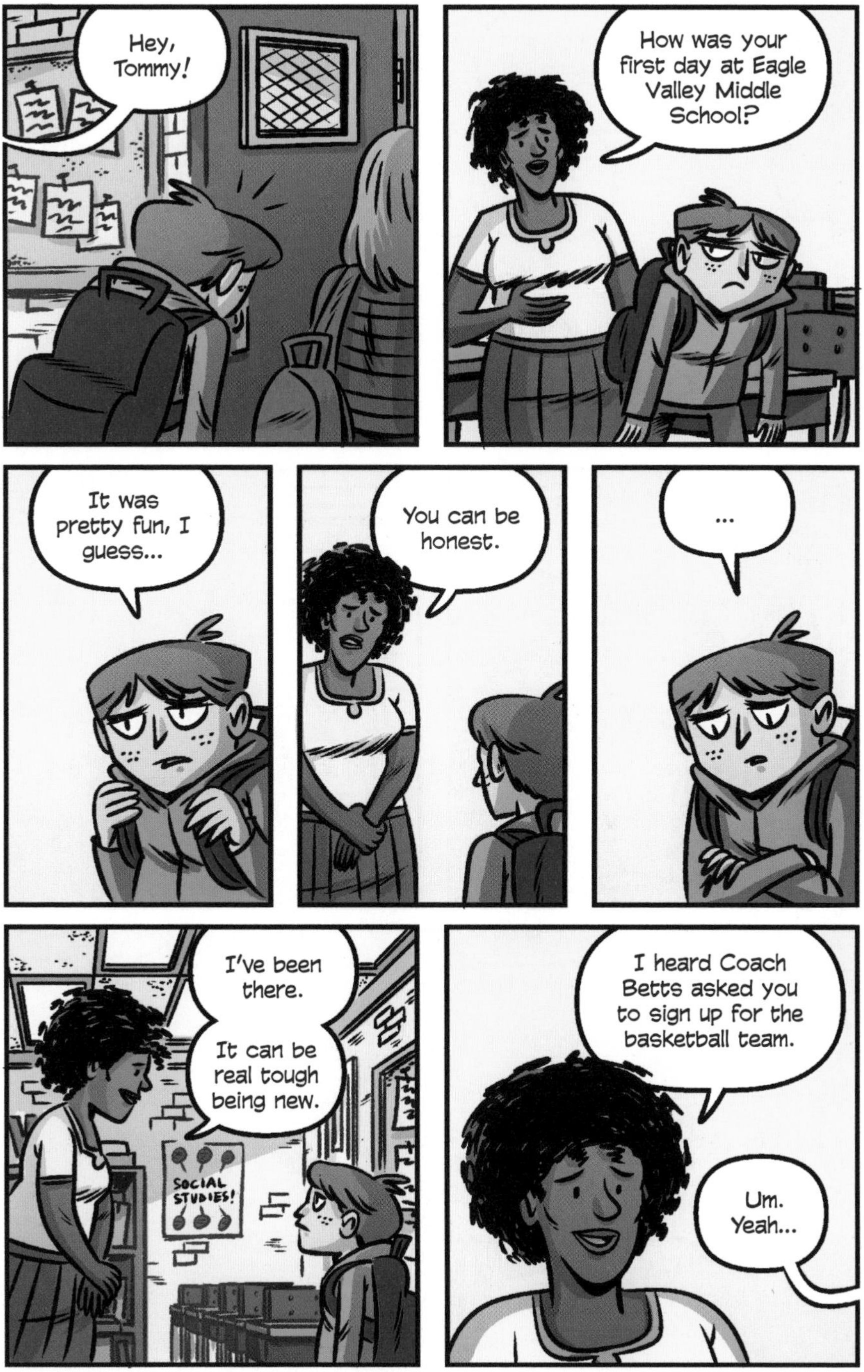
Hey, Tommy!
How was your first day at Eagle Valley Middle School?
It was pretty fun, I guess...
You can be honest.
...
I've been there.
It can be real tough being new.
SOCIAL STUDIES!
I heard Coach Betts asked you to sign up for the basketball team.
Um. Yeah...

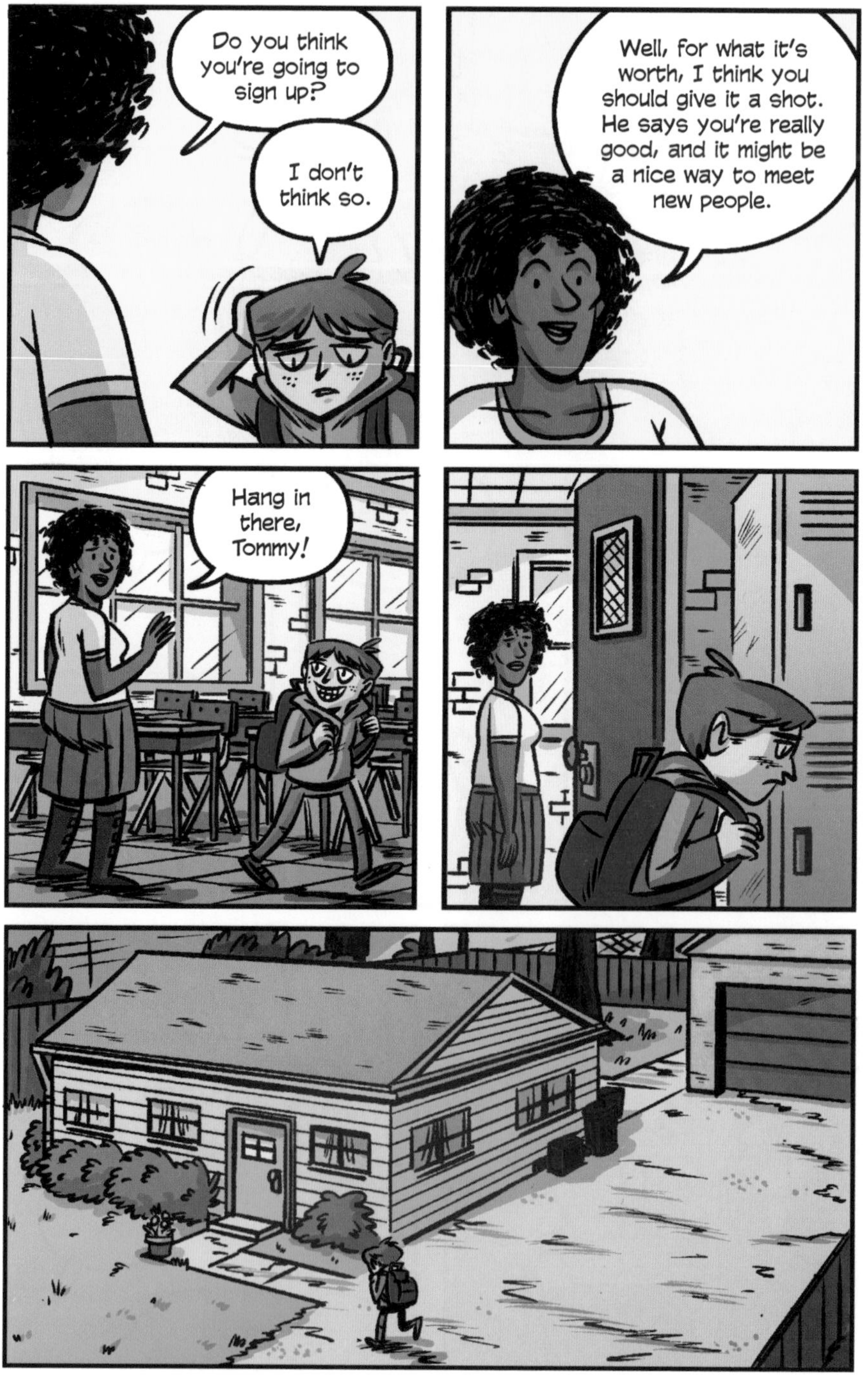
Do you think you're going to sign up?
I don't think so.
Well, for what it's worth, I think you should give it a shot. He says you're really good, and it might be a nice way to meet new people.
Hang in there, Tommy!

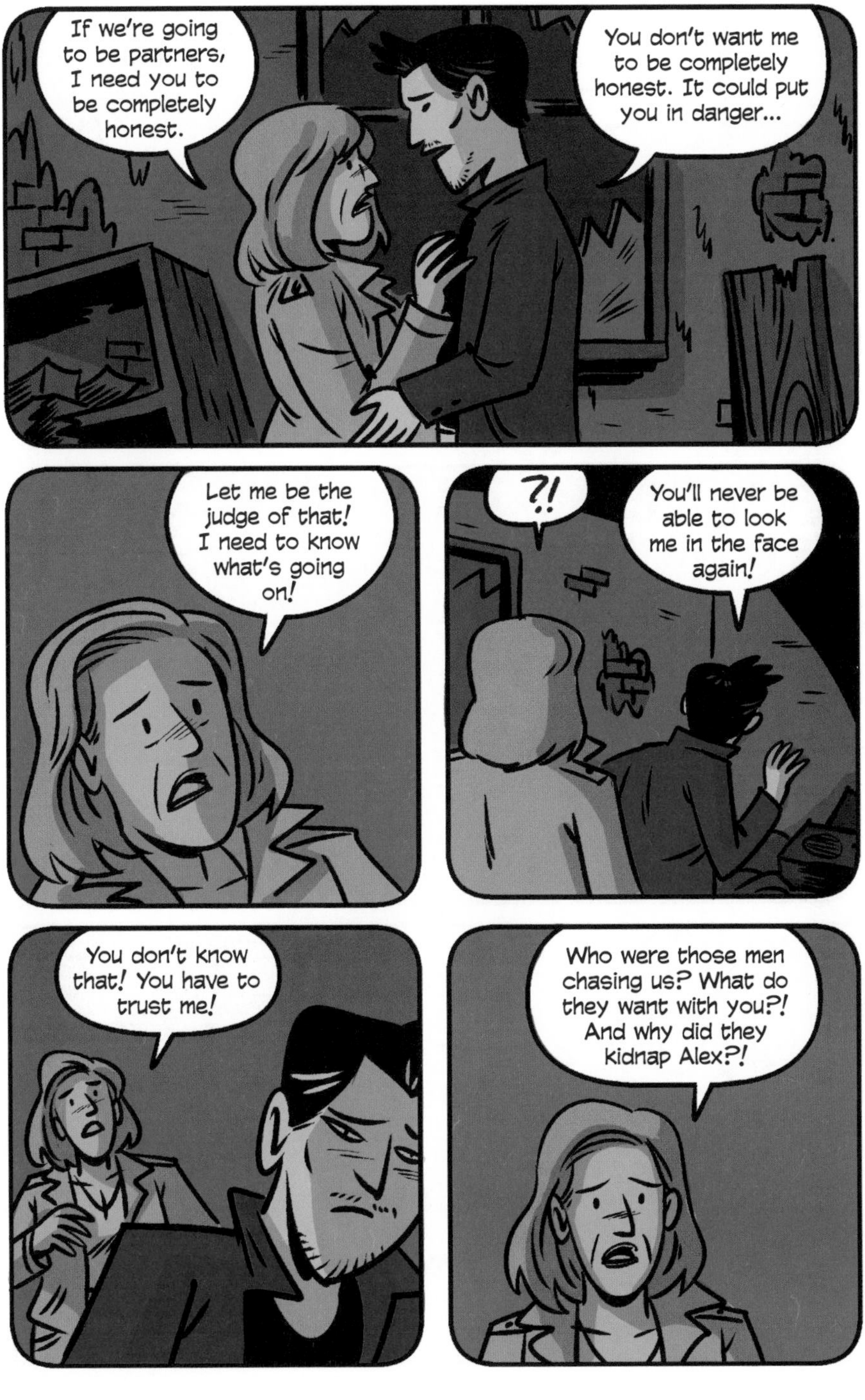
If we're going to be partners, I need you to be completely honest.
You don't want me to be completely honest. It could put you in danger...
Let me be the judge of that! I need to know what's going on!
?!
You'll never be able to look me in the face again!
You don't know that! You have to trust me!
Who were those men chasing us? What do they want with you?! And why did they kidnap Alex?!

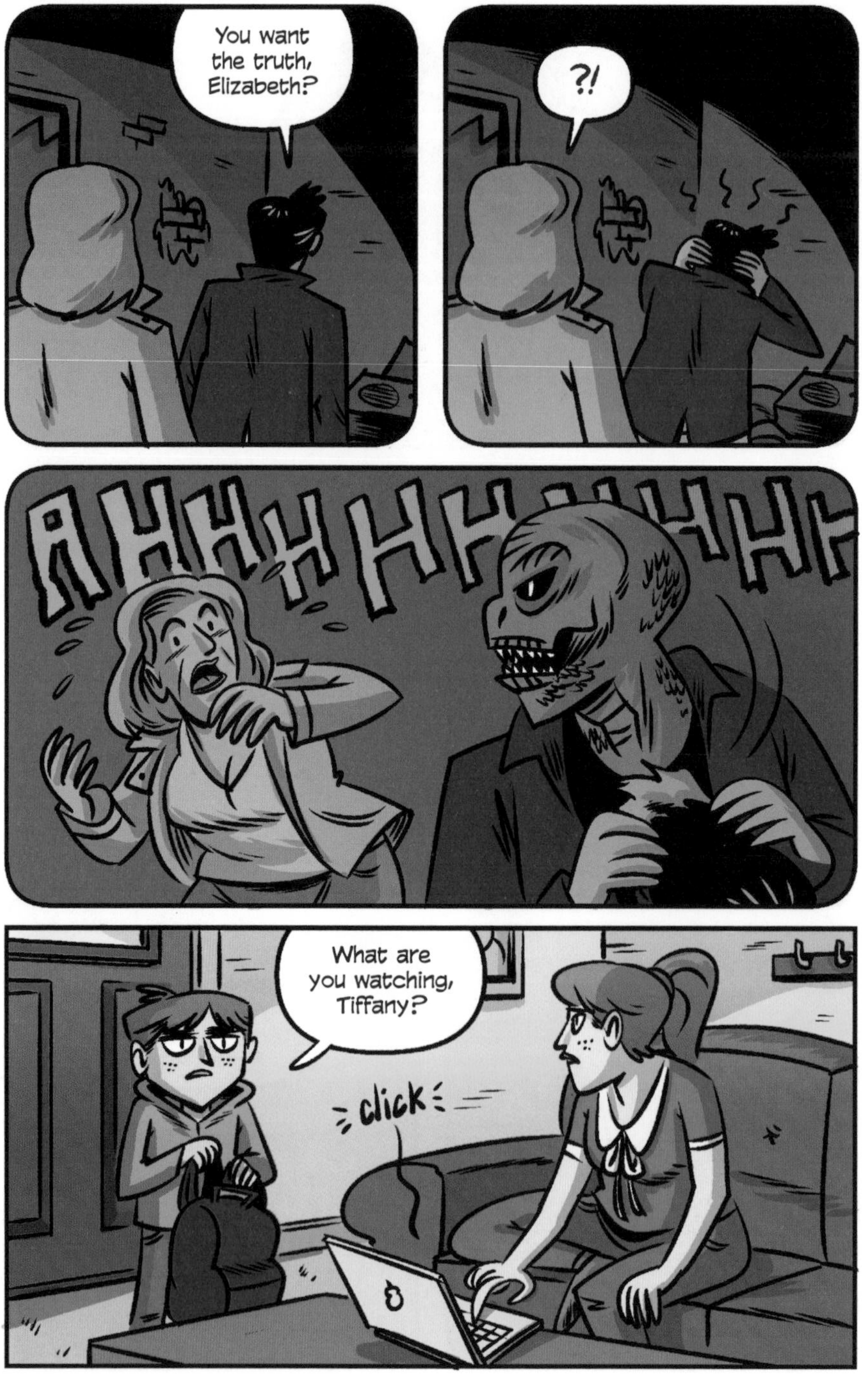
You want the truth, Elizabeth?
?!
AHHHHHHHHHHH
What are you watching, Tiffany?
click

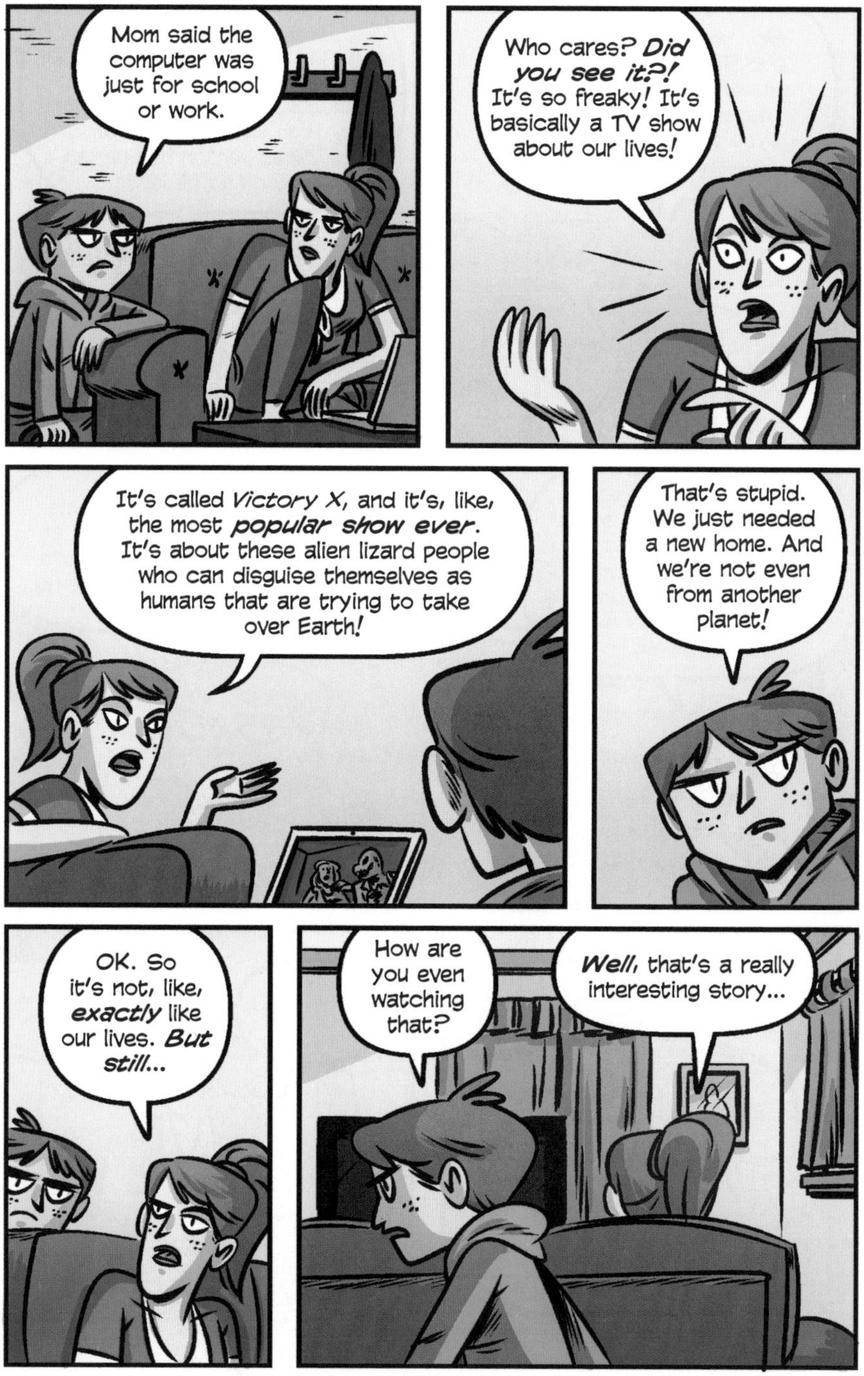
Mom said the computer was just for school or work.
Who cares? Did you see it?! It's so freaky! It's basically a TV show about our lives!
It's called Victory X, and it's, like, the most popular show ever. It's about these alien lizard people who can disguise themselves as humans that are trying to take over Earth!
That's stupid. We just needed a new home. And we're not even from another planet!
OK. So it's not, like, exactly like our lives. But still...
How are you even watching that?
Well, that's a really interesting story...

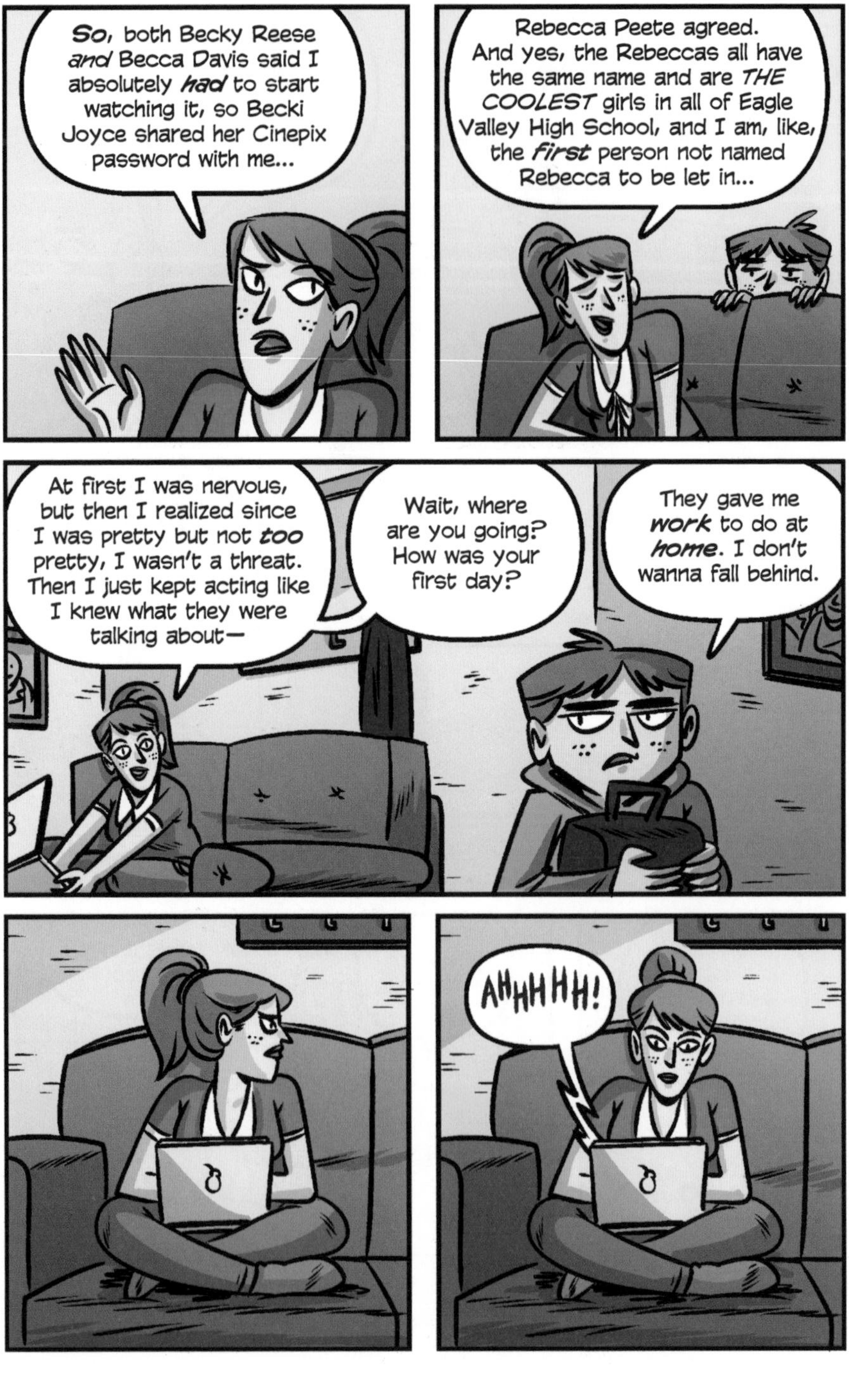
So, both Becky Reese and Becca Davis said I absolutely had to start watching it, so Becki Joyce shared her Cinepix password with me...
Rebecca Peete agreed. And yes, the Rebeccas all have the same name and are THE COOLEST girls in all of Eagle Valley High School, and I am, like, the first person not named Rebecca to be let in...
At first I was nervous, but then I realized since I was pretty but not too pretty, I wasn't a threat. Then I just kept acting like I knew what they were talking about—
Wait, where are you going? How was your first day?
They gave me work to do at home. I don't wanna fall behind.
AHHHHH!

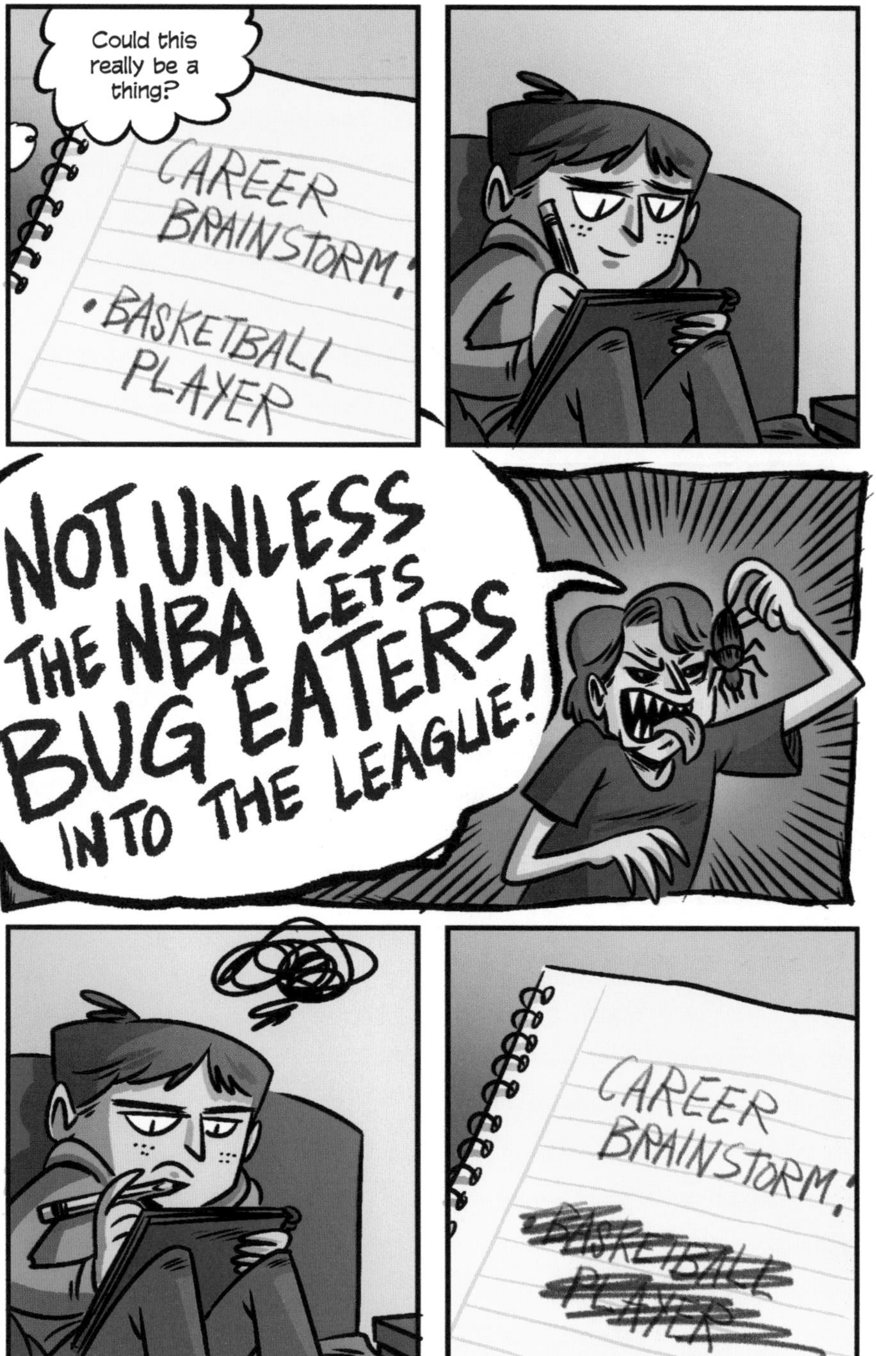
Could this really be a thing?
CAREER BRAINSTORM:
• BASKETBALL PLAYER
NOT UNLESS THE NBA LETS BUG EATERS INTO THE LEAGUE!
CAREER BRAINSTORM:
BASKETBALL PLAYER

CHAPTER 3

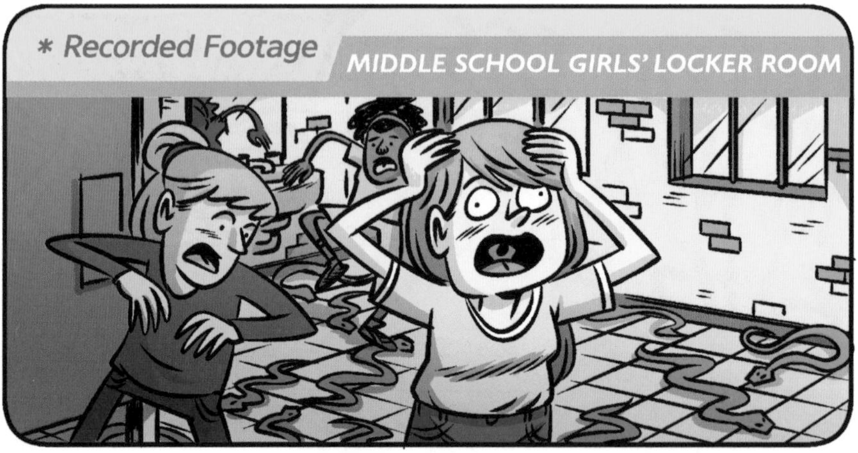
* Recorded Footage
MIDDLE SCHOOL GIRLS' LOCKER ROOM

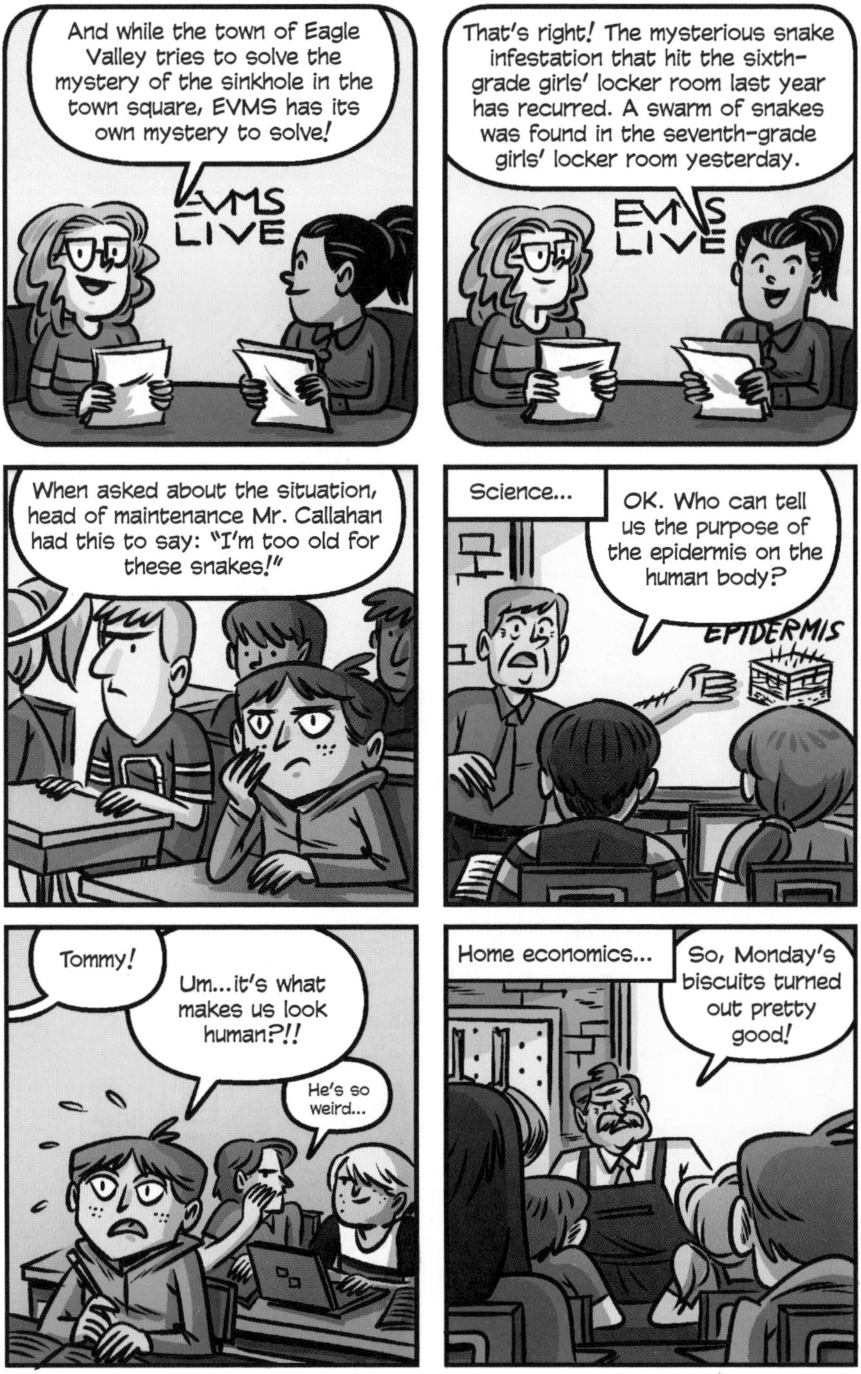
And while the town of Eagle Valley tries to solve the mystery of the sinkhole in the town square, EVMS has its own mystery to solve!
EVMS LIVE
That's right! The mysterious snake infestation that hit the sixth-grade girls' locker room last year has recurred. A swarm of snakes was found in the seventh-grade girls' locker room yesterday.
EVMS LIVE
When asked about the situation, head of maintenance Mr. Callahan had this to say: "I'm too old for these snakes!"
Science...
OK. Who can tell us the purpose of the epidermis on the human body?
EPIDERMIS
Tommy!
Um...it's what makes us look human?!!
He's so weird...
Home economics...
So, Monday's biscuits turned out pretty good!

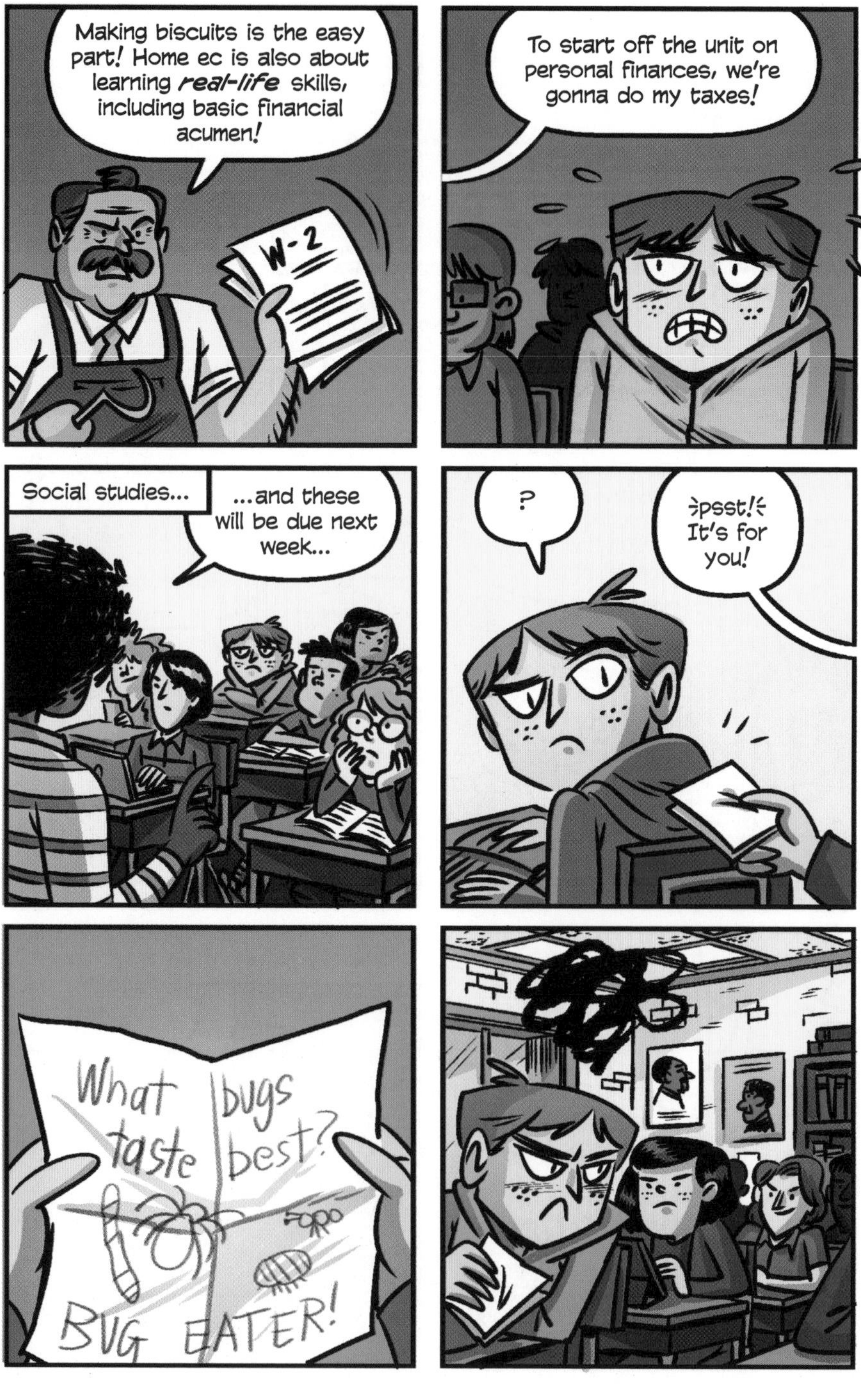
Making biscuits is the easy part! Home ec is also about learning real-life skills, including basic financial acumen!
W-2
To start off the unit on personal finances, we're gonna do my taxes!
Social studies...
...and these will be due next week...
?
psst! It's for you!
What bugs taste best?
BUG EATER!

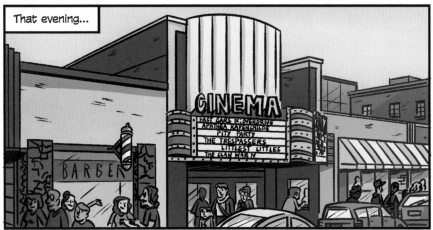

That evening...
CINEMA
FAST CARS IX: OVERDRIVE
APATHEA RAVENCHILDE
PITY PARTY
THE TRESPASSERS
LITTLEST LITTLES
THE CLAN WAR IV
BARBER
Well, that certainly was... LOUD.
What did everyone else think?
I need to know which bald muscle man was hotter so I know how to talk to the Rebeccas on Monday.
The movies in Elberon were way better...
!
!

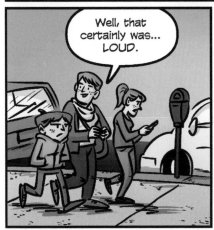

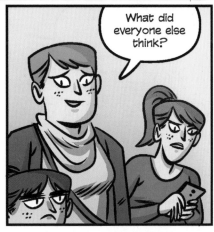

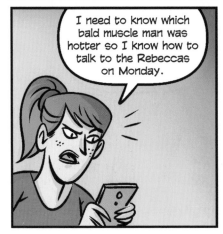

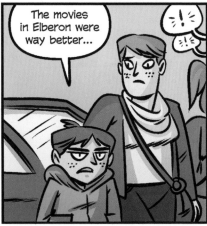

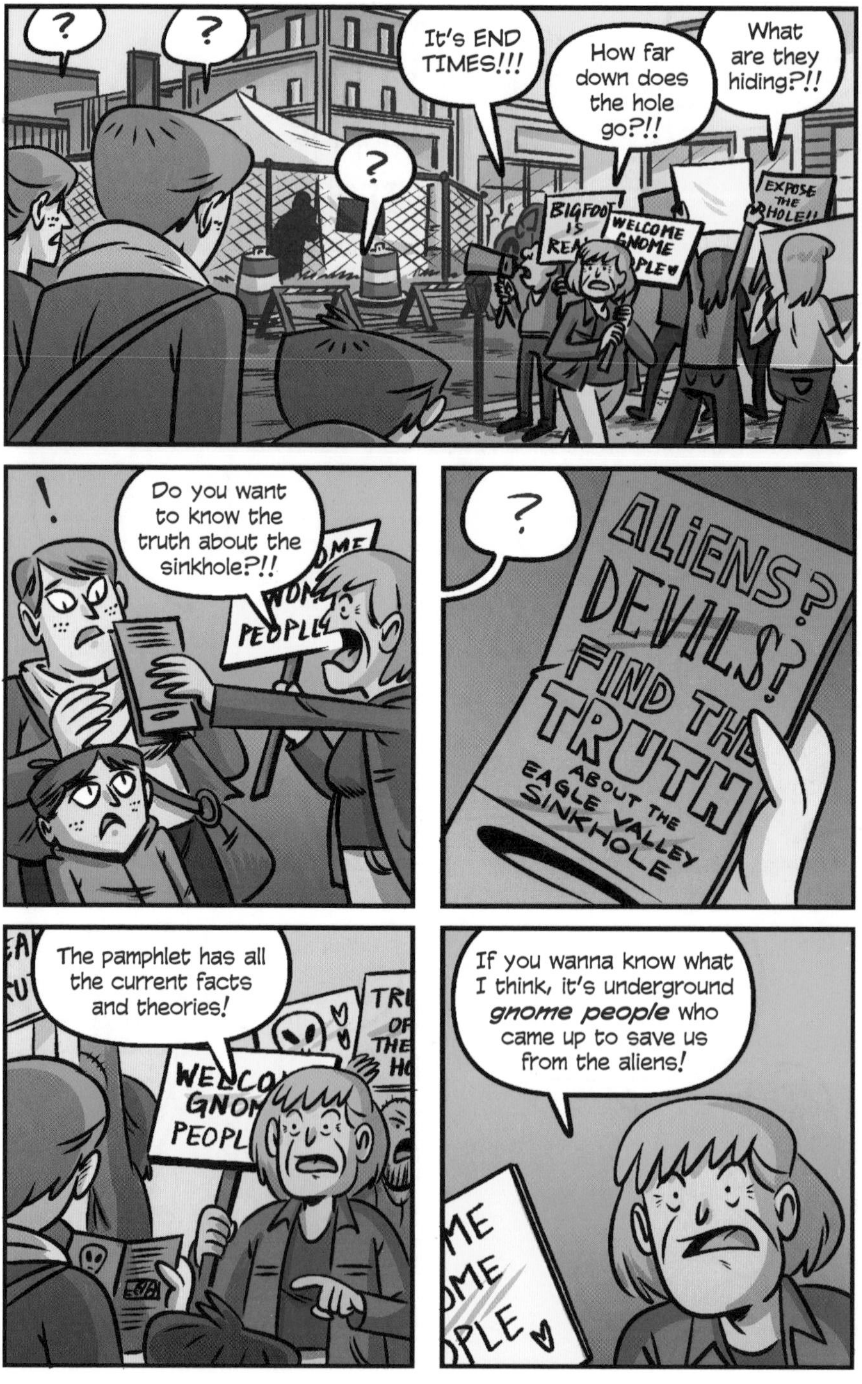
?
?
It's END TIMES!!!
How far down does the hole go?!!
What are they hiding?!!
?
BIGFOOT IS REA
WELCOME GNOME PLE
EXPOSE THE HOLE!!
!
Do you want to know the truth about the sinkhole?!!
PEOPLE
?
ALIENS? DEVILS? FIND THE TRUTH ABOUT THE EAGLE VALLEY SINKHOLE
The pamphlet has all the current facts and theories!
WELCO GNOM PEOPL
If you wanna know what I think, it's underground *gnome people* who came up to save us from the aliens!
ME OME PLE

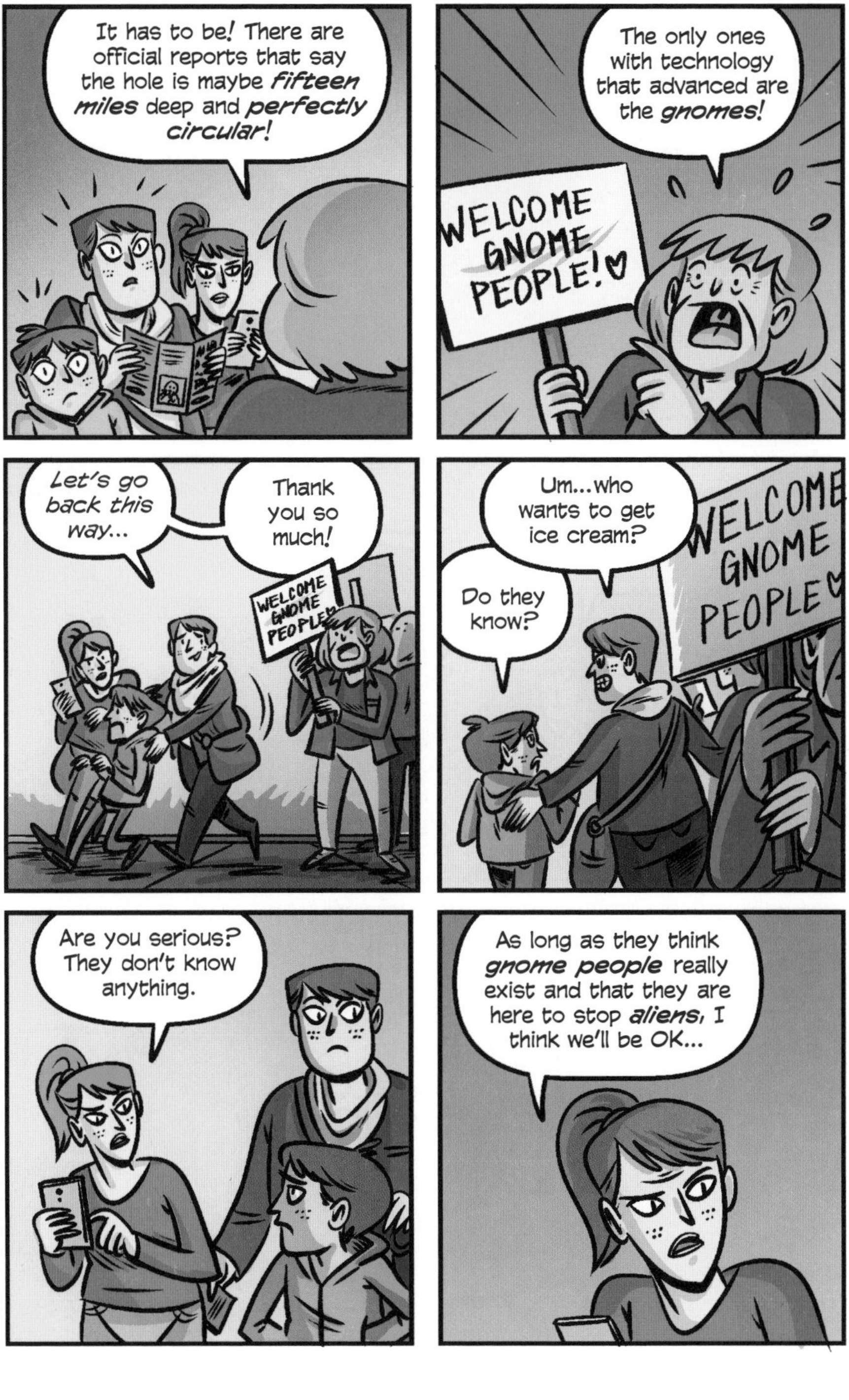
It has to be! There are official reports that say the hole is maybe *fifteen miles* deep and *perfectly circular*!
The only ones with technology that advanced are the *gnomes*!
WELCOME GNOME PEOPLE!
Let's go back this way...
Thank you so much!
WELCOME GNOME PEOPLE
Um...who wants to get ice cream?
Do they know?
WELCOME GNOME PEOPLE
Are you serious? They don't know anything.
As long as they think *gnome people* really exist and that they are here to stop *aliens*, I think we'll be OK...

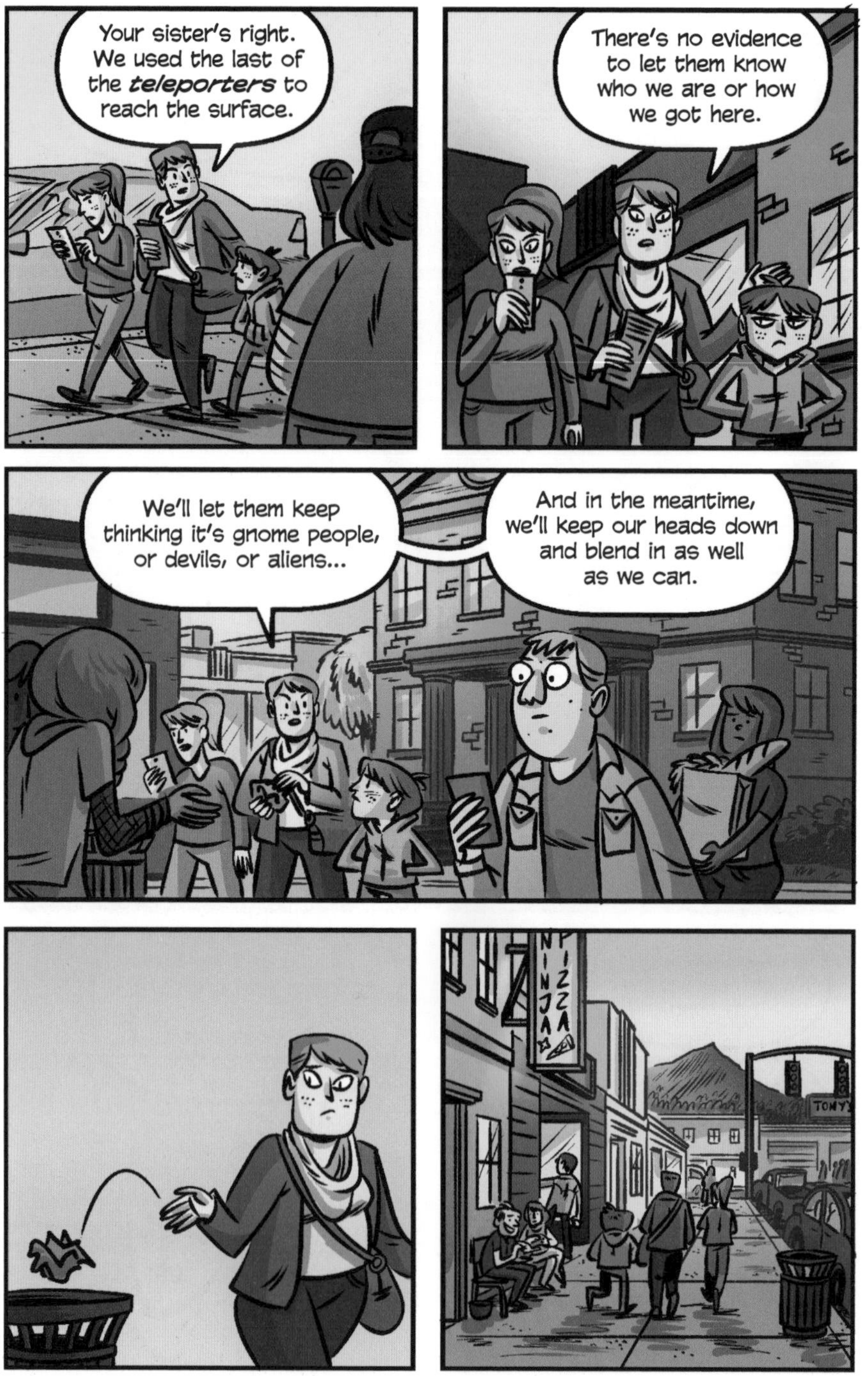
Your sister's right. We used the last of the *teleporters* to reach the surface.
There's no evidence to let them know who we are or how we got here.
We'll let them keep thinking it's gnome people, or devils, or aliens...
And in the meantime, we'll keep our heads down and blend in as well as we can.
NINJA
PIZZA

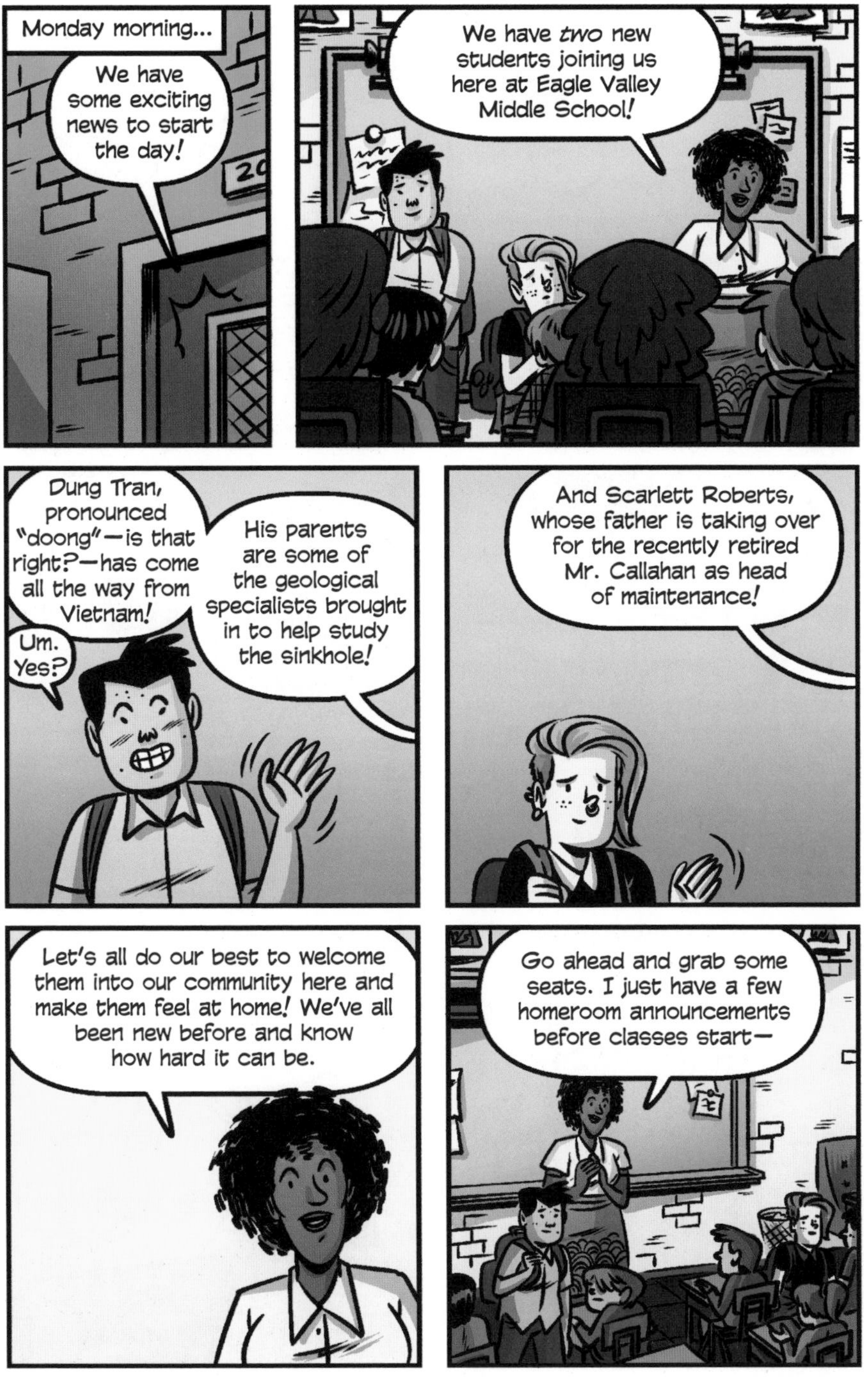
Monday morning...
We have some exciting news to start the day!
We have *two* new students joining us here at Eagle Valley Middle School!
Dung Tran, pronounced "doong"—is that right?—has come all the way from Vietnam!
Um. Yes?
His parents are some of the geological specialists brought in to help study the sinkhole!
And Scarlett Roberts, whose father is taking over for the recently retired Mr. Callahan as head of maintenance!
Let's all do our best to welcome them into our community here and make them feel at home! We've all been new before and know how hard it can be.
Go ahead and grab some seats. I just have a few homeroom announcements before classes start—

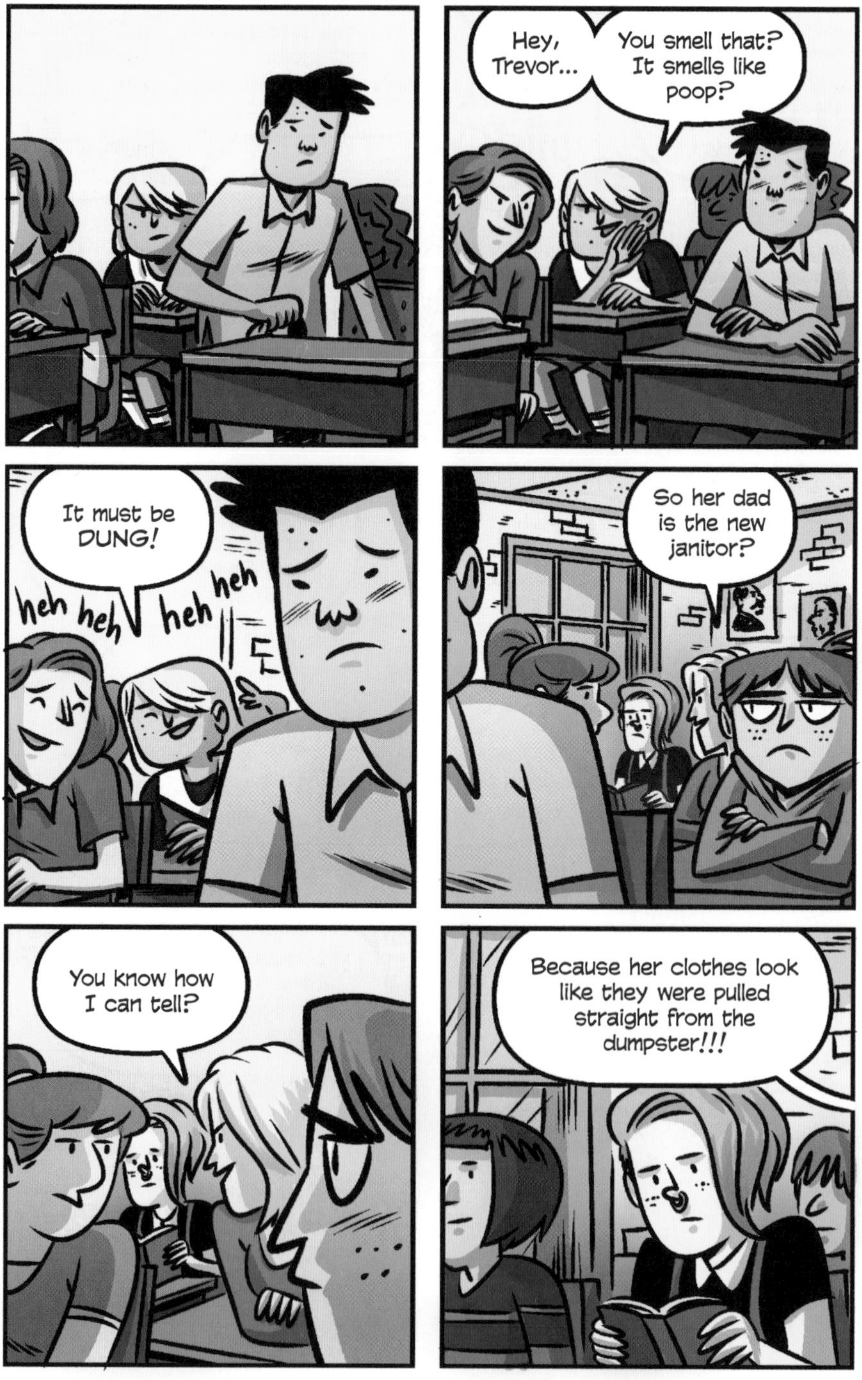
Hey, Trevor...
You smell that? It smells like poop?
It must be DUNG!
heh heh heh heh
So her dad is the new janitor?
You know how I can tell?
Because her clothes look like they were pulled straight from the dumpster!!!

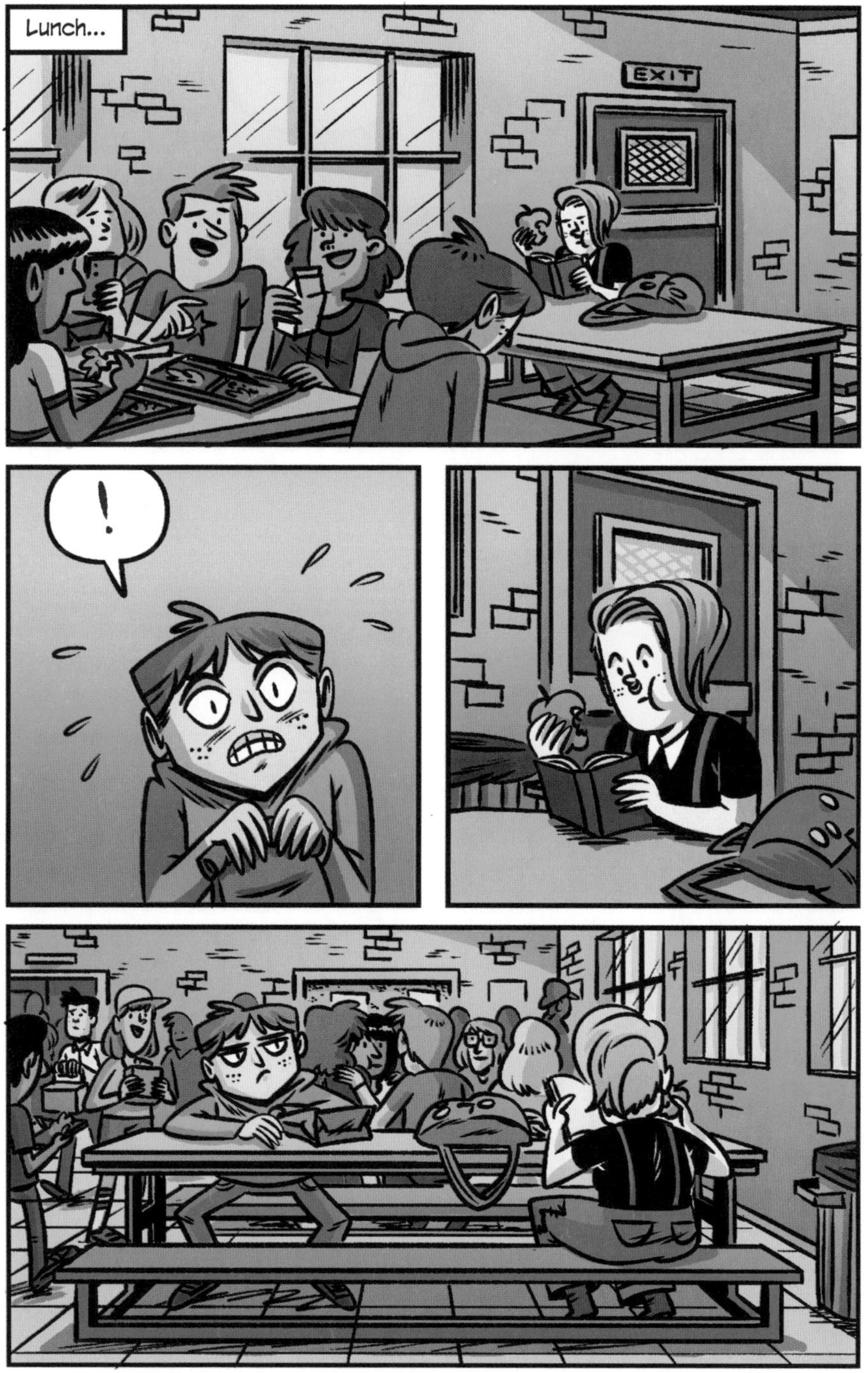
Lunch...
EXIT
!

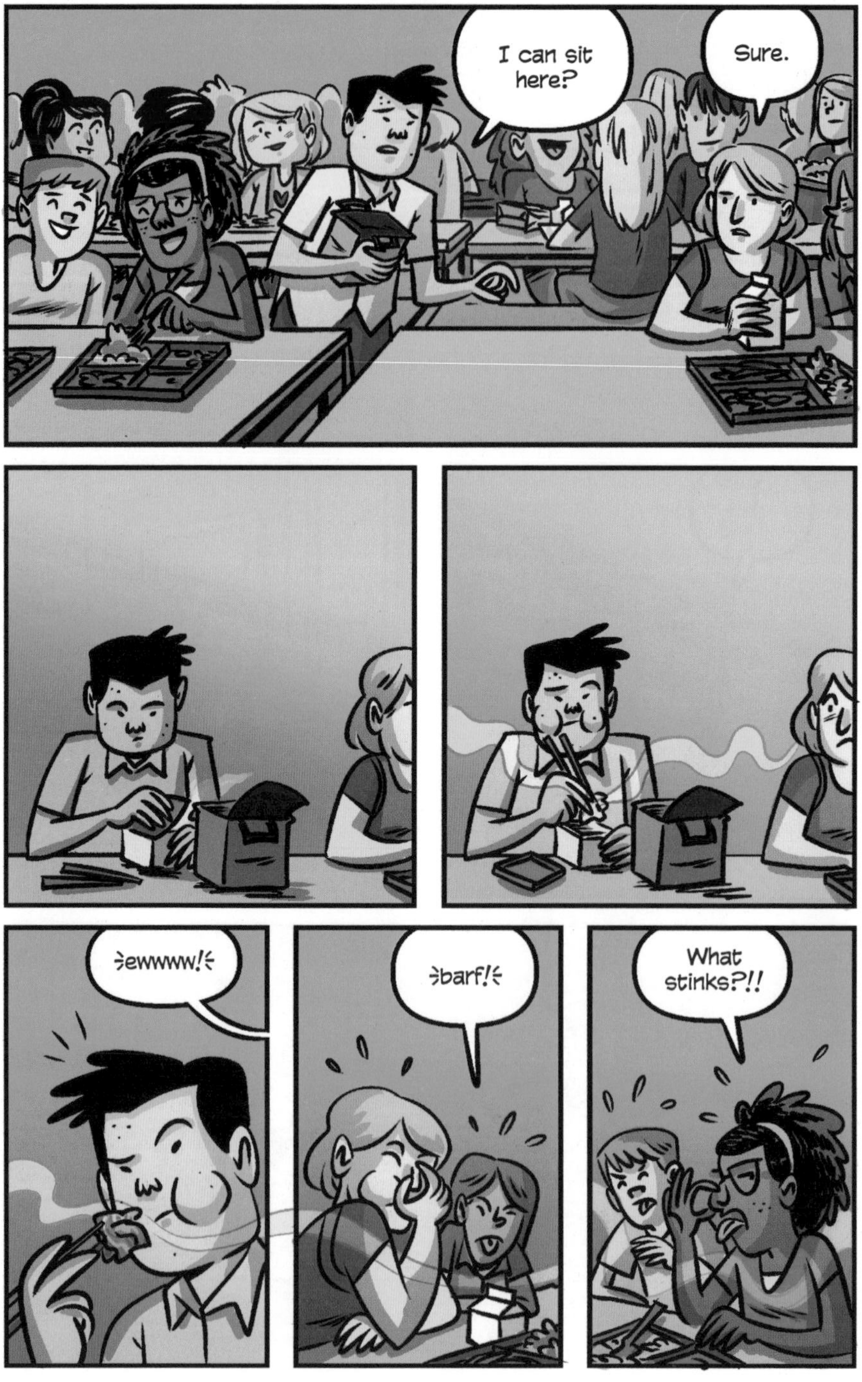
I can sit here?
Sure.
ewwww!
barf!
What stinks?!!

I can sit here?

Um... yeah.

!

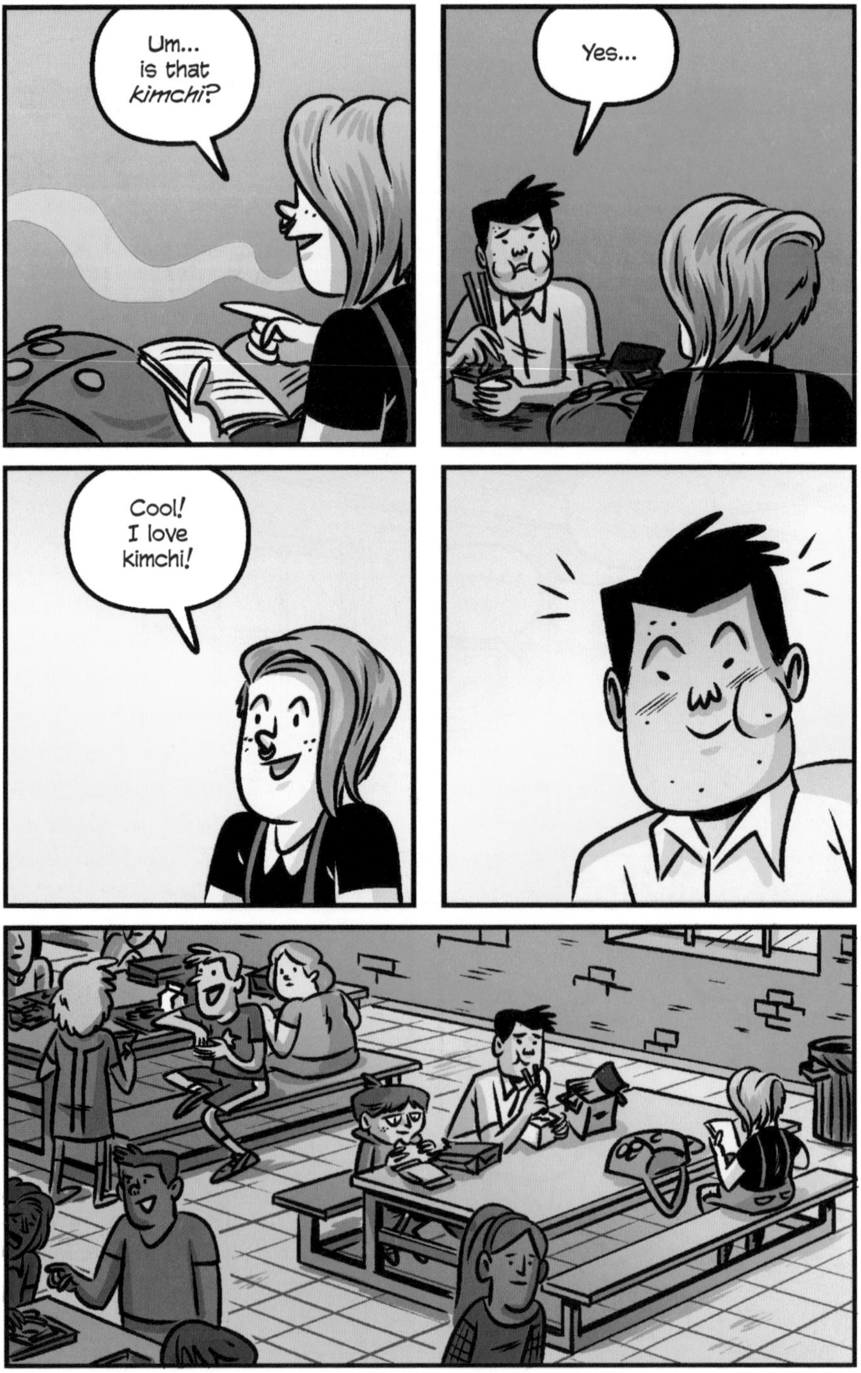
Um... is that *kimchi*?
Yes...
Cool! I love kimchi!

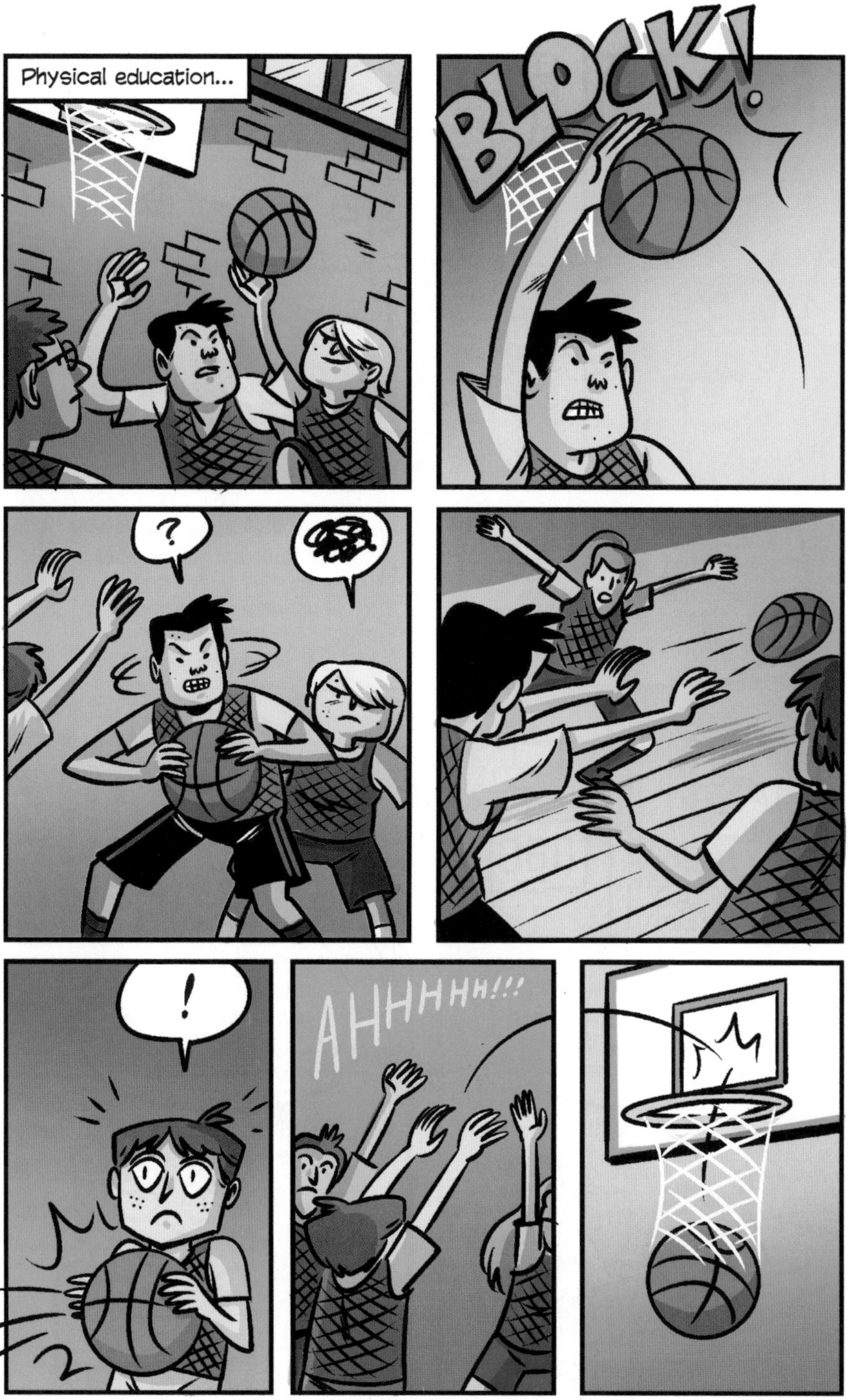
Physical education...
BLOCK!
?
!
AHHHHH!!!

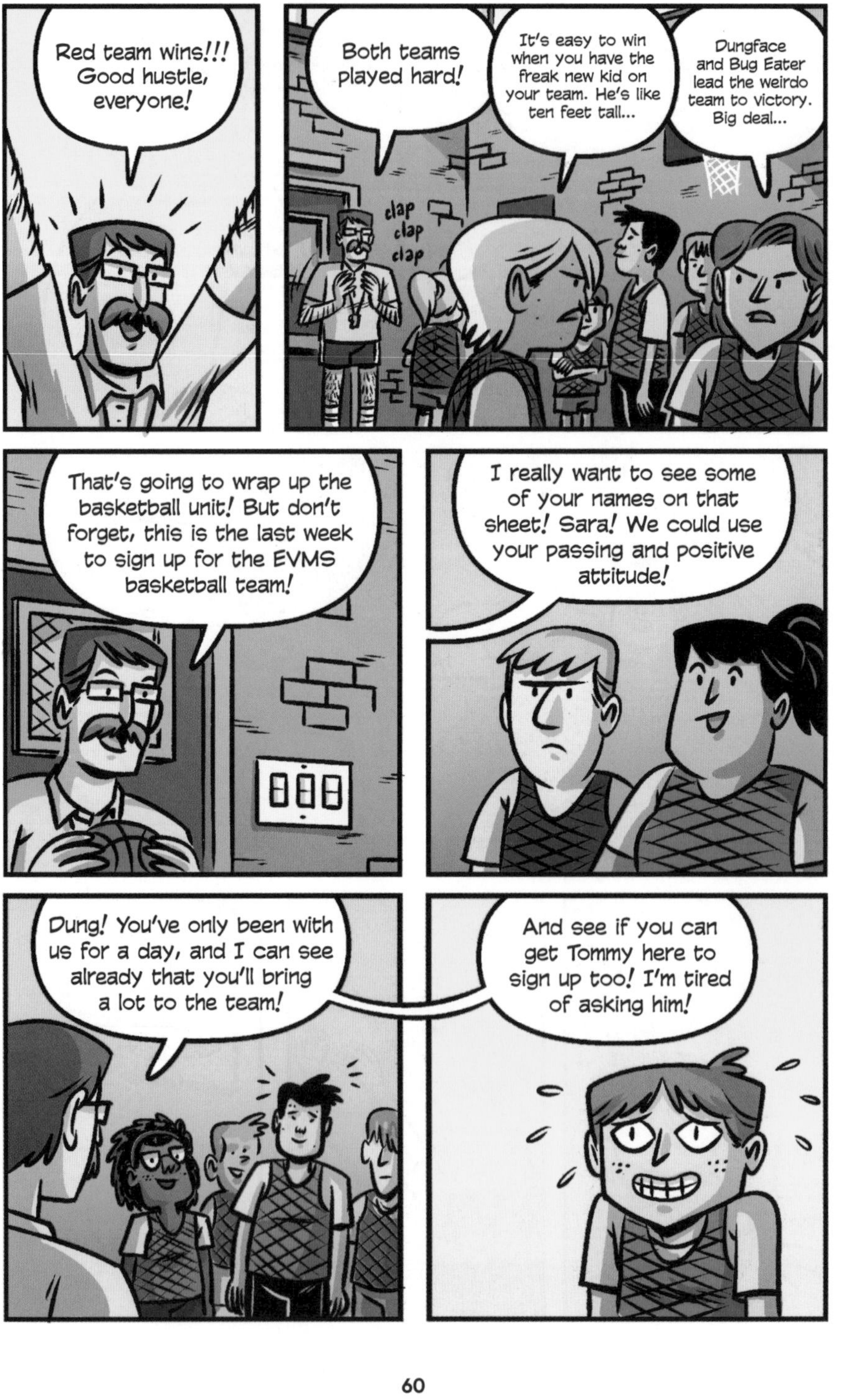
Red team wins!!! Good hustle, everyone!
Both teams played hard!
It's easy to win when you have the freak new kid on your team. He's like ten feet tall...
Dungface and Bug Eater lead the weirdo team to victory. Big deal...
clap clap clap
That's going to wrap up the basketball unit! But don't forget, this is the last week to sign up for the EVMS basketball team!
I really want to see some of your names on that sheet! Sara! We could use your passing and positive attitude!
Dung! You've only been with us for a day, and I can see already that you'll bring a lot to the team!
And see if you can get Tommy here to sign up too! I'm tired of asking him!

Social studies...

Here's your career brainstorming homework back with some notes. There was a lot of good stuff here.

Greg, I particularly loved your deep dive into the work of ice resurfacing operators.

That's Zambonis...

Here you go, Tommy.

See me after class. —Miss S. TOMMY T.

BRAINSTORM

• DOCTOR
• MAIL PERSON
• GROCERY PERSON
• POLICE
• LAWYER
• FIREFIGHTER

RINNNGGGGGGGGGGGGGG

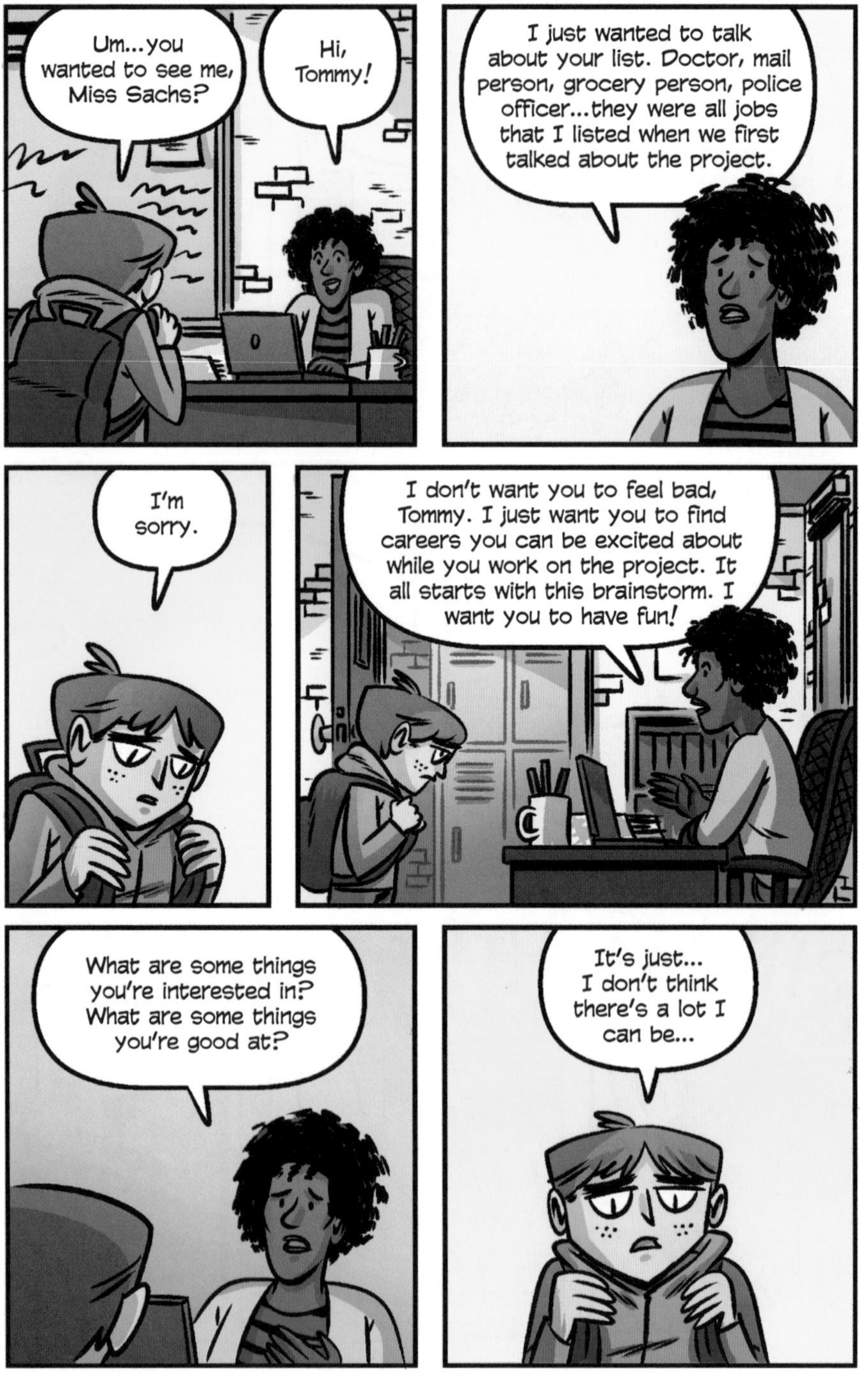
Um...you wanted to see me, Miss Sachs?
Hi, Tommy!
I just wanted to talk about your list. Doctor, mail person, grocery person, police officer...they were all jobs that I listed when we first talked about the project.
I'm sorry.
I don't want you to feel bad, Tommy. I just want you to find careers you can be excited about while you work on the project. It all starts with this brainstorm. I want you to have fun!
What are some things you're interested in? What are some things you're good at?
It's just... I don't think there's a lot I can be...

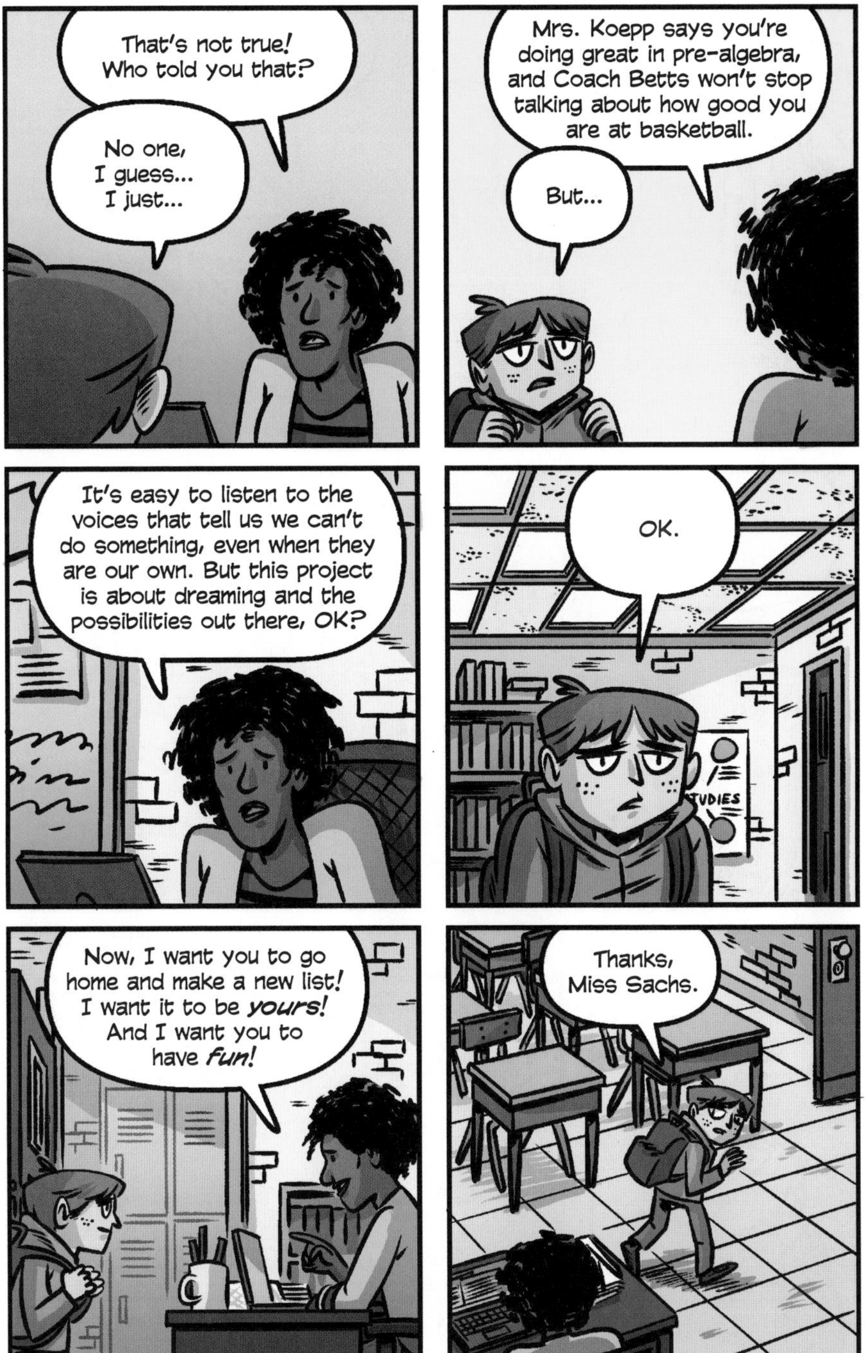
That's not true! Who told you that?
No one, I guess... I just...
Mrs. Koepp says you're doing great in pre-algebra, and Coach Betts won't stop talking about how good you are at basketball.
But...
It's easy to listen to the voices that tell us we can't do something, even when they are our own. But this project is about dreaming and the possibilities out there, OK?
OK.
Now, I want you to go home and make a new list! I want it to be *yours*! And I want you to have *fun*!
Thanks, Miss Sachs.

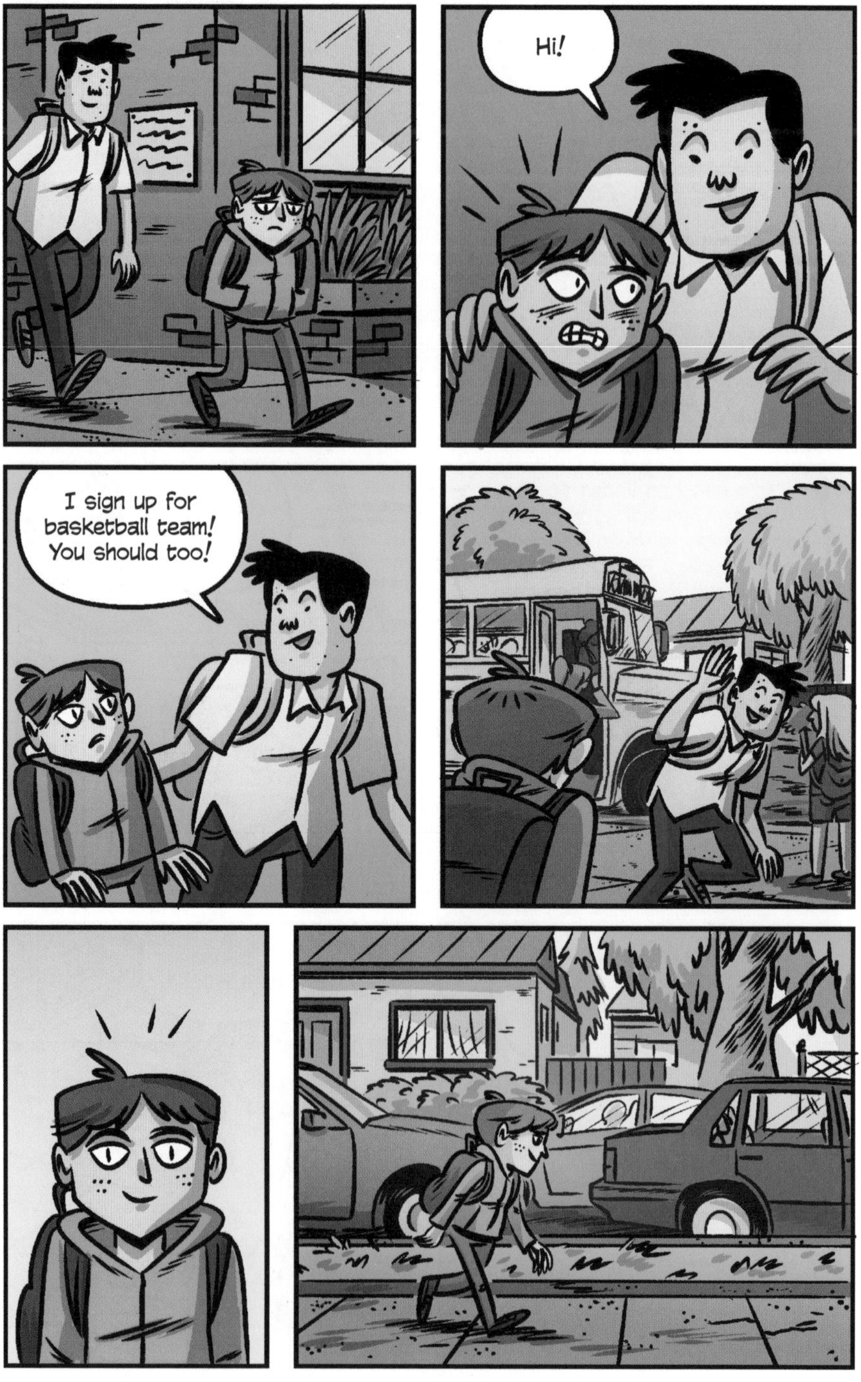
Hi!
I sign up for basketball team! You should too!

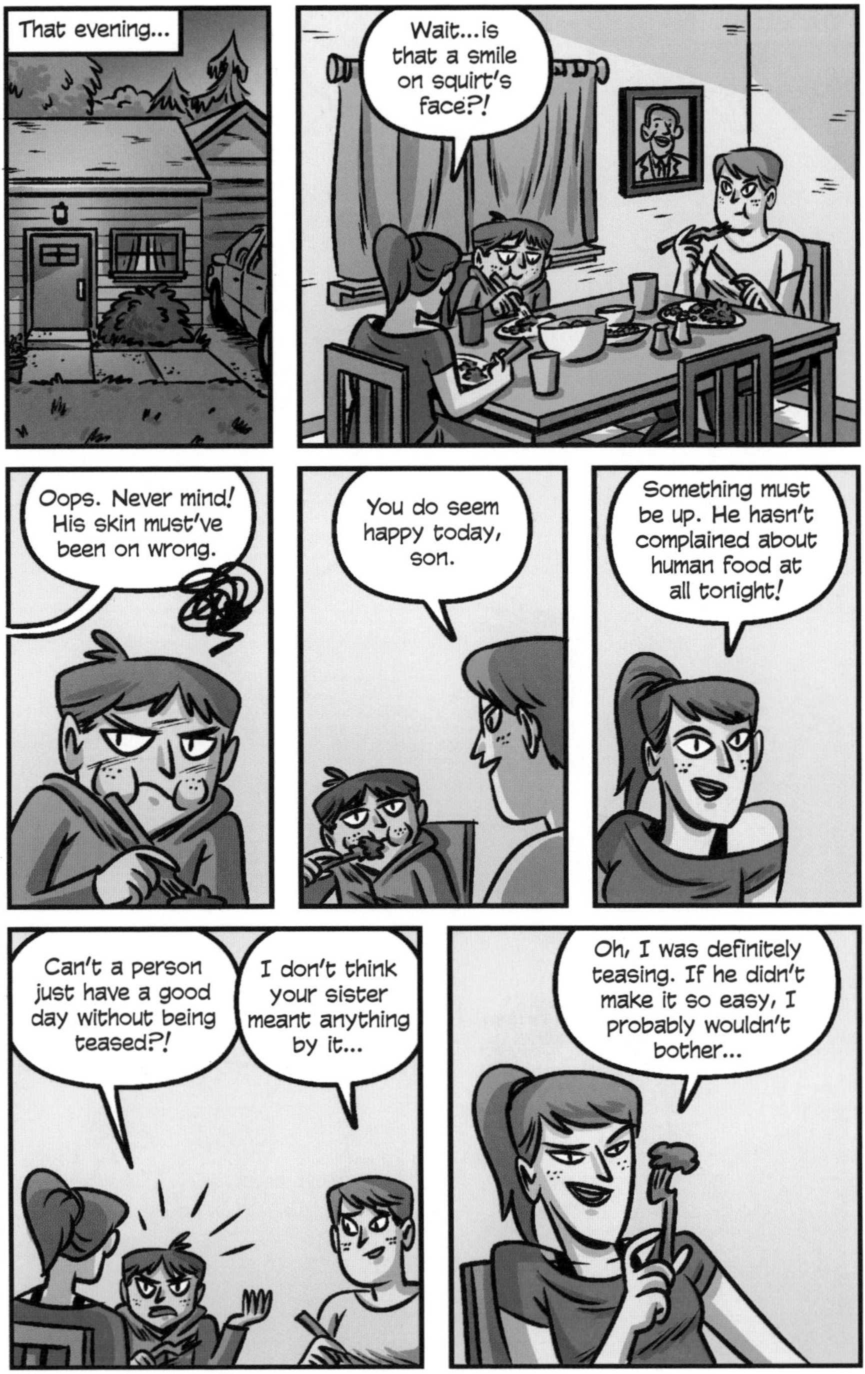
That evening...
Wait...is that a smile on squirt's face?!
Oops. Never mind! His skin must've been on wrong.
You do seem happy today, son.
Something must be up. He hasn't complained about human food at all tonight!
Can't a person just have a good day without being teased?!
I don't think your sister meant anything by it...
Oh, I was definitely teasing. If he didn't make it so easy, I probably wouldn't bother...

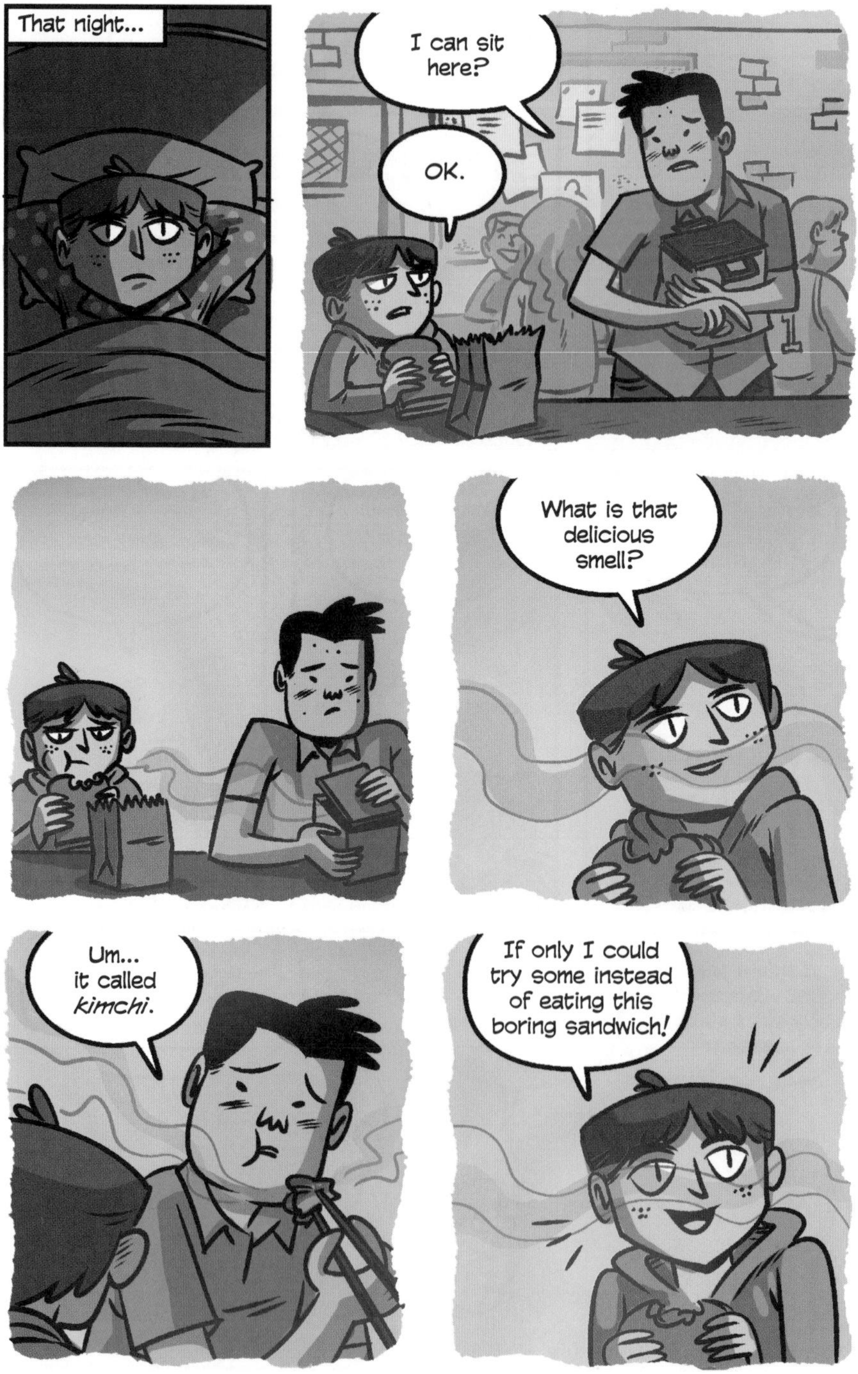
That night...
I can sit here?
OK.
What is that delicious smell?
Um... it called *kimchi*.
If only I could try some instead of eating this boring sandwich!

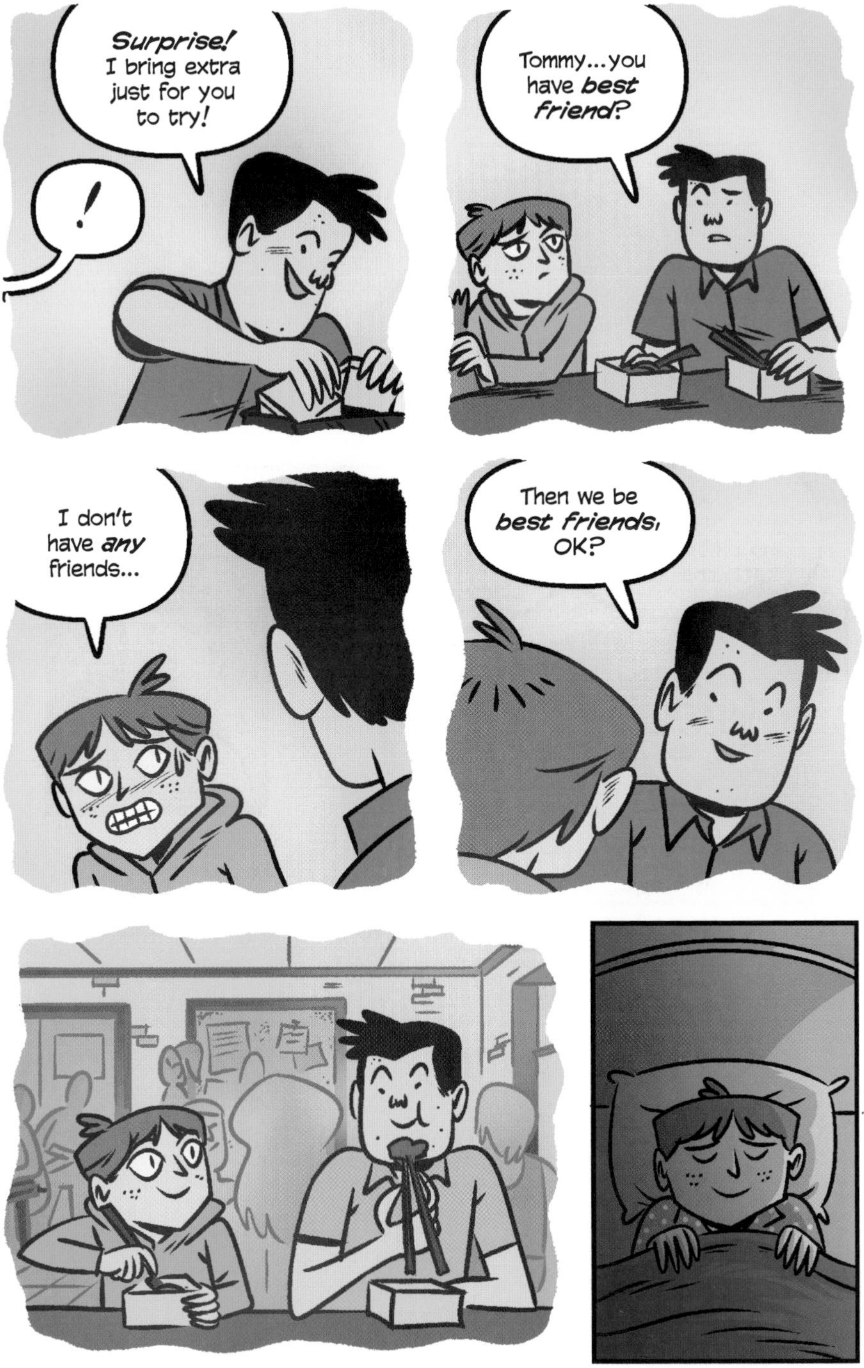

Surprise! I bring extra just for you to try!
!
Tommy...you have best friend?
I don't have any friends...
Then we be best friends, OK?

CHAPTER 4

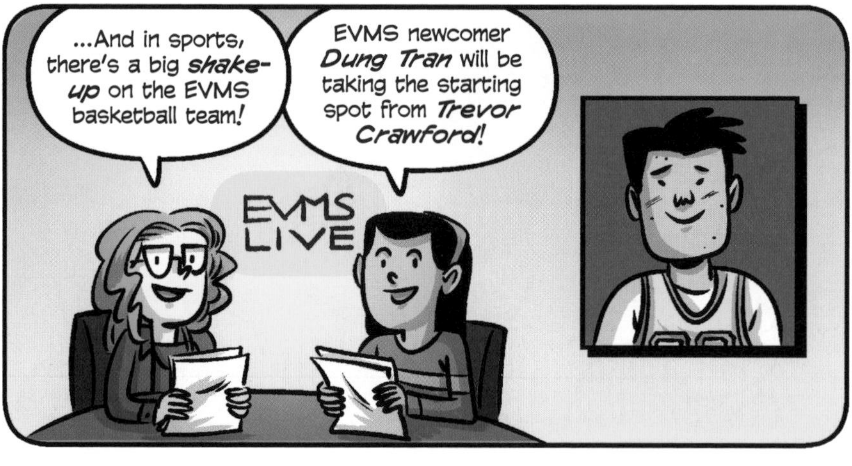

...And in sports, there's a big *shake-up* on the EVMS basketball team!
EVMS newcomer *Dung Tran* will be taking the starting spot from *Trevor Crawford*!
EVMS LIVE

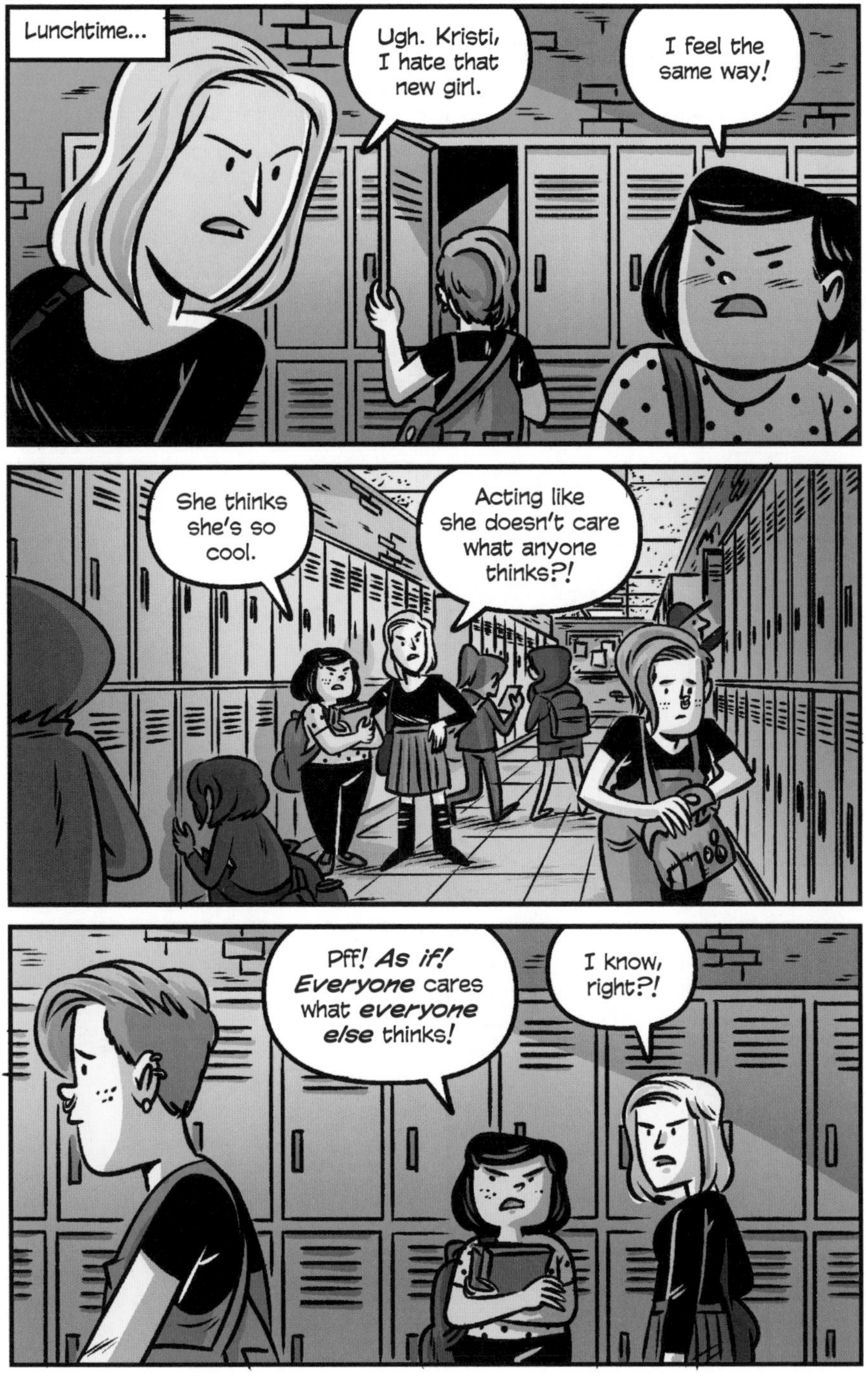
Lunchtime...
Ugh. Kristi, I hate that new girl.
I feel the same way!
She thinks she's so cool.
Acting like she doesn't care what anyone thinks?!
Pff! As if! Everyone cares what everyone else thinks!
I know, right?!

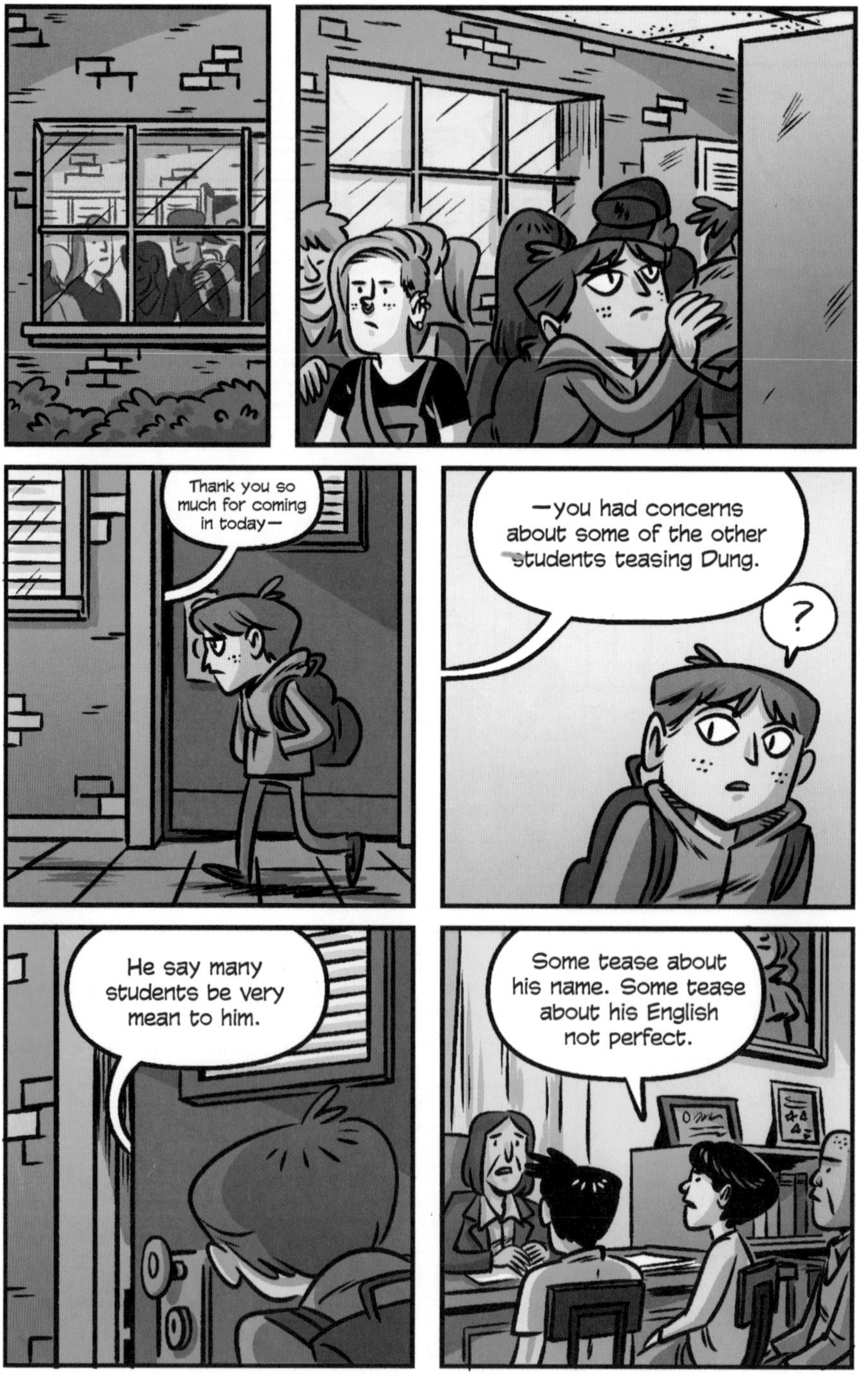
Thank you so much for coming in today—
—you had concerns about some of the other students teasing Dung.
?
He say many students be very mean to him.
Some tease about his name. Some tease about his English not perfect.

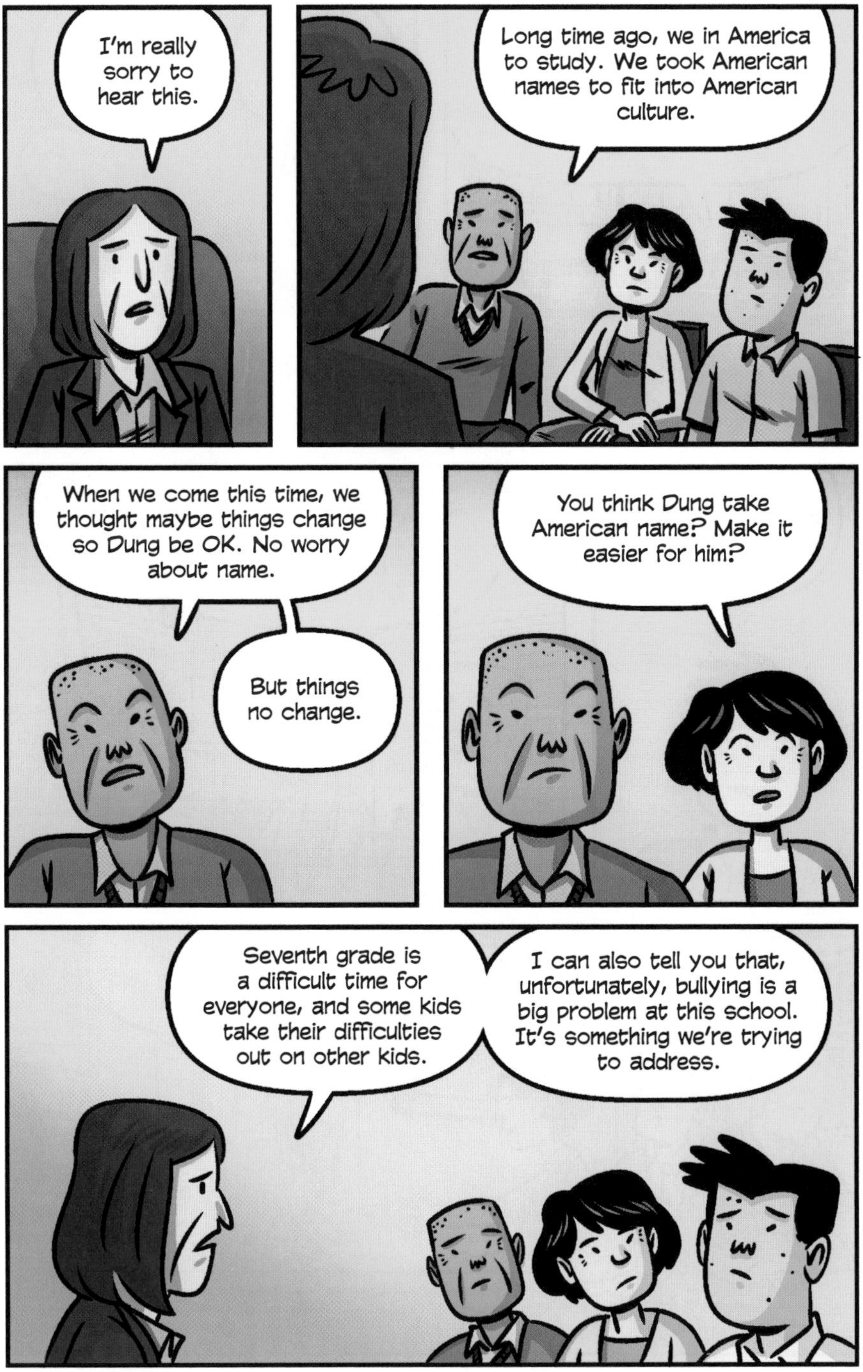
I'm really sorry to hear this.
Long time ago, we in America to study. We took American names to fit into American culture.
When we come this time, we thought maybe things change so Dung be OK. No worry about name.
But things no change.
You think Dung take American name? Make it easier for him?
Seventh grade is a difficult time for everyone, and some kids take their difficulties out on other kids.
I can also tell you that, unfortunately, bullying is a big problem at this school. It's something we're trying to address.

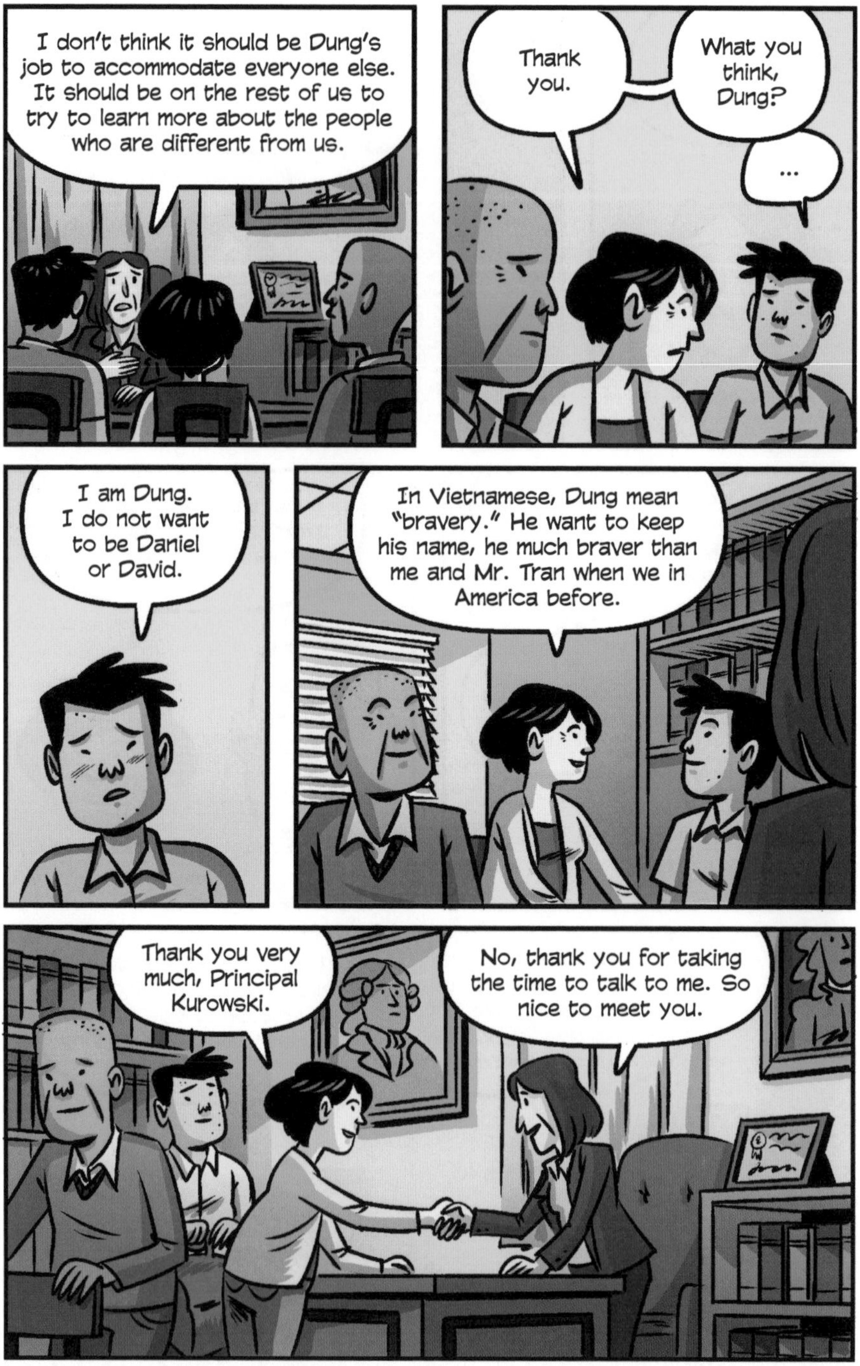
I don't think it should be Dung's job to accommodate everyone else. It should be on the rest of us to try to learn more about the people who are different from us.
Thank you.
What you think, Dung?
...
I am Dung. I do not want to be Daniel or David.
In Vietnamese, Dung mean "bravery." He want to keep his name, he much braver than me and Mr. Tran when we in America before.
Thank you very much, Principal Kurowski.
No, thank you for taking the time to talk to me. So nice to meet you.

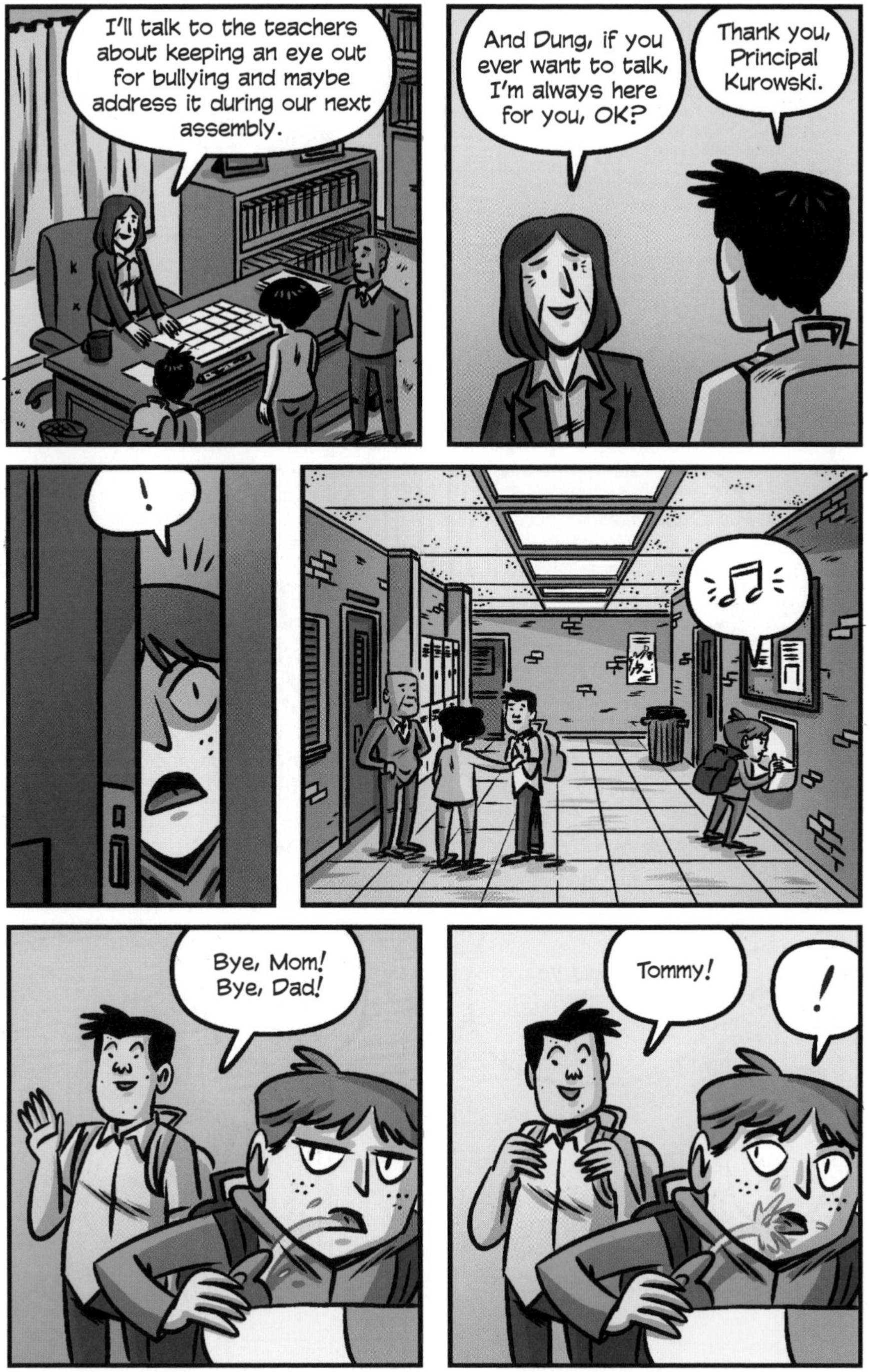
I'll talk to the teachers about keeping an eye out for bullying and maybe address it during our next assembly.
And Dung, if you ever want to talk, I'm always here for you, OK?
Thank you, Principal Kurowski.
!
Bye, Mom! Bye, Dad!
Tommy!
!

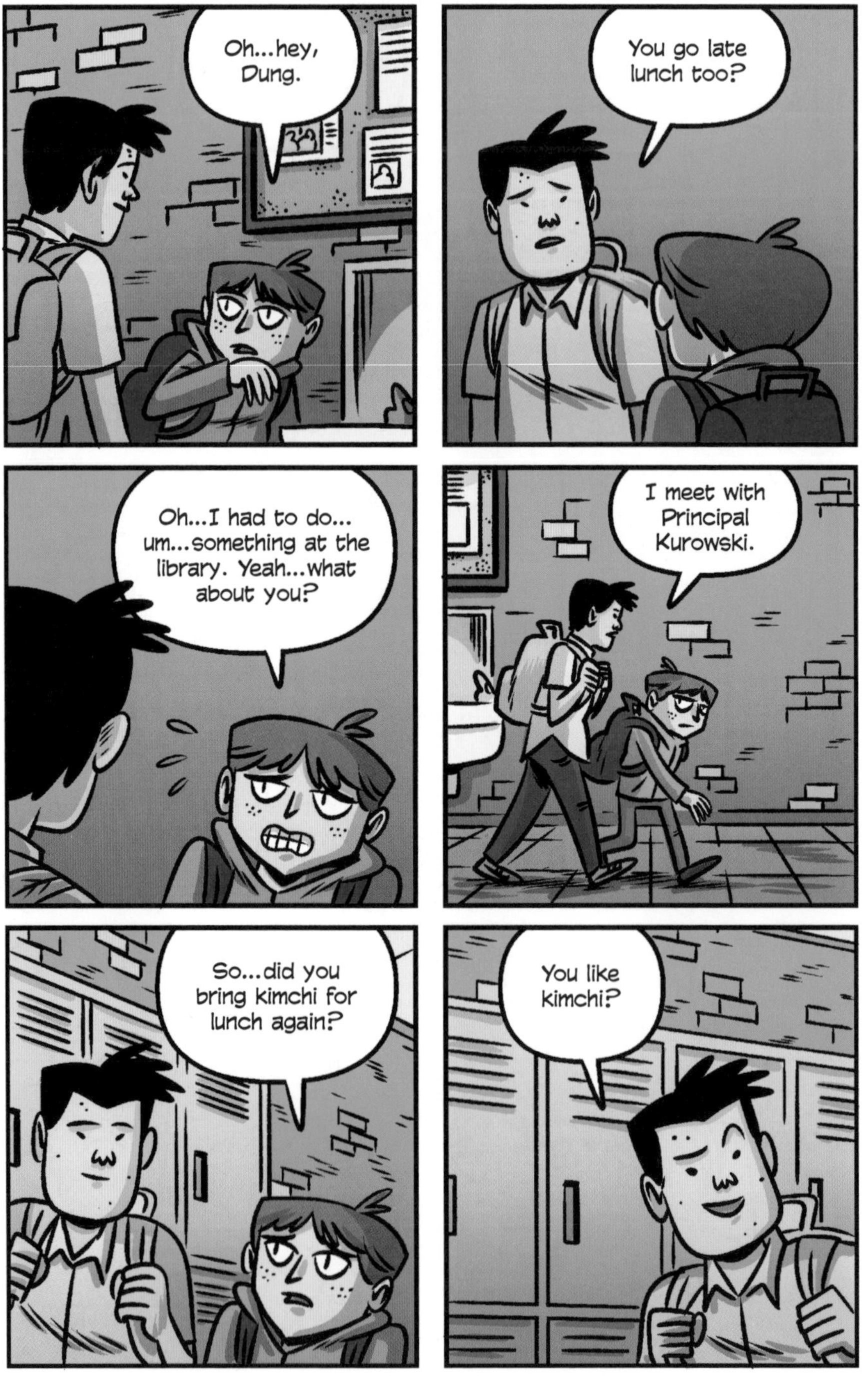
Oh...hey, Dung.
You go late lunch too?
Oh...I had to do... um...something at the library. Yeah...what about you?
I meet with Principal Kurowski.
So...did you bring kimchi for lunch again?
You like kimchi?

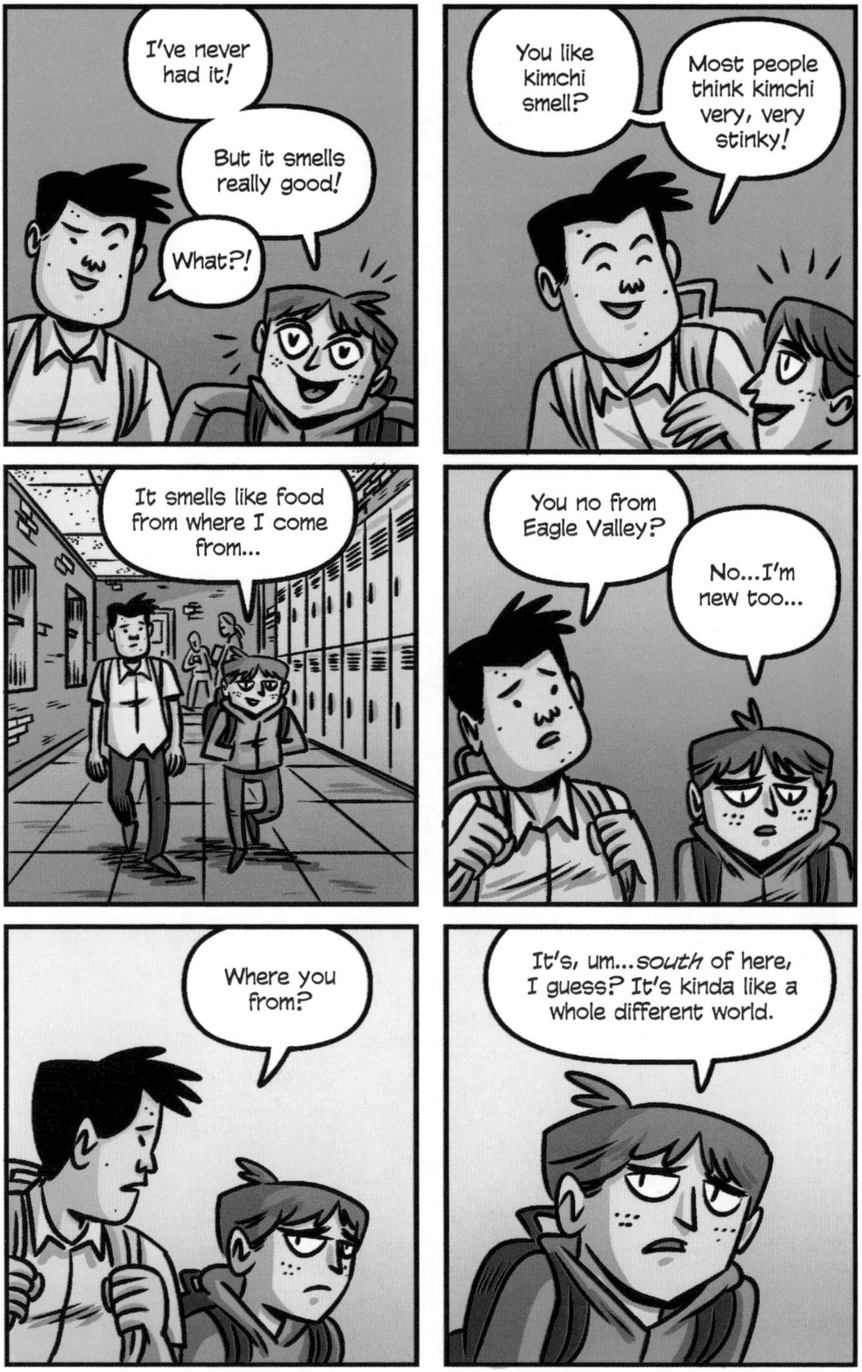
I've never had it!
But it smells really good!
What?!
You like kimchi smell?
Most people think kimchi very, very stinky!
It smells like food from where I come from...
You no from Eagle Valley?
No...I'm new too...
Where you from?
It's, um...*south* of here, I guess? It's kinda like a whole different world.

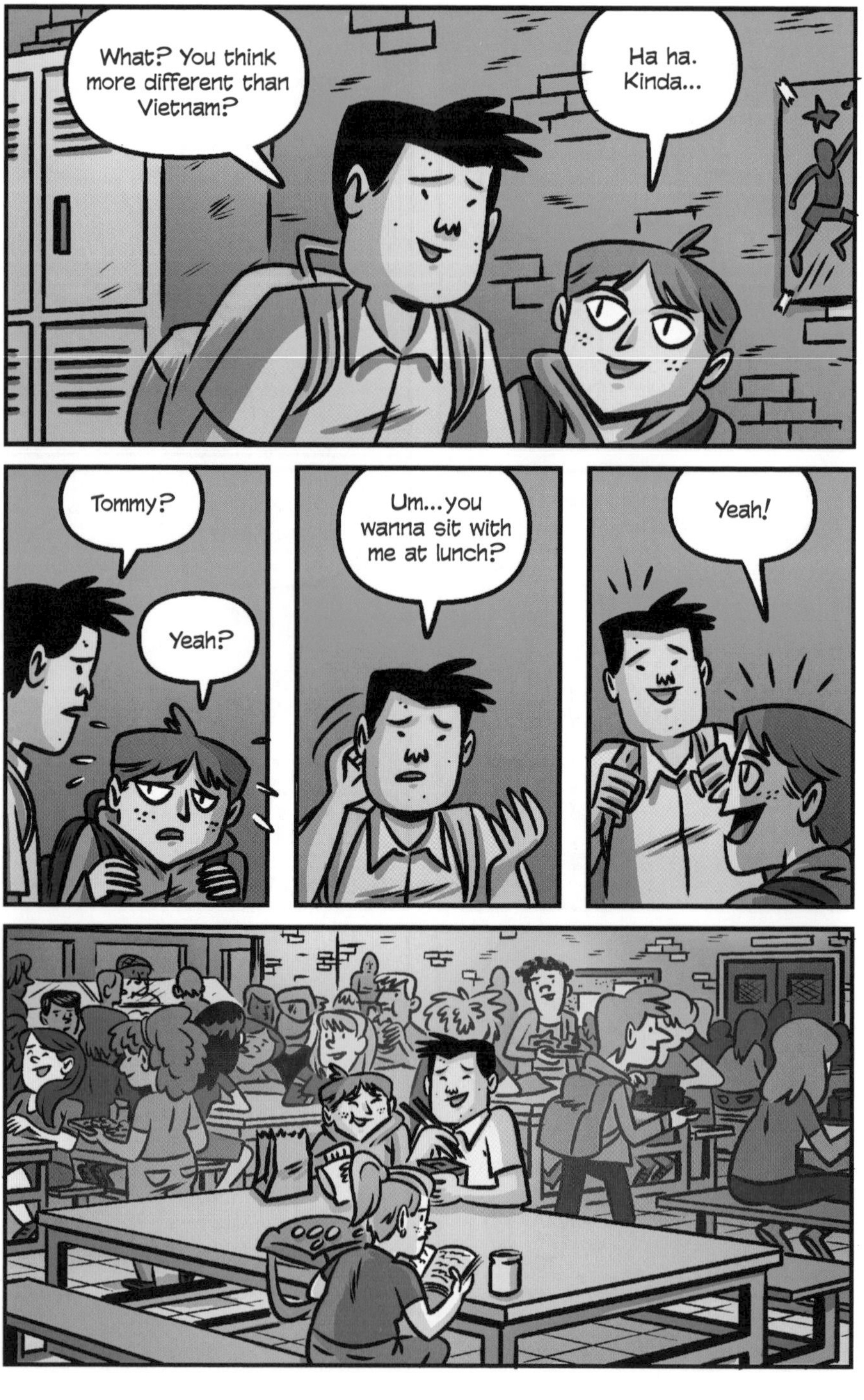
What? You think more different than Vietnam?
Ha ha. Kinda...
Tommy?
Yeah?
Um...you wanna sit with me at lunch?
Yeah!

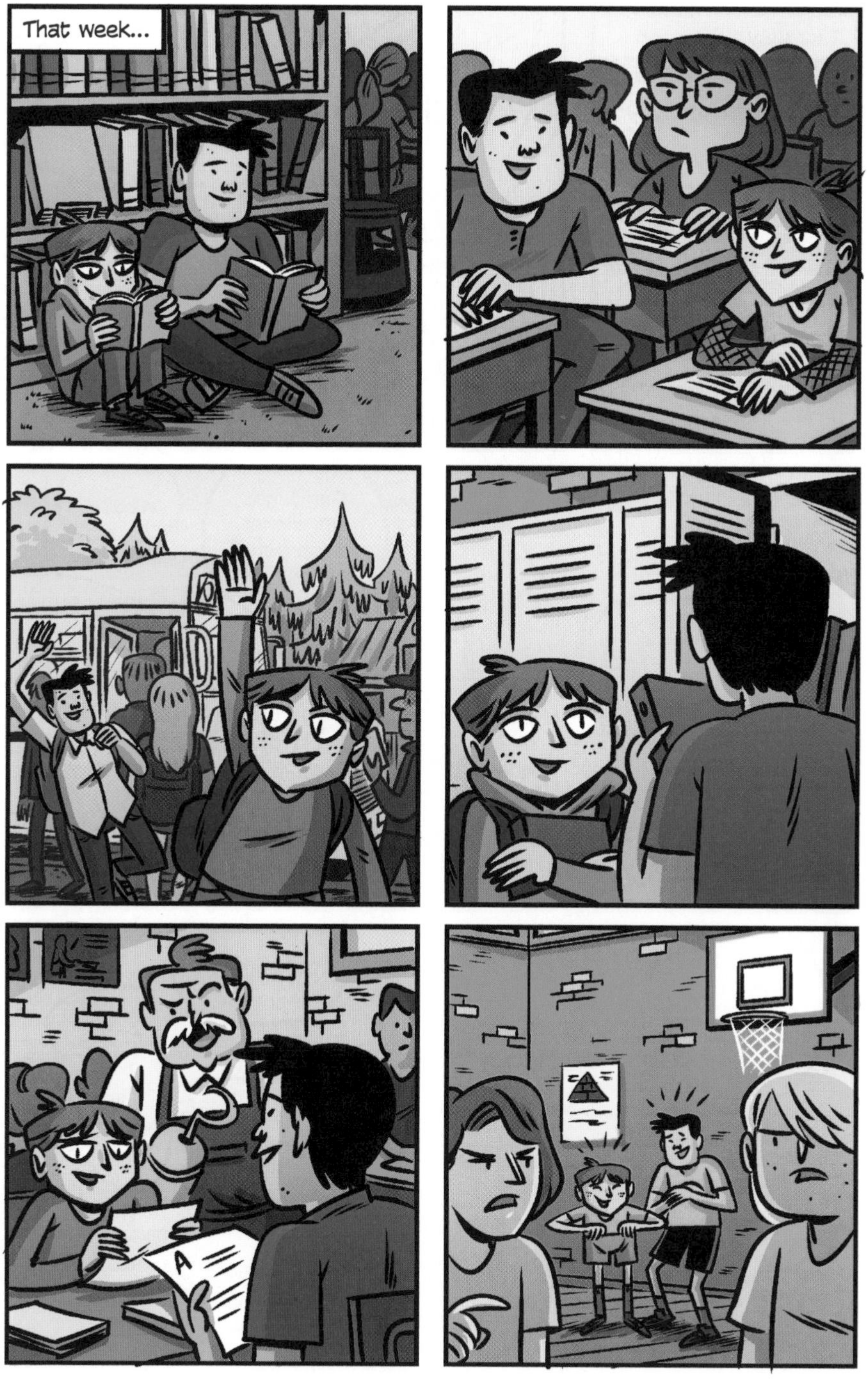
That week...
A

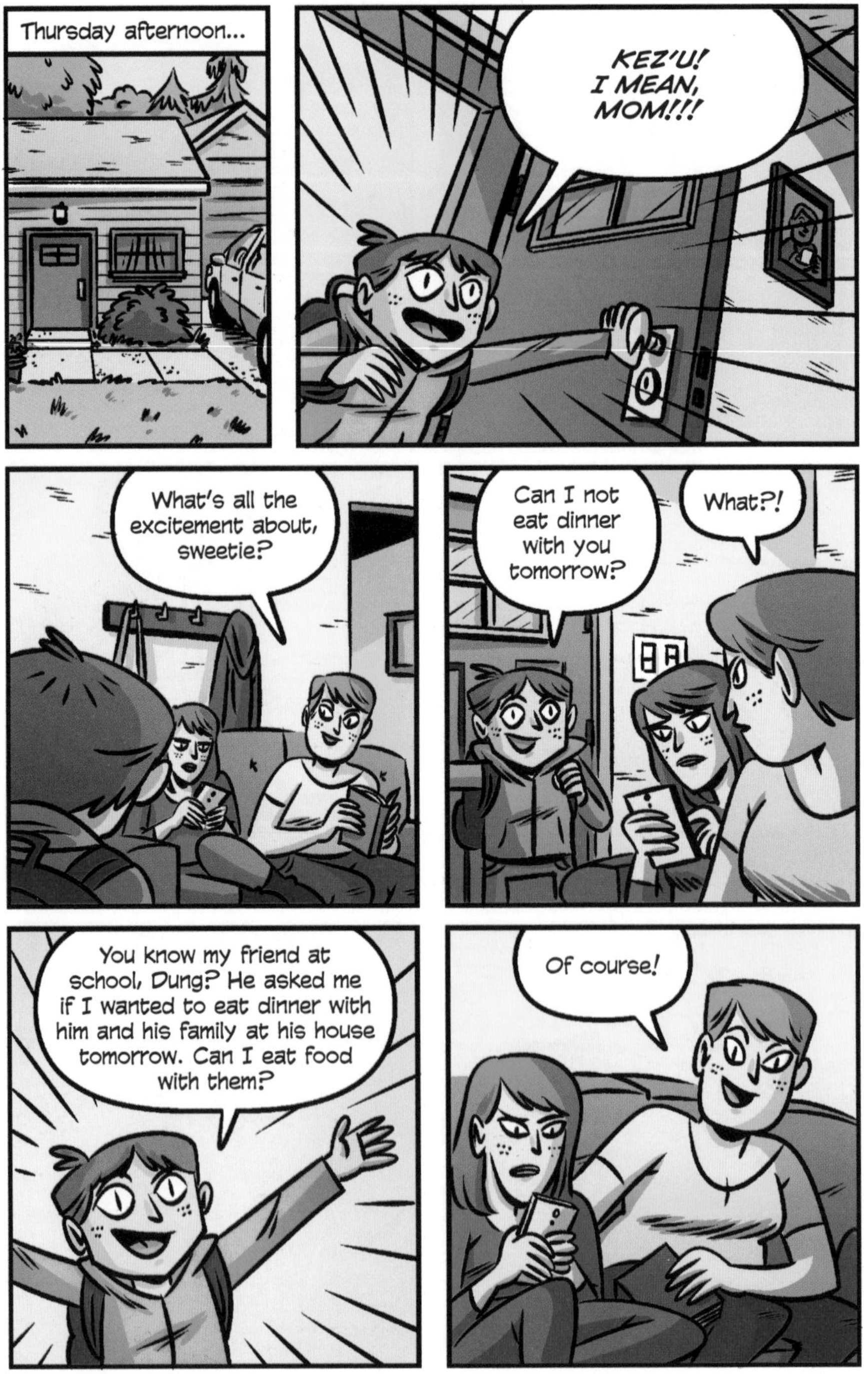
Thursday afternoon...
KEZ'U! I MEAN, MOM!!!
What's all the excitement about, sweetie?
Can I not eat dinner with you tomorrow?
What?!
You know my friend at school, Dung? He asked me if I wanted to eat dinner with him and his family at his house tomorrow. Can I eat food with them?
Of course!

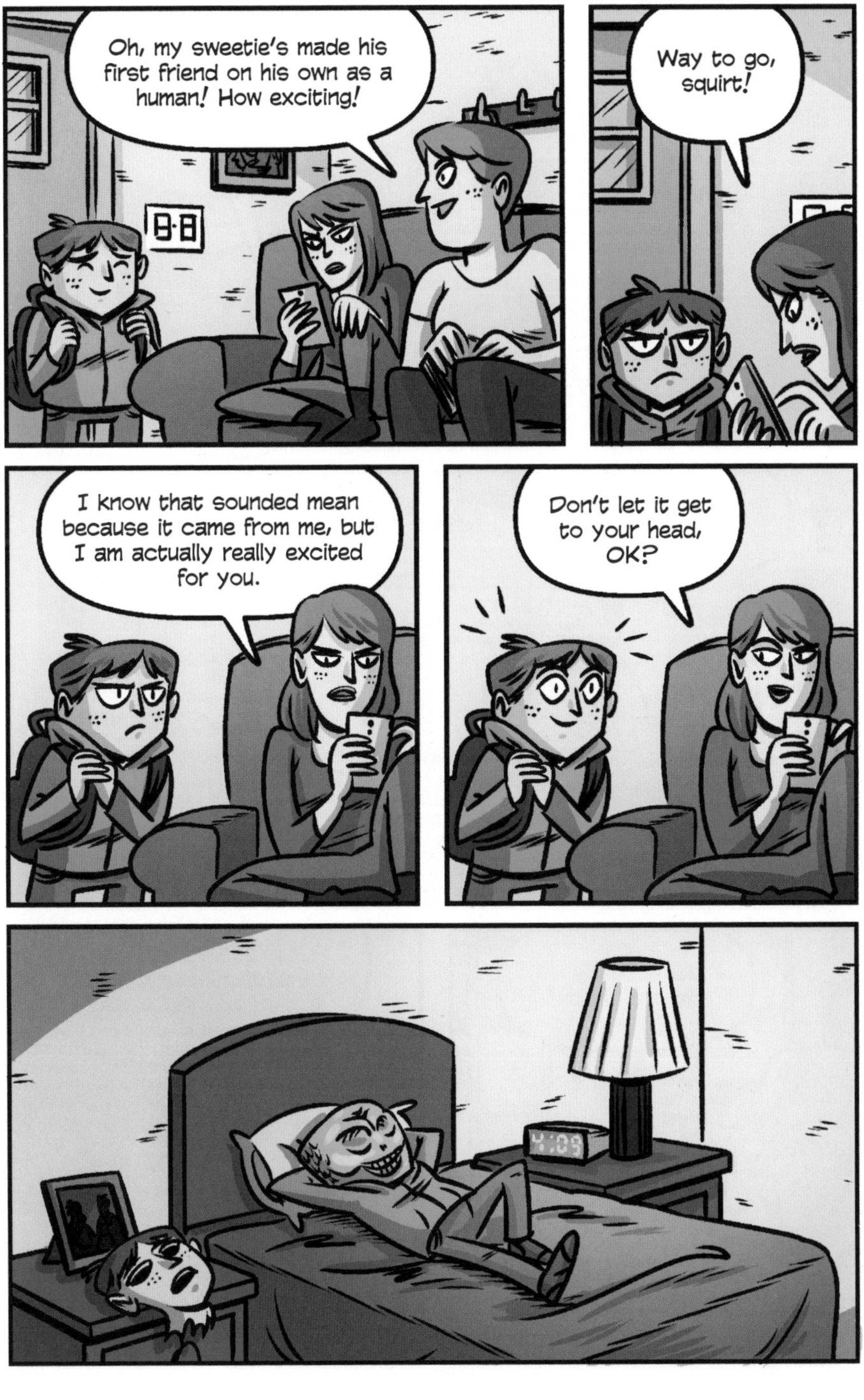
Oh, my sweetie's made his first friend on his own as a human! How exciting!
Way to go, squirt!
I know that sounded mean because it came from me, but I am actually really excited for you.
Don't let it get to your head, OK?

<Dung! Your cousins called today. They'll be up from California this weekend to visit!>

<speaking Vietnamese>

<OK, Mom.>

Your house is so big and fancy!

Ha ha. This not our house! Company rent for us while we stay in Eagle Valley and work.

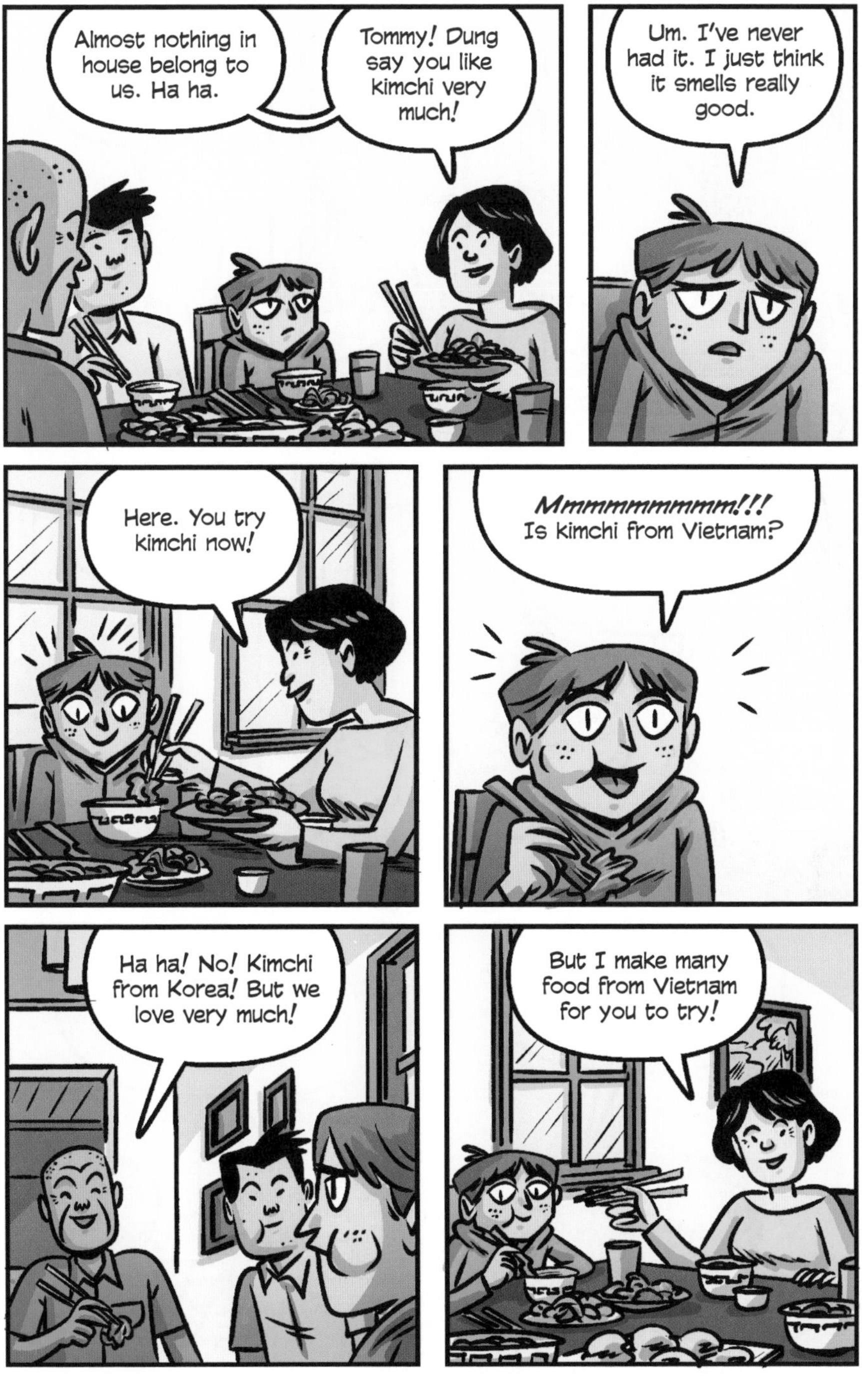
Almost nothing in house belong to us. Ha ha.
Tommy! Dung say you like kimchi very much!
Um. I've never had it. I just think it smells really good.
Here. You try kimchi now!
Mmmmmmmmmm!!!
Is kimchi from Vietnam?
Ha ha! No! Kimchi from Korea! But we love very much!
But I make many food from Vietnam for you to try!

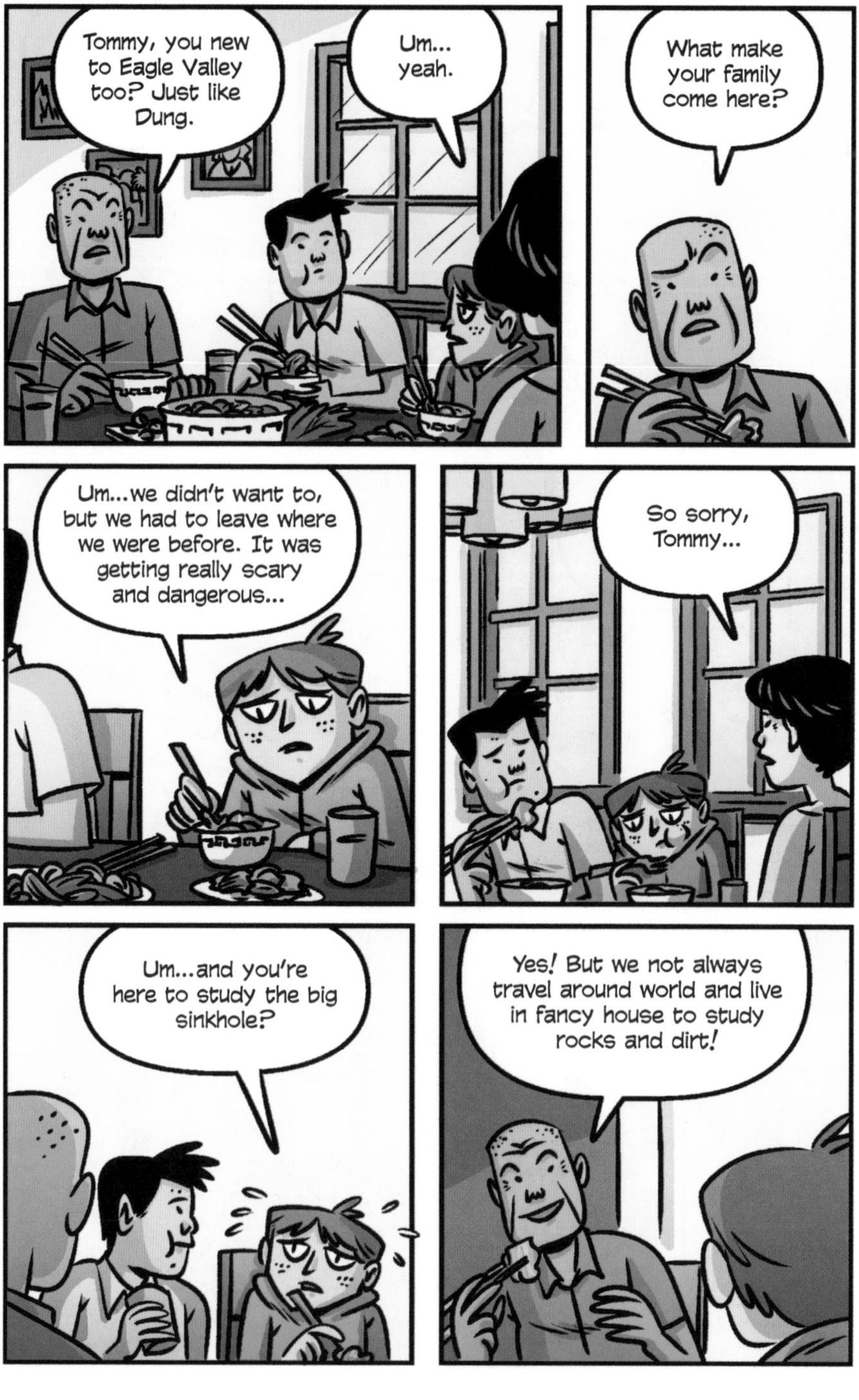
Tommy, you new to Eagle Valley too? Just like Dung.
Um... yeah.
What make your family come here?
Um...we didn't want to, but we had to leave where we were before. It was getting really scary and dangerous...
So sorry, Tommy...
Um...and you're here to study the big sinkhole?
Yes! But we not always travel around world and live in fancy house to study rocks and dirt!

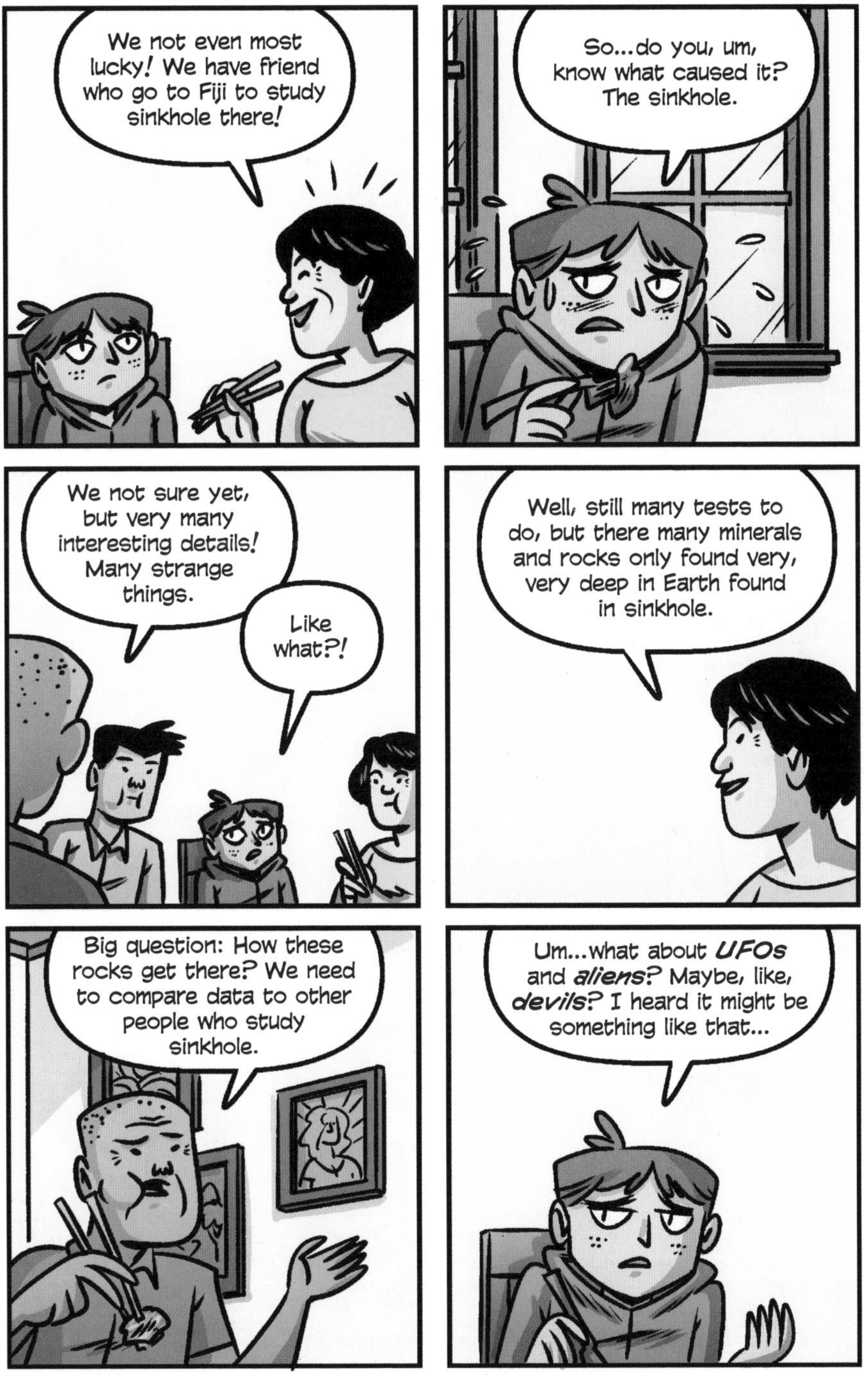

We not even most lucky! We have friend who go to Fiji to study sinkhole there!
So...do you, um, know what caused it? The sinkhole.
We not sure yet, but very many interesting details! Many strange things.
Like what?!
Well, still many tests to do, but there many minerals and rocks only found very, very deep in Earth found in sinkhole.
Big question: How these rocks get there? We need to compare data to other people who study sinkhole.
Um...what about *UFOs* and *aliens*? Maybe, like, *devils*? I heard it might be something like that...

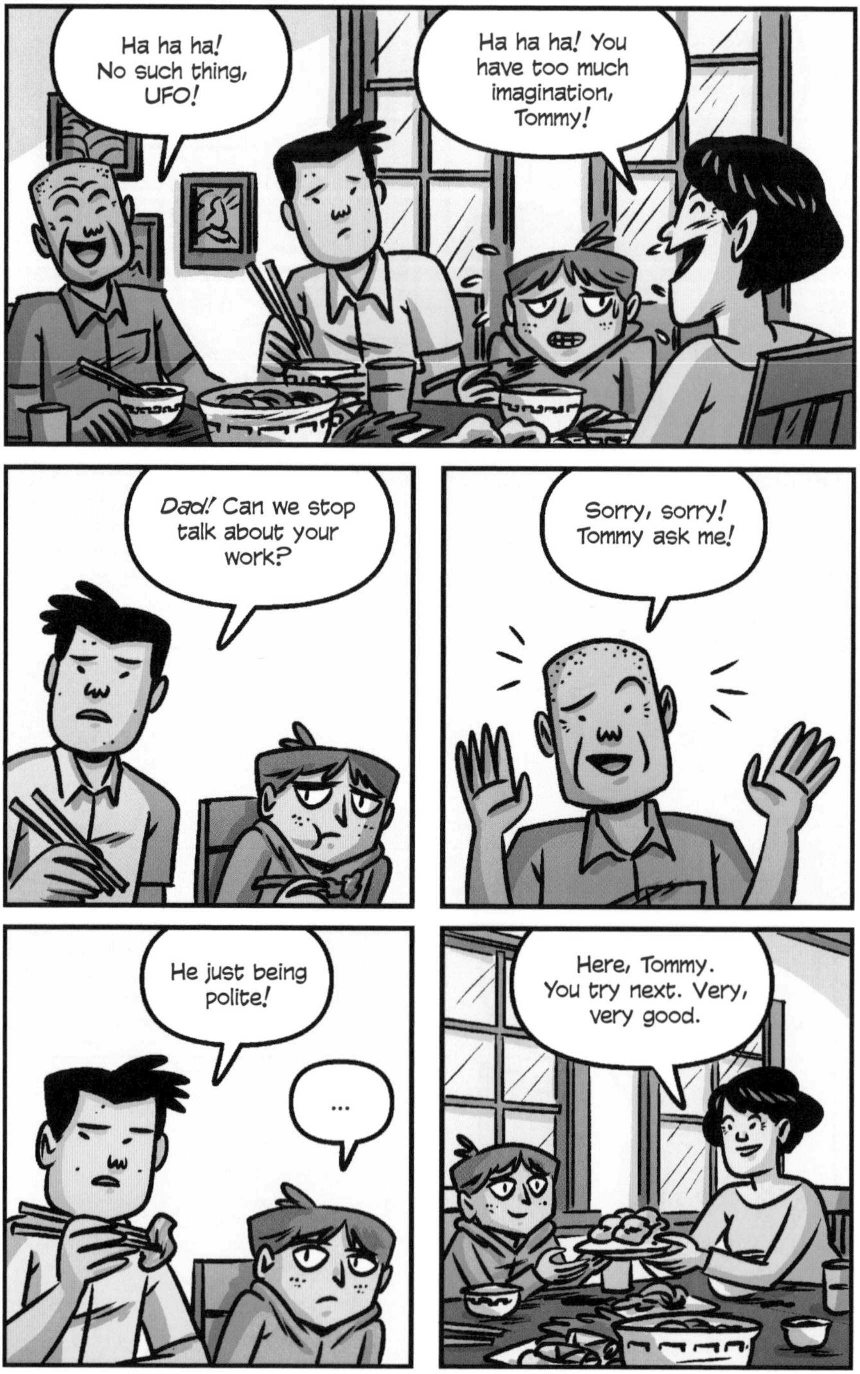

Ha ha ha! No such thing, UFO!
Ha ha ha! You have too much imagination, Tommy!
Dad! Can we stop talk about your work?
Sorry, sorry! Tommy ask me!
He just being polite!
...
Here, Tommy. You try next. Very, very good.

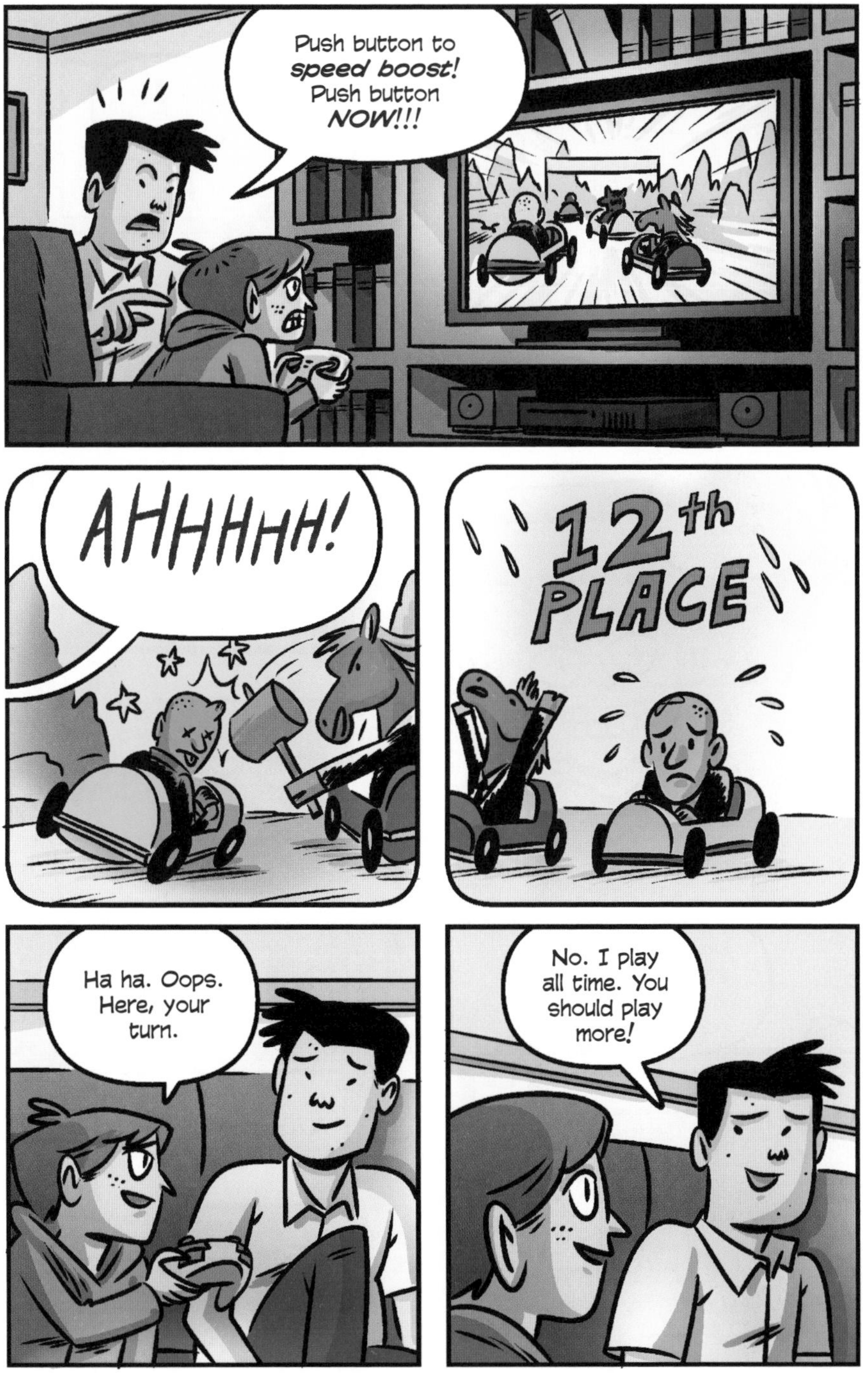
Push button to *speed boost!* Push button *NOW!!!*
AHHHHH!
12th PLACE
Ha ha. Oops. Here, your turn.
No. I play all time. You should play more!

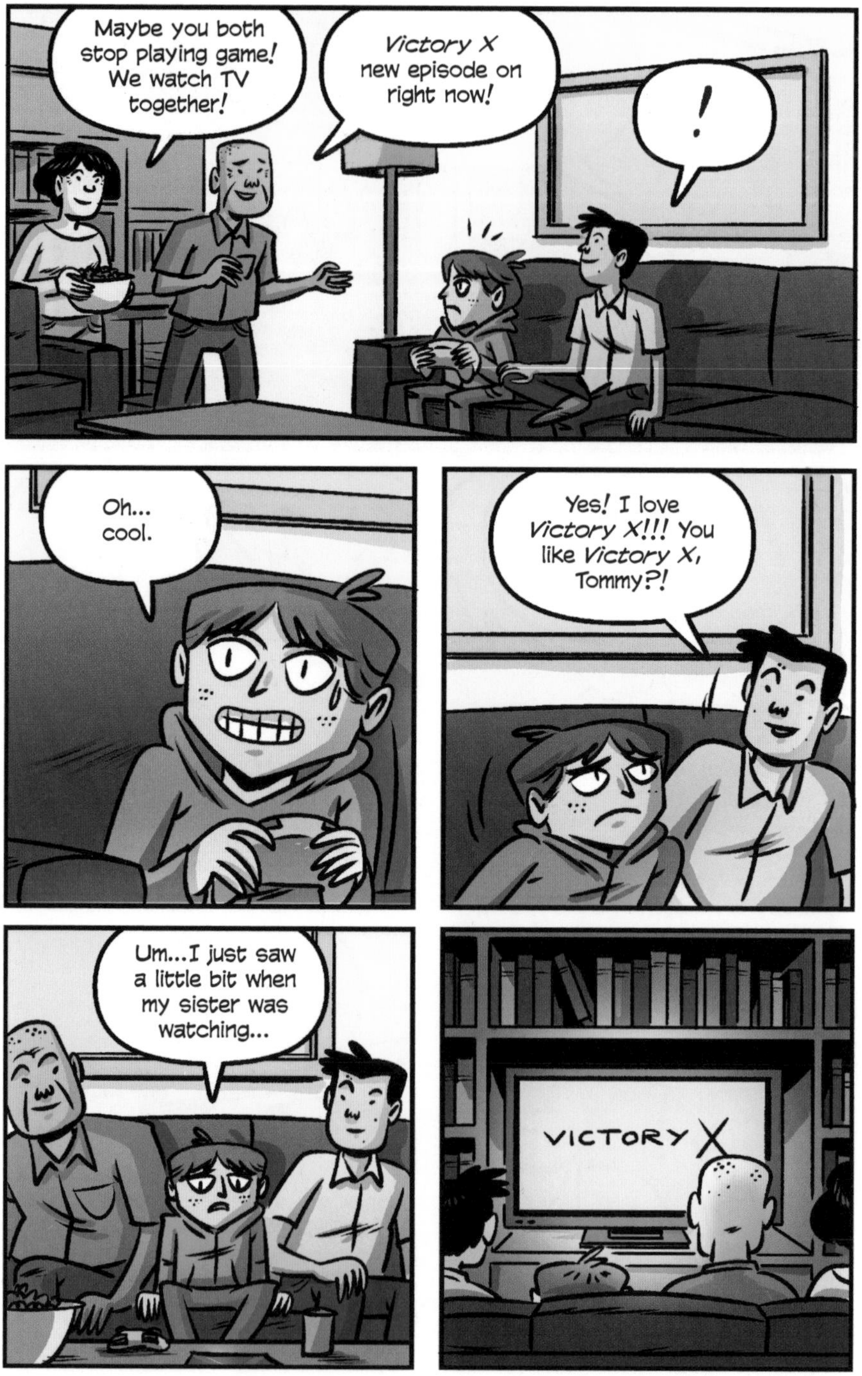
Maybe you both stop playing game! We watch TV together!
Victory X new episode on right now!
!
Oh... cool.
Yes! I love *Victory X*!!! You like *Victory X*, Tommy?!
Um...I just saw a little bit when my sister was watching...
VICTORY X

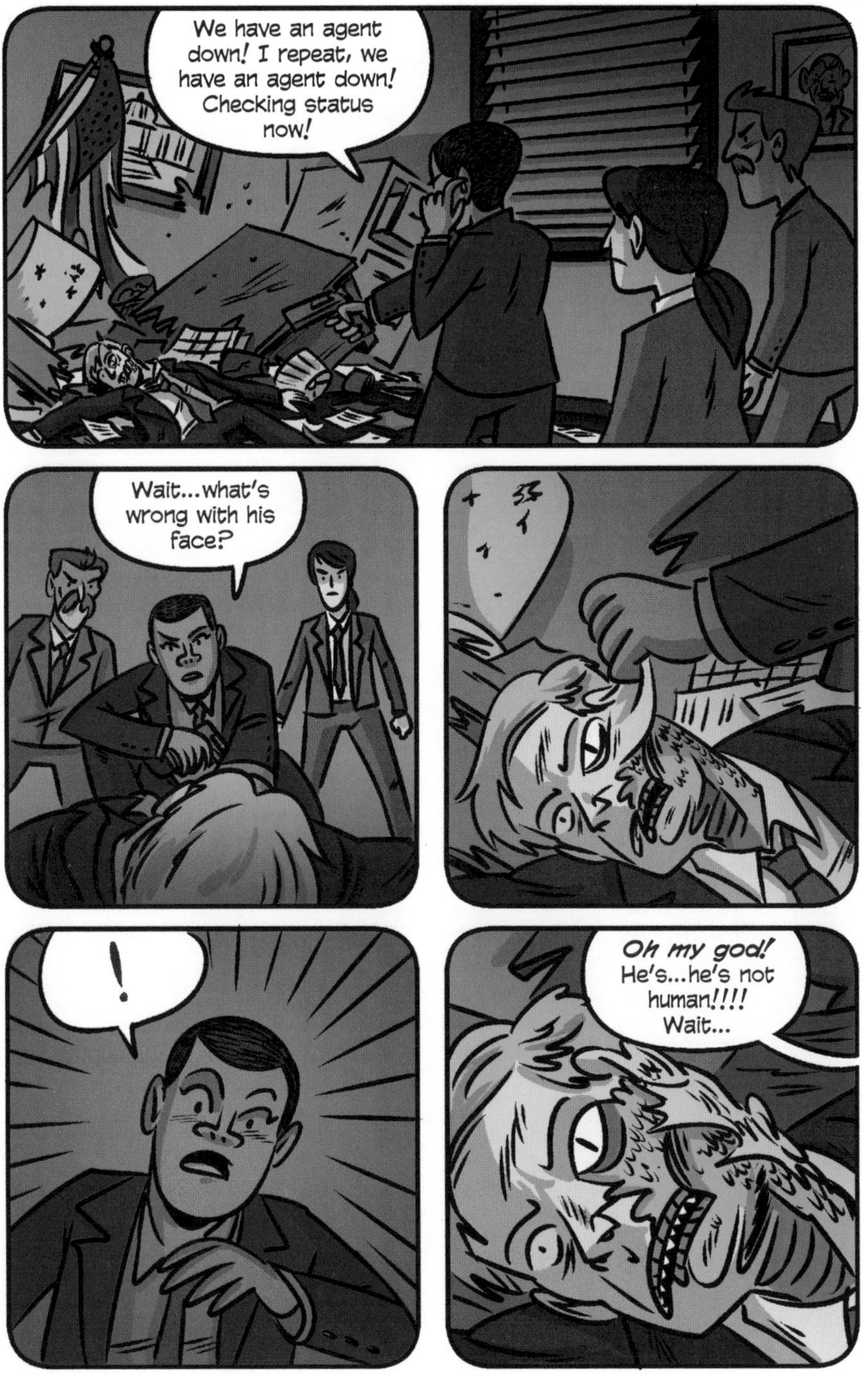
We have an agent down! I repeat, we have an agent down! Checking status now!
Wait...what's wrong with his face?
!
Oh my god! He's...he's not human!!!! Wait...

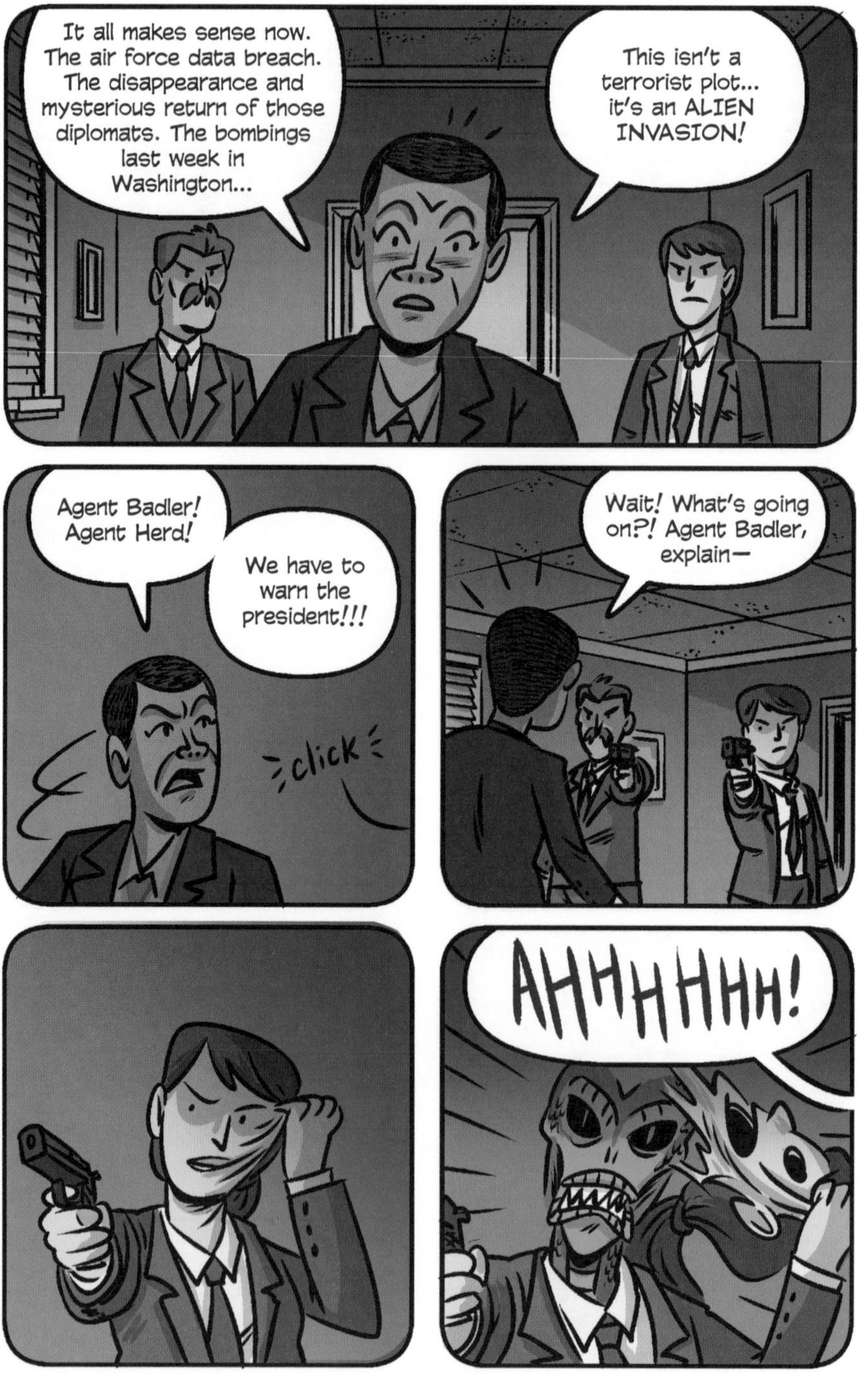
It all makes sense now. The air force data breach. The disappearance and mysterious return of those diplomats. The bombings last week in Washington...
This isn't a terrorist plot... it's an ALIEN INVASION!
Agent Badler! Agent Herd!
We have to warn the president!!!
click
Wait! What's going on?! Agent Badler, explain—
AHHHHHH!

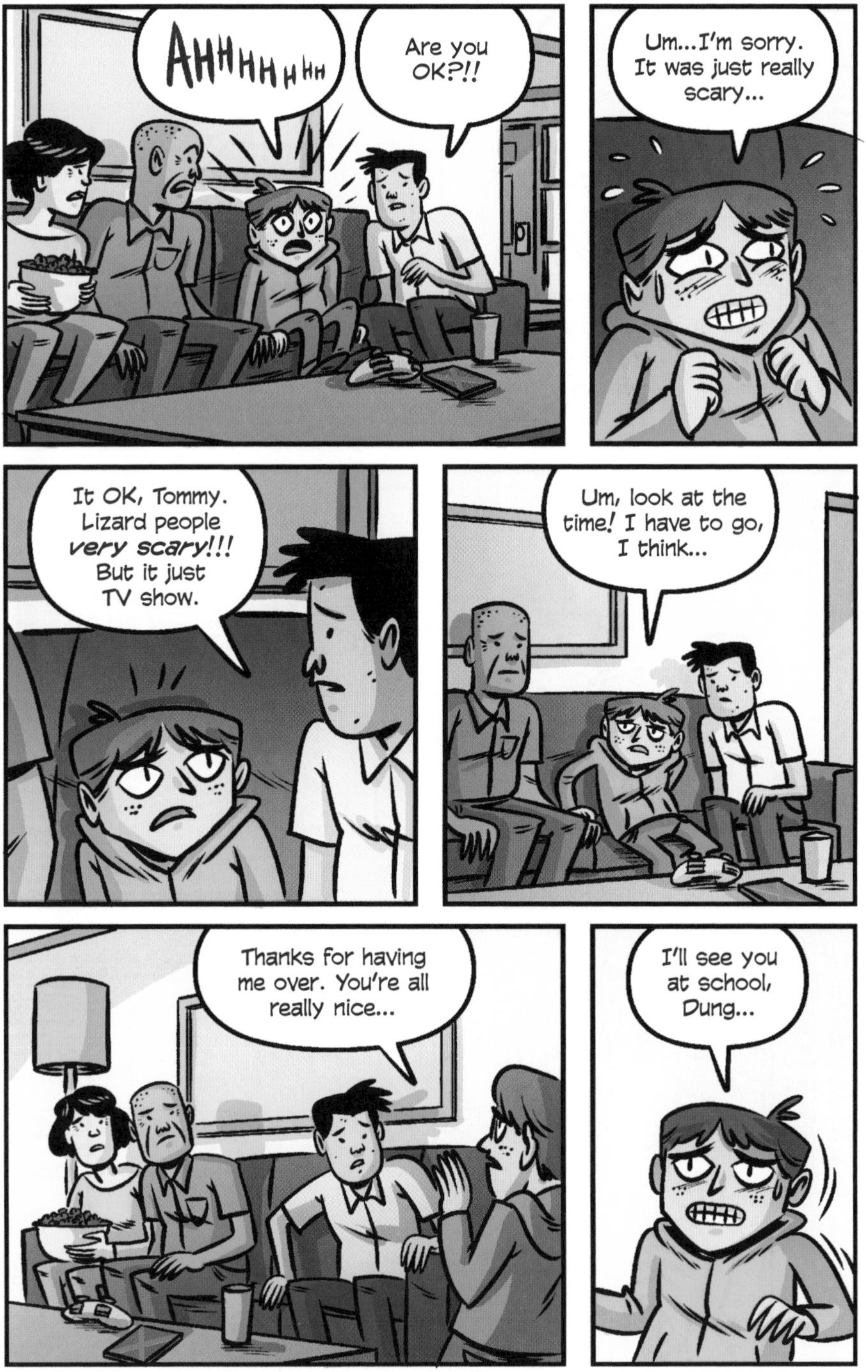
AHHHHHHHH
Are you OK?!!
Um...I'm sorry. It was just really scary...
It OK, Tommy. Lizard people very scary!!! But it just TV show.
Um, look at the time! I have to go, I think...
Thanks for having me over. You're all really nice...
I'll see you at school, Dung...

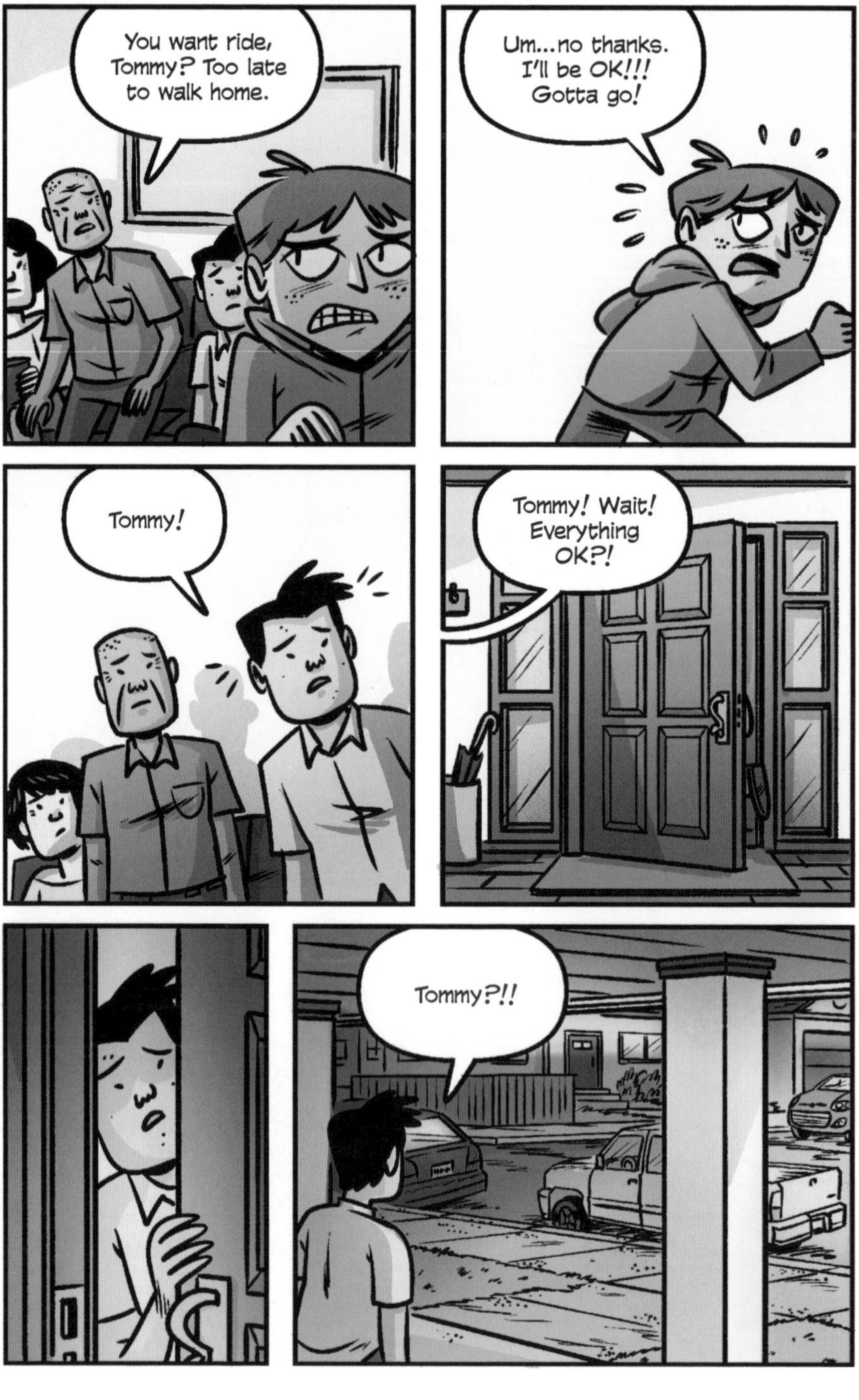
You want ride, Tommy? Too late to walk home.
Um...no thanks. I'll be OK!!! Gotta go!
Tommy!
Tommy! Wait! Everything OK?!
Tommy?!!

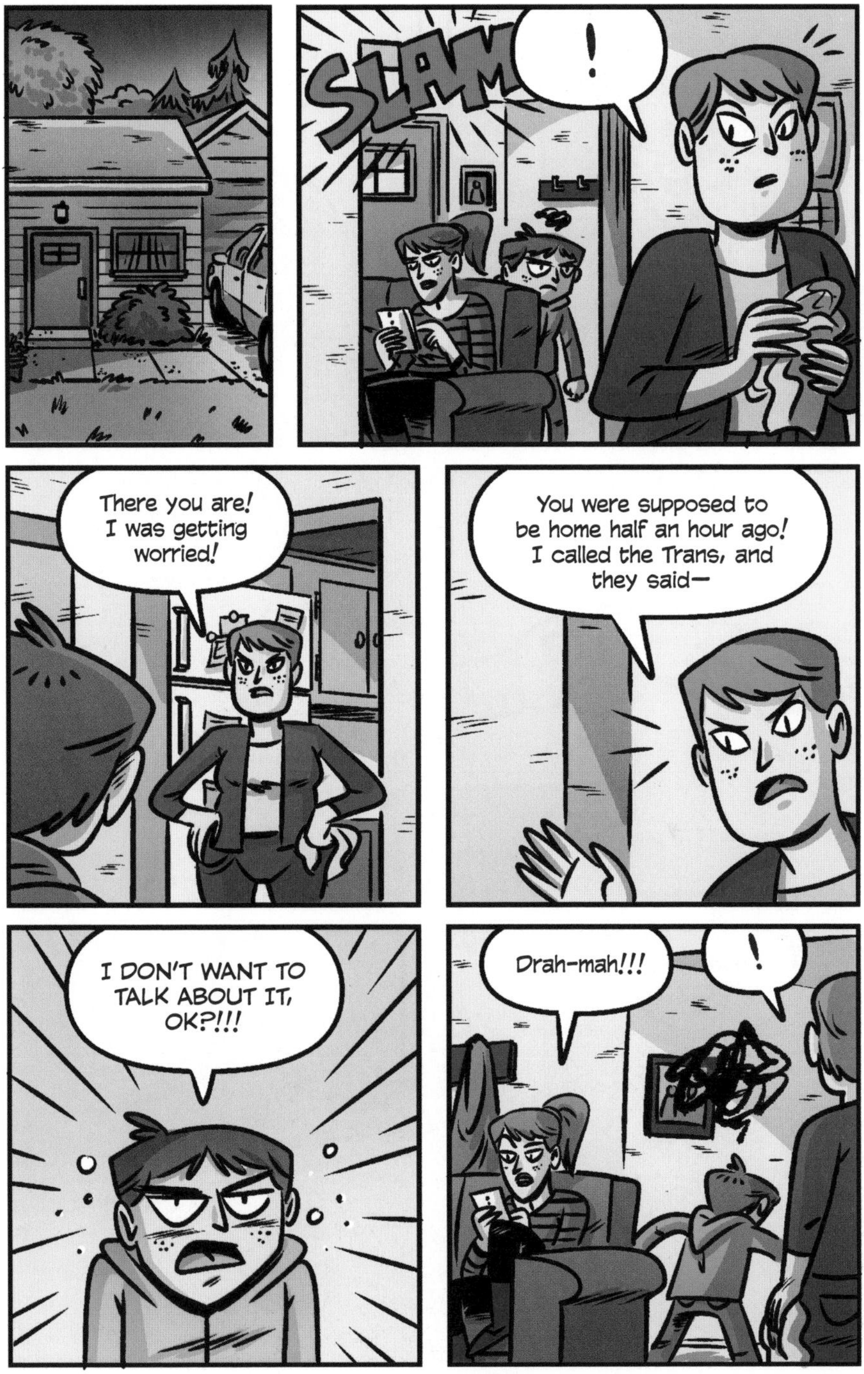
SLAM
!
There you are! I was getting worried!
You were supposed to be home half an hour ago! I called the Trans, and they said—
I DON'T WANT TO TALK ABOUT IT, OK?!!!
Drah-mah!!!
!

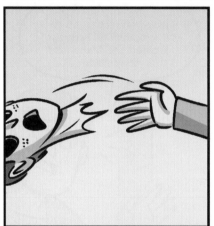

꒓sob!꒔
꒓sob!꒔

CHAPTER 5

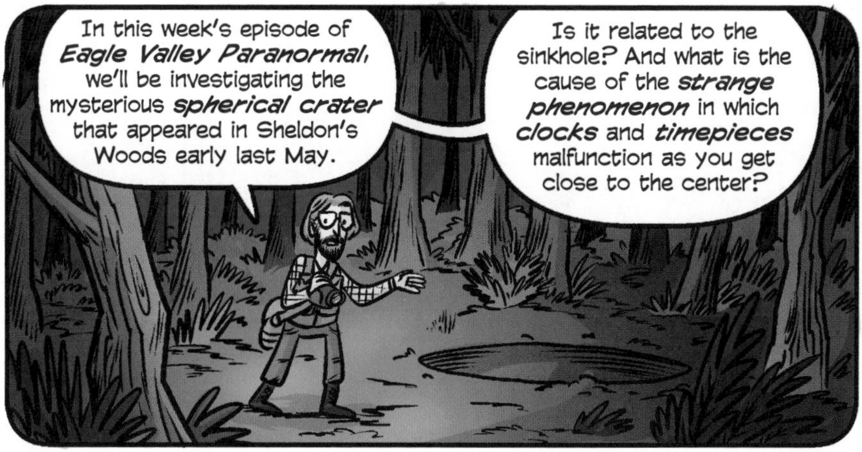

In this week's episode of *Eagle Valley Paranormal*, we'll be investigating the mysterious ***spherical crater*** that appeared in Sheldon's Woods early last May.
Is it related to the sinkhole? And what is the cause of the ***strange phenomenon*** in which ***clocks*** and ***timepieces*** malfunction as you get close to the center?

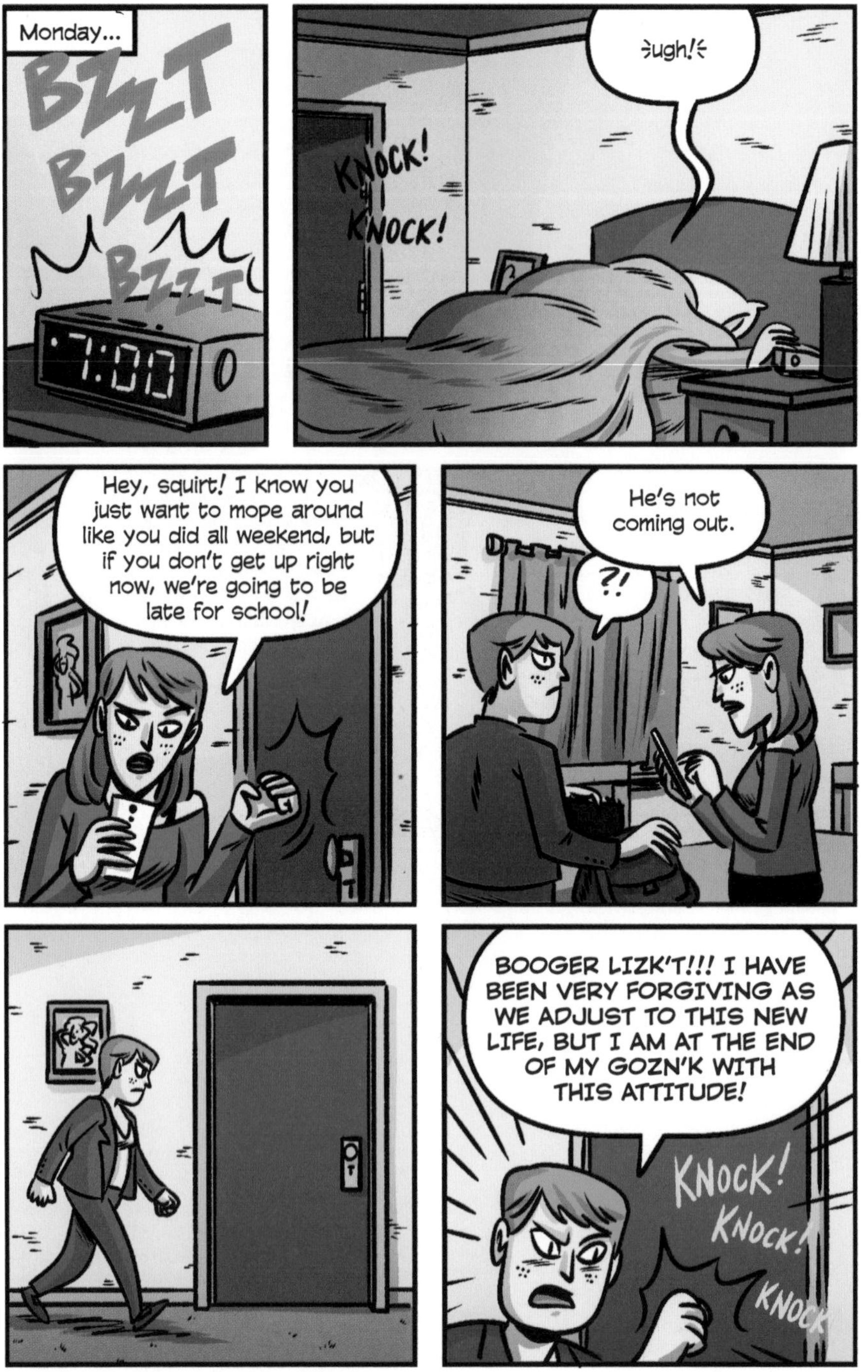
Monday...
BZZZT
BZZZT
BZZZT
7:00
ugh!
KNOCK!
KNOCK!
Hey, squirt! I know you just want to mope around like you did all weekend, but if you don't get up right now, we're going to be late for school!
He's not coming out.
?!
BOOGER LIZK'T!!! I HAVE BEEN VERY FORGIVING AS WE ADJUST TO THIS NEW LIFE, BUT I AM AT THE END OF MY GOZN'K WITH THIS ATTITUDE!
KNOCK!
KNOCK!
KNOCK

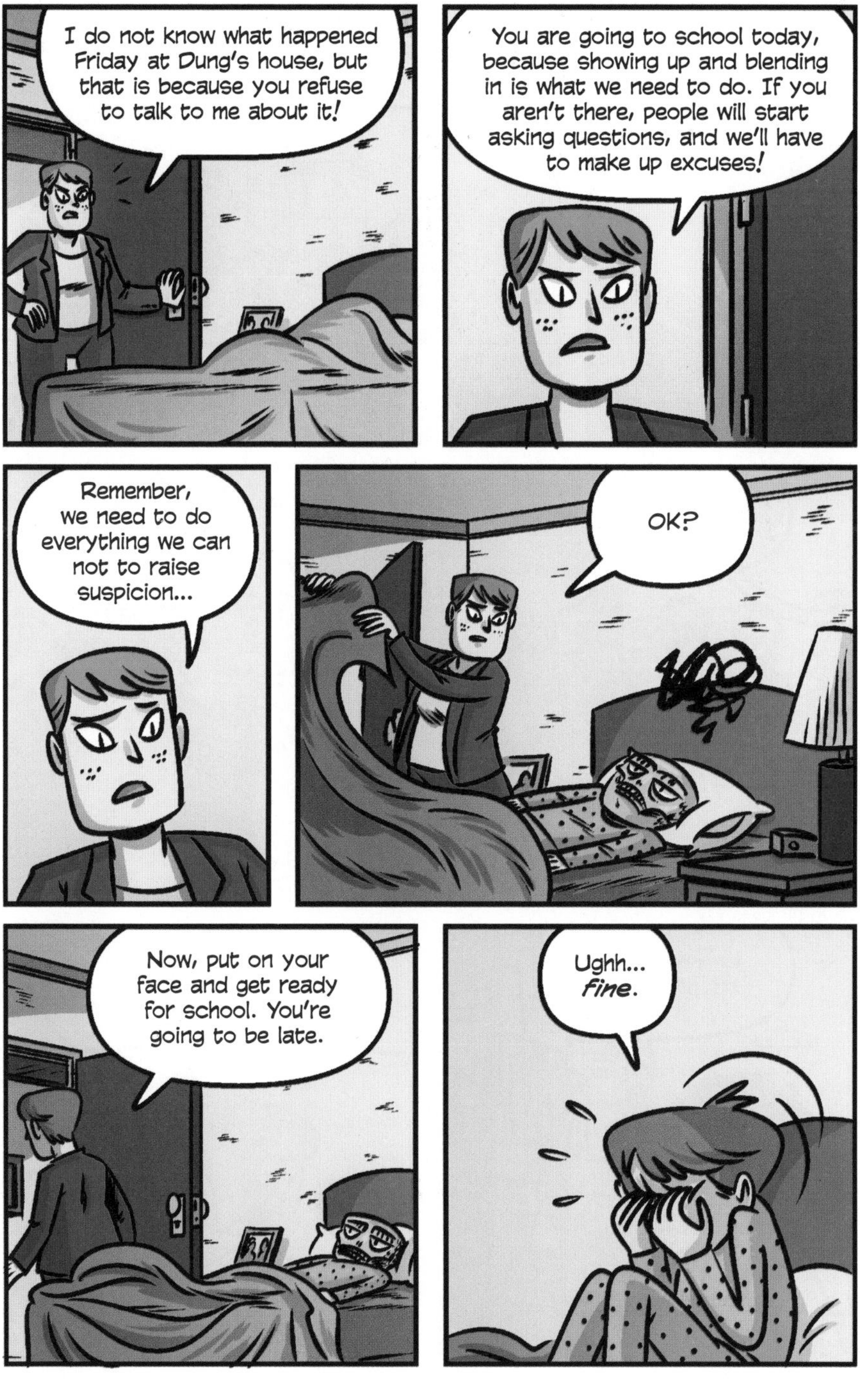

I do not know what happened Friday at Dung's house, but that is because you refuse to talk to me about it!
You are going to school today, because showing up and blending in is what we need to do. If you aren't there, people will start asking questions, and we'll have to make up excuses!
Remember, we need to do everything we can not to raise suspicion...
OK?
Now, put on your face and get ready for school. You're going to be late.
Ughh... *fine*.

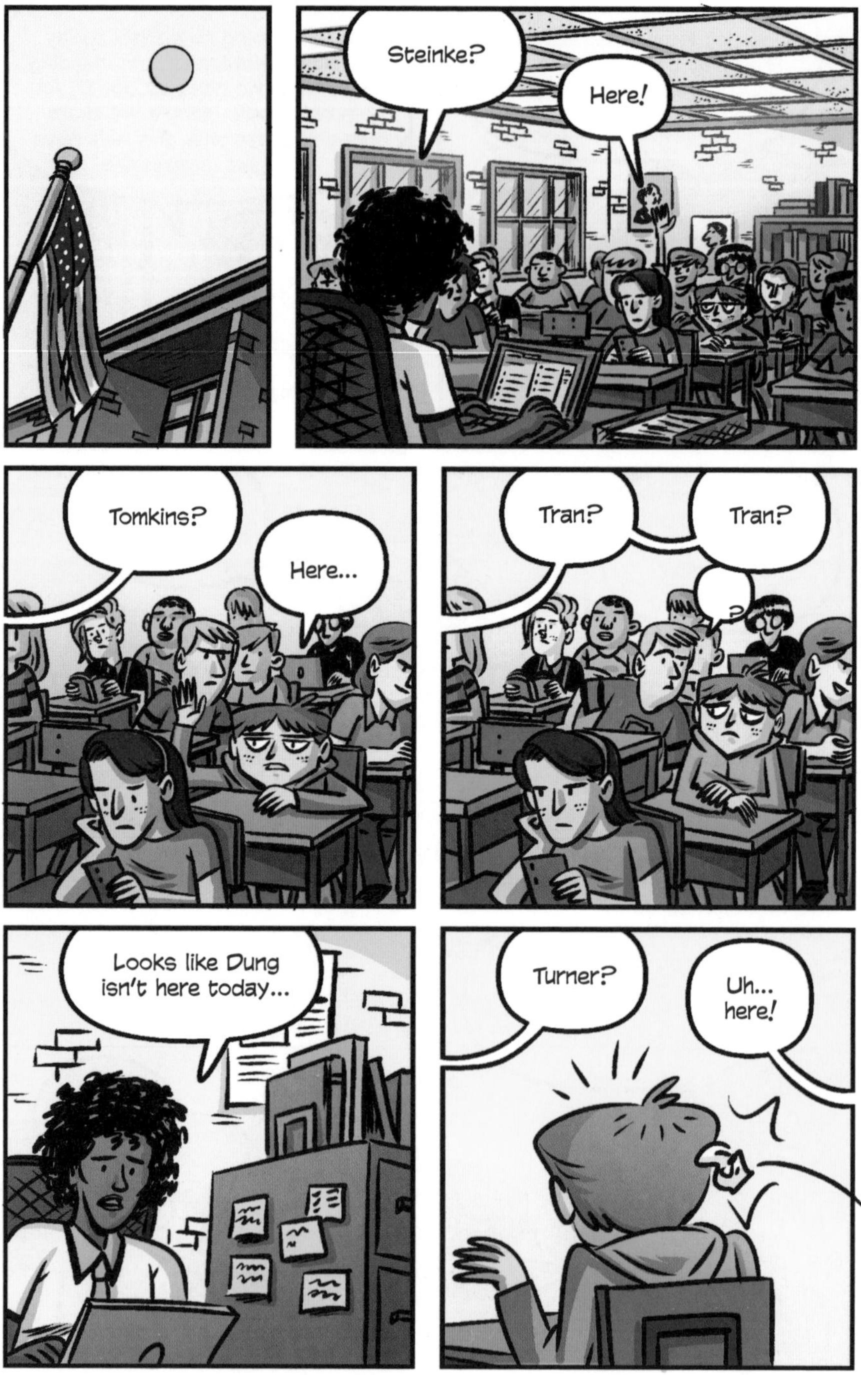
Steinke?
Here!
Tomkins?
Here...
Tran?
Tran?
Looks like Dung isn't here today...
Turner?
Uh... here!

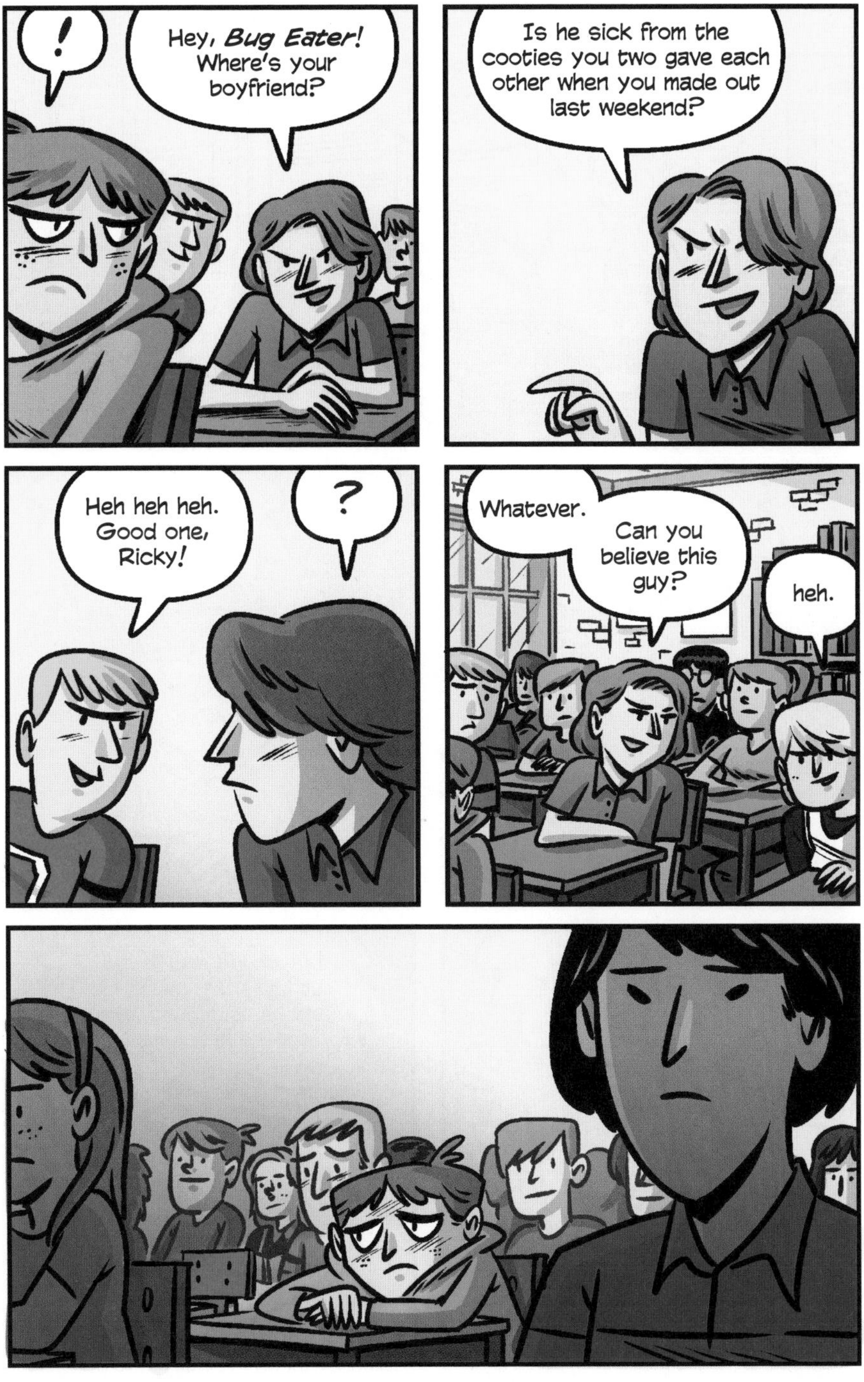
!
Hey, Bug Eater! Where's your boyfriend?
Is he sick from the cooties you two gave each other when you made out last weekend?
Heh heh heh. Good one, Ricky!
?
Whatever.
Can you believe this guy?
heh.

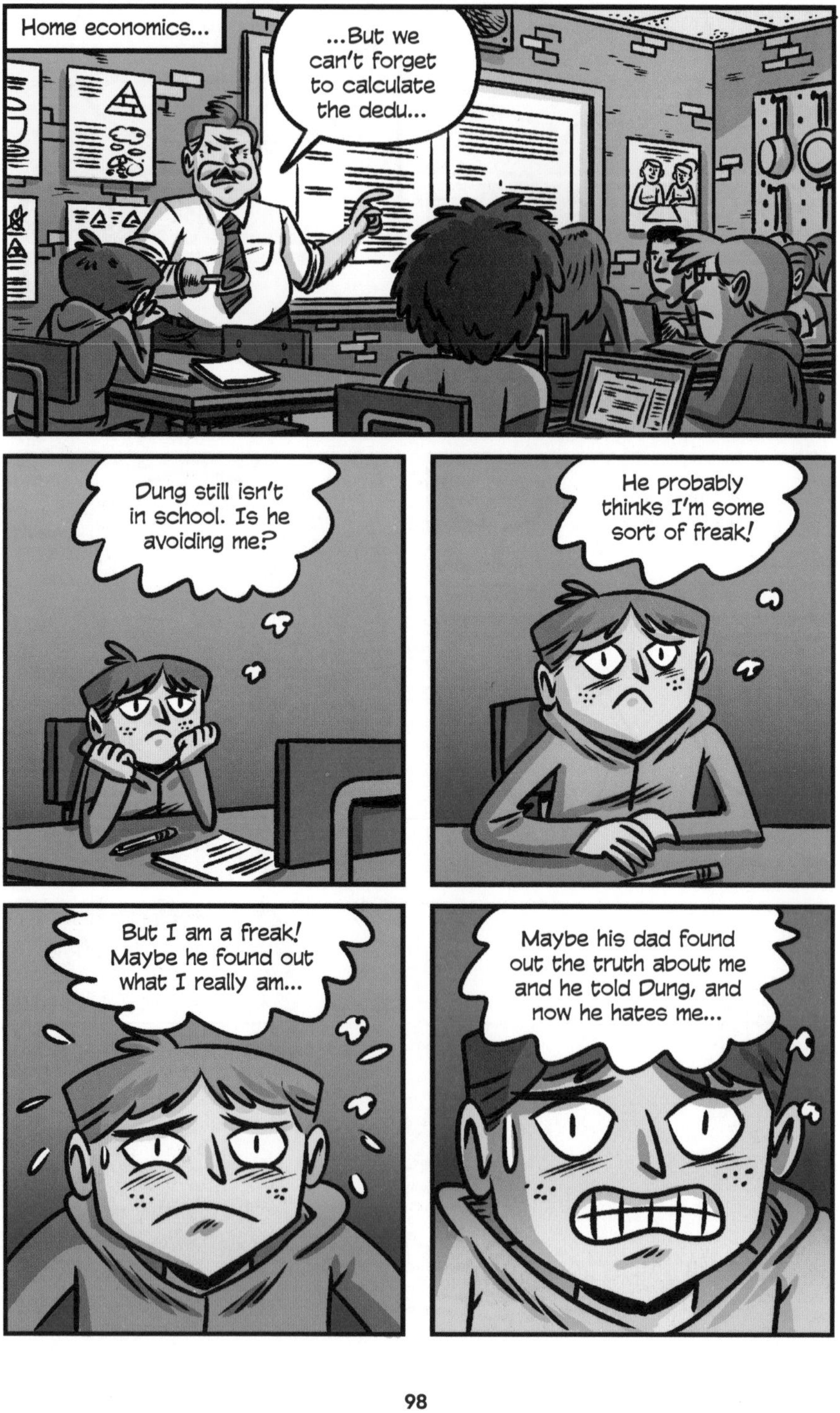
Home economics...
...But we can't forget to calculate the dedu...
Dung still isn't in school. Is he avoiding me?
He probably thinks I'm some sort of freak!
But I am a freak! Maybe he found out what I really am...
Maybe his dad found out the truth about me and he told Dung, and now he hates me...

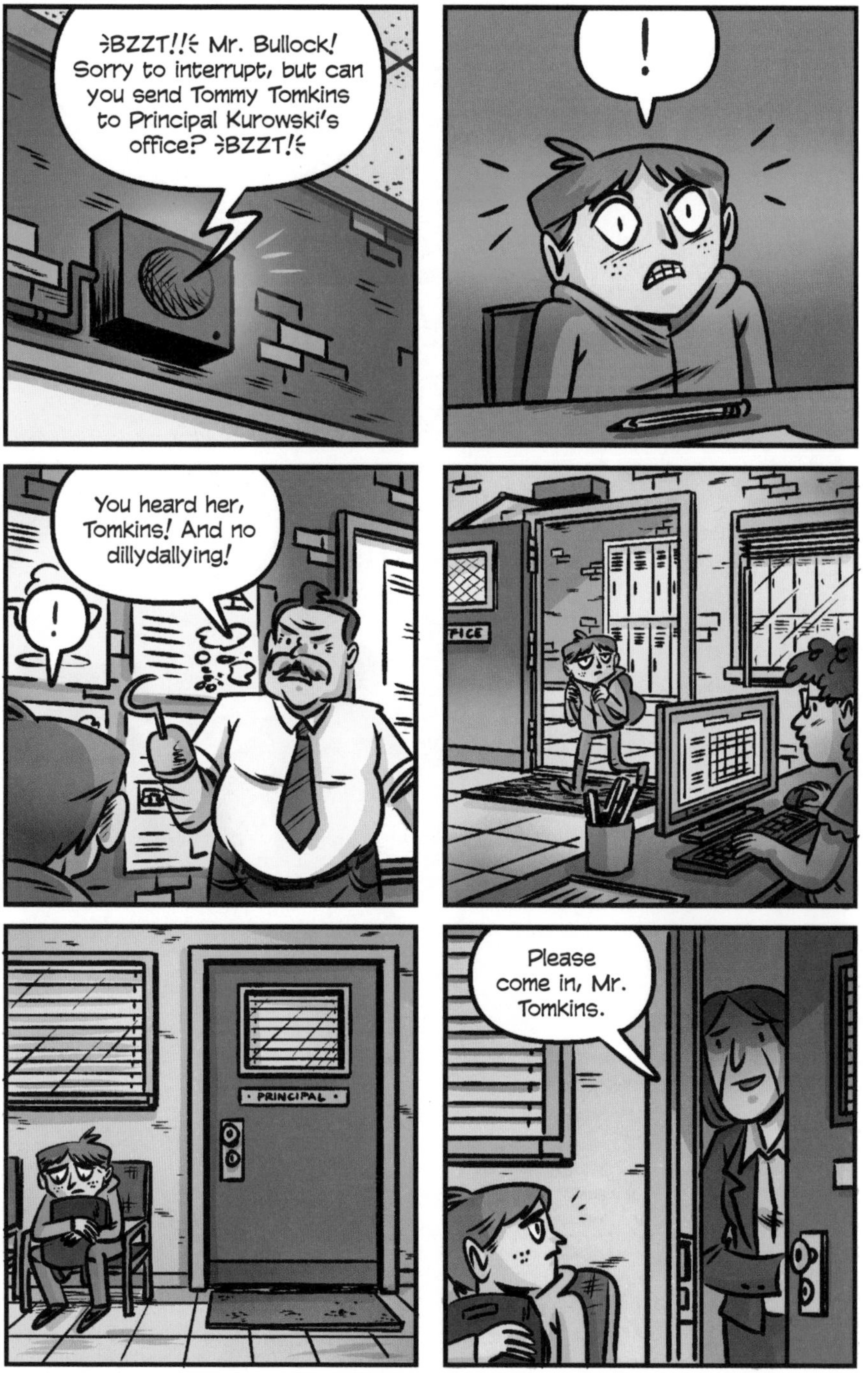

⊰BZZT!!⊱ Mr. Bullock! Sorry to interrupt, but can you send Tommy Tomkins to Principal Kurowski's office? ⊰BZZT!⊱
!
You heard her, Tomkins! And no dillydallying!
!
FICE
PRINCIPAL
Please come in, Mr. Tomkins.

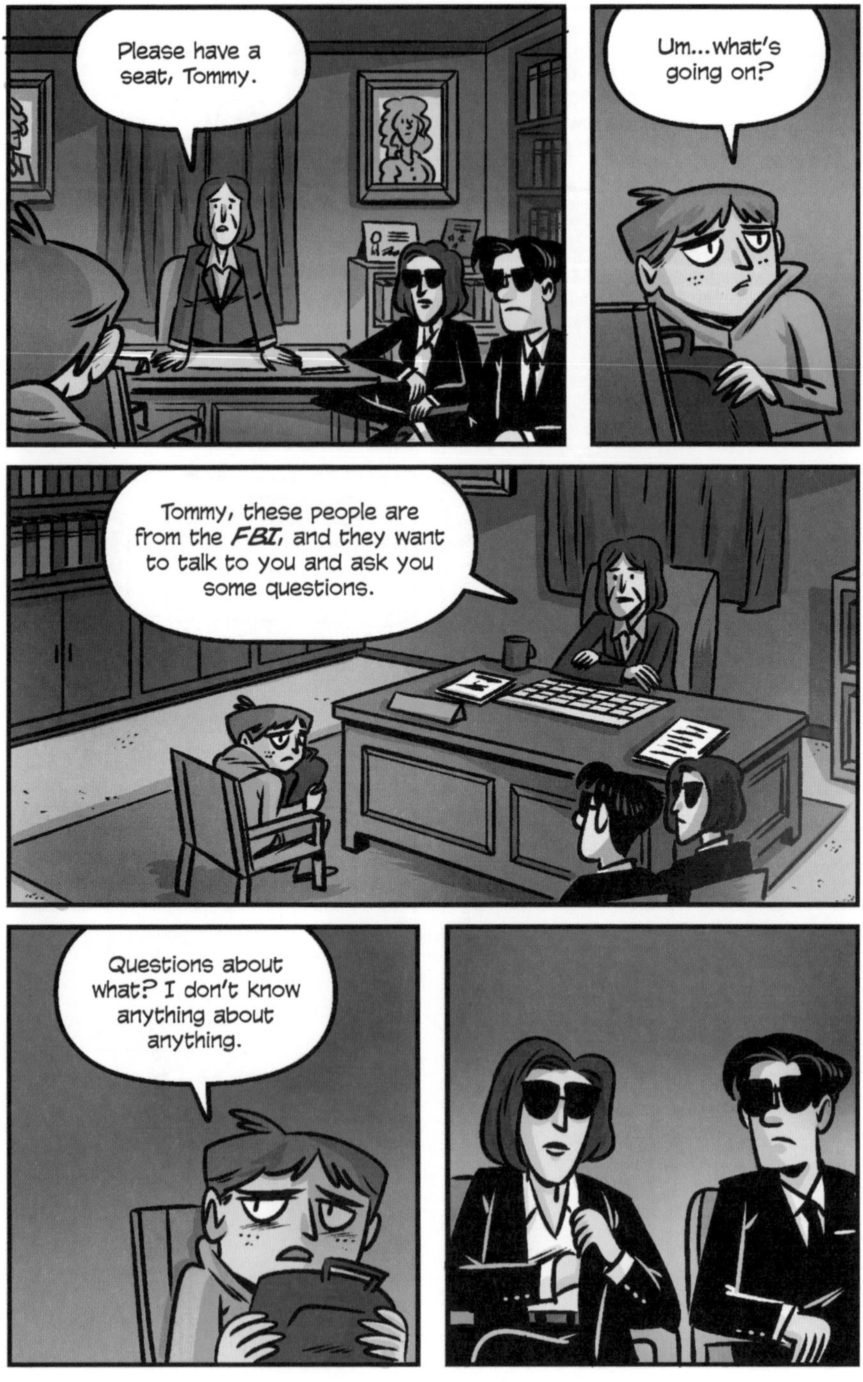

Please have a seat, Tommy.
Um...what's going on?
Tommy, these people are from the FBI, and they want to talk to you and ask you some questions.
Questions about what? I don't know anything about anything.

Do you know what this is, Tommy?

Uh... it looks like a rock.

It's not just any rock.

It's *Elberonium*. It's one of the rarest materials on the planet. It can only be found deep in the earth's crust.

So why are you asking me about it?

Have you ever seen *Elberonium* before, Tommy?

Uh... no.

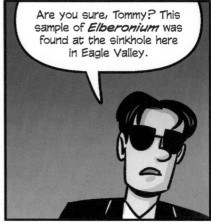

Are you sure, Tommy? This sample of *Elberonium* was found at the sinkhole here in Eagle Valley.

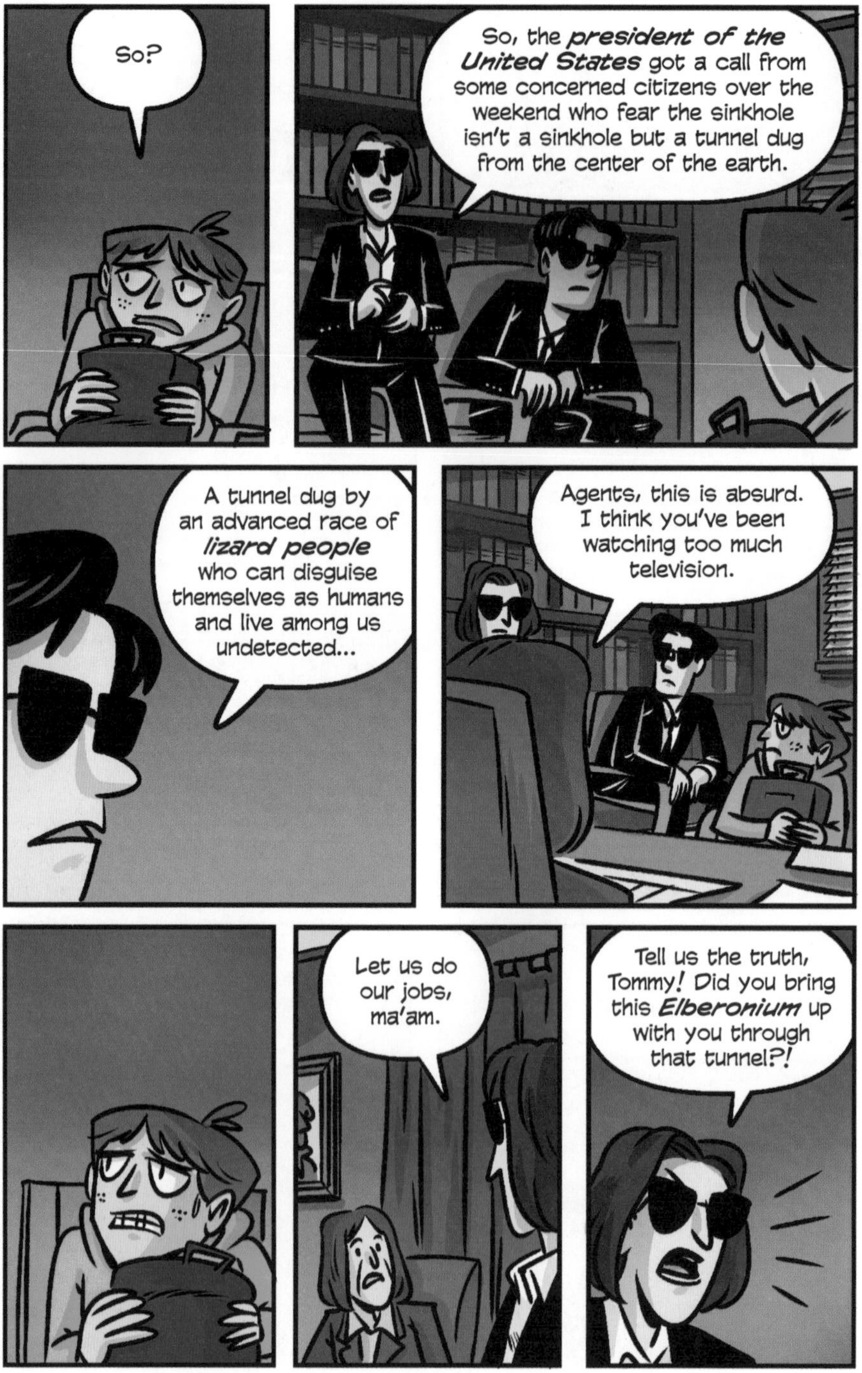
So?
So, the president of the United States got a call from some concerned citizens over the weekend who fear the sinkhole isn't a sinkhole but a tunnel dug from the center of the earth.
A tunnel dug by an advanced race of lizard people who can disguise themselves as humans and live among us undetected...
Agents, this is absurd. I think you've been watching too much television.
Let us do our jobs, ma'am.
Tell us the truth, Tommy! Did you bring this Elberonium up with you through that tunnel?!

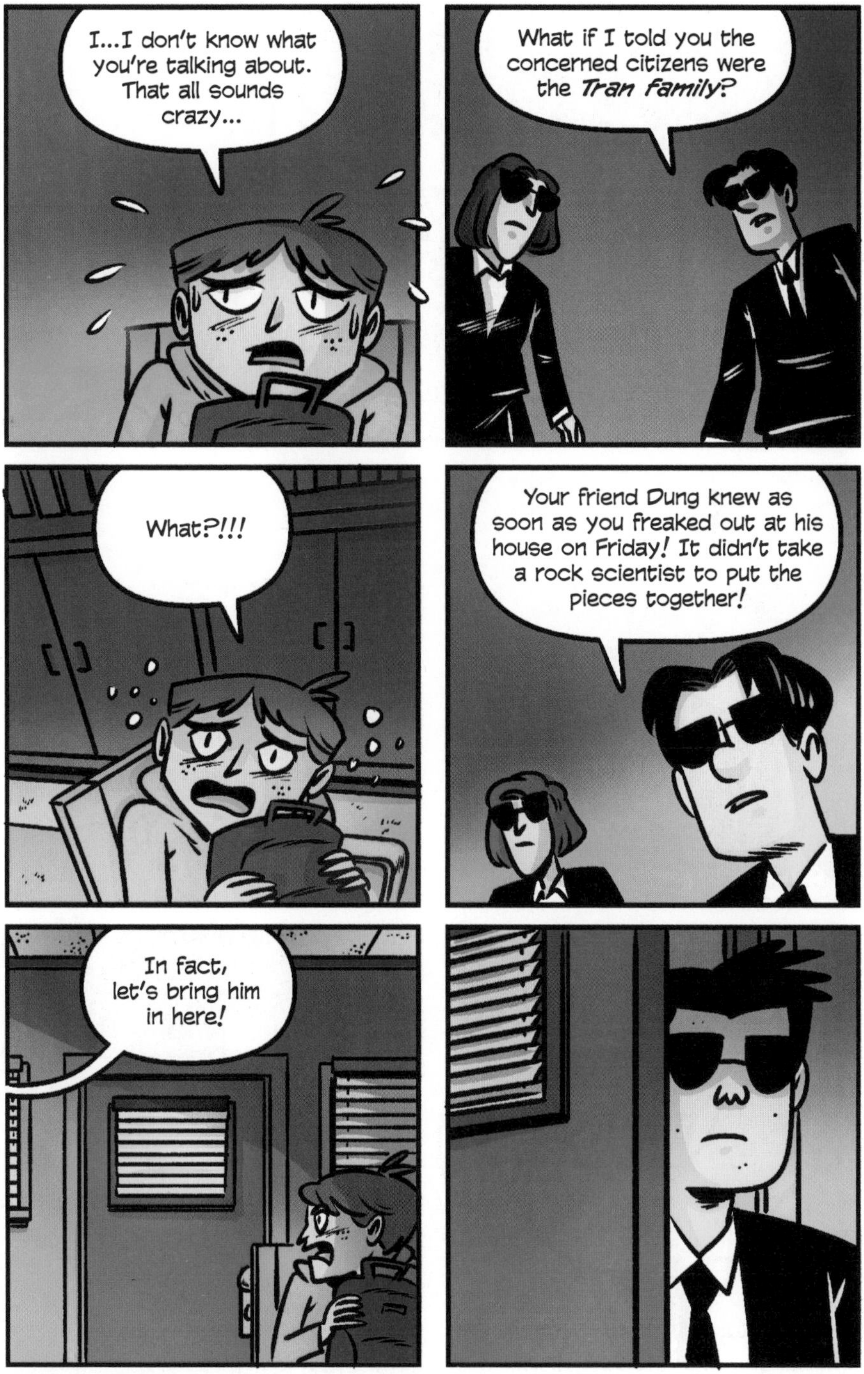

I...I don't know what you're talking about. That all sounds crazy...
What if I told you the concerned citizens were the *Tran family*?
What?!!!
Your friend Dung knew as soon as you freaked out at his house on Friday! It didn't take a rock scientist to put the pieces together!
In fact, let's bring him in here!

Lizard people are scary, Tommy. Are you *lizard people?!!*

No, no, no...I thought we were friends. Why would you—

Let's find out what's behind that face...

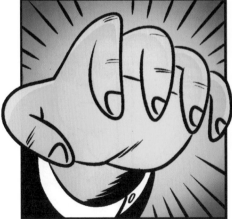

AHHHHH

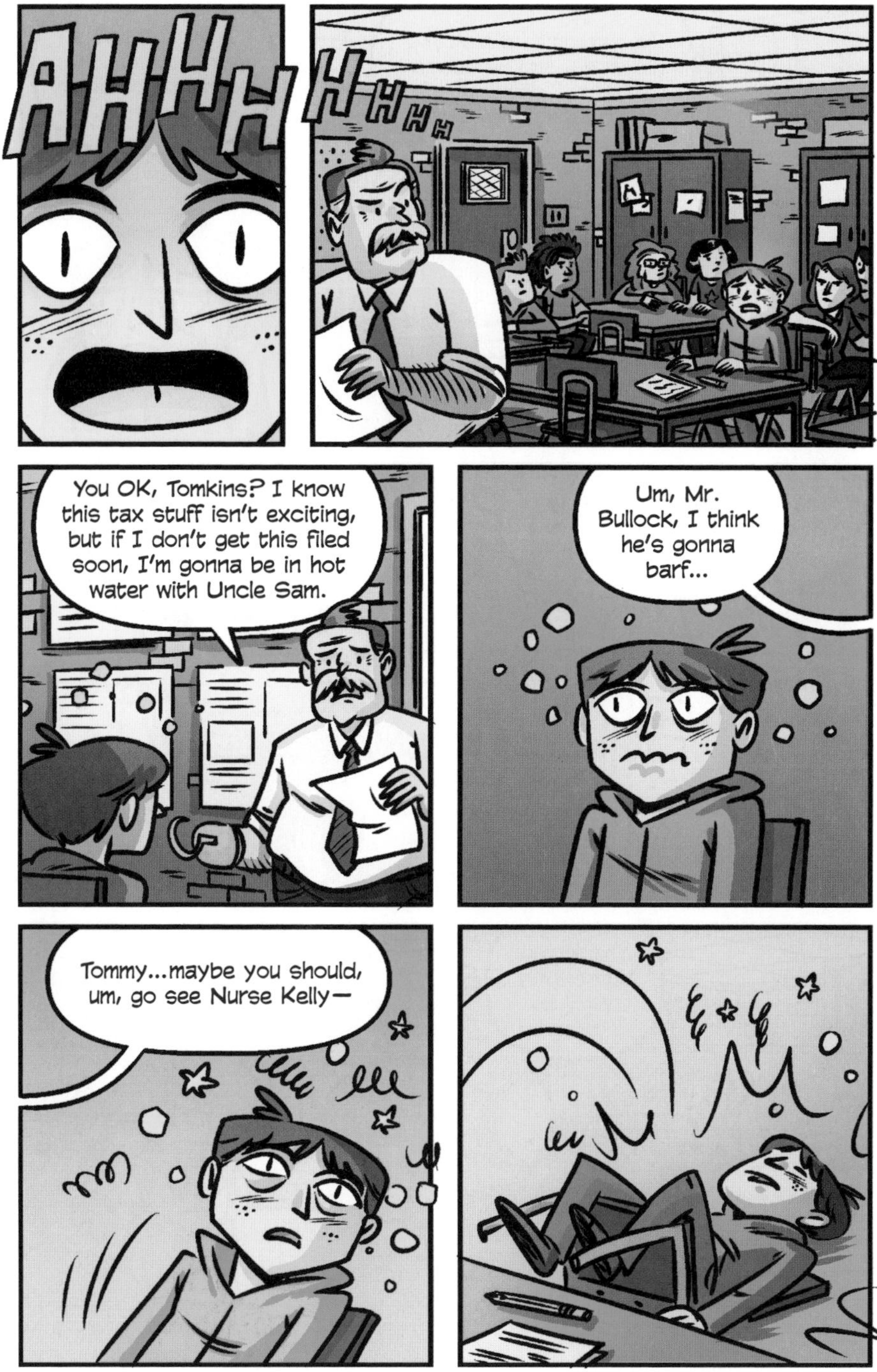
AHHHHHHHHH
You OK, Tomkins? I know this tax stuff isn't exciting, but if I don't get this filed soon, I'm gonna be in hot water with Uncle Sam.
Um, Mr. Bullock, I think he's gonna barf...
Tommy...maybe you should, um, go see Nurse Kelly—

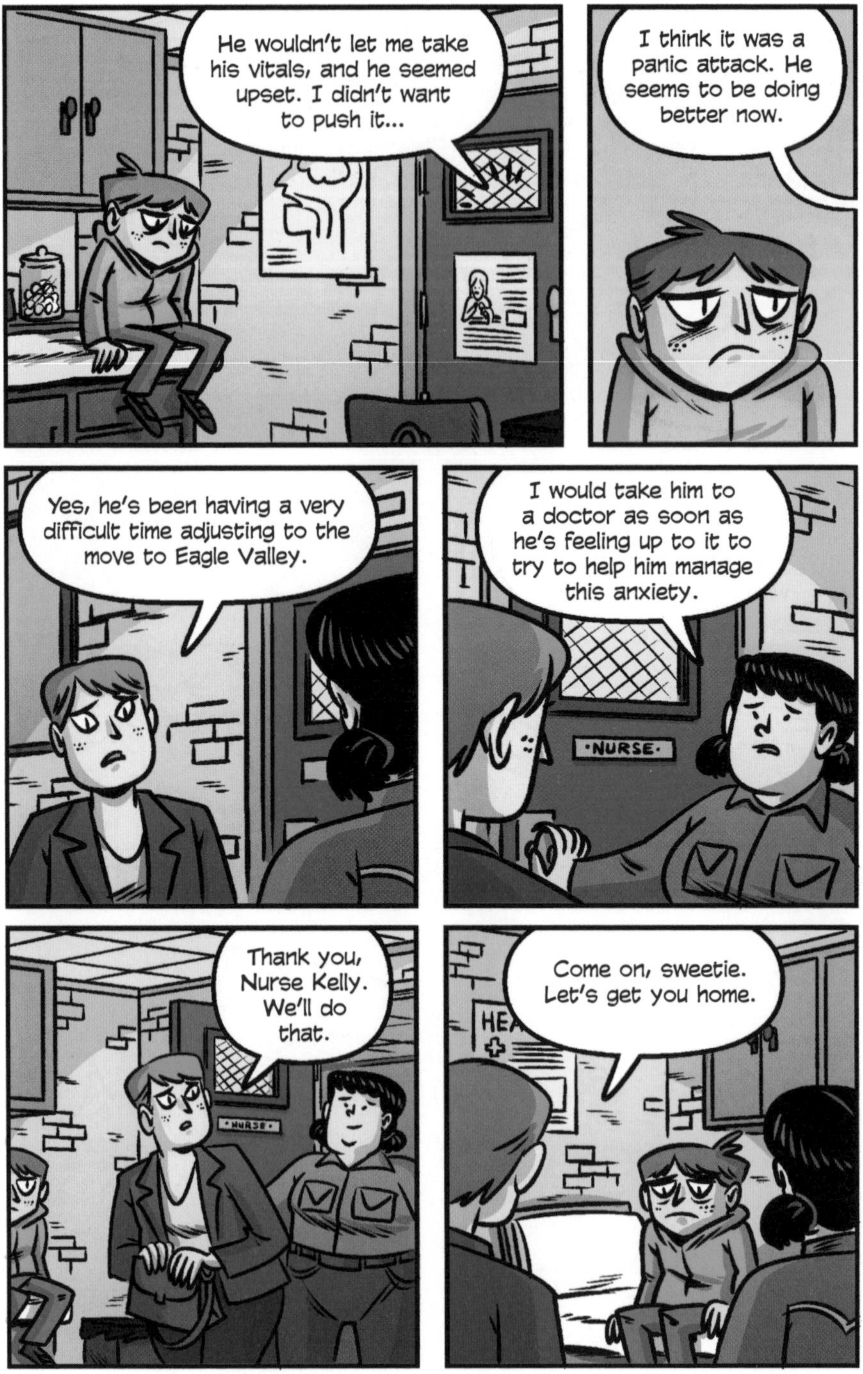
He wouldn't let me take his vitals, and he seemed upset. I didn't want to push it...
I think it was a panic attack. He seems to be doing better now.
Yes, he's been having a very difficult time adjusting to the move to Eagle Valley.
I would take him to a doctor as soon as he's feeling up to it to try to help him manage this anxiety.
NURSE
Thank you, Nurse Kelly. We'll do that.
NURSE
Come on, sweetie. Let's get you home.

CHAPTER 6

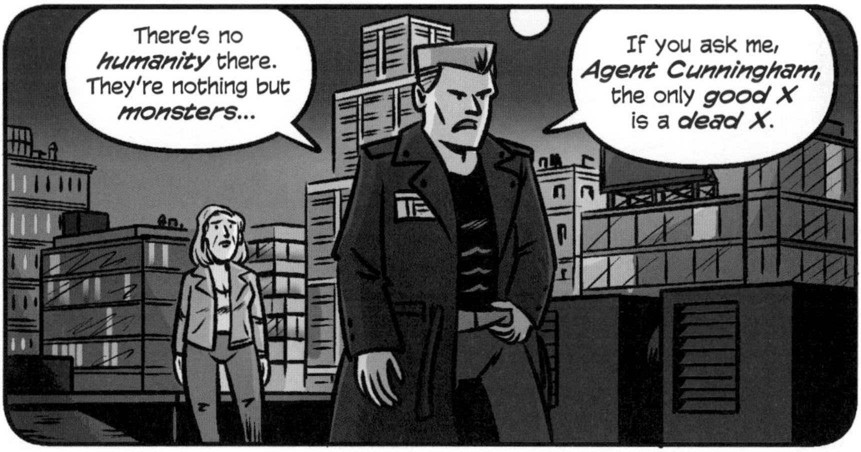

There's no *humanity* there. They're nothing but *monsters*...
If you ask me, *Agent Cunningham,* the only *good X* is a *dead X*.

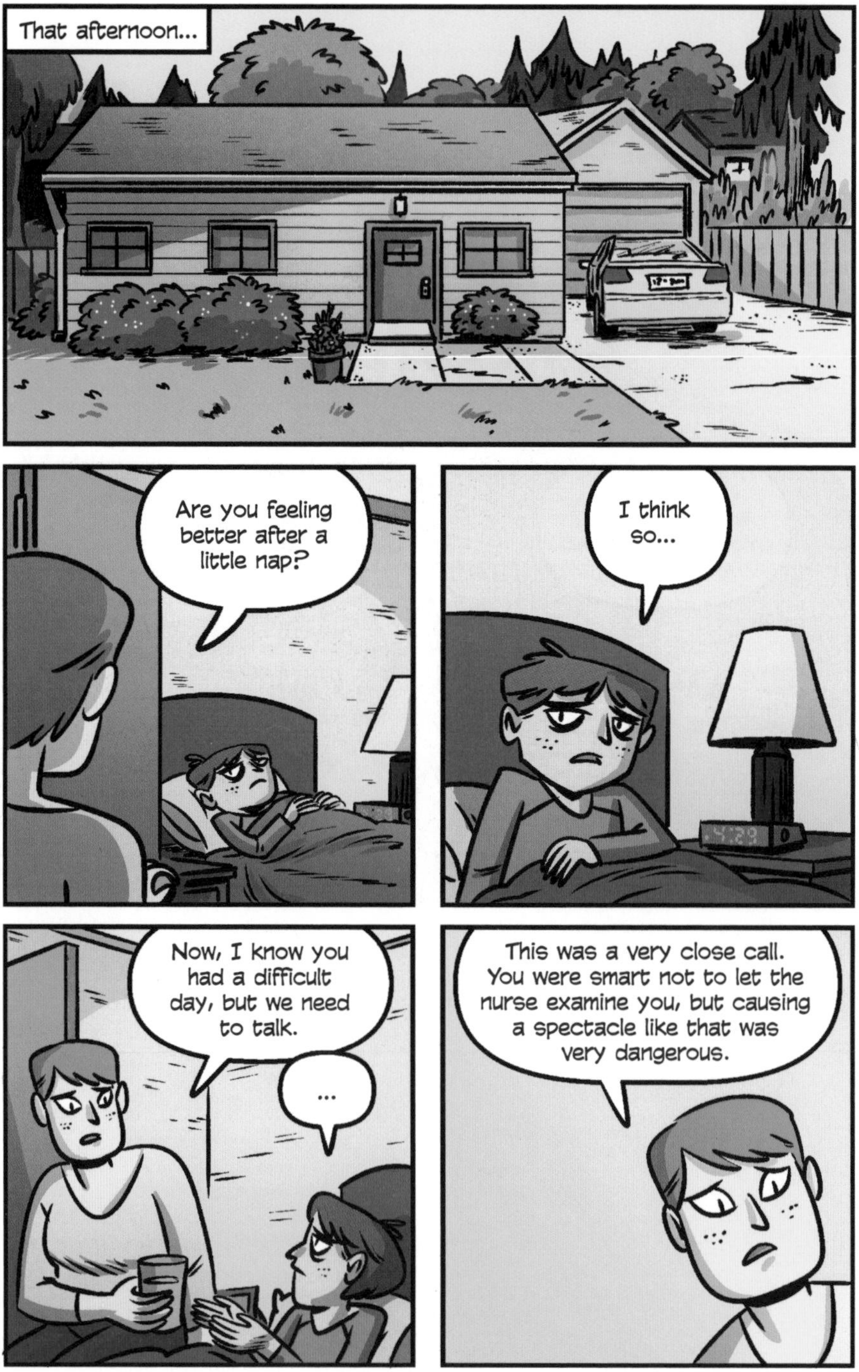
That afternoon...
Are you feeling better after a little nap?
I think so...
Now, I know you had a difficult day, but we need to talk.
...
This was a very close call. You were smart not to let the nurse examine you, but causing a spectacle like that was very dangerous.

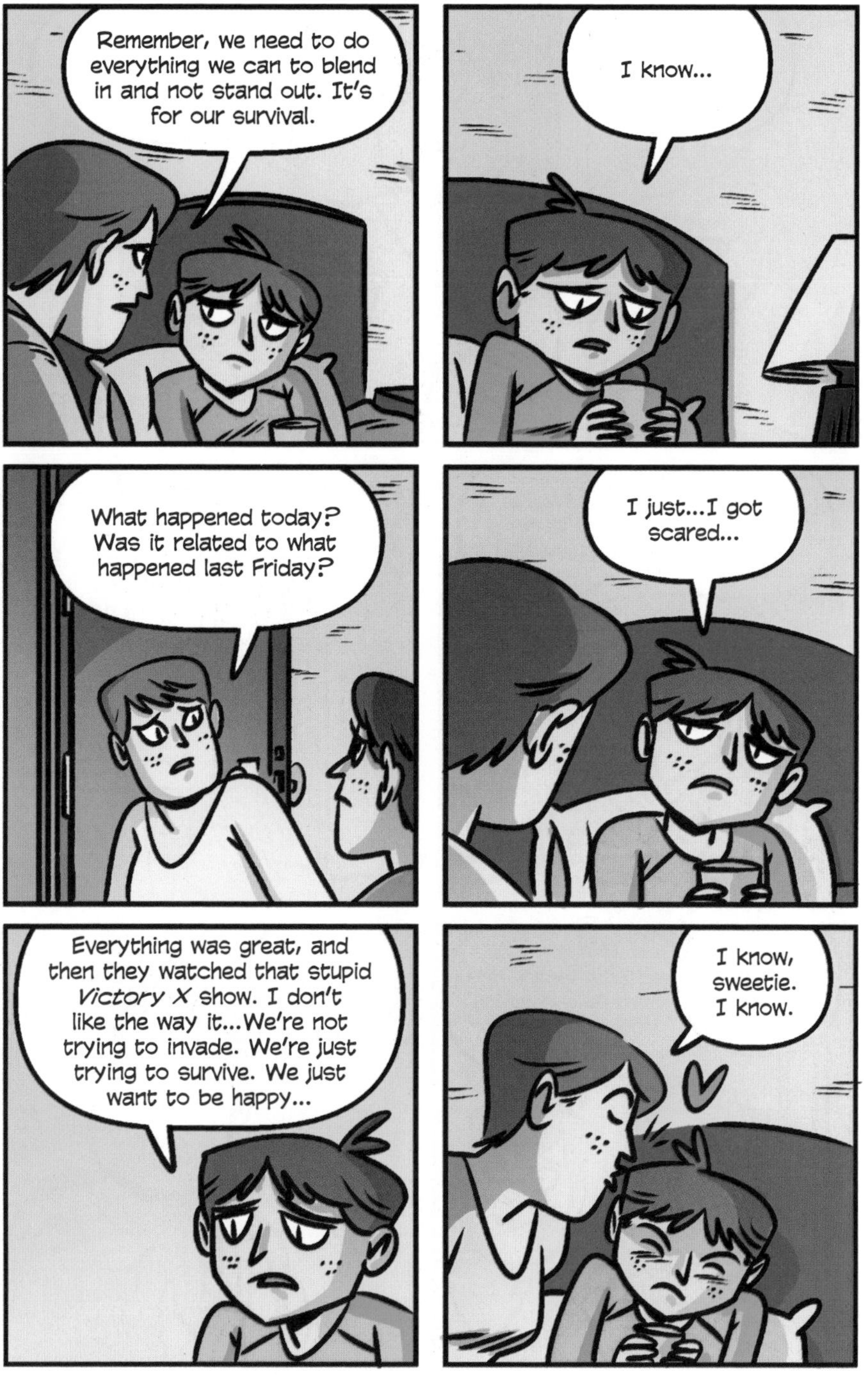
Remember, we need to do everything we can to blend in and not stand out. It's for our survival.
I know...
What happened today? Was it related to what happened last Friday?
I just...I got scared...
Everything was great, and then they watched that stupid *Victory X* show. I don't like the way it...We're not trying to invade. We're just trying to survive. We just want to be happy...
I know, sweetie. I know.

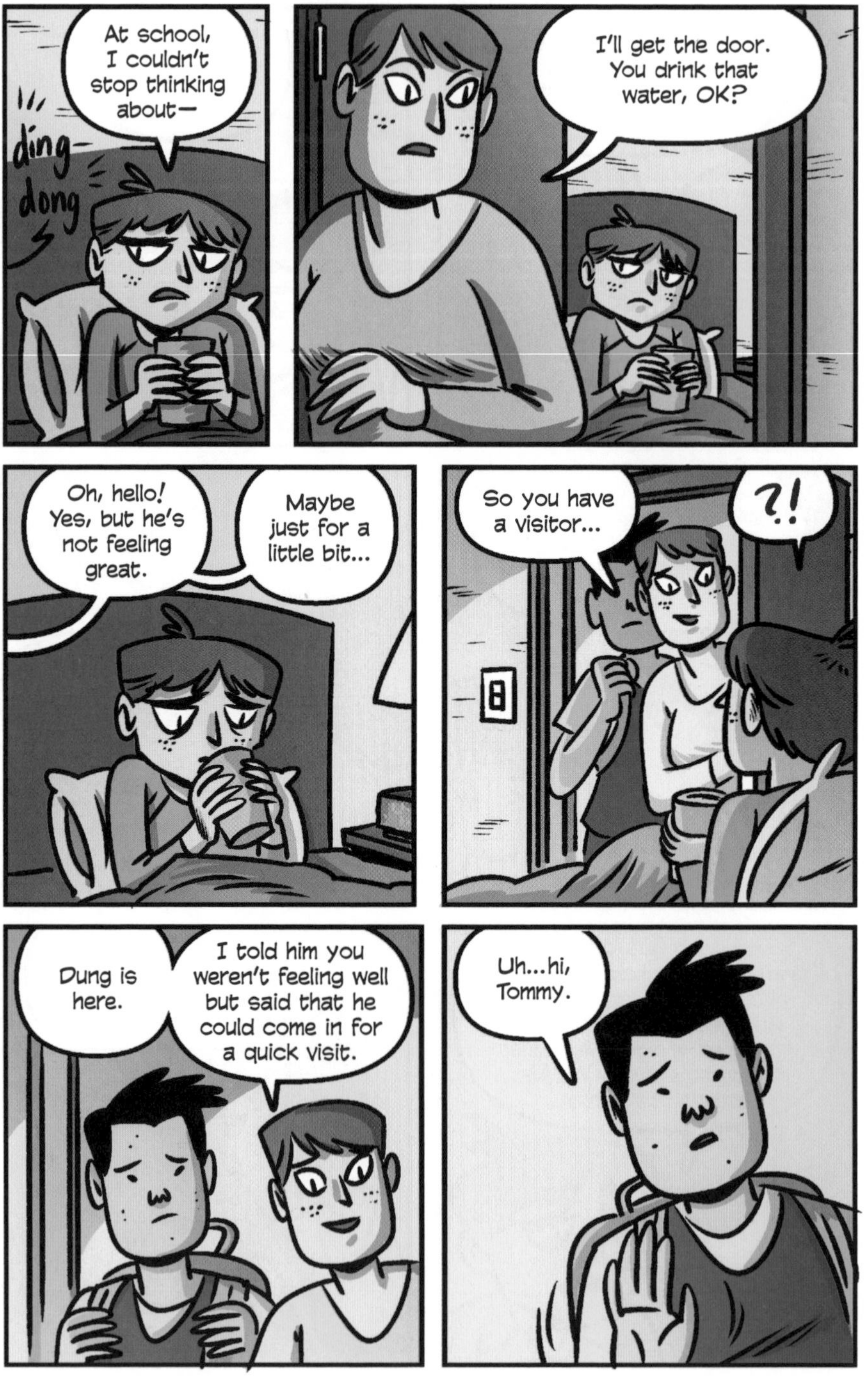
At school, I couldn't stop thinking about—
ding-dong
I'll get the door. You drink that water, OK?
Oh, hello! Yes, but he's not feeling great.
Maybe just for a little bit...
So you have a visitor...
?!
Dung is here.
I told him you weren't feeling well but said that he could come in for a quick visit.
Uh...hi, Tommy.

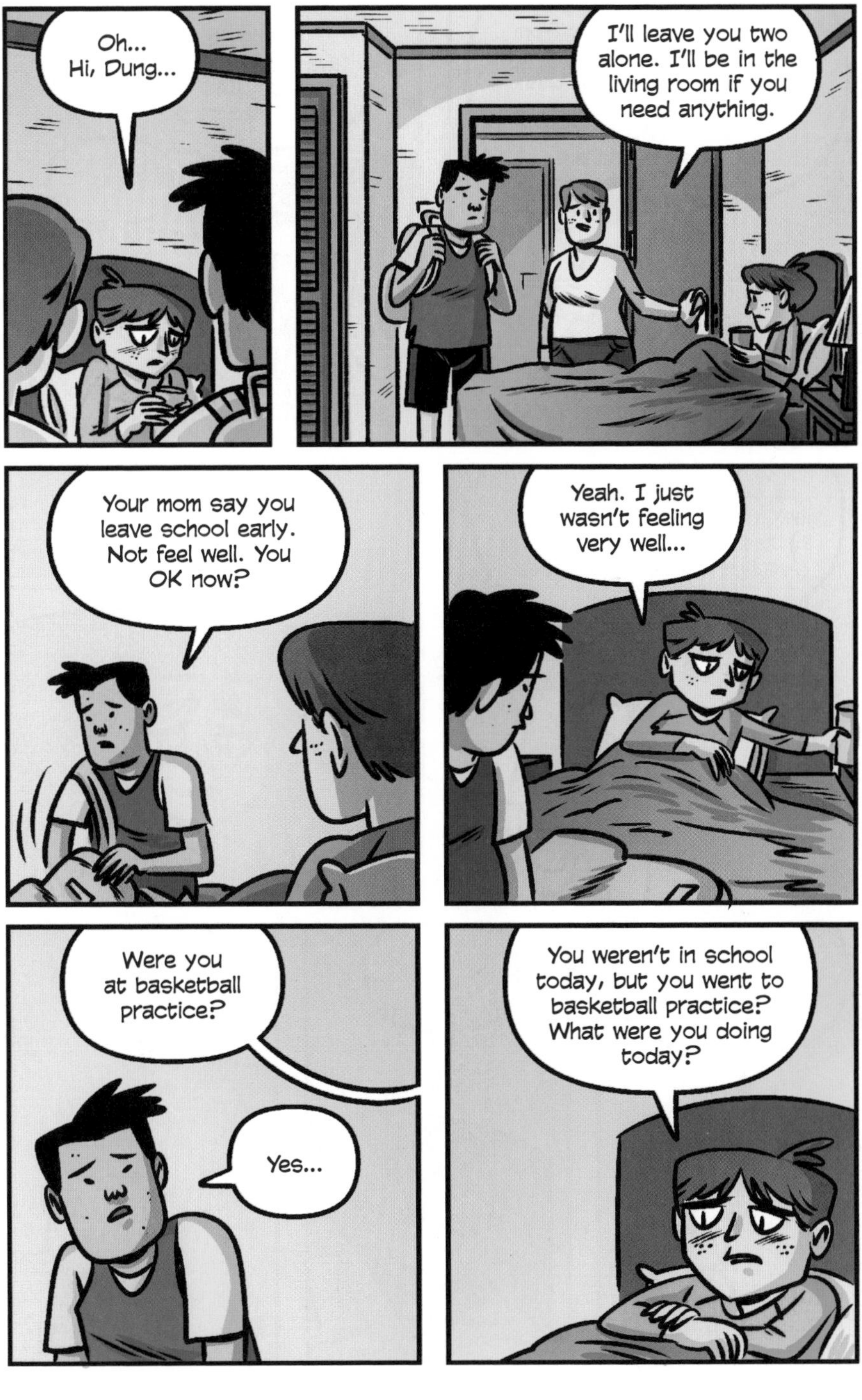
Oh... Hi, Dung...
I'll leave you two alone. I'll be in the living room if you need anything.
Your mom say you leave school early. Not feel well. You OK now?
Yeah. I just wasn't feeling very well...
Were you at basketball practice?
Yes...
You weren't in school today, but you went to basketball practice? What were you doing today?

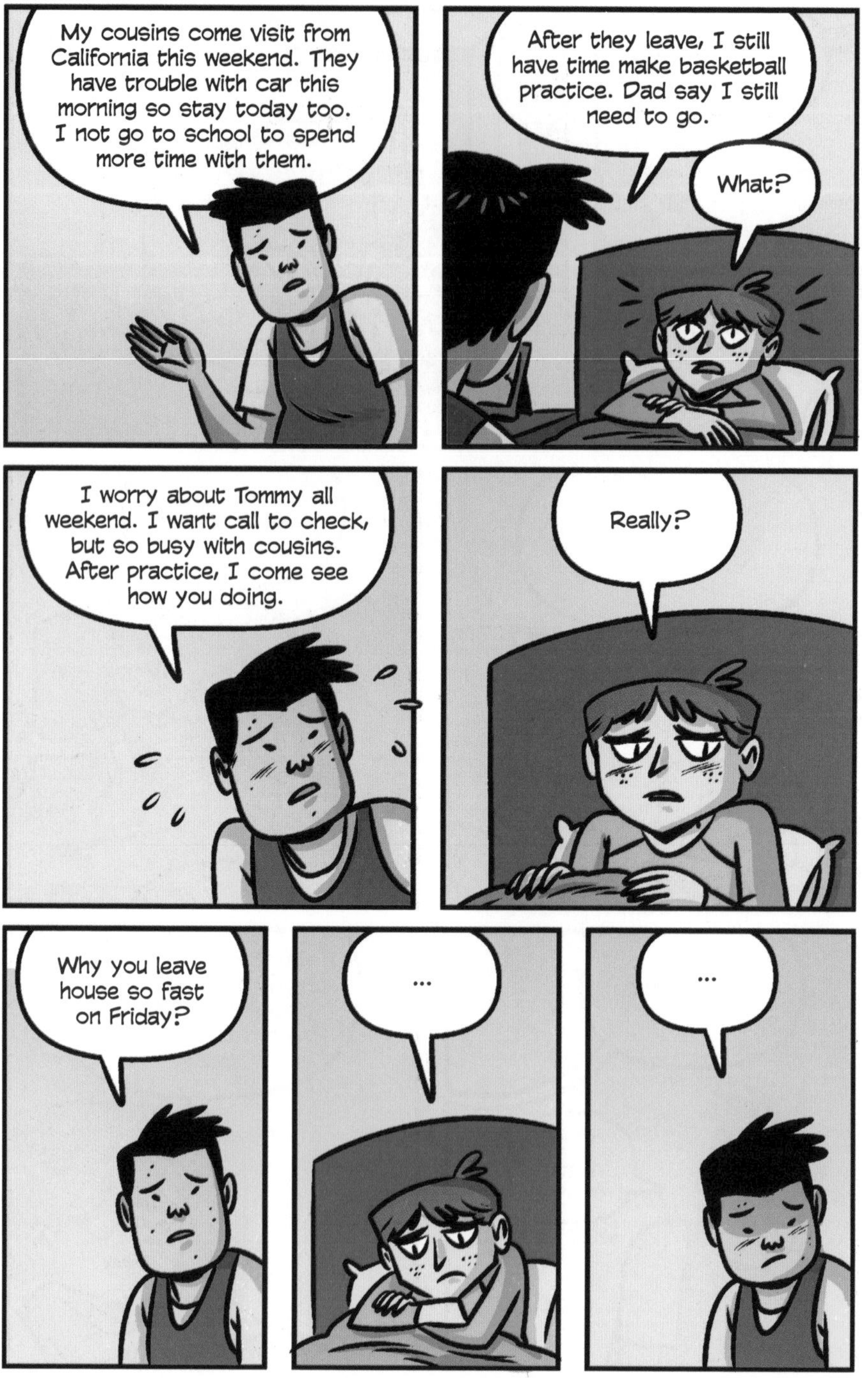
My cousins come visit from California this weekend. They have trouble with car this morning so stay today too. I not go to school to spend more time with them.
After they leave, I still have time make basketball practice. Dad say I still need to go.
What?
I worry about Tommy all weekend. I want call to check, but so busy with cousins. After practice, I come see how you doing.
Really?
Why you leave house so fast on Friday?
...
...

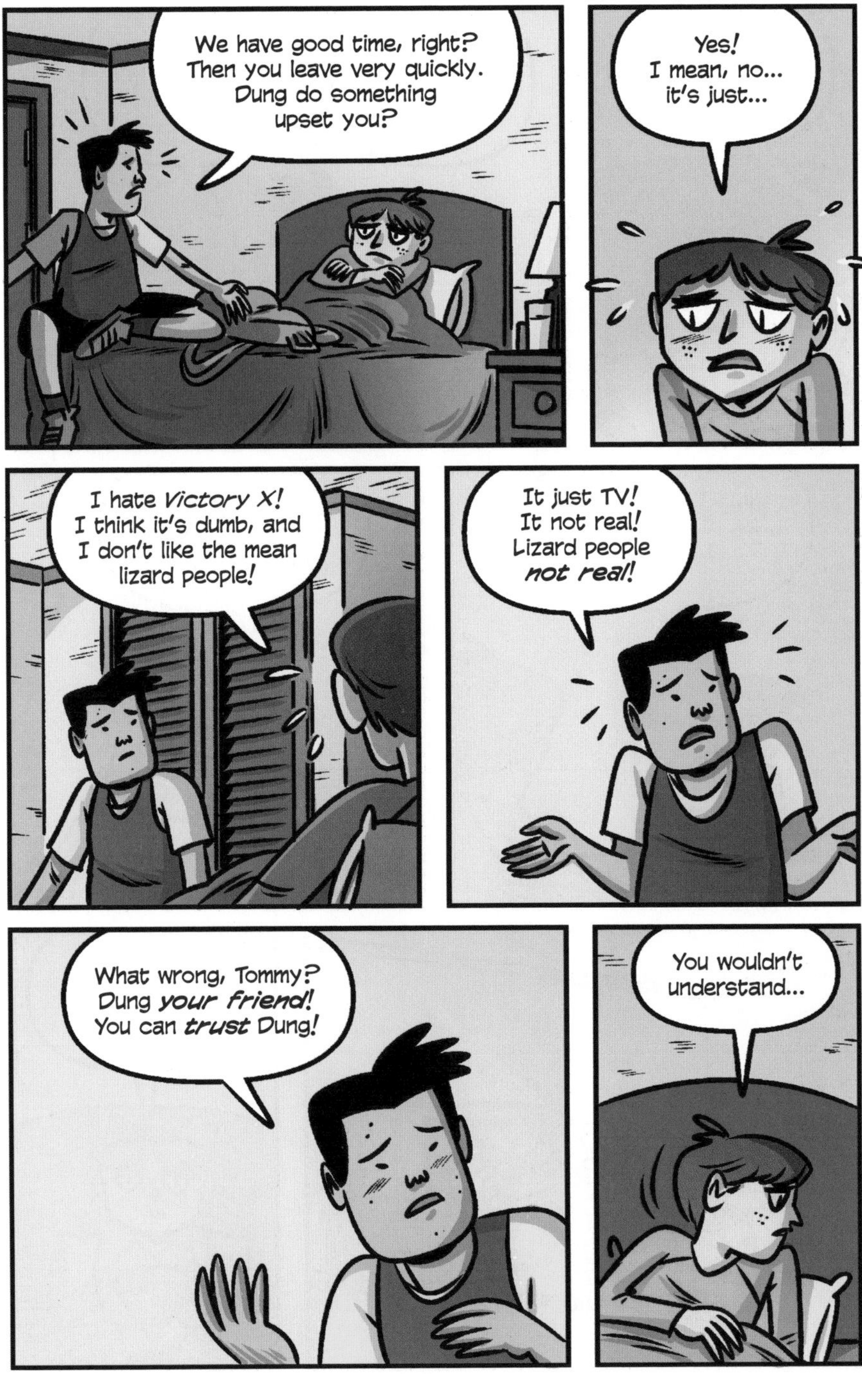
We have good time, right? Then you leave very quickly. Dung do something upset you?
Yes! I mean, no... it's just...
I hate *Victory X*! I think it's dumb, and I don't like the mean lizard people!
It just TV! It not real! Lizard people ***not real***!
What wrong, Tommy? Dung ***your friend***! You can ***trust*** Dung!
You wouldn't understand...

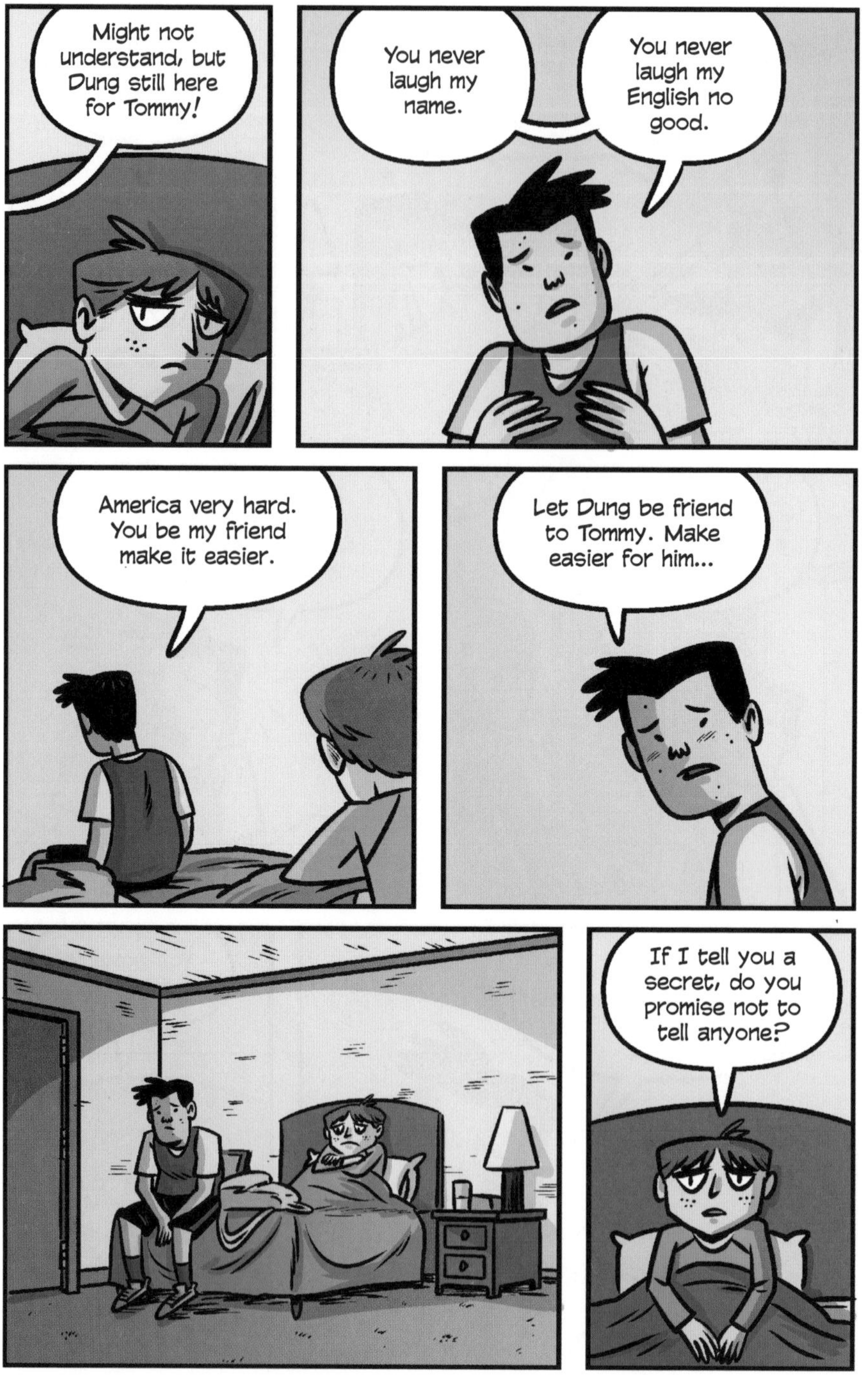
Might not understand, but Dung still here for Tommy!
You never laugh my name.
You never laugh my English no good.
America very hard. You be my friend make it easier.
Let Dung be friend to Tommy. Make easier for him...
If I tell you a secret, do you promise not to tell anyone?

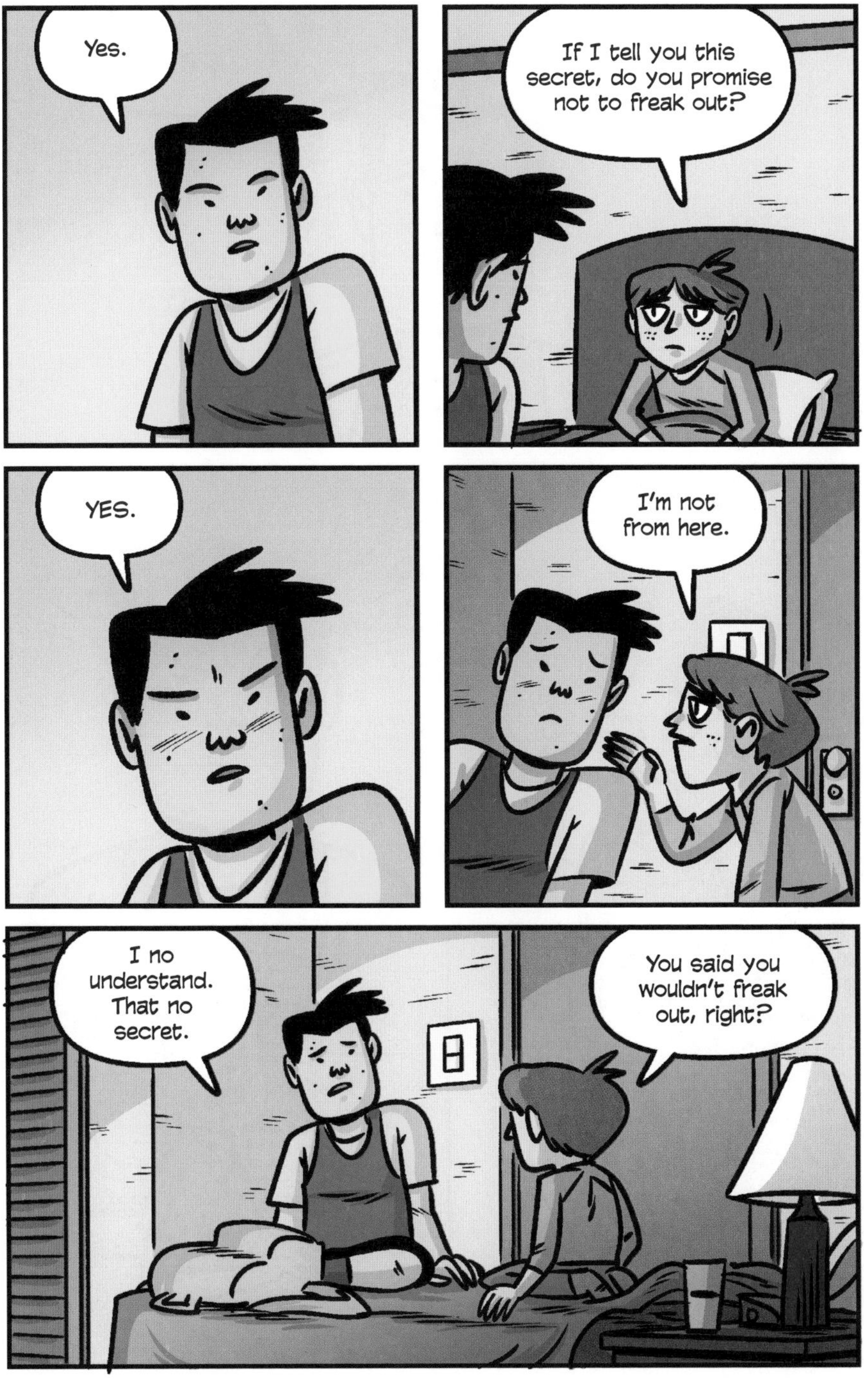
Yes.
If I tell you this secret, do you promise not to freak out?
YES.
I'm not from here.
I no understand. That no secret.
You said you wouldn't freak out, right?

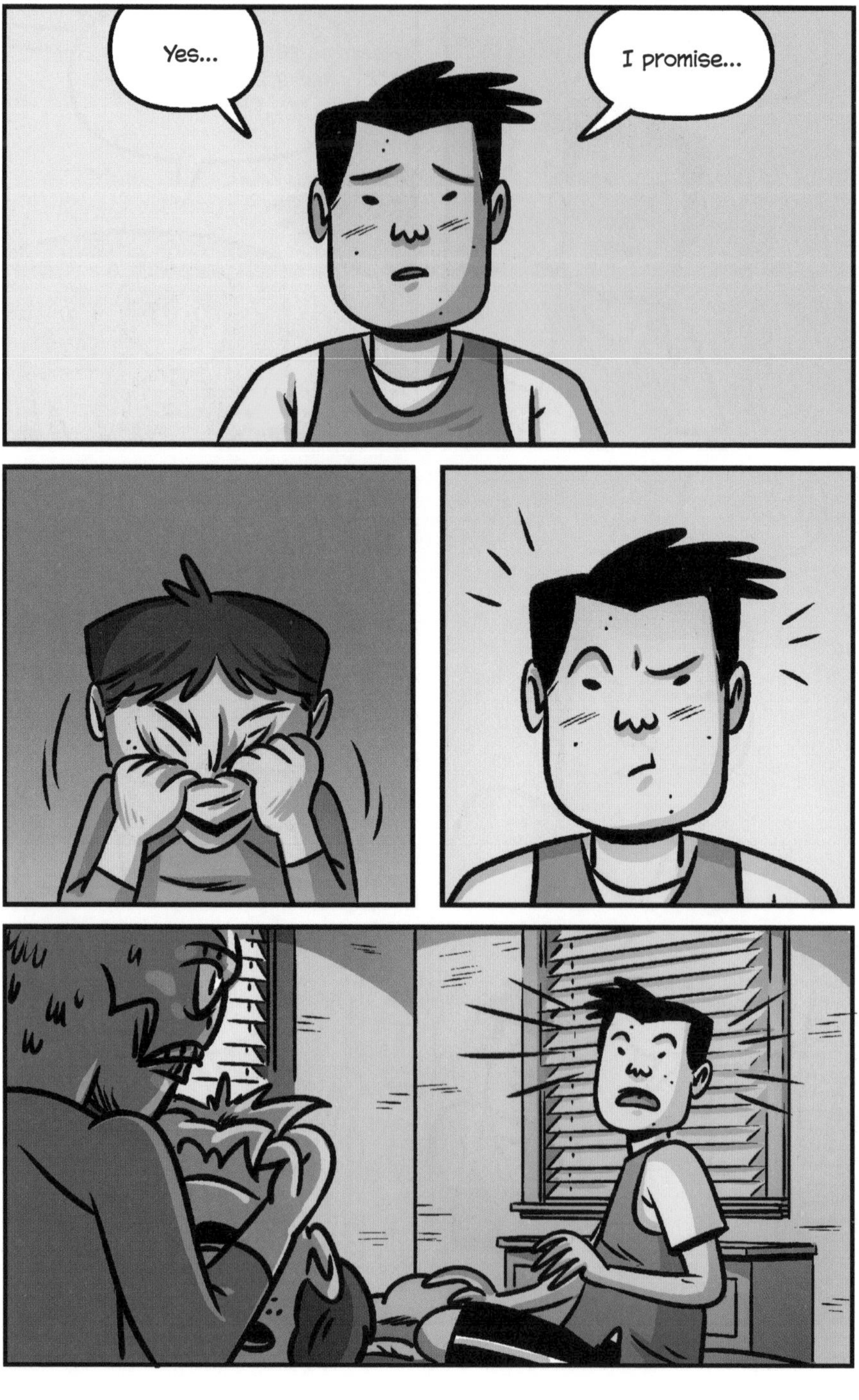
Yes...
I promise...

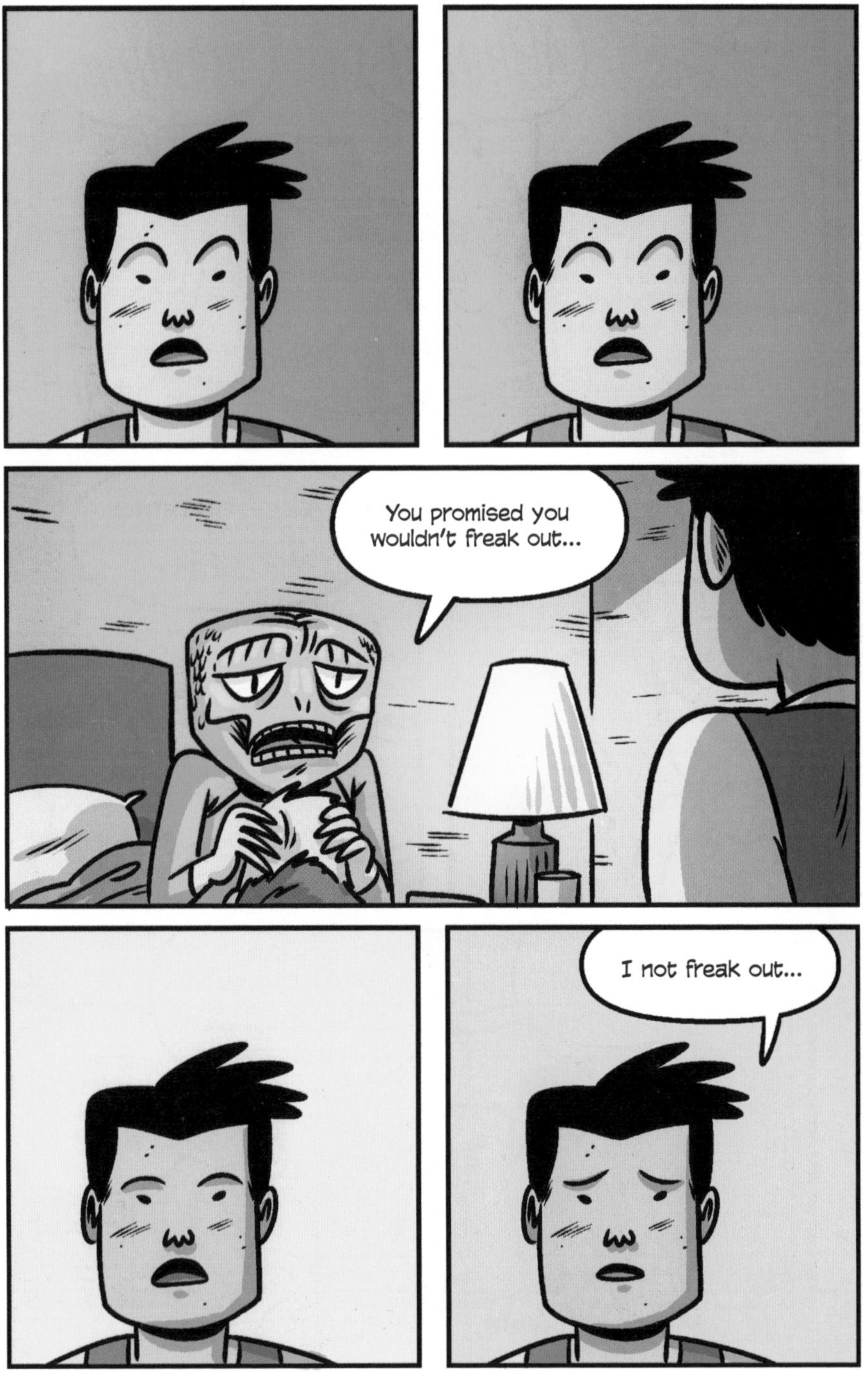
You promised you wouldn't freak out...
I not freak out...

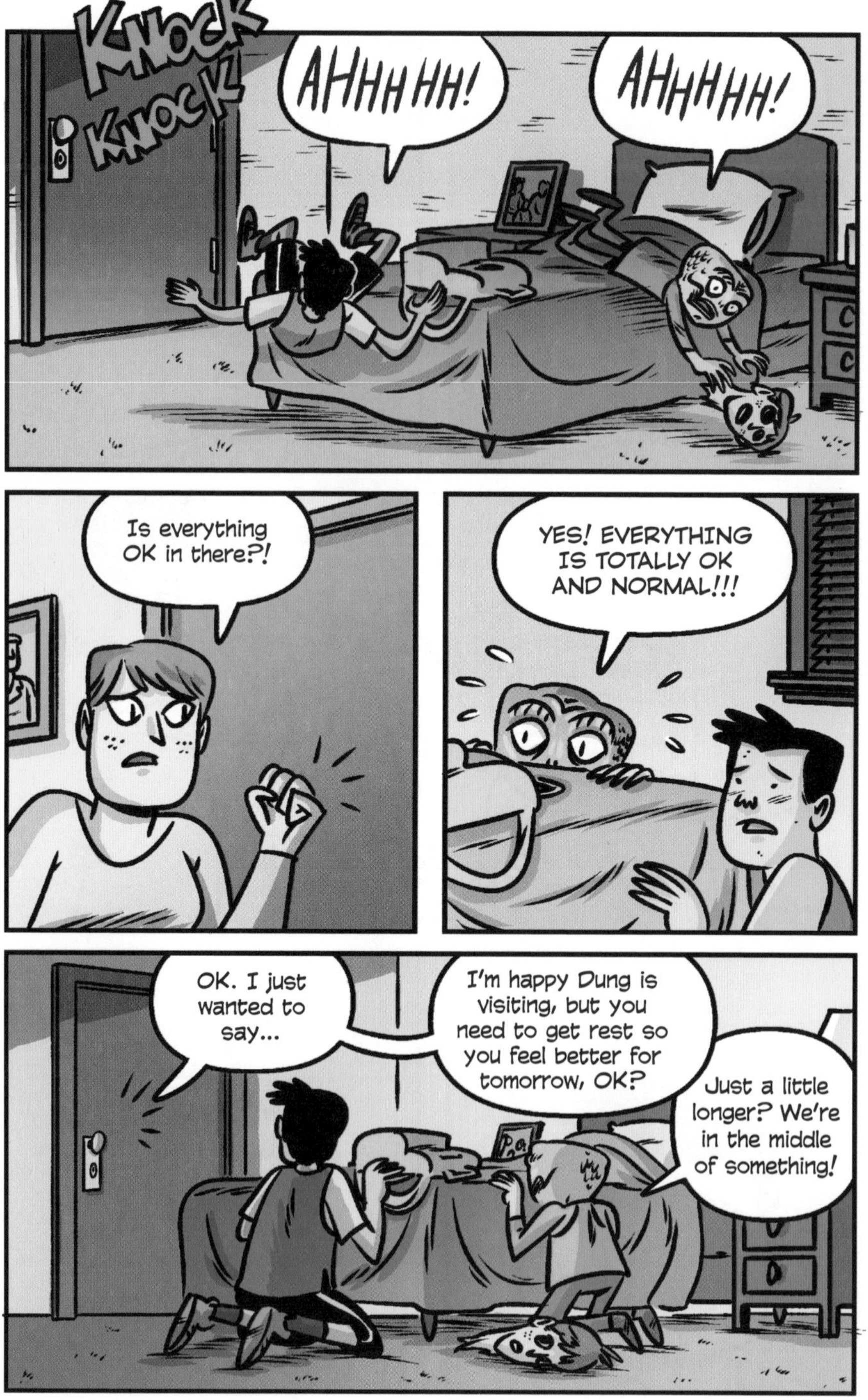
KNOCK
KNOCK
AHHHHH!
AHHHHH!
Is everything OK in there?!
YES! EVERYTHING IS TOTALLY OK AND NORMAL!!!
OK. I just wanted to say...
I'm happy Dung is visiting, but you need to get rest so you feel better for tomorrow, OK?
Just a little longer? We're in the middle of something!

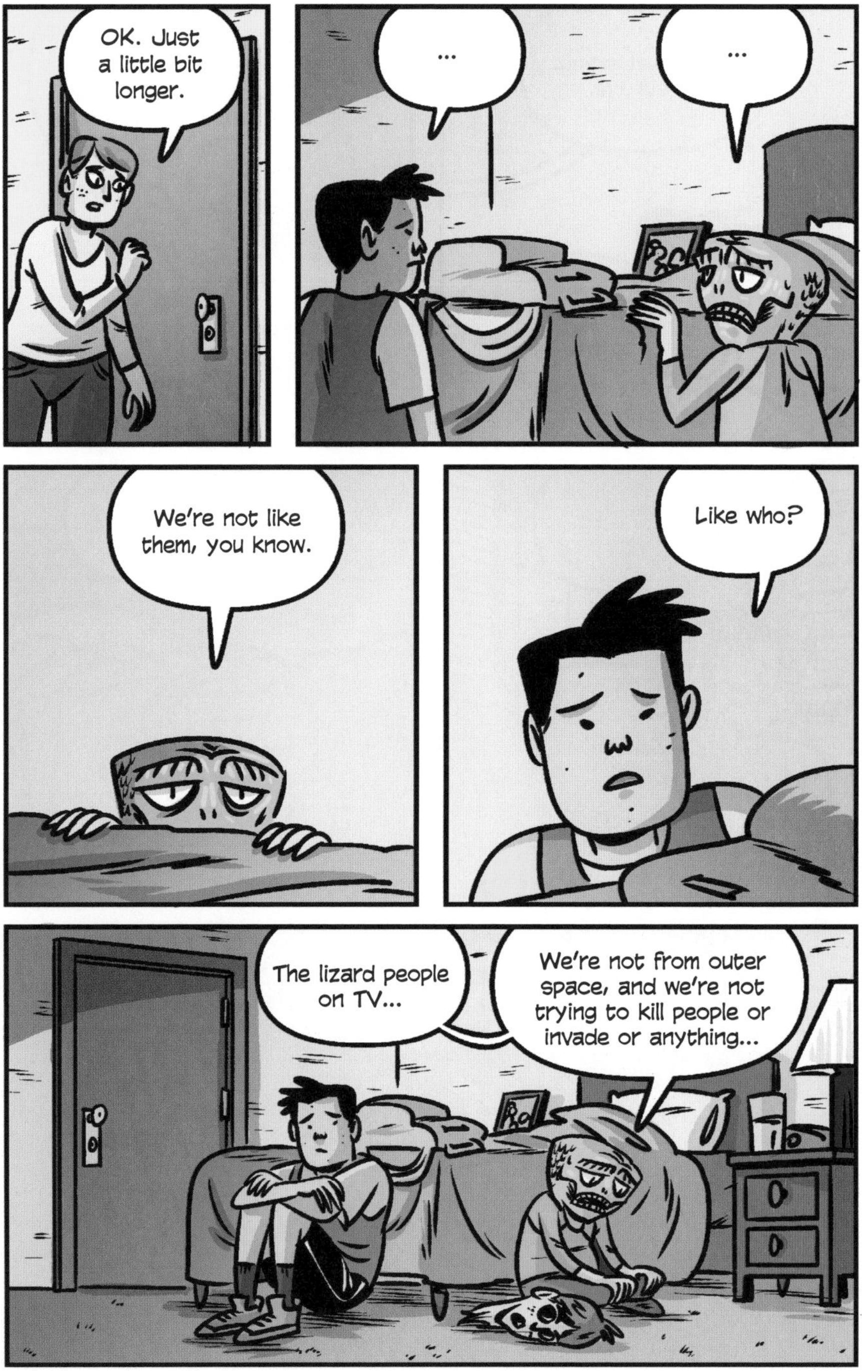

OK. Just a little bit longer.
...
...
We're not like them, you know.
Like who?
The lizard people on TV...
We're not from outer space, and we're not trying to kill people or invade or anything...

We're just trying to survive.

You tell Dung you not from here. You say your home very, very different. More different from Vietnam...

What you mean?

Well...

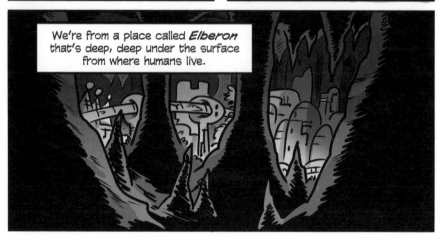

We're from a place called *Elberon* that's deep, deep under the surface from where humans live.

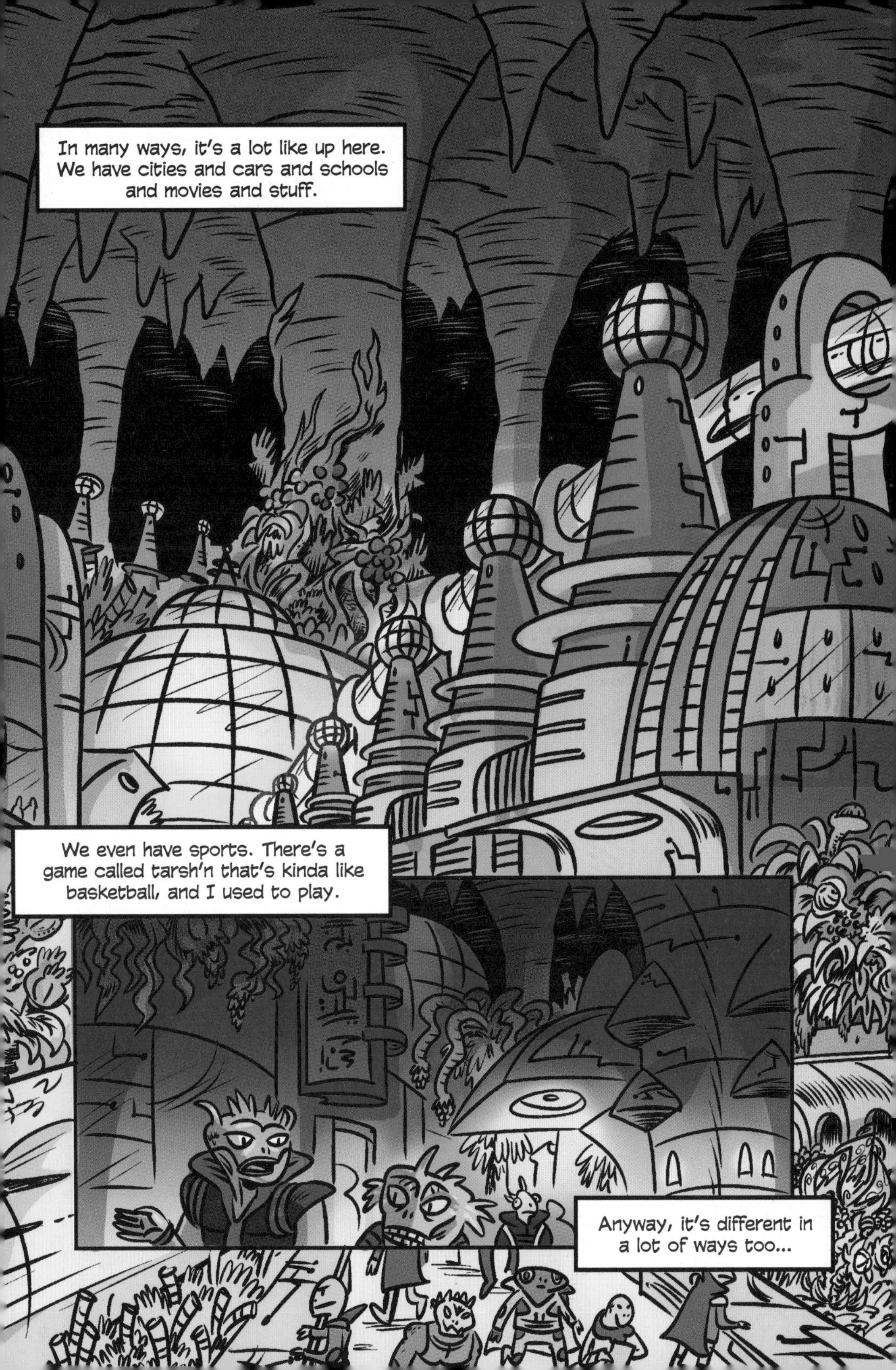
In many ways, it's a lot like up here. We have cities and cars and schools and movies and stuff.
We even have sports. There's a game called tarsh'n that's kinda like basketball, and I used to play.
Anyway, it's different in a lot of ways too...

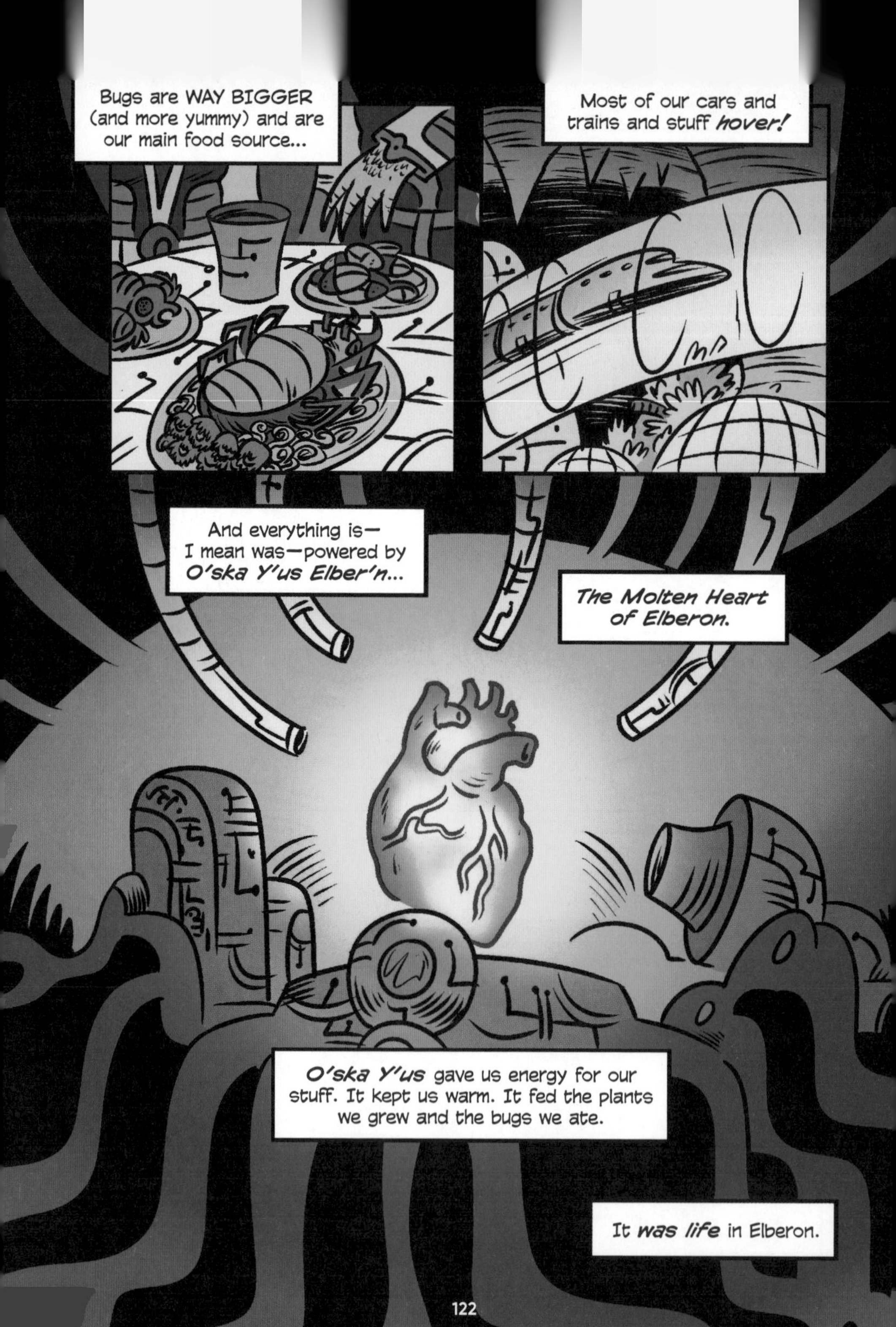

Bugs are WAY BIGGER (and more yummy) and are our main food source...
Most of our cars and trains and stuff *hover!*
And everything is— I mean was—powered by *O'ska Y'us Elber'n*...
The Molten Heart of Elberon.
O'ska Y'us gave us energy for our stuff. It kept us warm. It fed the plants we grew and the bugs we ate.
It *was life* in Elberon.

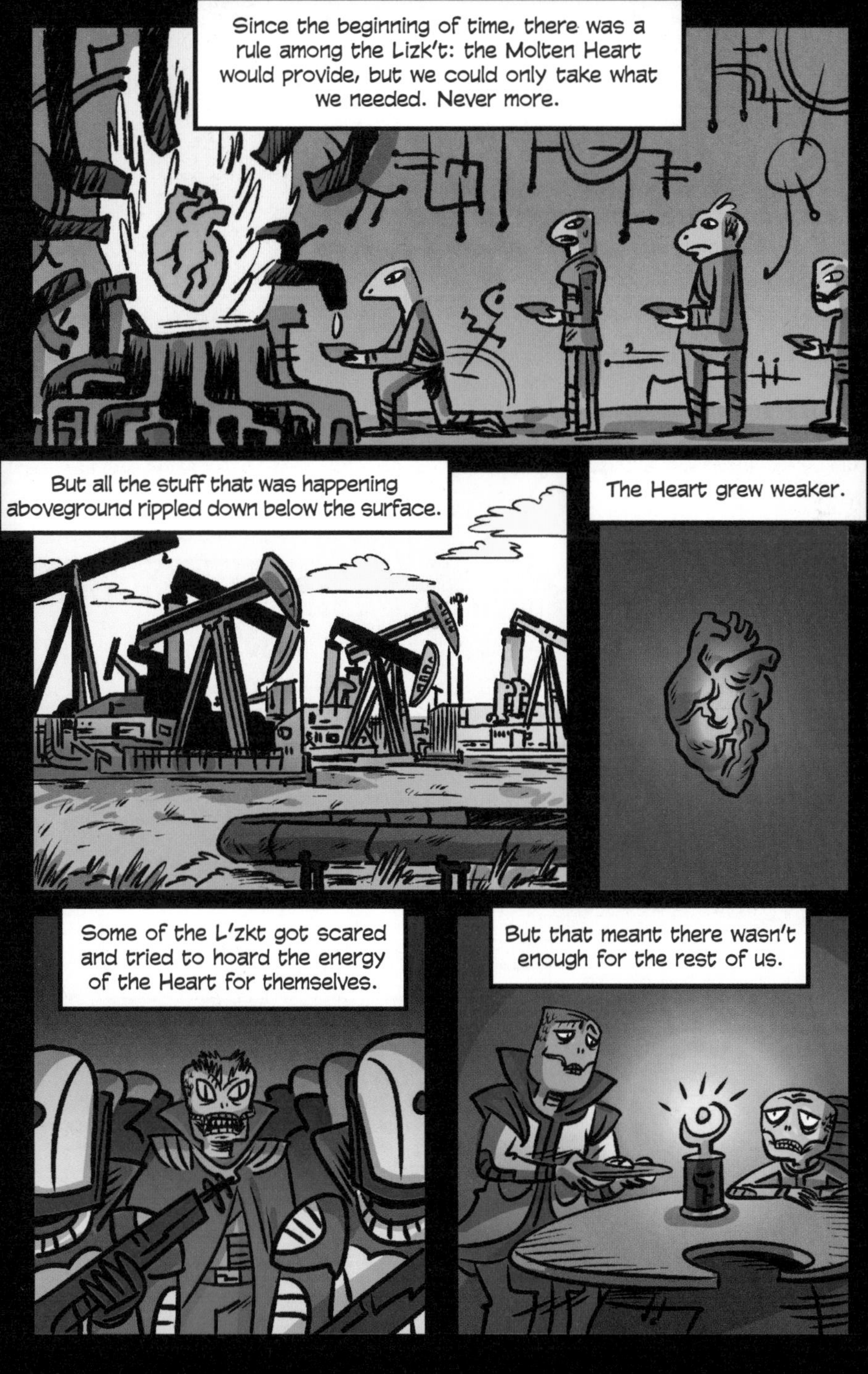

Since the beginning of time, there was a rule among the Lizk't: the Molten Heart would provide, but we could only take what we needed. Never more.
But all the stuff that was happening aboveground rippled down below the surface.
The Heart grew weaker.
Some of the L'zkt got scared and tried to hoard the energy of the Heart for themselves.
But that meant there wasn't enough for the rest of us.

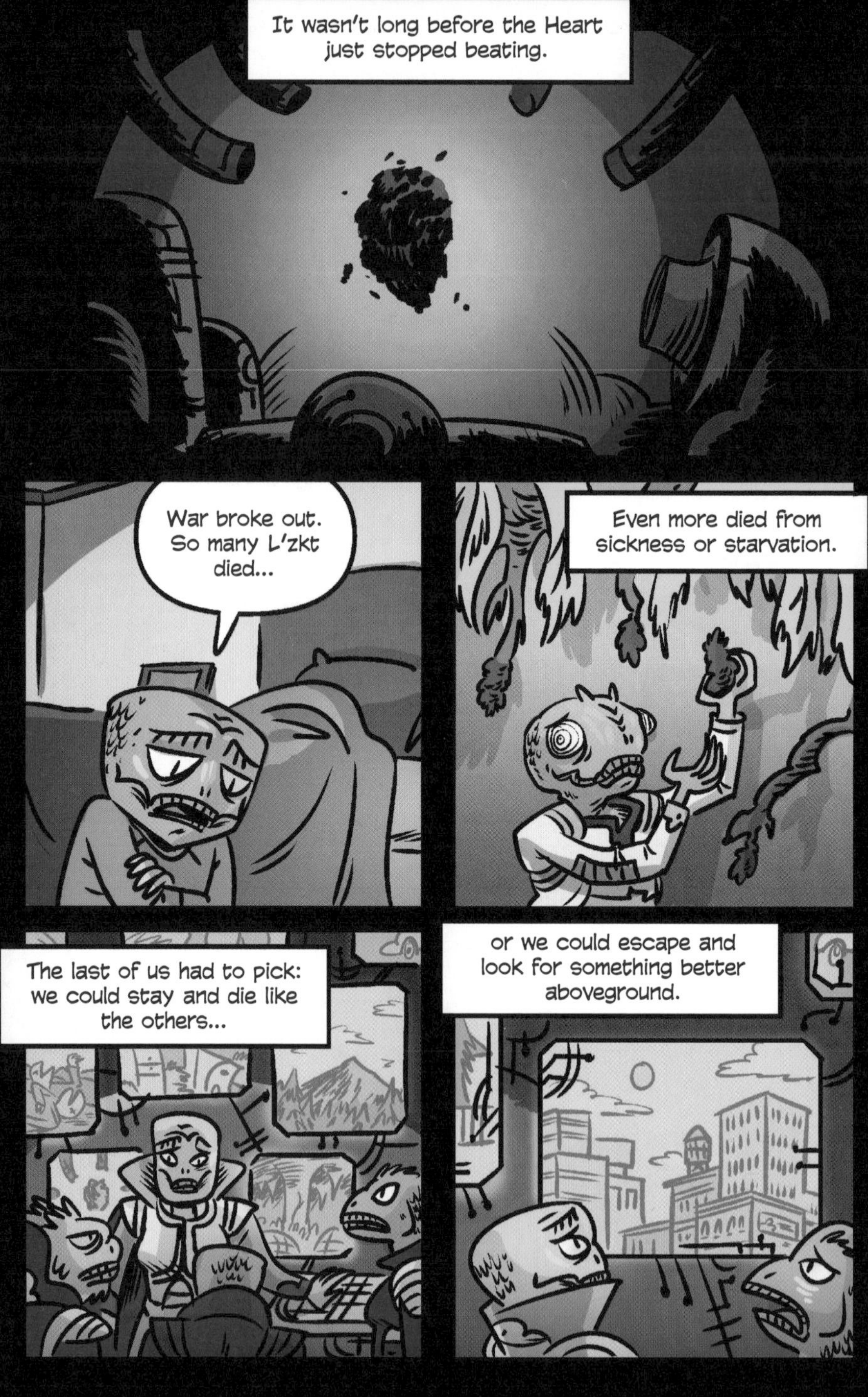
It wasn't long before the Heart just stopped beating.
War broke out. So many L'zkt died...
Even more died from sickness or starvation.
The last of us had to pick: we could stay and die like the others...
or we could escape and look for something better aboveground.

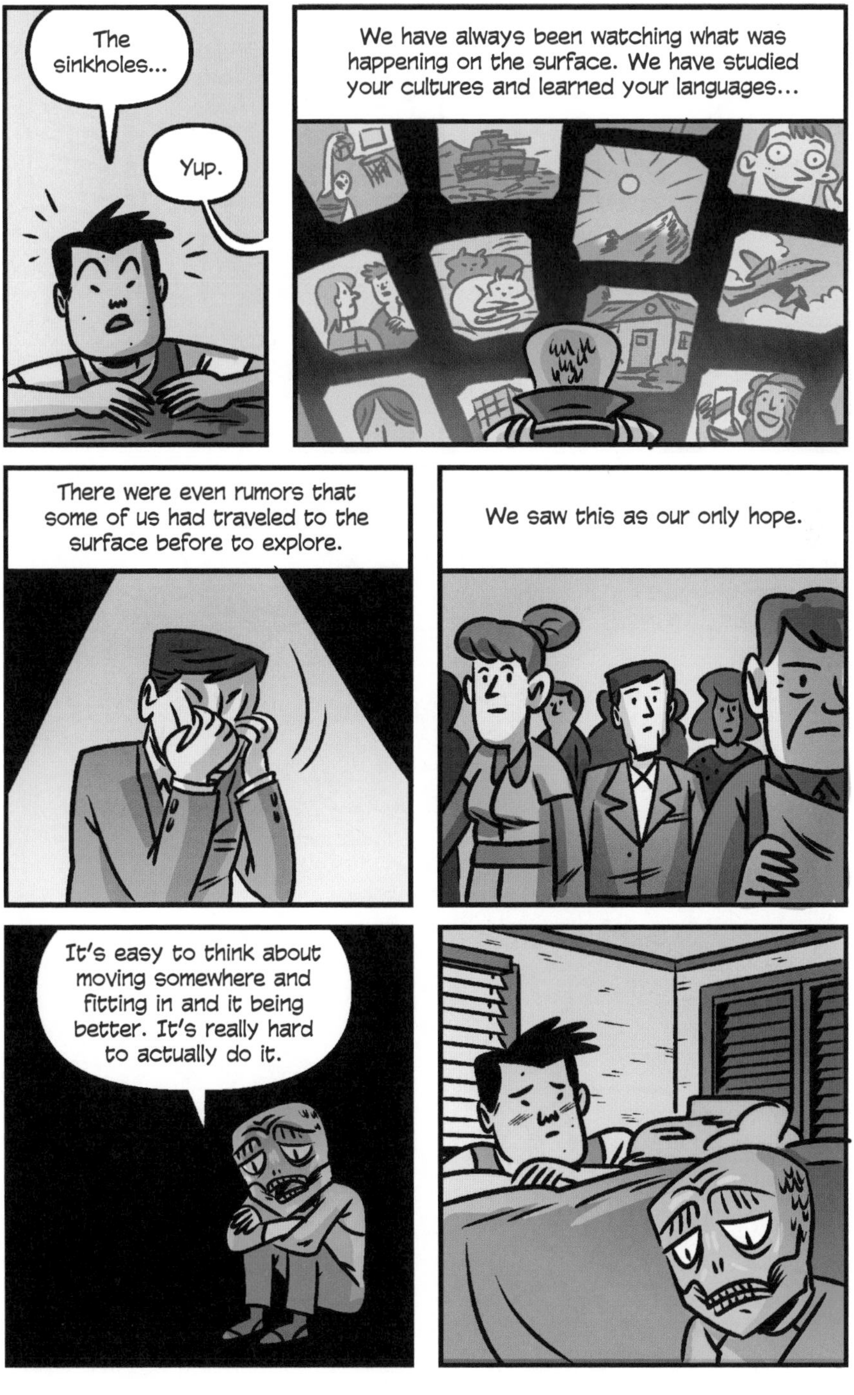
The sinkholes...
Yup.
We have always been watching what was happening on the surface. We have studied your cultures and learned your languages...
There were even rumors that some of us had traveled to the surface before to explore.
We saw this as our only hope.
It's easy to think about moving somewhere and fitting in and it being better. It's really hard to actually do it.

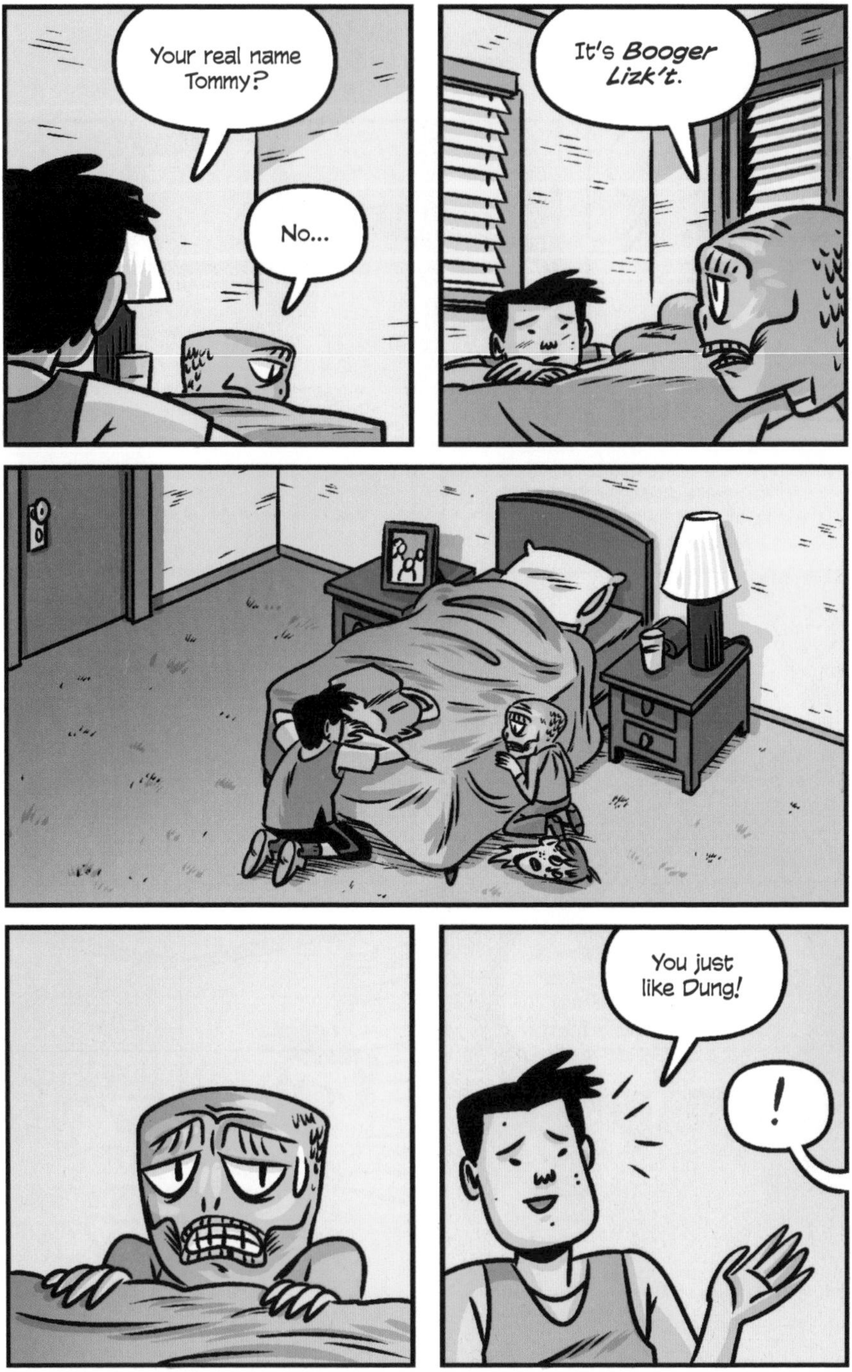
Your real name Tommy?
No...
It's *Booger Lizk't.*
You just like Dung!
!

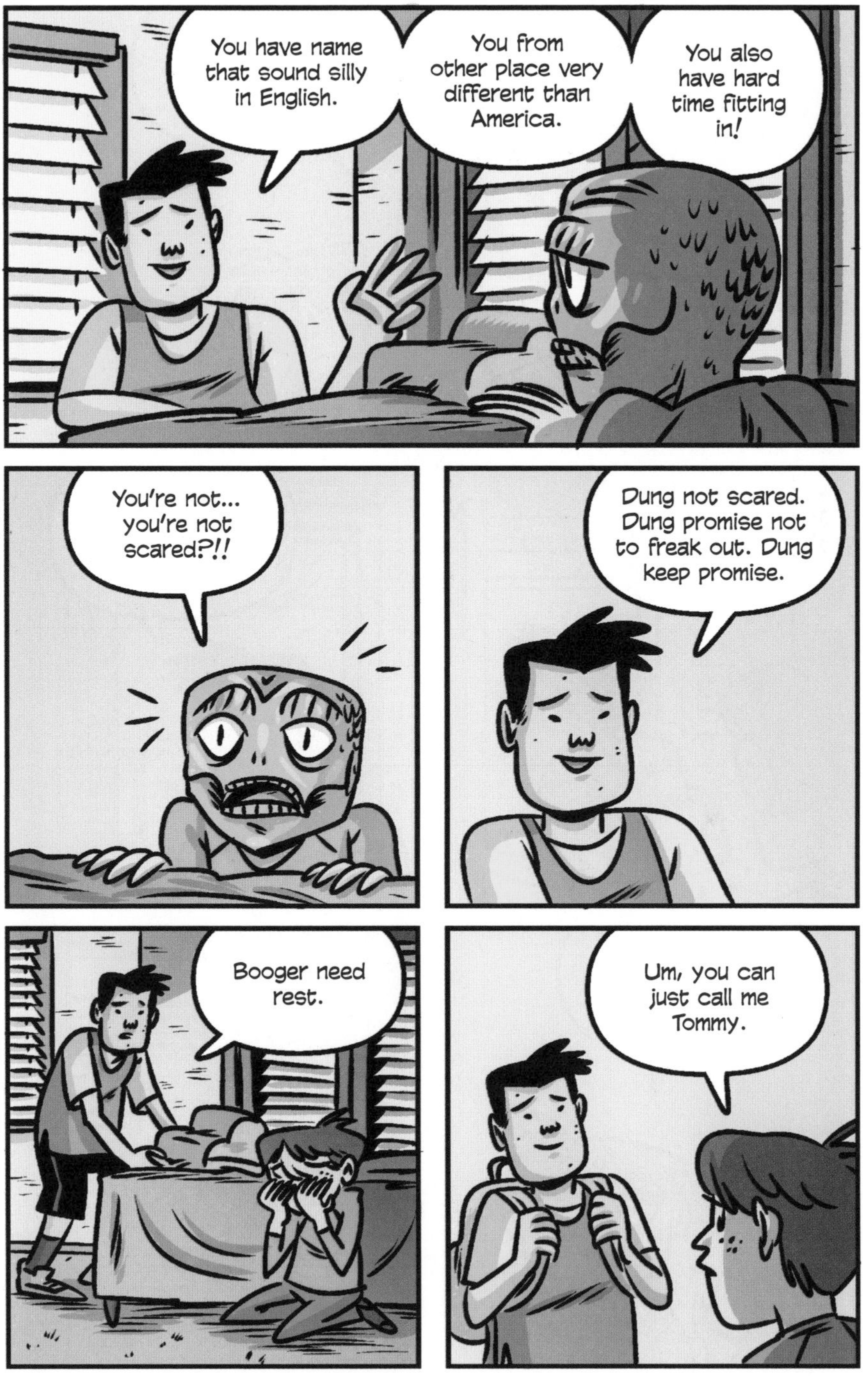
You have name that sound silly in English.
You from other place very different than America.
You also have hard time fitting in!
You're not... you're not scared?!!
Dung not scared. Dung promise not to freak out. Dung keep promise.
Booger need rest.
Um, you can just call me Tommy.

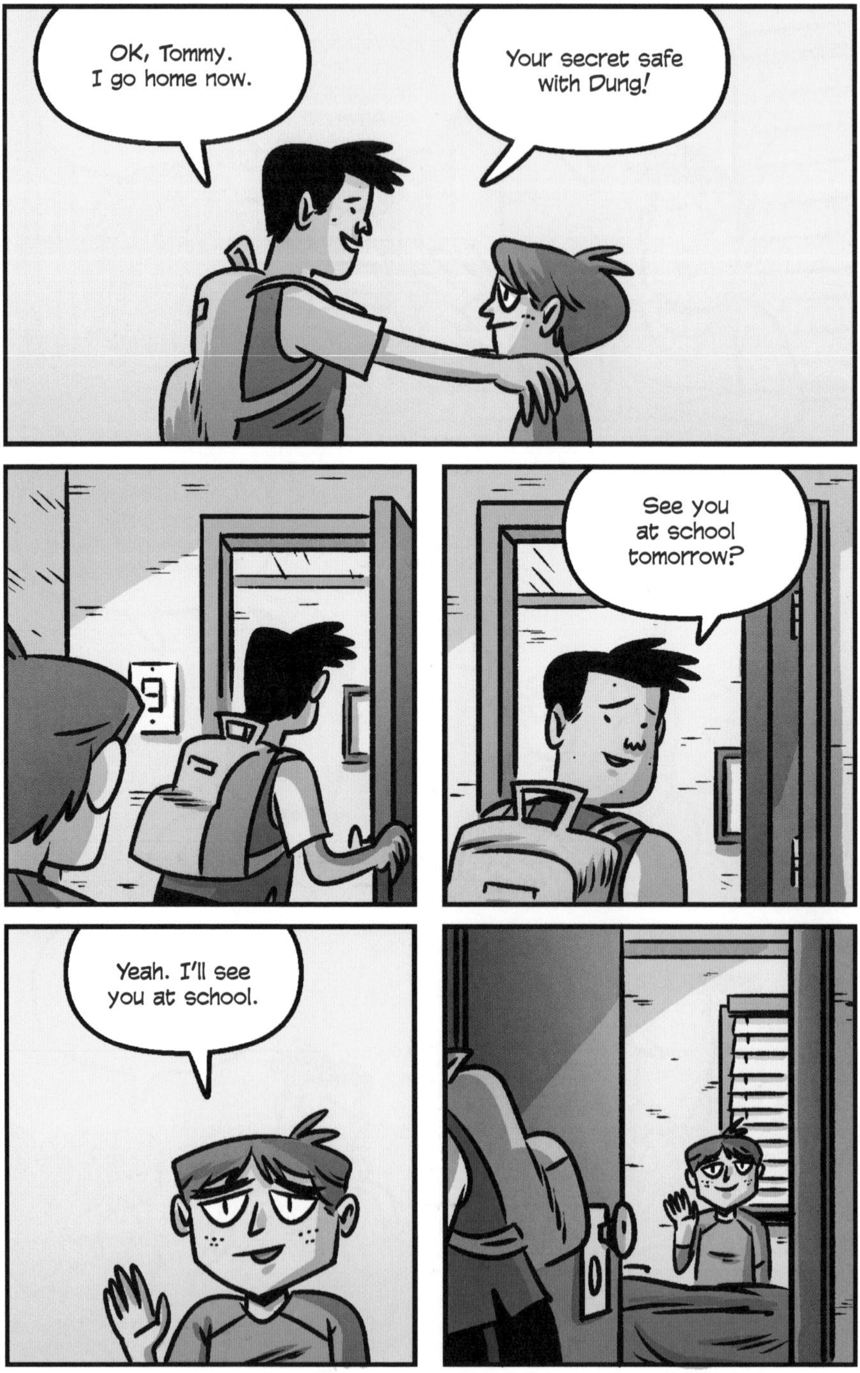
OK, Tommy.
I go home now.
Your secret safe
with Dung!
See you
at school
tomorrow?
Yeah. I'll see
you at school.

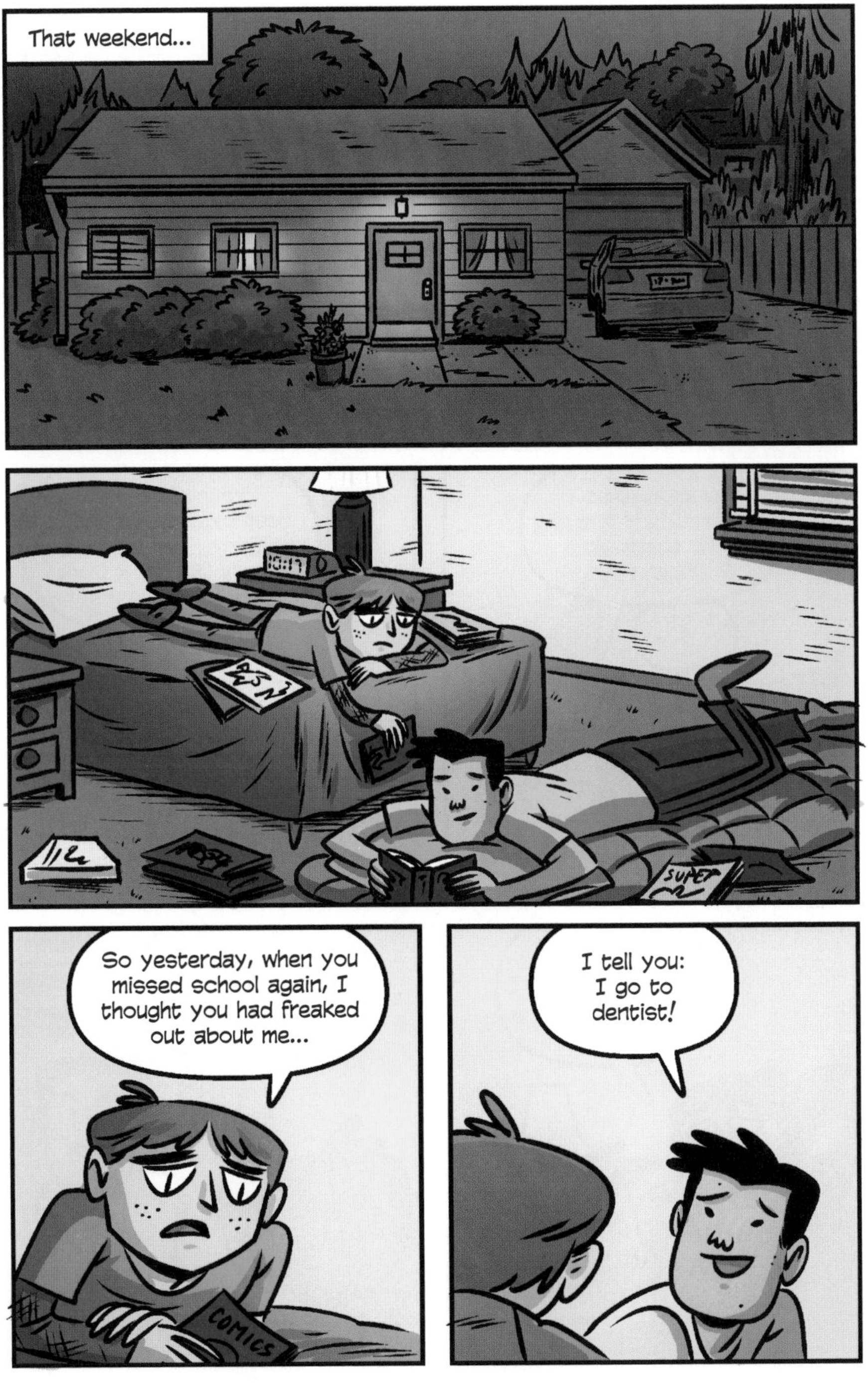
That weekend...
So yesterday, when you missed school again, I thought you had freaked out about me...
I tell you: I go to dentist!

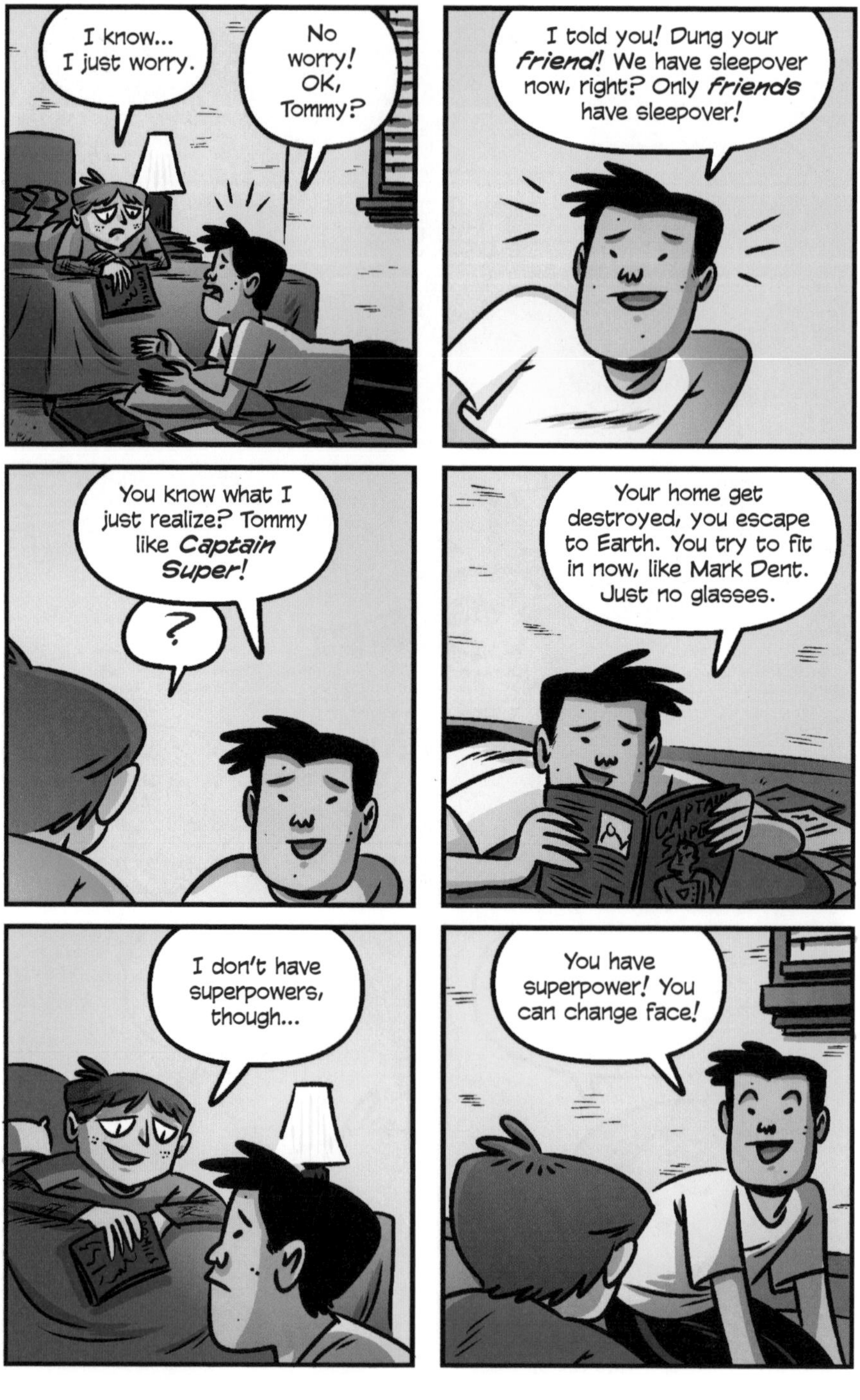
I know... I just worry.
No worry! OK, Tommy?
I told you! Dung your *friend*! We have sleepover now, right? Only *friends* have sleepover!
You know what I just realize? Tommy like *Captain Super*!
?
Your home get destroyed, you escape to Earth. You try to fit in now, like Mark Dent. Just no glasses.
I don't have superpowers, though...
You have superpower! You can change face!

It's not really a superpower...

In Elberon, we change the skin on our faces to let each other know how we are feeling...

Happiness	Anger	Sadness

Fear	Love	Disgust

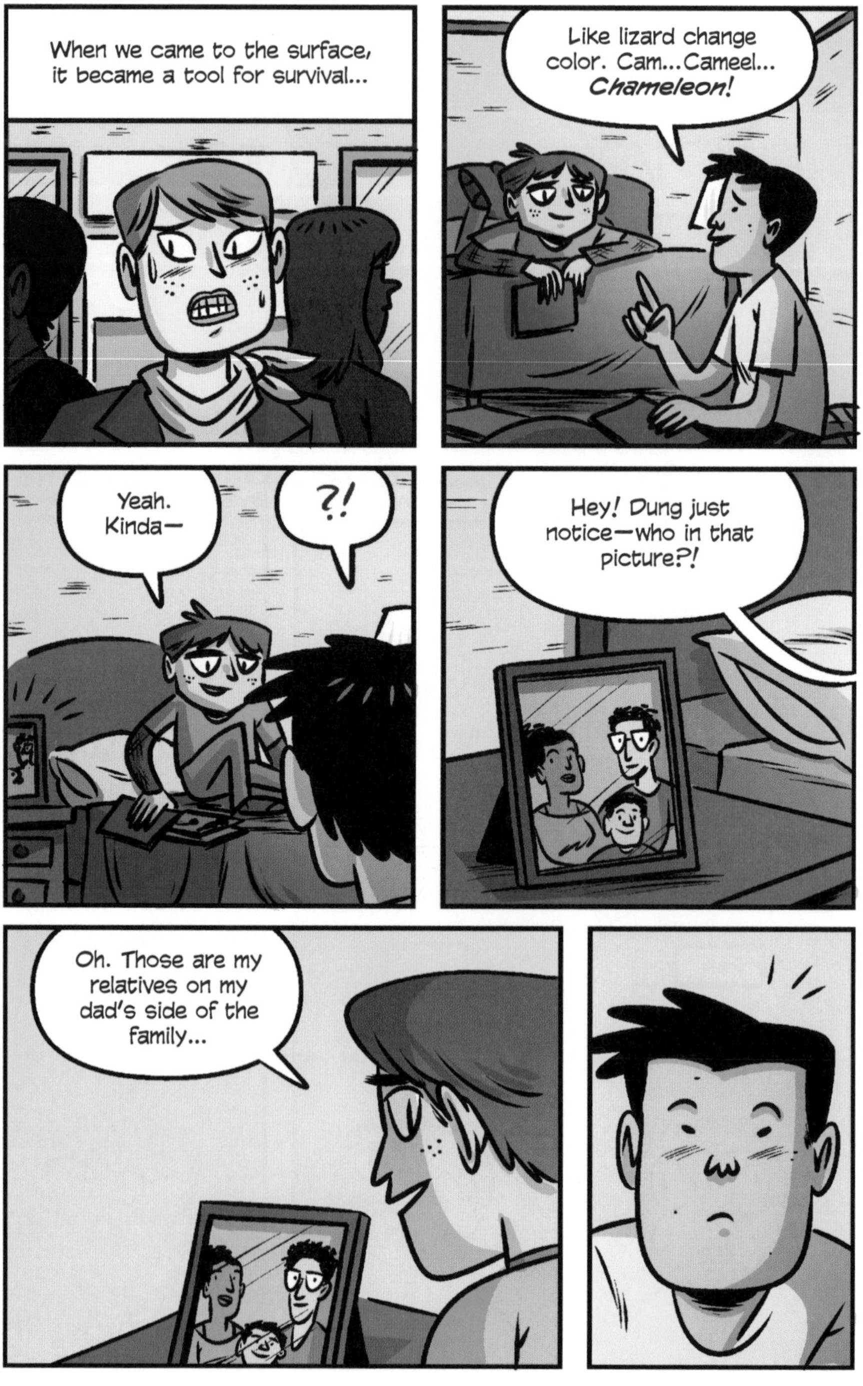
When we came to the surface, it became a tool for survival...
Like lizard change color. Cam...Cameel... *Chameleon!*
Yeah. Kinda—
?!
Hey! Dung just notice—who in that picture?!
Oh. Those are my relatives on my dad's side of the family...

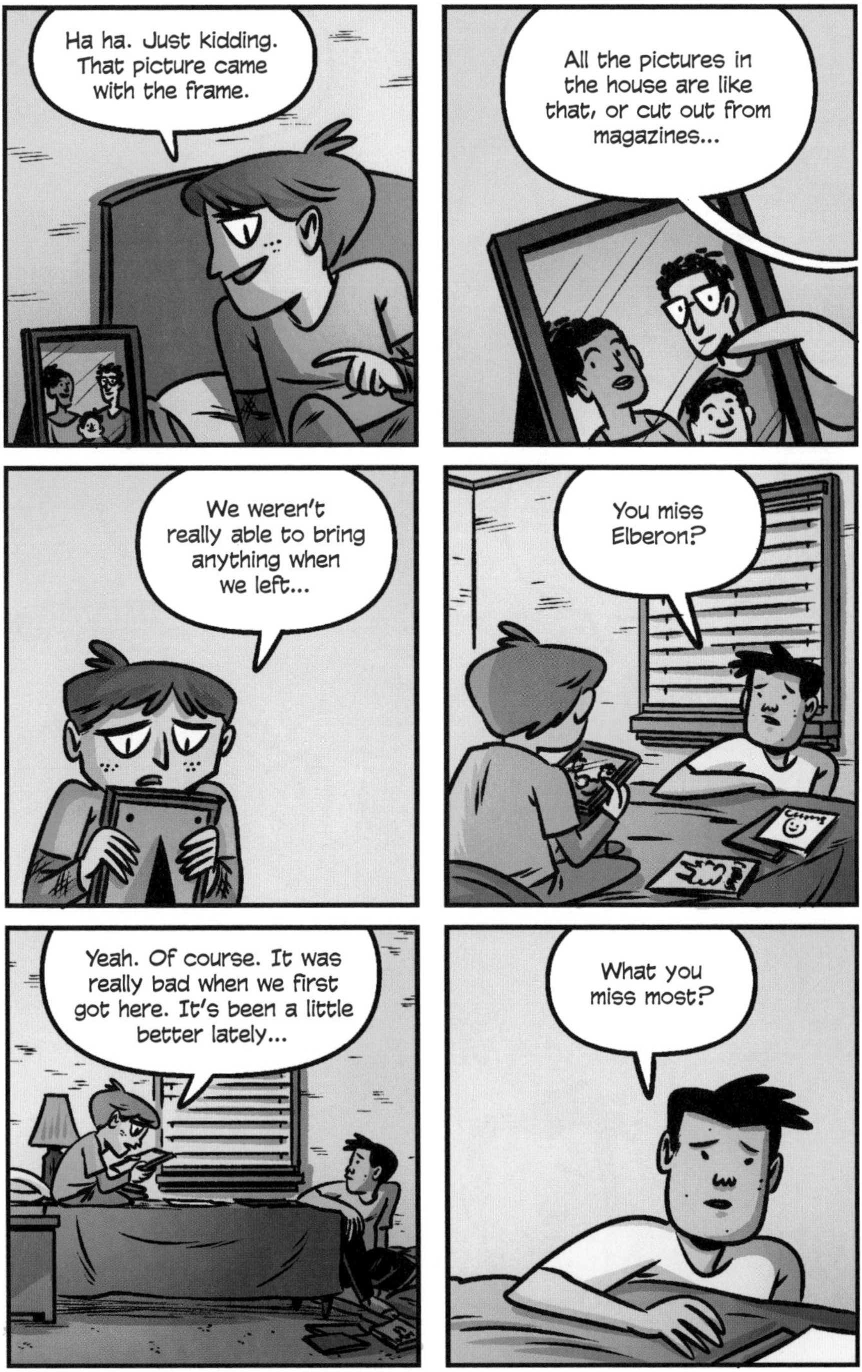
Ha ha. Just kidding. That picture came with the frame.
All the pictures in the house are like that, or cut out from magazines...
We weren't really able to bring anything when we left...
You miss Elberon?
Yeah. Of course. It was really bad when we first got here. It's been a little better lately...
What you miss most?

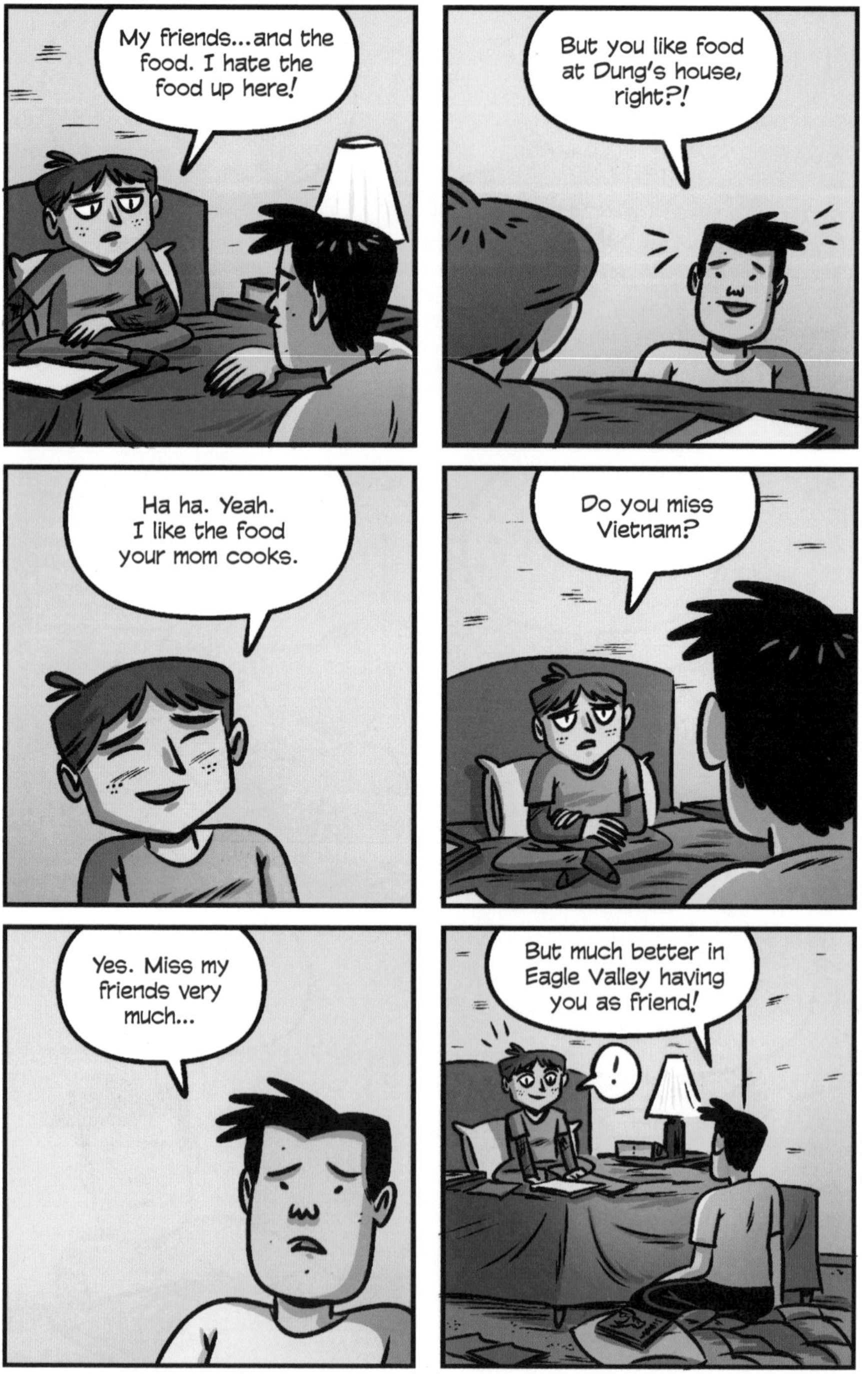
My friends...and the food. I hate the food up here!
But you like food at Dung's house, right?!
Ha ha. Yeah. I like the food your mom cooks.
Do you miss Vietnam?
Yes. Miss my friends very much...
But much better in Eagle Valley having you as friend!
!

KNOCK KNOCK

I love that you boys are having fun, but it's getting pretty late. If you don't get *some* sleep tonight, I bet Dung's mom will be real upset with me!

OK, Mom.

OK, Miss Tomkins.

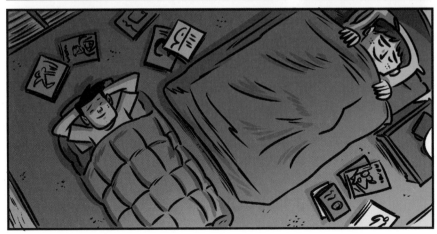

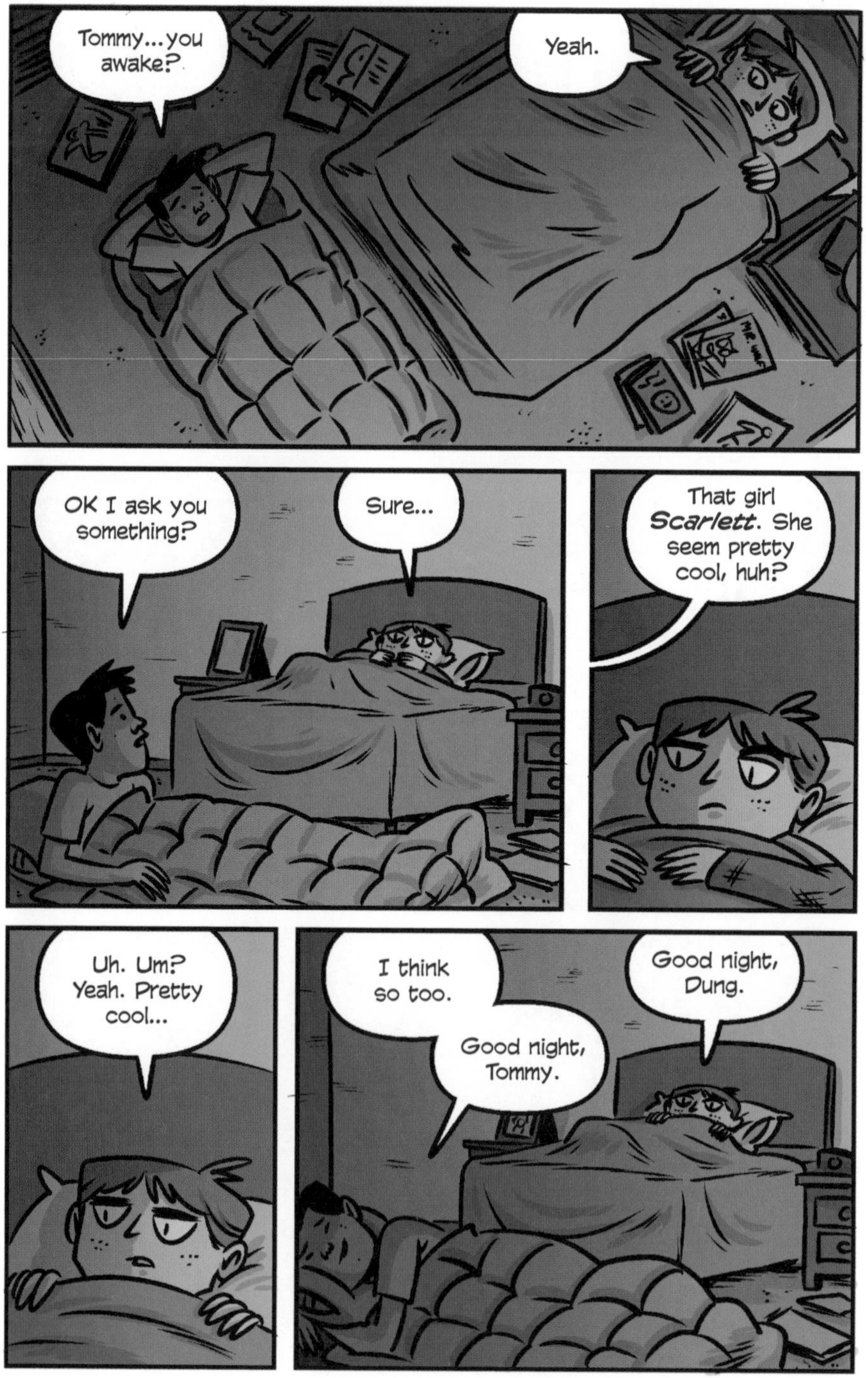
Tommy...you awake?
Yeah.
OK I ask you something?
Sure...
That girl *Scarlett*. She seem pretty cool, huh?
Uh. Um? Yeah. Pretty cool...
I think so too.
Good night, Tommy.
Good night, Dung.

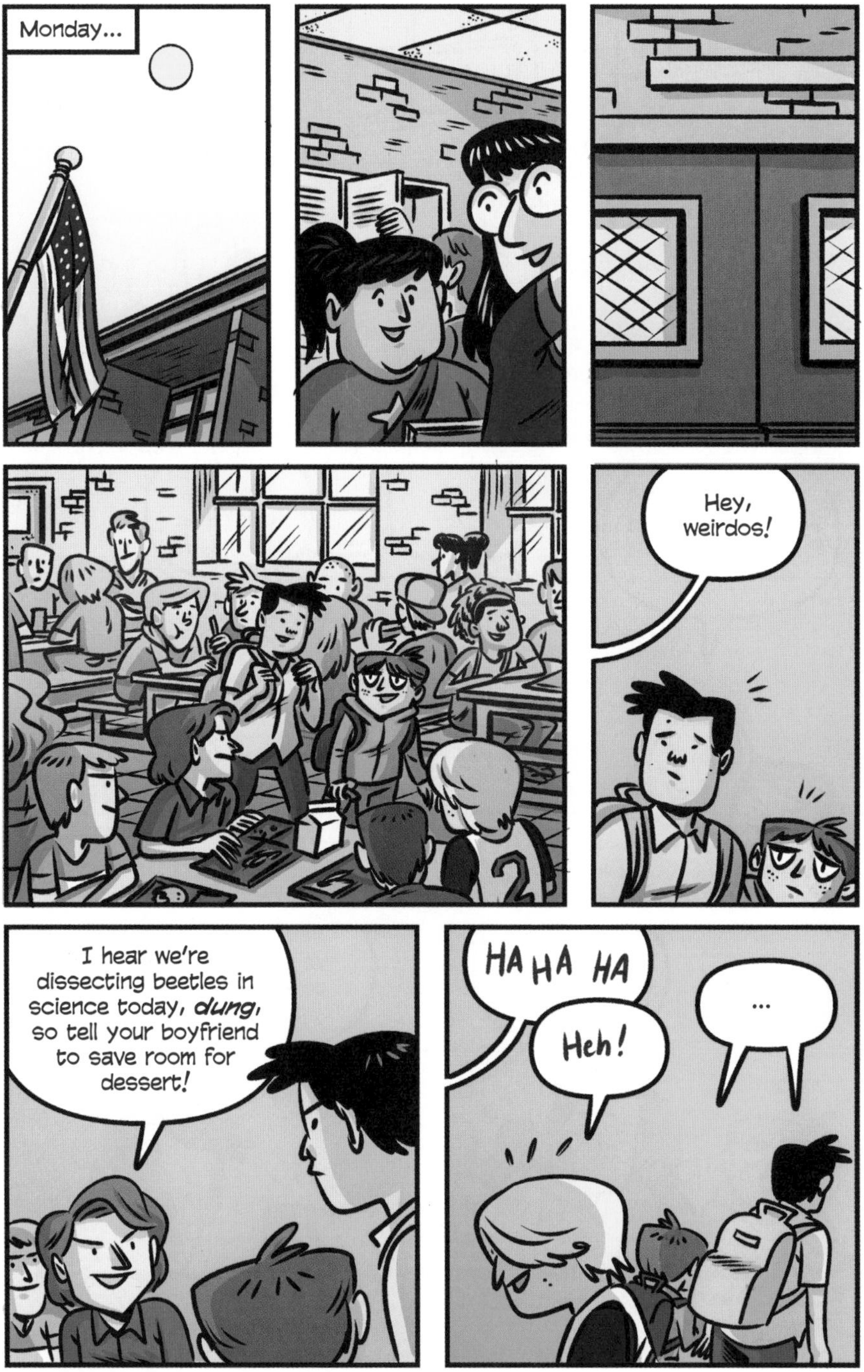
Monday...
Hey, weirdos!
I hear we're dissecting beetles in science today, *dung*, so tell your boyfriend to save room for dessert!
HA HA HA
Heh!
...

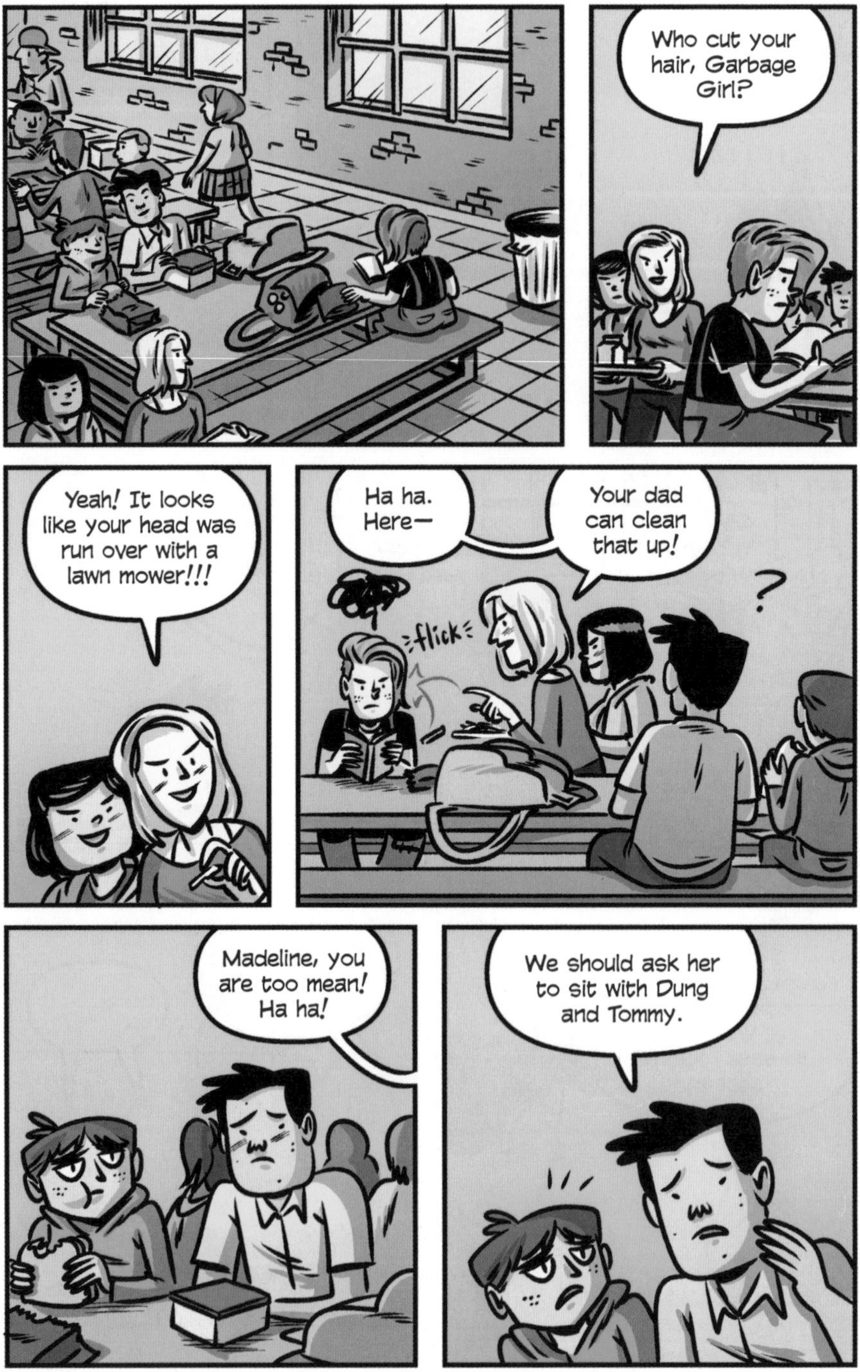

Who cut your hair, Garbage Girl?
Yeah! It looks like your head was run over with a lawn mower!!!
Ha ha. Here—
Your dad can clean that up!
flick
?
Madeline, you are too mean! Ha ha!
We should ask her to sit with Dung and Tommy.

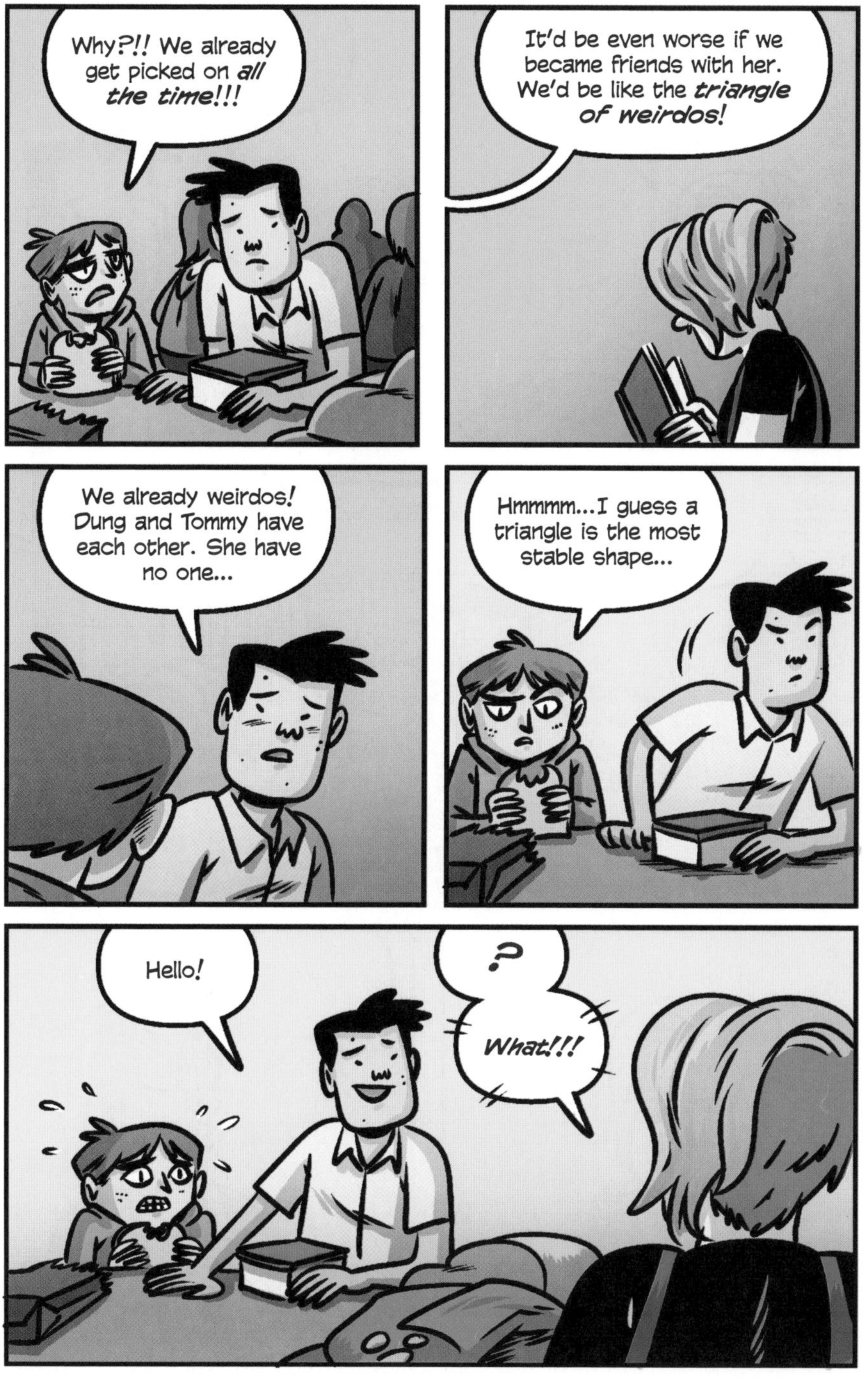
Why?!! We already get picked on *all the time*!!!
It'd be even worse if we became friends with her. We'd be like the *triangle of weirdos*!
We already weirdos! Dung and Tommy have each other. She have no one...
Hmmmm...I guess a triangle is the most stable shape...
Hello!
?
What!!!

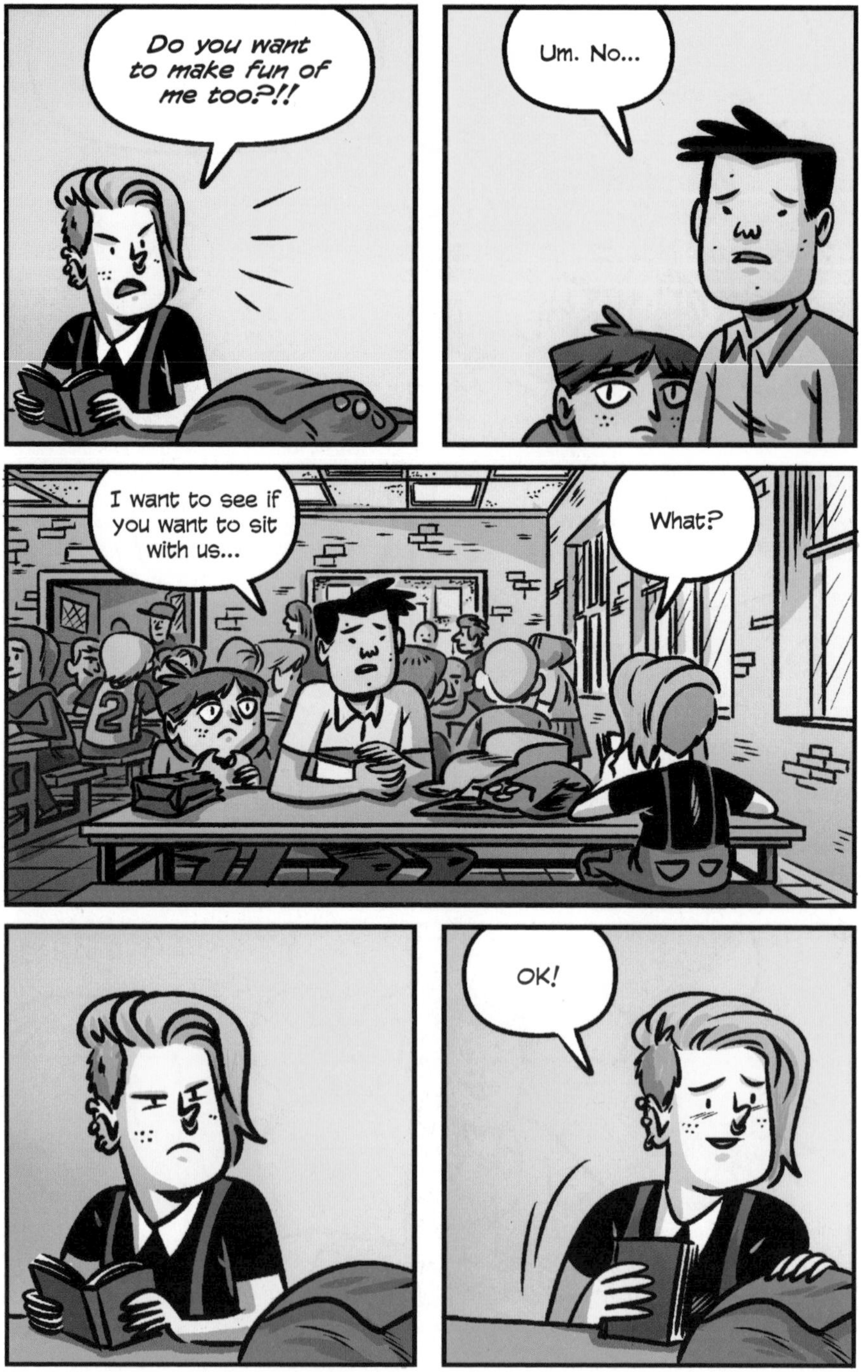
Do you want to make fun of me too?!!
Um. No...
I want to see if you want to sit with us...
What?
OK!

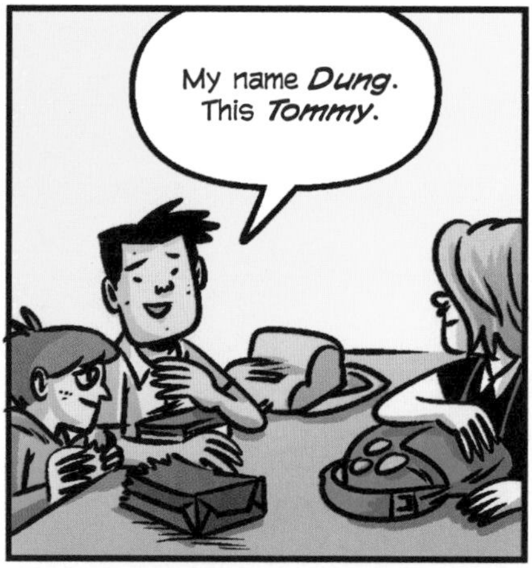
My name Dung. This Tommy.

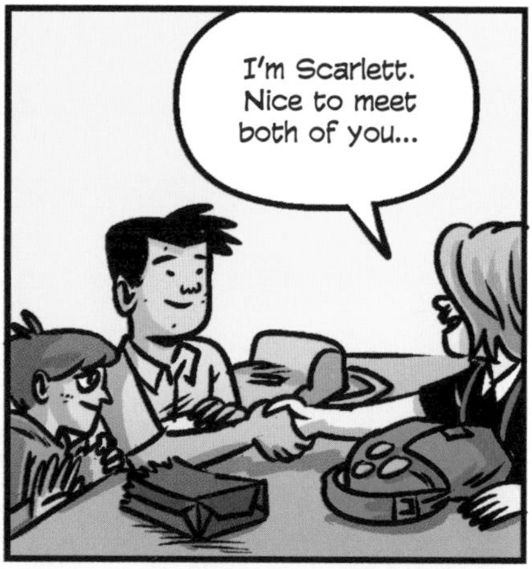
I'm Scarlett. Nice to meet both of you...

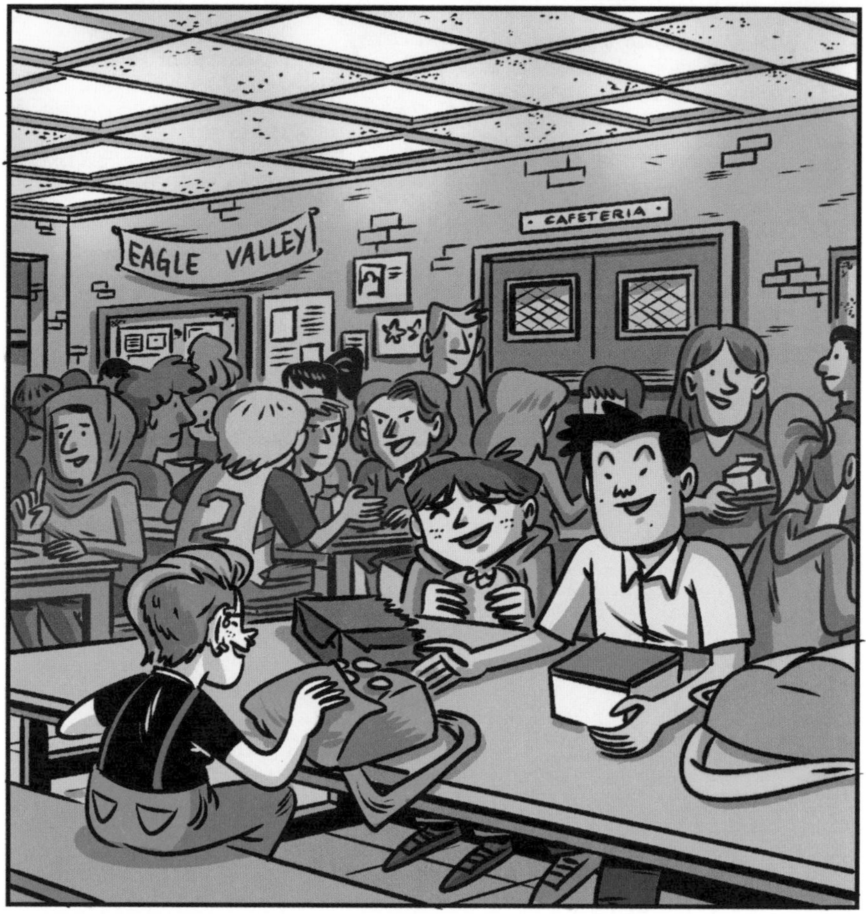
EAGLE VALLEY
CAFETERIA

CHAPTER 7

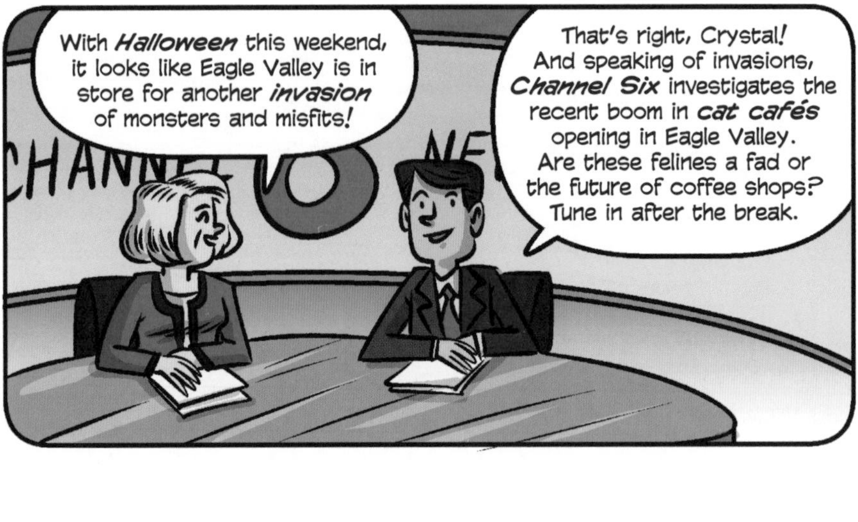

With *Halloween* this weekend, it looks like Eagle Valley is in store for another *invasion* of monsters and misfits!
That's right, Crystal! And speaking of invasions, *Channel Six* investigates the recent boom in *cat cafés* opening in Eagle Valley. Are these felines a fad or the future of coffee shops? Tune in after the break.

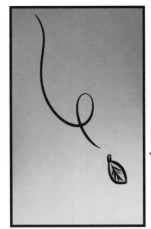

So what are you guys going to be for Halloween?

I've never really done Halloween...

⇃shrug⇂

YOU GUYS HAVE TO BE KIDDING ME!!!

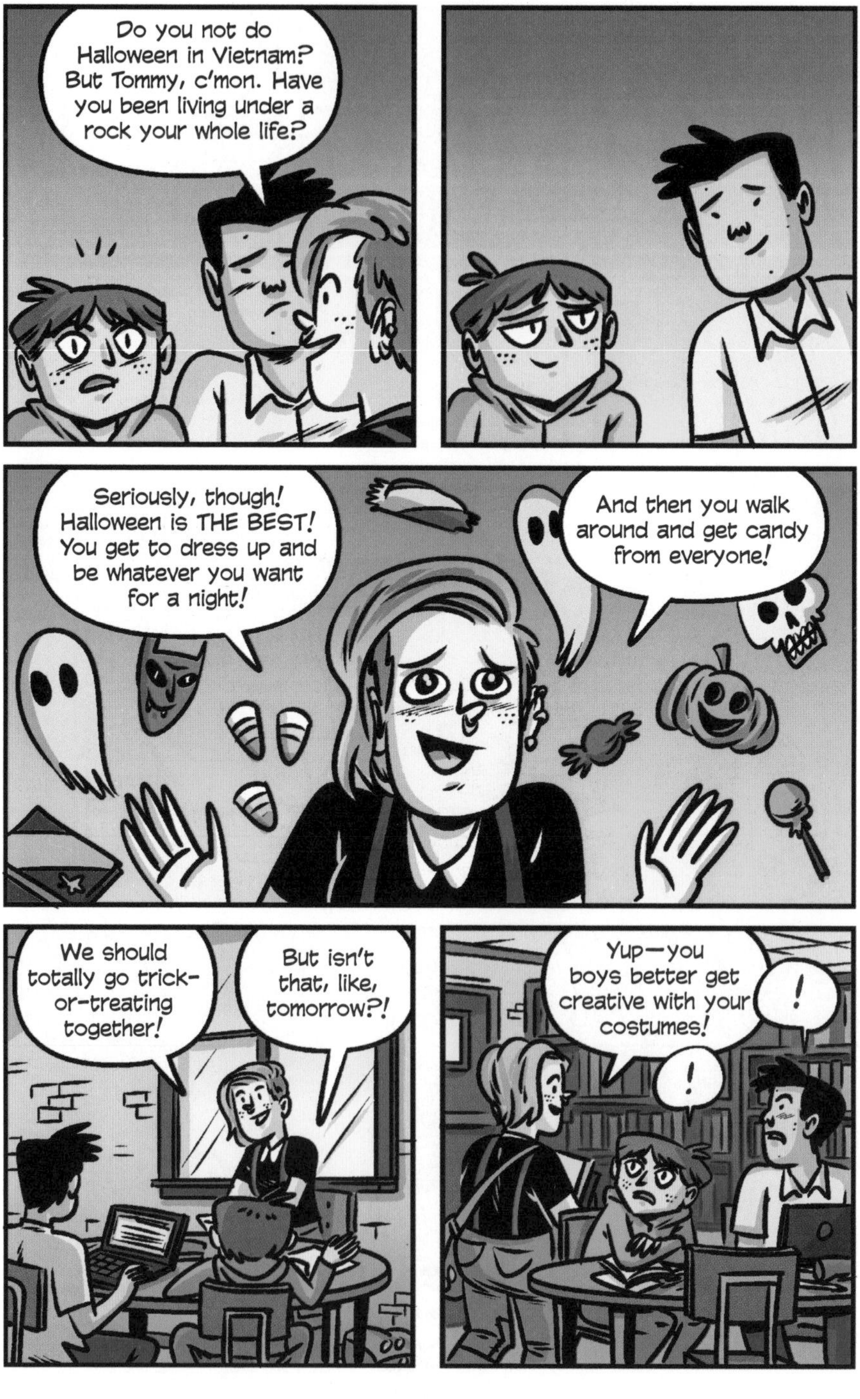
Do you not do Halloween in Vietnam? But Tommy, c'mon. Have you been living under a rock your whole life?
Seriously, though! Halloween is THE BEST! You get to dress up and be whatever you want for a night!
And then you walk around and get candy from everyone!
We should totally go trick-or-treating together!
But isn't that, like, tomorrow?!
Yup—you boys better get creative with your costumes!
!
!

Next night...

≥sob≤

≥sob≤ It's just not... ≥sob≤...*fair!!!* All the Rebeccas got boyfriends, and...≥sob≤ they just *abandoned* me! ≥sob≤≥sob≤

There, there. It's just part of growing up. Even in Elberon, I was left behind while my friends found their mates.

≥sob≤ ≥sob≤ It's just not fair...I'm so much *hotter* than all of them...≥sob≤

ding! dong!

!

Oh! These must be our first trickster treaters! How exciting!

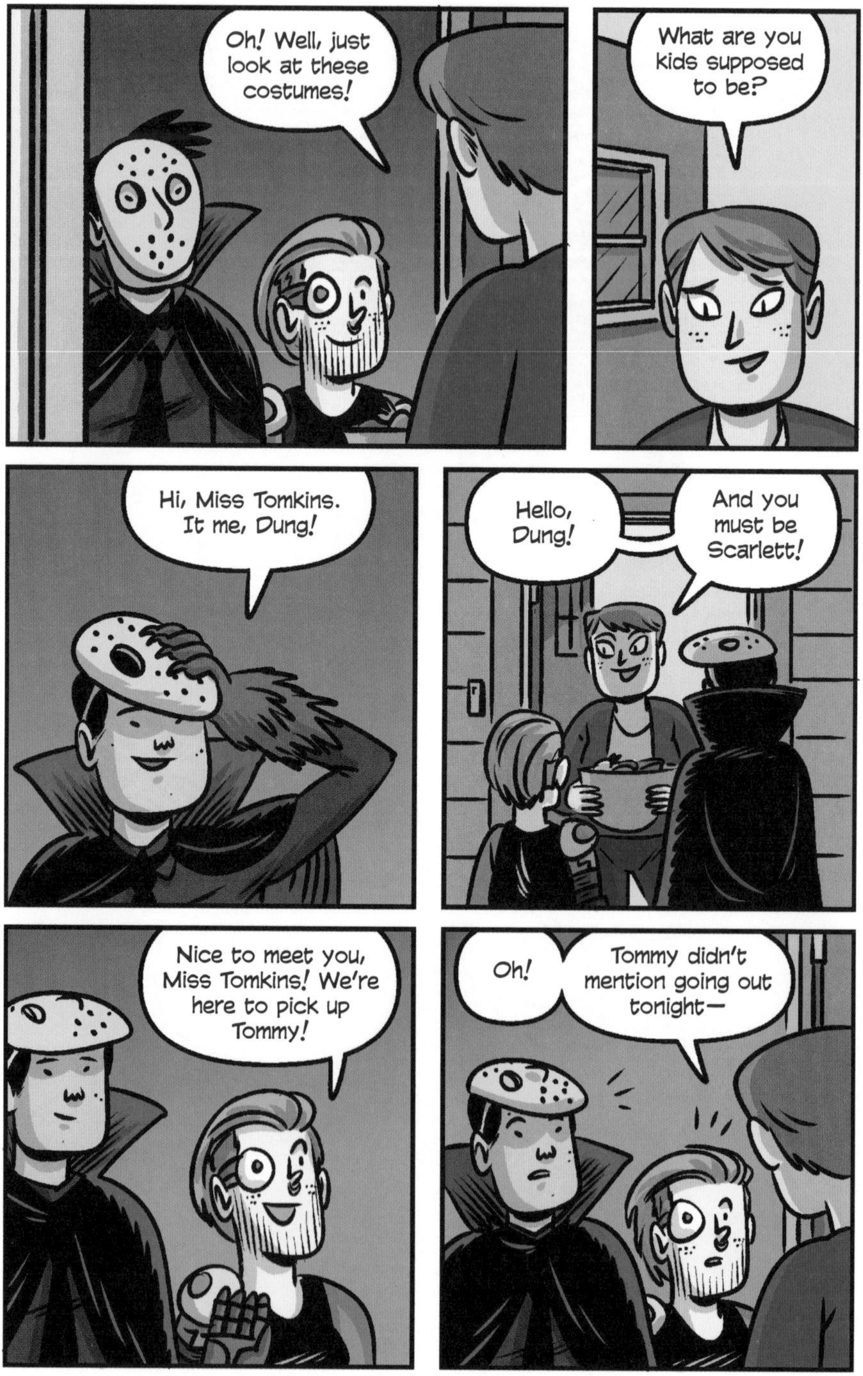
Oh! Well, just look at these costumes!
What are you kids supposed to be?
Hi, Miss Tomkins. It me, Dung!
Hello, Dung!
And you must be Scarlett!
Nice to meet you, Miss Tomkins! We're here to pick up Tommy!
Oh!
Tommy didn't mention going out tonight—

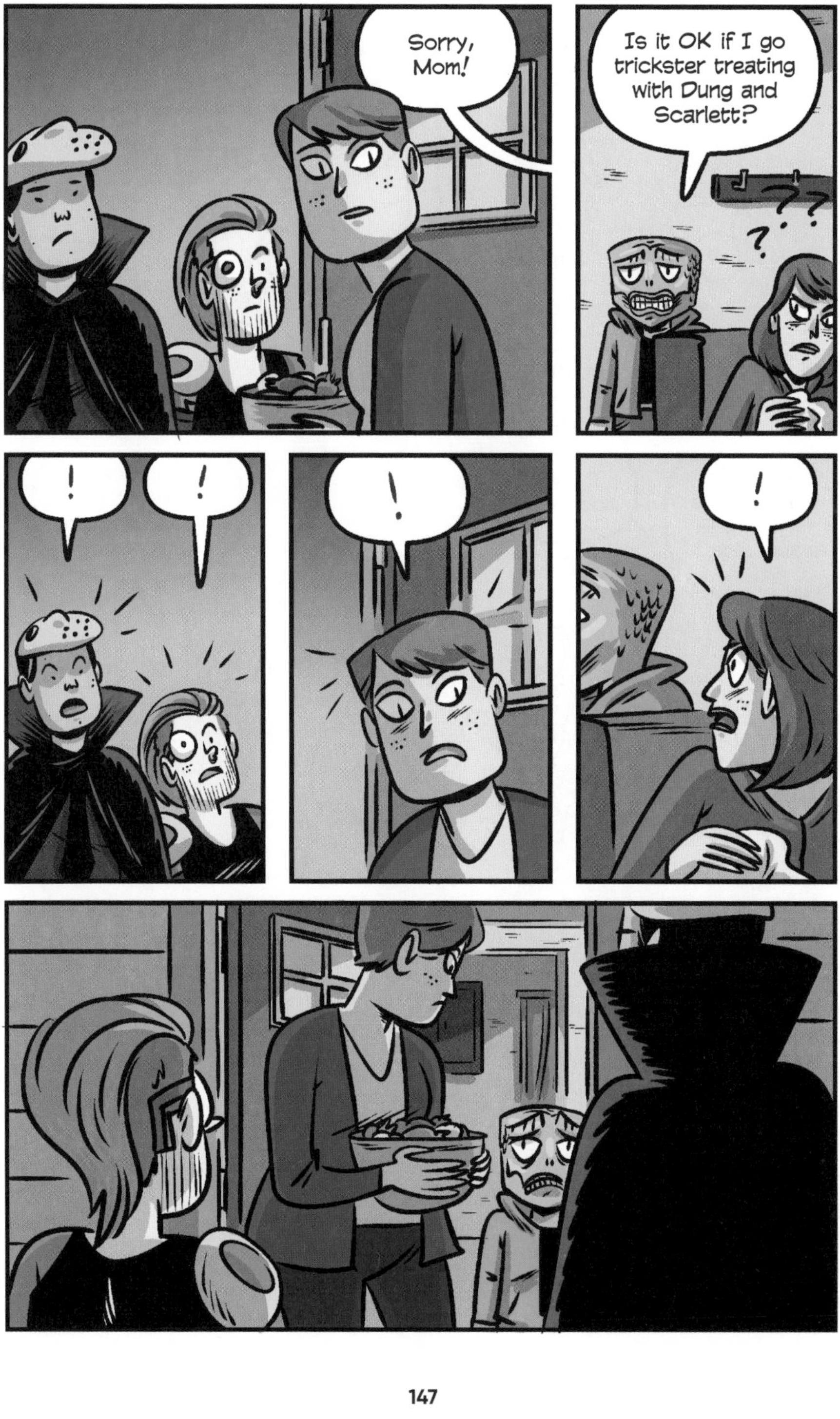
Sorry, Mom!
Is it OK if I go trickster treating with Dung and Scarlett?
?
?
?
!
!
!
!

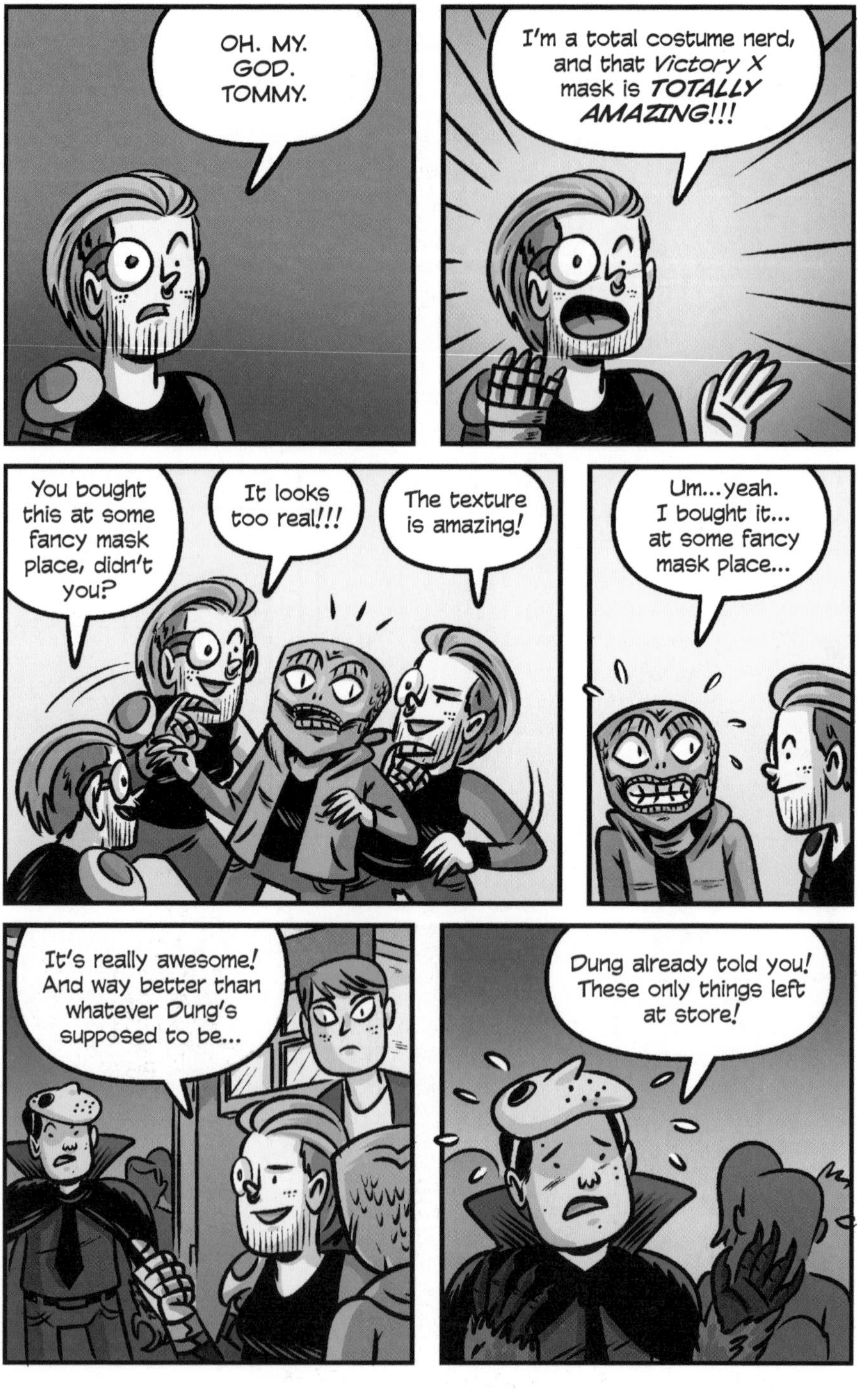
OH. MY. GOD. TOMMY.
I'm a total costume nerd, and that *Victory X* mask is ***TOTALLY AMAZING!!!***
You bought this at some fancy mask place, didn't you?
It looks too real*!!!*
The texture is amazing*!*
Um...yeah. I bought it... at some fancy mask place...
It's really awesome*!* And way better than whatever Dung's supposed to be...
Dung already told you*!* These only things left at store*!*

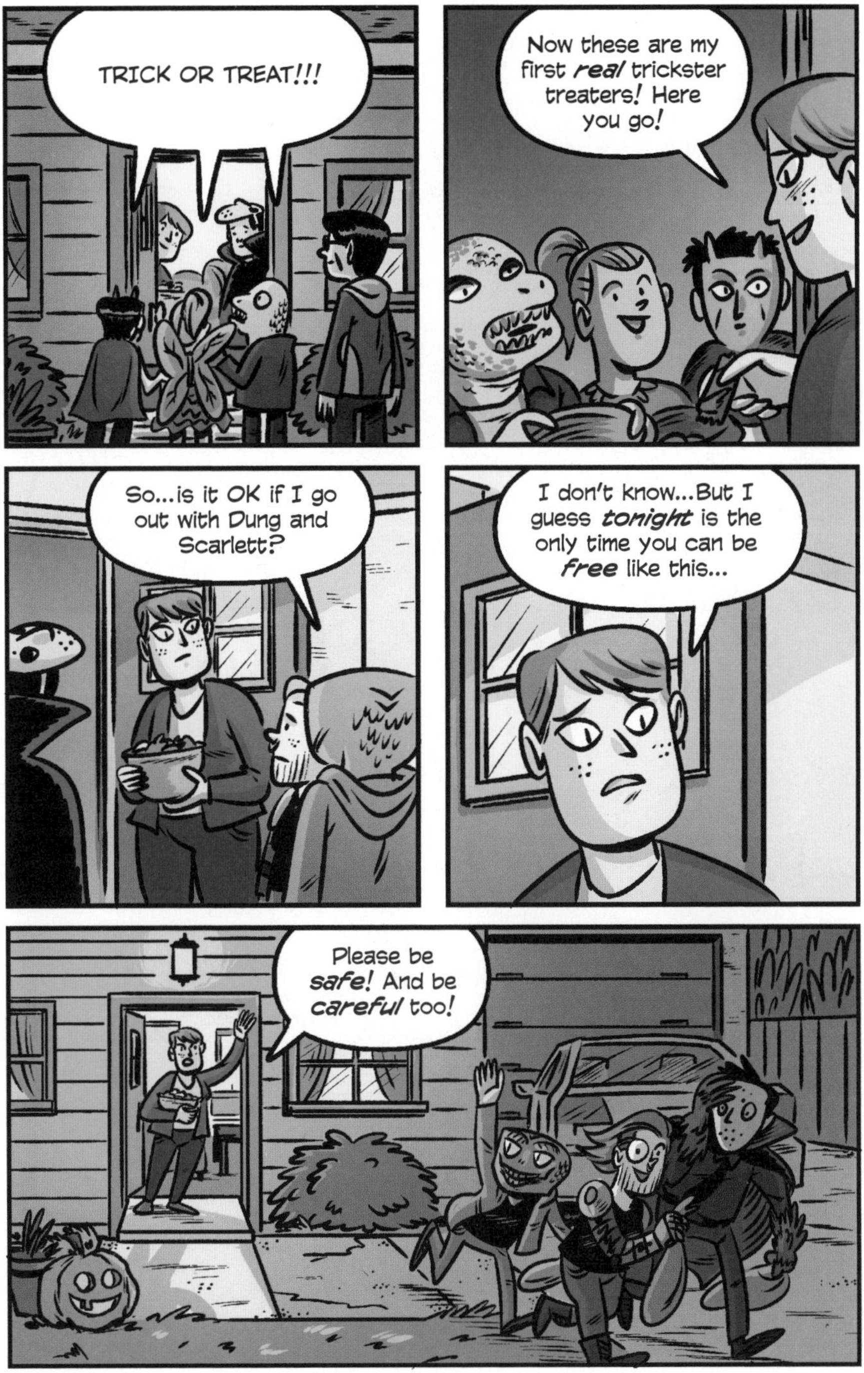
TRICK OR TREAT!!!
Now these are my first *real* trickster treaters! Here you go!
So...is it OK if I go out with Dung and Scarlett?
I don't know...But I guess *tonight* is the only time you can be *free* like this...
Please be *safe!* And be *careful* too!

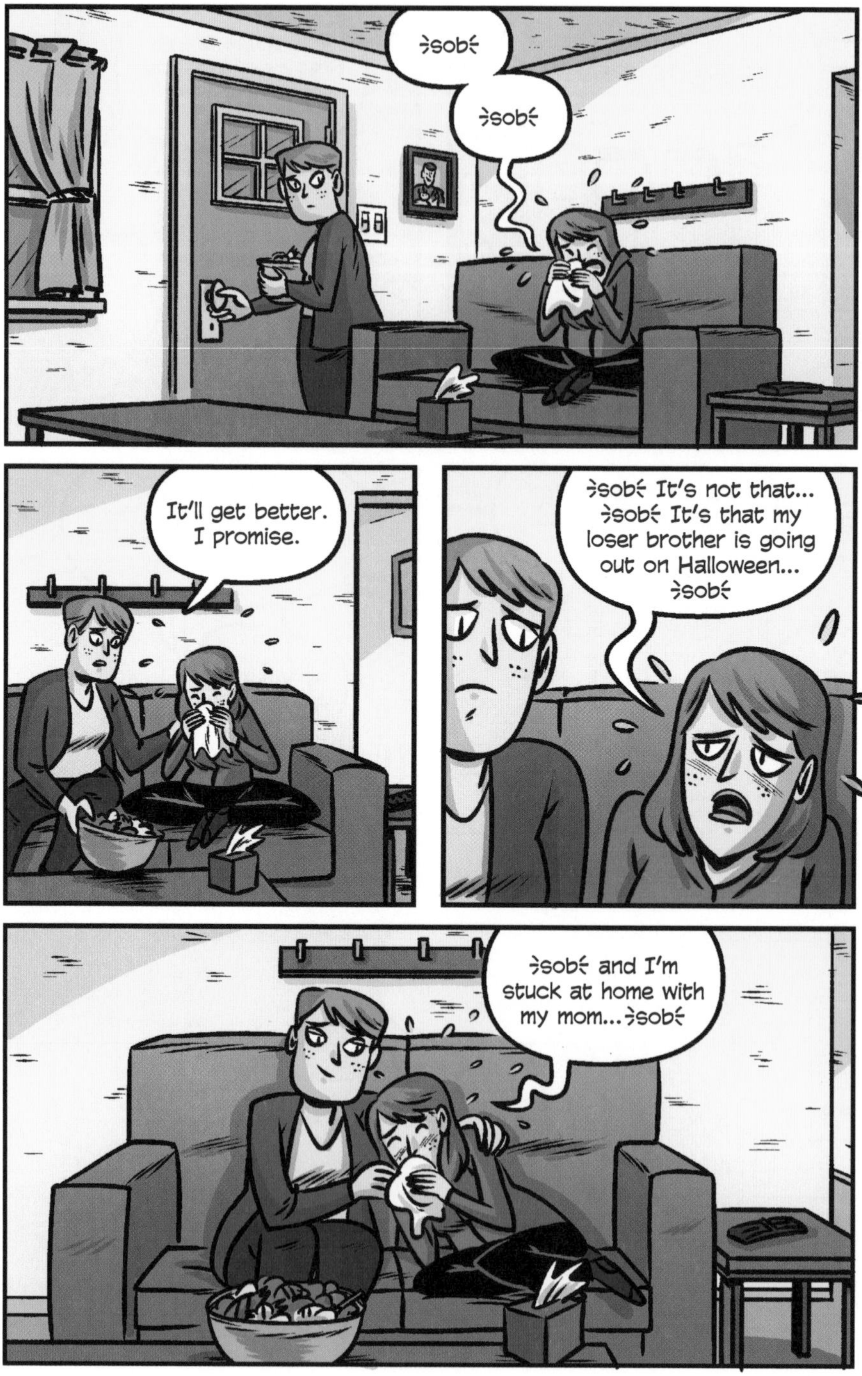

⋝sob⋜
⋝sob⋜
It'll get better. I promise.
⋝sob⋜ It's not that... ⋝sob⋜ It's that my loser brother is going out on Halloween... ⋝sob⋜
⋝sob⋜ and I'm stuck at home with my mom... ⋝sob⋜

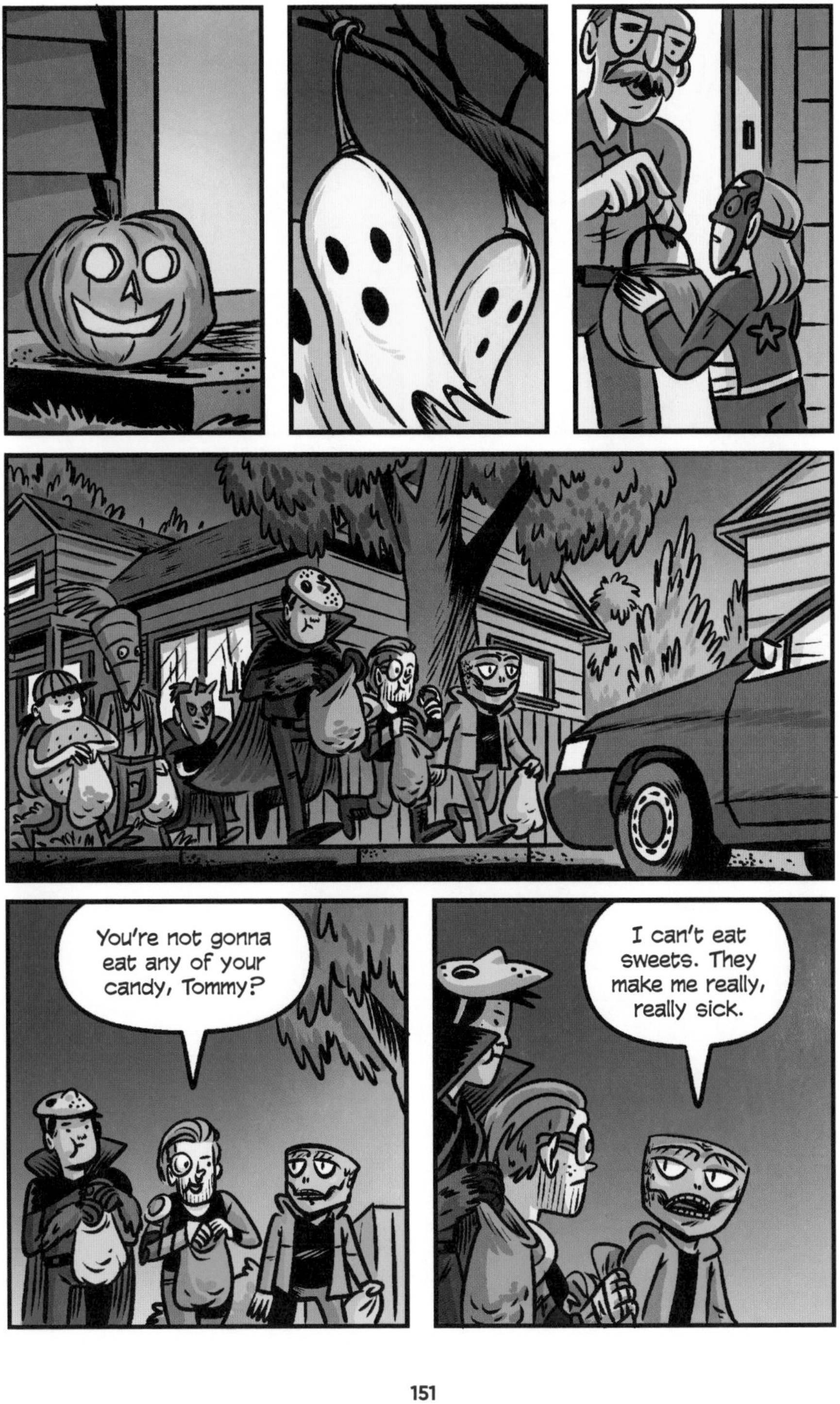
You're not gonna eat any of your candy, Tommy?
I can't eat sweets. They make me really, really sick.

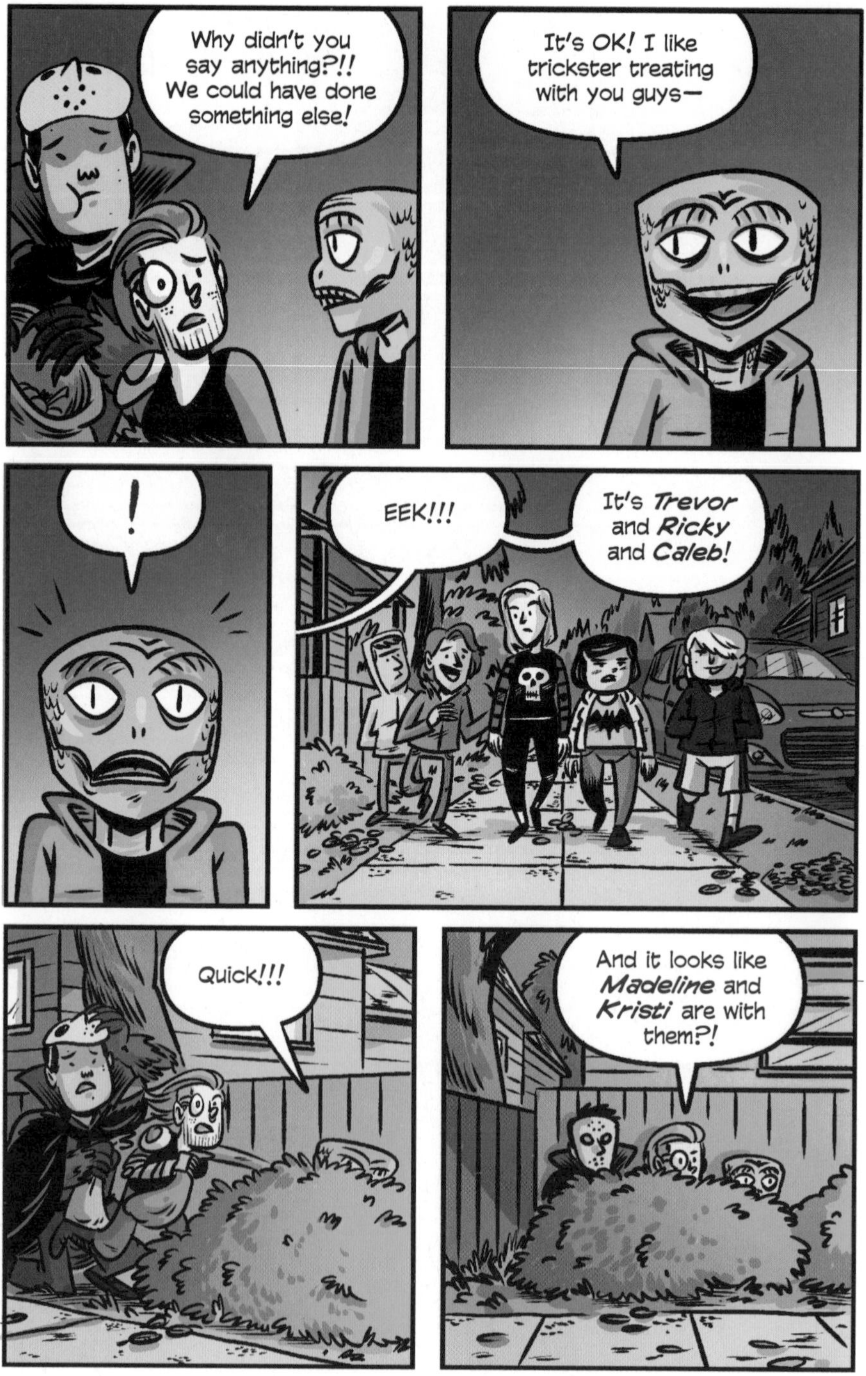
Why didn't you say anything?!! We could have done something else!
It's OK! I like trickster treating with you guys—
!
EEK!!!
It's *Trevor* and *Ricky* and *Caleb*!
Quick!!!
And it looks like *Madeline* and *Kristi* are with them?!

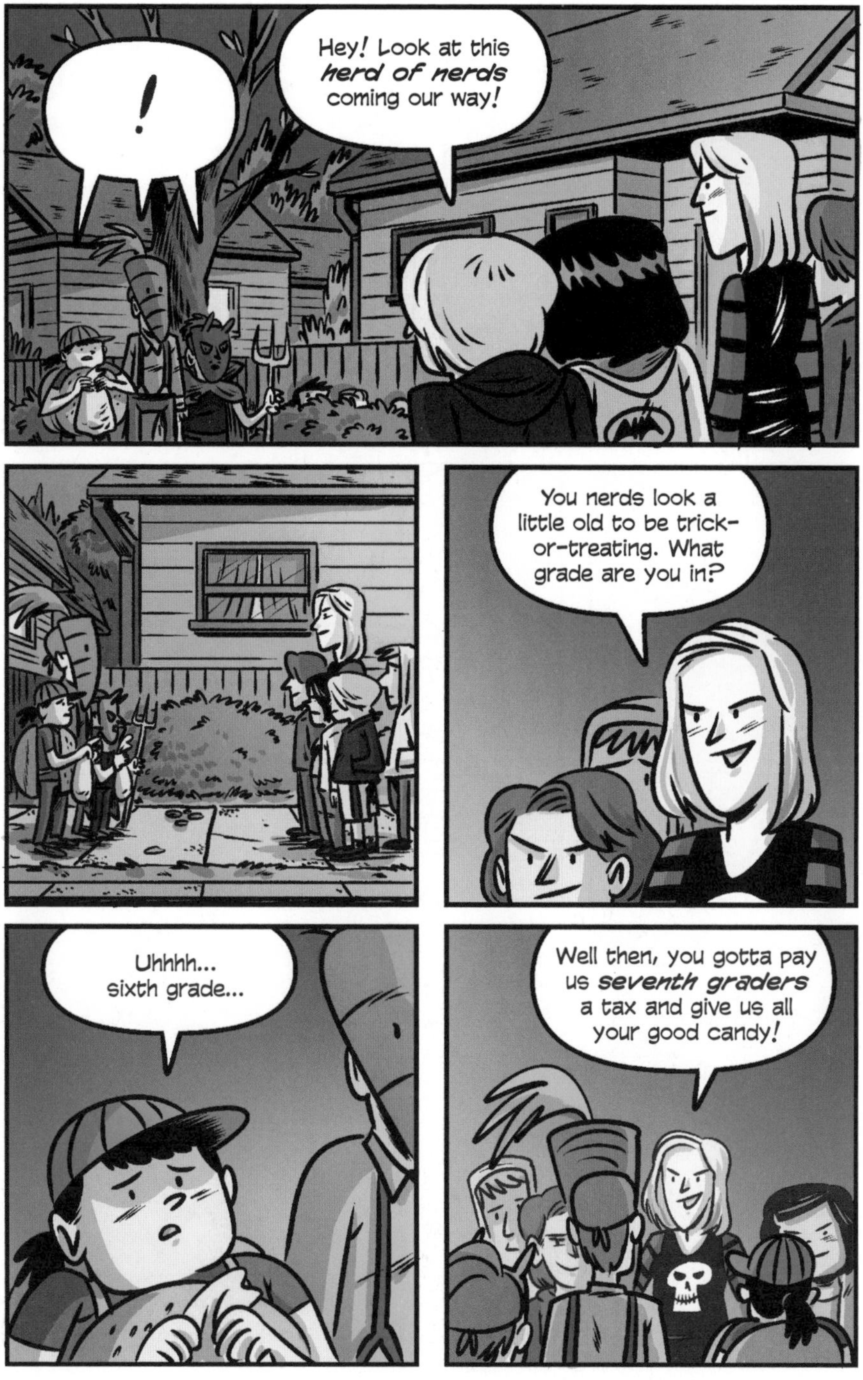
!
Hey! Look at this *herd of nerds* coming our way!
You nerds look a little old to be trick-or-treating. What grade are you in?
Uhhhh... sixth grade...
Well then, you gotta pay us *seventh graders* a tax and give us all your good candy!

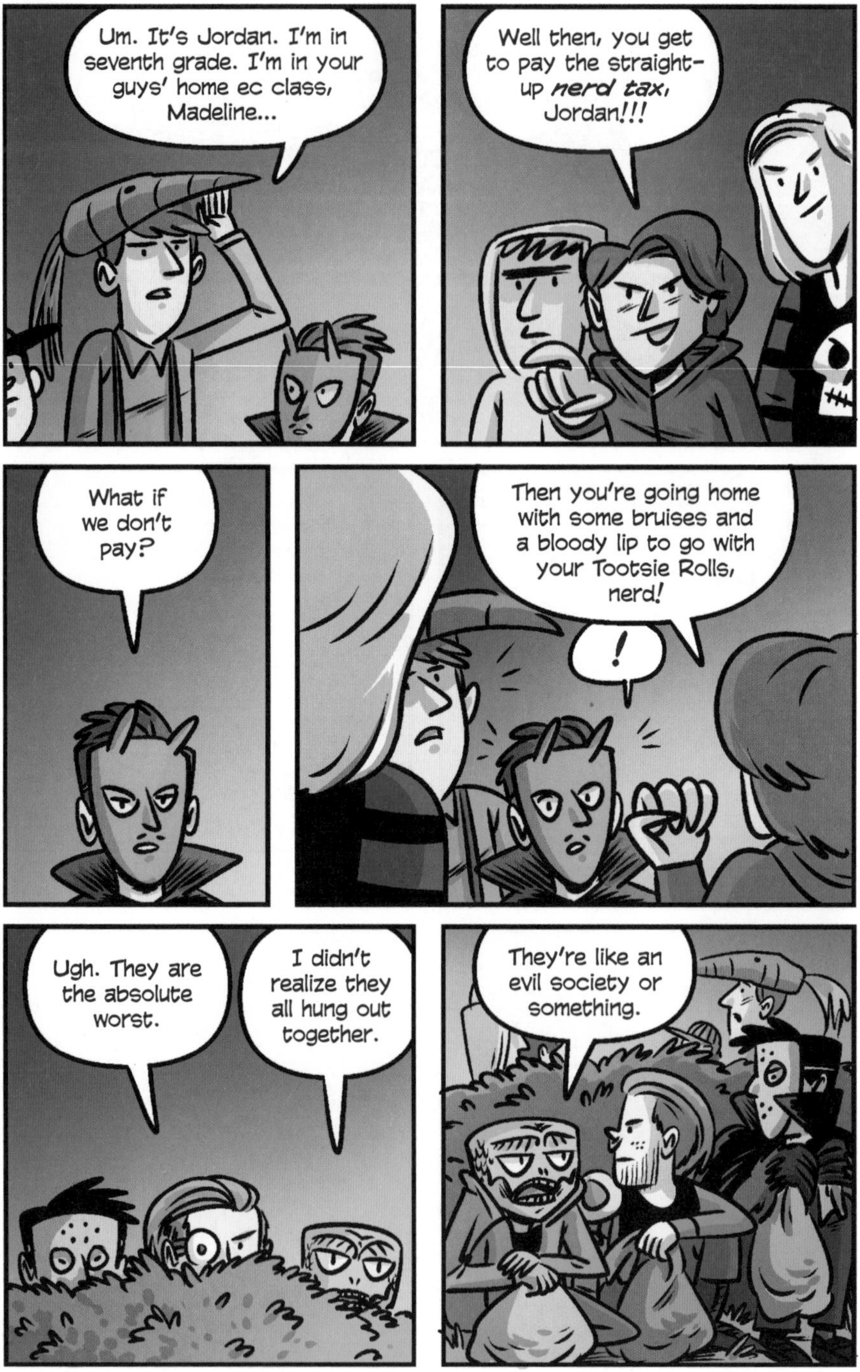
Um. It's Jordan. I'm in seventh grade. I'm in your guys' home ec class, Madeline...
Well then, you get to pay the straight-up *nerd tax*, Jordan!!!
What if we don't pay?
Then you're going home with some bruises and a bloody lip to go with your Tootsie Rolls, nerd!
!
Ugh. They are the absolute worst.
I didn't realize they all hung out together.
They're like an evil society or something.

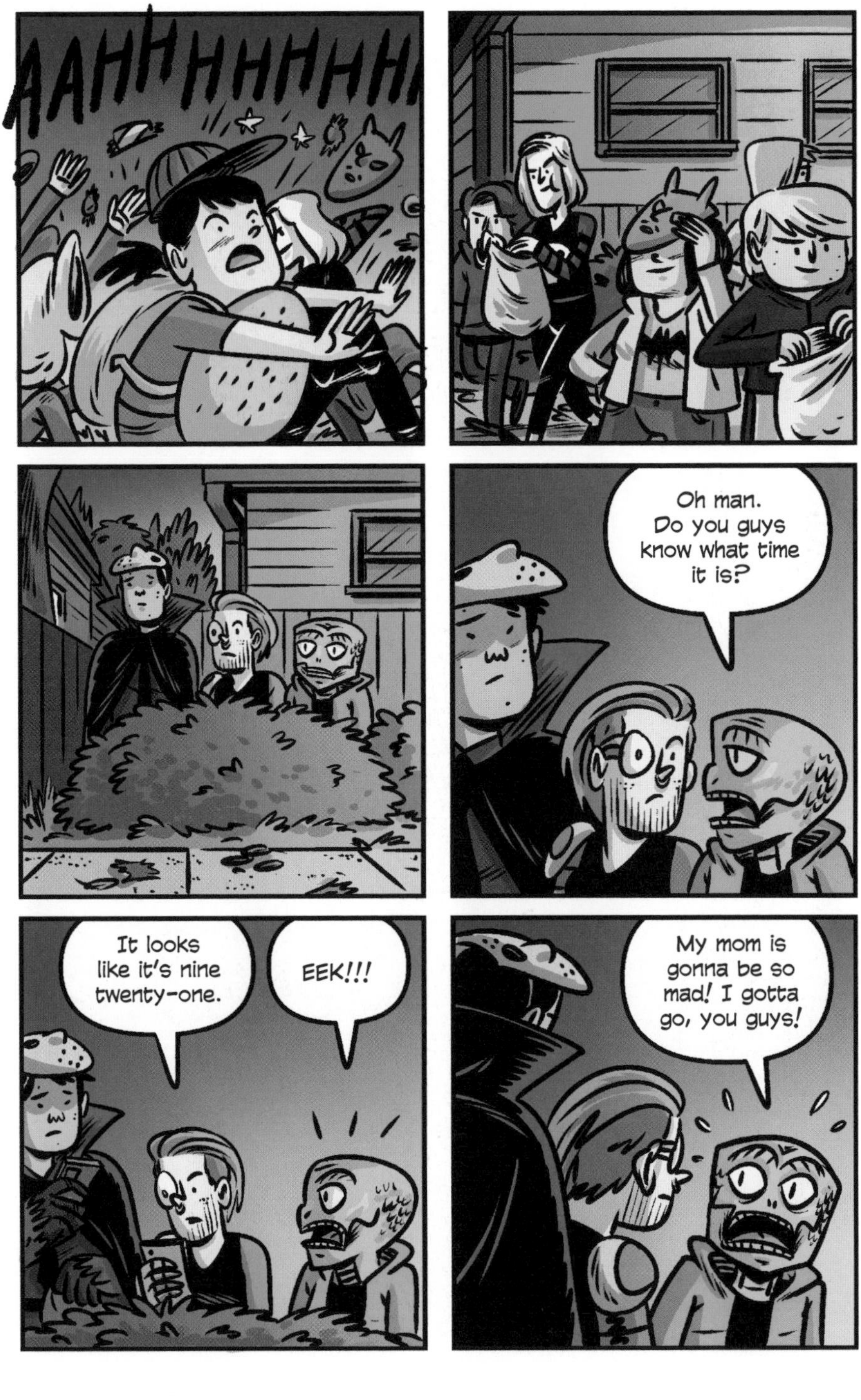
AAHHHHHHHH
Oh man.
Do you guys
know what time
it is?
It looks
like it's nine
twenty-one.
EEK!!!
My mom is
gonna be so
mad! I gotta
go, you guys!

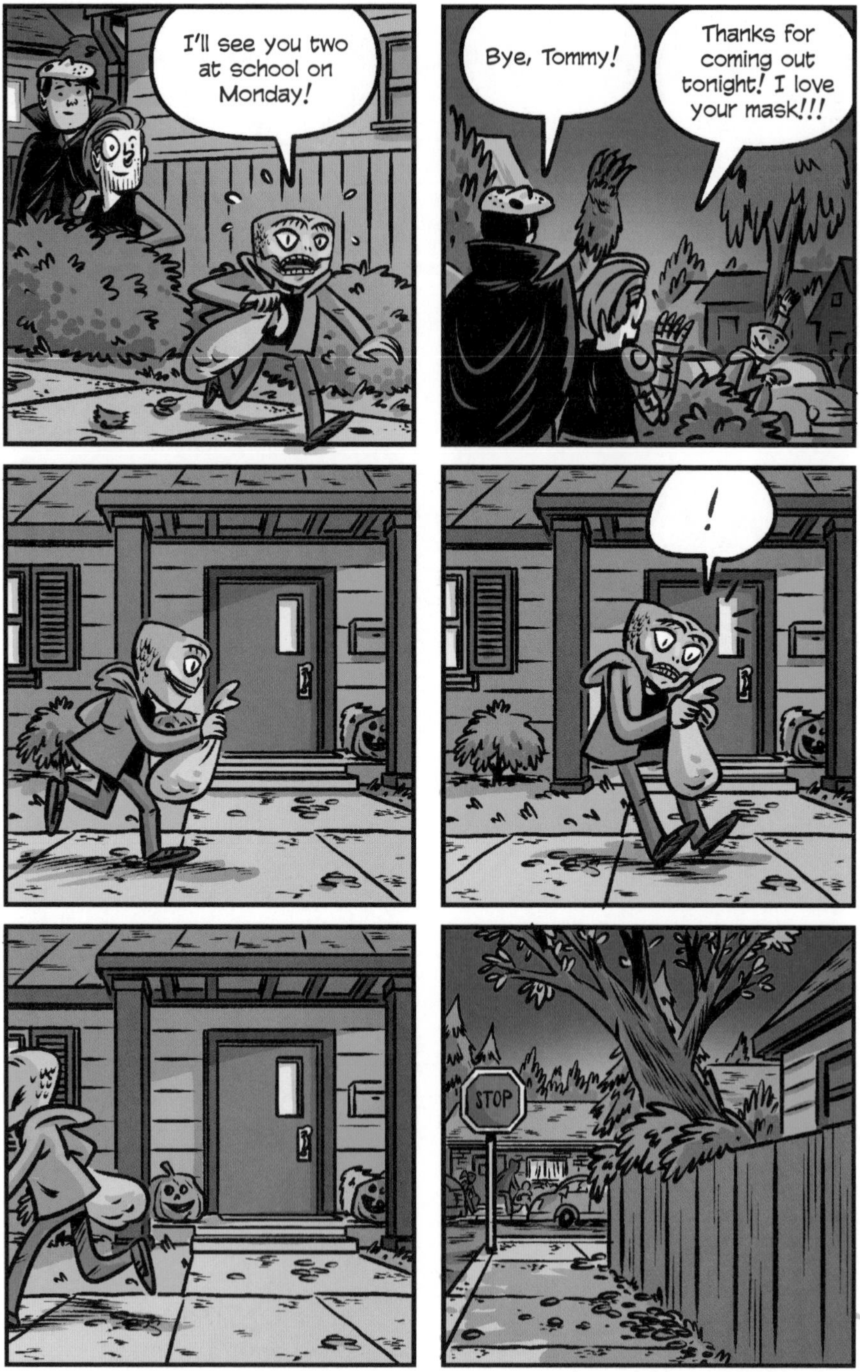
I'll see you two at school on Monday!
Bye, Tommy!
Thanks for coming out tonight! I love your mask!!!
!
STOP

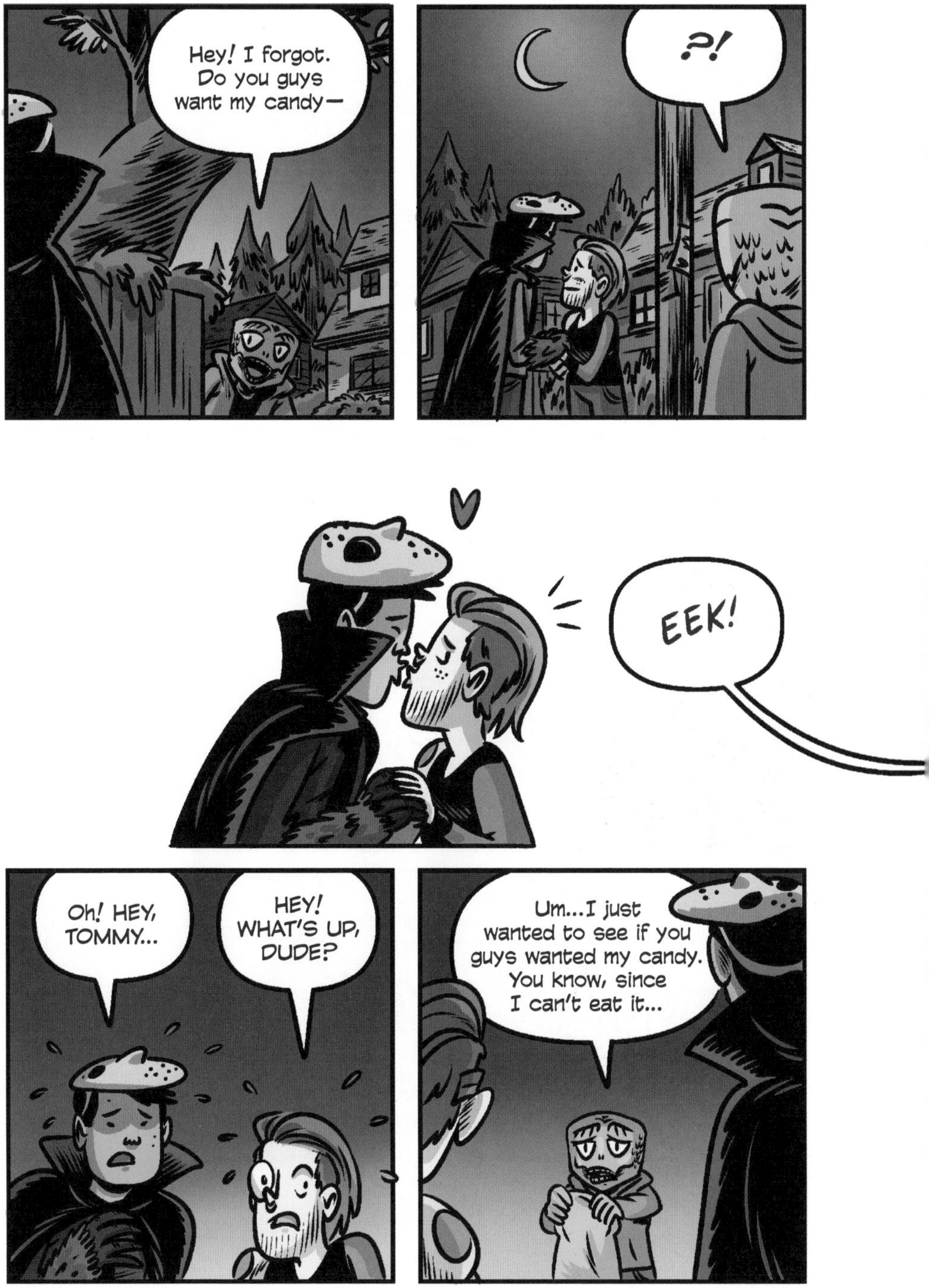
Hey! I forgot. Do you guys want my candy—
?!
EEK!
Oh! HEY, TOMMY...
HEY! WHAT'S UP, DUDE?
Um...I just wanted to see if you guys wanted my candy. You know, since I can't eat it...

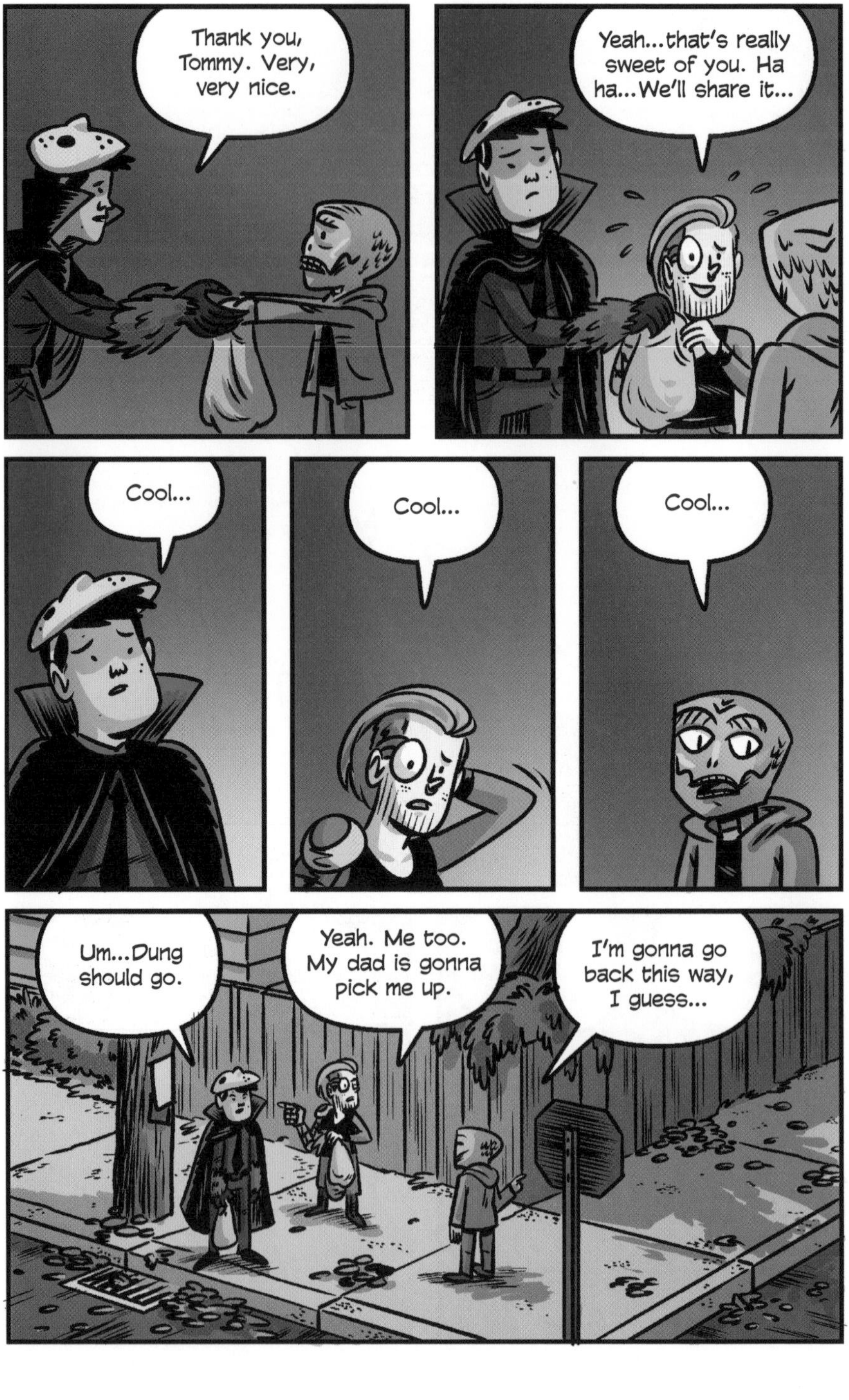
Thank you, Tommy. Very, very nice.
Yeah...that's really sweet of you. Ha ha...We'll share it...
Cool...
Cool...
Cool...
Um...Dung should go.
Yeah. Me too. My dad is gonna pick me up.
I'm gonna go back this way, I guess...

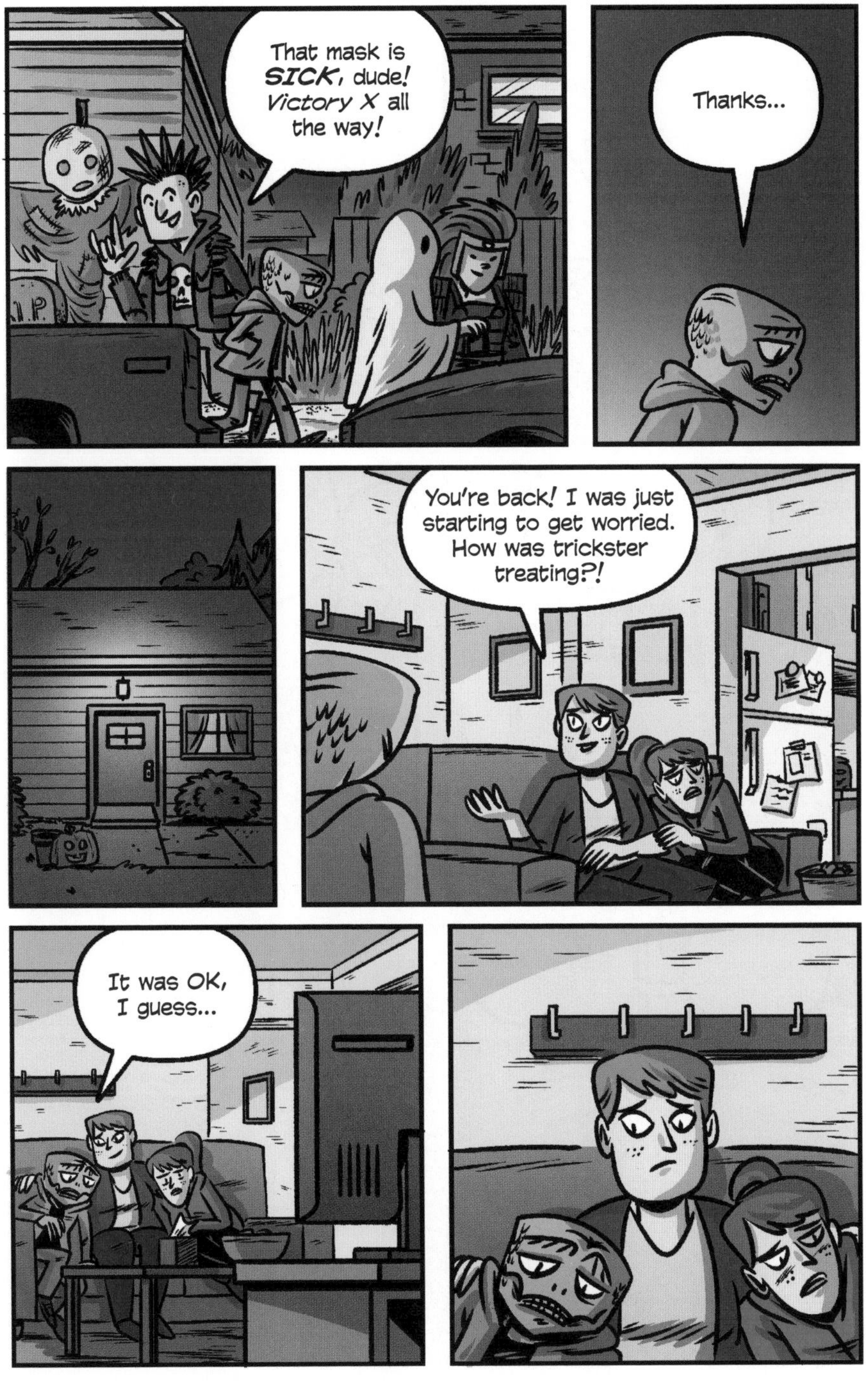

That mask is SICK, dude! Victory X all the way!
Thanks...
You're back! I was just starting to get worried. How was trickster treating?!
It was OK, I guess...

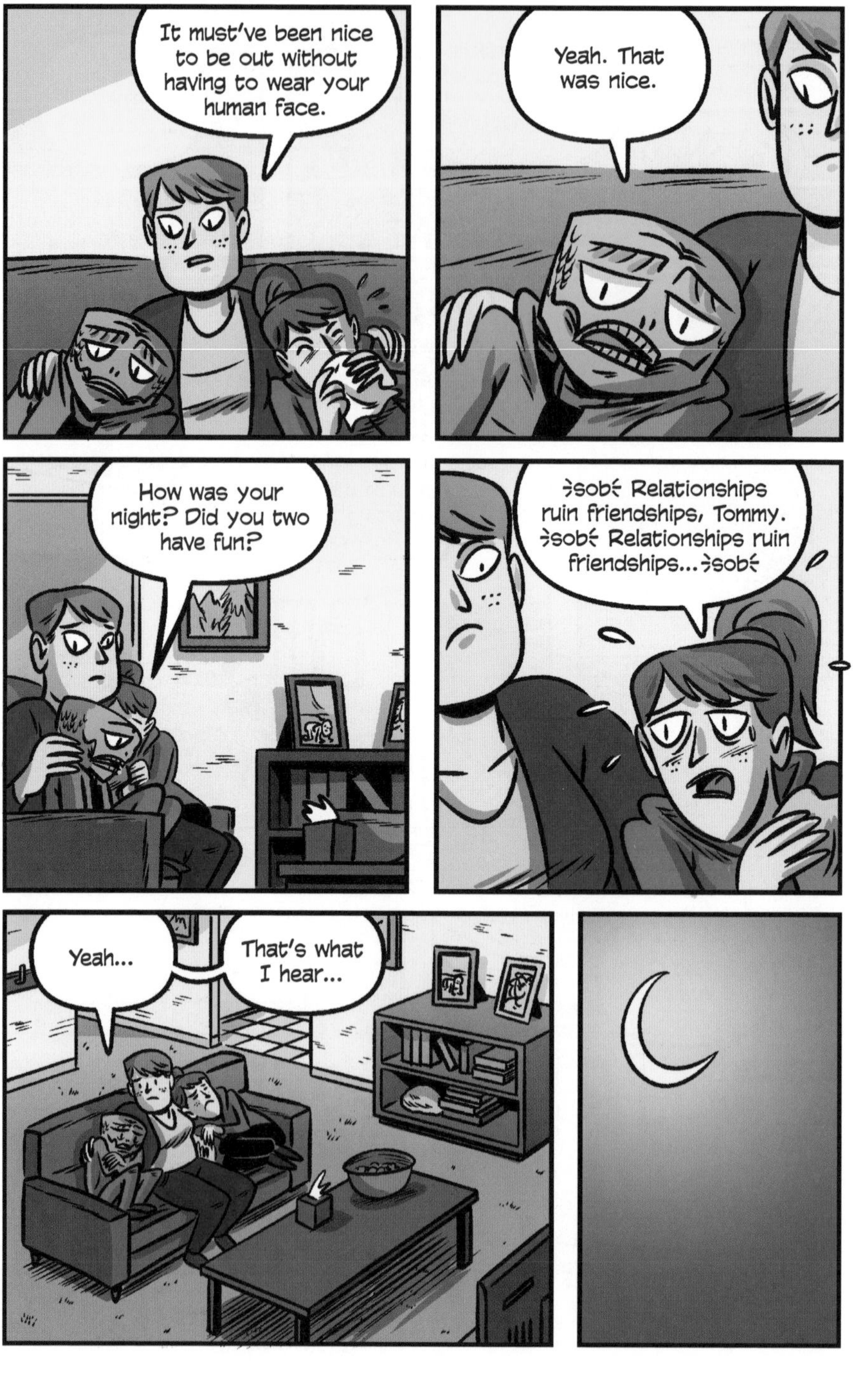
It must've been nice to be out without having to wear your human face.
Yeah. That was nice.
How was your night? Did you two have fun?
⪢sob⪡ Relationships ruin friendships, Tommy. ⪢sob⪡ Relationships ruin friendships... ⪢sob⪡
Yeah...
That's what I hear...

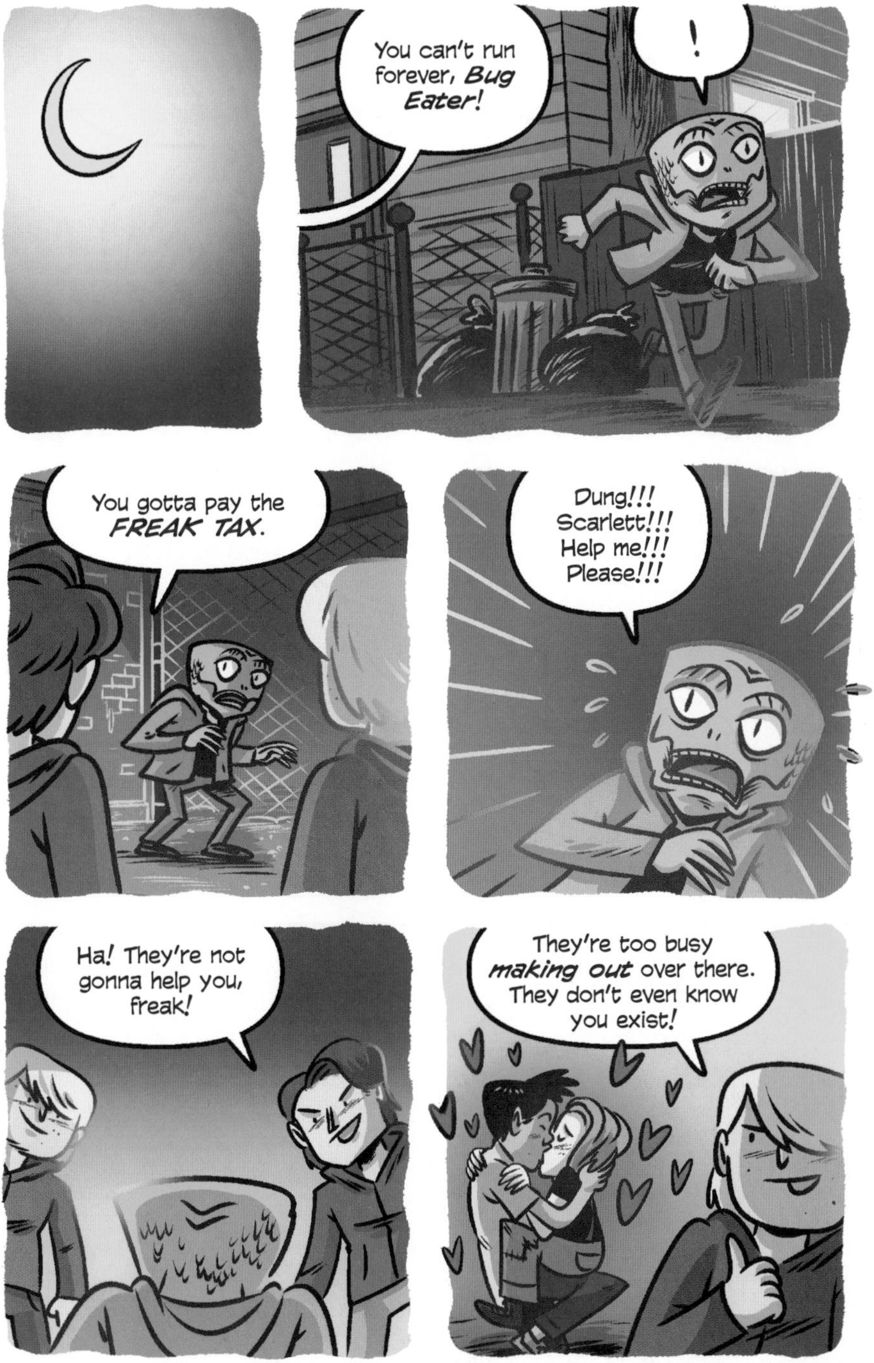
You can't run forever, Bug Eater!
!
You gotta pay the FREAK TAX.
Dung!!! Scarlett!!! Help me!!! Please!!!
Ha! They're not gonna help you, freak!
They're too busy making out over there. They don't even know you exist!

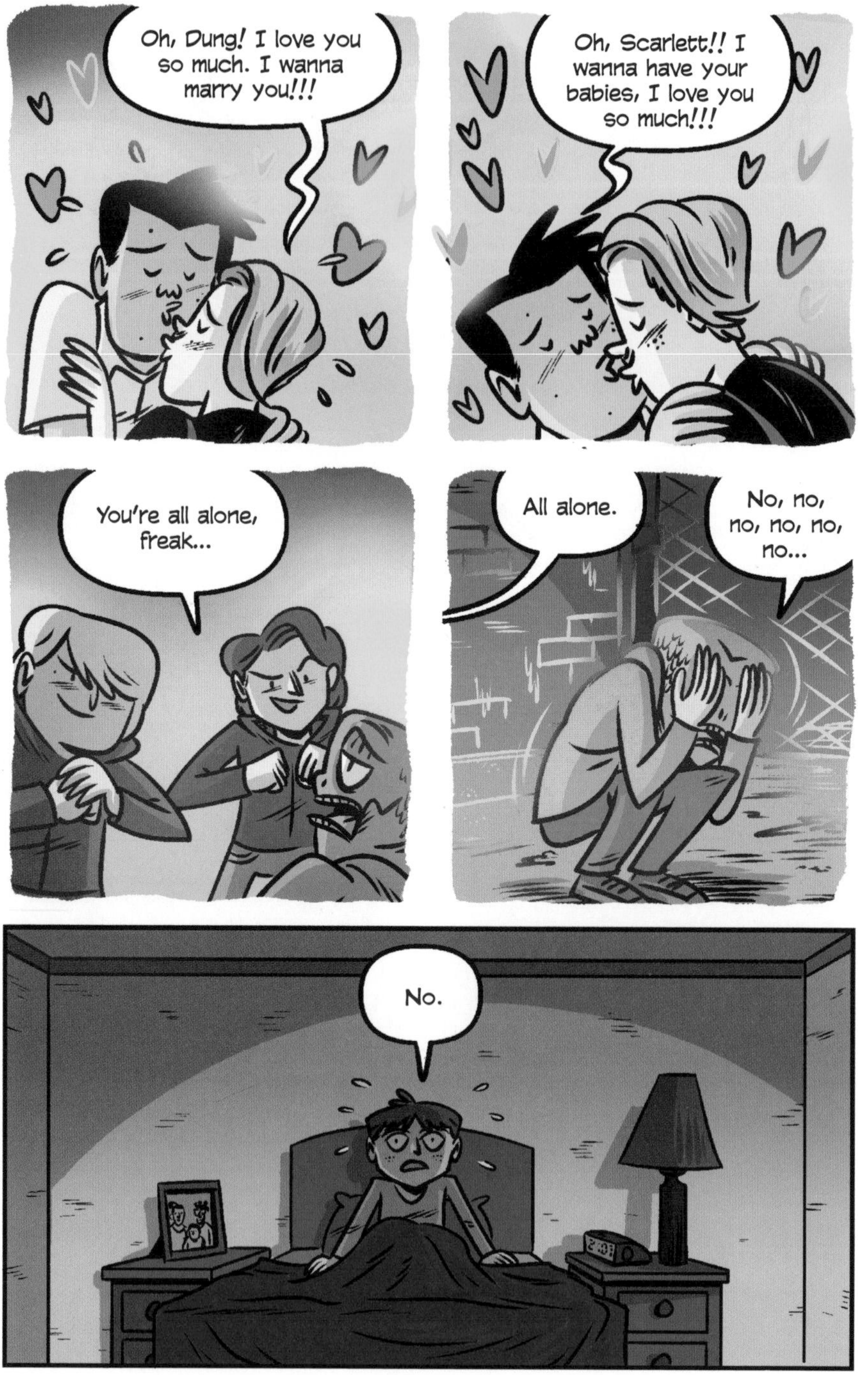
Oh, Dung! I love you so much. I wanna marry you!!!
Oh, Scarlett!! I wanna have your babies, I love you so much!!!
You're all alone, freak...
All alone.
No, no, no, no, no, no...
No.

CHAPTER 8

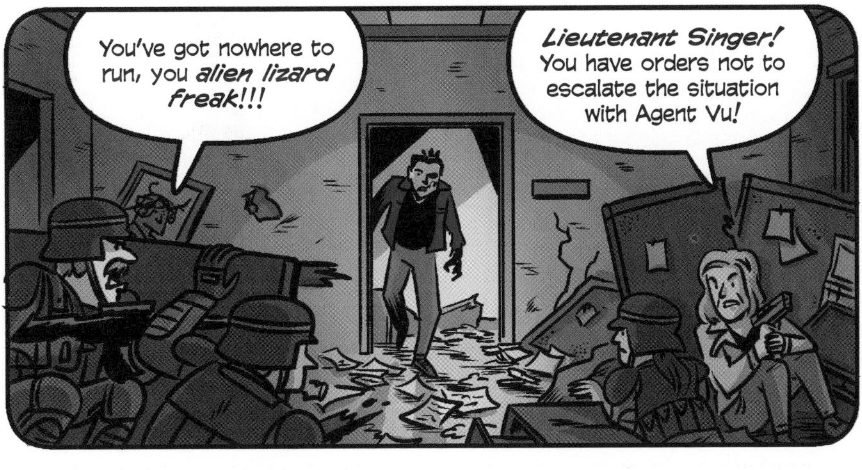
You've got nowhere to run, you *alien lizard freak*!!!
Lieutenant Singer! You have orders not to escalate the situation with Agent Vu!

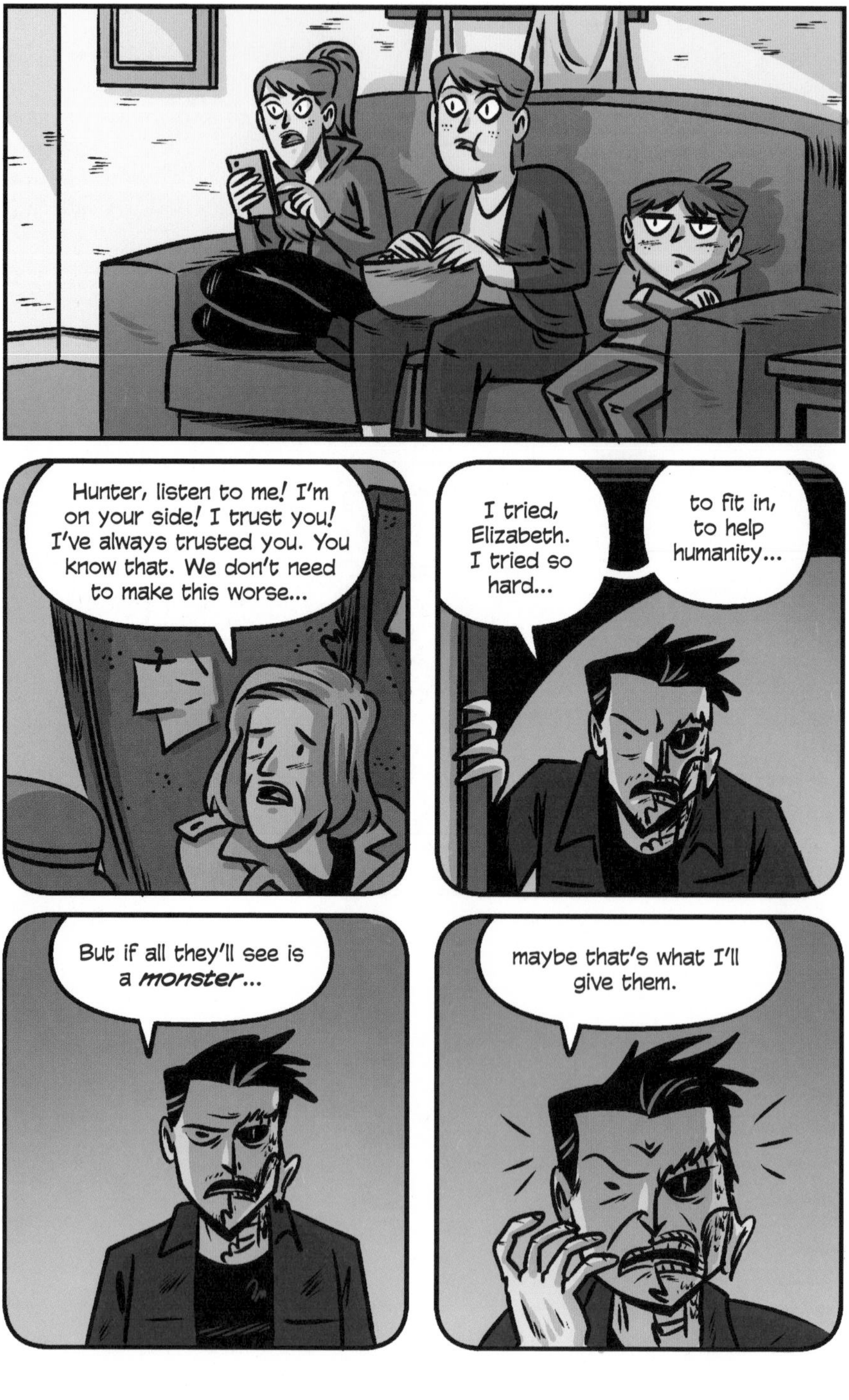
Hunter, listen to me! I'm on your side! I trust you! I've always trusted you. You know that. We don't need to make this worse...
I tried, Elizabeth. I tried so hard...
to fit in, to help humanity...
But if all they'll see is a *monster*...
maybe that's what I'll give them.

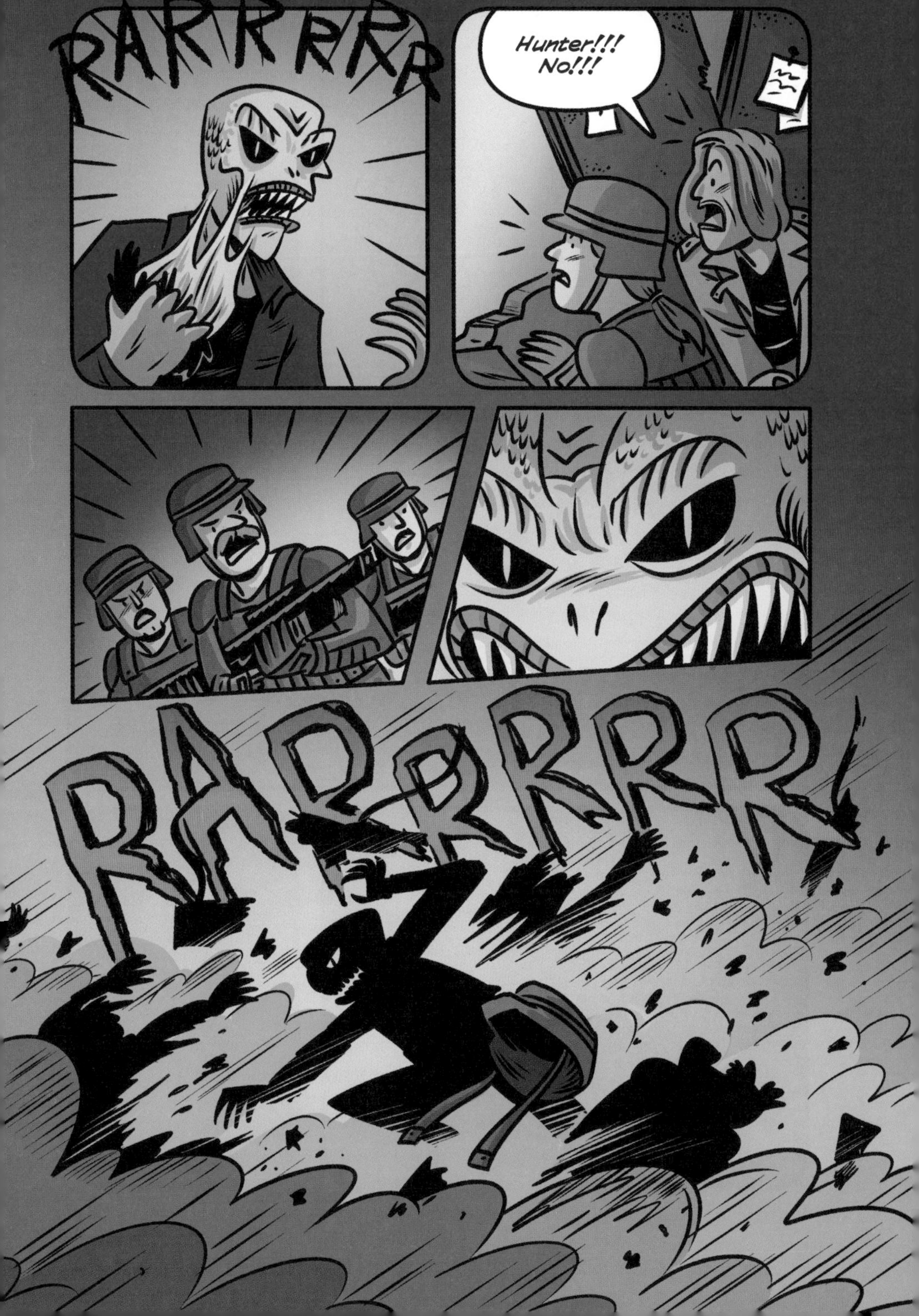
RARRRRRR
Hunter!!!
No!!!
RARRRRR

Elizabeth!!!

No, no, no...

I'm so sorry. I never meant for you to get hurt...

click

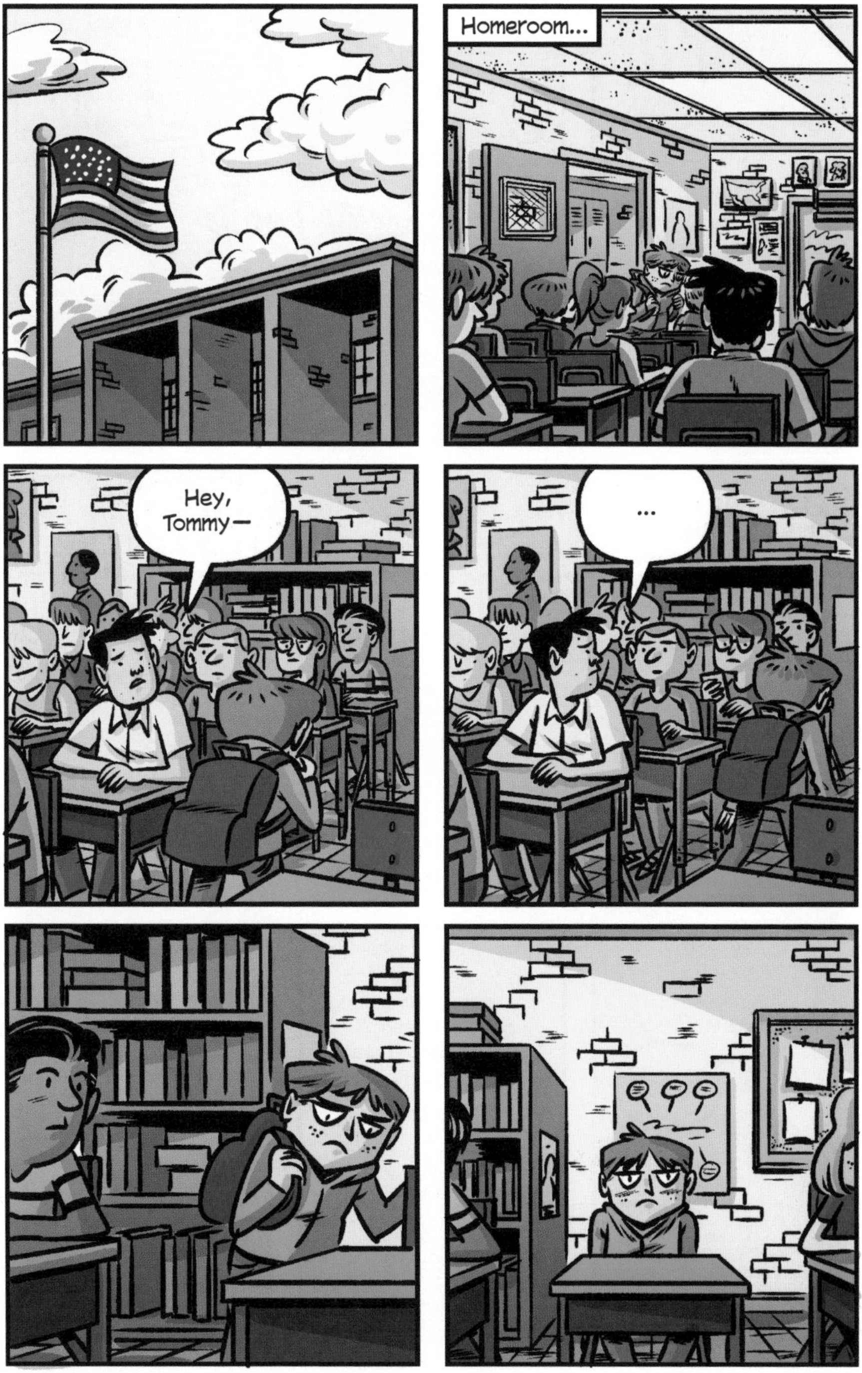
Homeroom...
Hey, Tommy—
...

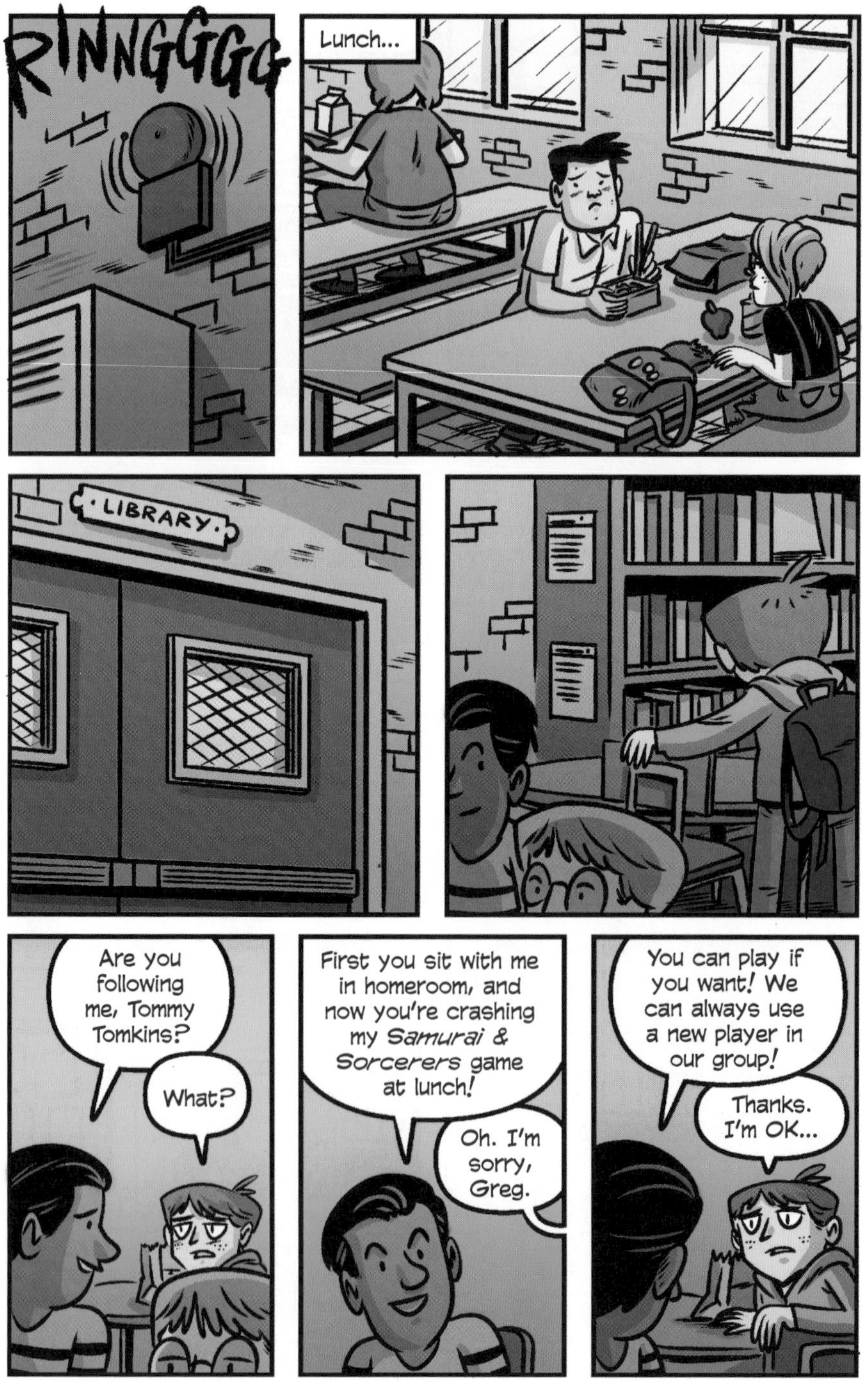
RINNGGGG
Lunch...
LIBRARY
Are you following me, Tommy Tomkins?
What?
First you sit with me in homeroom, and now you're crashing my *Samurai & Sorcerers* game at lunch!
Oh. I'm sorry, Greg.
You can play if you want! We can always use a new player in our group!
Thanks. I'm OK...

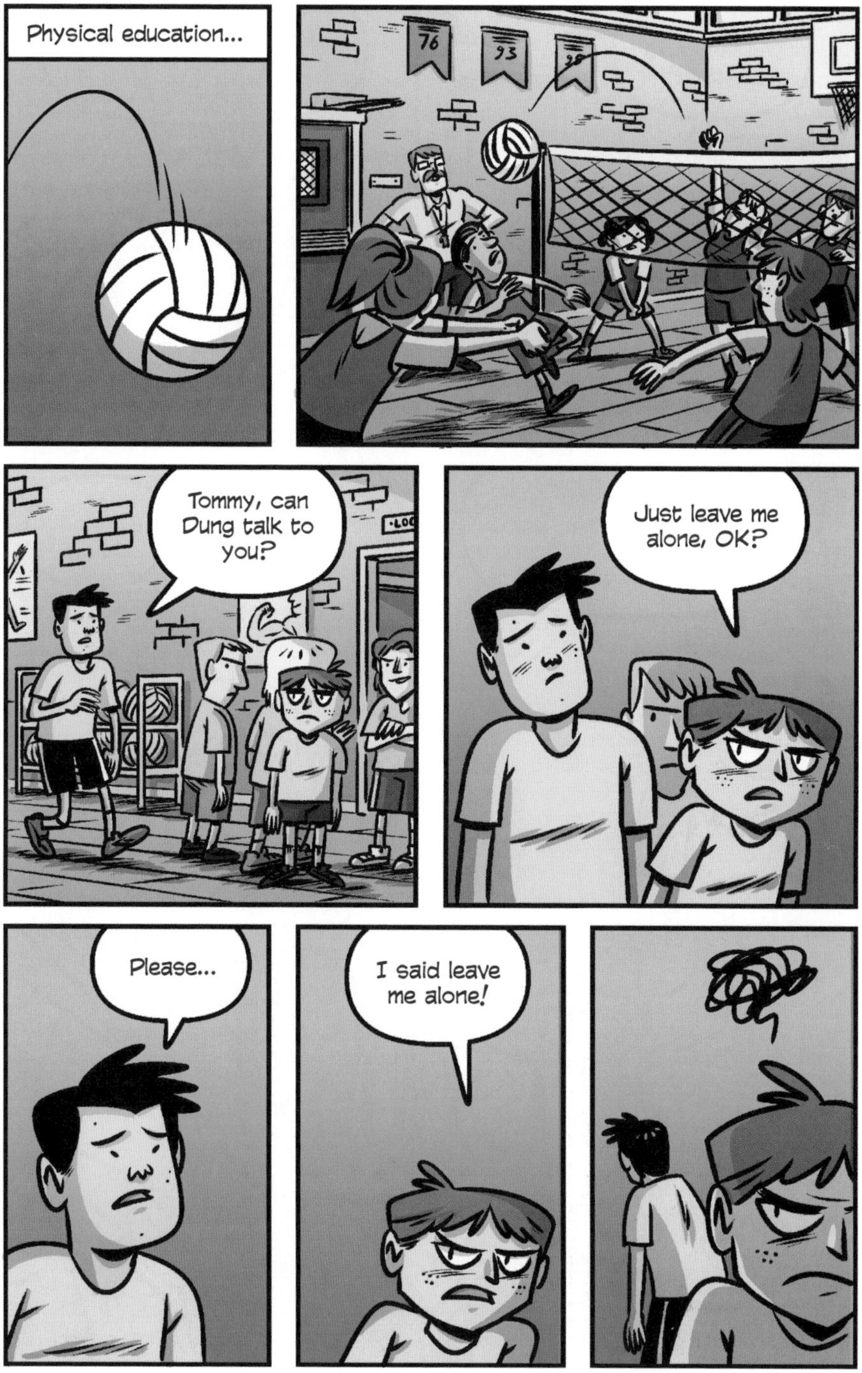
Physical education...
76
93
Tommy, can Dung talk to you?
Just leave me alone, OK?
Please...
I said leave me alone!

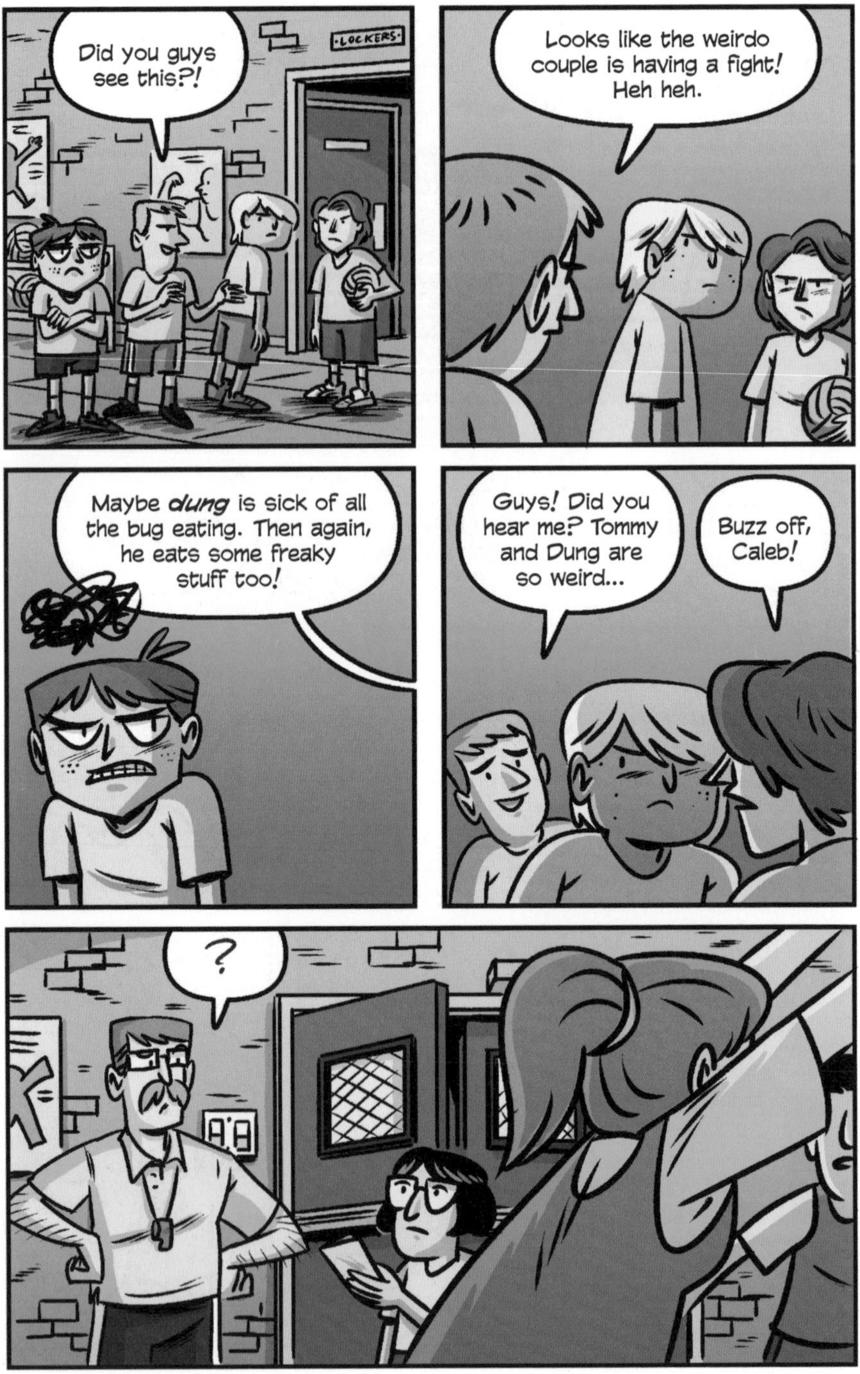

Did you guys see this?!
LOCKERS
Looks like the weirdo couple is having a fight! Heh heh.
Maybe dung is sick of all the bug eating. Then again, he eats some freaky stuff too!
Guys! Did you hear me? Tommy and Dung are so weird...
Buzz off, Caleb!
?

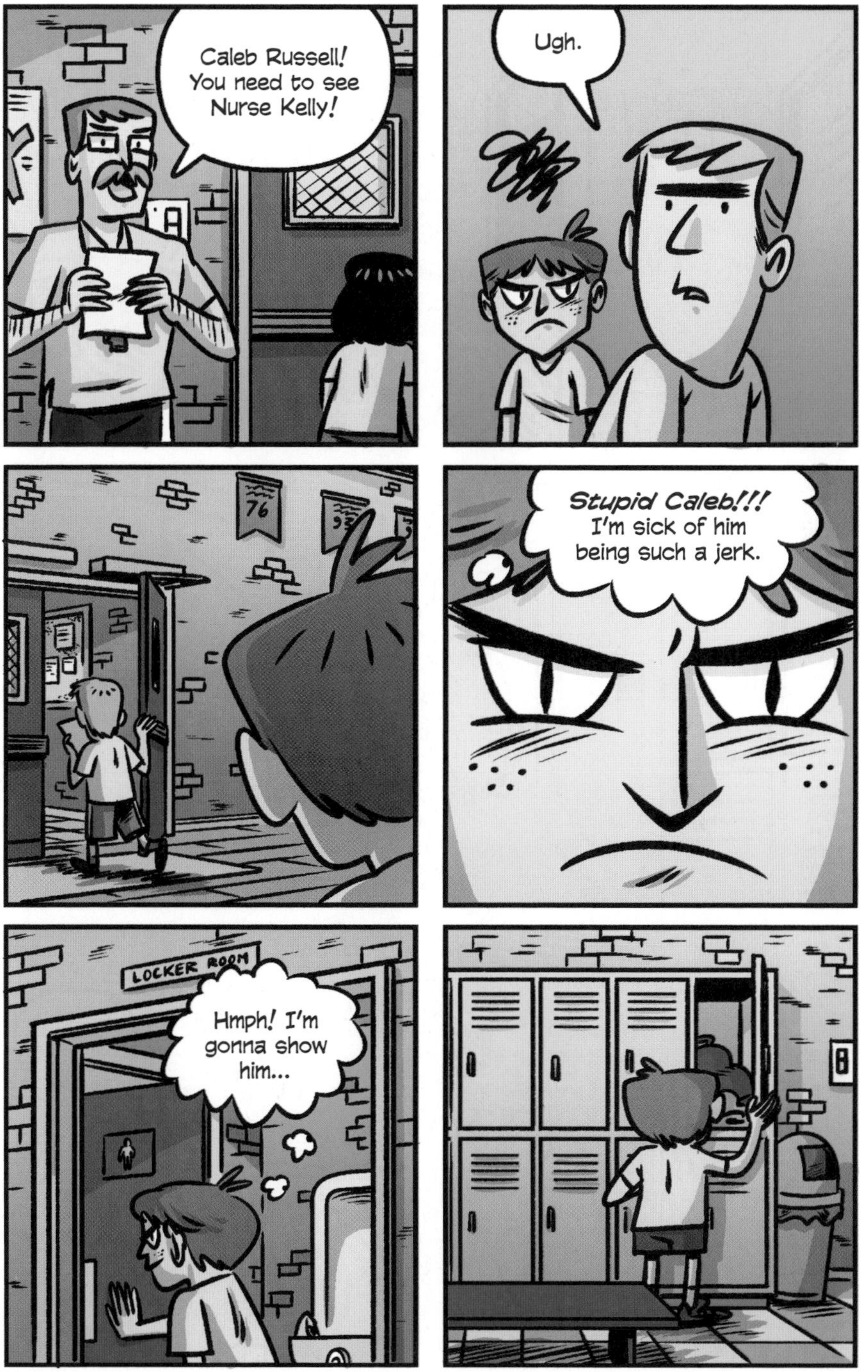
Caleb Russell! You need to see Nurse Kelly!
Ugh.
Stupid Caleb!!! I'm sick of him being such a jerk.
LOCKER ROOM
Hmph! I'm gonna show him...

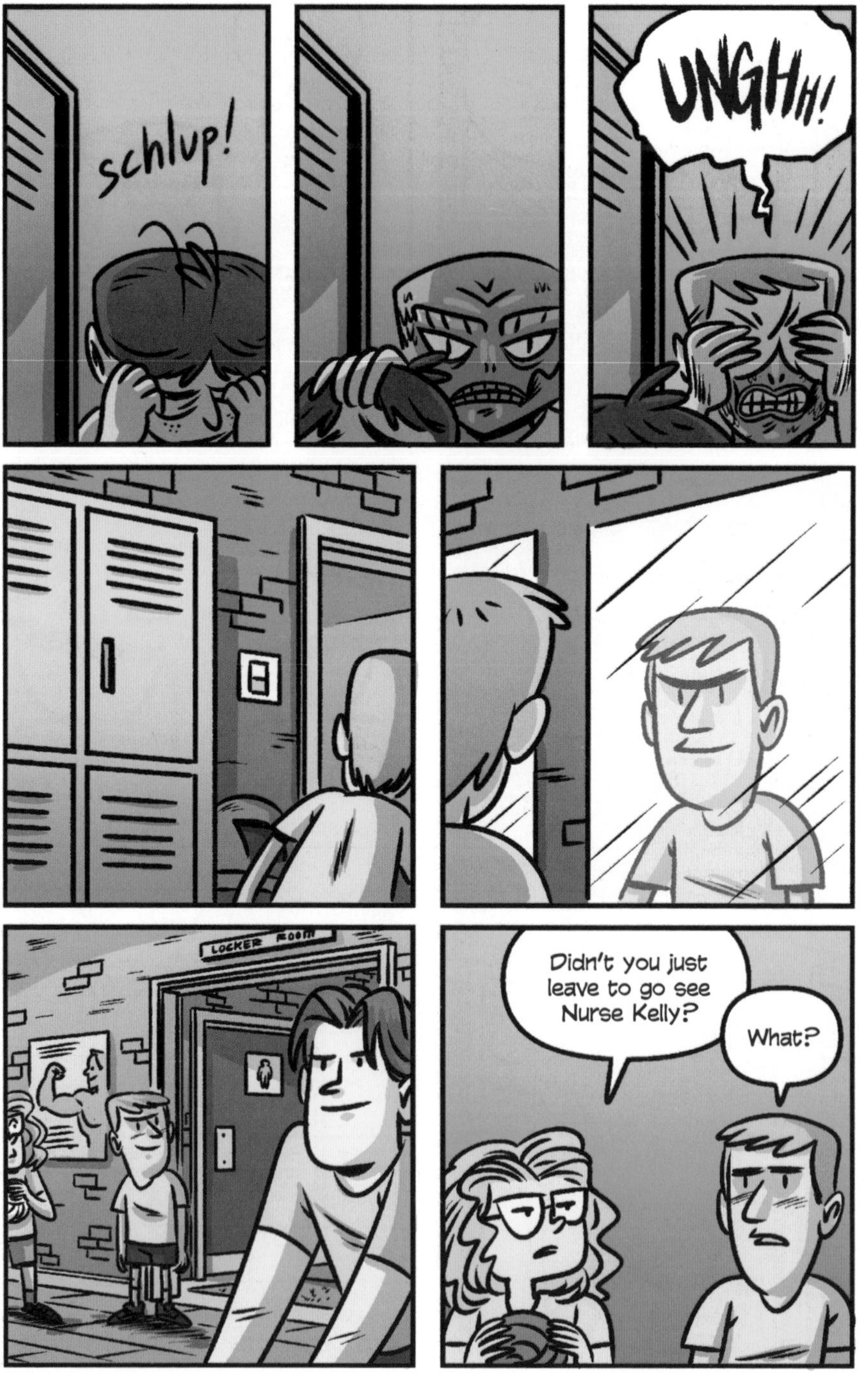
schlup!
UNGHH!
LOCKER ROOM
Didn't you just leave to go see Nurse Kelly?
What?

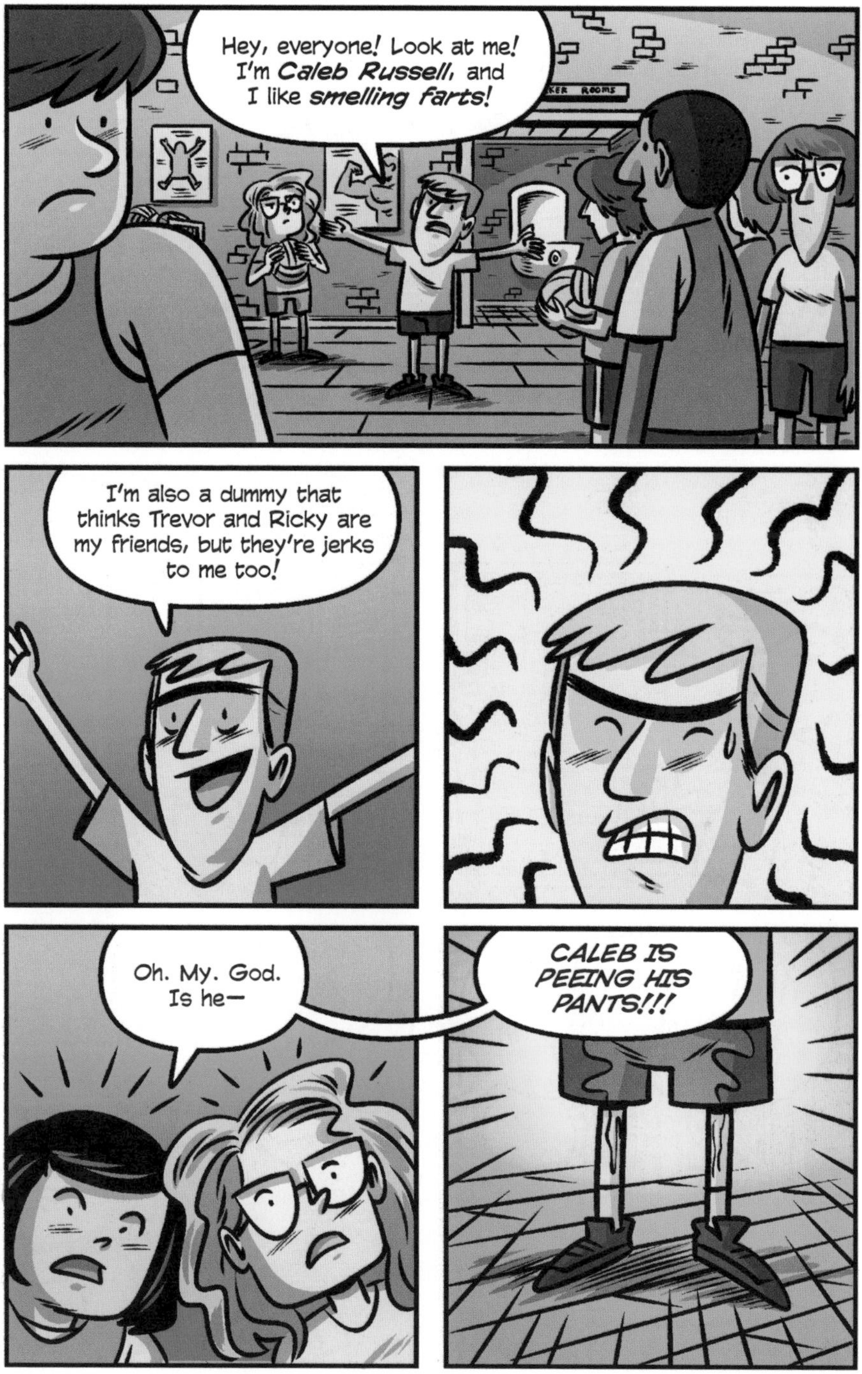

Hey, everyone! Look at me! I'm *Caleb Russell*, and I like *smelling farts*!
I'm also a dummy that thinks Trevor and Ricky are my friends, but they're jerks to me too!
Oh. My. God. Is he—
CALEB IS PEEING HIS PANTS!!!

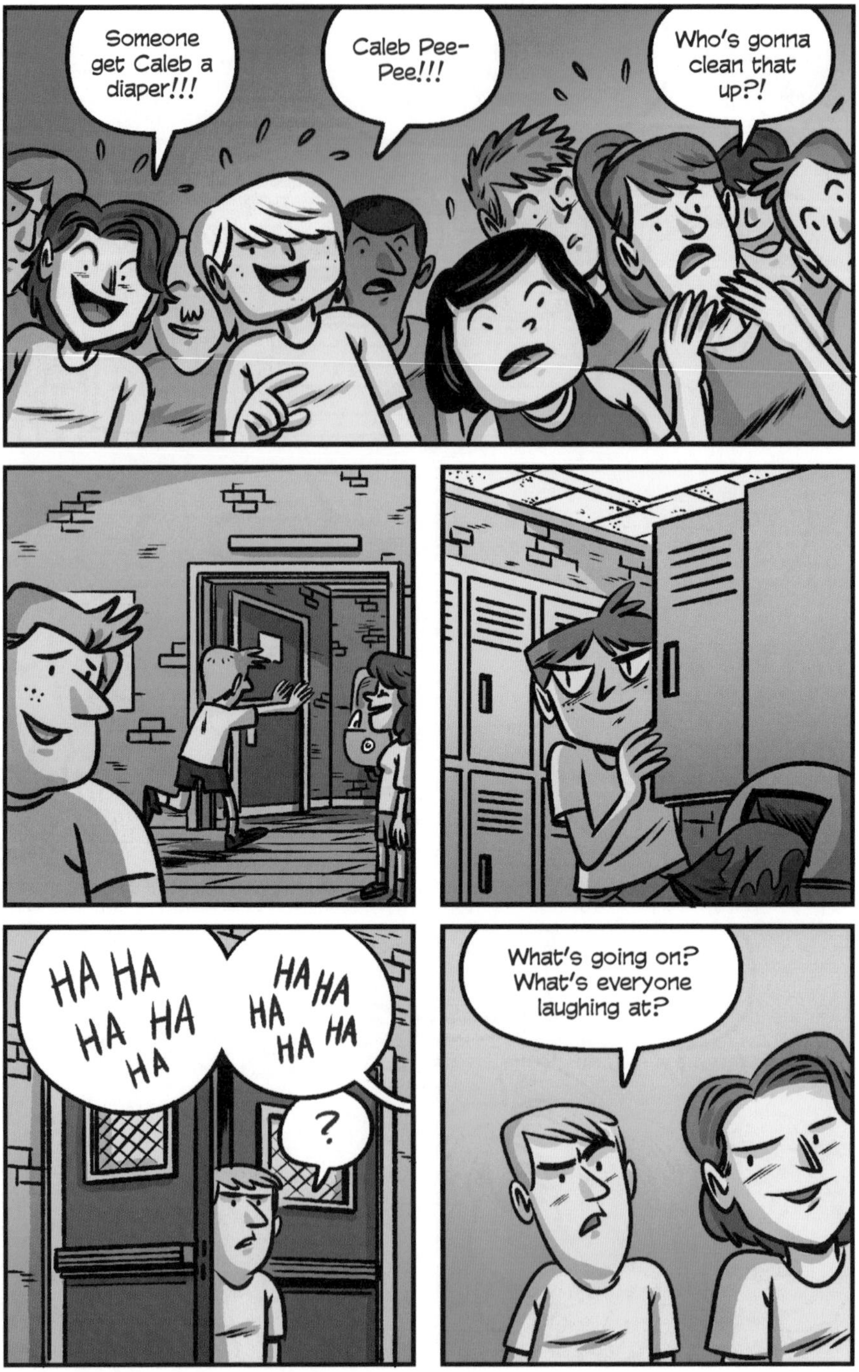
Someone get Caleb a diaper!!!
Caleb Pee-Pee!!!
Who's gonna clean that up?!
HA HA HA HA HA
HA HA HA HA HA HA
?
What's going on? What's everyone laughing at?

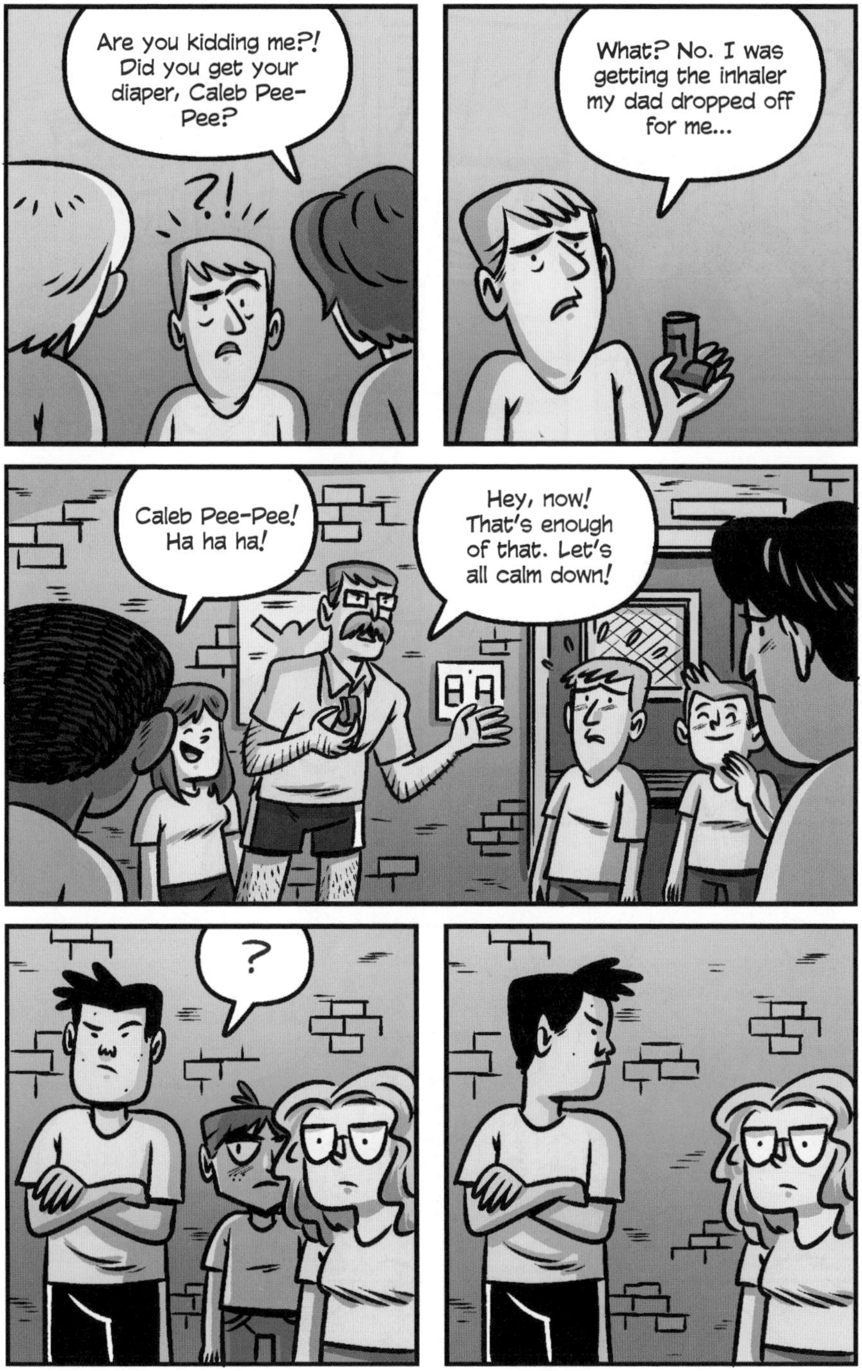

Are you kidding me?! Did you get your diaper, Caleb Pee-Pee?
?!
What? No. I was getting the inhaler my dad dropped off for me...
Caleb Pee-Pee! Ha ha ha!
Hey, now! That's enough of that. Let's all calm down!
?

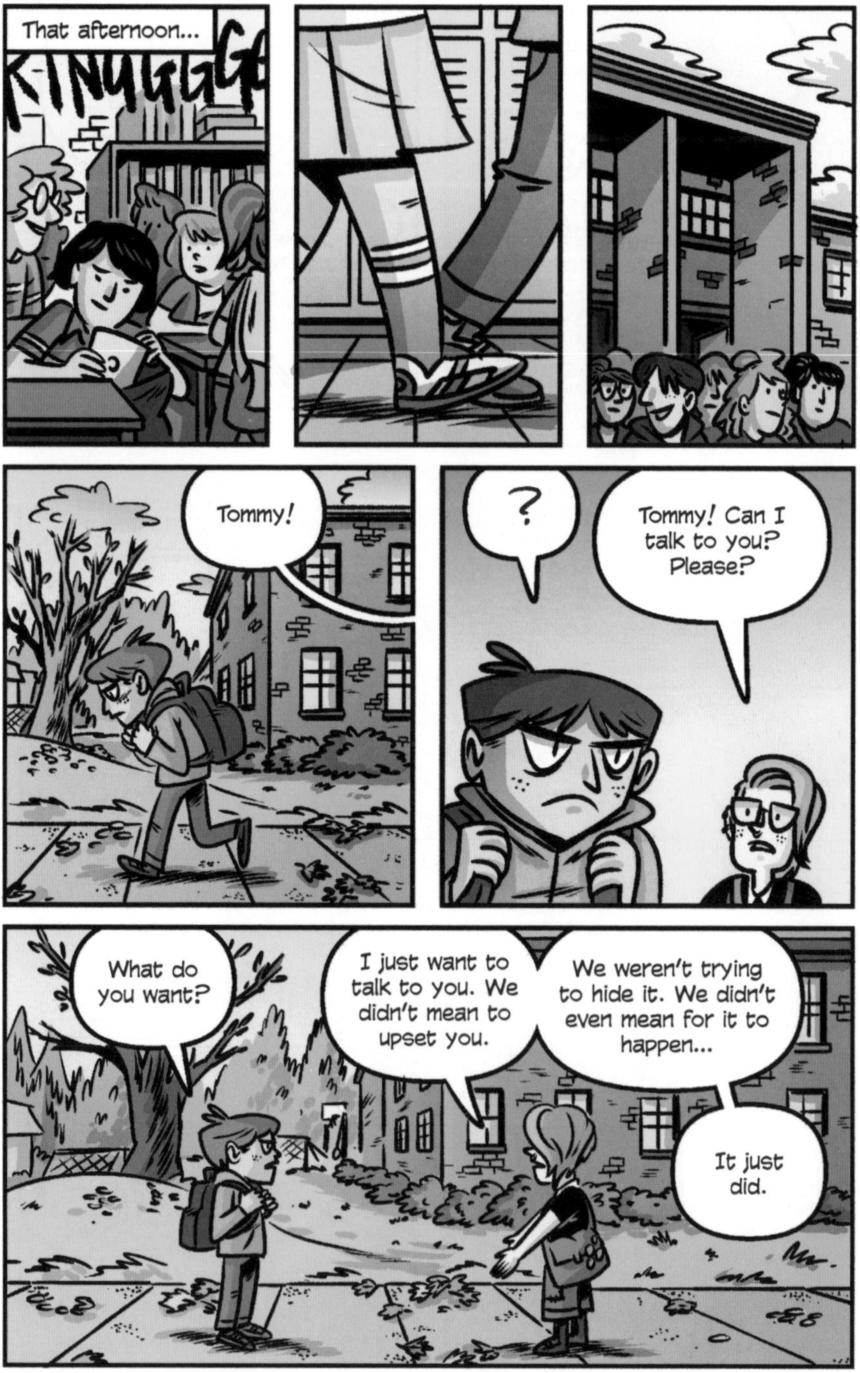
That afternoon...
KINGGGG
Tommy!
?
Tommy! Can I talk to you? Please?
What do you want?
I just want to talk to you. We didn't mean to upset you.
We weren't trying to hide it. We didn't even mean for it to happen...
It just did.

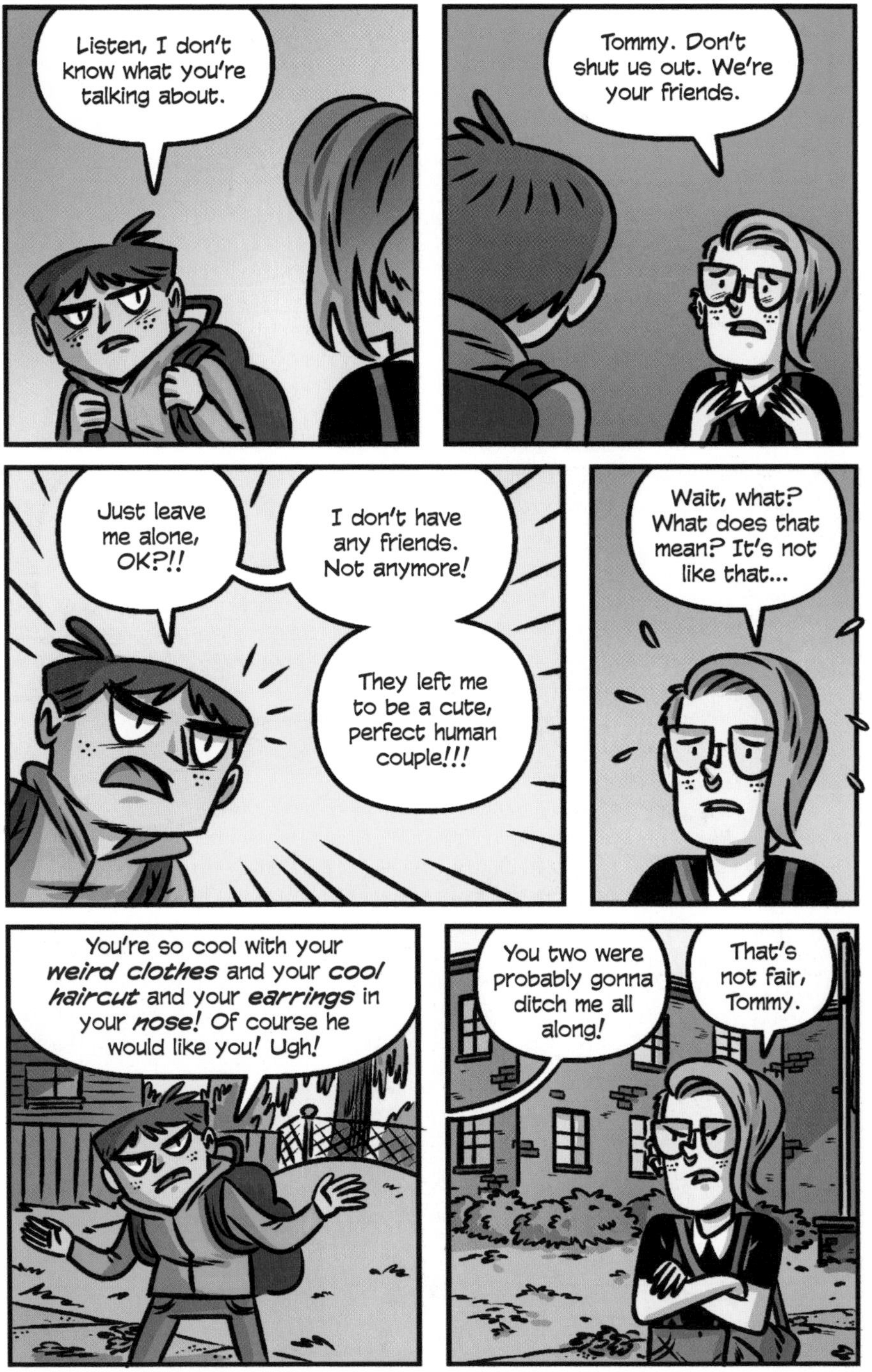

Listen, I don't know what you're talking about.
Tommy. Don't shut us out. We're your friends.
Just leave me alone, OK?!!
I don't have any friends. Not anymore!
They left me to be a cute, perfect human couple!!!
Wait, what? What does that mean? It's not like that...
You're so cool with your *weird clothes* and your *cool haircut* and your *earrings* in your *nose*! Of course he would like you! Ugh!
You two were probably gonna ditch me all along!
That's not fair, Tommy.

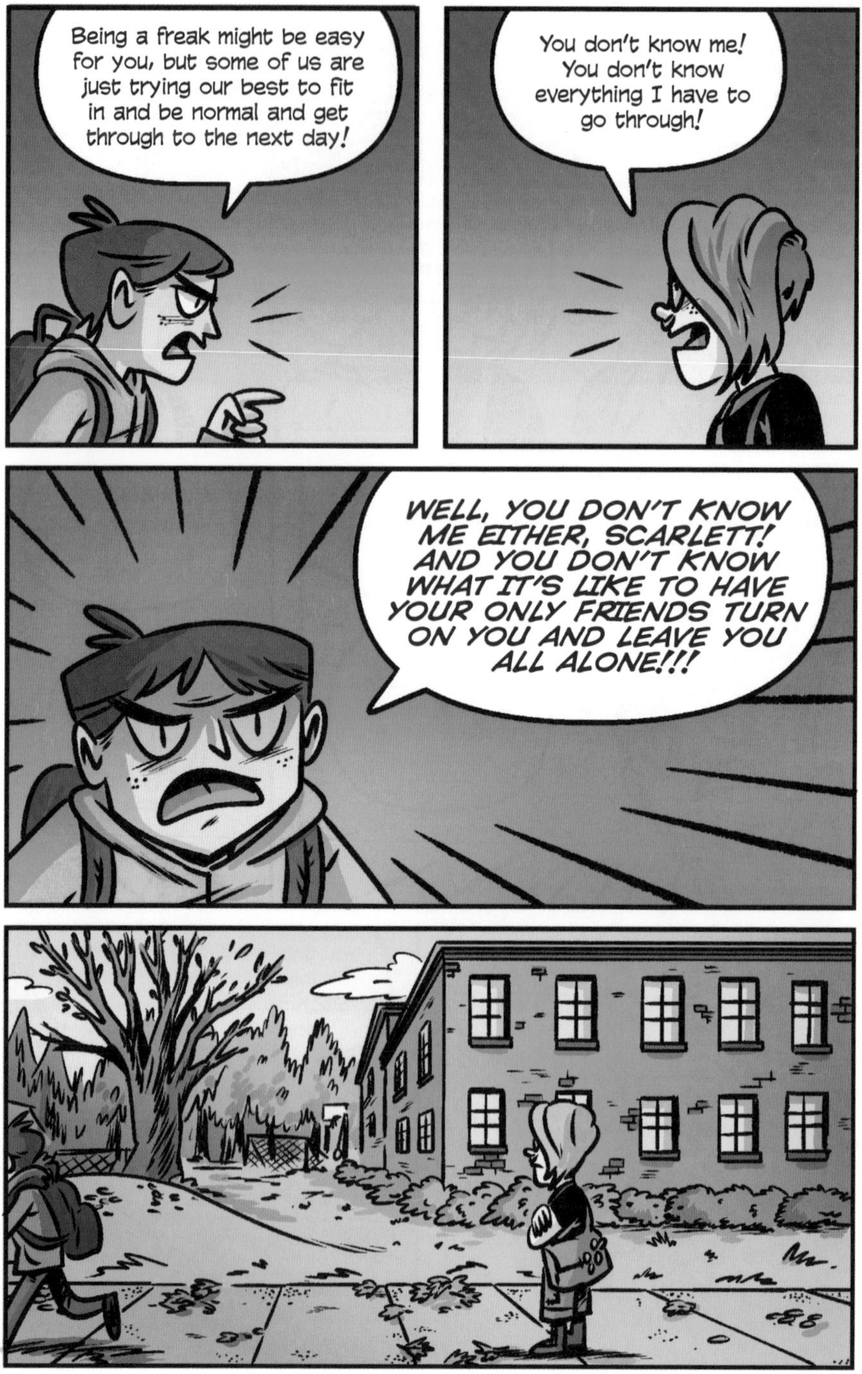
Being a freak might be easy for you, but some of us are just trying our best to fit in and be normal and get through to the next day!
You don't know me! You don't know everything I have to go through!
WELL, YOU DON'T KNOW ME EITHER, SCARLETT! AND YOU DON'T KNOW WHAT IT'S LIKE TO HAVE YOUR ONLY FRIENDS TURN ON YOU AND LEAVE YOU ALL ALONE!!!

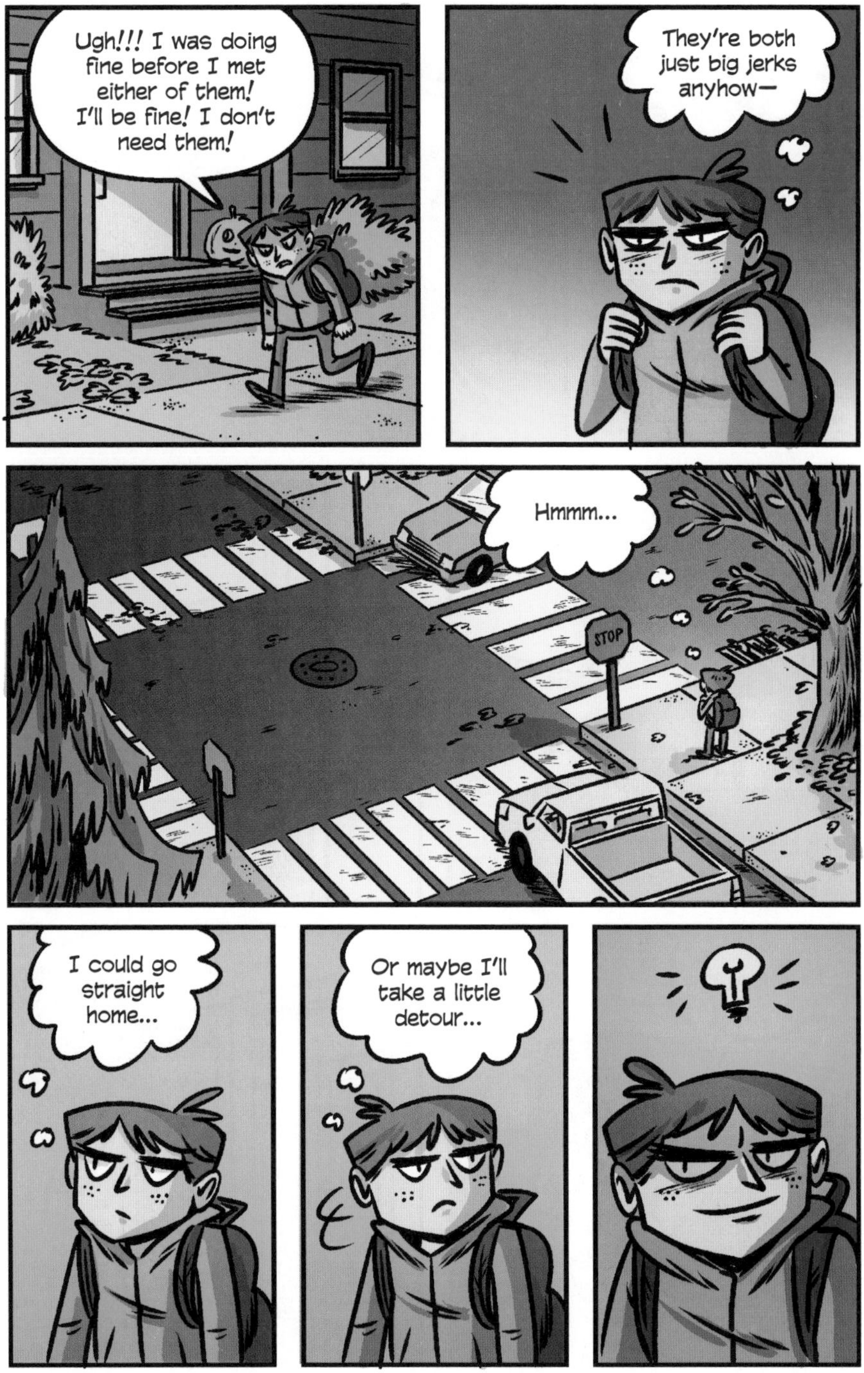
Ugh!!! I was doing fine before I met either of them! I'll be fine! I don't need them!
They're both just big jerks anyhow—
Hmmm...
STOP
I could go straight home...
Or maybe I'll take a little detour...

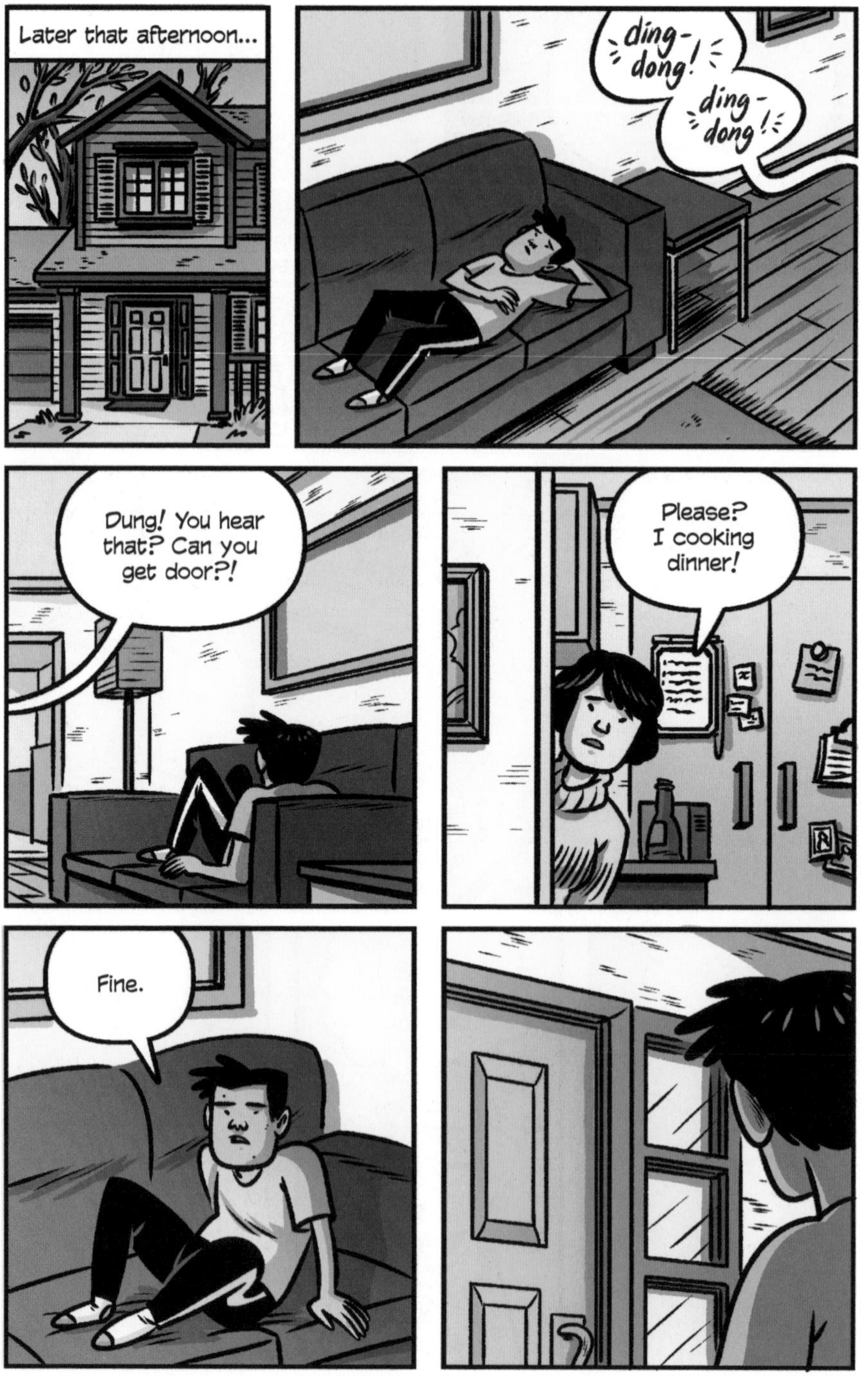
Later that afternoon...
ding-dong!
ding-dong!
Dung! You hear that? Can you get door?!
Please? I cooking dinner!
Fine.

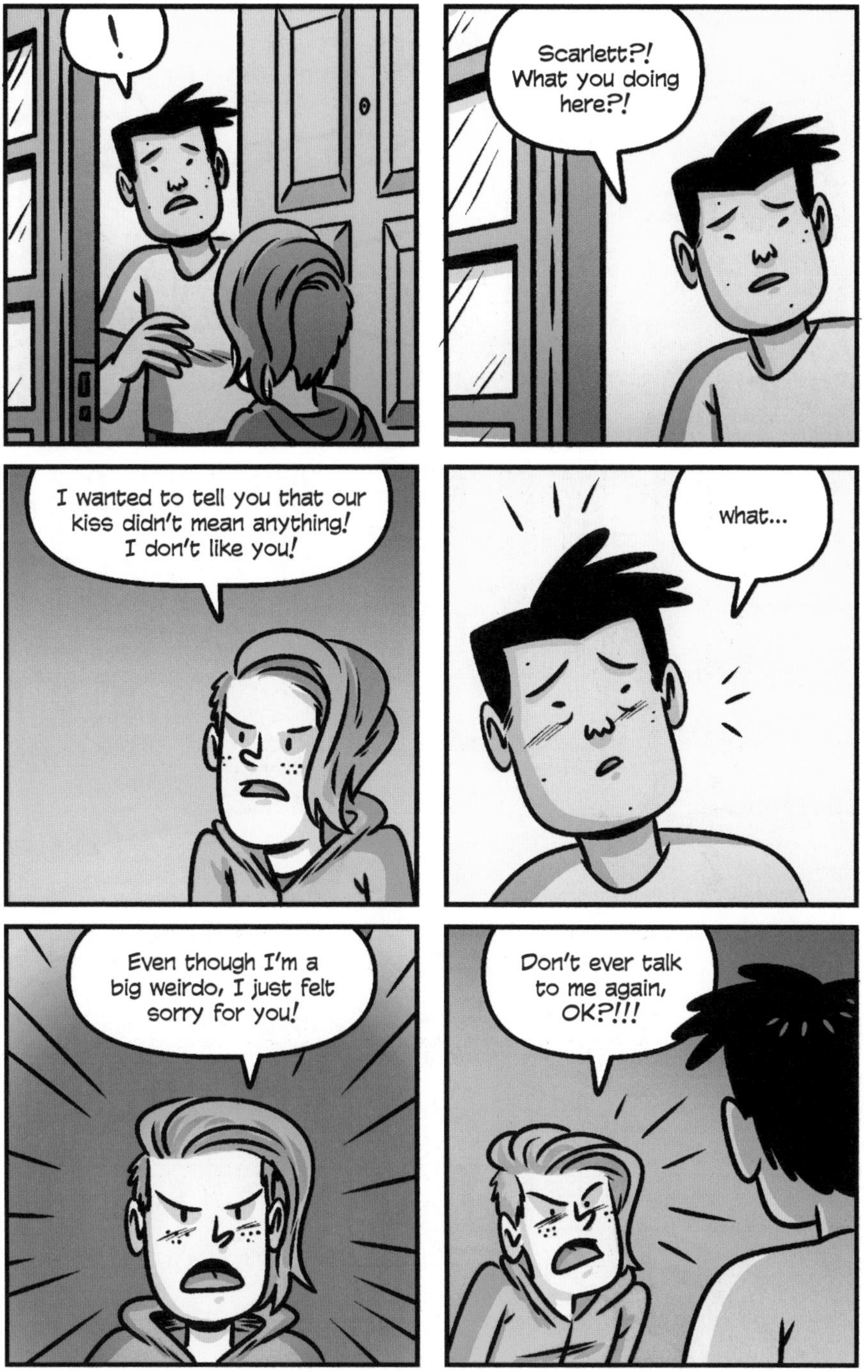
!
Scarlett?! What you doing here?!
I wanted to tell you that our kiss didn't mean anything! I don't like you!
what...
Even though I'm a big weirdo, I just felt sorry for you!
Don't ever talk to me again, OK?!!!

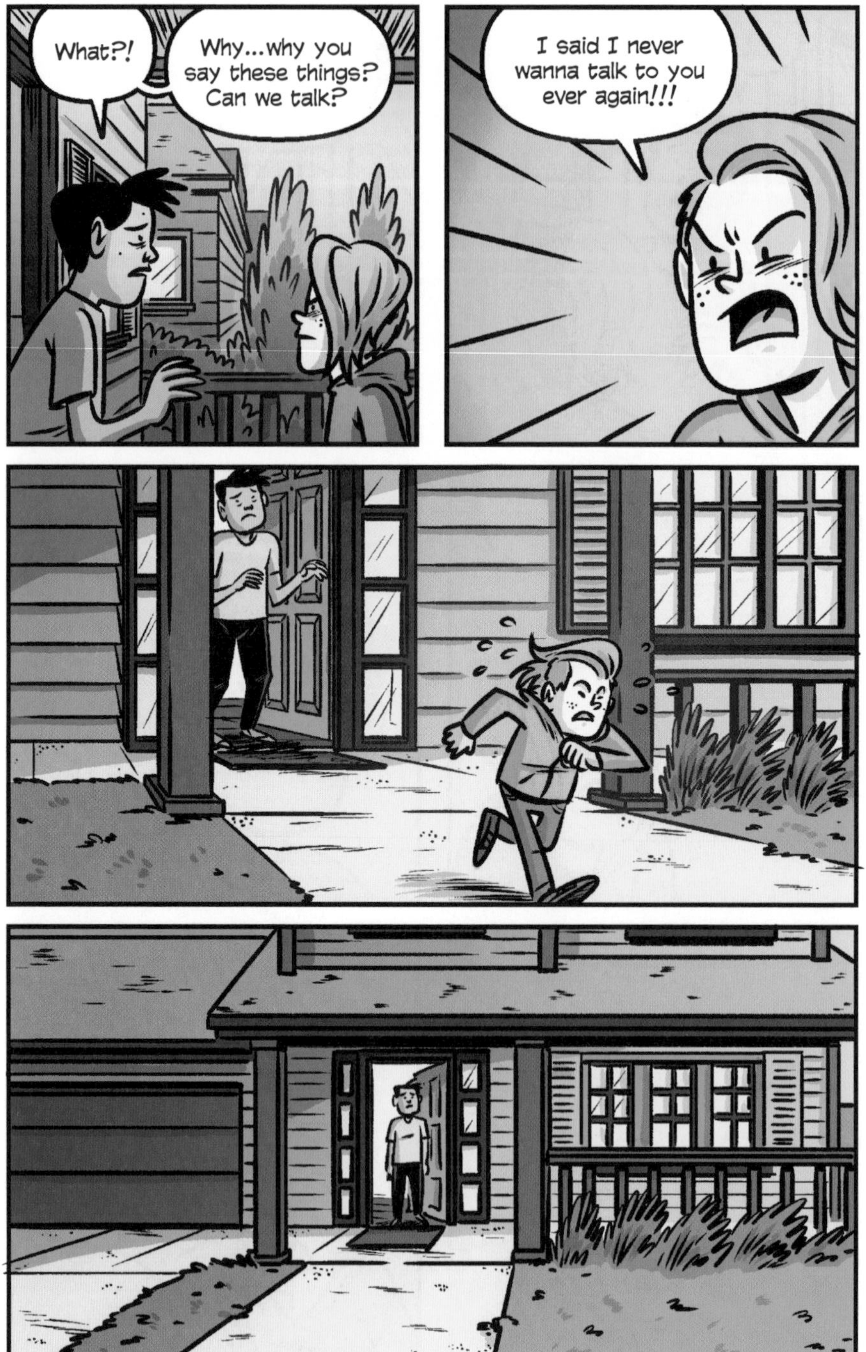
What?!
Why...why you say these things? Can we talk?
I said I never wanna talk to you ever again!!!

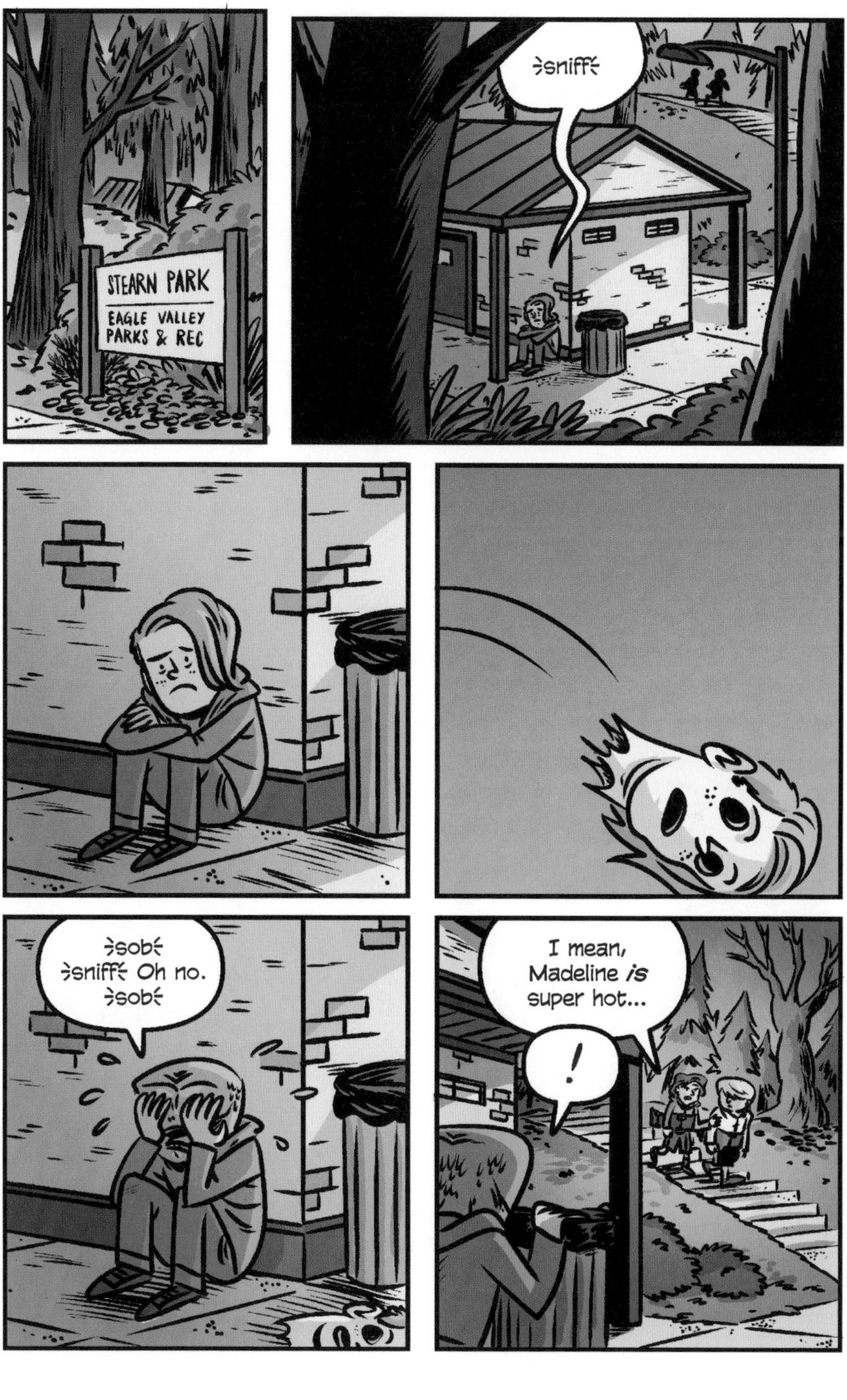
STEARN PARK
EAGLE VALLEY PARKS & REC
sniff
sob
sniff Oh no.
sob
I mean, Madeline *is* super hot...
!

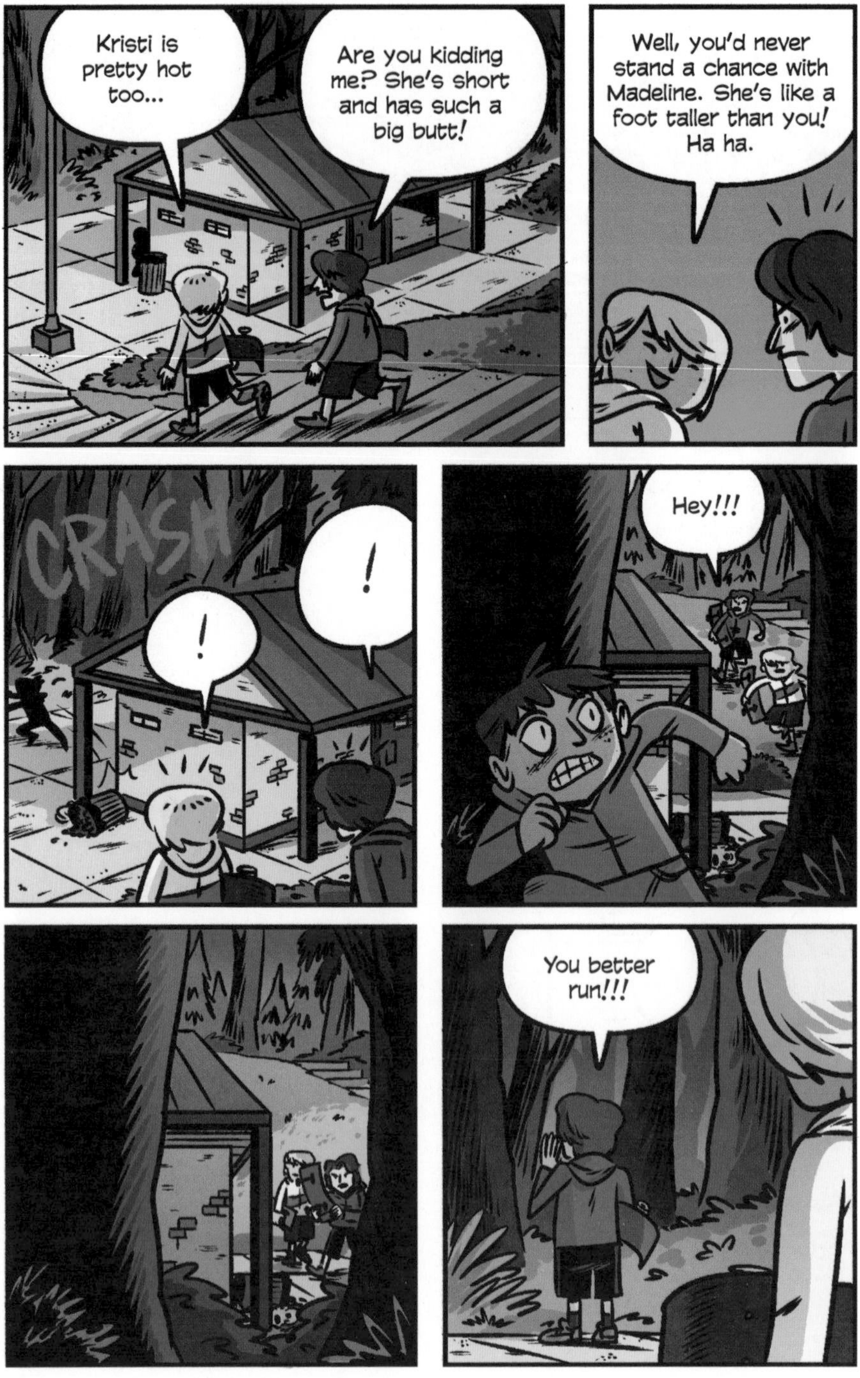
Kristi is pretty hot too...
Are you kidding me? She's short and has such a big butt!
Well, you'd never stand a chance with Madeline. She's like a foot taller than you! Ha ha.
CRASH
!
!
Hey!!!
You better run!!!

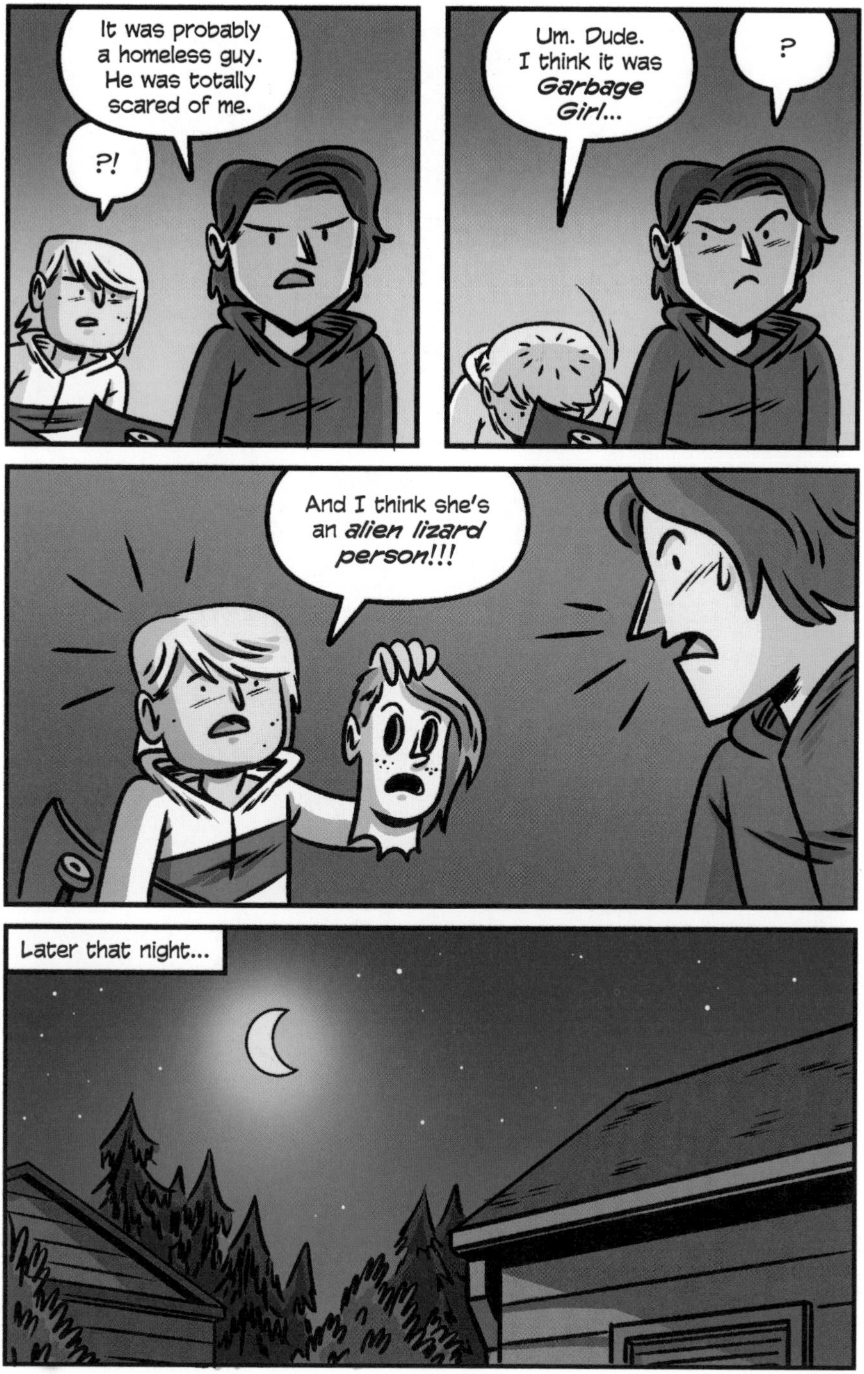
It was probably a homeless guy. He was totally scared of me.
?!
Um. Dude. I think it was *Garbage Girl*...
?
And I think she's an *alien lizard person*!!!
Later that night...

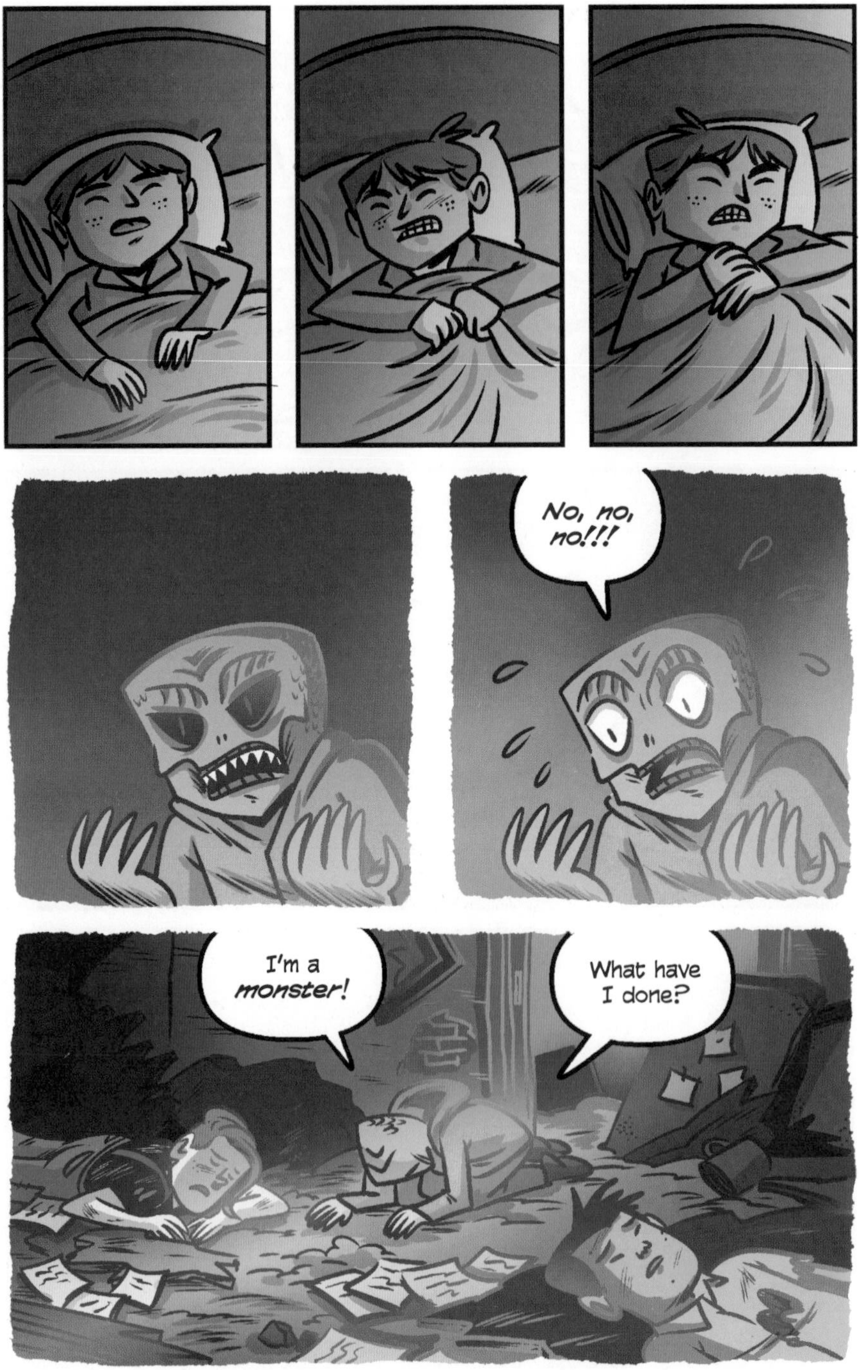
No, no, no!!!
I'm a *monster*!
What have I done?

CHAPTER 9

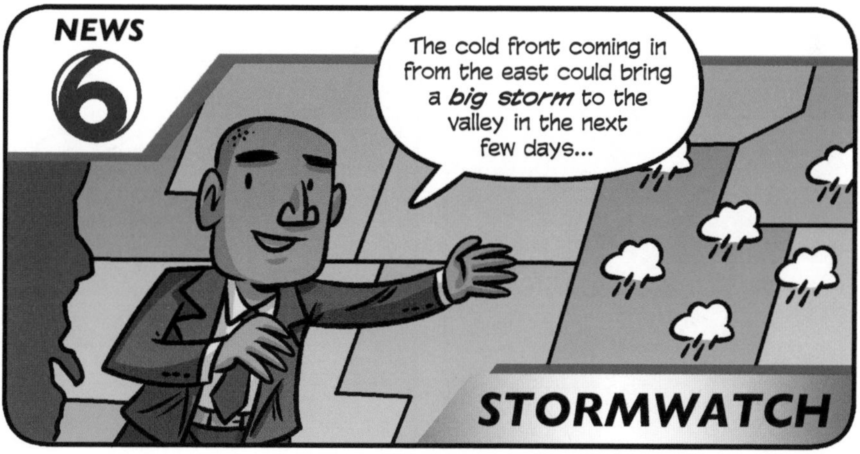
NEWS 6
The cold front coming in from the east could bring a *big storm* to the valley in the next few days...
STORMWATCH

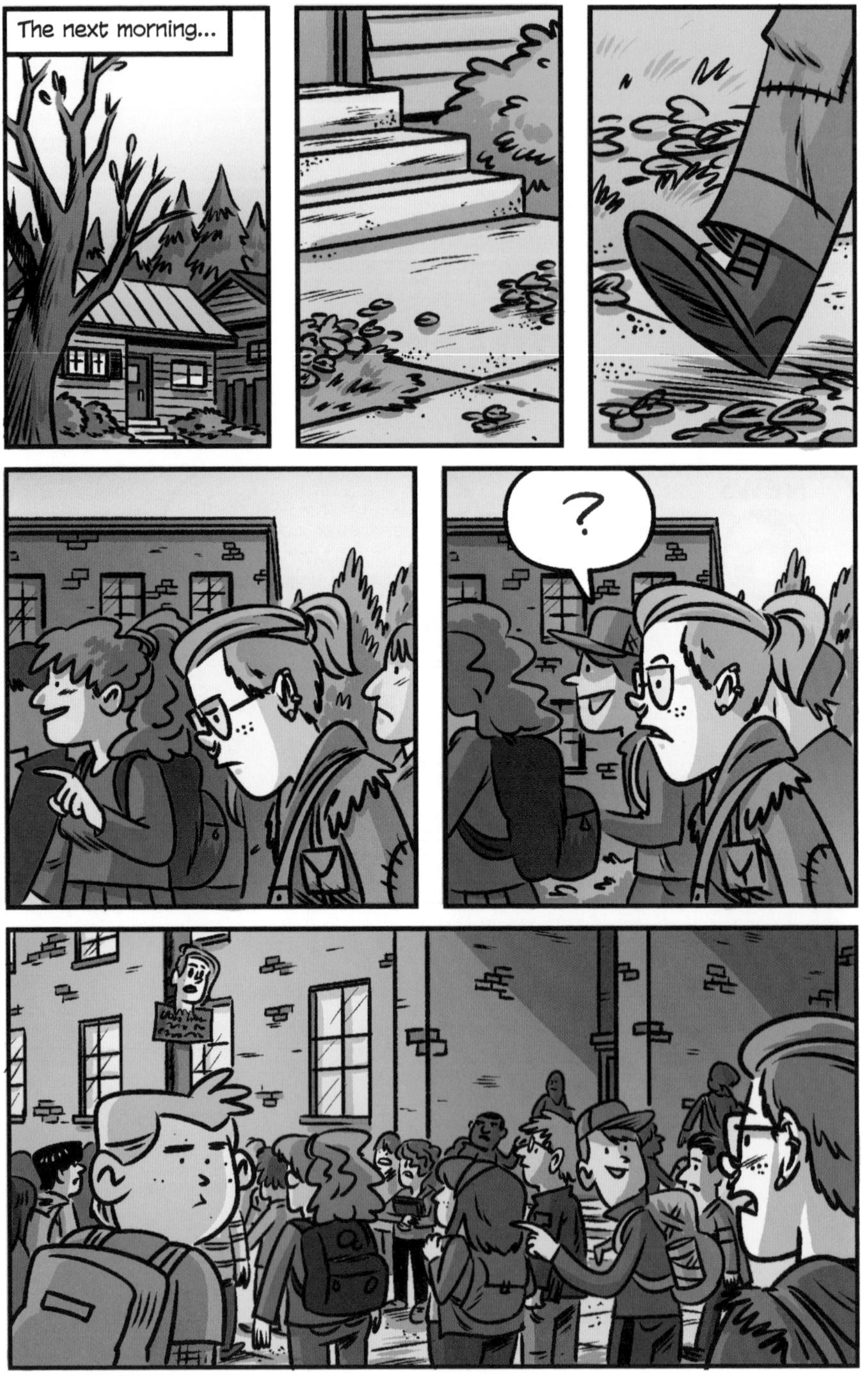
The next morning...
?

HA HA HA HA HA HA HA HA HA HA HA HA
...
GARBAGE GIRL IS AN ALIEN LIZARD FREAK!
GARBAGE GIRL IS AN ALIEN LIZARD FREAK!

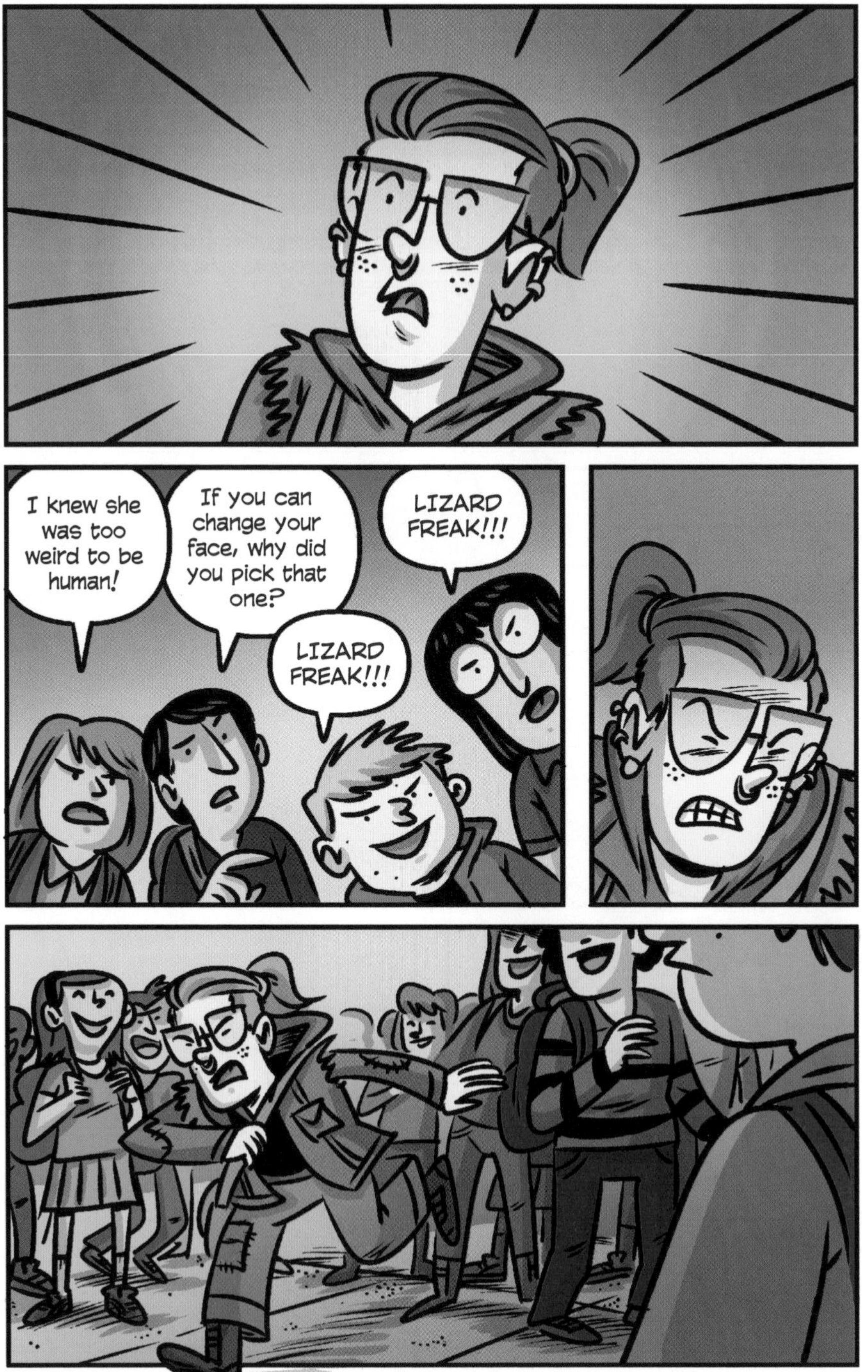
I knew she was too weird to be human!
If you can change your face, why did you pick that one?
LIZARD FREAK!!!
LIZARD FREAK!!!

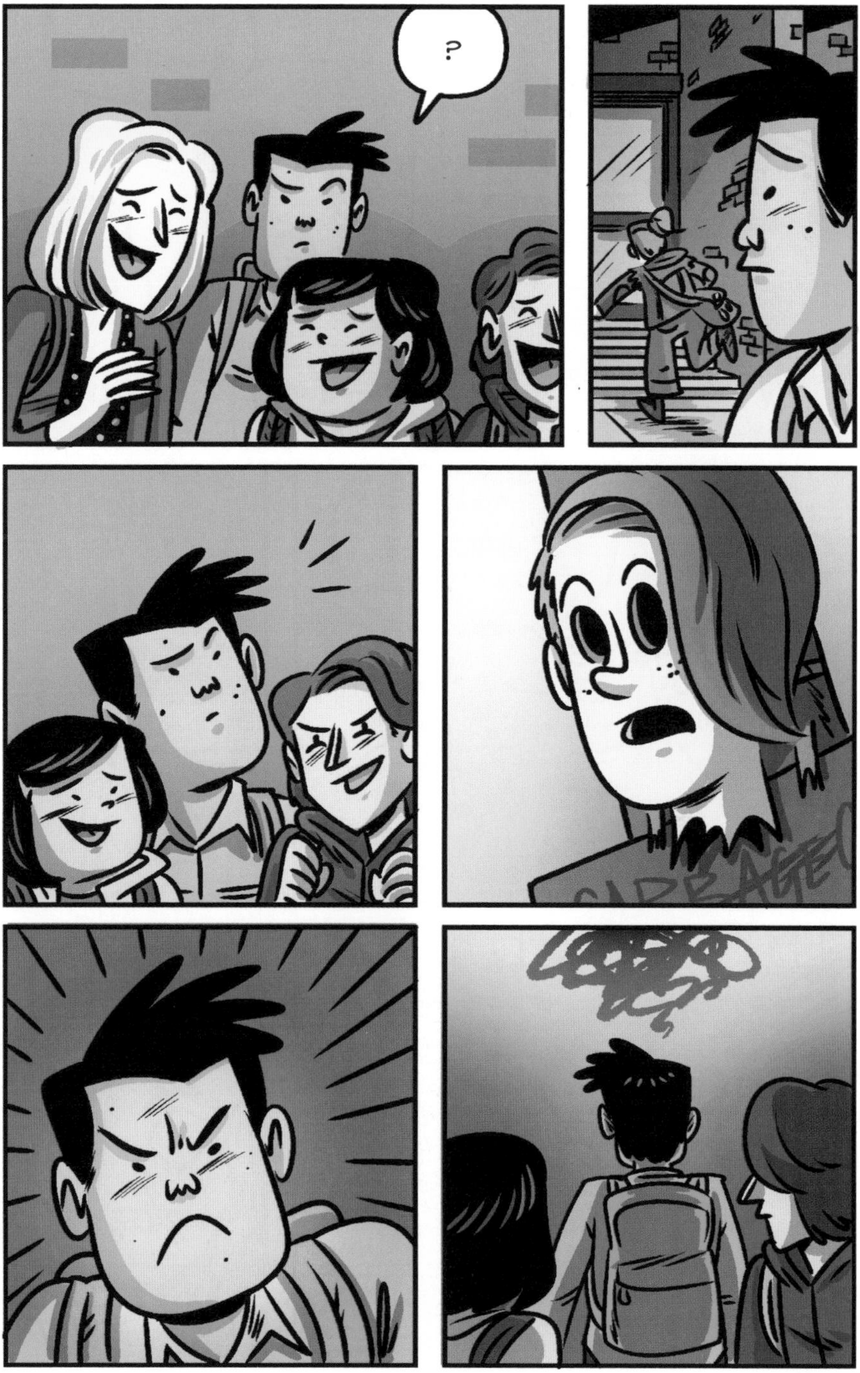
?

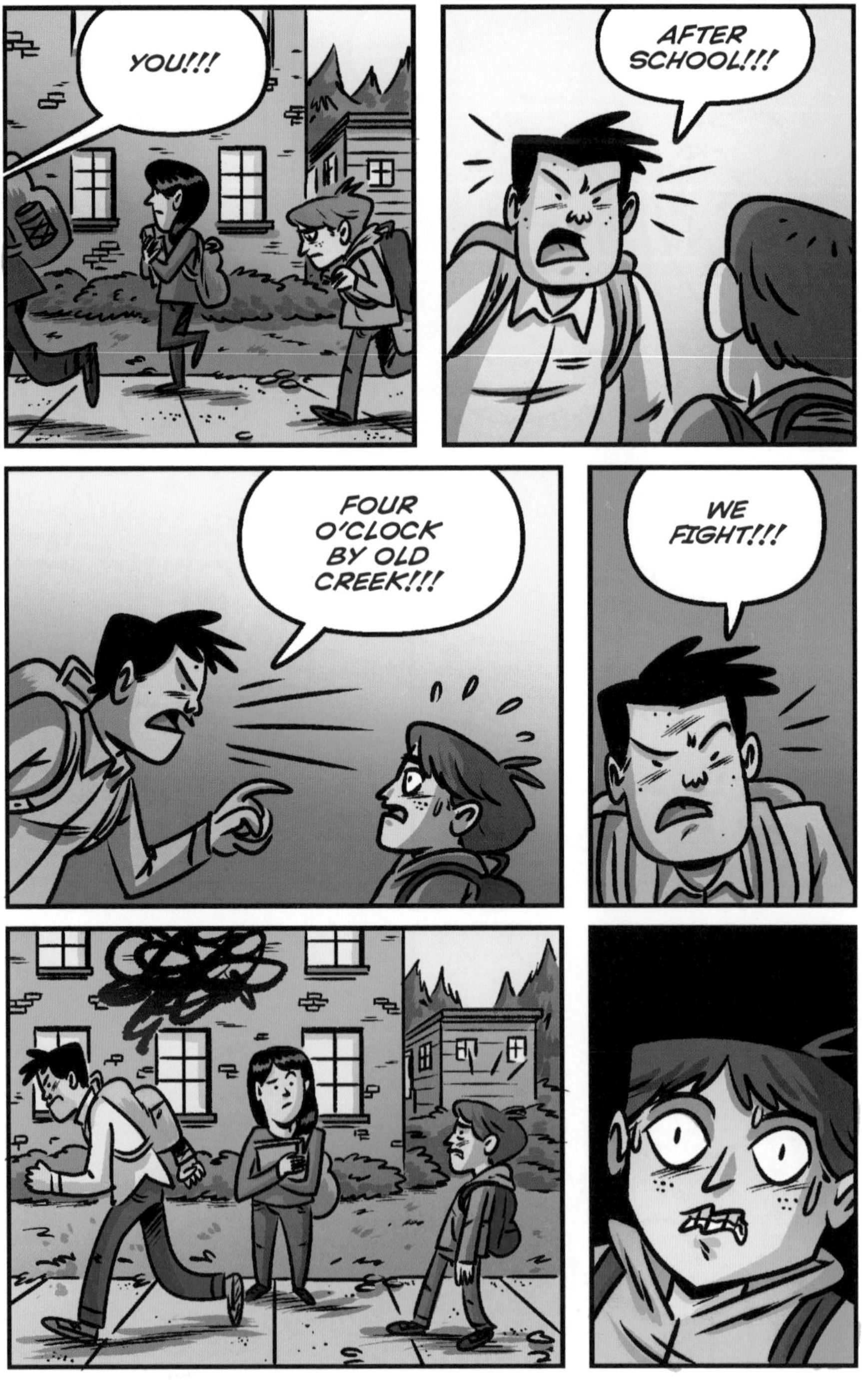
YOU!!!
AFTER SCHOOL!!!
FOUR O'CLOCK BY OLD CREEK!!!
WE FIGHT!!!

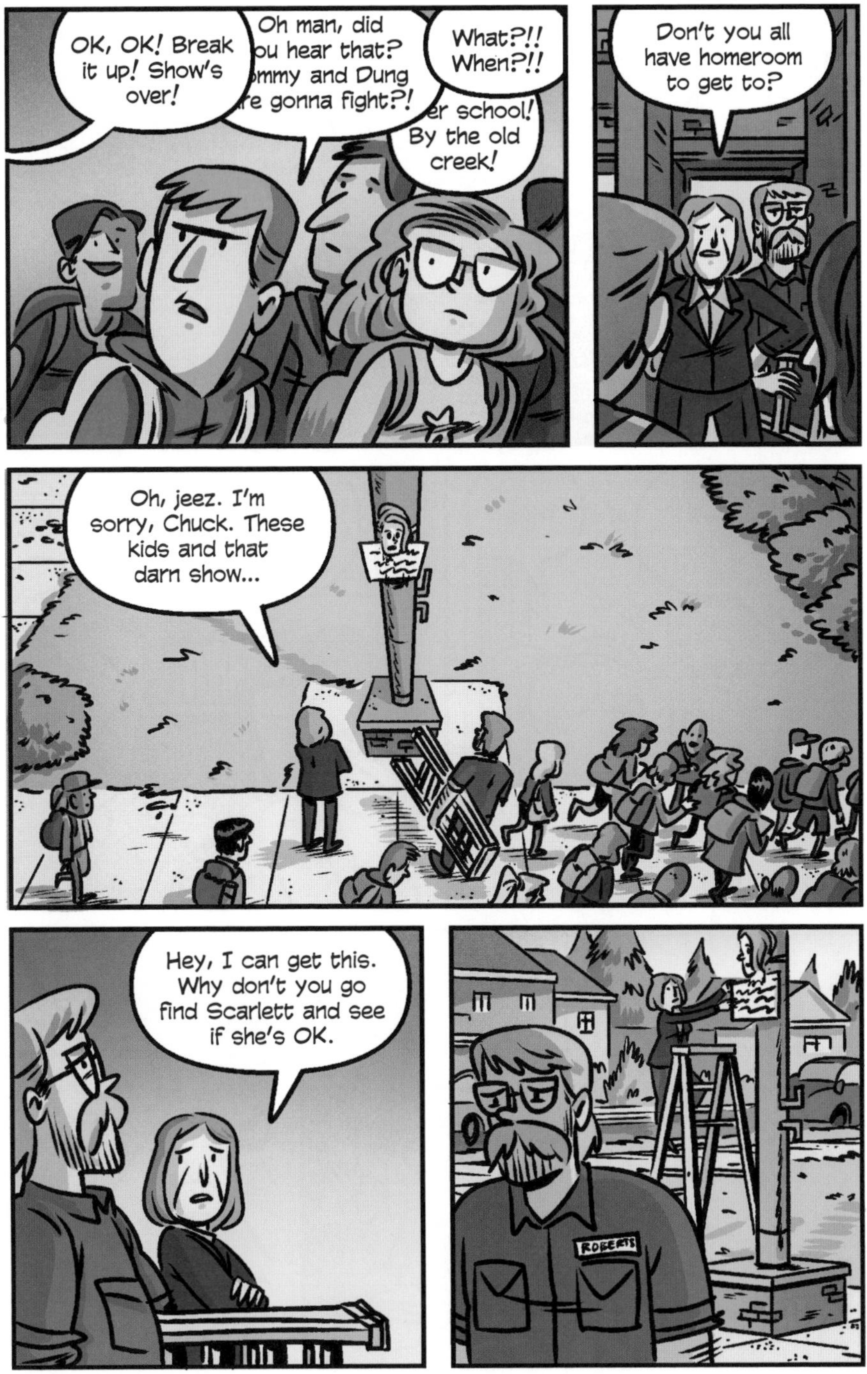
OK, OK! Break it up! Show's over!
Oh man, did ou hear that? ommy and Dung re gonna fight?!
What?!! When?!!
er school! By the old creek!
Don't you all have homeroom to get to?
Oh, jeez. I'm sorry, Chuck. These kids and that darn show...
Hey, I can get this. Why don't you go find Scarlett and see if she's OK.
ROBERTS

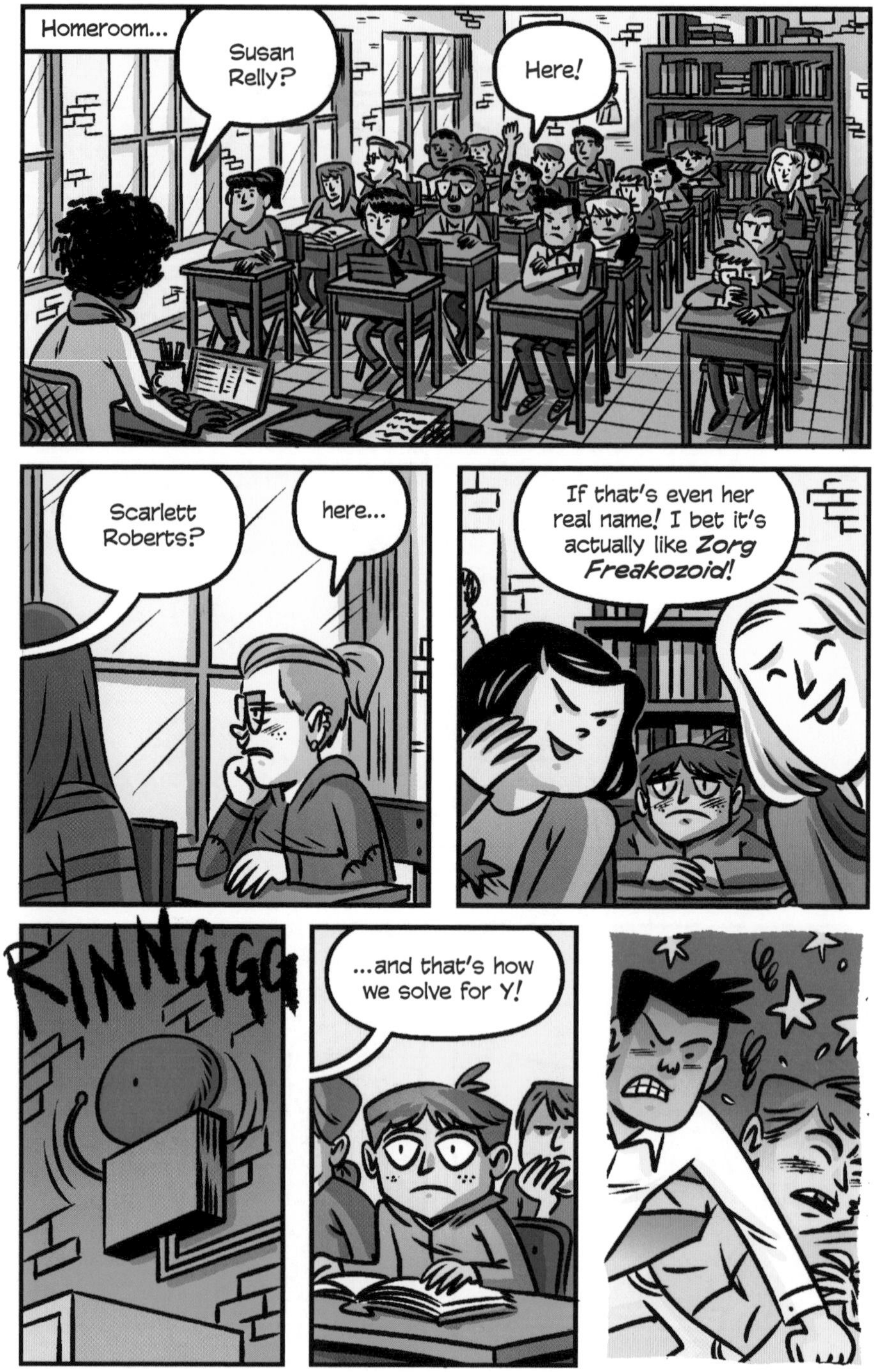
Homeroom...
Susan Relly?
Here!
Scarlett Roberts?
here...
If that's even her real name! I bet it's actually like *Zorg Freakozoid*!
RINNGGG
...and that's how we solve for Y!

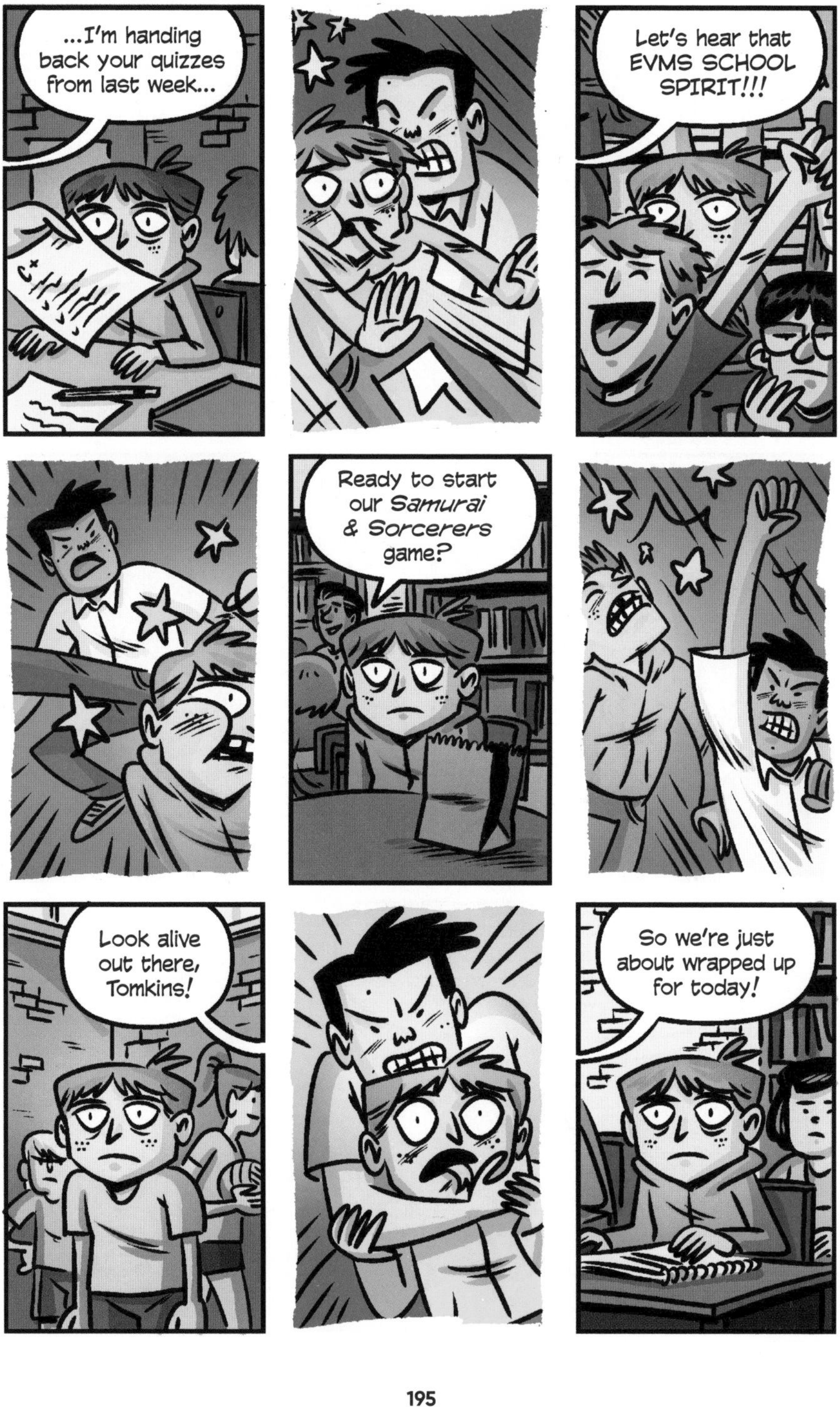
...I'm handing back your quizzes from last week...
C+
Let's hear that EVMS SCHOOL SPIRIT!!!
Ready to start our *Samurai & Sorcerers* game?
Look alive out there, Tomkins!
So we're just about wrapped up for today!

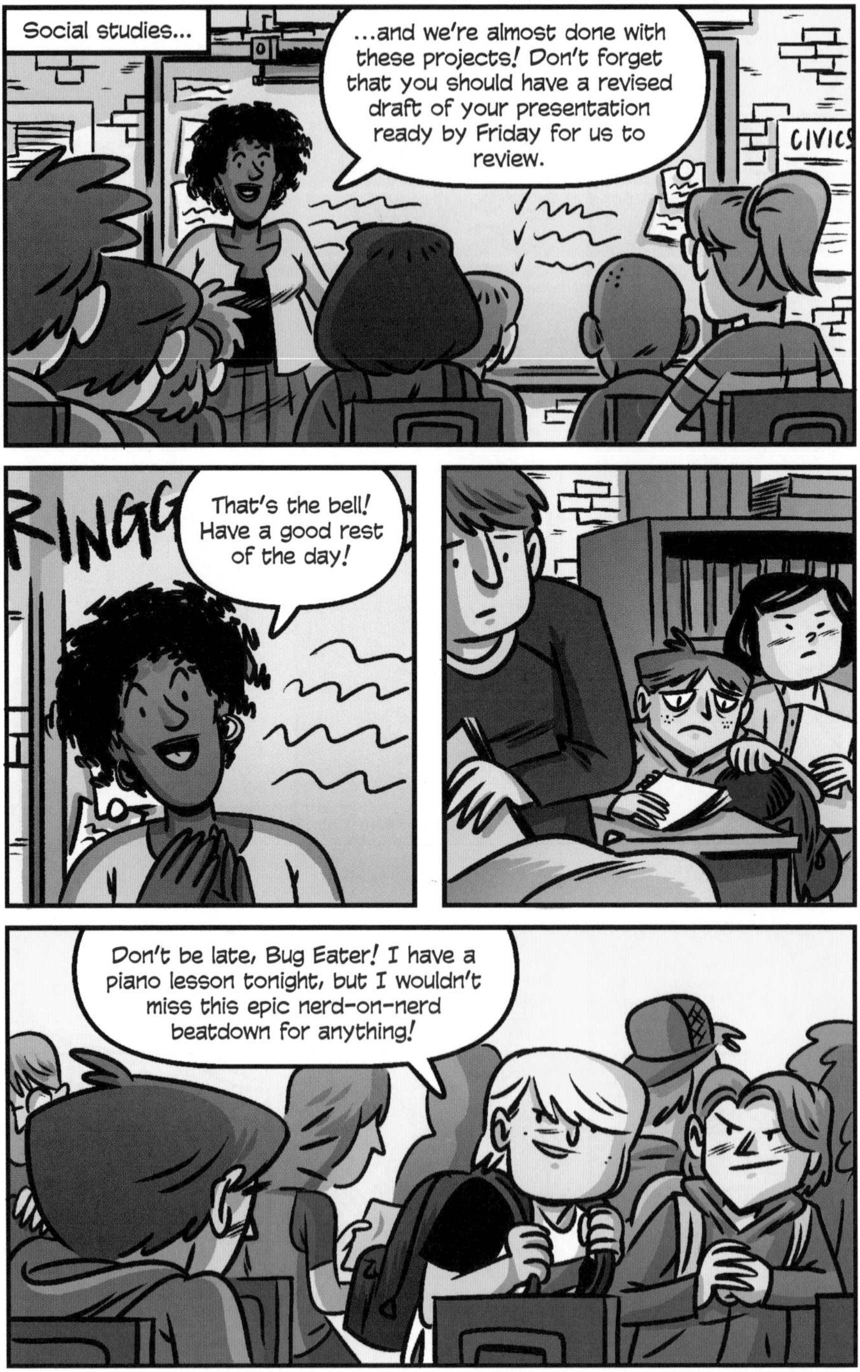
Social studies...
...and we're almost done with these projects! Don't forget that you should have a revised draft of your presentation ready by Friday for us to review.
CIVICS
RINGG
That's the bell! Have a good rest of the day!
Don't be late, Bug Eater! I have a piano lesson tonight, but I wouldn't miss this epic nerd-on-nerd beatdown for anything!

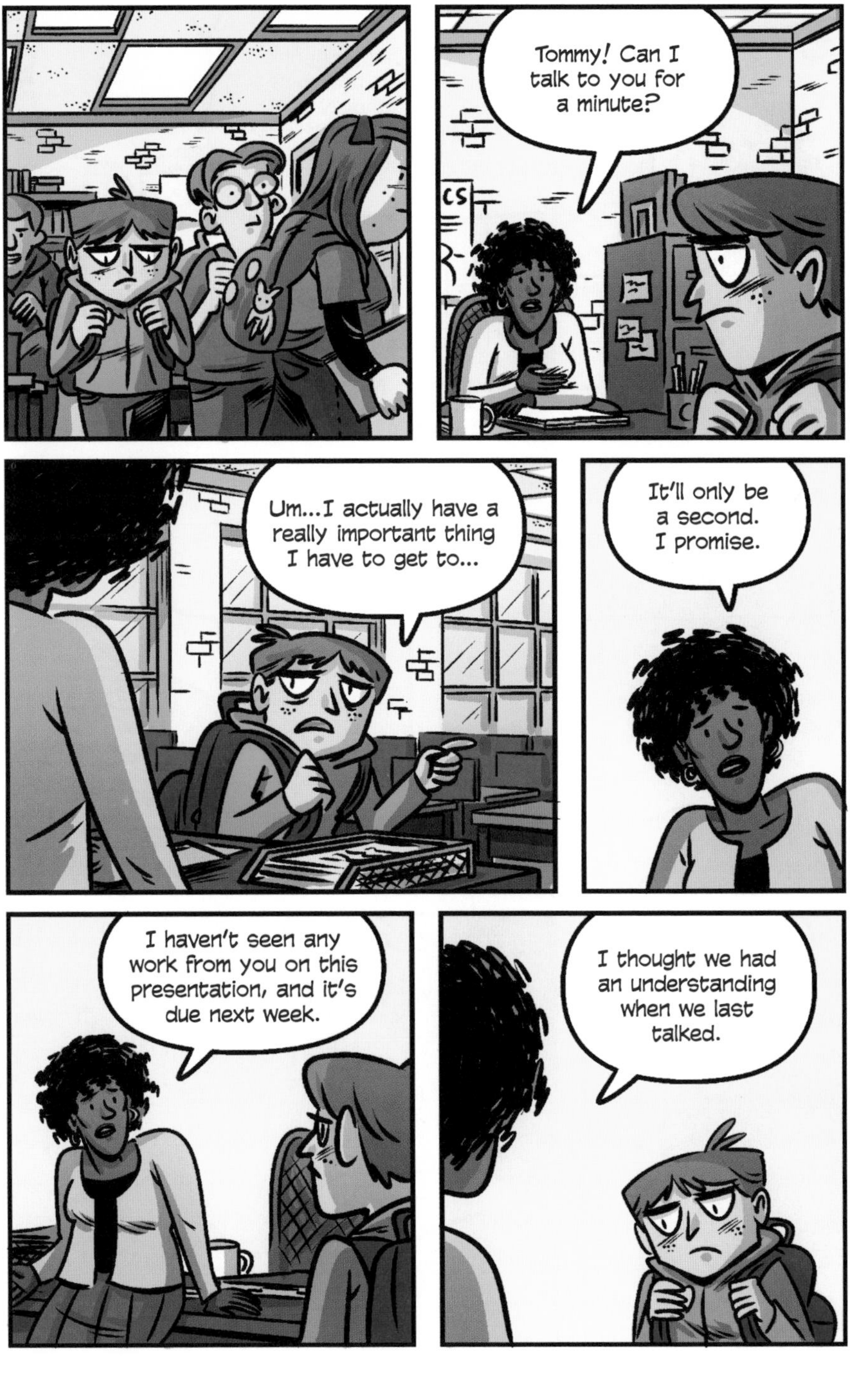
Tommy! Can I talk to you for a minute?
Um...I actually have a really important thing I have to get to...
It'll only be a second. I promise.
I haven't seen any work from you on this presentation, and it's due next week.
I thought we had an understanding when we last talked.

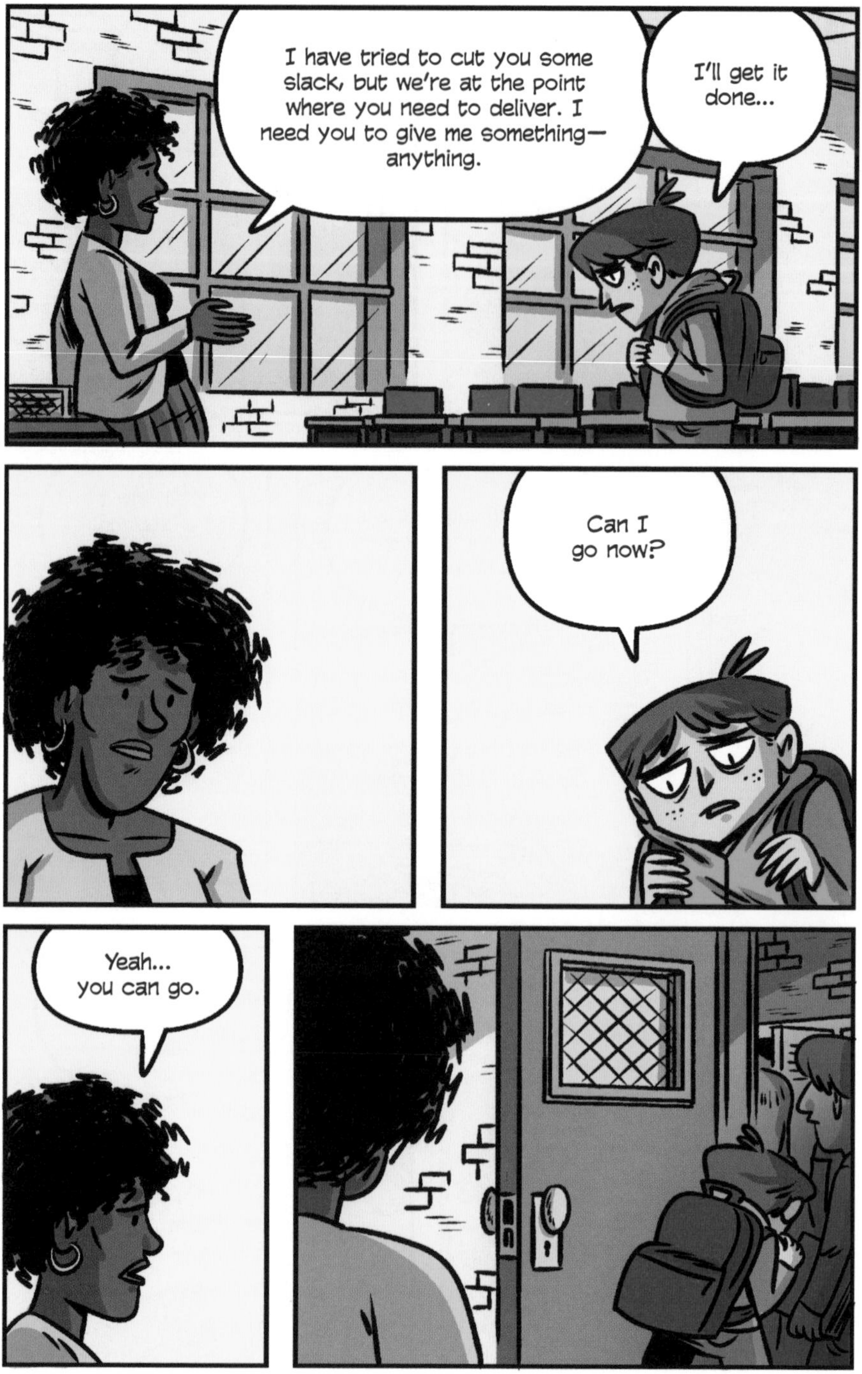
I have tried to cut you some slack, but we're at the point where you need to deliver. I need you to give me something—anything.
I'll get it done...
Can I go now?
Yeah... you can go.

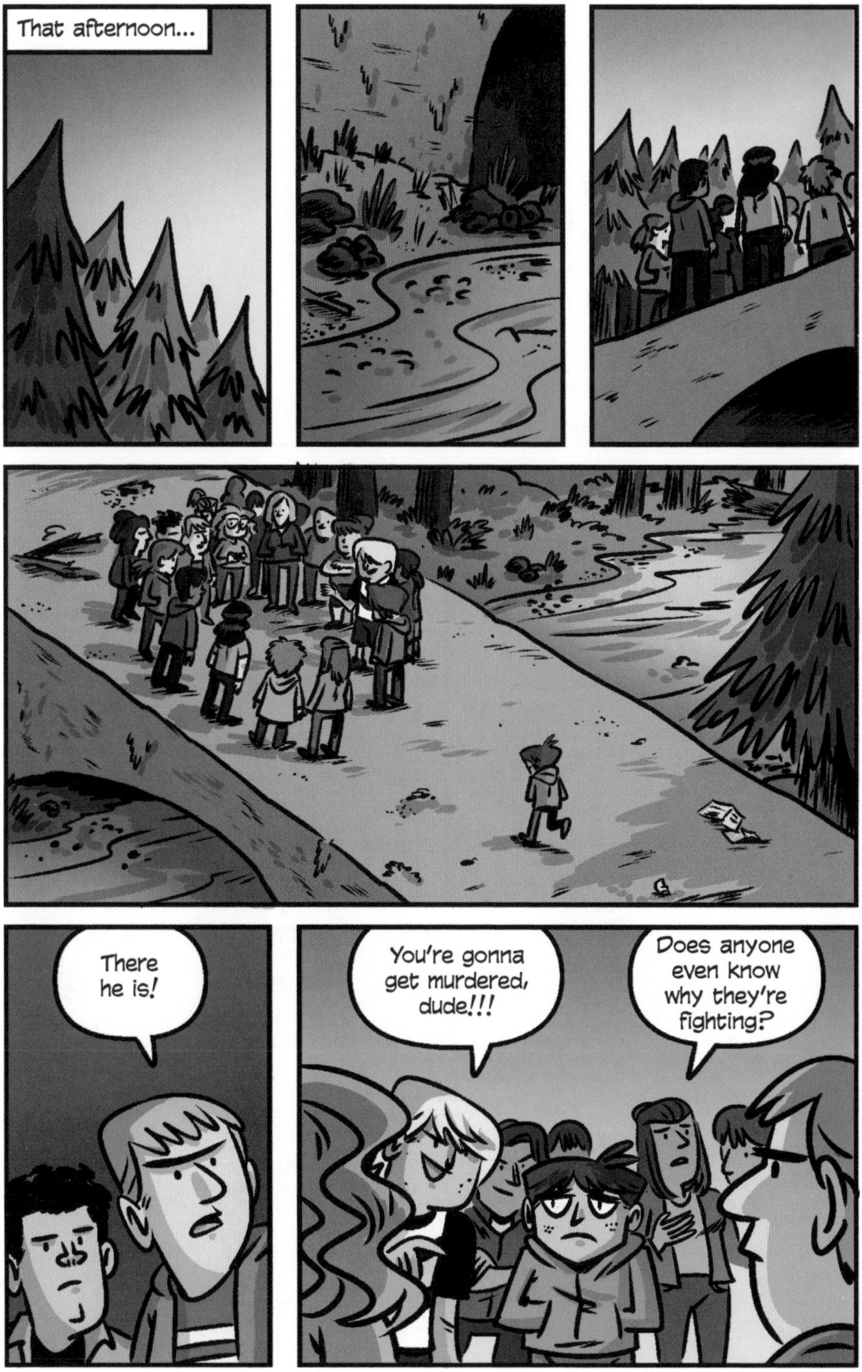
That afternoon...
There he is!
You're gonna get murdered, dude!!!
Does anyone even know why they're fighting?

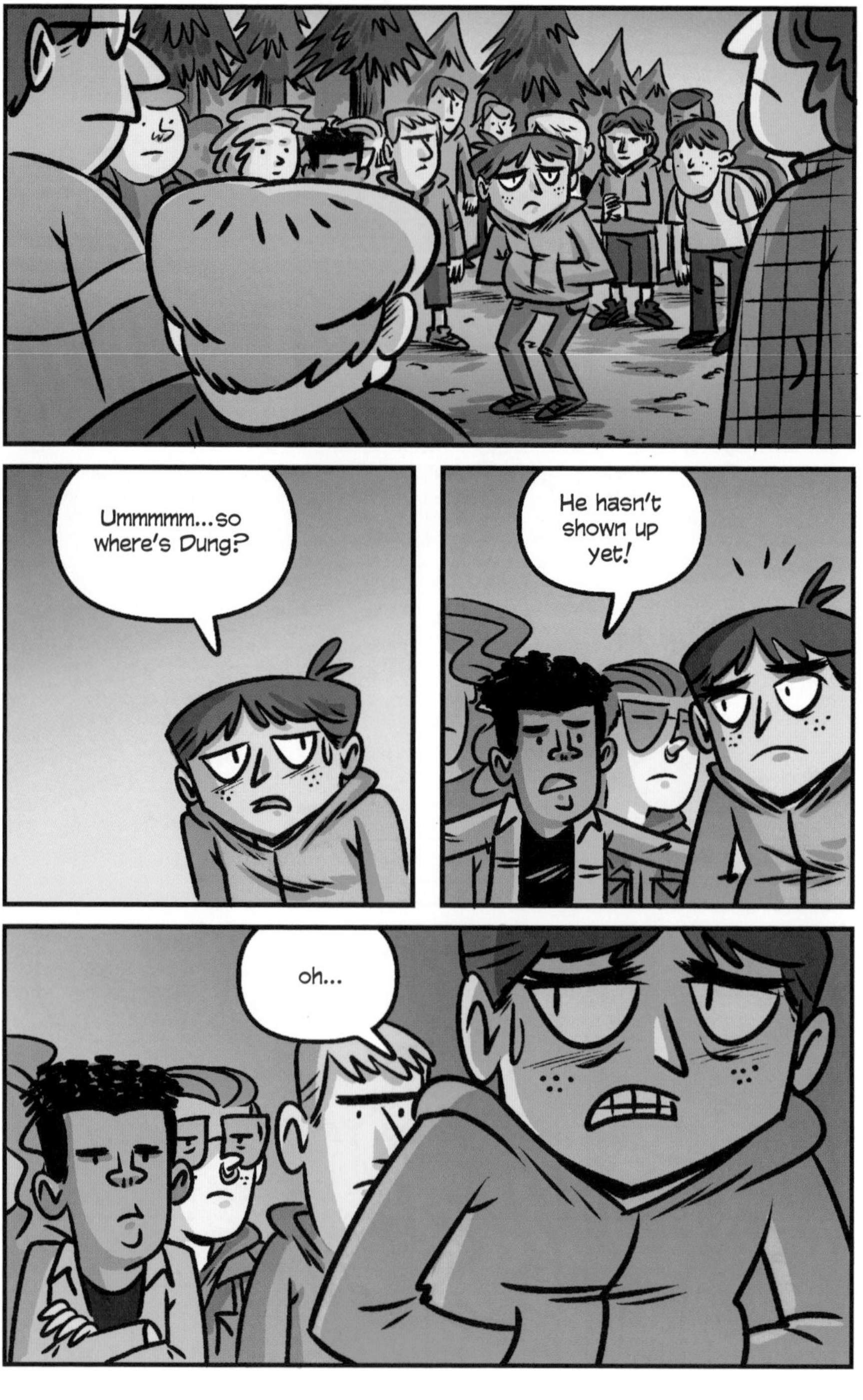
Ummmmm...so where's Dung?
He hasn't shown up yet!
oh...

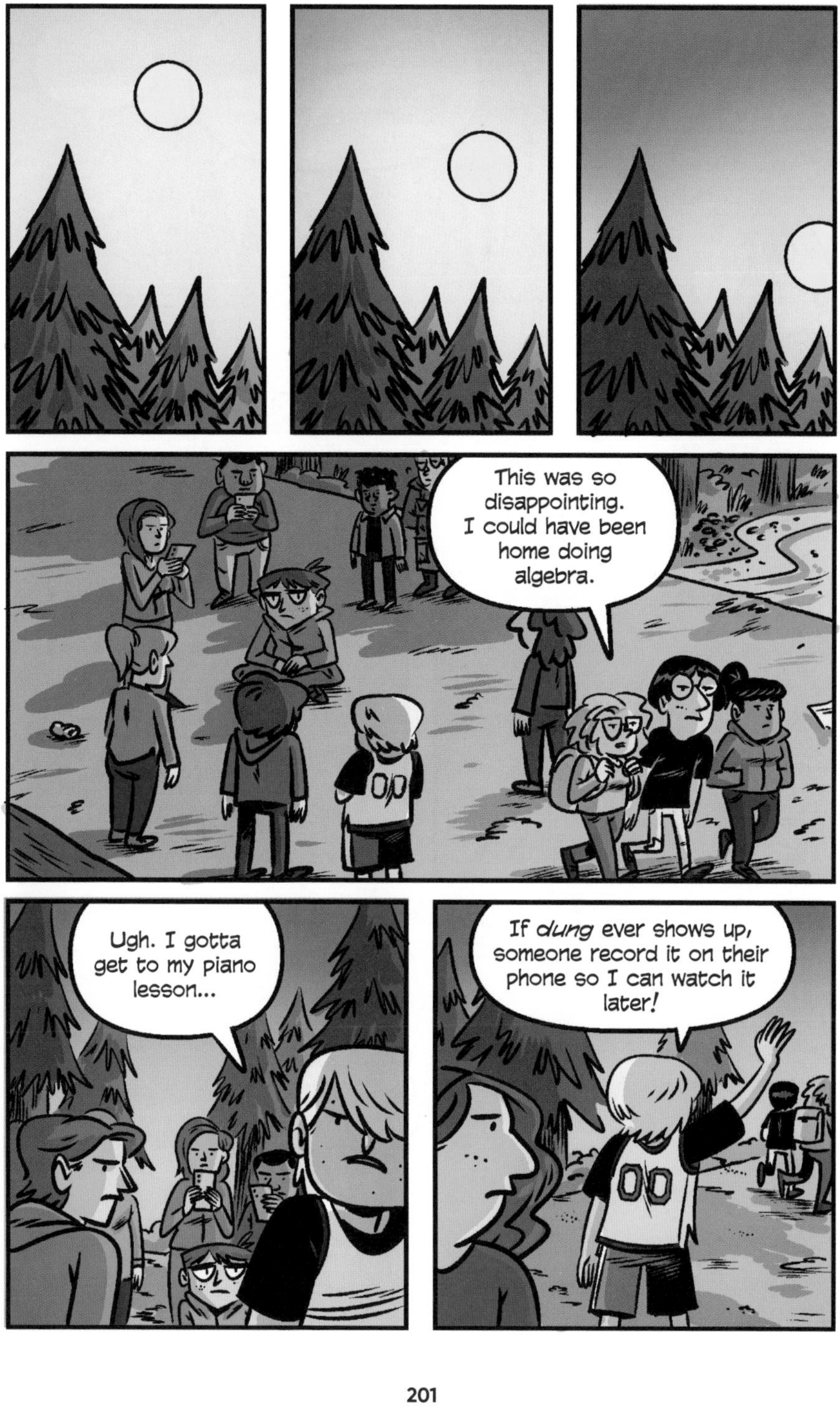
This was so disappointing. I could have been home doing algebra.
Ugh. I gotta get to my piano lesson...
If *dung* ever shows up, someone record it on their phone so I can watch it later!

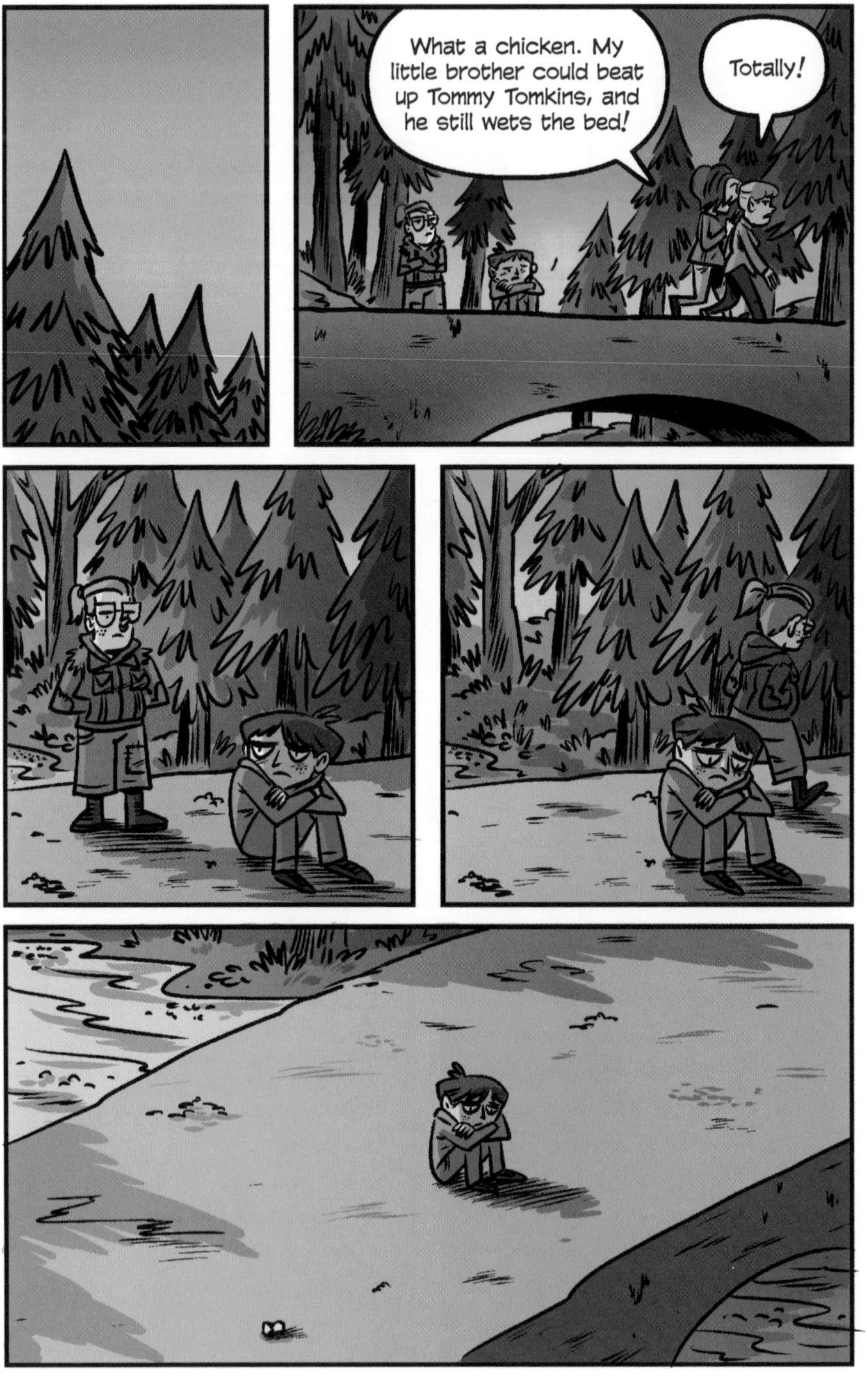
What a chicken. My little brother could beat up Tommy Tomkins, and he still wets the bed!
Totally!

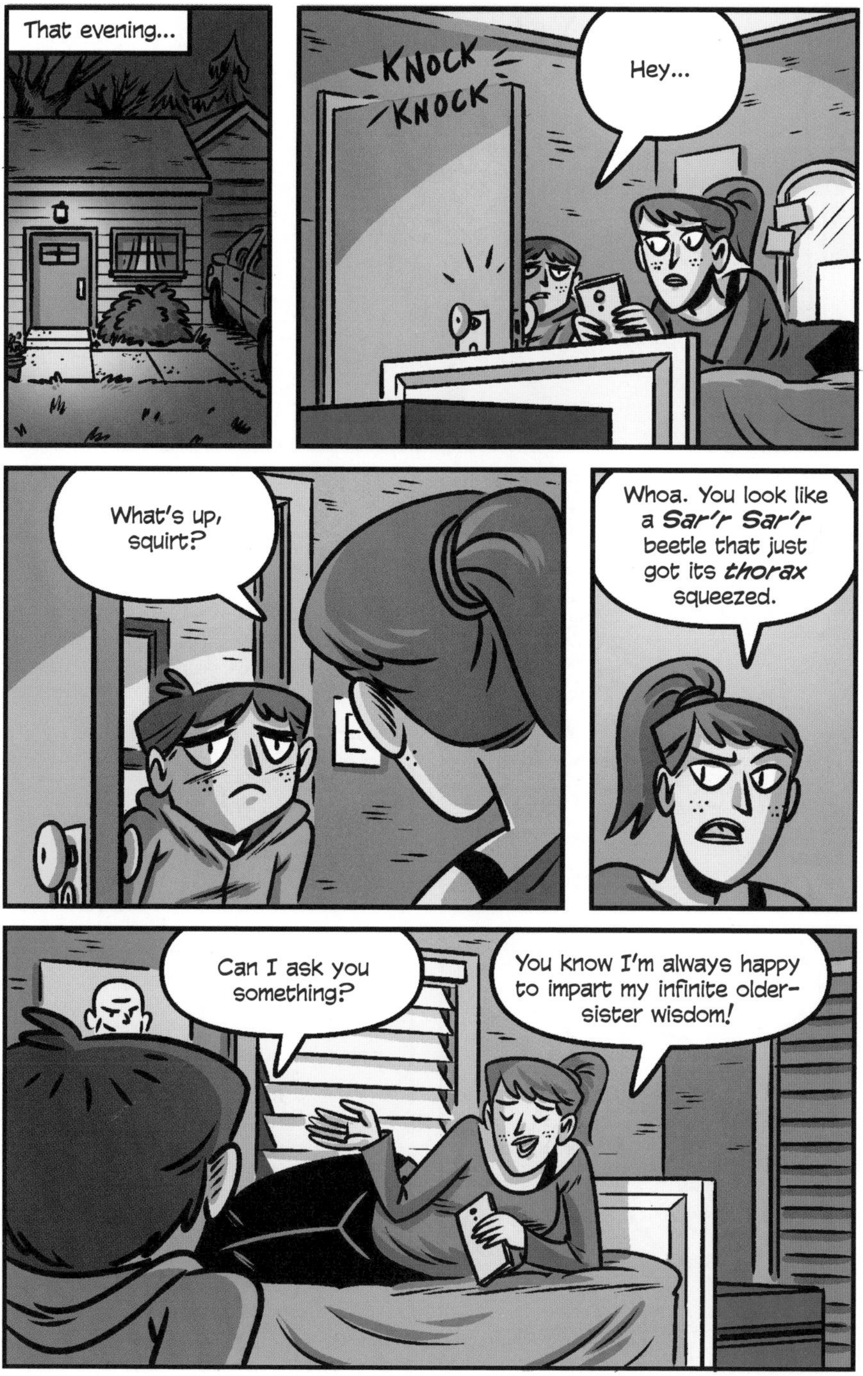
That evening...
KNOCK KNOCK
Hey...
What's up, squirt?
Whoa. You look like a *Sar'r Sar'r* beetle that just got its *thorax* squeezed.
Can I ask you something?
You know I'm always happy to impart my infinite older-sister wisdom!

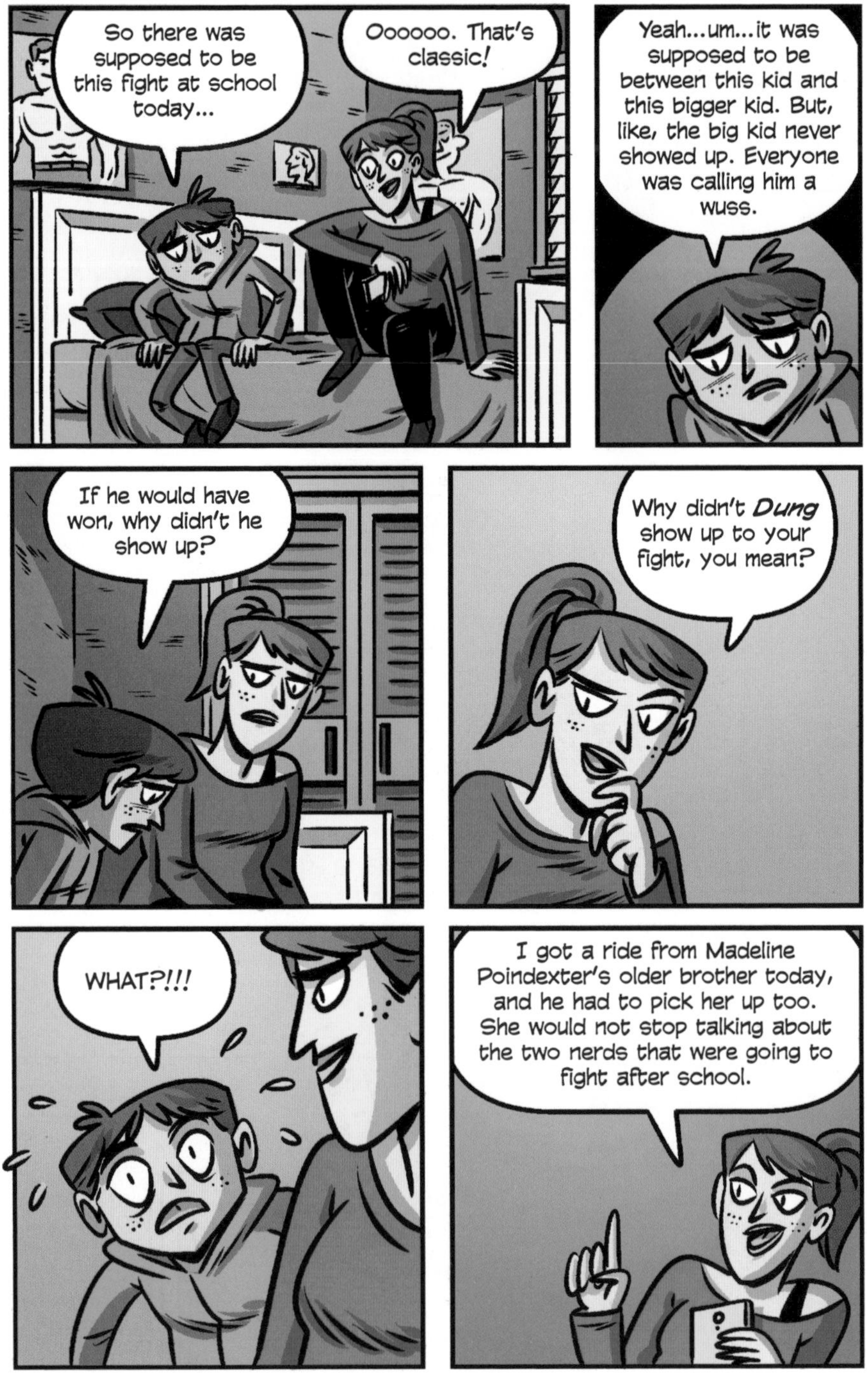

So there was supposed to be this fight at school today...
Oooooo. That's classic!
Yeah...um...it was supposed to be between this kid and this bigger kid. But, like, the big kid never showed up. Everyone was calling him a wuss.
If he would have won, why didn't he show up?
Why didn't *Dung* show up to your fight, you mean?
WHAT?!!!
I got a ride from Madeline Poindexter's older brother today, and he had to pick her up too. She would not stop talking about the two nerds that were going to fight after school.

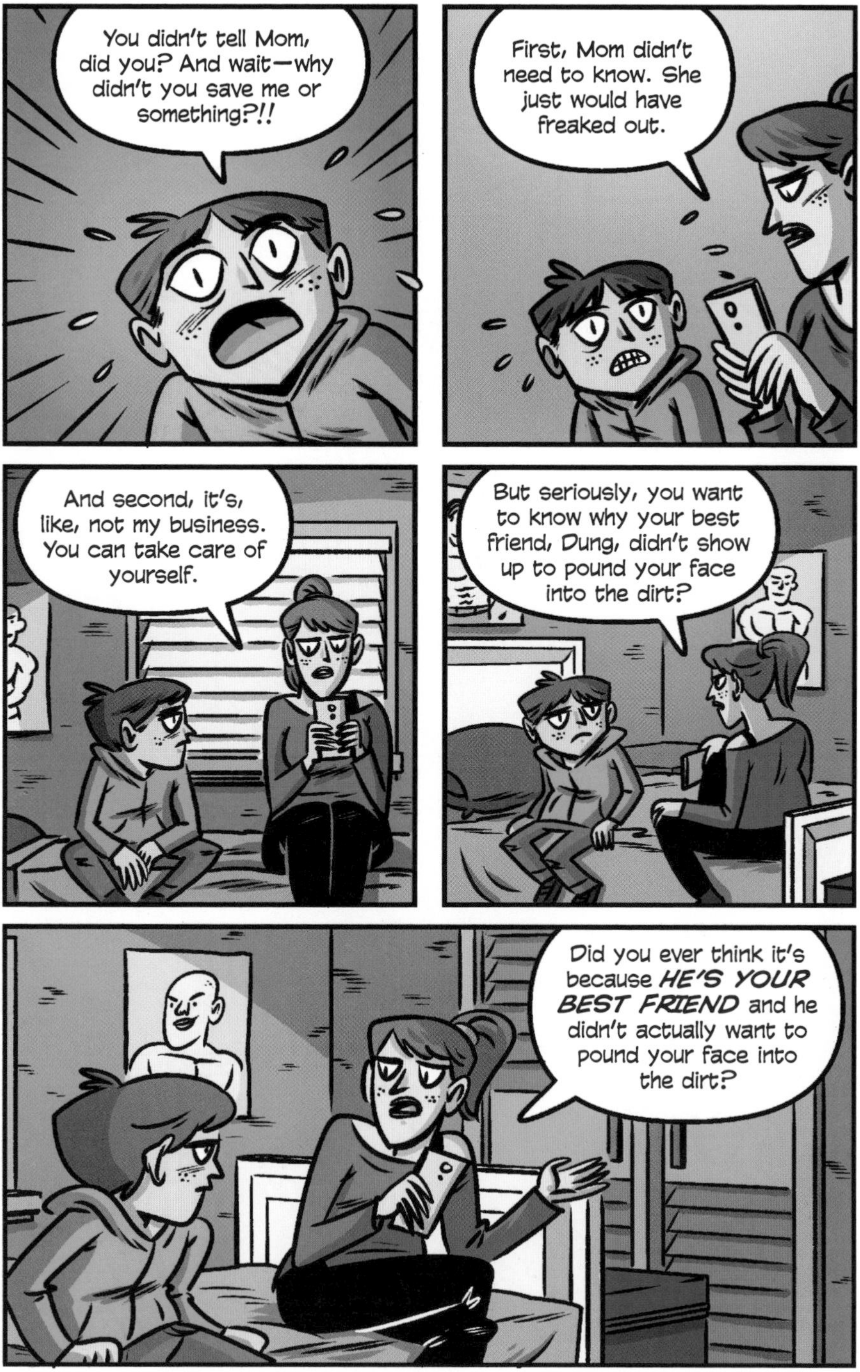
You didn't tell Mom, did you? And wait—why didn't you save me or something?!!
First, Mom didn't need to know. She just would have freaked out.
And second, it's, like, not my business. You can take care of yourself.
But seriously, you want to know why your best friend, Dung, didn't show up to pound your face into the dirt?
Did you ever think it's because HE'S YOUR BEST FRIEND and he didn't actually want to pound your face into the dirt?

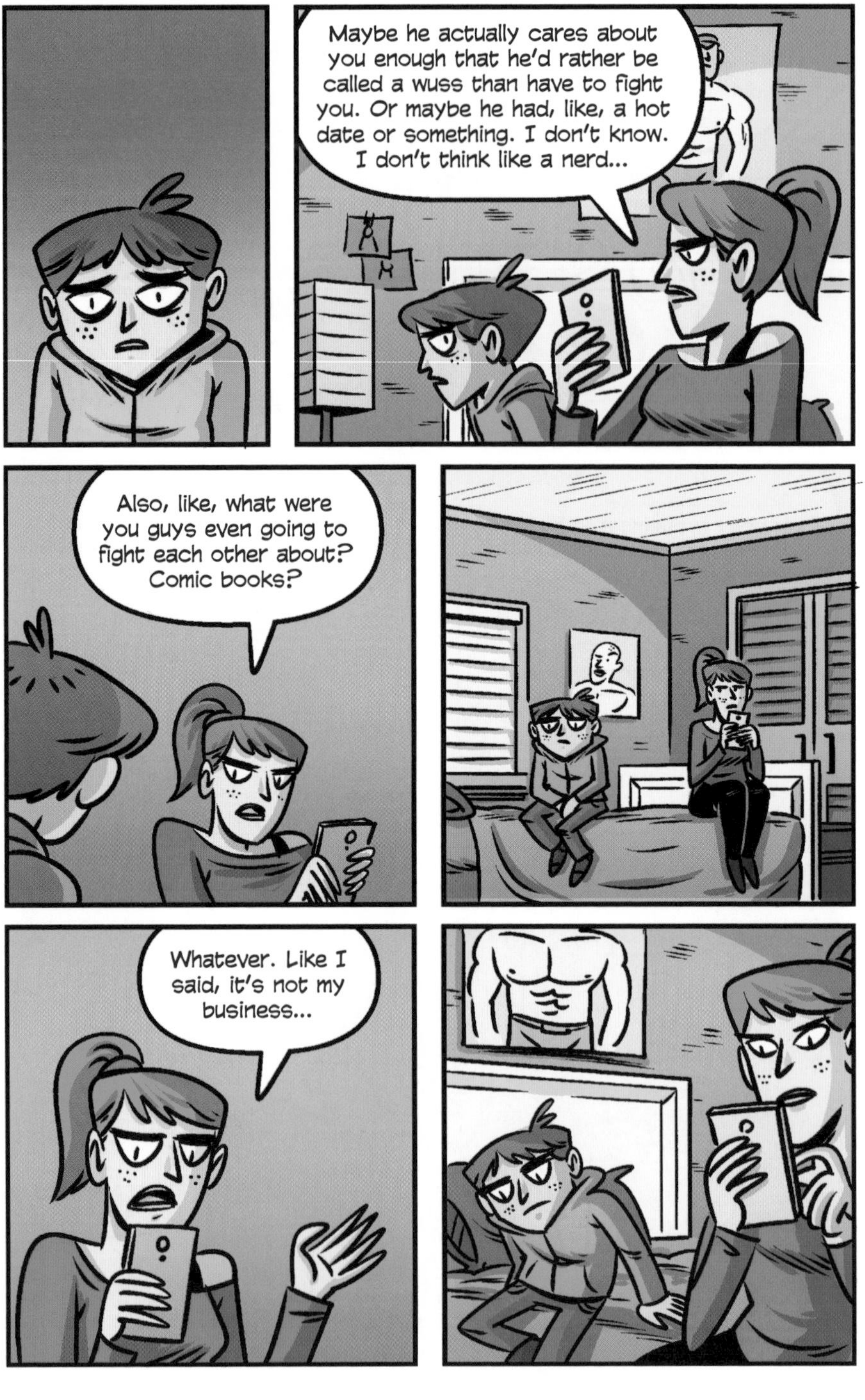
Maybe he actually cares about you enough that he'd rather be called a wuss than have to fight you. Or maybe he had, like, a hot date or something. I don't know. I don't think like a nerd...
Also, like, what were you guys even going to fight each other about? Comic books?
Whatever. Like I said, it's not my business...

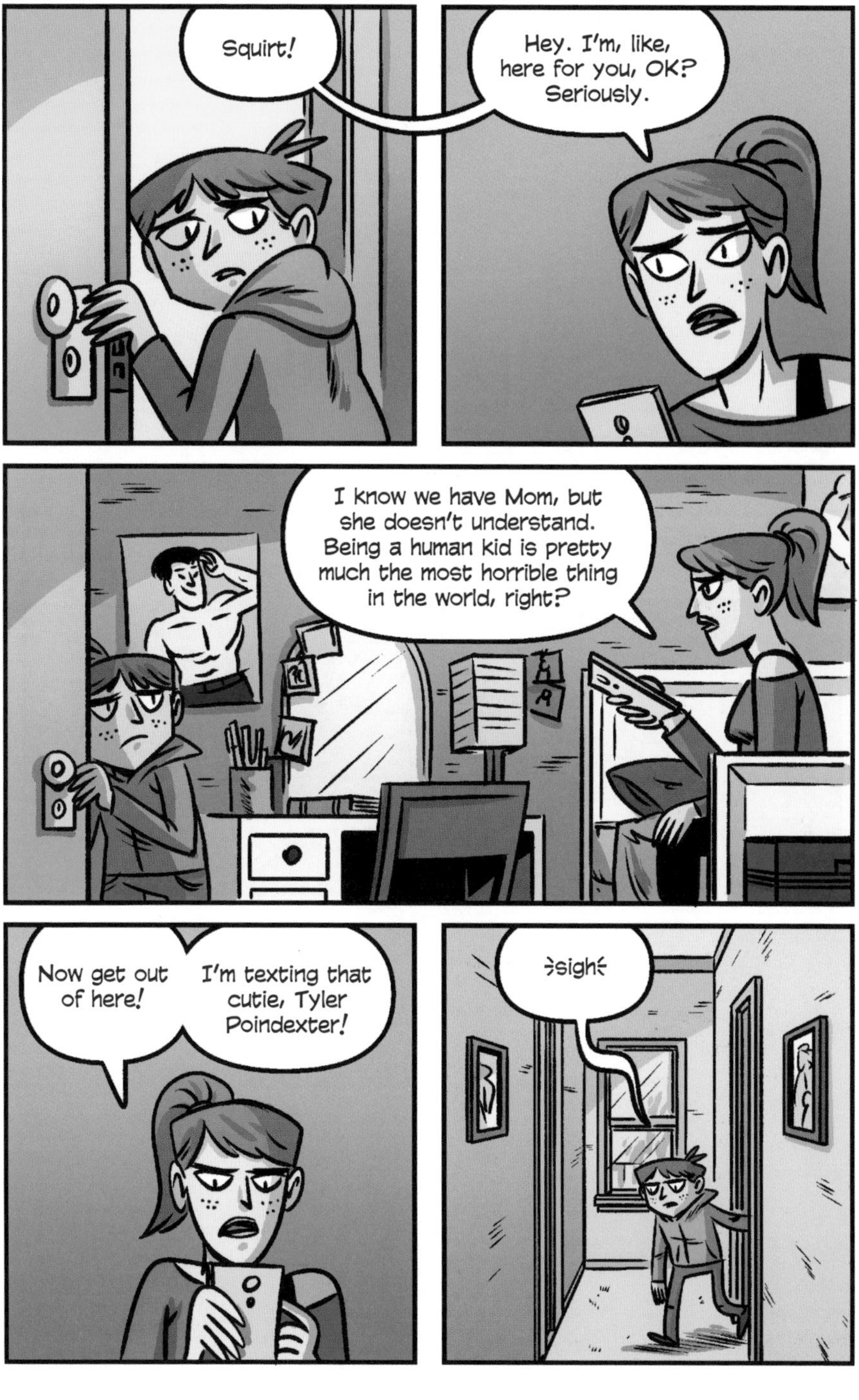

Squirt!
Hey. I'm, like, here for you, OK? Seriously.
I know we have Mom, but she doesn't understand. Being a human kid is pretty much the most horrible thing in the world, right?
I'm texting that cutie, Tyler Poindexter!
Now get out of here!
sigh

CHAPTER 10

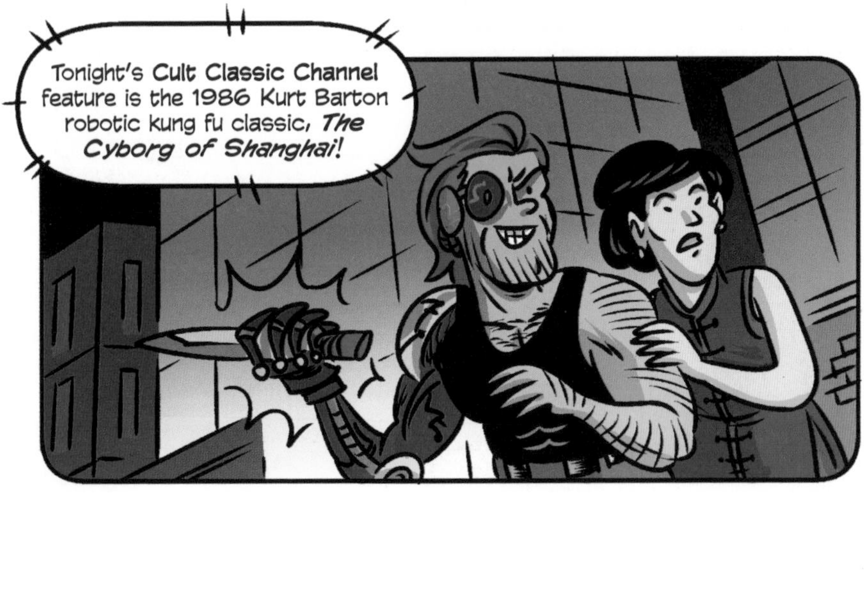
Tonight's Cult Classic Channel feature is the 1986 Kurt Barton robotic kung fu classic, *The Cyborg of Shanghai*!

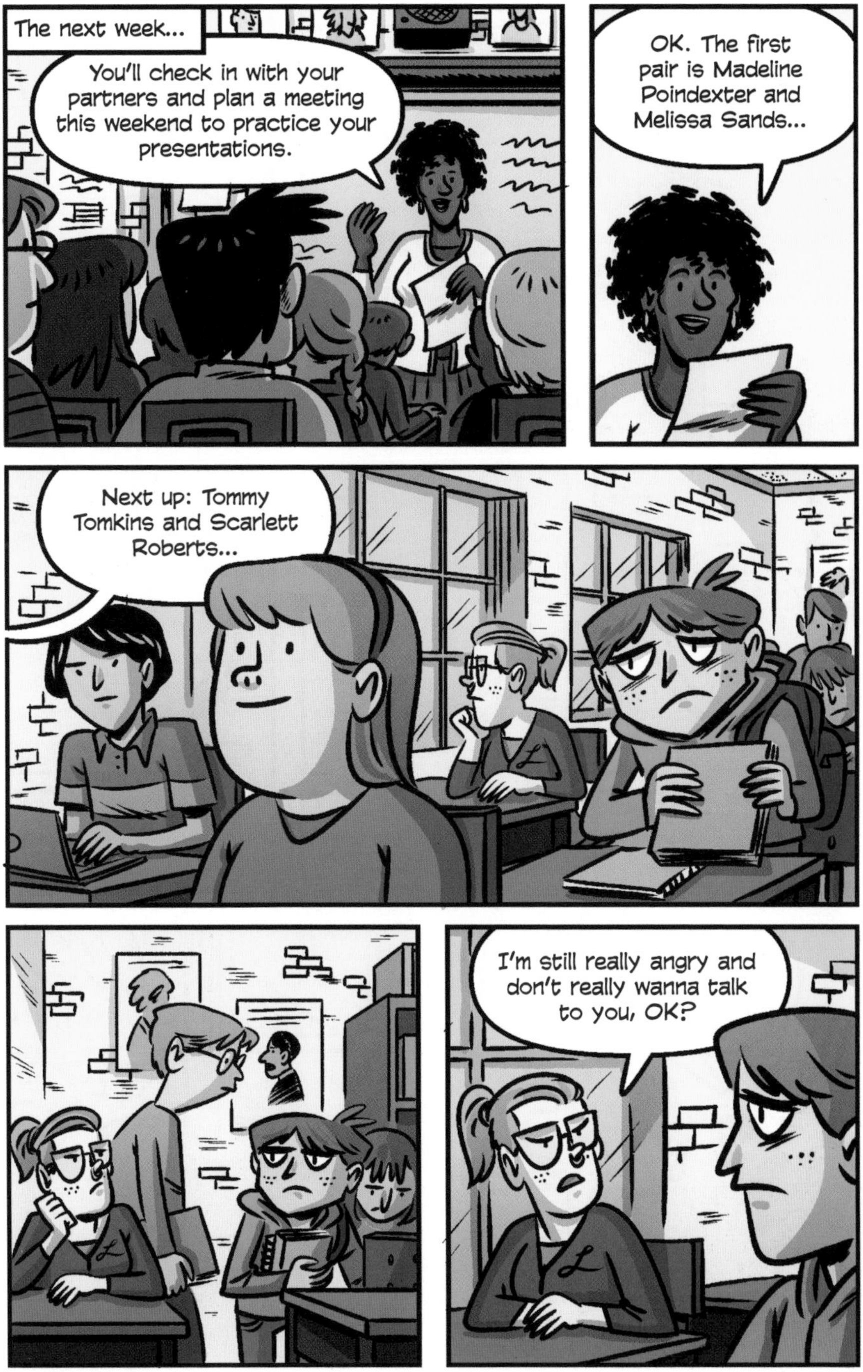
The next week...
You'll check in with your partners and plan a meeting this weekend to practice your presentations.
OK. The first pair is Madeline Poindexter and Melissa Sands...
Next up: Tommy Tomkins and Scarlett Roberts...
I'm still really angry and don't really wanna talk to you, OK?

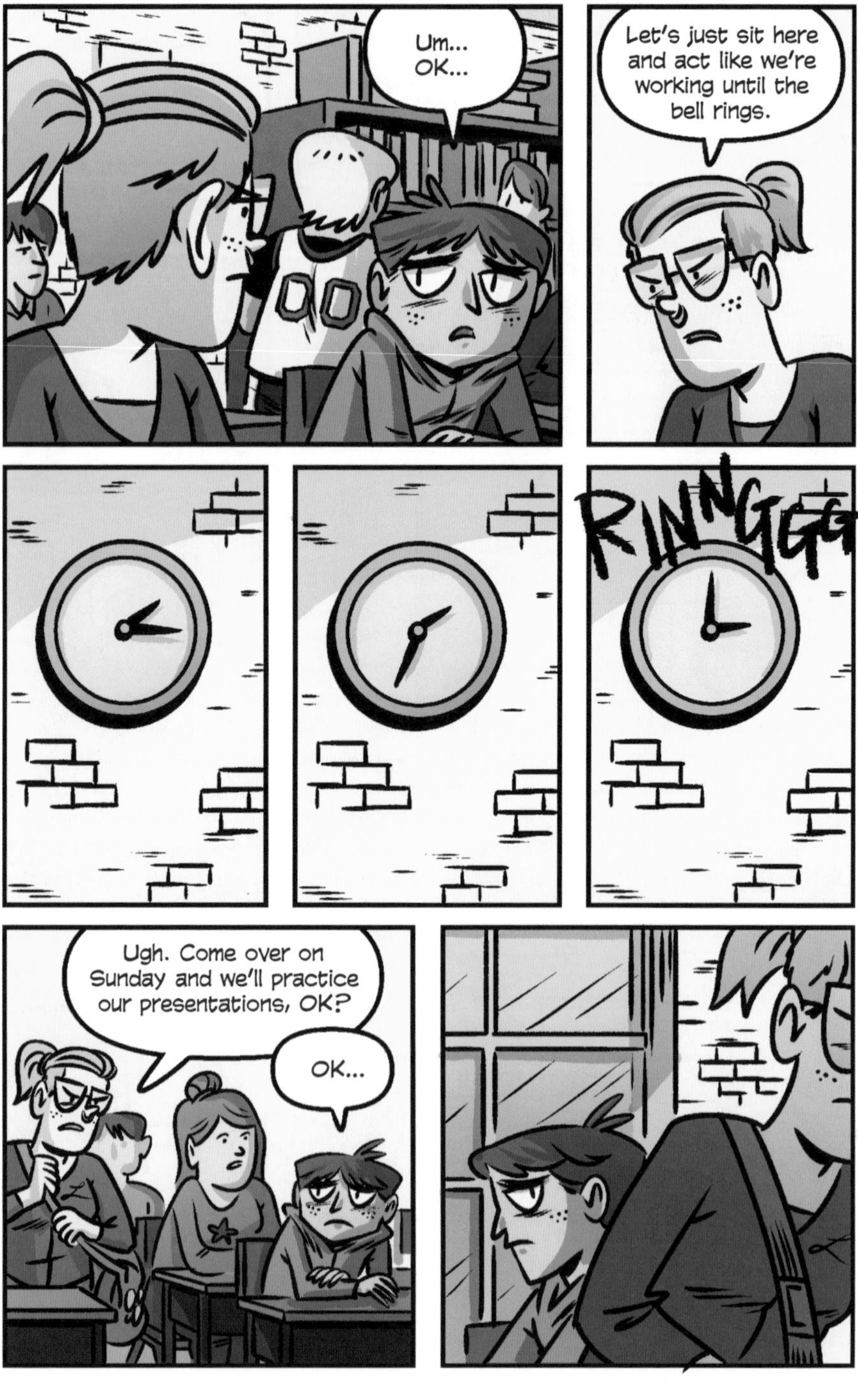
Um...
OK...
Let's just sit here and act like we're working until the bell rings.
RINNGGG
Ugh. Come over on Sunday and we'll practice our presentations, OK?
OK...

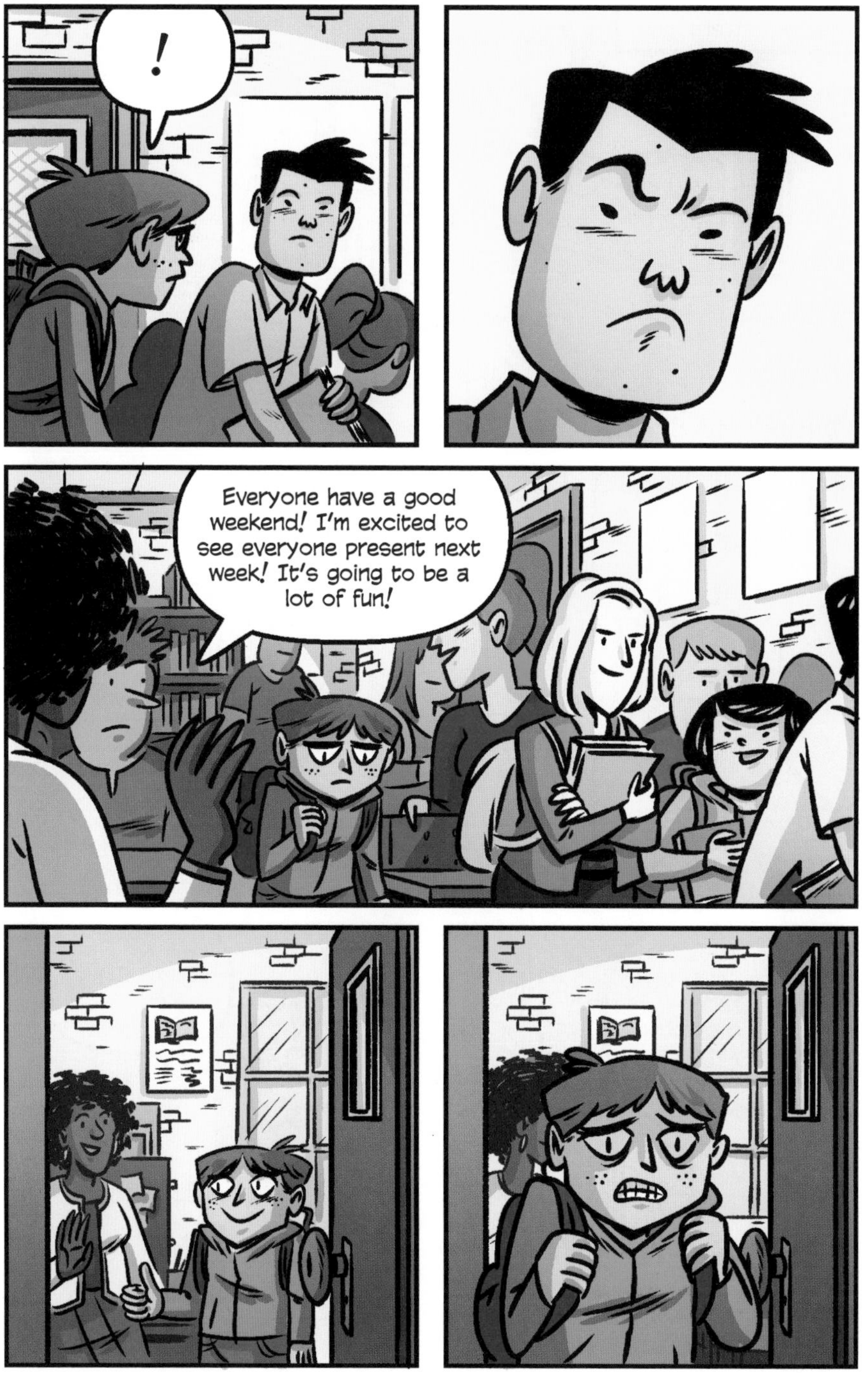
!
Everyone have a good weekend! I'm excited to see everyone present next week! It's going to be a lot of fun!

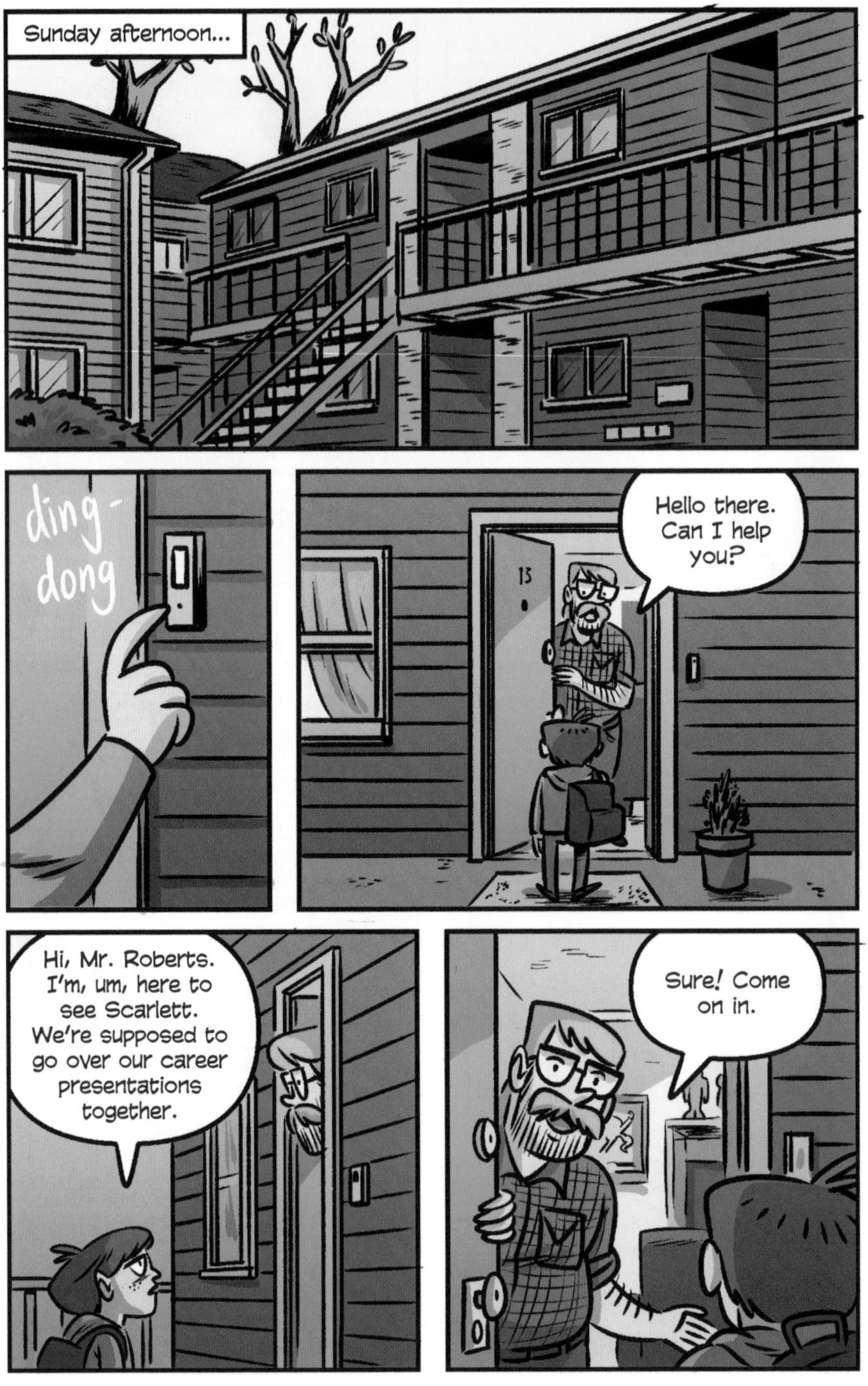
Sunday afternoon...
ding-dong
Hello there. Can I help you?
Hi, Mr. Roberts. I'm, um, here to see Scarlett. We're supposed to go over our career presentations together.
Sure! Come on in.

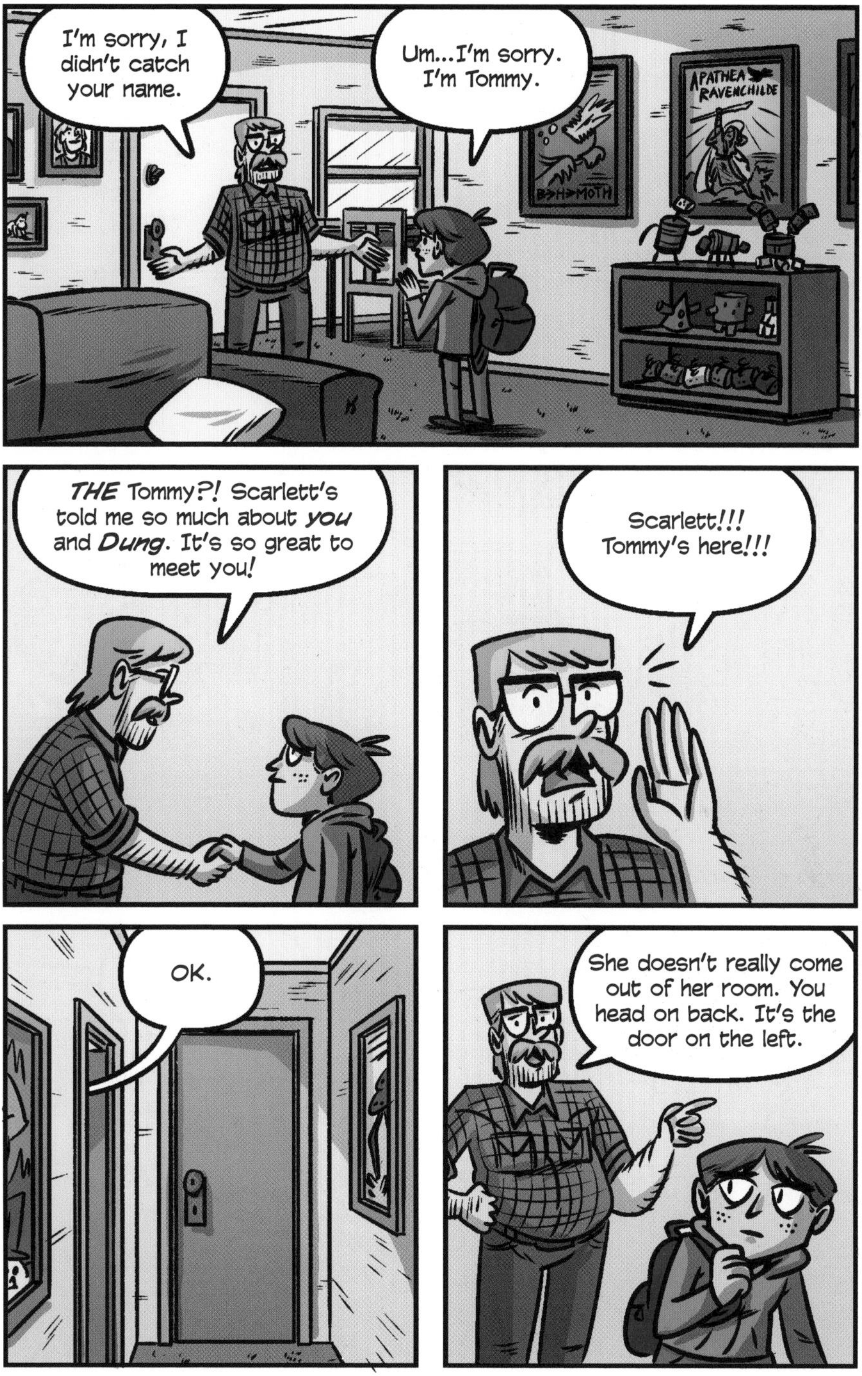
I'm sorry, I didn't catch your name.
Um...I'm sorry. I'm Tommy.
APATHEA RAVENCHILDE
THE Tommy?! Scarlett's told me so much about *you* and *Dung*. It's so great to meet you!
Scarlett!!! Tommy's here!!!
OK.
She doesn't really come out of her room. You head on back. It's the door on the left.

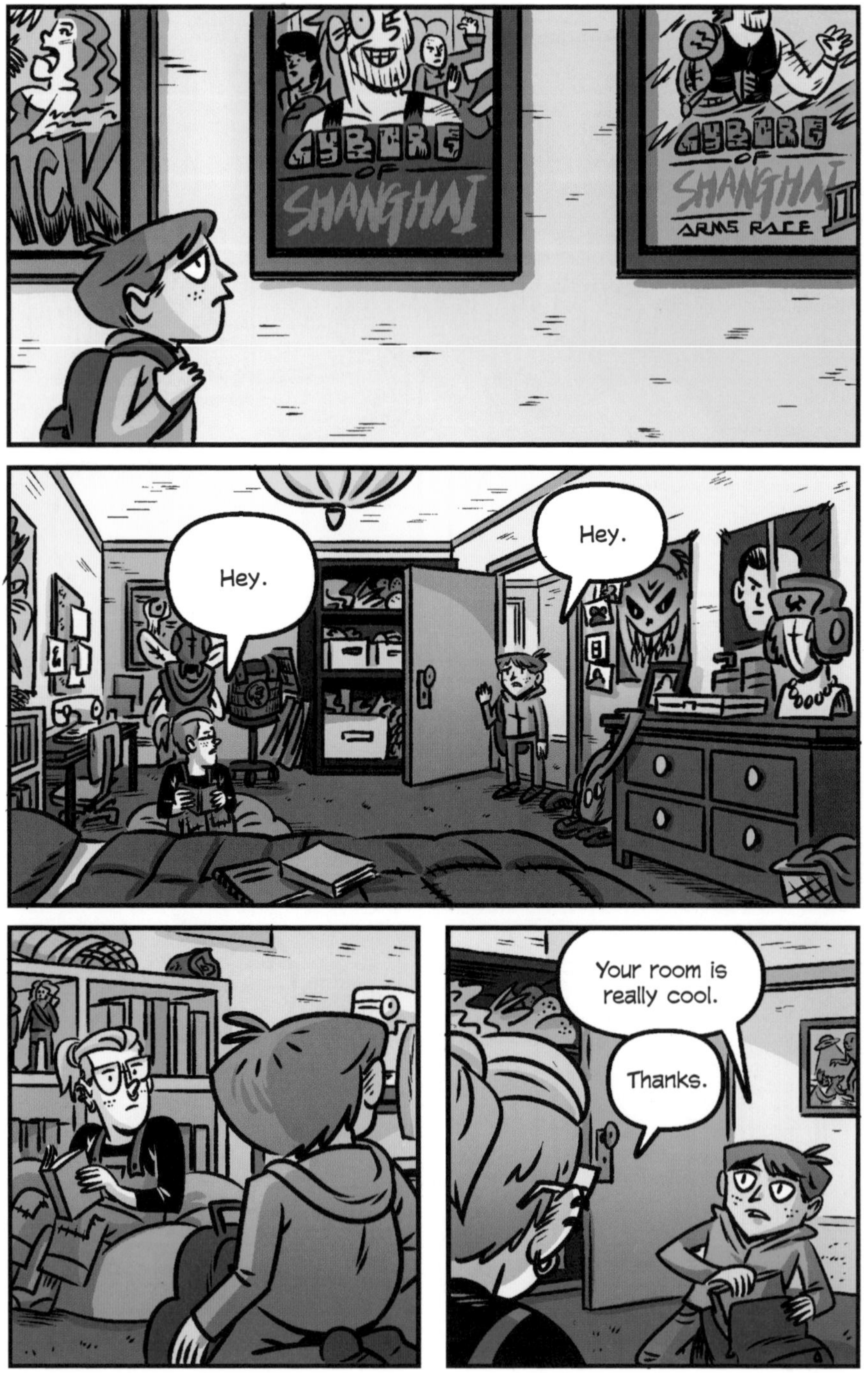
Hey.
Hey.
Your room is really cool.
Thanks.

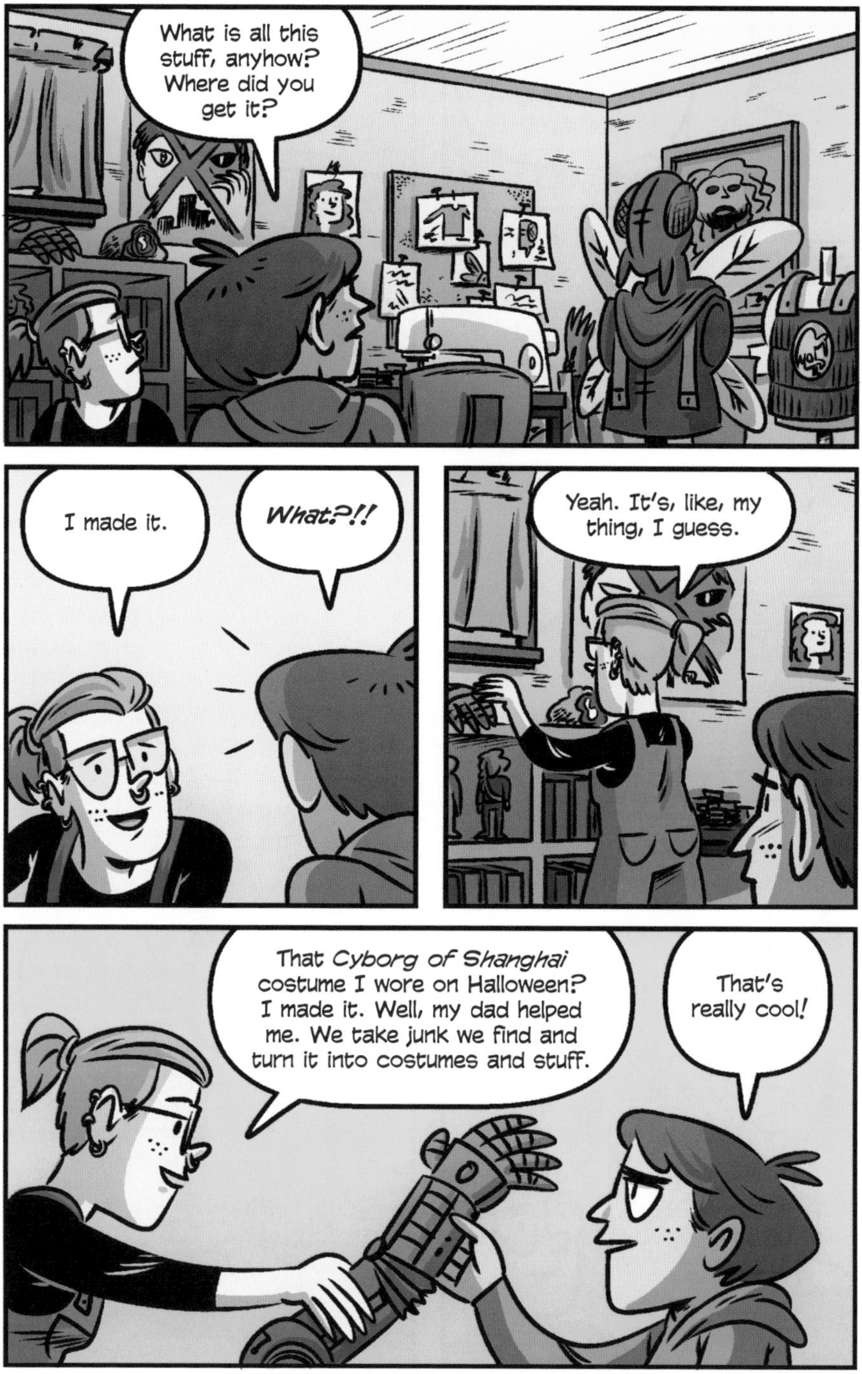
What is all this stuff, anyhow? Where did you get it?
I made it.
What?!!
Yeah. It's, like, my thing, I guess.
That *Cyborg of Shanghai* costume I wore on Halloween? I made it. Well, my dad helped me. We take junk we find and turn it into costumes and stuff.
That's really cool!

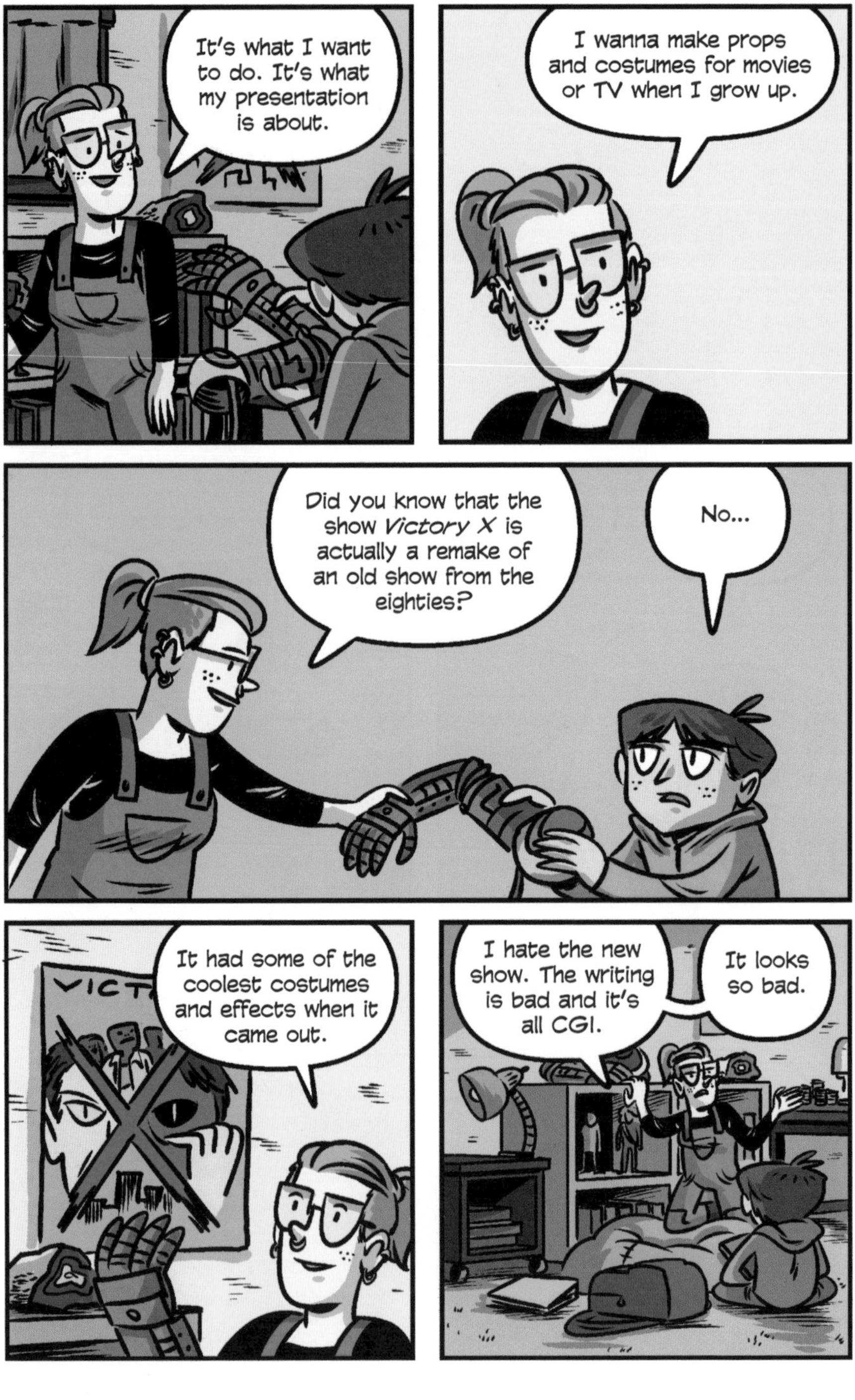
It's what I want to do. It's what my presentation is about.
I wanna make props and costumes for movies or TV when I grow up.
Did you know that the show *Victory X* is actually a remake of an old show from the eighties?
No...
VICT
It had some of the coolest costumes and effects when it came out.
I hate the new show. The writing is bad and it's all CGI.
It looks so bad.

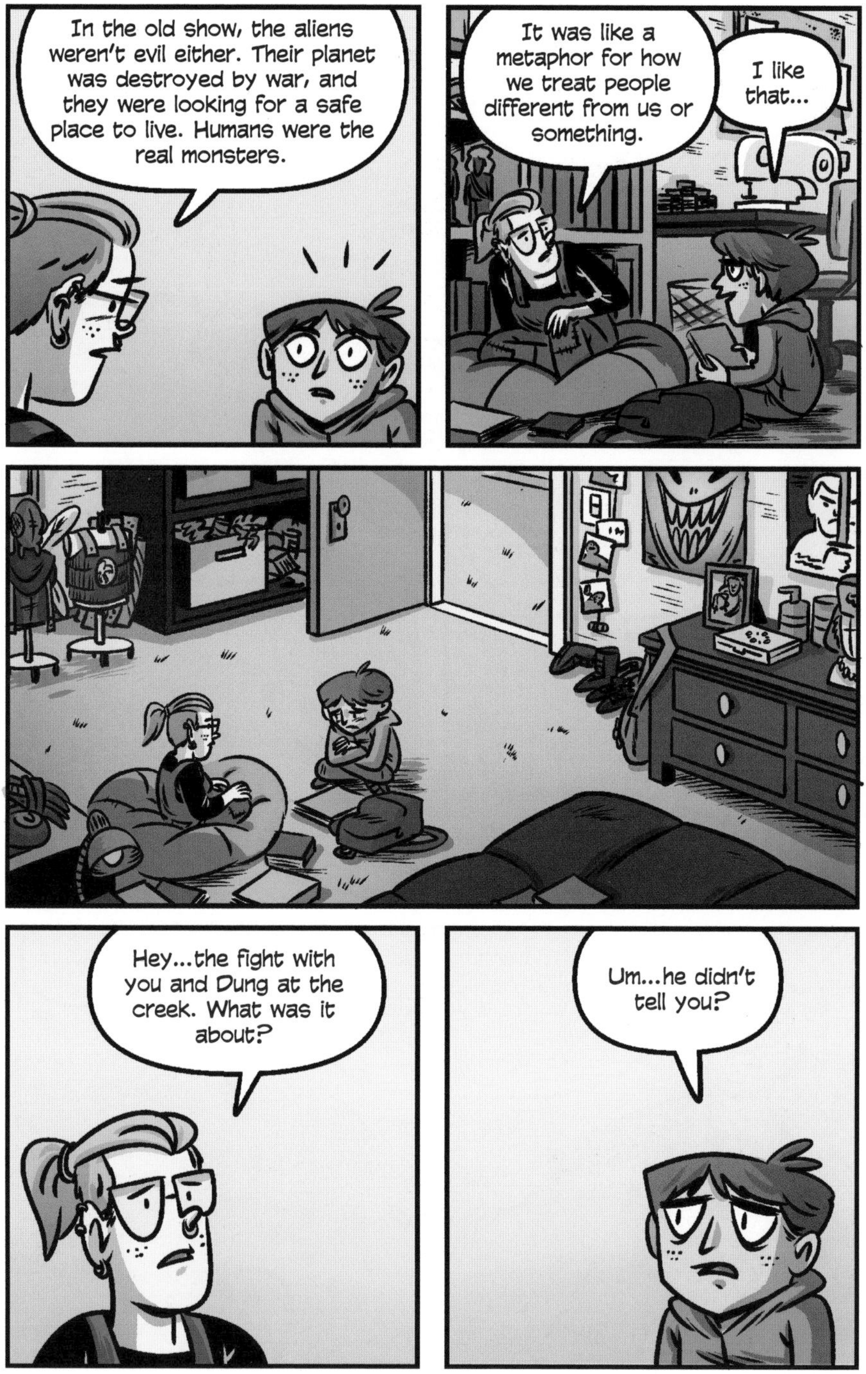
In the old show, the aliens weren't evil either. Their planet was destroyed by war, and they were looking for a safe place to live. Humans were the real monsters.
It was like a metaphor for how we treat people different from us or something.
I like that...
Hey...the fight with you and Dung at the creek. What was it about?
Um...he didn't tell you?

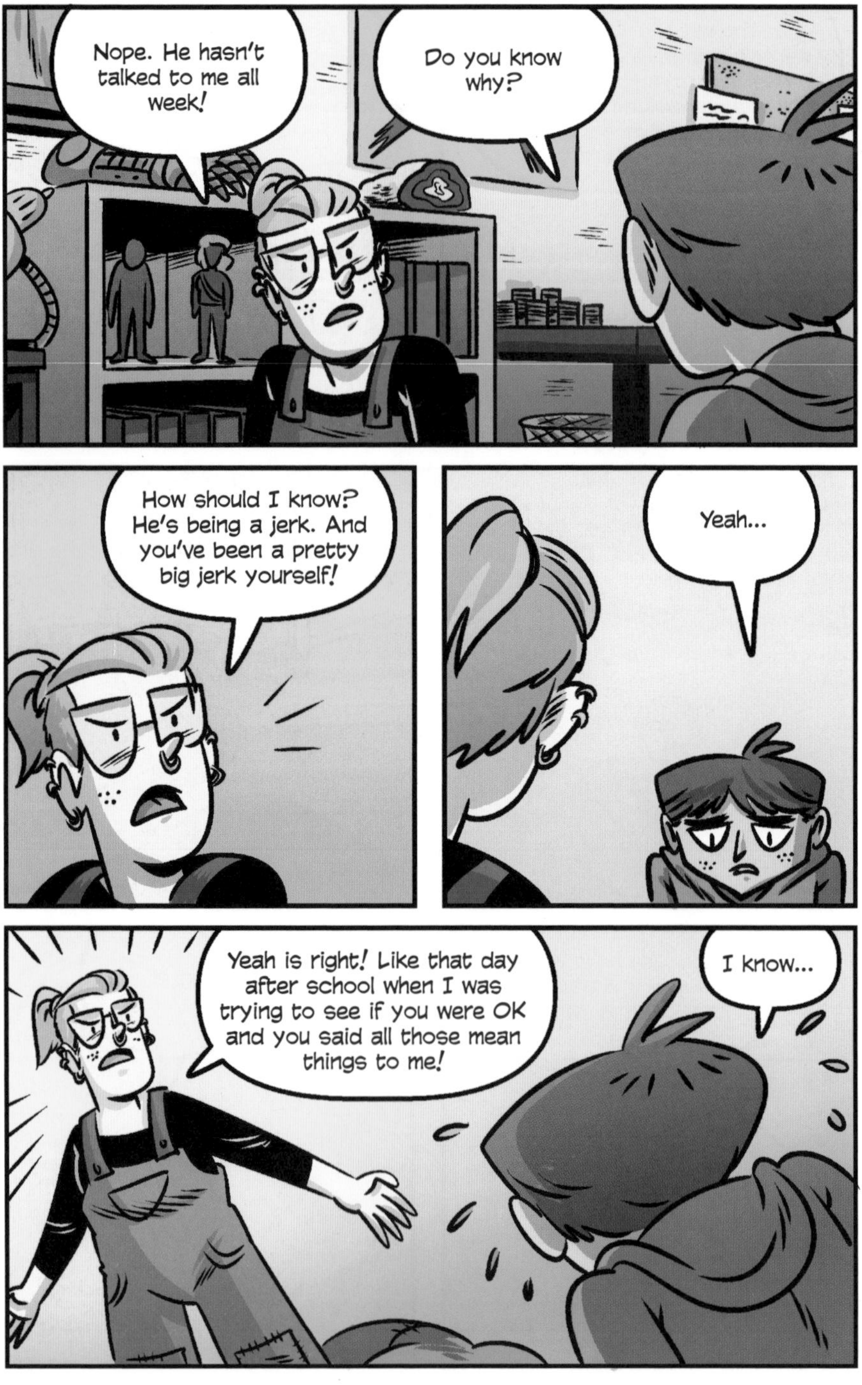
Nope. He hasn't talked to me all week!
Do you know why?
How should I know? He's being a jerk. And you've been a pretty big jerk yourself!
Yeah...
Yeah is right! Like that day after school when I was trying to see if you were OK and you said all those mean things to me!
I know...

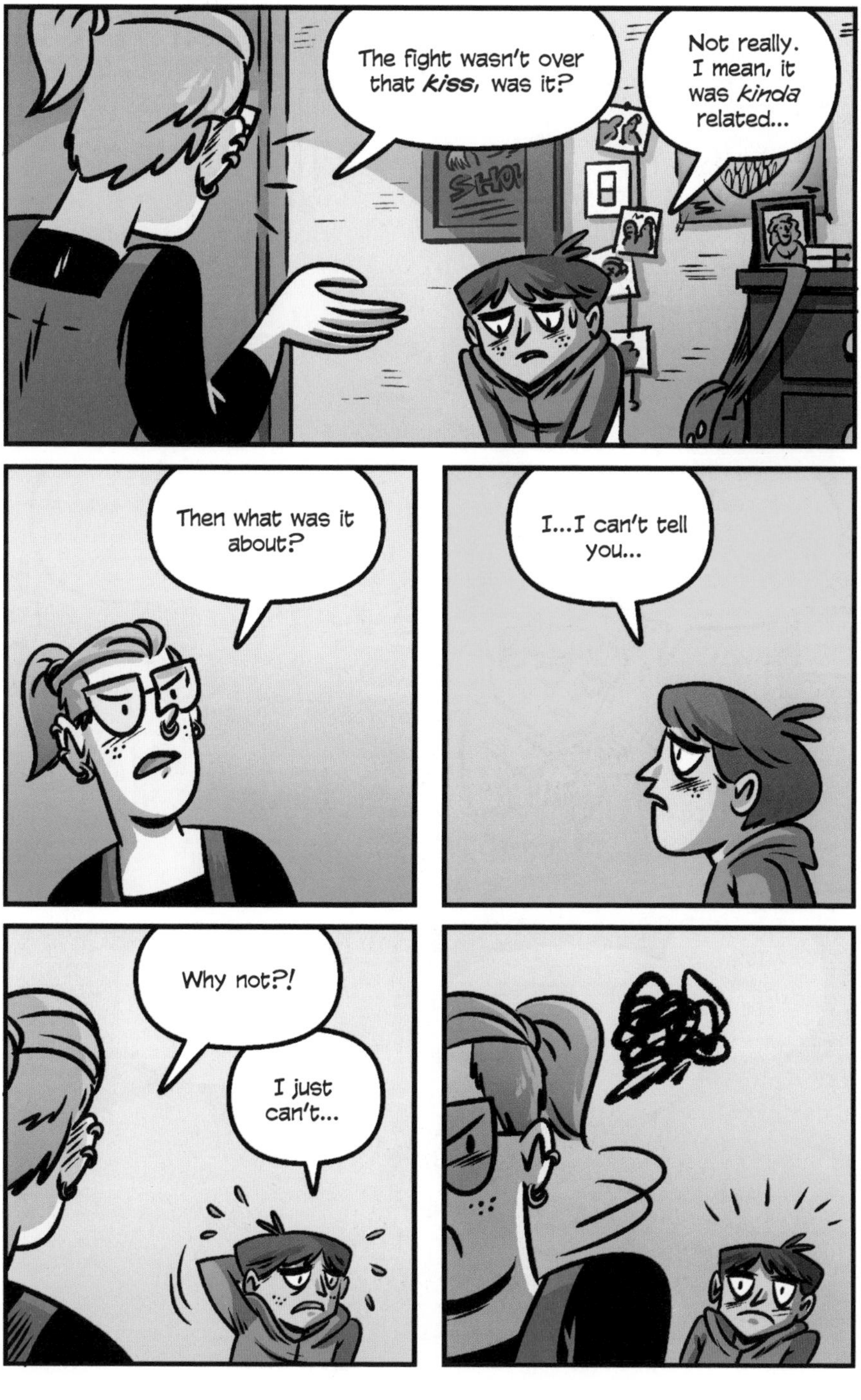
The fight wasn't over that *kiss*, was it?
Not really. I mean, it was *kinda* related...
Then what was it about?
I...I can't tell you...
Why not?!
I just can't...

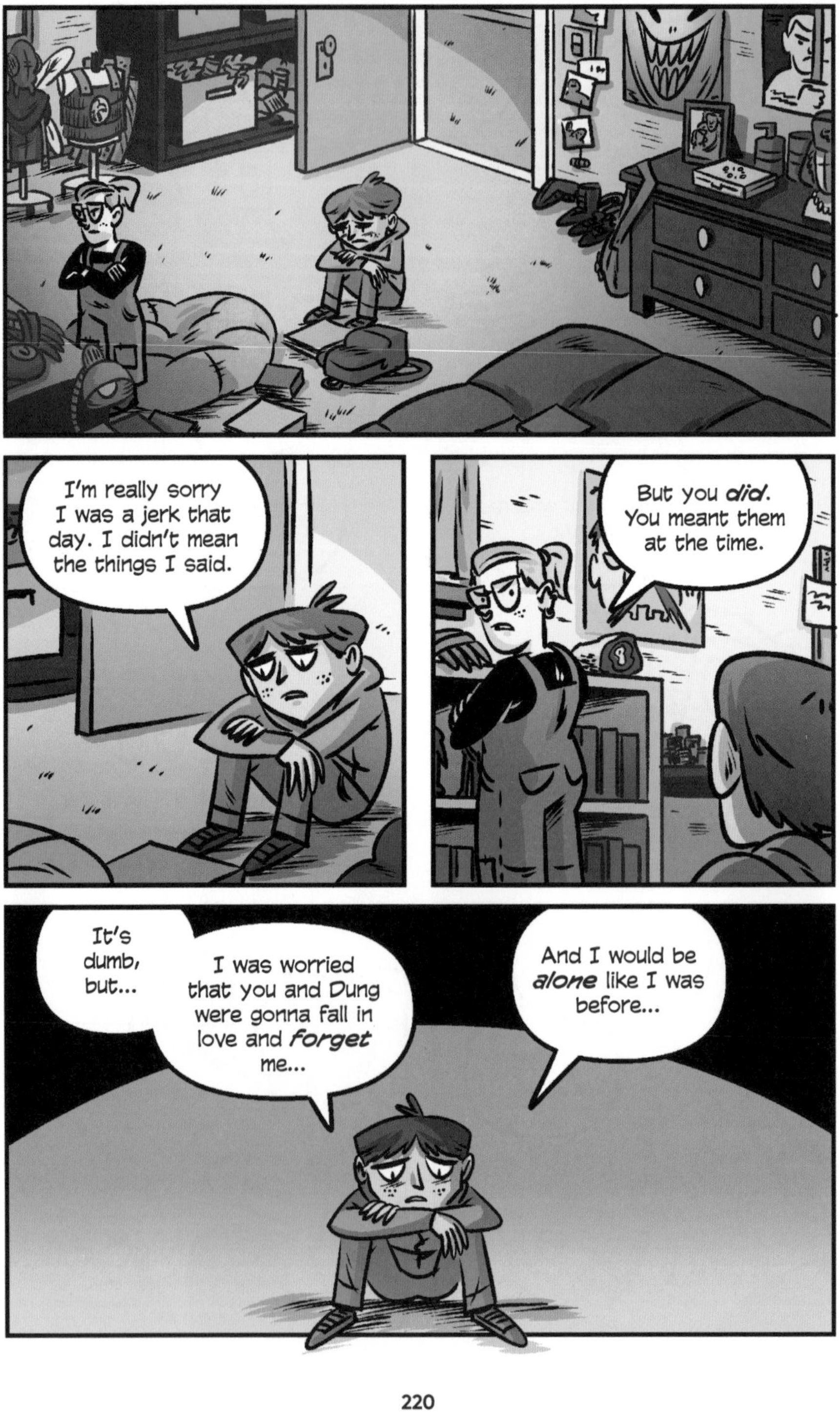
I'm really sorry I was a jerk that day. I didn't mean the things I said.
But you *did*. You meant them at the time.
It's dumb, but...
I was worried that you and Dung were gonna fall in love and *forget* me...
And I would be *alone* like I was before...

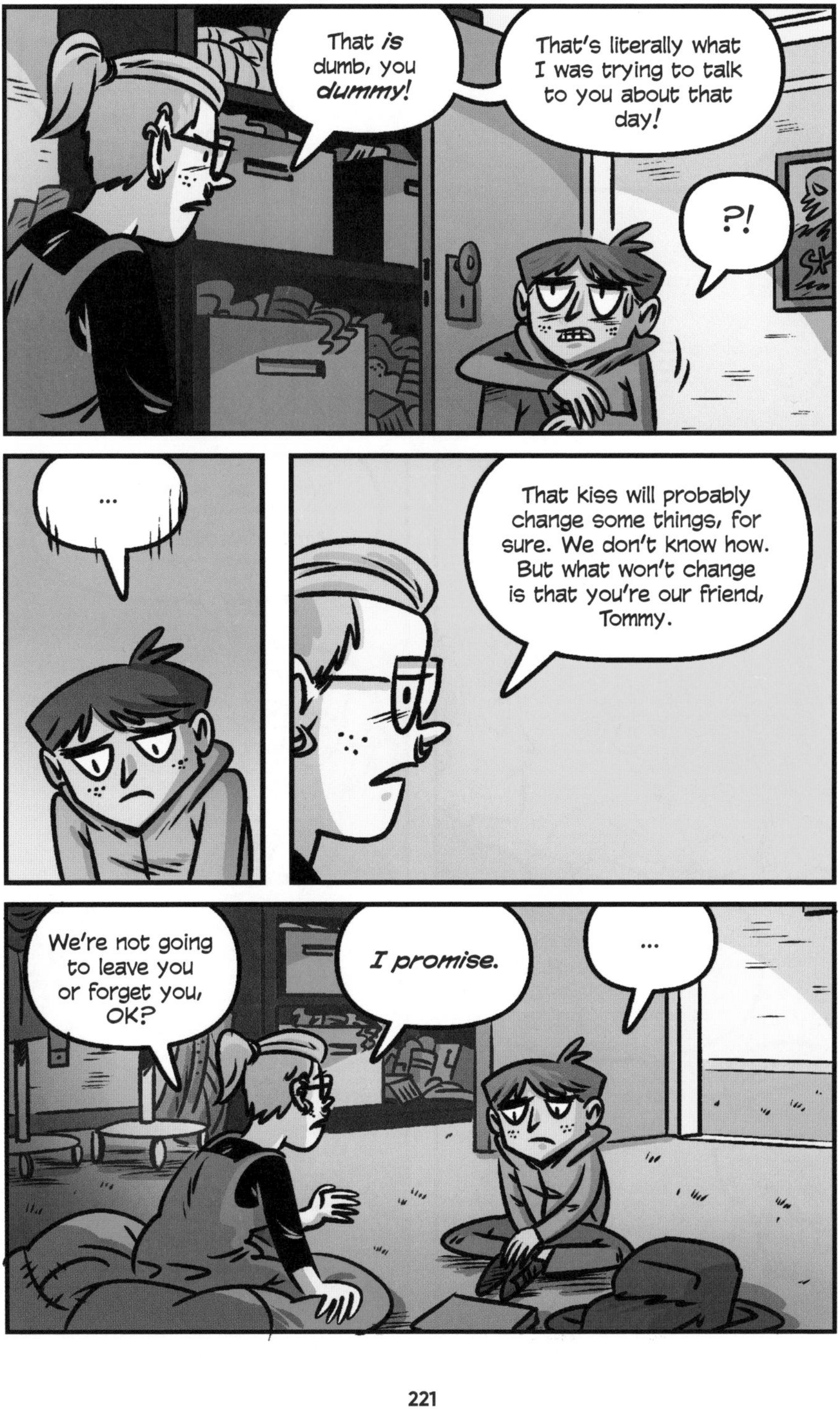

That *is* dumb, you *dummy*!
That's literally what I was trying to talk to you about that day!
?!
...
That kiss will probably change some things, for sure. We don't know how. But what won't change is that you're our friend, Tommy.
We're not going to leave you or forget you, OK?
I promise.
...

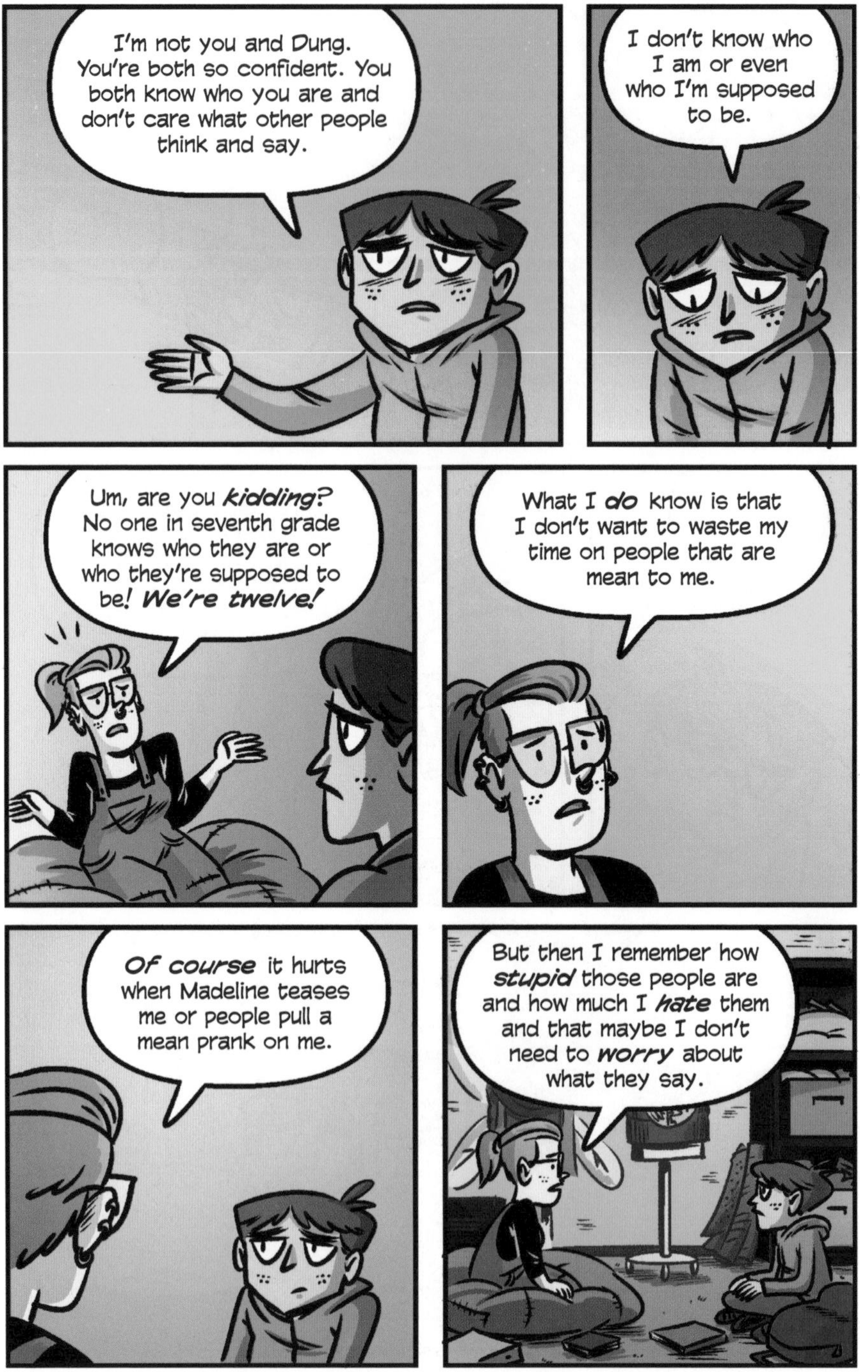
I'm not you and Dung. You're both so confident. You both know who you are and don't care what other people think and say.
I don't know who I am or even who I'm supposed to be.
Um, are you *kidding*? No one in seventh grade knows who they are or who they're supposed to be! *We're twelve!*
What I *do* know is that I don't want to waste my time on people that are mean to me.
Of course it hurts when Madeline teases me or people pull a mean prank on me.
But then I remember how *stupid* those people are and how much I *hate* them and that maybe I don't need to *worry* about what they say.

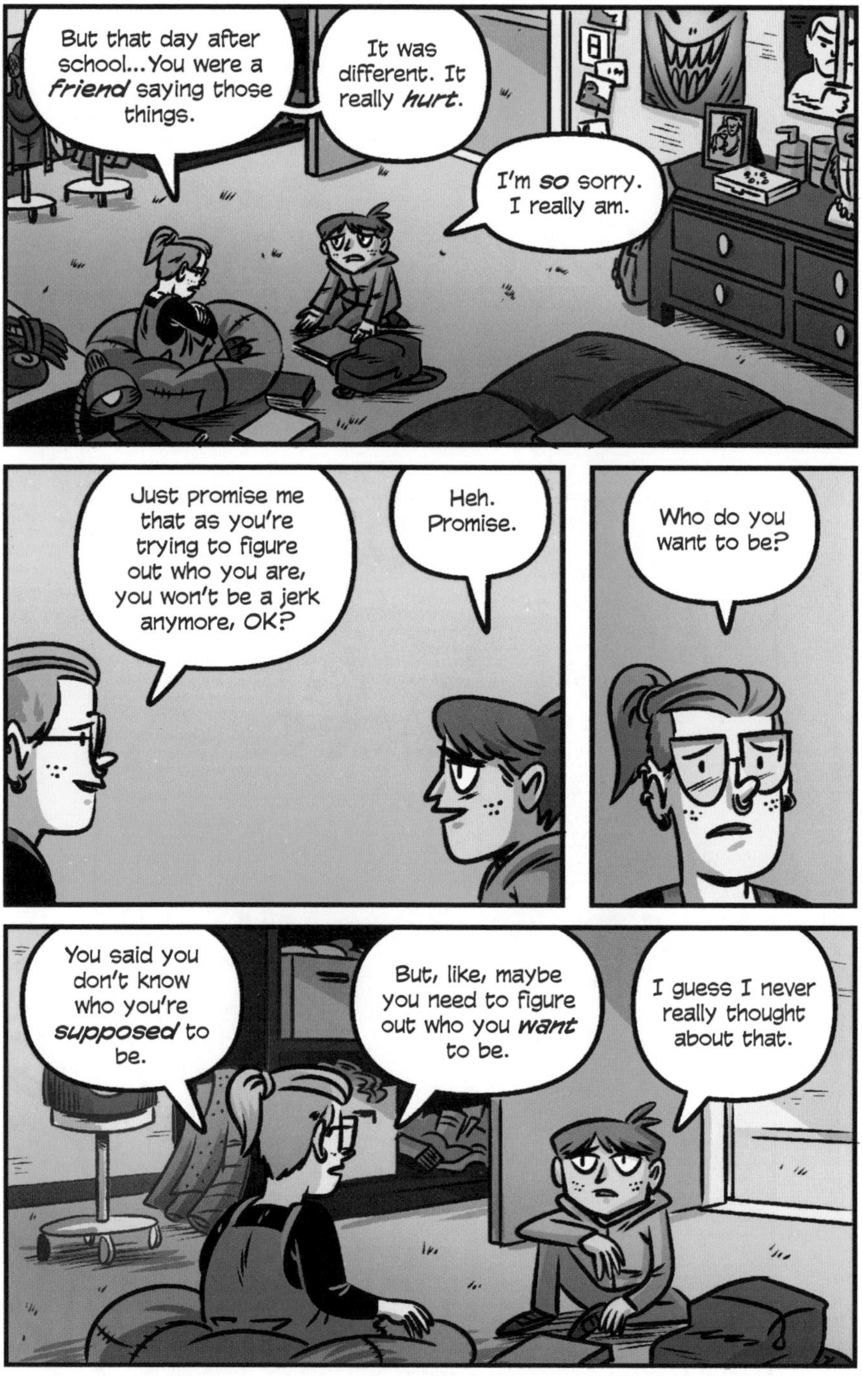

But that day after school...You were a *friend* saying those things.
It was different. It really *hurt*.
I'm *so* sorry. I really am.
Just promise me that as you're trying to figure out who you are, you won't be a jerk anymore, OK?
Heh. Promise.
Who do you want to be?
You said you don't know who you're *supposed* to be.
But, like, maybe you need to figure out who you *want* to be.
I guess I never really thought about that.

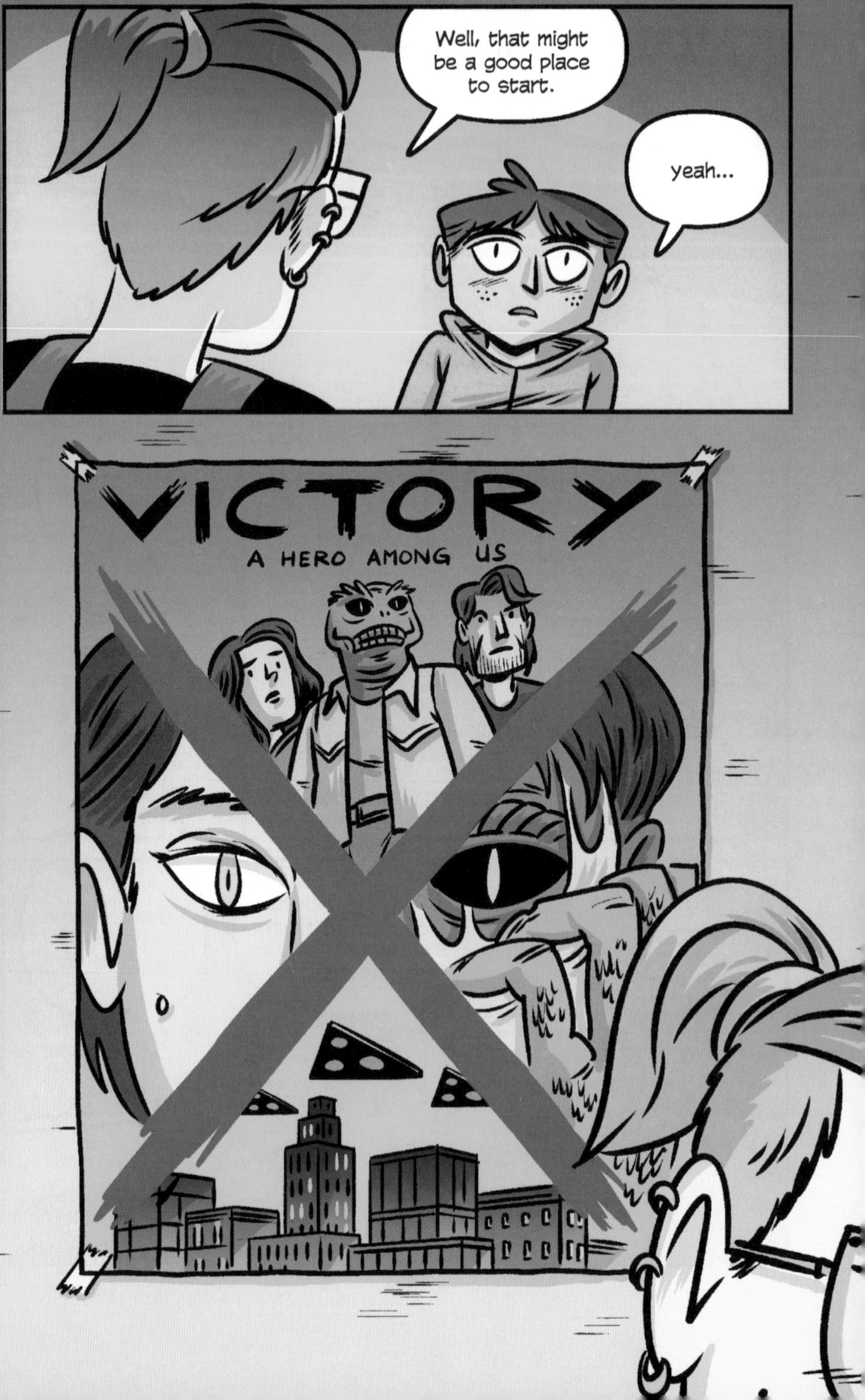
Well, that might be a good place to start.
yeah...
VICTORY
A HERO AMONG US

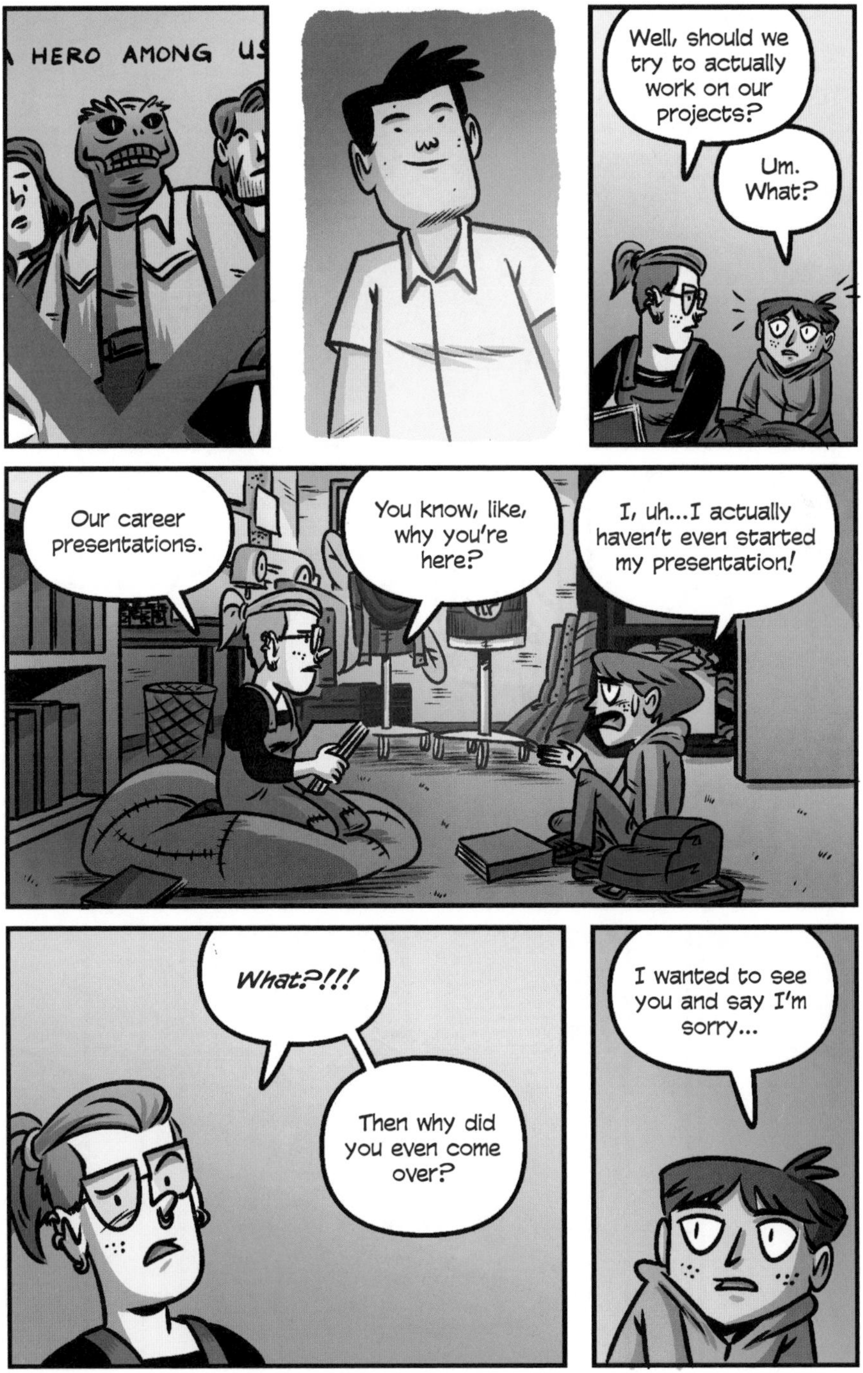
A HERO AMONG US
Well, should we try to actually work on our projects?
Um. What?
Our career presentations.
You know, like, why you're here?
I, uh...I actually haven't even started my presentation!
What?!!!
Then why did you even come over?
I wanted to see you and say I'm sorry...

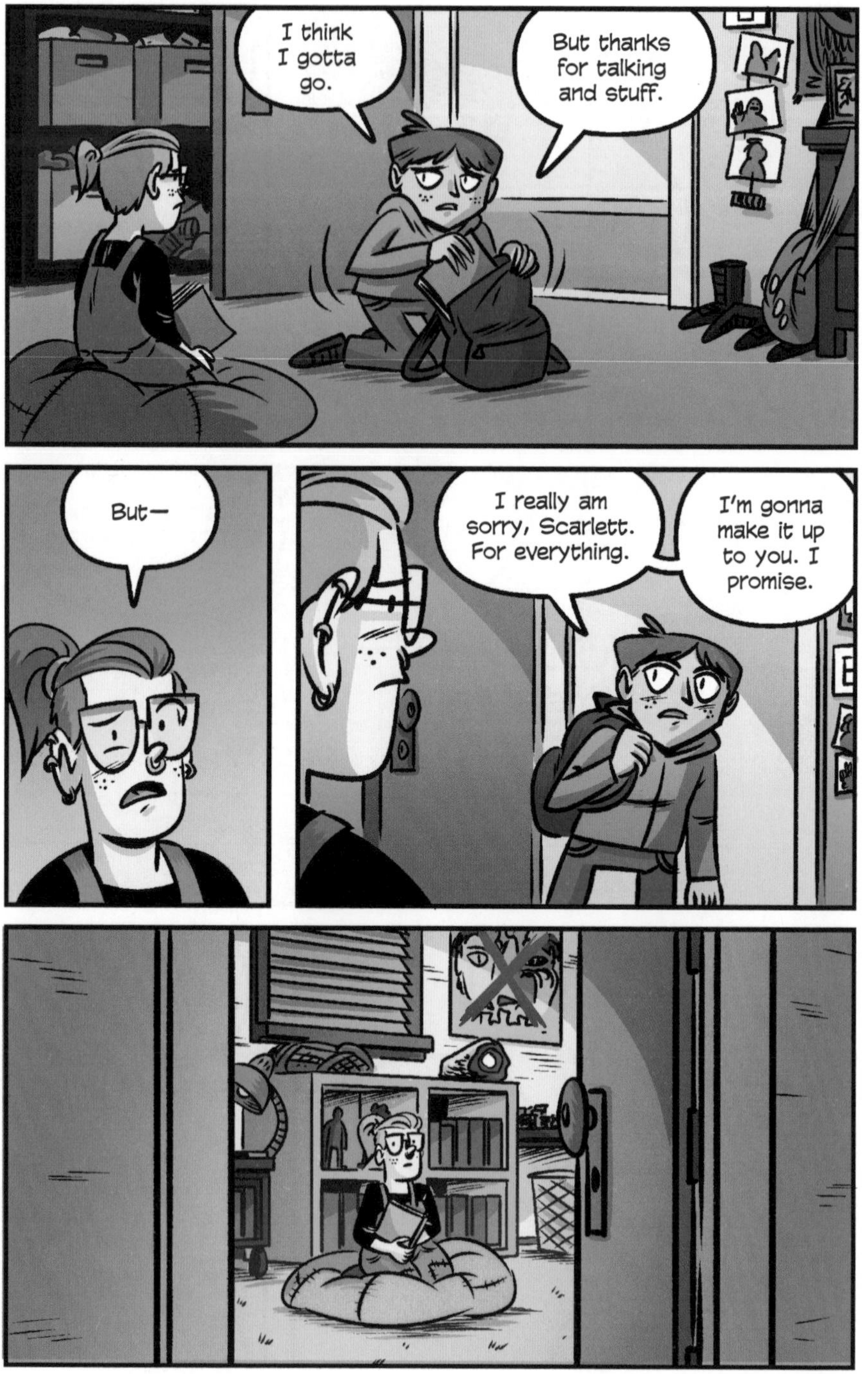
I think I gotta go.
But thanks for talking and stuff.
But—
I really am sorry, Scarlett. For everything.
I'm gonna make it up to you. I promise.

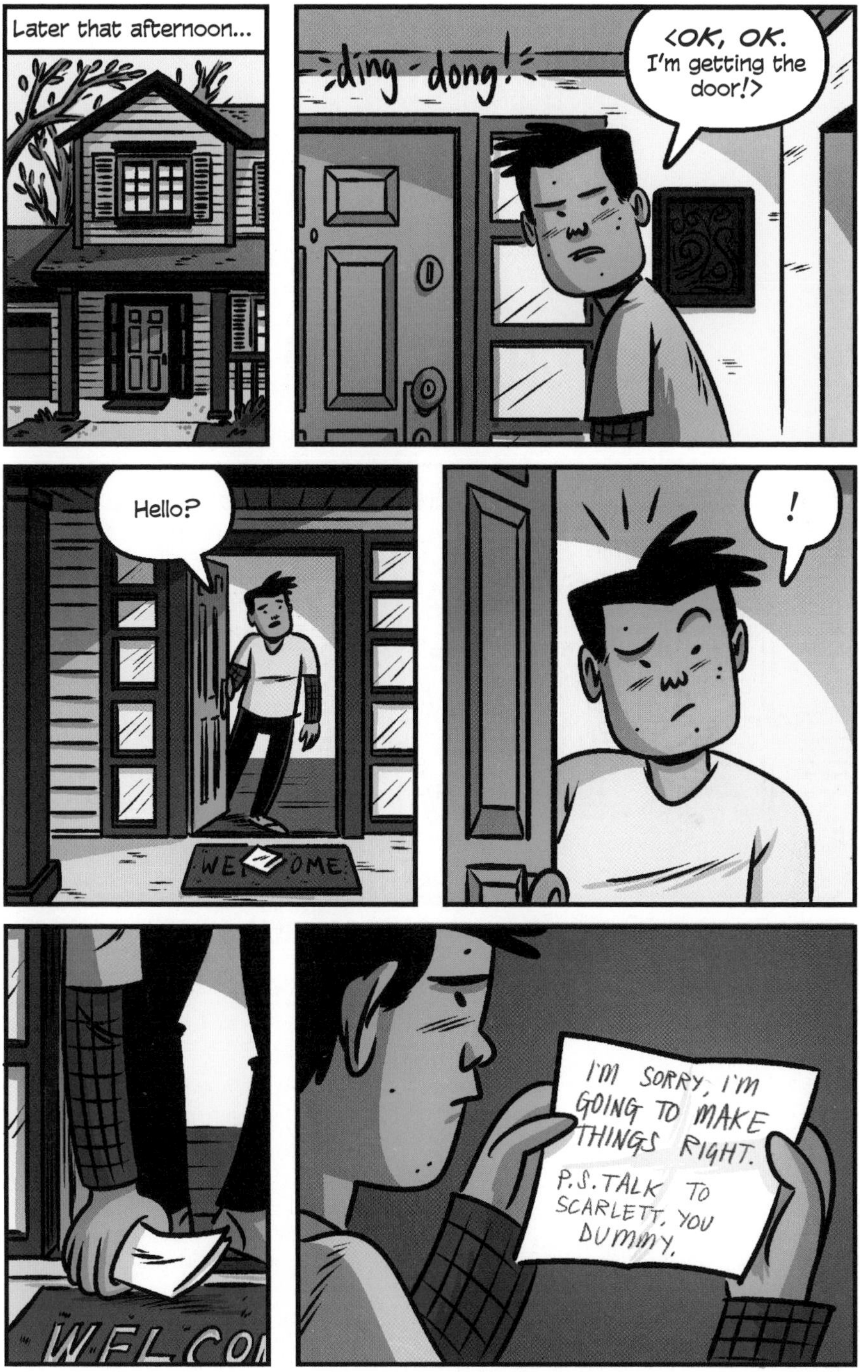
Later that afternoon...
ding dong!
<OK, OK. I'm getting the door!>
Hello?
WE OME
!
I'M SORRY, I'M GOING TO MAKE THINGS RIGHT.
P.S. TALK TO SCARLETT, YOU DUMMY.
WELCOM

CHAPTER 11

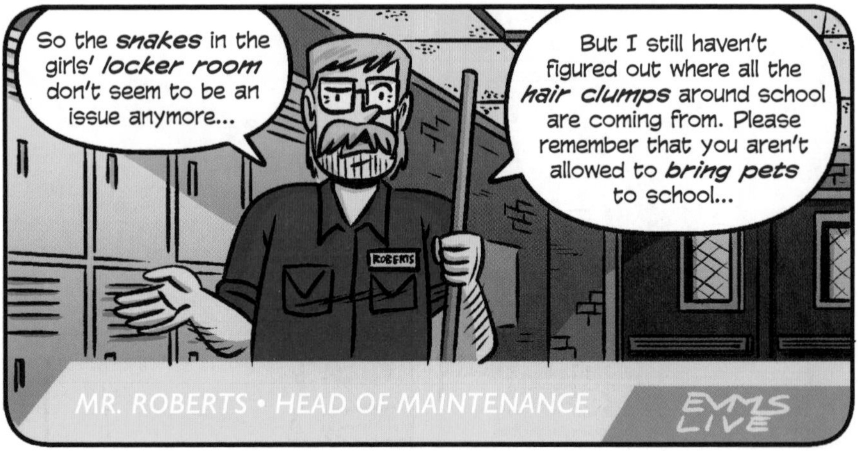
So the *snakes* in the girls' *locker room* don't seem to be an issue anymore...
But I still haven't figured out where all the *hair clumps* around school are coming from. Please remember that you aren't allowed to *bring pets* to school...
ROBERTS
MR. ROBERTS • HEAD OF MAINTENANCE
EVMS LIVE

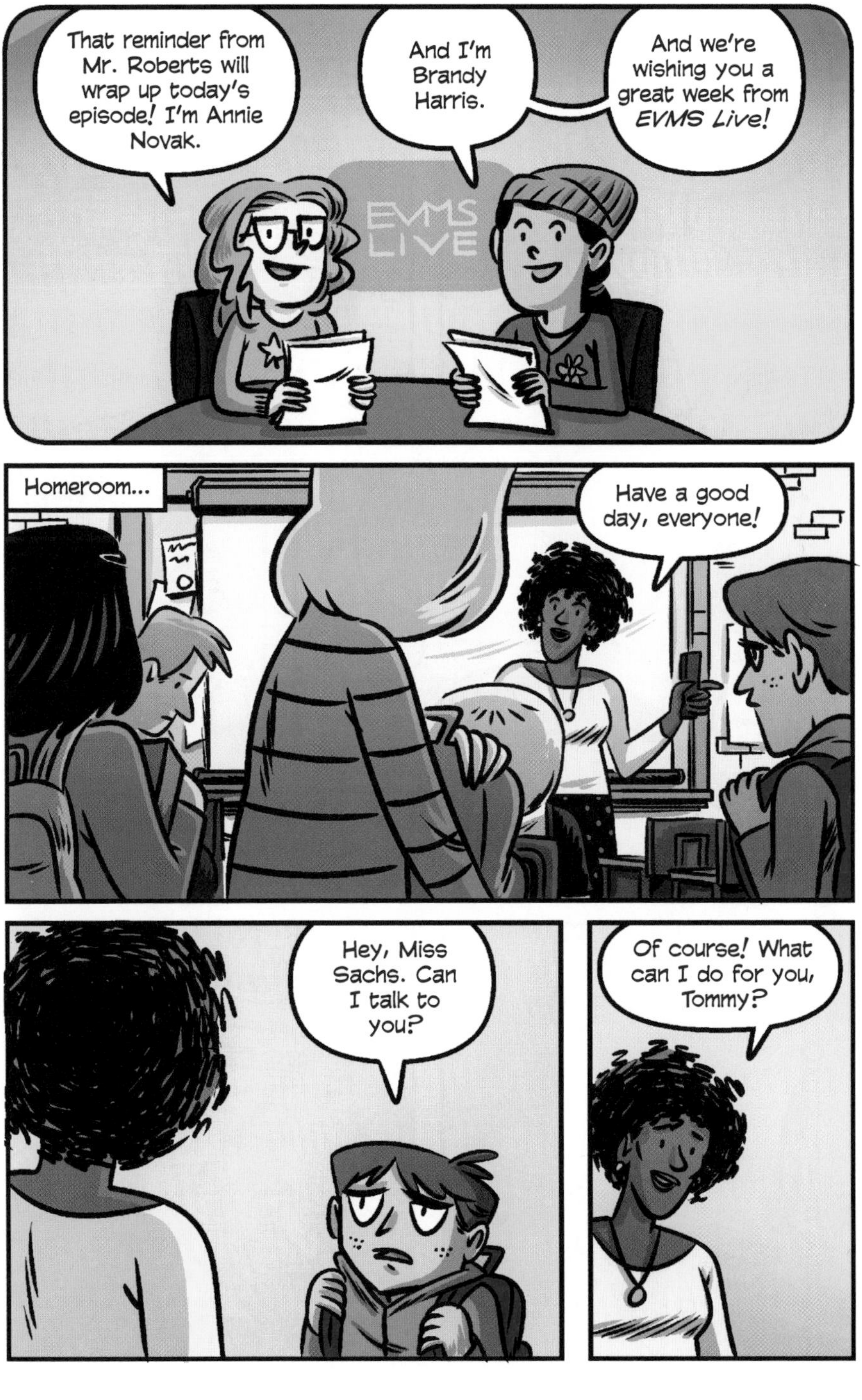
That reminder from Mr. Roberts will wrap up today's episode! I'm Annie Novak.
And I'm Brandy Harris.
And we're wishing you a great week from *EVMS Live!*
EVMS LIVE
Homeroom...
Have a good day, everyone!
Hey, Miss Sachs. Can I talk to you?
Of course! What can I do for you, Tommy?

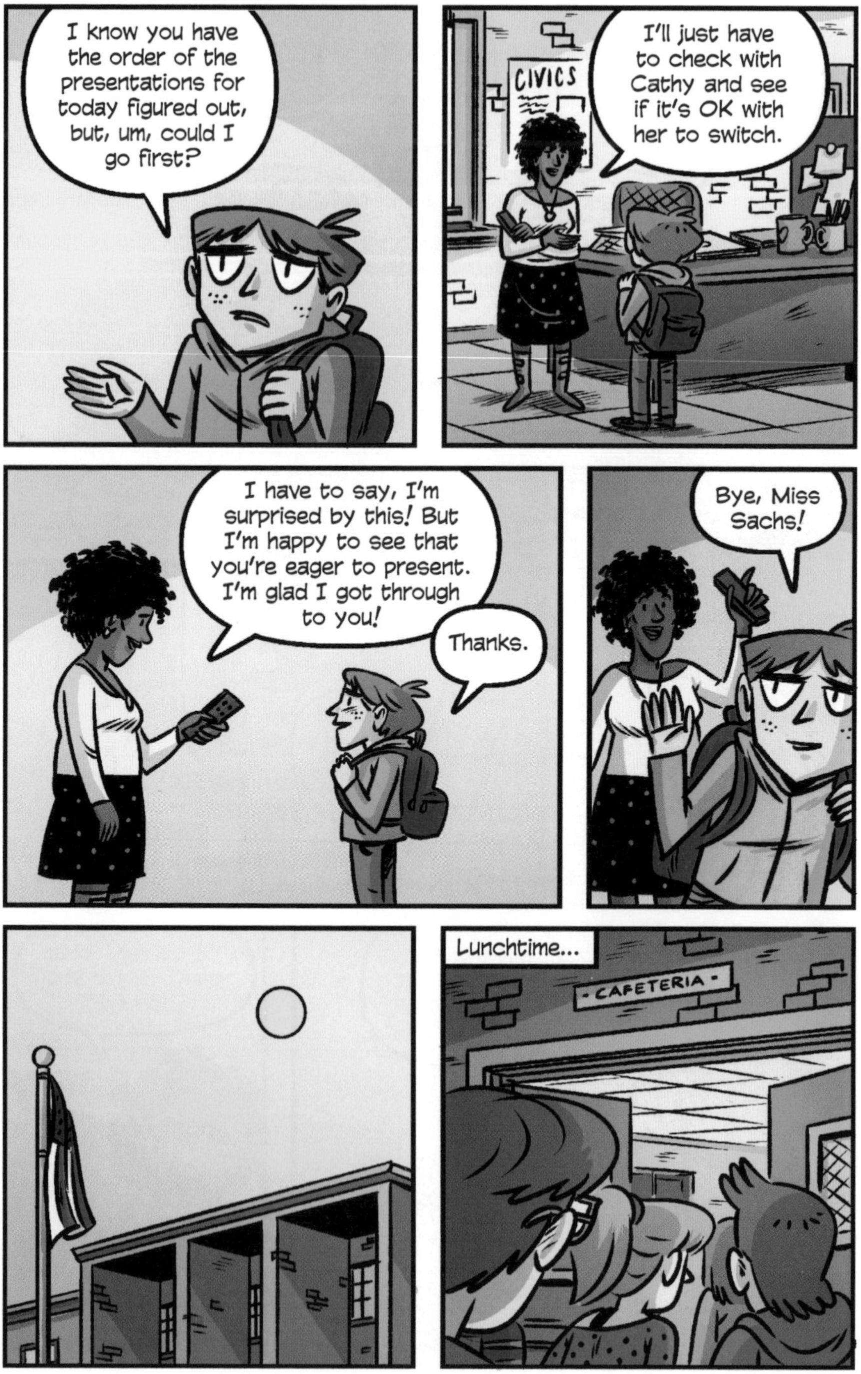
I know you have the order of the presentations for today figured out, but, um, could I go first?
CIVICS
I'll just have to check with Cathy and see if it's OK with her to switch.
I have to say, I'm surprised by this! But I'm happy to see that you're eager to present. I'm glad I got through to you!
Thanks.
Bye, Miss Sachs!
Lunchtime...
CAFETERIA

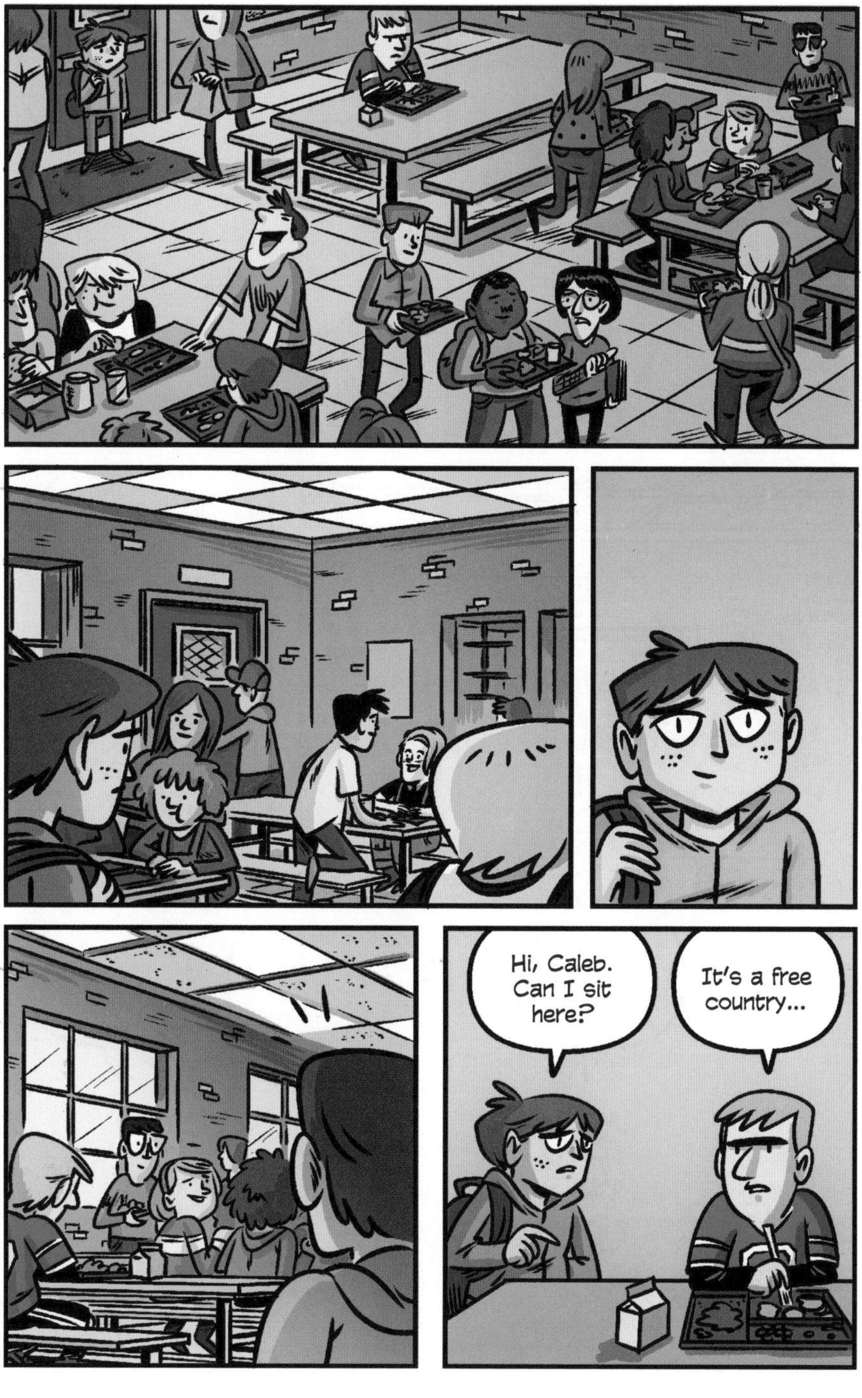
Hi, Caleb.
Can I sit
here?
It's a free
country...

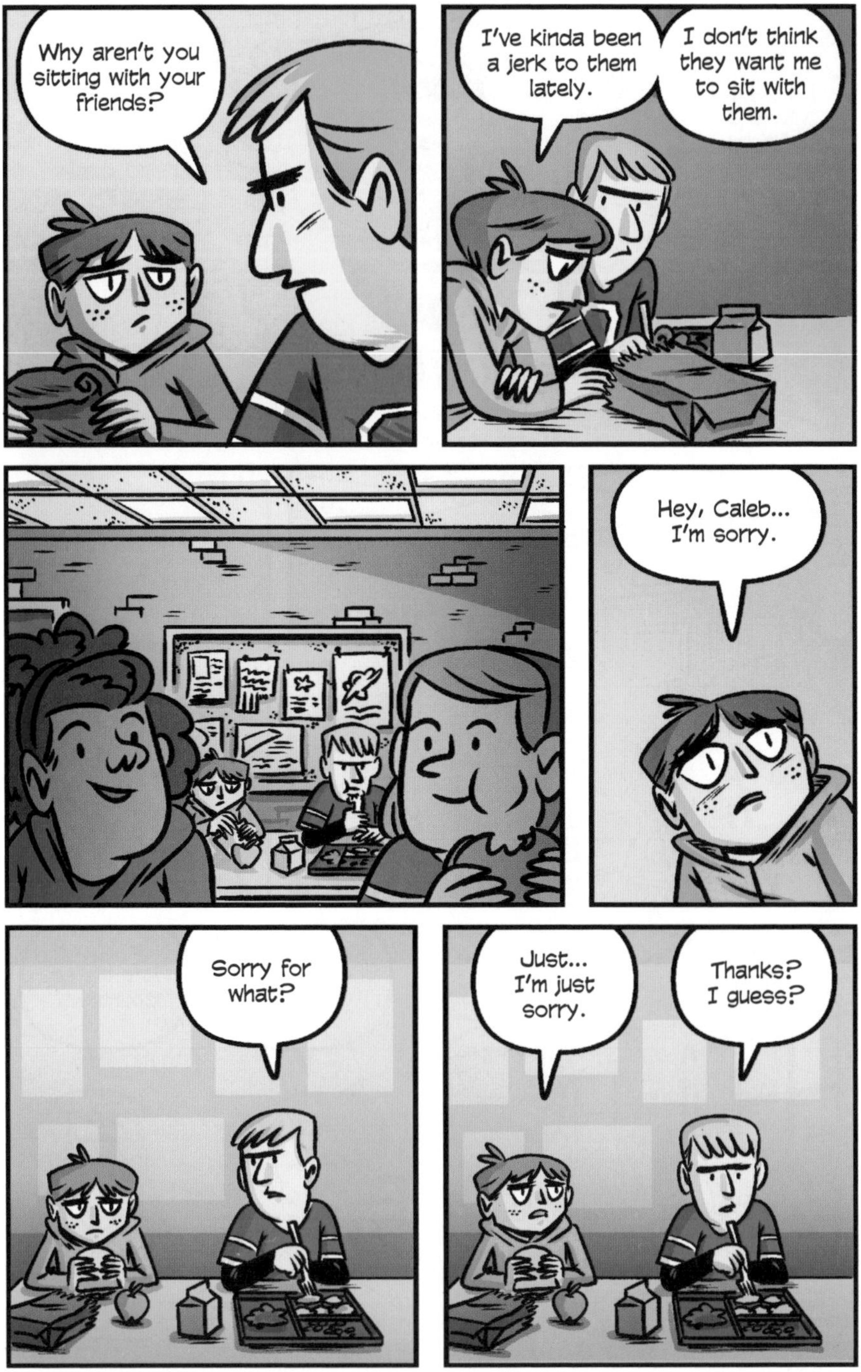
Why aren't you sitting with your friends?
I've kinda been a jerk to them lately.
I don't think they want me to sit with them.
Hey, Caleb... I'm sorry.
Sorry for what?
Just... I'm just sorry.
Thanks? I guess?

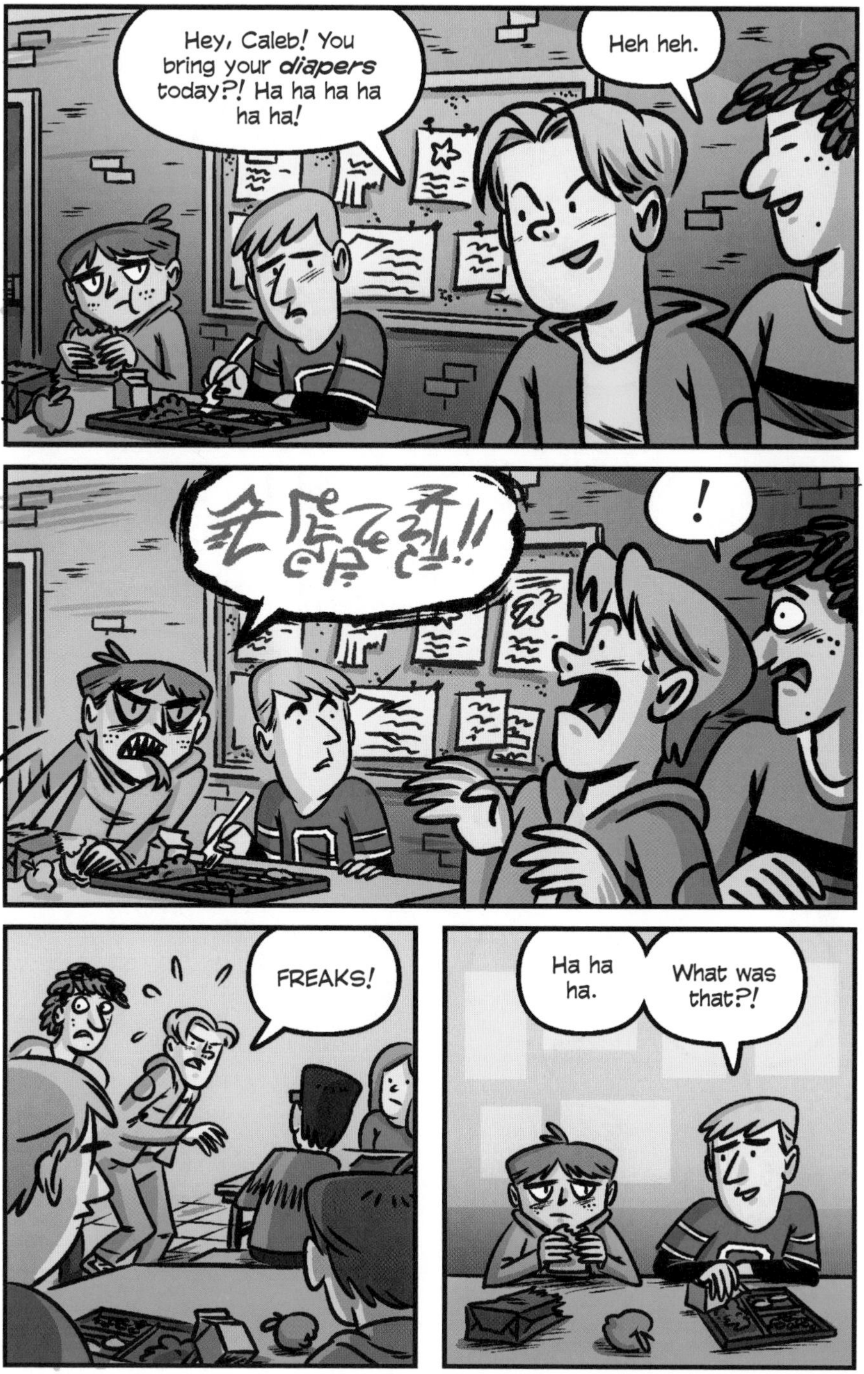
Hey, Caleb! You bring your *diapers* today?! Ha ha ha ha ha ha!
Heh heh.
!
FREAKS!
Ha ha ha.
What was that?!

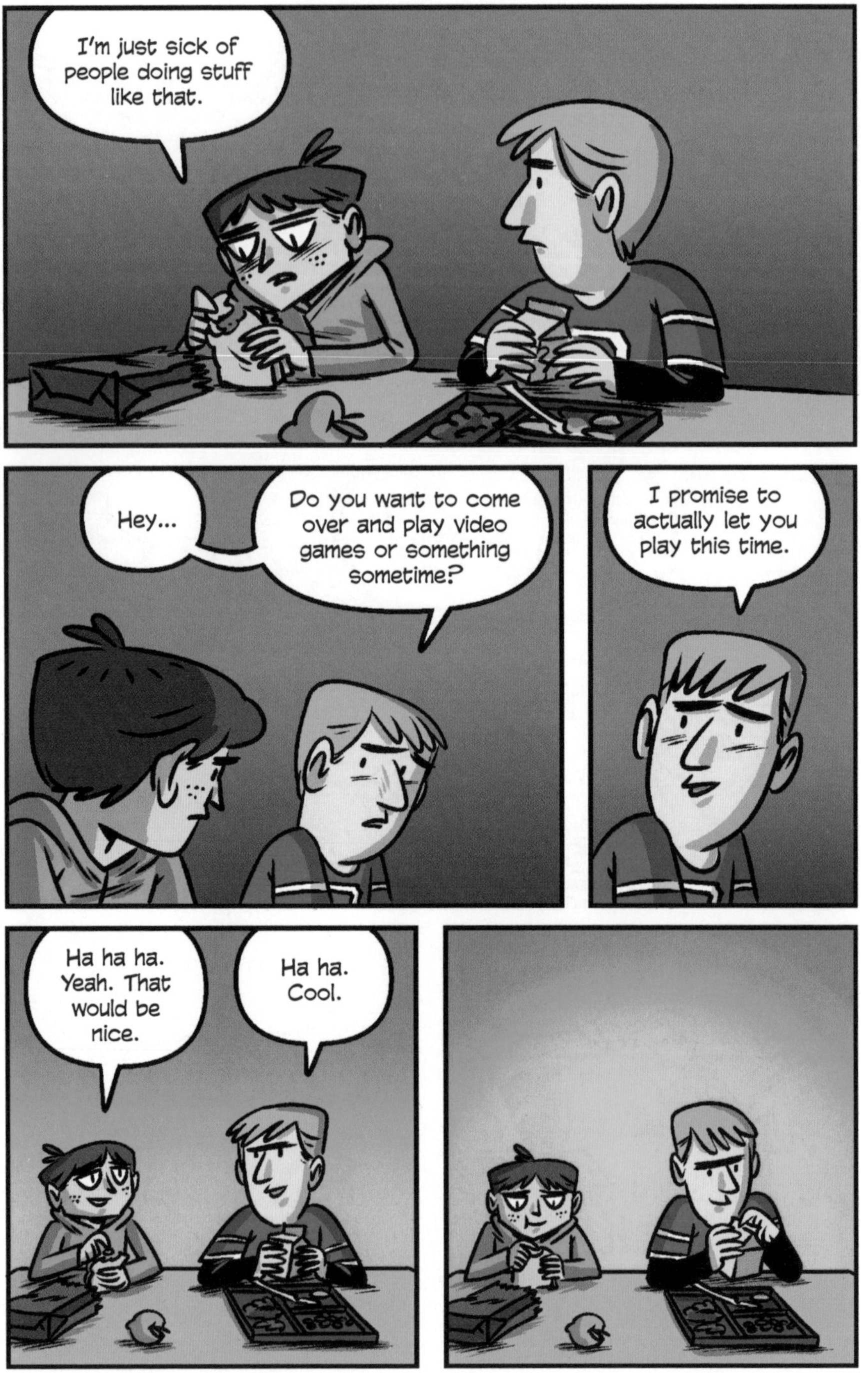
I'm just sick of people doing stuff like that.
Hey...
Do you want to come over and play video games or something sometime?
I promise to actually let you play this time.
Ha ha ha. Yeah. That would be nice.
Ha ha. Cool.

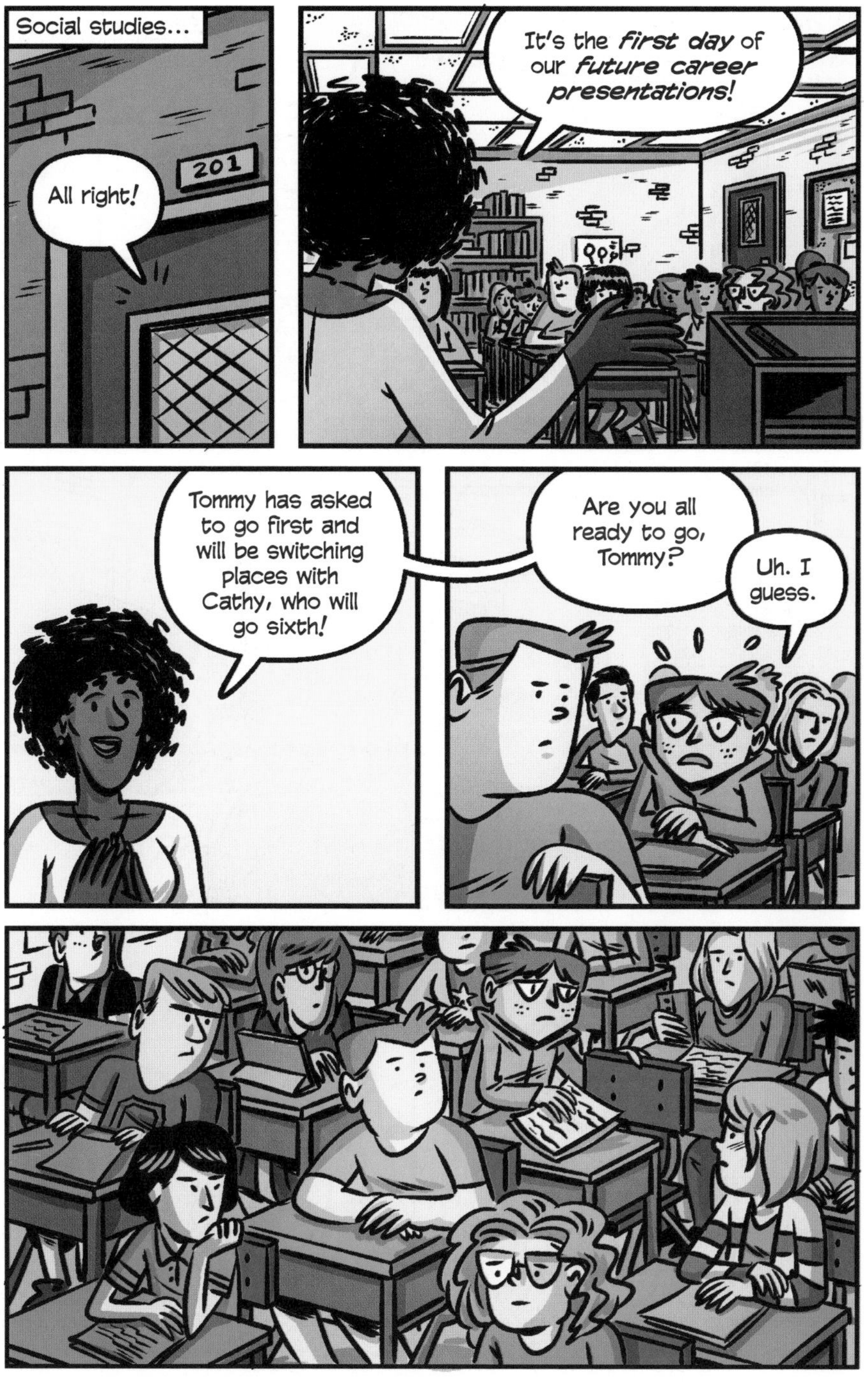
Social studies...
All right!
201
It's the *first day* of our *future career presentations!*
Tommy has asked to go first and will be switching places with Cathy, who will go sixth!
Are you all ready to go, Tommy?
Uh. I guess.

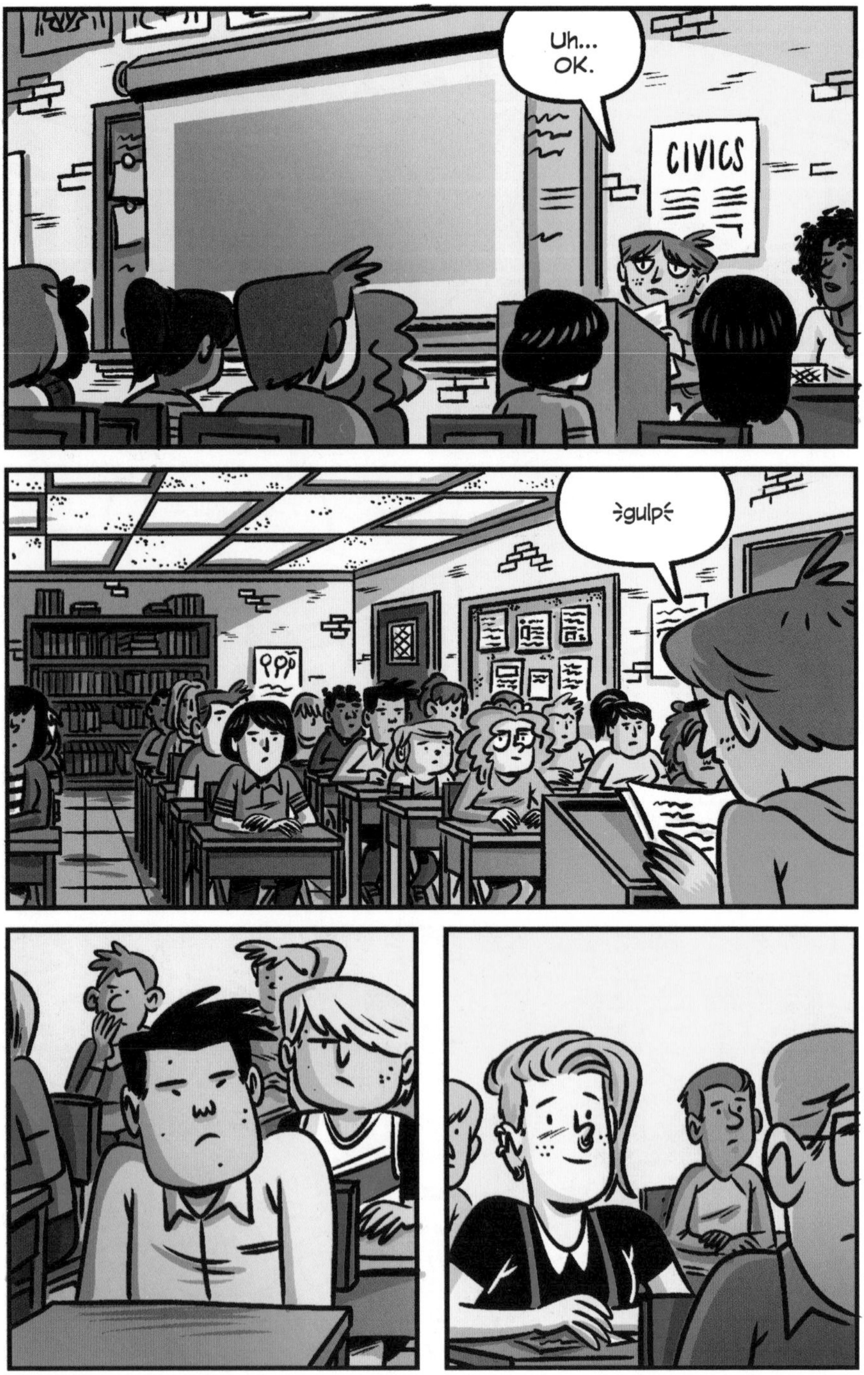
Uh... OK.
CIVICS
gulp

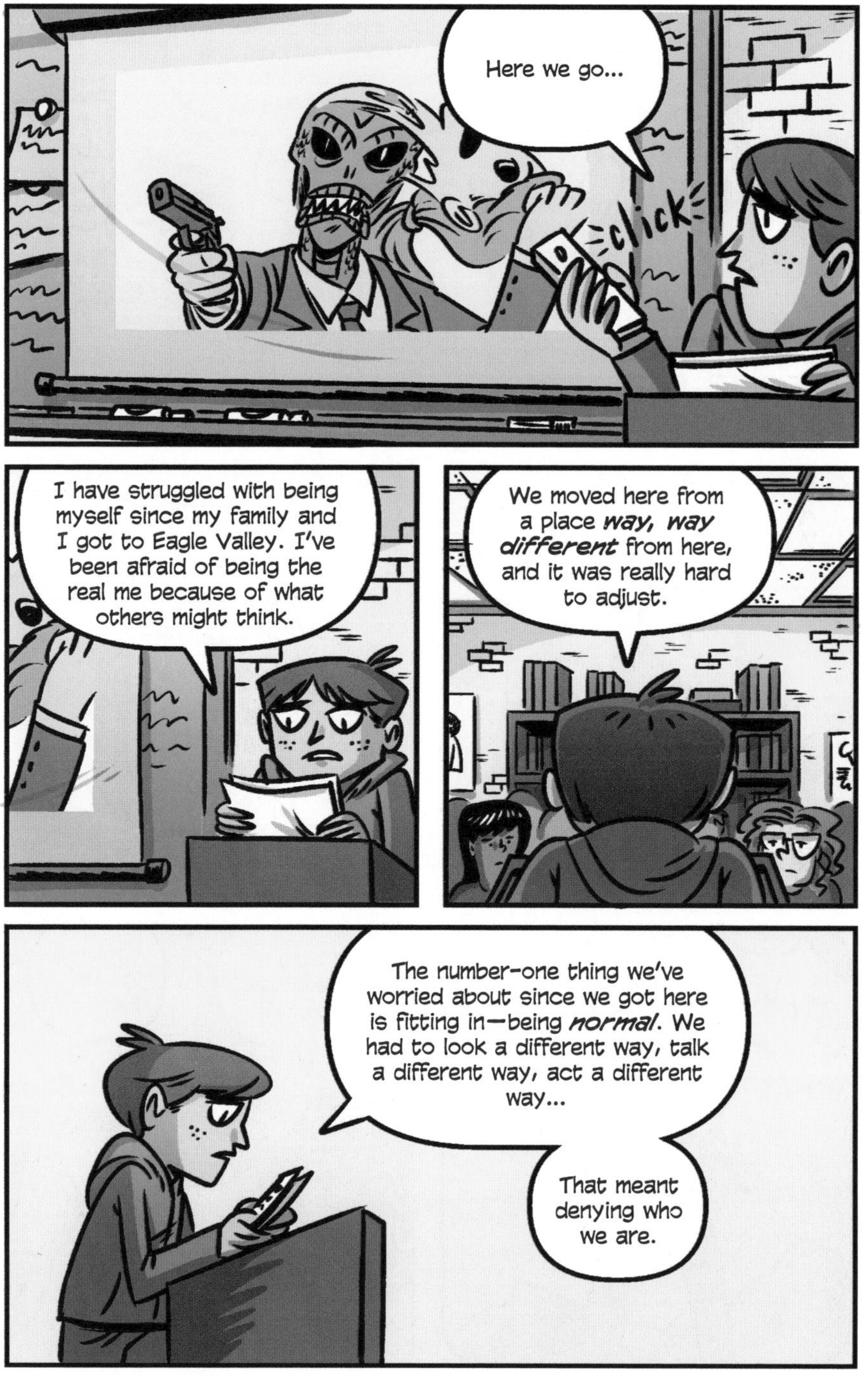
Here we go...
click
I have struggled with being myself since my family and I got to Eagle Valley. I've been afraid of being the real me because of what others might think.
We moved here from a place *way, way different* from here, and it was really hard to adjust.
The number-one thing we've worried about since we got here is fitting in—being *normal*. We had to look a different way, talk a different way, act a different way...
That meant denying who we are.

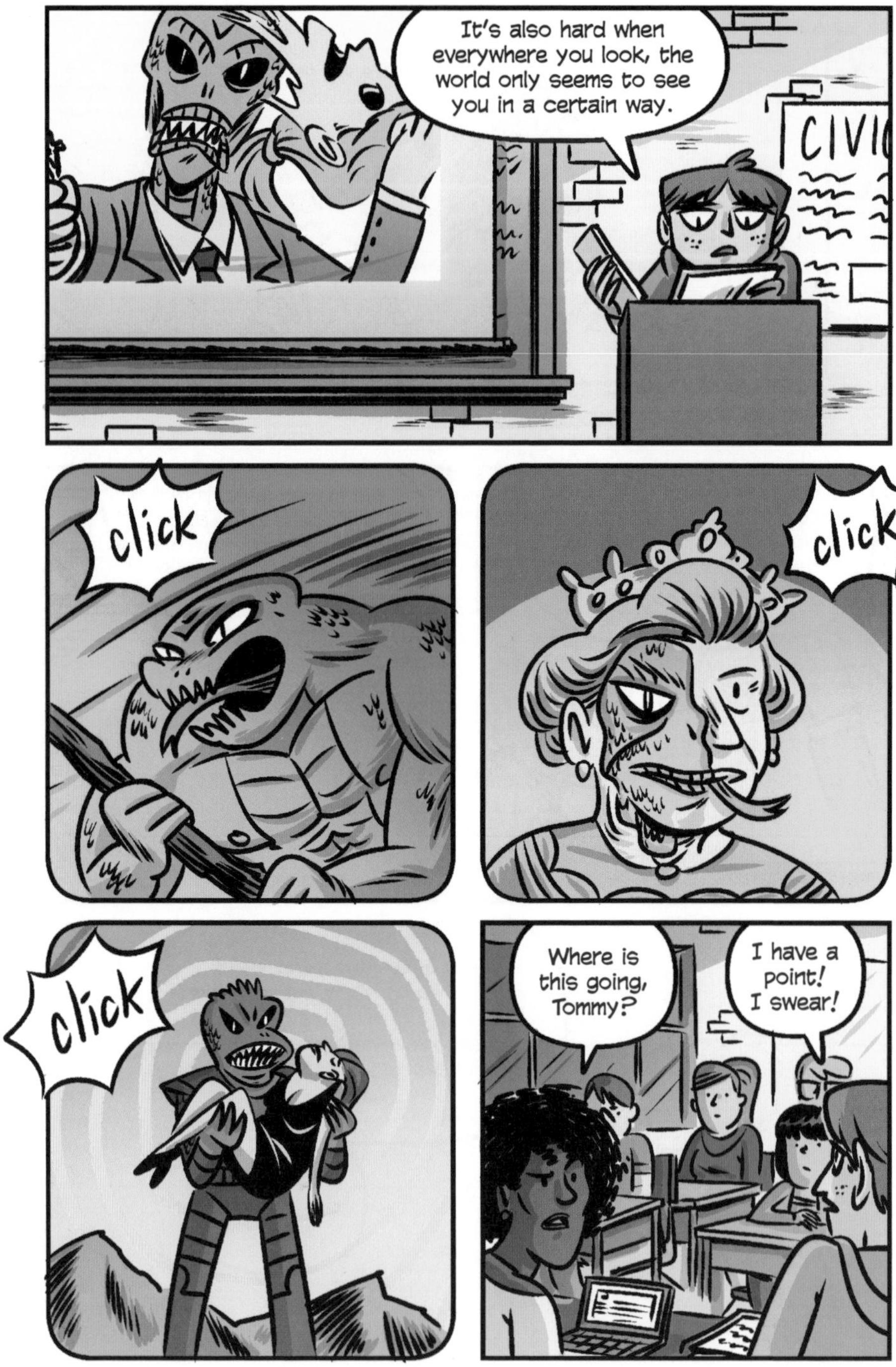
It's also hard when everywhere you look, the world only seems to see you in a certain way.
CIVI
click
click
click
Where is this going, Tommy?
I have a point! I swear!

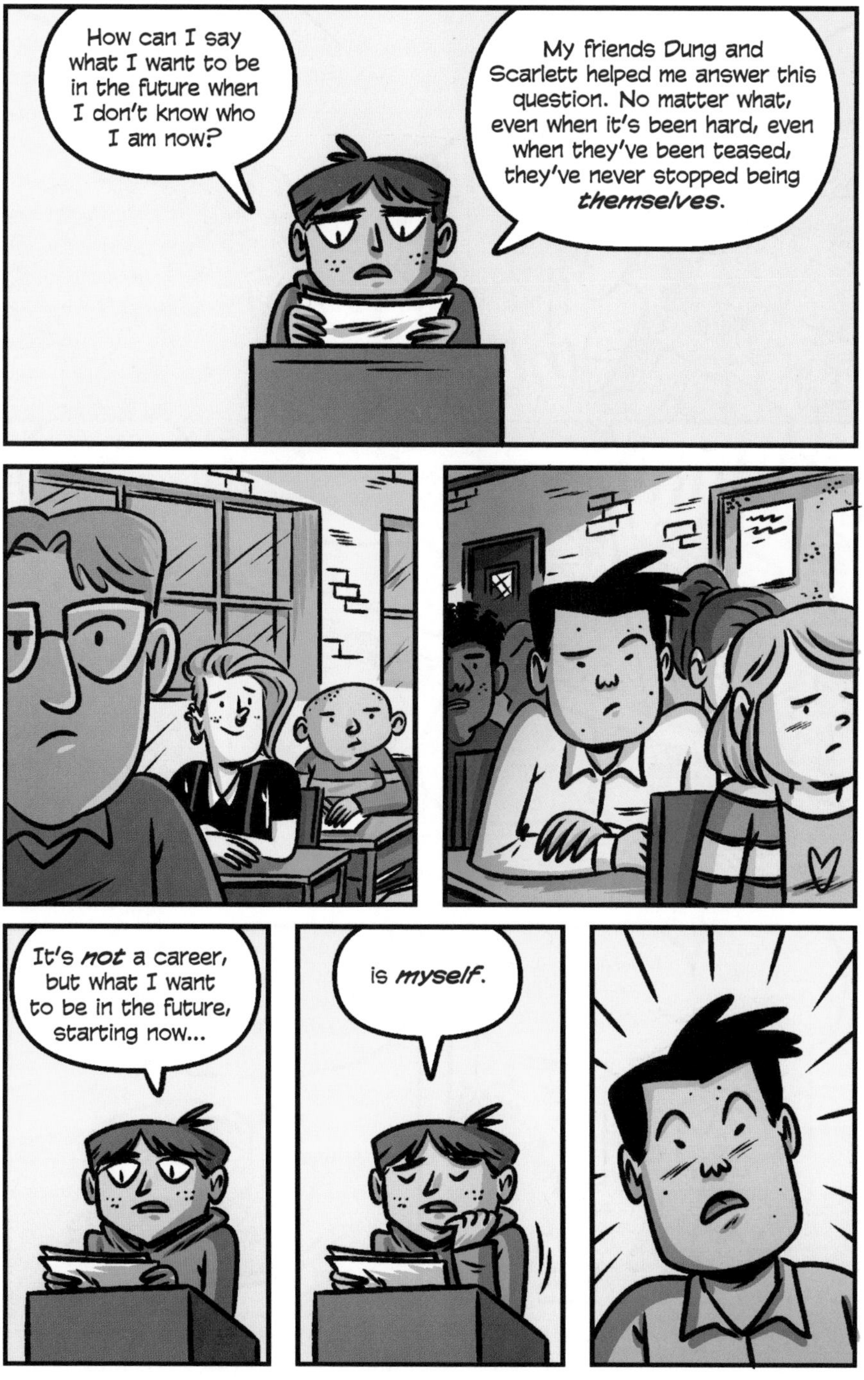
How can I say what I want to be in the future when I don't know who I am now?
My friends Dung and Scarlett helped me answer this question. No matter what, even when it's been hard, even when they've been teased, they've never stopped being *themselves*.
It's *not* a career, but what I want to be in the future, starting now...
is *myself*.

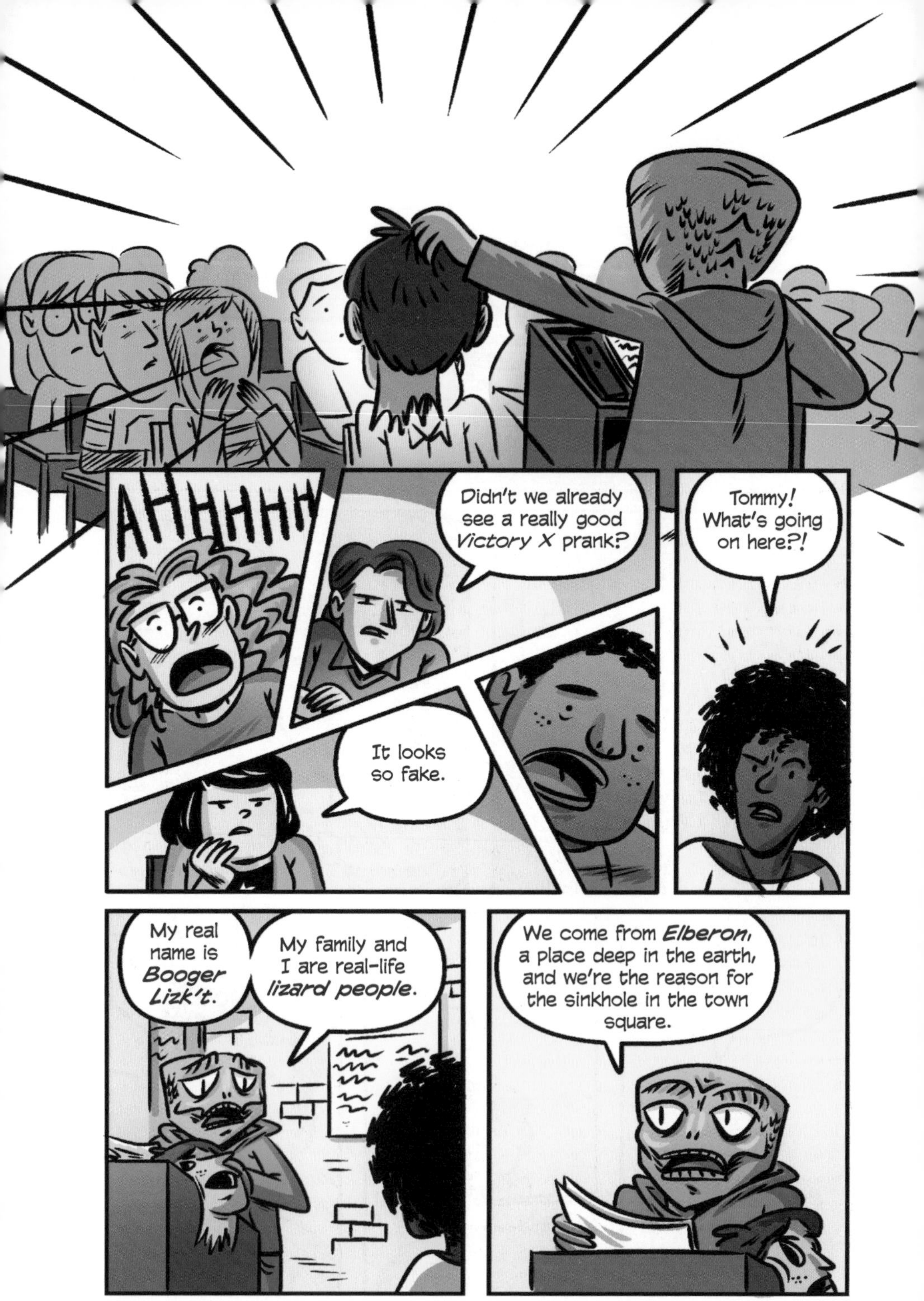
AHHHHH
Didn't we already see a really good *Victory X* prank?
It looks so fake.
Tommy! What's going on here?!
My real name is ***Booger Lizk't***.
My family and I are real-life ***lizard people***.
We come from ***Elberon***, a place deep in the earth, and we're the reason for the sinkhole in the town square.

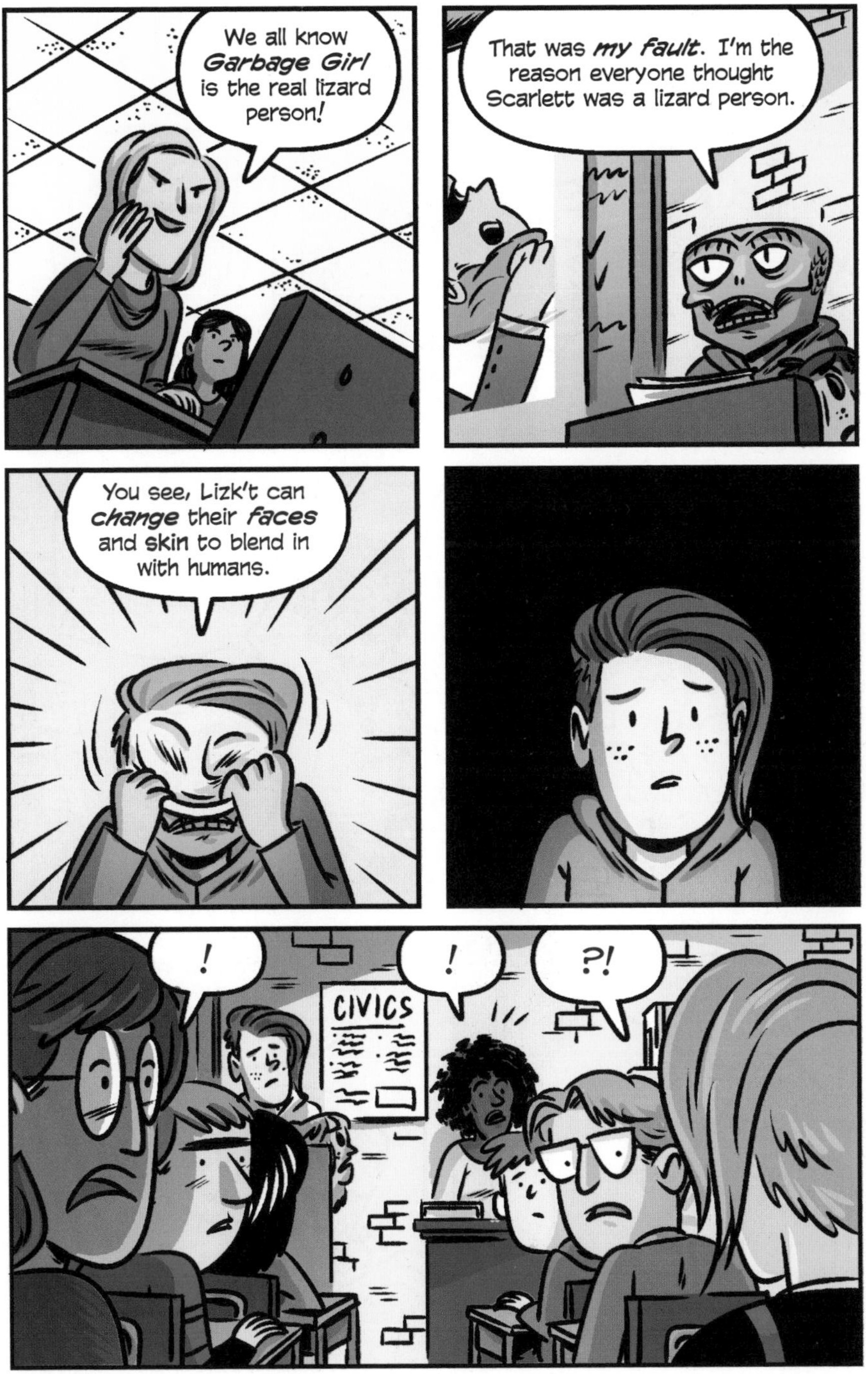
We all know Garbage Girl is the real lizard person!
That was my fault. I'm the reason everyone thought Scarlett was a lizard person.
You see, Lizk't can change their faces and skin to blend in with humans.
!
!
?!
CIVICS

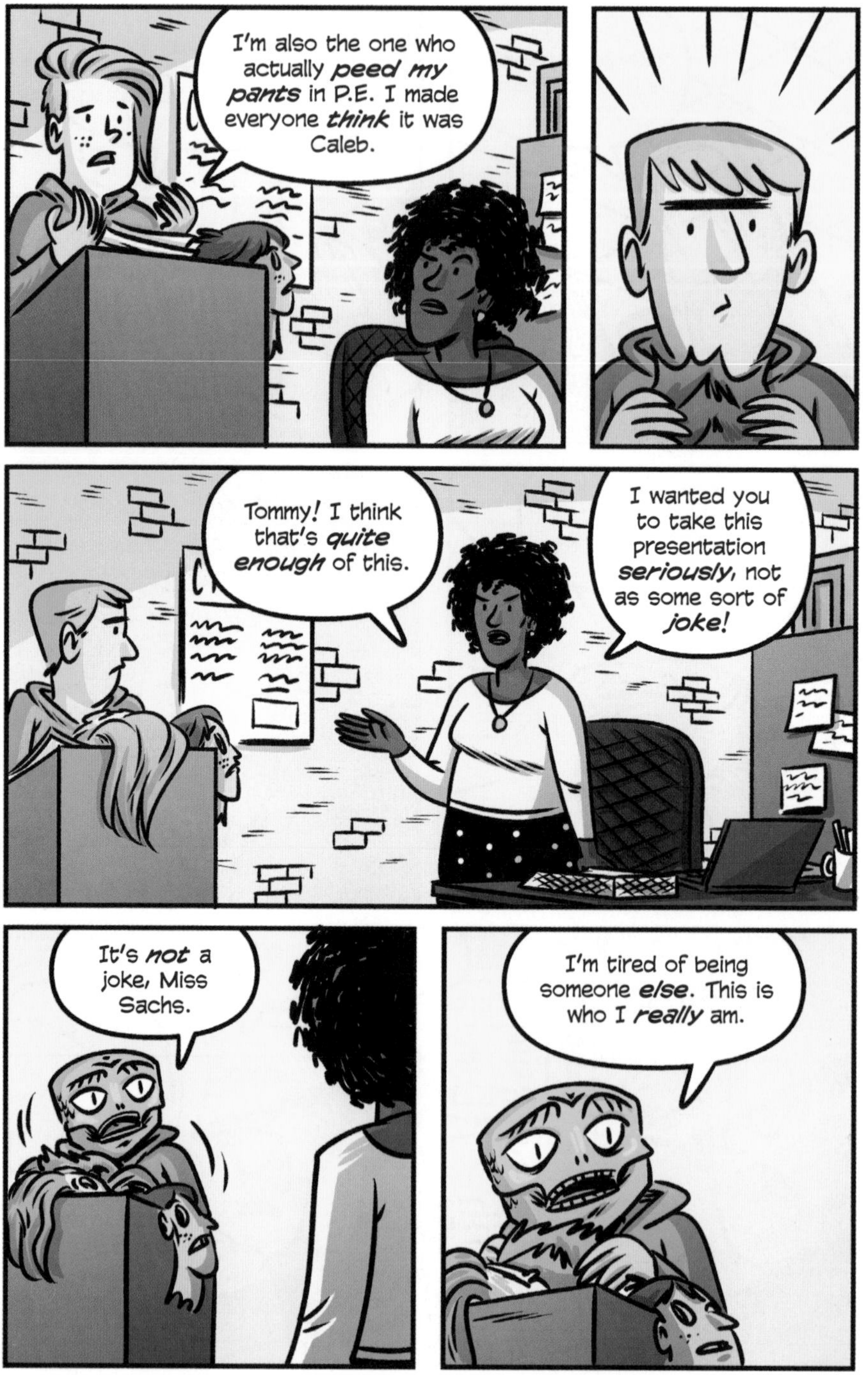
I'm also the one who actually *peed my pants* in P.E. I made everyone *think* it was Caleb.
Tommy! I think that's *quite enough* of this.
I wanted you to take this presentation *seriously*, not as some sort of *joke!*
It's *not* a joke, Miss Sachs.
I'm tired of being someone *else*. This is who I *really* am.

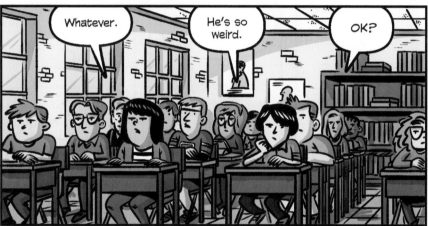

Whatever.

He's so weird.

OK?

Thank you, Tommy.

Don't forget to, um, take your faces with you.

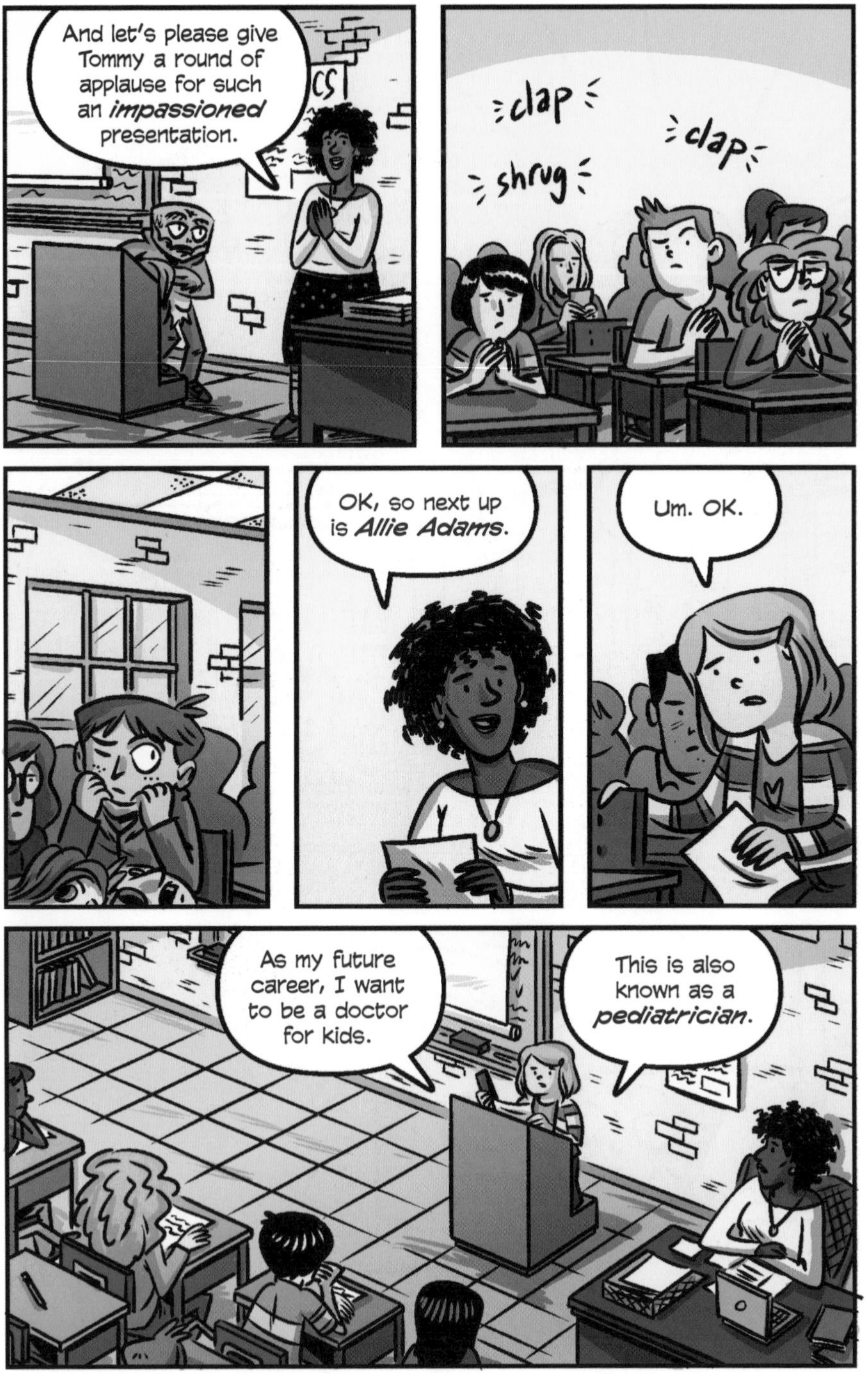
And let's please give Tommy a round of applause for such an *impassioned* presentation.
clap
clap
shrug
OK, so next up is *Allie Adams*.
Um. OK.
As my future career, I want to be a doctor for kids.
This is also known as a *pediatrician*.

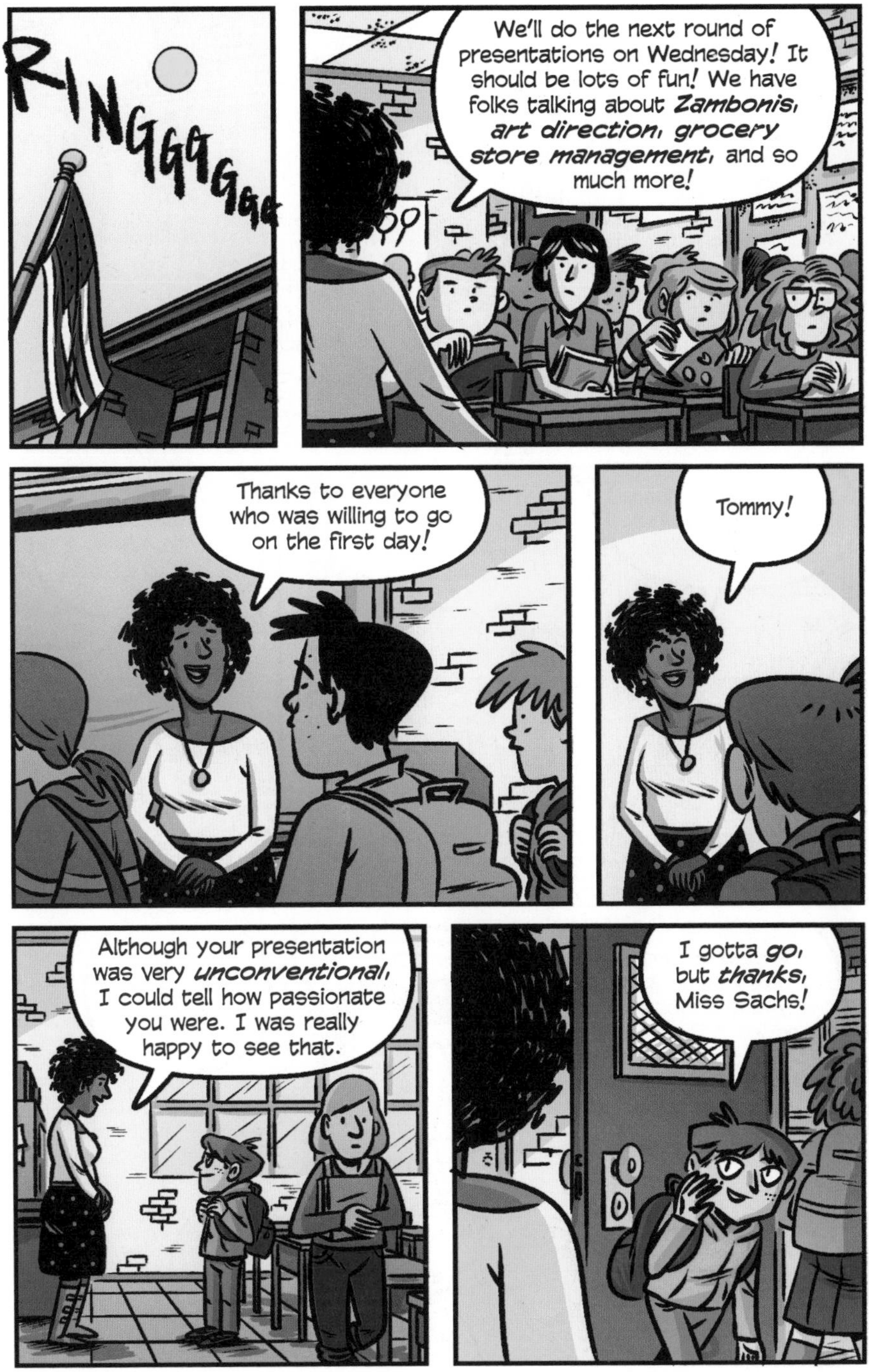
RINGGGGGG
We'll do the next round of presentations on Wednesday! It should be lots of fun! We have folks talking about *Zambonis*, *art direction*, *grocery store management*, and so much more!
Thanks to everyone who was willing to go on the first day!
Tommy!
Although your presentation was very *unconventional*, I could tell how passionate you were. I was really happy to see that.
I gotta *go*, but *thanks*, Miss Sachs!

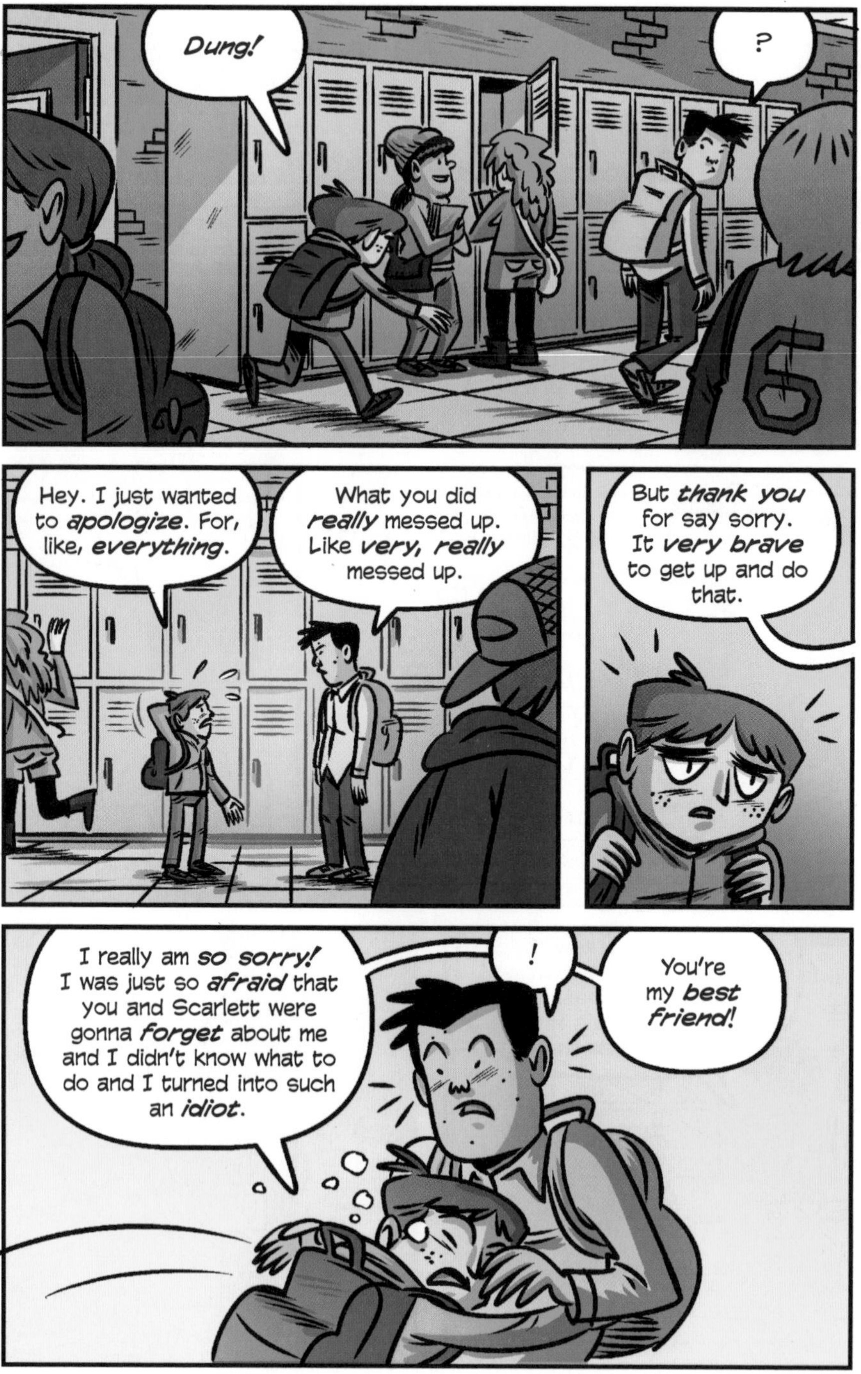
Dung!
?
Hey. I just wanted to apologize. For, like, everything.
What you did really messed up. Like very, really messed up.
But thank you for say sorry. It very brave to get up and do that.
I really am so sorry! I was just so afraid that you and Scarlett were gonna forget about me and I didn't know what to do and I turned into such an idiot.
!
You're my best friend!

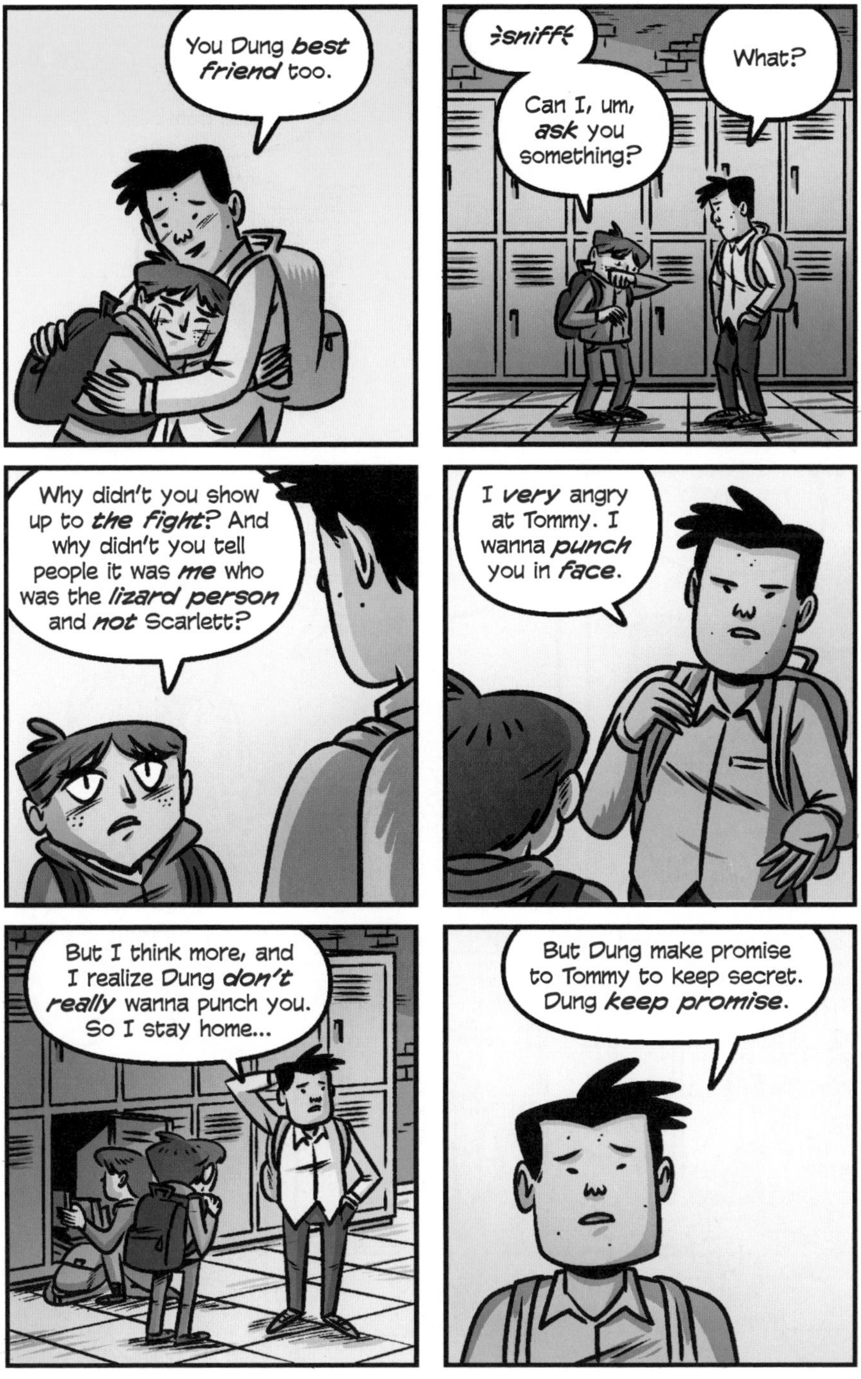
You Dung best friend too.
sniff
Can I, um, ask you something?
What?
Why didn't you show up to the fight? And why didn't you tell people it was me who was the lizard person and not Scarlett?
I very angry at Tommy. I wanna punch you in face.
But I think more, and I realize Dung don't really wanna punch you. So I stay home...
But Dung make promise to Tommy to keep secret. Dung keep promise.

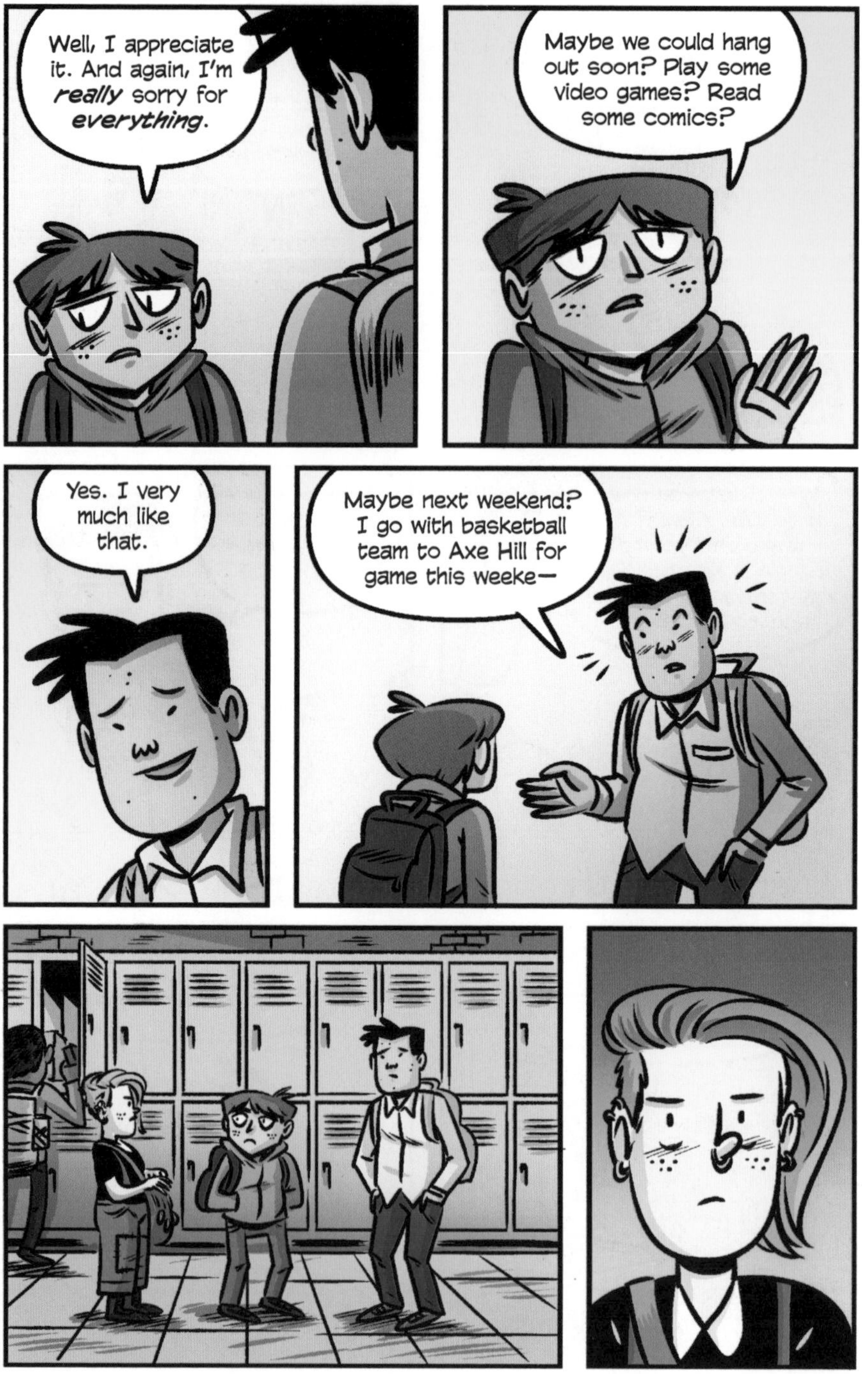
Well, I appreciate it. And again, I'm *really* sorry for *everything*.
Maybe we could hang out soon? Play some video games? Read some comics?
Yes. I very much like that.
Maybe next weekend? I go with basketball team to Axe Hill for game this weeke—

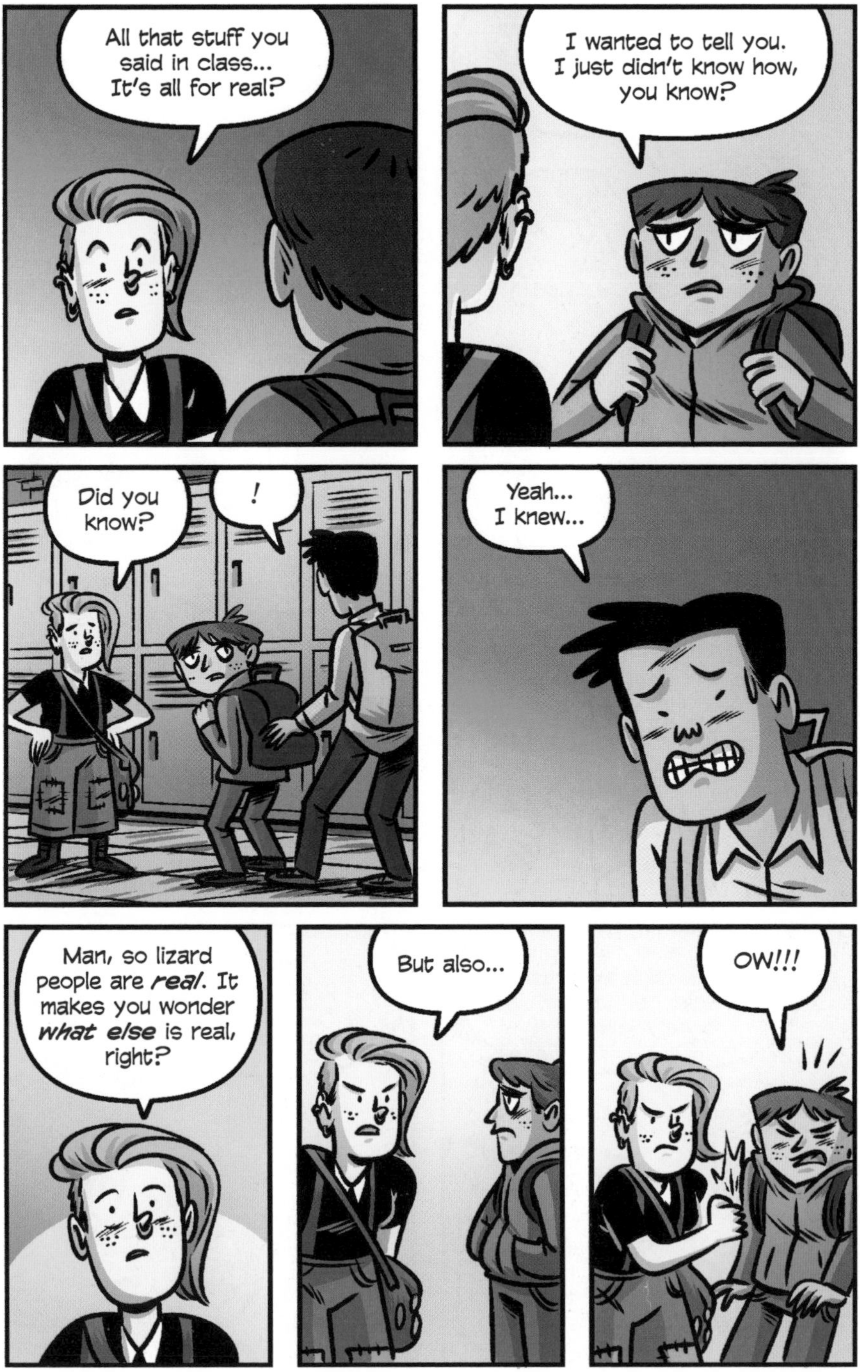
All that stuff you said in class... It's all for real?
I wanted to tell you. I just didn't know how, you know?
Did you know?
!
Yeah... I knew...
Man, so lizard people are *real*. It makes you wonder ***what else*** is real, right?
But also...
OW!!!

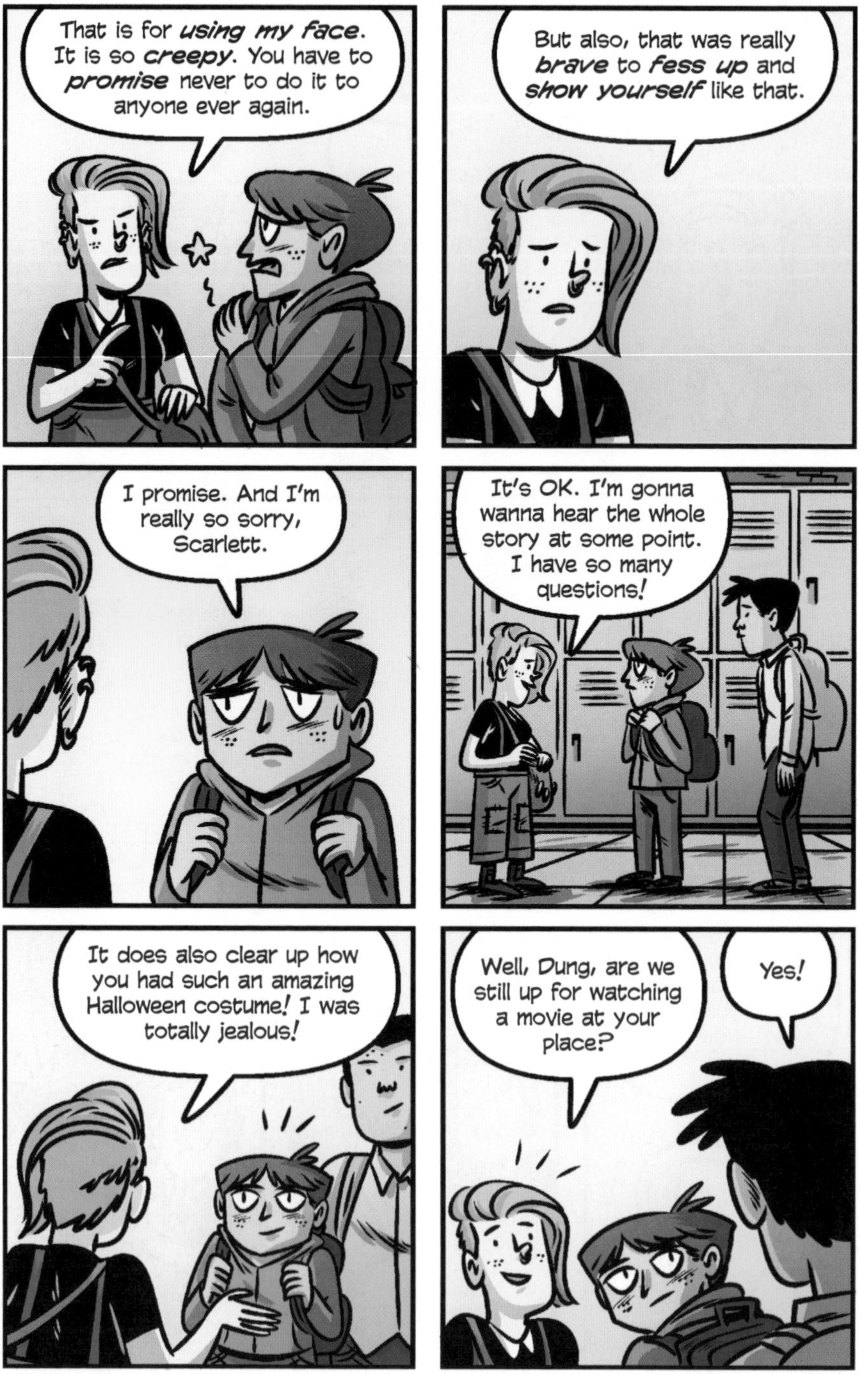
That is for *using my face*. It is so *creepy*. You have to *promise* never to do it to anyone ever again.
But also, that was really *brave* to *fess up* and *show yourself* like that.
I promise. And I'm really so sorry, Scarlett.
It's OK. I'm gonna wanna hear the whole story at some point. I have so many questions!
It does also clear up how you had such an amazing Halloween costume! I was totally jealous!
Well, Dung, are we still up for watching a movie at your place?
Yes!

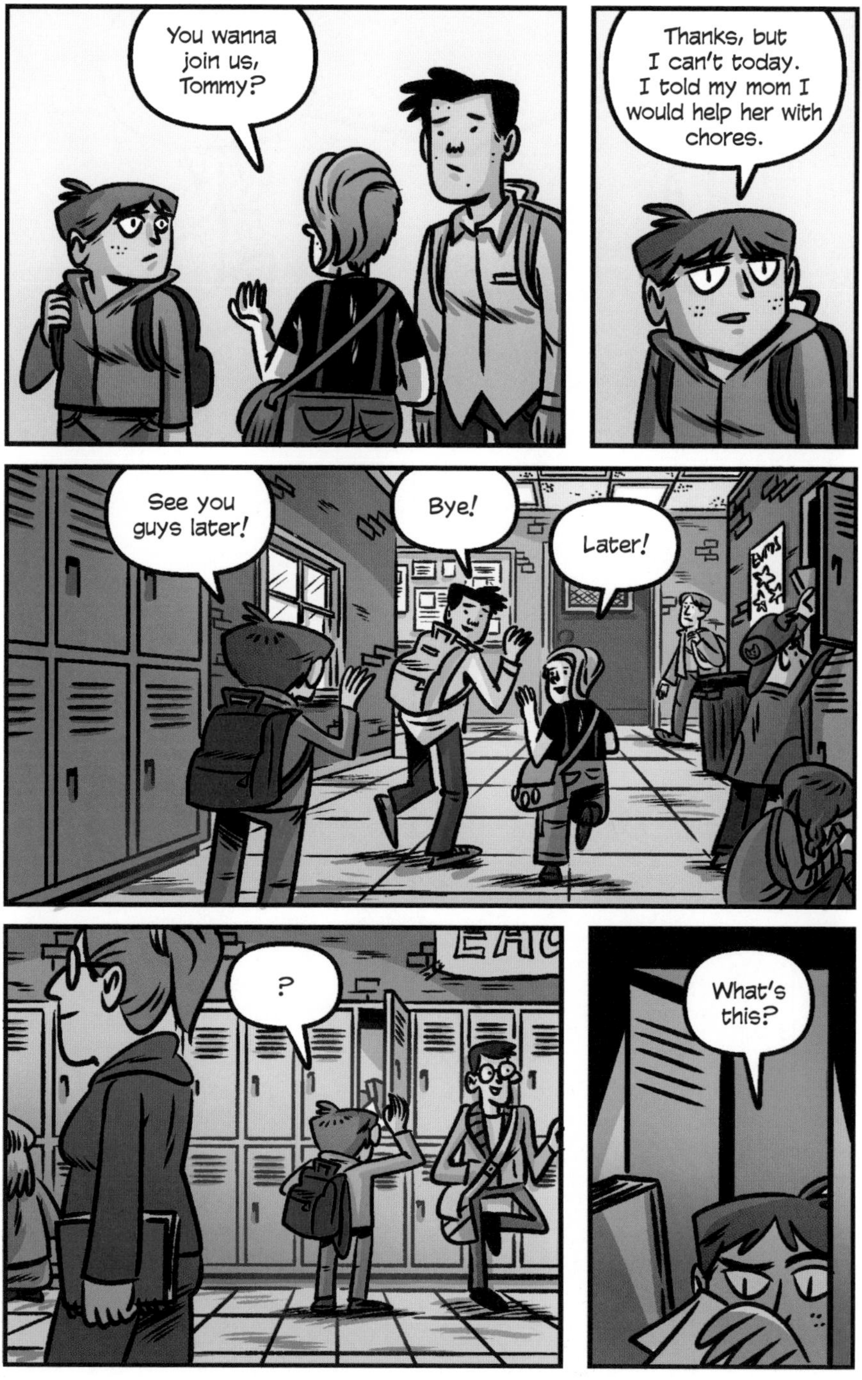
You wanna join us, Tommy?
Thanks, but I can't today. I told my mom I would help her with chores.
See you guys later!
Bye!
Later!
?
What's this?

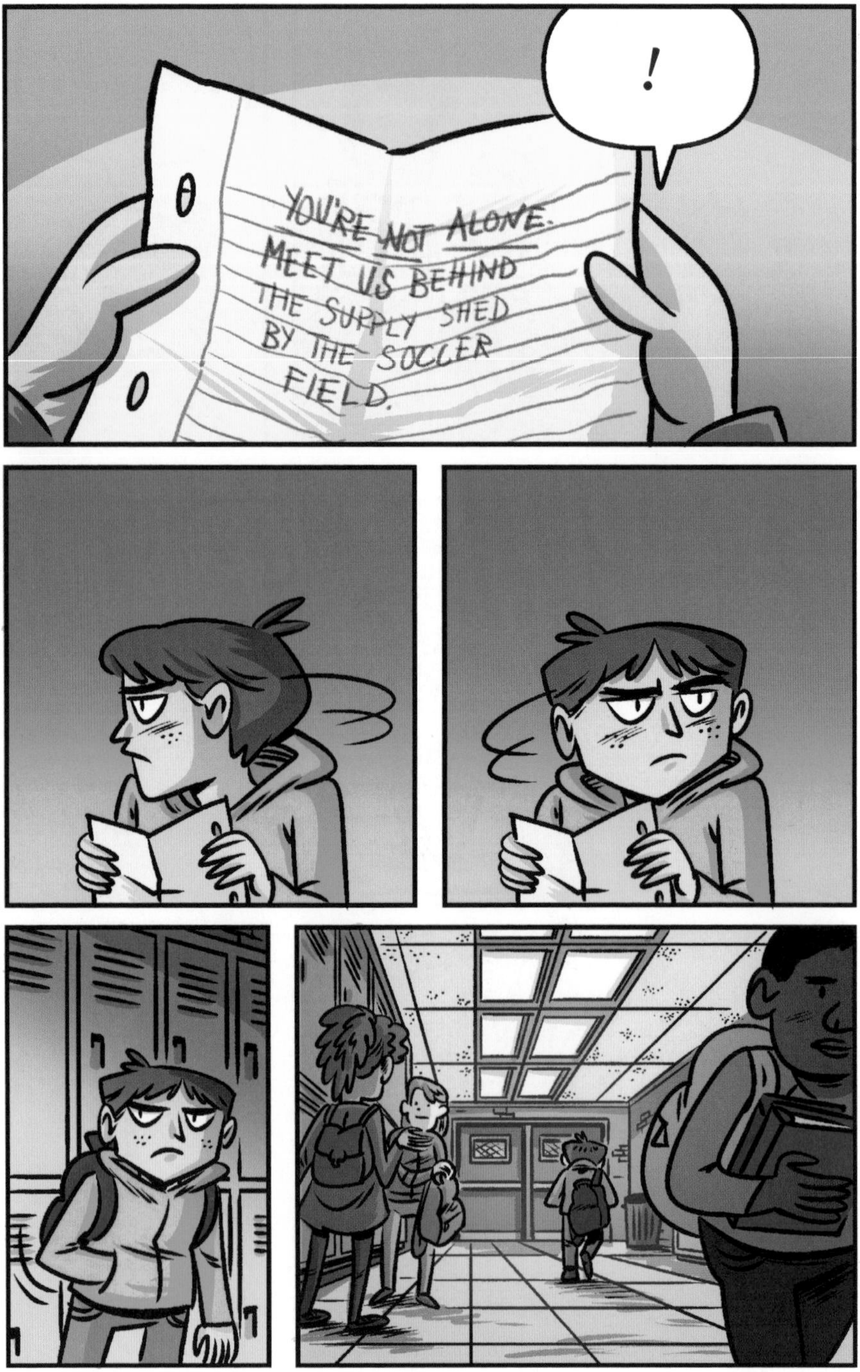
!
YOU'RE NOT ALONE. MEET US BEHIND THE SUPPLY SHED BY THE SOCCER FIELD.

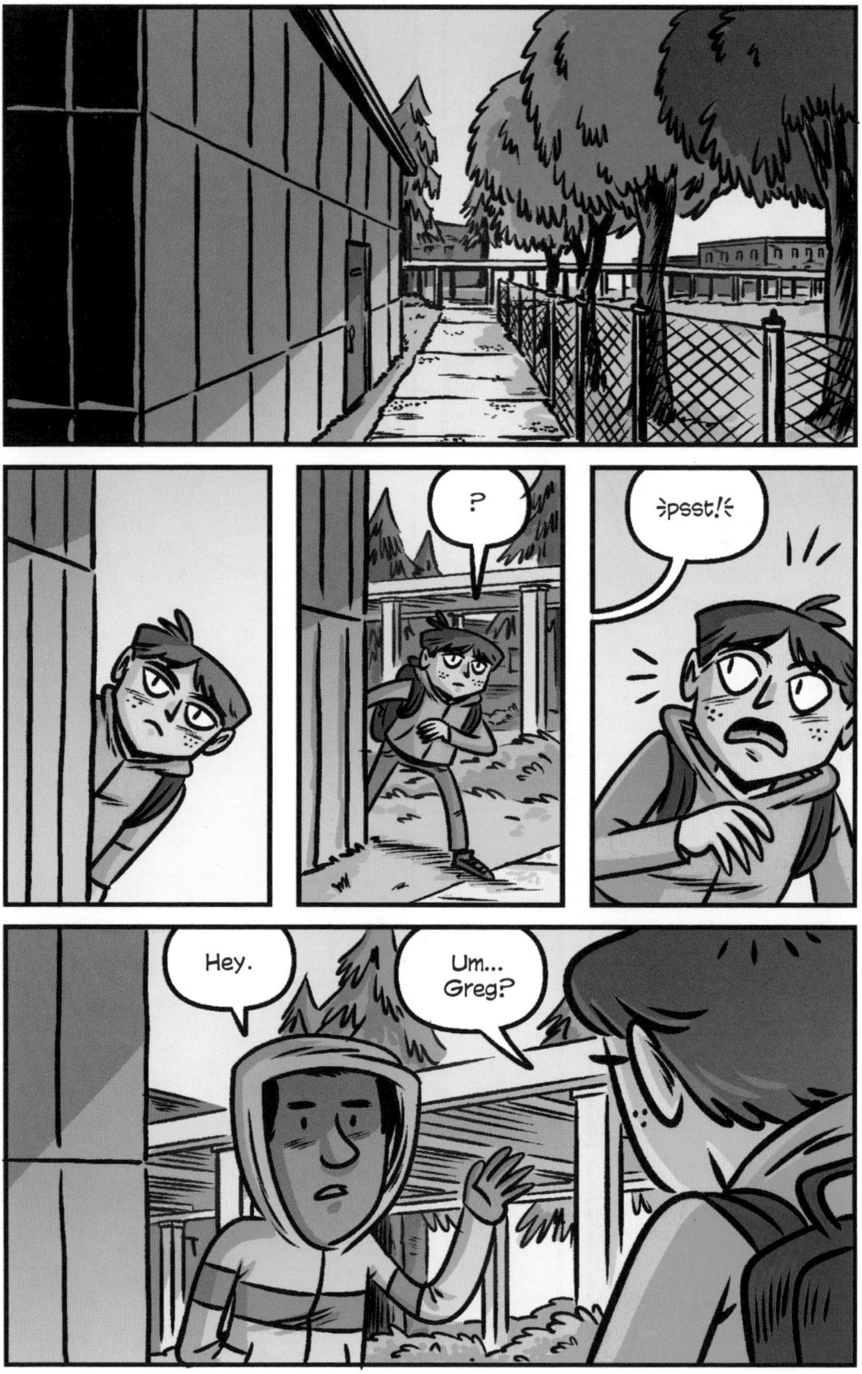
?
psst!
Hey.
Um... Greg?

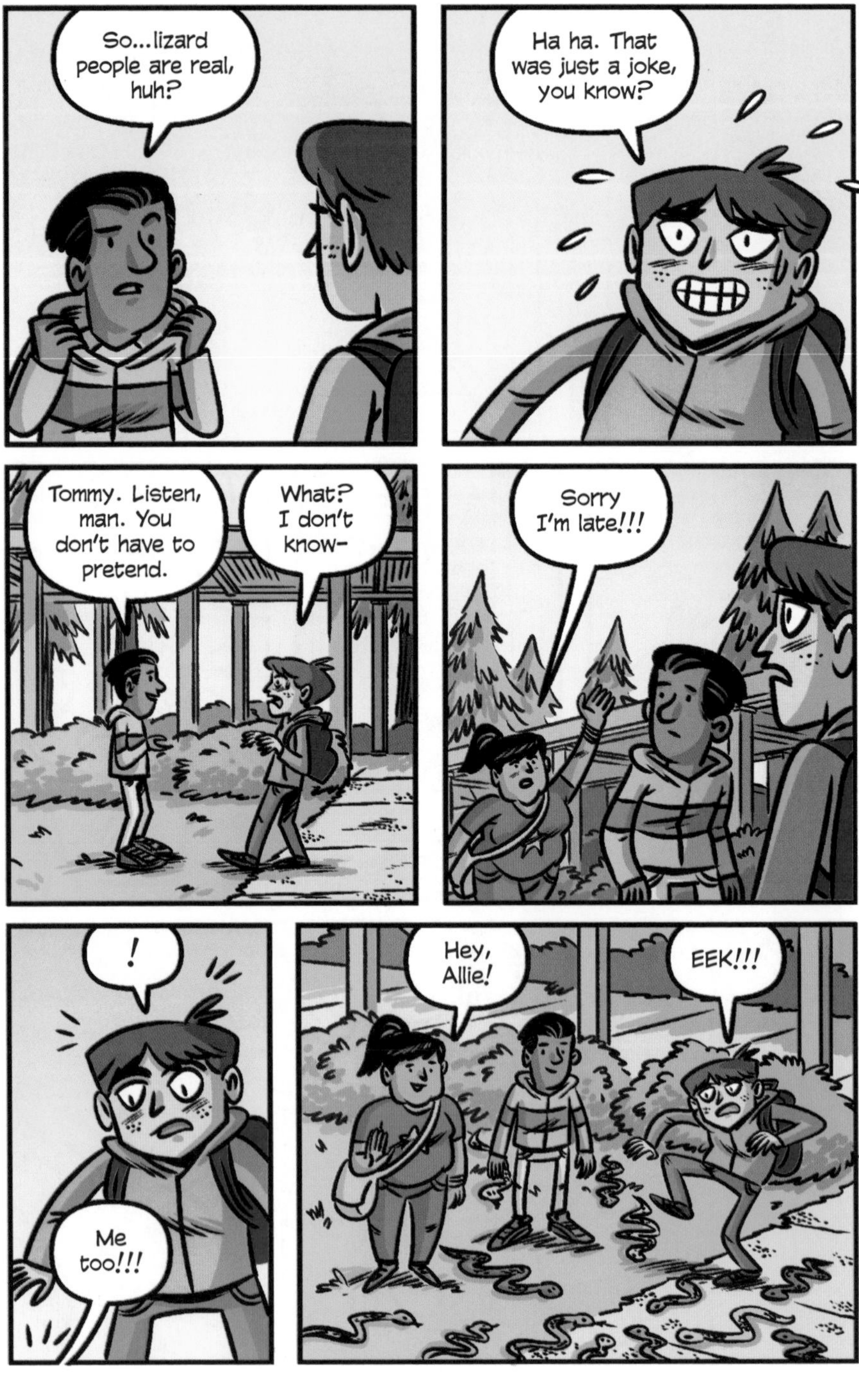
So...lizard people are real, huh?
Ha ha. That was just a joke, you know?
Tommy. Listen, man. You don't have to pretend.
What? I don't know-
Sorry I'm late!!!
!
Me too!!!
Hey, Allie!
EEK!!!

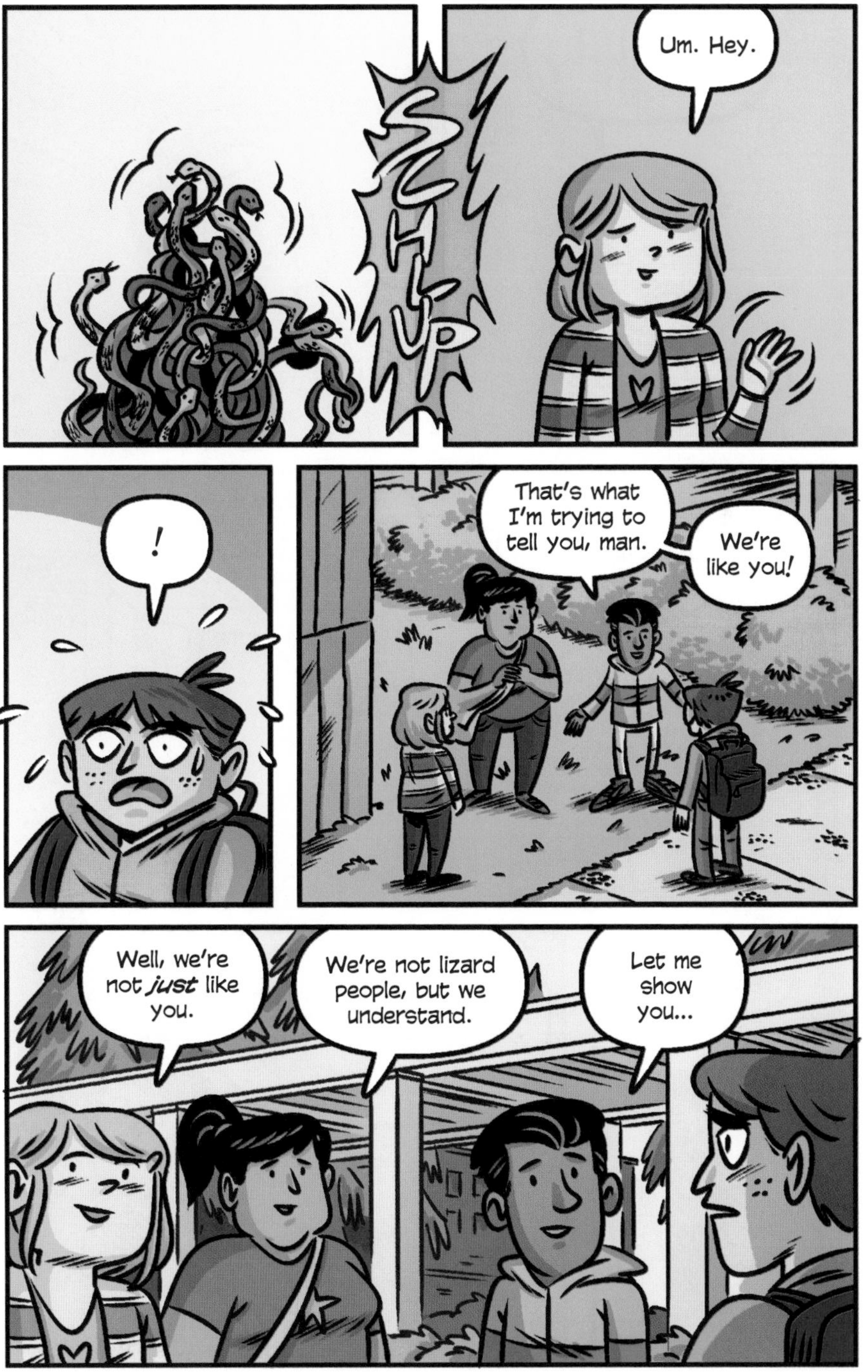
SHLIP
Um. Hey.
!
That's what I'm trying to tell you, man.
We're like you!
Well, we're not *just* like you.
We're not lizard people, but we understand.
Let me show you...

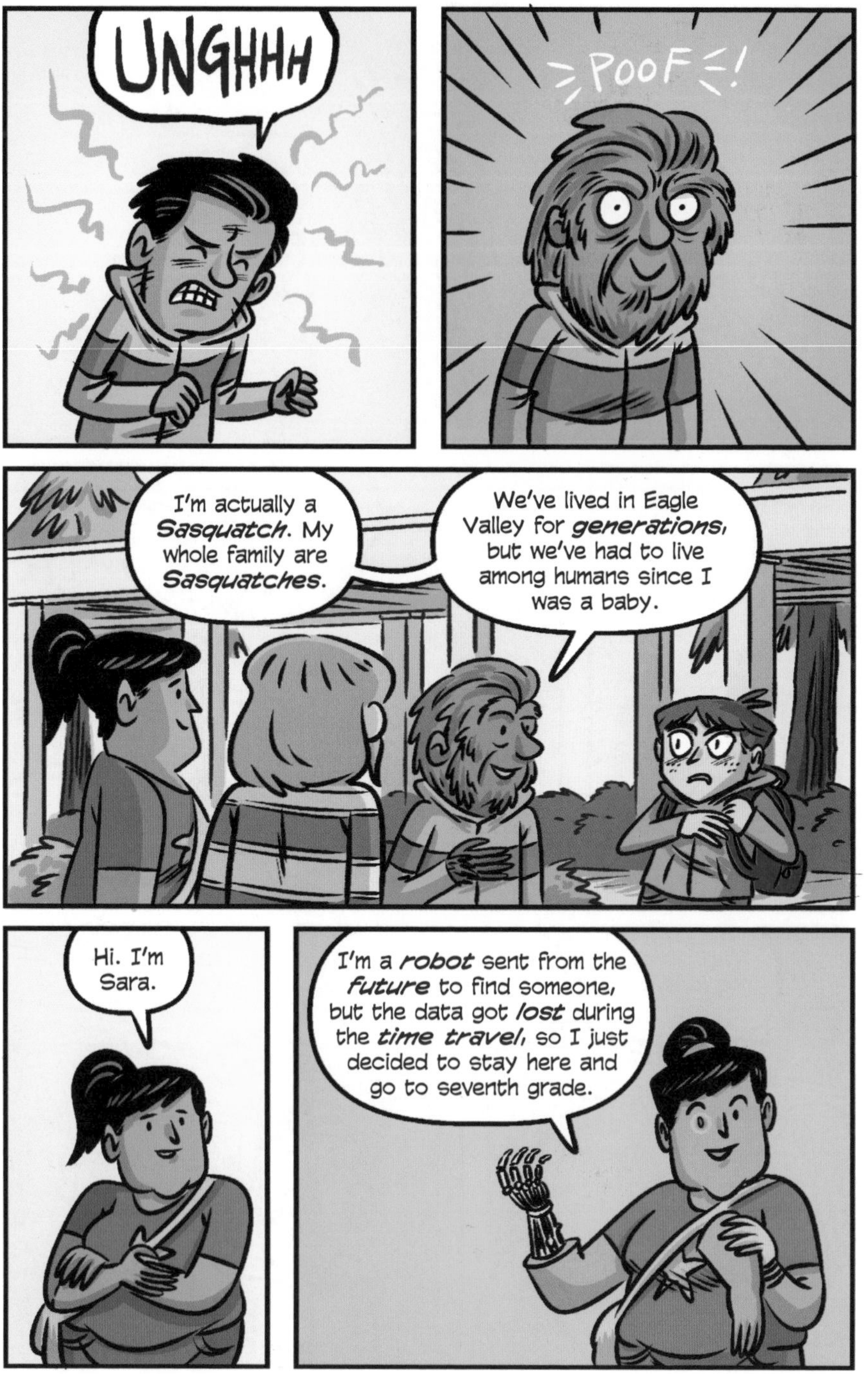
UNGHHH
POOF!
I'm actually a *Sasquatch*. My whole family are *Sasquatches*.
We've lived in Eagle Valley for *generations*, but we've had to live among humans since I was a baby.
Hi. I'm Sara.
I'm a *robot* sent from the *future* to find someone, but the data got *lost* during the *time travel*, so I just decided to stay here and go to seventh grade.

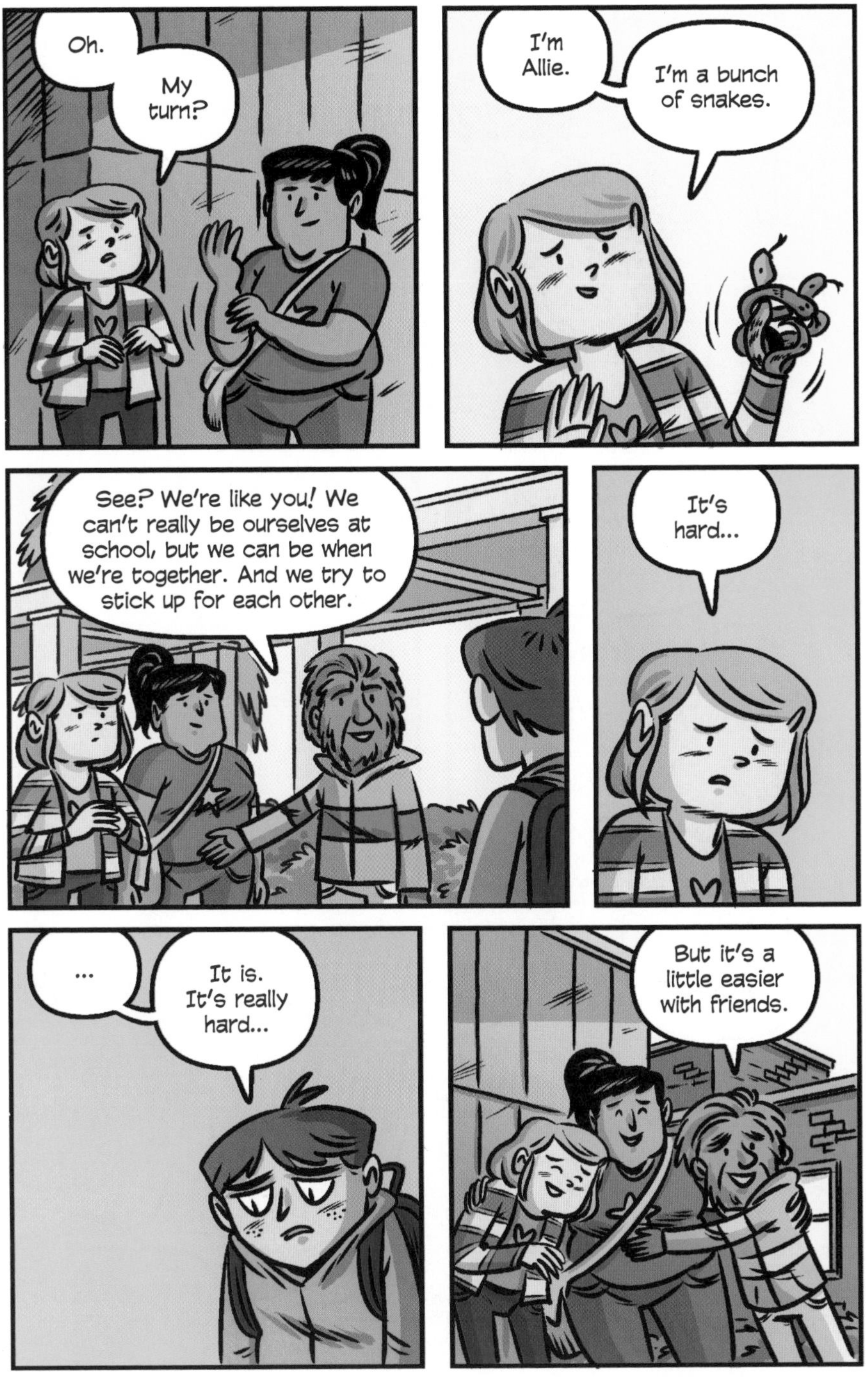
Oh.
My turn?
I'm Allie.
I'm a bunch of snakes.
See? We're like you! We can't really be ourselves at school, but we can be when we're together. And we try to stick up for each other.
It's hard...
...
It is. It's really hard...
But it's a little easier with friends.

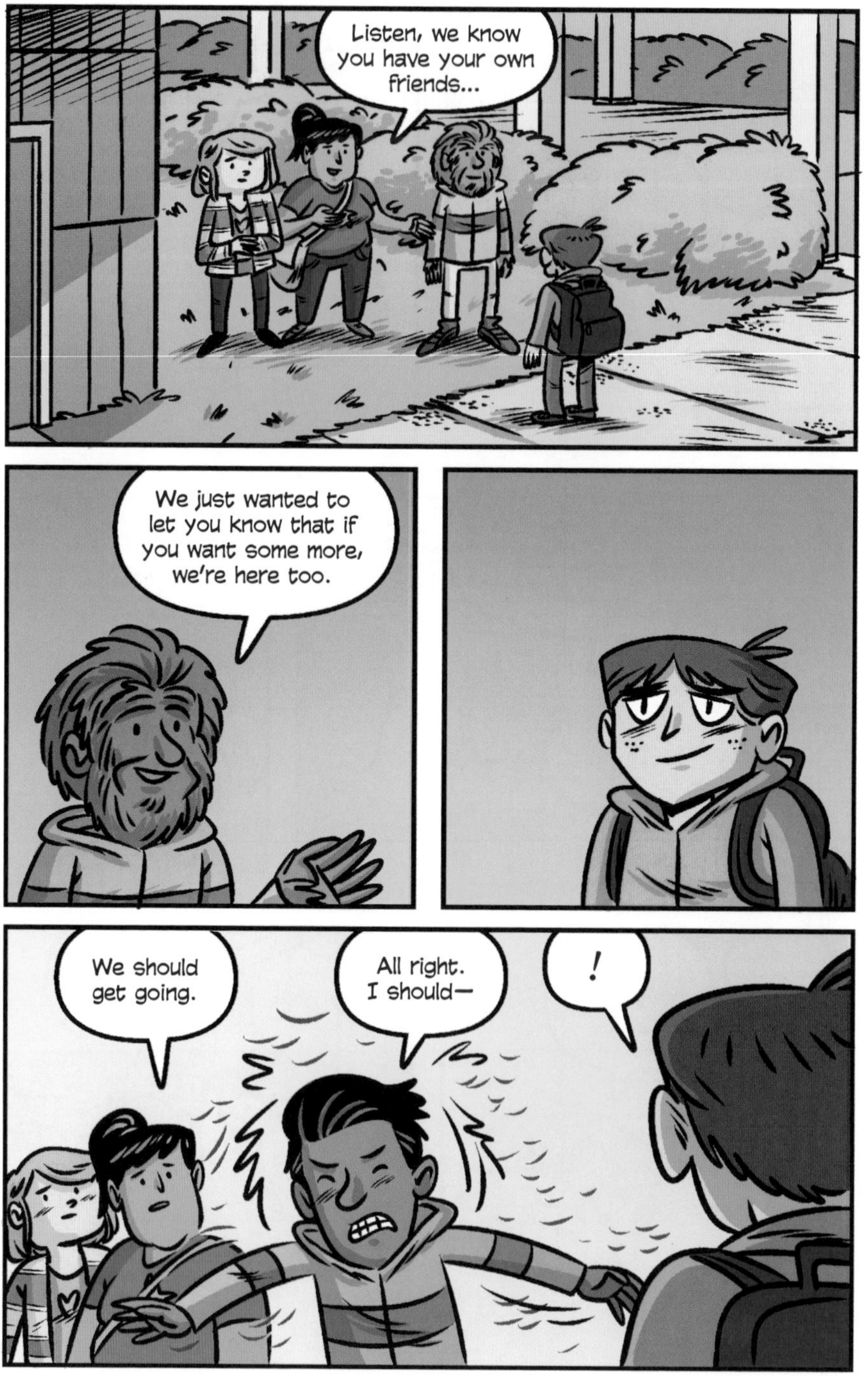
Listen, we know you have your own friends...
We just wanted to let you know that if you want some more, we're here too.
We should get going.
All right. I should—
!

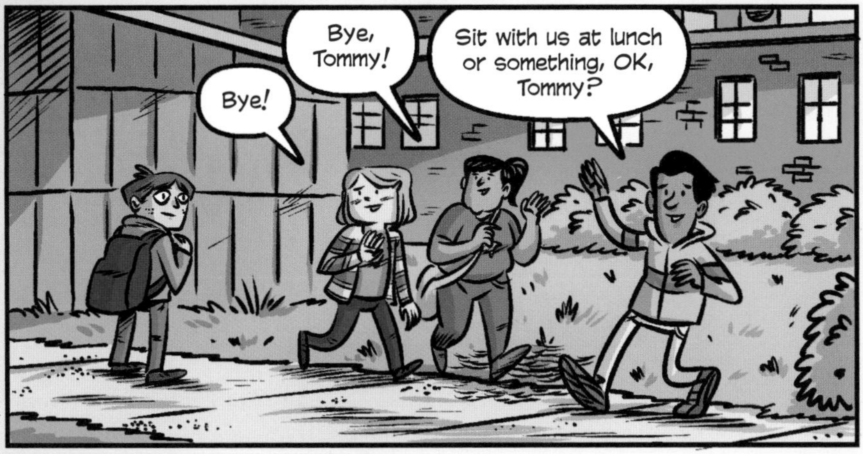
Bye!
Bye, Tommy!
Sit with us at lunch or something, OK, Tommy?

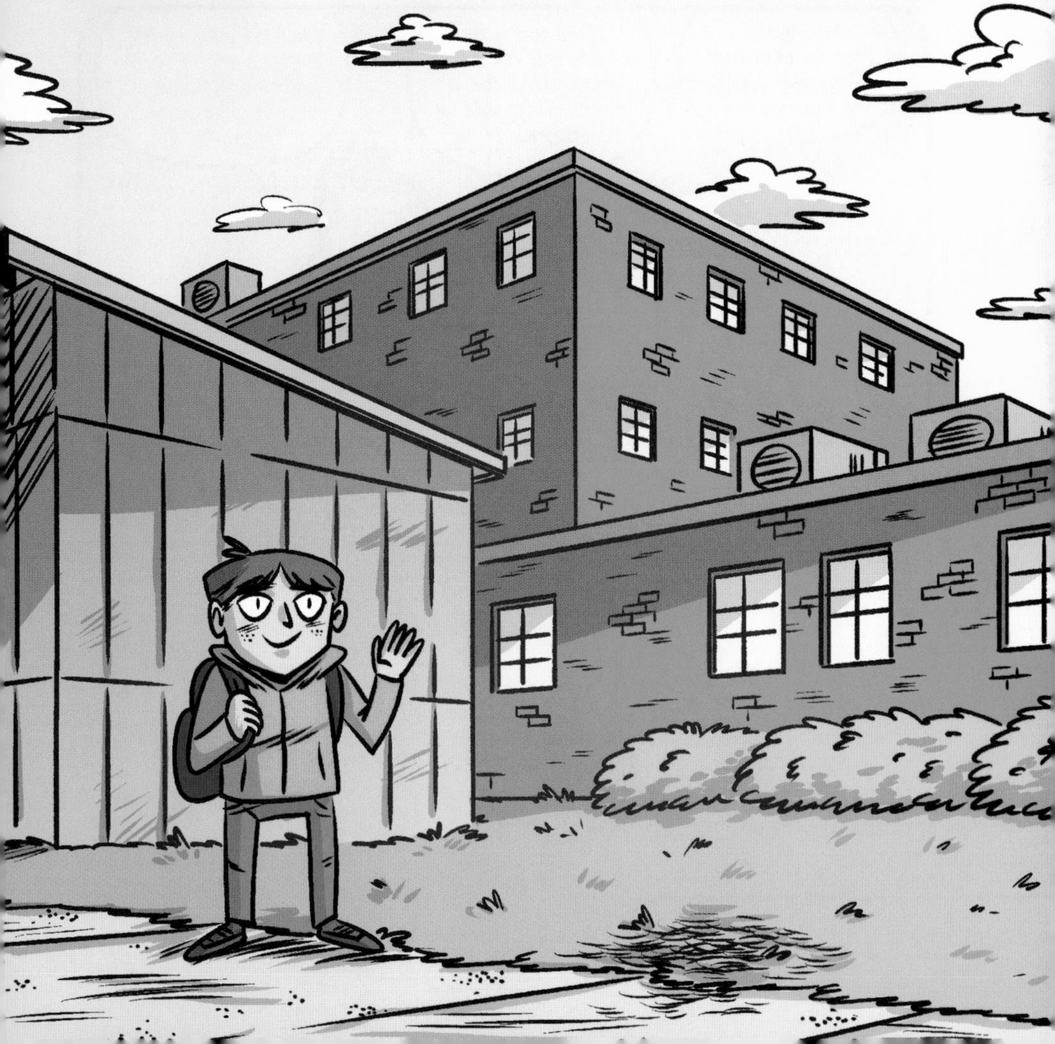

EPILOGUE

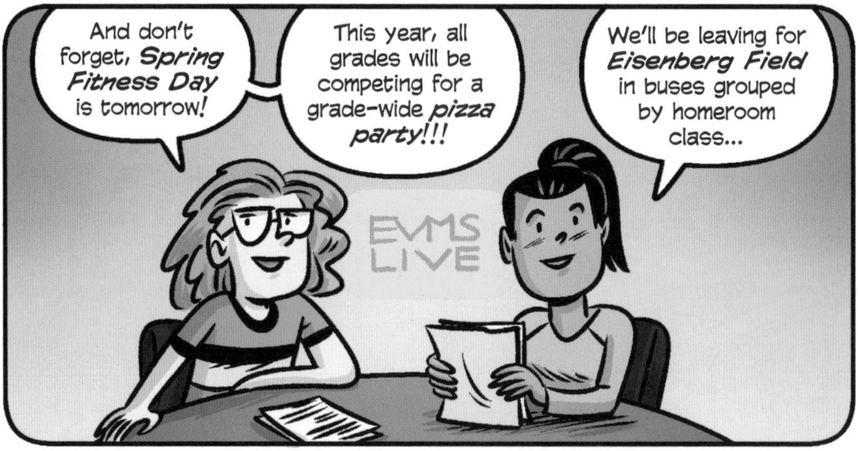

And don't forget, *Spring Fitness Day* is tomorrow!
This year, all grades will be competing for a grade-wide *pizza party*!!!
We'll be leaving for *Eisenberg Field* in buses grouped by homeroom class...
EVMS LIVE

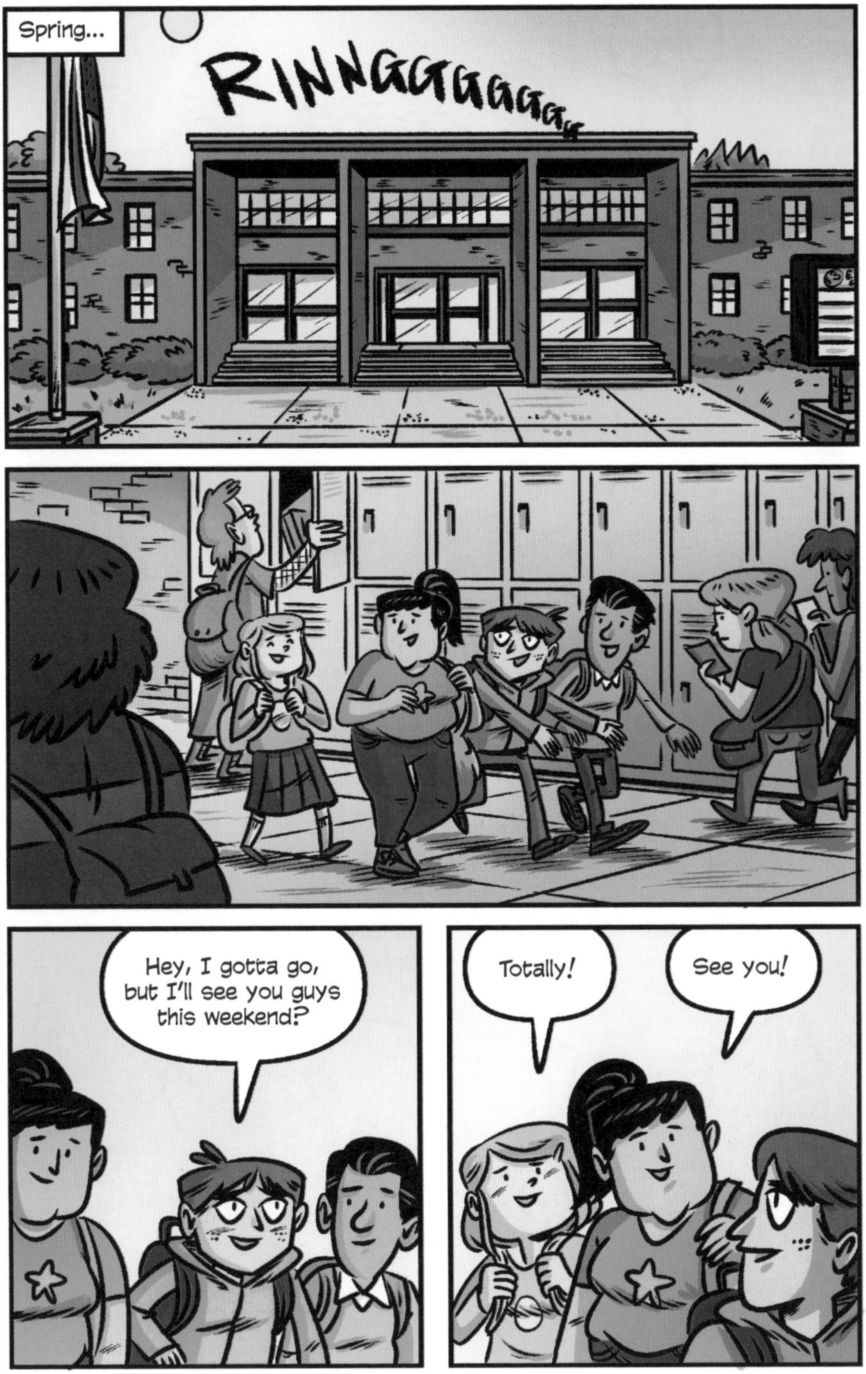
Spring...
RINNGGGGGGG
Hey, I gotta go, but I'll see you guys this weekend?
Totally!
See you!

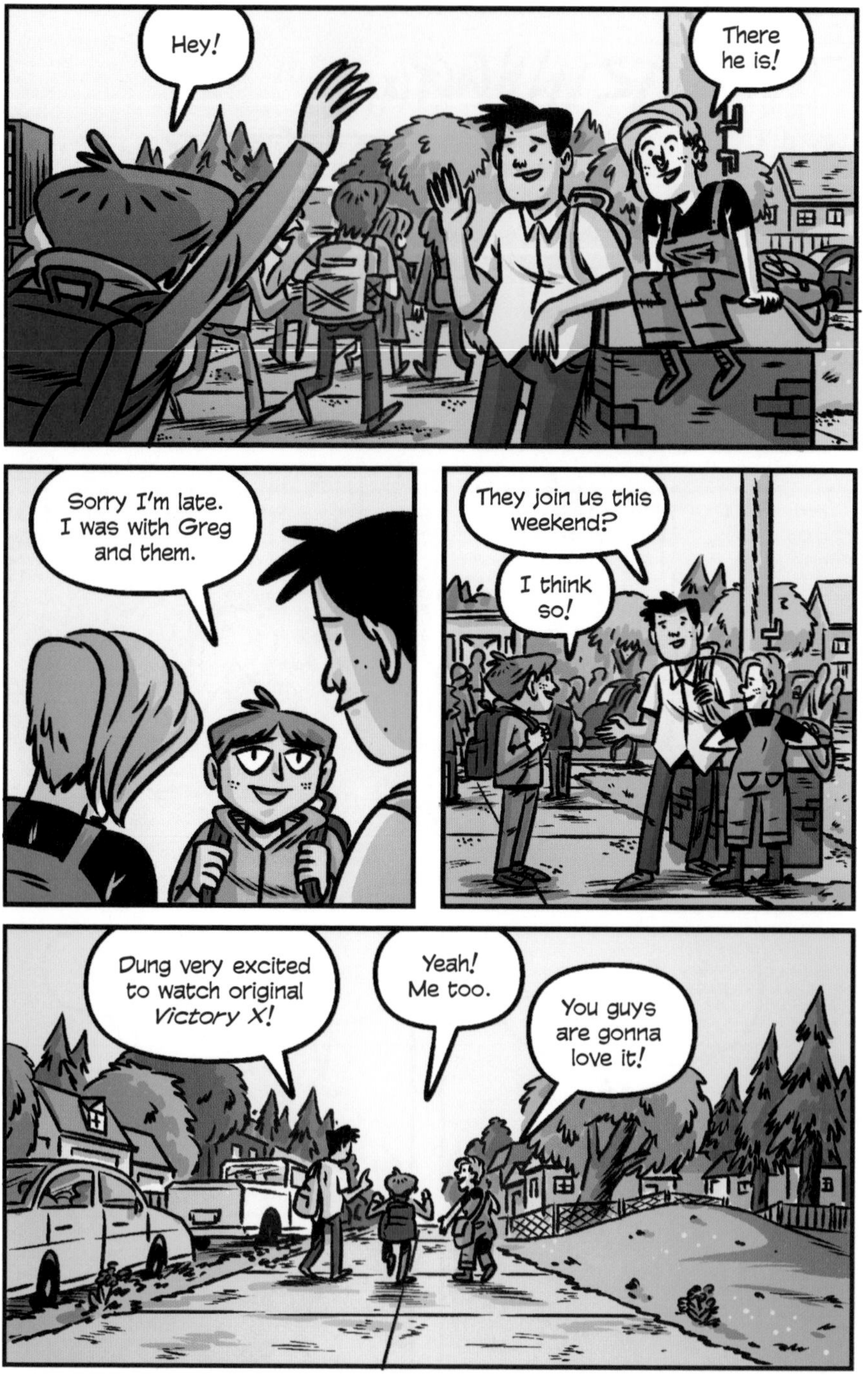
Hey!
There he is!
Sorry I'm late. I was with Greg and them.
They join us this weekend?
I think so!
Dung very excited to watch original *Victory X*!
Yeah! Me too.
You guys are gonna love it!

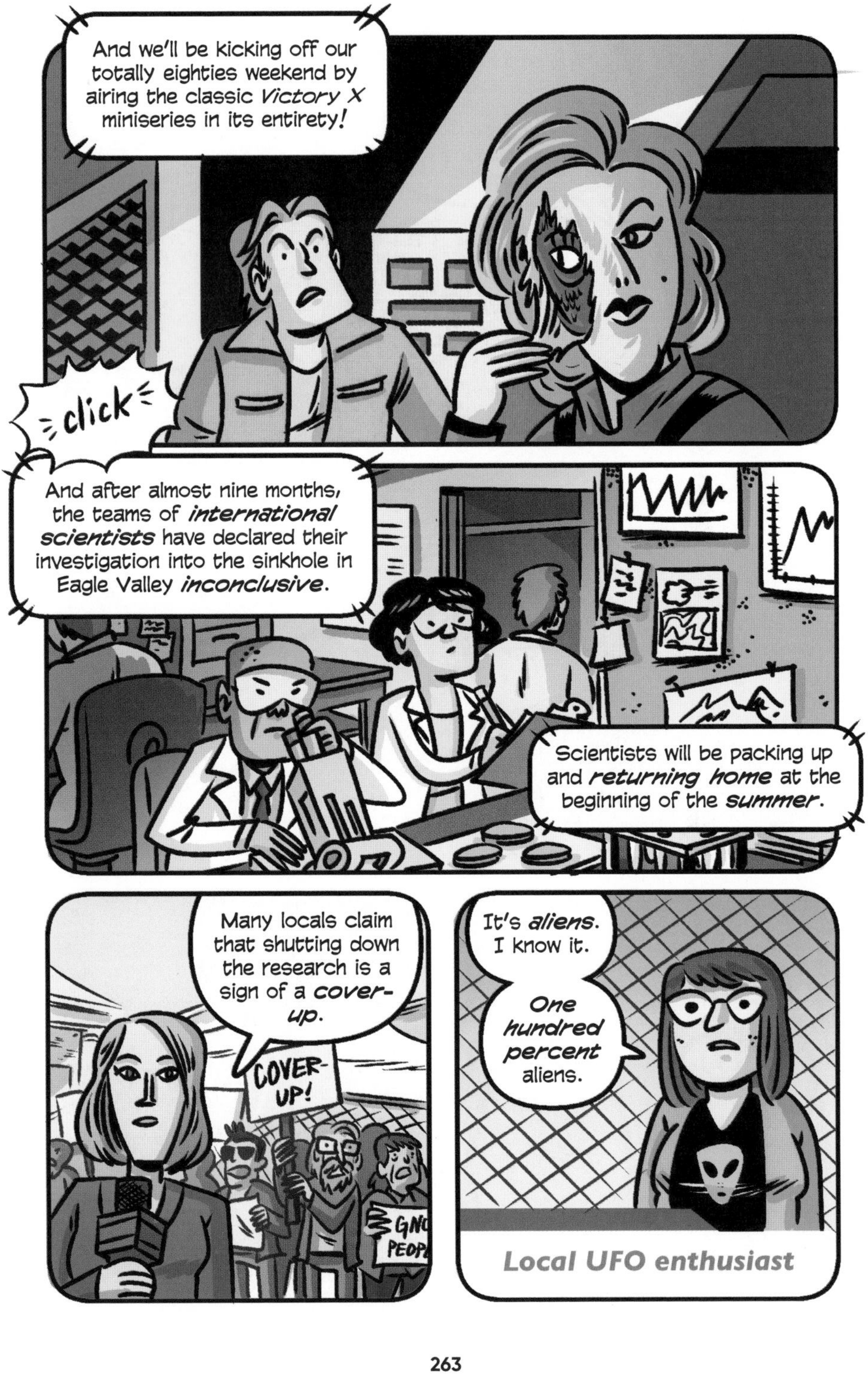

And we'll be kicking off our totally eighties weekend by airing the classic *Victory X* miniseries in its entirety!
click
And after almost nine months, the teams of *international scientists* have declared their investigation into the sinkhole in Eagle Valley *inconclusive*.
Scientists will be packing up and *returning home* at the beginning of the *summer*.
Many locals claim that shutting down the research is a sign of a *cover-up*.
COVER-UP!
It's *aliens*. I know it.
One hundred percent aliens.
Local UFO enthusiast

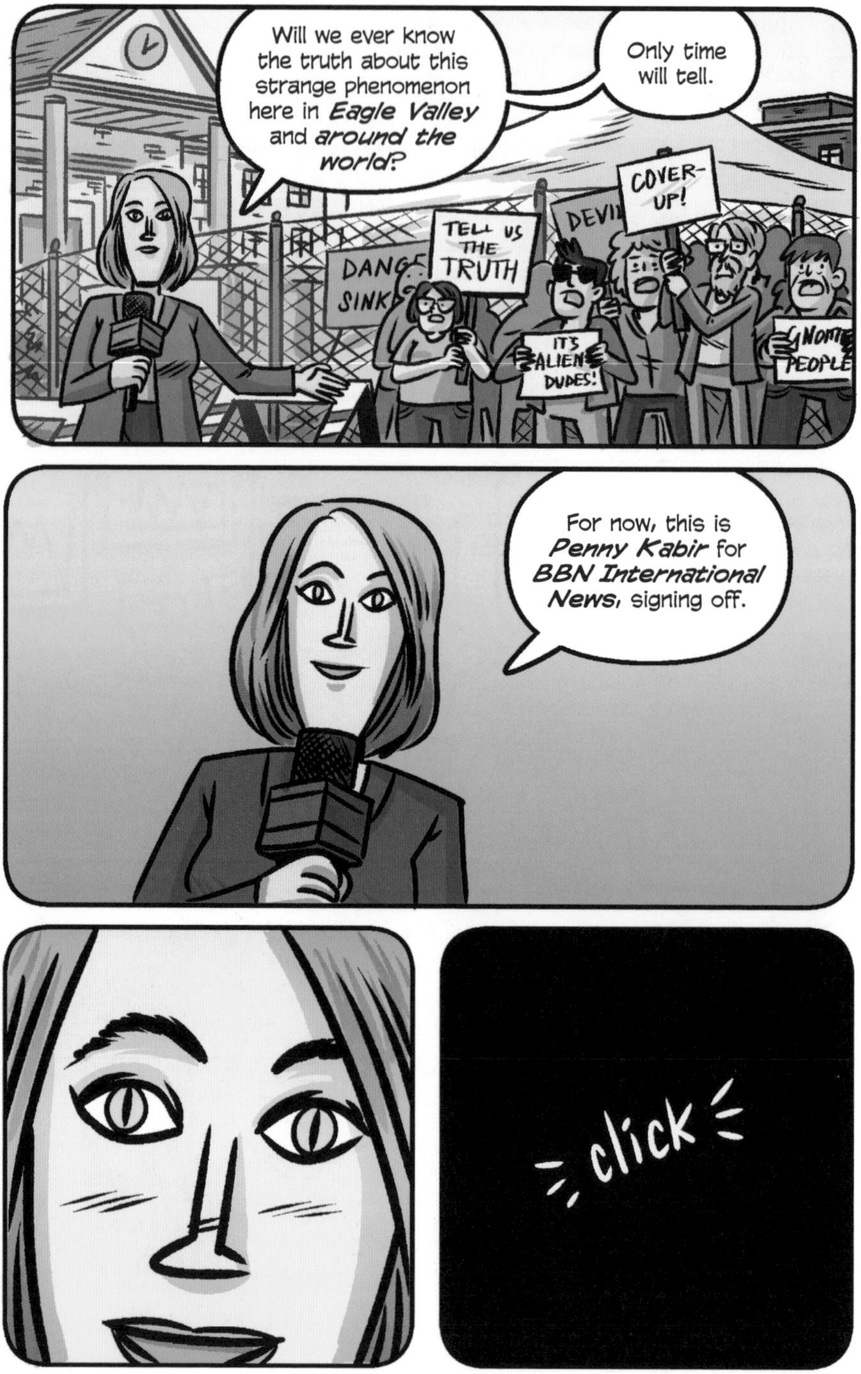

Will we ever know the truth about this strange phenomenon here in *Eagle Valley* and *around the world?*
Only time will tell.
TELL US THE TRUTH
COVER-UP!
IT'S ALIEN DUDES!
PEOPLE
For now, this is *Penny Kabir* for *BBN International News*, signing off.
click

AUTHOR'S NOTE

The hope is always that the work will speak for itself, but there are a few things in the book that I wanted to talk about a little more.

Dung, Vietnamese Names, and Compromises

One of the biggest inspirations for the book is my family's experiences as Vietnamese immigrants and the decisions that they, like many immigrants, faced in adapting to their new home.

My uncle Phuc is a huge part of my life. He helped raise me and my brothers, and we have always been very, very close. The character of Dung is based, in part, on his early experiences as a refugee from Vietnam, arriving in the US in the 1970s.

Growing up, I was told the story of how he was thrown into a public school in Connecticut, not knowing the language, being the only non-white student, and with a name that stood out as much as he did—Phuc Vu.

Phuc Vu, age 16

Although many immigrants change their names slightly or give themselves Western names to fit in more easily, my uncle chose not to. All my life this decision has been an inspiration to me and a reminder that we decide who we get to be in the world.

So it came as a surprise to me when I was working on this book and listening to the audiobook of Phuc Tran's autobiographical novel, *Sigh, Gone*, that I realized that I had been saying my uncle's name wrong my whole life. It was not "*Phuc*, rhymes with *hook*," as I would often tell my friends, but something slightly different that my American tongue is unable to reproduce accurately.

Here is Phuc Tran discussing the pronunciation of his name in *Sigh, Gone*:

In Vietnamese, my name is phonetically pronounced fuhp. *It sounds like a baseball clapping into the lithe, oiled leather of a catcher's glove.* Fuhp. *Also, because Vietnamese is tonal (like its northern neighbor, Chinese), there's a rising tone to it, so your voice upswings like a Valley girl if you say it correctly.* FUHp?

The letter c *at the end of my name isn't even pronounced like a* c *(thanks to archaic orthography and sound changes in the language)—it's a* p *sound.*

This was incredibly confusing to me. In my head I had a narrative of my uncle not compromising his name in order to stay true to himself, despite the difficulty he would face. But upon learning this, I wondered if he *was* having to compromise in some way, and not just to strangers but to some of his closest family. Is compromise just an inevitable part of being an immigrant? Of being different from the dominant culture?

Vivian, one of our sensitivity readers for this book, brought up a similar issue with Dung and the pronunciation of his name. I had seen the name "Dung" as a good stand-in for my uncle's name—both unfortunately close in sound to unpleasant English words. But Vivian said, "Dung's name sounds more like 'yoong' than 'doong' because *D*s in Vietnamese are different."

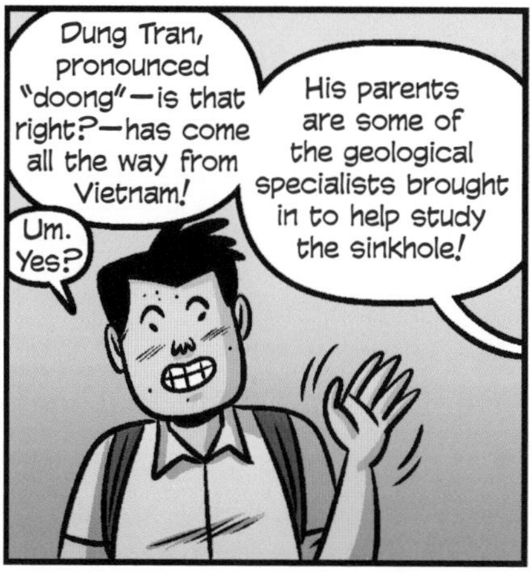
Dung Tran, pronounced "doong"—is that right?—has come all the way from Vietnam!
His parents are some of the geological specialists brought in to help study the sinkhole!
Um. Yes?

And yet, when I was listening to Viet Thanh Nguyen's *The Committed* on audiobook, narrator François Chau pronounced the name, shared by one of the characters in the book, as "doong." Which pronunciation was "right"?

I talked to my uncle about compromise. He had this to say:

"You're right in having to compromise. It's about how you can get through life easier. For me that's kind of how I view it. I mean, I sort of accept it—you guys are my nephews, you're born and raised here in America. That's the best you can do. Now, if you never pronounced my name at all, I would be more offended ...

So yeah, there's a lot of compromising.

I do want to tell you a story why I never thought about changing my name.

So when I was born, for the first month I did not have a name. And your mom and my older sisters, they were quite angry with our dad. 'He's the only boy, how come he doesn't have a name?'

Your grandpa was highly educated. He wanted to give a name befitting his only boy and that I could kinda carry with me through life. So him and my godfather, who are best friends, are like, 'Yeah. We're gonna have to get this right. This is our only chance to get right.'"

My uncle went on to explain that Vietnamese is like Chinese in that you combine characters to make different

Me and my brothers with Uncle Phuc, 1986

words or phrases. The name Phúc is a character that, when combined with the names of his father and godfather, created new meanings. His father's name was Hạnh, pronounced with a short "a" so it sounds more like "hun" instead of "hawn." When you put Hạnh and Phúc together, you get Hạnh Phúc, or "happiness." His godfather's name was Hậu, pronounced "how." When you put Phúc and Hậu together, you get Phúc Hậu, and it means "good fortune will always follow." So Phúc sits between their names and makes happiness and good fortune.

"In this way, between them, they were going to carry me through life. When I got my citizenship in Michigan in

'83, they gave me an opportunity to change my name. They were like, 'OK, what do you want to be called? Do you want an American name?' And I decided against it. I said, 'No. I don't want to.' Because when I left Vietnam with your mom, my father didn't give us anything except the name I carried with me. I think it would have been a great disservice for him if I would have picked a different name.

That's the importance of identity. I always believe you lose your identity, you lose who you are, and then your culture after that. I think the name to me is everything because it's followed by retaining your culture and your language and things like that."

Dung's Speech

Growing up Vietnamese-American in the eighties, the only Asian-Americans I saw in mainstream media were comic relief characters, with thick accents and broken English. And worse, these characters were sometimes portrayed by a white actor in "yellow face." I didn't realize then how harmful those portrayals were and how in so many ways they shaped the way I saw myself and the way I felt I could exist in the world.

When I was making *Tales of a Seventh-Grade Lizard Boy*, it was important to me to give Dung an authentic way of speaking. I didn't want him to sound like those eighties characters, but I also didn't want his English to be perfect. I wanted it to reflect the speech of my family and the people

Family Christmas, 1989

I knew growing up. To me this is an act of defiance against the media I saw when I was younger, where the broken English was intended to lessen and ridicule those characters. Speaking a second language, however imperfectly, is a huge strength! How many of us speak a second language? By portraying Dung's speech with respect and intention, I hope I have created a fully realized character instead of a comic relief one.

There was difficulty in handling this in a medium that doesn't allow for sound. How do you create an accent on the page for the reader to "hear" accurately? For this, I consulted some friends and family who speak both Vietnamese and English to make sure Dung's cadence reflected that of someone who speaks Vietnamese as their first language and also speaks English well enough to get by, but might struggle with the consistency of getting it perfect from time to time.

Thank you so much to Vivian Dang, Lisa Tran, and Phuc Vu for their help with bringing Dung to life in a thoughtful and respectful way.

A Note About Food

In the story Tommy is attracted to the smell of Dung's kimchi at lunch, and although Dung is Vietnamese, it is explained later that it's actually a Korean dish. Tommy eventually comes over to Dung's house to try kimchi and a variety of Vietnamese dishes.

One of the sensitivity readers, my "big sister" Lisa Tran, had a question for me: Why didn't I use that moment as an opportunity to showcase Vietnamese food? Maybe the strong smell that deterred other kids but appealed to Tommy could have been that of nước mắm (Vietnamese fish sauce)? I chose kimchi because I wanted to show the worldliness and openness of Dung's family. But I think another reason is that I still struggle with feeling between cultures myself. I often feel too Vietnamese to be American and too American to really be Vietnamese. Maybe I didn't feel Vietnamese enough to talk about Vietnamese food? Who knows? But I *am* part Vietnamese, and I grew up with many Vietnamese dishes that I want to share with you now. Some of these have become ubiquitous in the US, but others not so much. I have loved sharing these foods with my friends and my found family, and would love to share them here with you!

phở bò: This beef noodle soup is my all-time, number one, MVP comfort food. This dish is so important to me, I am almost at a loss for words. To share a bowl of phở with you means that you are family in my eyes. I had a friend who, hesitant to try it, asked, "Would you say that phở is something everyone loves?" After the meal, she told me confidently, "You can tell people that phở is something that everyone will love." I know that's probably not the case, but that's how I see it.

bánh mì: This Vietnamese sandwich is probably as popular, if not more popular, than phở. When I was in my twenties and would visit my mom in Southern California, she would always stop at a Vietnamese market on our way to the airport so she could load me up with a few of these to take home on the plane. Sometimes I worried that the pickled vegetables would stink up the plane and I would be too embarrassed to eat the sandwiches, no matter how hungry I got!

chả giò: These Vietnamese fried egg rolls are the perfect appetizer. Eat them wrapped in lettuce and dipped in nước mắm, the above-mentioned fish sauce. They're a perfect blend of warm, cool, crispy, and flavorful! Whenever we visit my mom she makes like fifty of these and freezes them and sends them home with us (whether we are driving or flying). If you can't tell, my mom's love language is making sure we're fed.

bún thịt nướng: We probably had this dish second most often after phở. It's a salad of lettuce, cucumber, and vermicelli rice noodles served with grilled pork on top. We would often eat it with cut-up chả giò too. Then you pour the nước mắm over it. It's the perfect summer dish that is cool and refreshing with the added warmth and saltiness of the pork and egg rolls!

thịt kho trứng: I honestly didn't know the name of this dish until writing this section. It's a salty pork braise with hard-boiled eggs. The pork melts in your mouth. It's something I always ask my mom to make when I visit her, but I just say, "Can you cook the pork dish with the eggs in it?" I have never tried to order this at a restaurant because in my head it's something only Mom can make.

bò lúc lắc: The translation means "shaken beef." It's a dish of cubed, sauteed beef that my mom would serve over a bed of romaine lettuce, tomatoes, hard-boiled eggs, and onions soaked in vinegar. This is another dish that we grew up with and I always ask my mom to cook up for me when I visit. This one is easy enough for me to make, but I can never get it to taste as good as when she makes it.

ACKNOWLEDGMENTS

I am nothing without the people in my life, and there are so many I'd like to thank for helping me make this book. Thank you to my agent, Alex, for being a most excellent dude and for helping me get to the next place in my journey. To Nyssa, for breathing life into my line art with their colors in a way no one else could. The folks at Candlewick: my editor, Susan, for seeing what I hoped someone would see in this weird book about lizard people and giving me the chance to make it, and Maria for being such a joy to collaborate and work with. Thanks to my cousin Vivian and my "big sis," Lisa, for their insight and for making sure we portrayed Dung and his family as respectfully as possible. MK, Greg, and Jason have listened to me talk about making a book about lizard people for as long as I can remember and have encouraged me every single time. Thank you to Clive and Seaerra for the remote work dates, feedback, and helping me brainstorm Tommy's real name in those early days, and to Aron, Breena, and Lisa for your close friendship and community over the years. And last, my family: Jen,

for your unwavering love and support and for being someone I can absolutely, truly, take my mask off and be myself
with, and my mom and my uncle Phuc—there are no words
that will properly acknowledge or thank you for everything
you have so kindly given me over the years, the weight of
which is unbearable at times. I love you both so much. And
of course, you, dear reader! Thank you for your support!

JONATHAN HILL is a cartoonist, illustrator, and educator who has been nominated for an Ignatz Award. This is the first graphic novel he has written and illustrated for children. He lives in Portland, Oregon.

NYSSA ORU is a media illustrator in Portland, Oregon. They enjoy rain, bright colors, and stories about misfits.

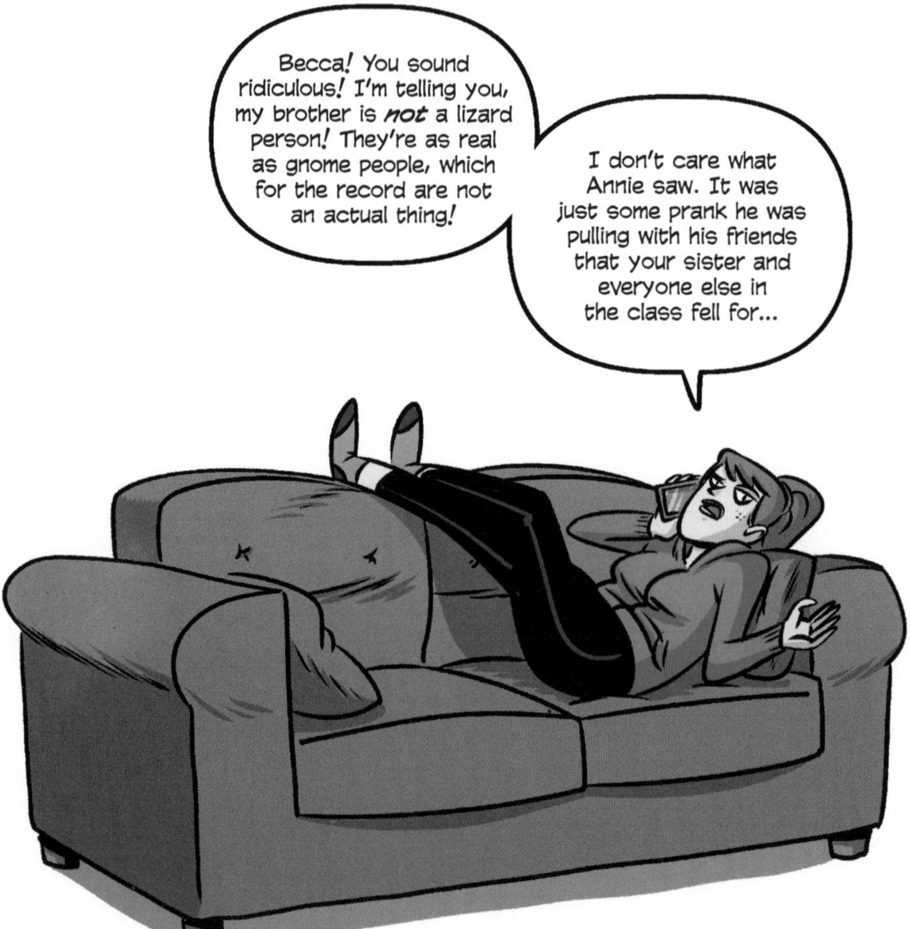
Becca! You sound ridiculous! I'm telling you, my brother is *not* a lizard person! They're as real as gnome people, which for the record are not an actual thing!
I don't care what Annie saw. It was just some prank he was pulling with his friends that your sister and everyone else in the class fell for...